The English Novels
Part B

The Collected Novels of P. C. Wren
Volume 6B

Fiction Titles by P. C. Wren

Dew and Mildew. 1912
Father Gregory. 1913
The Snake and Sword. 1914.
Driftwood Spars. 1916
The Wages of Virtue. 1916
The Young Stagers. 1917
Stepsons of France. 1917
Cupid in Africa. 1920
Beau Geste. 1924
Beau Sabreur. 1926
Beau Ideal. 1928
Good Gestes. 1929
Soldiers of Misfortune. 1929
The Mammon of Righteousness. 1930 (U.S. title: Mammon)
Mysterious Waye. 1930
Sowing Glory. 1931
Valiant Dust. 1932
Flawed Blades. 1933
Action and Passion. 1933
Port o' Missing Men. 1934
Beggars' Horses. 1934 (U.S. title: The Dark Woman)
Sinbad the Soldier. 1935
Explosion. 1935
Spanish Maine. 1935 (U.S. title: The Desert Heritage)
Bubble Reputation. 1936 (U.S. title: The Cortenay Treasure)
Fort in the Jungle. 1936
The Man of a Ghost. 1937 (U.S. title: The Spur of Pride)
Worth Wile. 1937 (U.S. title: To the Hilt)
Cardboard Castle. 1938
Rough Shooting. 1938
Paper Prison. 1939 (U.S. Title: The Man the Devil Didn't
    Want)
The Disappearance of General Jason. 1940
Two Feet From Heaven. 1940
The Uniform of Glory. 1941
Odd—But Even So. 1941

The English Novels

Part B

by

Percival Christopher Wren

THE MAMMON OF RIGHTEOUSNESS

TWO FEET FROM HEAVEN

Edited

by

John L. Espley

Riner Publishing Company
Culpeper Virginia
2020

ISBN
9780999074978

The text of *The Mammon of Righteousness* will be in the Public Domain as of 1 January 2026 since it was originally published in 1930

The text of *Two Feet From Heaven* will be in the Public Domain as of 1 January 2036 since it was originally published in 1940

CONTENTS

PREFACE

The English Novels Part A and *The English Novels Part B* by Percival Christopher Wren are the sixth of a multi-volume series, *The Collected Novels of P. C. Wren.* The purpose of publishing this series is to make the novels written by P. C. Wren more available to the reading public. His novel, *Beau Geste*, is usually recognized by most of the book dealers I have met over the years, but his other works are not so easily remembered.

I have been collecting P. C. Wren for over fifty years, and have been working on a comprehensive bibliography for almost as long. The text of the twenty-eight novels was easily obtained from copies in my own collection. For that collection, I certainly need to thank the hundreds of used book dealers I have purchased items from, and I need to thank some by name: Steven Temple, David Mason, Walt Barrie and, especially, the late Denis McDonnell for the advice and help they have provided over the years.

With regard to Wren himself, Mr. John Venmore and Mr. Philip Fairweather, have been very helpful in providing additional biographical information. Both of them are descendants of the late Mr. Richard Alan Graham-Smith, Wren's stepson and executor of Wren's estate.

As it has been over seventy years since the death of P. C. Wren (November 22, 1941), Wren's works have passed into the public domain in the United Kingdom. In the United States, fourteen of the twenty-eight novels are still under copyright. Thanks to information provided by Messrs. Venmore and Fairweather, the heirs to Wren's literary estate, Mr. Danny Adekoya Campbell and Mr. Christopher Oladipo Graham-Smith, were located and permission has been granted to reprint Wren's works.

I also need to acknowledge the help and guidance of my family members: my daughter and son-in-law, Dawn and Andrew; my son and daughter-in-law, Jared and Claudia; and my long-suffering wife, Cathy. Thank you.

In conclusion, I need to thank Percival Christopher Wren for the many years of great enjoyment that his stories have provided. I know that Wren is not a literary or critical success, but, for me, he is one of the great storytellers of the early twentieth century.

John L. Espley
Culpeper, Virginia
February 2, 2020

INTRODUCTION

Percival Christopher Wren is best known as a novelist, publishing twenty-eight novels from 1912 to 1941, the most famous being *Beau Geste* (1924). Wren also published seven short story collections; *Stepsons of France* (1917), *The Young Stagers* (1917), *Good Gestes* (1929), *Flawed Blades* (1933), *Port o' Missing Men* (1934), *Rough Shooting* (1938), and *Odd—But Even So* (1941), containing a total of 116 stories. There were also two omnibus collections, *Stories of the Foreign Legion* (1947) and *Dead Men's Boots* (1949), containing stories selected from *Stepsons of France*, *Good Gestes*, *Flawed Blades*, and *Port o' Missing Men*. All 116 short stories can be found in the five volume collection, *The Collected Short Stories of Percival Christopher Wren*.[1]

Wren was a man of mystery in that the majority of biographical statements about him seem to be more fiction than fact. A typical biography places his birth in Devon in 1885, his education at Oxford, and his career as that of world traveler, hunter, journalist, tramp, British cavalry trooper, legionnaire in the French Foreign Legion, assistant director of education in Bombay, and a Justice of the Peace. Most of the above biography, however, is false or has not been verified.

Wren was born Percy Wren on November 1, 1875 in Deptford, a district of South London on the banks of the Thames. He did attend Oxford University, graduating in 1898 with a 3rd class

---

[1] For further information on *The Collected Short Stories of Percival Christopher Wren* see rinerpublishing.wordpress.com

honours in History leading to a Bachelor of Arts degree. He attained his "M.A." in 1901. In those days, a person acquired a "M.A." after a certain number of years (three in Wren's case) and upon payment of a fee.

After leaving Oxford, he married Alice Lucie Shovelier in December 1899 with whom he had a daughter, Estelle Lenore Wren, born in February 1901, and a son, Percival Rupert Christopher Wren, born in February 1904. Percy worked as a teacher at various commercial schools until 1903, when he and his family left England for India.

From 1903 to approximately 1919, Wren was employed as an educator by the Indian Education-al Service (I.E.S.). During that time he published a number of educational textbooks, some of which are still in use in Indian schools today. It was during this period that he started using the name Percival C. and Percival Christopher on the text-books.

From 1905 to 1915, he also served in the Volunteer Corps (Sind and Poona) in India (see the novel *Driftwood Spars*, which contains a descrip-tion of a Volunteer Corps), and was appointed a Captain in the Indian Army Reserve of Officers, the 101st Grenadiers of the Indian Infantry, in November 1914. He probably saw action in the East African campaign of World War I (see the novel *Cupid in Africa*, which takes place in East Africa during the War), and resigned from the Indian Army Reserve of Officers in November 1915.[2]

---

[2] Most of the biographical information about Wren has been obtained through certificates, documents, and original research at the British Library, Bodleian Library, and the India Office papers. Further information on Wren and his works was obtained during a three week research visit in September 2018 at the John Murray Archives in the National Library of Scotland. Detailed documentation and sources will be cited in the biographical essay to be included in the forthcoming publication, *An Annotated Bibliography of Percival Christopher Wren*.

Wren's first novel, *Dew and Mildew*, was published by Longmans, Green in 1912. His first novel of the French Foreign Legion, *The Wages of Virtue*, was written in 1913 and published by John Murray in 1916. One of the many questions about Wren is whether he did serve in the French Foreign Legion. Given the chronology of his documented biography it is difficult to see where he had time to actually serve in the Legion.[3] Wren himself always maintained that he had served and his stepson, Richard Alan Graham-Smith, who died in 2006, "strongly maintained that Wren had indeed served in the French Foreign Legion and was always quick to refute those who said otherwise."[4]

*   *   *   *   *   *   *

The series, *The Collected Novels of P. C. Wren*, is intended to include all twenty-eight novels in seven thematic omnibus volumes. The number of physical volumes will be fourteen, with each thematic volume divided into Part A and Part B. The individual titles will not be in Wren's original publication order, but will instead have a connecting theme such as characters or locale. The seven volumes are:[5]

v. 1 - The Geste Novels
Part A:
Beau Geste
Beau Sabreur

---

[3] After examining just over half of the available files at the John Murray Archives, it is evident that Wren was consistent about serving in the Legion. The only available time though would have been between 1891, when Wren was fifteen and 1894 when he entered Oxford, shortly before he was nineteen.

[4] wikipedia.org/wiki/P._C._Wren

[5] The order of volumes four through seven has been modified since the publication of volume two.

Part B:
  Beau Ideal
  Spanish Maine
v. 2 - The Sinbad Novels
  Part A:
    Action and Passion
    Sinbad the Soldier
  Part B:
    Fort in the Jungle
    The Disappearance of General Jason
v. 3 - The Foreign Legion Novels
  Part A:
    The Wages of Virtue
    Sowing Glory
  Part B:
    The Uniform of Glory
    Paper Prison
v. 4 - The Earlier India Novels
  Part A:
    Dew and Mildew
    Father Gregory
  Part B:
    The Snake and the Sword
    Driftwood Spars
v. 5 - The Later India Novels
  Part A:
    Beggars' Horses
    Explosion
  Part B:
    The Man of a Ghost
    Worth Wile
v. 6 - The English Novels
  Part A:
    Bubble Reputation
    Cardboard Castle
  Part B:
    The Mammon of Righteousness
    Two Feet From Heaven

v. 7 - A Mixed Bag of Novels[6]
    Part A:
        Soldiers of Misfortune
        Valiant Dust
    Part B:
        Cupid in Africa
        Mysterious Waye

*   *   *   *   *   *   *

Volume Six of *The Collected Novels of P. C. Wren*, *The English Novels*, contains four novels with a different setting than that of his other novels. The action takes place almost entirely in England, which is why the title of this omnibus edition is *The English Novels*.

*   *   *   *   *   *   *

The English Novels Part B

The English Novels Part B contains two novels, *The Mammon of Righteousness* and *Two Feet From Heaven*, that are more psychological, versus mystery and adventure, than the rest of Wren's novels.

The Mammon of Righteousness, with a subtitle of *The Story of Coxe and the Box*, was published in the Spring of 1930 and is the story of Algernon Coxe, a neurotic young man under the heavy influence of his over-domineering mother, Miranda. He meets and falls in love with a young woman, Giovanna Blayton, of whom his mother disapproves. Algernon's mother persuades him to marry another young woman, but before he does, Giovanna asks him to look after a large traveling trunk or box while she goes away for a while. He

---

[6] Previous to May 2019 volume seven's title was "The Other Novels".

does so, but shortly thereafter his new wife discovers the dead body of Giovanna in the box and Algernon is arrested for Giovanna's murder. This story is framed by an account, twenty years earlier, of five young men who are friends at school and college, and their interactions with Miranda.

Wren was working on the manuscript of *The Mammon of Righteousness*, originally titled "Coxe and the Box," in May 1929 when in a letter to his publisher he stated that the story was turning out better then he expected, and that "it won't be another *Beau Geste*, but it may well be another *Mystery of a Hansom Cab*,"[7] referring to a bestseller mystery novel by Fergus Hume published in 1896.

The Mammon of Righteousness was published by Frederick A. Stokes, under the title of *Mammon, a Mystery Novel*, on March 6, 1930, with the British edition available, a month later on April 9, 1930. It was, however, a dismal failure in sales, and agents around the world requested permission to return copies.[8] Despite the lack of sales, less expensive reprint editions were published in 1932 by John Murray in the United Kingdom and A. L. Burt in the United States.

The second novel in *The English Novels Part B* is *Two Feet From Heaven* which Wren described, when submitting the manuscript in March 1940, as "quite a new departure, and more of an orthodox novel than a 'rattling good yarn', as the lowest form of review calls the story of action and

---

[7] John Murray Archive, National Library of Scotland (cited hereafter as JMA), file Acc. 12927/379 BG25. Italics added.
[8] JMA, file Acc. 12927/228 CH14, date 7 April 1930, file Acc. 13328/74 DG32, date 3 Jun 1931, file Acc. 12927/228 CH14 dates 14 and 16 January, 9 May, and 8 July 1932.

romantic adventure."[9] The novel is essentially the story of a vicar, Richard Neystoke, of a small village in the country, and his mental illness.

On April 10, 1940, John Murray responded to the manuscript stating that he enjoyed the novel, but had some criticisms and suggested changes. The changes included not having Neystoke know that he killed anybody, and that he [Murray] does not like books which have characters with the names of Goering, Goebbels and Hitler, which were the names of three displaced and poor young refugees from London. Also that the Nursing home and school incidents were overdone with much of them being "like a study of a clinic for psycho-analysis [. . .]"[10]

Wren responded the next day with

> "the book is, of course, mainly a pathological study, and the 'hero' an abnormal neurotic and something of a Jekyll-and-Hyde. His character on the whole, is admirable, but infirm of purpose and with a weak and cowardly streak. Like all my characters, he is drawn from life. [. . .] He is, however the victim of an equally fundamental weakness of character—unstable temperament and an injurious mother complex."

Wren goes on to state that he will follow Sir John's suggestions, and that he

> "sketched his boyhood at some length because such episodes as his sudden and complete falling out of love with

---

[9] JMA, file Acc. 12927/140 BH40, date 18 March 1940.
[10] JMA, file Acc. 12927/140 BH40, date 10 April 1940.

Claire Bell, adultery with Johnstone, and his battering of the rabbit as he killed it, were highly significant and pathologically symptomatic. [. . .] I can embark on a new book, but after living for four months on bromo-choral, digitalis, cermain, strophanthus, vegenin, opium, and injections of (to me) unknown poisons, I find it incredibly difficult to re-cast a book already written. If you remember, 'Beau Geste' was constructed on the same principle."

Wren goes on to state that he will change the names of Goering and Goebbels, but wants to retain Itler [sic] as he is one of the main characters. Wren will also sharpen the clinic and school parts, and he wanted Sir John to know that he

"spent a long time after the war in Crichton Miller's Clinic. He, being then —and again now—head of the Government R.A.M.C. department of the treatment of shell-shock and war-neurosis causes. My trouble being tropical cerebral-anemia, after prolonged combined malaria and dysentery, contracted in the Umba Valley. I saw a great deal of the incredibly interesting working of psycho-therapeutics."

On the same day, 11 April, Sir John wrote to Wren concerned that Wren might be too depressed over his criticism and comments, and that "perhaps I have not sufficiently expressed my pleasure with much of it."[11]

Two Feet From Heaven was published by John Murray on October 9, 1940, and on January 6, 1941 by Macrae-Smith. Almost immediately there was trouble with the American edition of *Two Feet From Heaven*. The earliest reference to the trouble was on January 17, when Curtis-Brown, Wren's American agent, sent John Murray two newspaper clippings of advertisements for *Two Feet From Heaven* and stated that Macrae-Smith had been threatened with a lawsuit because of a book with a similar title. The book was *One Foot in Heaven*, a memoir, by Hartzell Spence published in 1940. The book was not the problem; the lawsuit was initiated by the Warner Brothers film studio, fearing that Wren's fiction book about a British vicar would confuse the American public with a non-fiction book and film about an American clergyman.

The final official decree was issued on July 3, 1941, with the result being that Wren's book, *Two Feet From Heaven*, could not be sold in the United States after January 6, 1942, even if there were copies available. The estimation of the number of remaining copies was about 1,300. In addition there would be no publication of a reprint (cheap) edition.

There is a large amount of correspondence in the John Murray Archives regarding the unfairness of the lawsuit, but the small publishing company of Macrae-Smith could not afford a vigorous defense against a large corporation such as Warner Brothers. Also, during this time period, Wren could not participate since he was very ill and in a nursing home, and eventually died on

---

[11] JMA, file Acc. 12927/140 BH40, date 11 April 1940

November 22, 1941.[12]

*   *   *   *   *   *   *

The original spelling, punctuation, and grammar of the British editions, except for obvious errors, has been preserved as found in the latest editions/printings of the stories during Wren's lifetime (1875-1941). The footnotes, in the novels, are also as found in the original source material.

---

[12] JMA, file Acc. 12927/140 BH40, dates 17 January through 20 October 1941.

THE MAMMON OF RIGHTEOUSNESS

THE STORY OF COXE AND THE BOX

"L'inglese italianato
'E il diavolo incarnato."

CONTENTS

THE OUTER BOOK

PART I. SERVING AS A PROLOGUE

THE INNER BOOK

PART I. INTRODUCING COXE AND ALSO THE BOX

PART II. THE LIFE AND ADVENTURES OF ALGERNON
DASHWOOD COXE

THE OUTER BOOK
(Continued)

PART II. SERVING AS AN EPILOGUE

THE OUTER BOOK

PART I

SERVING AS A PROLOGUE

PROLOGUE

I

In the largest of the studies of the Head Master's House at one of the greatest English Public Schools, five boys, Mortimer, Tattinger, Fortescue, John Desart and Clarence Coxe, sat about the fire, one Saturday night, munching biscuits and drinking the cocoa that the two hosts, Mortimer and Tattinger, had brewed.

Mortimer, known for some long-forgotten reason as Milly, a tall thin dark youth, somewhat elegant of person, soft and suave of speech, Head of the House and Captain of Cricket, was also the acknowledged head and leader of this little coterie.

They, diverse of character as five boys could be, had come from the same Preparatory School and had together gone up the ladder of this their Public School, step by step, until, still united, they had reached the Sixth form and their last term.

Mortimer's close familiar friend and stable-companion, Richard Tattinger—known as Scrub by reason of the general scrubby effect achieved by short, wiry, sandy hair, snub nose, freckles, big mouth and ears, and general untidiness, was, according to John Desart, reminiscent of a thoroughbred fox-terrier; while Mortimer rather suggested a greyhound. In further pursuit of his doggy similes, he saw in the third of the Mortimer-Tattinger-Fortescue trio, an admirable specimen of the British bull-dog.

In this also was he justified, for Fortescue, affectionately known as Tub, was a powerfully-built thick-set youth, with bull-neck, bandy legs,

7

jutting chin and jaw, and a look of grim determination.

His pleasing and attractive smile disclosed small even teeth, the lower row of which protruded slightly beyond the upper.

Of the five, these three were the inner circle, the inseparables. The two others, John Desart and Clarence Coxe, had little in common with the trio and nothing with each other, save the accident of a decade of communal life and mutual experience.

Clarence Coxe, a pasty-faced pimply lumpish boy, was, according to John Desart, a poodle; in fact, a pooh-poodle; a good quiet house-trained dog, easily taught to sit up and beg, and to perform any other trick requiring little intelligence and less effort.

As that of young people is apt to be, John Desart's criticism was harsh and intolerant, albeit Clarence Coxe undeniably possessed more of the traits and attributes of the lap-dog than of the greyhound, terrier, or bull-dog.

Silent because he had little to say and less desire to say it; clumsy and bad at games because he was nervous and self-distrustful; only moderately good in class because he was rather unintelligent and somewhat lazy, Clarence Coxe was tolerated rather than beloved by the other four; and ignored, because overlooked rather than despised, by the remainder of the Sixth and the School in general.

Son of the Rector of Avesbury, his highest ambition—to scrape through school without being superannuated and to get a Fourth in Theology at Oxford—seemed likely to be fulfilled.

When, amused if not complimented, by John Desart's canine classifications, the others enquired as to what particular sort of dog he considered himself to be, Desart would reply that he was no special and particular kind of dog—just a dog—in the same sense that the House jam was no special particular and identifiable kind of jam, but just jam.

Clarence Coxe had somewhat surlily asked this question when kindly informed by Desart that he was an utter poodle, and, on learning that Desart was no particular kind of dog had, for him, quite brilliantly, observed:

"Certainly not a very particular dog . . . No; dirty dog, perhaps," introducing, as usual, the only jarring note; and, as usual, incurring a sharp rebuke from Scrub Tattinger, who, at times, quite obviously hated him.

This John Desart, son of a great and famous Edinburgh physician, by far the cleverest of the five, proposed to follow in his father's footsteps and, by way of Harley Street, attain rank, fame and fortune as King's Physician, Knight, Baronet, and Peer.

After exhaustive discussion of the afternoon's match, in which all but Clarence Coxe had played, a brief silence fell, as four comfortably tired and happily weary boys stared into the fire and fought the battle o'er again.

"Oh, for Heaven's sake, keep your foot still, Poodle," cried Scrub Tattinger suddenly and irritably, as he sat up and stared angrily at Clarence Coxe who, for the thousandth time, was offending by his unconquerable habit of crossing the left leg over the right and swinging the left foot up and down, swiftly, steadily and endlessly.

"Anyone got a bit of string?" continued Scrub Tattinger.

"I know where to put my hand on a piece of blind-cord," said Mortimer. "What do you want it for?"

"To tie Coxe's filthy foot to the coal-scuttle . . . Perhaps that'll keep his beastly hoof still for five minutes . . . Come on, get the cord, Milly."

Clarence Coxe arose and departed thence.

"A weak silent man," observed Scrub Tattinger, as the door closed. "Better than the strong silent sort, I suppose."

"You are hard on him, Scrub," observed Fortescue.

"Oh, Clarence Dashwood Coxe annoys me beyond speech."

"Not beyond speech, Scrub—unfortunately," remarked John Desart.

"Anyhow I could say a jolly sight more than I do," said Tattinger. "He reminds me of my mother's cook."

"In beauty or gentle femininity?"

"No. What I mean is—my mother's had our cook for twenty years. Hated her on sight when she engaged her, and has hated her more and more every day ever since."

The others laughed.

"Beauty!" continued Scrub Tattinger with a grunt. "Femininity I grant you. There's more of the makings of a man in his cousin Minerva Coxe's little finger than in our Clarence's whole body."

"Yes, they're changelings, I should think. Minerva certainly ought to have been a boy," observed Mortimer.

"Thank Heaven she isn't," observed Scrub Tattinger.

"No, that wouldn't do, Scrubby lad, would it?" laughed Fortescue.

"Did you hear that yarn that she's unofficially engaged to Clarence?" he continued mischievously. "Only a rumour, of course, but she had him in her pocket all last hols."

"A *canard*, as the learned say," remarked Mortimer softly.

"A damned lie," almost shouted Scrub Tattinger.

"Hoots, laddie, why this warmth, this wrath, this excitement?" jeered John Desart.

"Hush, Long John, your question is indiscreet. You tread on a hidden corn—I mean sacred ground," said Fortescue.

"Hidden corn growing in sacred ground, perhaps," murmured Mortimer.

"And fools rush in where poor old Scrub simply doesn't dare to tread."

"Sorry, Scrub," smiled John Desart. "You lads of the same village have your little local intrigues and scandals with which I am unacquent."

"What the devil d'you mean—intrigues and scandals?" asked Scrub Tattinger haughtily and with a dignity sadly marred by a heavy and well-aimed cushion.

"Chuck it, children," ordered Mortimer, "and let Poodle Coxe alone.

"For the old firm of Mortimer, Tattinger, Fortescue, Desart and Coxe is about to break up, alas," he continued . . . "You won't be troubled with him much longer, Scrub."

"You three will be at Sandhurst next year," said John Desart, "I shall be a medical student and Poodle Coxe an undergraduate. When shall we five meet again?"

"Tell you where we four will meet again, anyhow," put in Mortimer. "Look. Our three fathers—mine, Tattinger's and Fortescue's—are members of the Pelham, and we're down for it. In spite of its being a most exclusive club, we'll be able to squeeze you in, Long John. Then we're bound to meet from time to time."

"Yes," agreed Fortescue, "we'll have reunion dinners when Milly and Scrub are home from

Africa, and I from India. We're bound to coincide sometimes."

"Splendid," said John Desart. "I'll toddle round from Harley Street to your Loafers' Home. And we'll talk over old times . . . 'Forty Years On,' and all that."

"What about Poodle Coxe?" he added.

"Oh, leave him out of it," said Scrub Tattinger. "We've had all the Clarence Dashwood Coxe we want."

II

A runner had arrived with the mails at the stockaded post of Kinguna, a month's desert journey from the railway.

Clad only in a sleeveless khaki shirt, shorts, puttees, hob-nailed boots and a sun-helmet, Captain "Milly" Mortimer, of the King's African Rifles, crossed from his hut to where his comrade Scrub Tattinger sat outside his tent and stared at a letter that he held in his hand.

"Got one from Tubby Fortescue," said Mortimer, as he drew near, reading as he walked, and without looking at his friend.

"He's got his Ghurka Double Company. Says he'd love to 'pit them against a Double Company of our Nyassaland Yaos, who are supposed to be the Ghurkas of Africa, of course.'"

Still reading, and without looking at his companion, he seated himself beside him. Then, dropping the letter, he stared before him, absent-mindedly, out upon the dusty parade-ground where a coal-black Sergeant-Major was drilling a squad of African soldiers of fairer complexion.

"I'll tell you what it is, Scrub," he said, coming back to earth and the present. "It's all wrong, having these Soudanese non-commissioned officers in charge of Abyssinians and Somalis . . . 'Course they're just about the finest soldiers in the world, but they oughtn't to be put over those chaps. It's really almost on a par with putting Indian Mussalman or Hindu officers over British Tommies . . . Soudanese are looked upon as slave-people in Abyssinia and Somaliland. The Gallas absolutely despise them. I'm going to take jolly good care to get some Abyssinians promoted to Sergeant and . . . Hullo, what's up?"

Realizing that his friend had made no reply to any of his remarks, Mortimer turned to look at him, and saw that something was very wrong indeed.

"What is it, Dicky?" he asked softly.

Tattinger was staring straight before him, unseeing, unhearing, a look of stunned amazement on his set face, which had paled to a greyish pallor beneath its tan.

He looked stricken: as though he had received a mortal wound.

"What's up, Scrub? What's the matter?" asked Mortimer again, laying his hand on Tattinger's arm.

Tattinger made neither movement nor reply. Alarmed at the look upon his friend's face, Mortimer sprang up and gently shook him.

Had he been bitten by a *mamba* as he sat there?

"What's *wrong*, Dicky? What's up?"

And then Tattinger seemed to collapse upon himself, as he bowed his face into his hands.

"It isn't true . . ." he whispered. "It can't be . . . Minerva couldn't do *that* . . . Not *Minerva* . . ."

The letter that he had been holding fell to the ground, and Mortimer recognized its bold firm handwriting.

Scrub's girl . . . Minerva Coxe . . . Coming out to marry him as soon as it could be managed . . .

"What's happened, Dicky?" he asked.

"Go away, Milly," was the only reply; and rising, Tattinger entered his tent and closed the flap.

Of Scrub Tattinger it might be said, as once upon a time of a King of England, that he was not seen to smile again, nor ever heard to laugh.

Certainly not by his friend Mortimer, who was in fairly close touch with him for the next five-and-twenty years, and was with him when he died.

III

A tall lean brown-complexioned man, soldierly of face and figure, crossed from the Pelham Club dining-room to the huge lounge, and, as he stood stuffing his pipe, gazed around the well-remembered room which on that bright May morning he now entered again for the first time after a big-game shooting-trip in the beloved Africa from whose service he had retired.

Same great old leather arm-chairs; same great old leather-faced steward; same great old heads of lion, buffalo, ibex, oryx, eland and kudu . . . And, by Jove, great old Tubby Fortescue!

Striding across to where Tubby sat, deep in an arm-chair and a book, Colonel Mortimer murmured in his usual soft deceptive voice:

"Got a match, Tub?"

Major Fortescue gave one look and one leap from his chair.

"Well, I am d-d-d-d . . ." he stuttered, as he seized his friend's hand.

Colonel Mortimer nodded.

"You are, Tub," he whispered.

"Delighted, I was going to say," continued Major Fortescue. "When didjer get back, Milly? Have any luck? Got any genuine record heads?"

"Every one, Tub. Got the biggest mouse-deer antlers ever lassoed. Colossal. How's Mrs. Tub?"

Later it transpired that, throughout his last big-game shooting-trip, Colonel "Milly" Mortimer had had only one experience worth recording, and that a rather ghastly one. Very ghastly, in fact.

The elephants that he had shot had behaved in

16

the usual manner; no lion had laid an unkind claw upon him; every rhinoceros that had charged had done so with the usual impetuous enthusiasm and lack of finesse which so commonly lead to lack of result; no wounded buffalo had lain in wait for him; not a single *mamba* had bitten him; although he had fagged right across to the Belgian Congo and back to Mount Makeno in Tanganyika Territory, he had failed to find an okapi and had not encountered a single gorilla.

No, life had been rather dull, monotonous and uneventful until he had met Scrub Tattinger, and that had been the occasion of the one interesting experience of the three years' trip.

Yes, painfully interesting . . . Really most amazing . . . Astounding. And absolutely awful.

"Dear old Scrub's still alive and going strong, then, eh?" mused Major Fortescue, smiling reminiscently.

"No, that's just what he's not," replied Colonel Mortimer, gravely. "And on the whole you'll agree with me that it's a good job too—if he was going to live the rest of his life in the condition in which he was when I found him. Yes, poor Scrub's dead all right. I buried him myself."

"Drink?"

"No . . . No . . . No worse than you, Tub."

"What, not gone native?"

"No . . . No more than he'd been ever since he retired from the King's African Rifles. When I spoke of the condition he was in, I rather meant to imply mental condition. He'd got something truly appalling on his mind. Called himself a murderer and worse. Smote himself on the chest and groaned in the middle of the night—the night that I joined up with him—and the small hours of the morning, just when I was getting my beauty sleep. He wouldn't tell me about it, at first. Said he had only just found it out and must think—or try to. And he was in the greatest haste and hurry to reach a water-hole before the raiders did. But he was in absolute agony of mind for the next day or two, until he was killed."

"Don't wonder at it, either," he added. "Tell you by and by when we're a bit more private . . . Make you sit up."

"Good Lord! *Poor* old Scrub," said Major Fortescue. "Poor old Scrubby. I can't take it in.

"Our old Scrub *dead*," he added. "And calling himself a murderer. What had he been up to— giving way to that red-haired temper of his, and shooting-up the black brother? I've often felt like it myself on safari, and nearly done it, too, 'specially the faithful porter who pours away the petrol, totters along all day with an empty tin on his head, and fills it with water at night."

"Yes," smiled Colonel Mortimer, "or the stout lad who empties away your last bottle of gin, because why should the Bwana carry water about with him when he's trekking by a river?"

"No," he continued. "Scrub hadn't been shooting anybody, and . . .

"By Jove, here's old Long John," he interrupted himself, as another member, the great and famous neurologist, Doctor John Desart, approached, beaming, with outstretched hand.

"Well, well, well, so you're back, eh, Mortimer," said Long John Desart, as he warmly shook the hand of his old friend.

"Delighted to see you again, old chap. By Jove, you look fit! 'Pon my soul, I think I'll drop everything and come with you, next *time*."

"Splendid," whispered Colonel Mortimer. "Nothing I should like better. But what about the health of London if you abandon it for three years?"

"Oh, I couldn't make a three-year do of it. Wish

I could. But I might be able to come for long enough to miss a lion and then scuttle home and talk about it for the rest of my life."

"Meaning that that's what I do?" smiled Colonel Mortimer.

"Well, no . . . You may miss 'em, of course, but you certainly don't come home and talk about it . . . Now, sit you down and do a bit of talking just for once, and I'll give myself a whole hour's holiday. Tell us all about it."

"What, all I've done in three years?"

"No, skim the cream of it. Tell us about each record head . . . and its last words . . . and all about everything."

"Yes, go it, Milly," adjured Major Fortescue as he drew his cigar-case from the side-pocket of his coat.

"And tell us about poor Scrub Tattinger's murder," he added.

"Scrub Tattinger *murdered?*" exclaimed the doctor. "Why, it seems only the other day he was sitting in that chair!"

"No, no," replied Major Fortescue. "But Mortimer was just telling me that he's dead, poor chap. No, it isn't the murder of Tattinger, but a murder by, with, from or about . . . Milly was just going to tell me about it all when you arrived."

"Scrub *dead!*" ejaculated John Desart incredulously.

Colonel Mortimer nodded, frowning, with down-drawn lips.

"Look here, you chaps, it's pretty bad . . . pretty awful . . . Draw up a bit closer . . . I've been thinking about it for weeks, on my way home, and have decided to tell you both."

"Poor Scrub said:

" 'Tell Long John. He's a doctor and all that.'

"Then he said:

" 'If you and Long John don't agree, call in Tub-by Fortescue . . .' Sort of casting-vote idea.

"I needn't say that the story will die with us and not another soul will ever know. Part of the story, anyhow—where it concerns a woman. The other part must be blazoned abroad . . . In the Press . . .

"I suppose Clarence Coxe isn't in the Club, by the way?" he added.

"Yes, he is," replied Major Fortescue, "and he'll be in here any minute now. Always puts up in the club Chambers when he's in Town."

"Shouldn't have thought he'd have cared to show his face, poor devil, since that terrible business . . . Enough to kill a man like him. Should have thought he'd have buried himself alive, somewhere."

"Yes, one would," agreed Major Fortescue. "I rather fancy Minerva sends him here; makes him 'hold his head high' as she would say . . . Face it out, and live it down."

"Does *she* do any facing it out and living it down, herself?" enquired Colonel Mortimer.

"No . . . er . . . no; one can't say she does," replied John Desart. "I gather she's not been out of Melfont Parva Vicarage since it happened . . . Tell us about poor Scrub . . . I haven't really grasped it yet . . . Scrub *dead?*"

"Yes, and with a most shocking confession on his lips . . . Not exactly a confession, either, really. But terrible . . . terrible . . . About poor young Algernon Coxe."

"Look out," whispered Major Fortescue, touching Colonel Mortimer's ankle with his foot, as a grey-faced haggard-looking man, in clerical dress, approached.

"Good God! How the poor chap's aged," murmured Colonel Mortimer, rising and shaking the hand of his old school-fellow—or what he mentally termed the wreck of his old school-fellow—whose fine black beard and hair had, since he last saw him, turned almost white.

"Glad to see you back, Mortimer," said the Reverend Clarence Coxe. "Had a good time?" and he giggled foolishly and wrung his hands.

Seating himself and gnawing his nails, he added, with a painful nervous jerkiness of speech and manner:

"Tell us about your shooting trip. Come on, Milly, do tell us. All about the Best Beasts and Blackest Kings and Emperors."

And he cackled with mirthless laughter, uncomfortable to hear.

Doctor John Desart eyed him with sombre and professional interest. The man was evidently on the verge of a nervous breakdown.

"Come on, Milly, spin a great yarn. All about what you've seen and done and got," continued the reverend gentleman and began violently to swing his crossed leg.

"Oh, I don't know. Got one or two decent lions and two or three goodish heads and some tusks. Nothing much," replied the Colonel coldly.

"Exactly how many lions did you shoot?"

"Eight."

"Lions, large, black-maned, sportsmen for the use of, eight . . . Any records?" observed the Reverend Clarence Coxe with forced and feeble humour.

"Oh, I don't know . . . Goodish sable antelope . . ."

"Record?"

"Might be."

"Did you poach your elephants?"

"Yes . . . on toast."

"Did you get into the Reserve or Portuguese ter-

21

ritory and poach?"

"Oh, don't ask silly questions, Coxe," interrupted Major Fortescue impatiently. John Desart frowned at the Major, and shook his head in rebuke, for he knew something of what the pitiable man was suffering.

"Well," sighed the reverend gentleman, "that's about all we shall hear of your big-game shooting experience, I suppose. What about all your upper-class Kings and Emperors?"

"Oh, I don't know. I barged into Abyssinia a bit. But the most interestin' monarch I encountered wore a very natty gent's bowler hat with an ostrich feather sticking straight up in front," replied Colonel Mortimer.

"Anything else?" enquired the Reverend Clarence Coxe.

"Yes, of all things on this earth, a perfectly good cricket-pad."

"An old Blue?"

"No, an old devil."

"What did he do?"

"Oh, I don't know. Passed round the word for a boycott, cut off supplies and chucked things at us, at sunrise and evening star."

"What sort of things?"

"Spears. Nasty little arrows. Poisoned."

"What did you do? Shoot him up?" enquired Major Fortescue.

"Good Lord, no. I love those old-fashioned chaps. Not too many of 'em left nowadays. Gentlemen of the old school. What with aeroplanes, wireless, television and all that tripe, the place is getting spoilt.

"Why, I met a poor lad trekking with a load of alarm-clocks, dollar watches, mouth-organs, beads, brass-wire and red-flannel. Going to make his fortune. First tribal chief he came to offered him a cigar and a cocktail and said he'd cast an eye over his stock.

" 'Good,' said the lad. 'Plenty much good ju-ju got. Great big ting-a-ling loud watch-clock hang round neck. All people say Massa be one Big King . . .'

" '*Can* it!' said the Paramount Chief of the Wabobubo. 'Show us the doings.'

"And when the lad made his show-down of his best Brummagem trade-goods and near-gold and almost-diamond jewellery, the Chief laughed long and loud as he scratched his ribs.

" '*Hell*, Bo,' he said. 'Haven't you *one* portable wireless, or cine-camera, nor even a decent gramophone? Well, well, sit down a minute, while I send the kids along . . .'"

"How are the Masai behaving nowadays?" enquired Major Fortescue.

"Poor fellows! Going the way of the Zulus. No one to fight, and not even allowed to fight among themselves."

"Getting civilized. Soon have gorblimey caps and hobnailed boots, I expect."

"Well, now, plain answer to a plain question, Milly. Did you or did you not have any adventures with natives?" pursued the Reverend Clarence Coxe, his right foot oscillating with the speed and regularity of a pendulum.

"Oh, I don't know . . . Adventures . . . Natives of where?"

"Oh, you're hopeless."

"Well, I don't want to offer hope. How do you mean—adventures? . . . *Do* sit still, man . . ."

Again John Desart frowned, caught the Colonel's eye and shook his head. Clarence Coxe was to be humoured and handled gently.

"Well, did you or did your men ever have occasion to fire a single shot at a black brother?"

he asked.

"Oh, we had a bit of fun up Lake Rudolf way. The K.A.R. had got a couple of little columns out after the old firm that raids down from Southern Abyssinia to the Turkhana country. Besides slaughter, slavery, rape and arson they trap elephants in pits, leave them to starve, and then hack their tusks out—often before they are dead . . . Real choice band, that. Finest collection of prize stiffs on the face of the earth."

"What sort?"

"Oh, Abyssinian outlaws. Arab slave-traders and ivory-poachers, black hunters, soldiers, 'wanted' criminals, and bad lads from all the fighting tribes of those parts. Savage cruel devils. Regular bad hats."

"And you went along to see the fun, eh?" said Major Fortescue.

"Well, *I had got khubbar of* a white man with a big well-armed safari, and being a bit short on one or two things, we trekked for him. And blessed if it wasn't old Scrub Tattinger jogging along to take a hand.

"Quite unofficial of course, but old Scrub wasn't going to be out of it when the K.A.R. were up against his old pals the Abyssinian border-raiders, who did-in Scrub's best subaltern and dozens of his beloved askaris at one time and another.

"No, old Scrub was off on his own, to get between the raiders and their base over the border. Quite a big safari he'd got, and every man of them an old K.A.R. askari. And with personal scores to settle with the raiders, too."

"Scrub's private war, eh?" smiled Major Fortescue.

"Just that."

"And you chipped in?"

"Oh, I joined up with old Scrub, for any fun that might be going . . . By Jove, the old lad was a great bush-whacker."

"Yes," agreed Major Fortescue. "There isn't much he didn't know about native warfare."

"Did you get in the way of the raiders?"

"Rather, somewhat. Old Scrub laid a lovely ambush. Got 'em on toast. Looked as though we might get a surfeit of Arab on toast, at one time."

"How did he know which way they'd return from the raid?" enquired the doctor. "I suppose there were hundreds of miles of border where they . . ."

"Water," was the reply. "Got to steer by the water-holes in desert country, John. Scrub knew one they'd simply have to come to."

"Well, then, it seems to me they'd simply have to defeat you and drive you from the water, or die of thirst," observed John Desart.

"Just Scrub's point," replied Colonel Mortimer. "He knew they'd got to come there, and he knew they'd got to fight—and that was all he wanted."

"Well, well, tell us all about it," begged John Desart.

"Oh, we got there in time, and dossed down, and along they came, and barged into us."

"Yes, well?"

"We scrapped."

"Oh Lord! Be not like dumb driven cattle . . . Have a heart man, and tell a tale."

"Well, what d'you want to know?" enquired Colonel Mortimer, glancing meaningly at the Reverend Clarence Coxe, who sat twitching, fidgeting, and biting his nails nervously.

Clarence Coxe must not hear the tale that poor Scrub Tattinger had told ere he died.

"Everything. What time of day was it?"

"Peaceful eventide."

25

"What did they do when you opened fire?"

"Those who were hit fell down."

"And the rest?"

"Fell down even quicker."

"And then?"

"Spread out and crawled all round us in a circle."

"You were outnumbered, then?"

"About twenty to one."

"And then?"

"Rushed us at dawn."

"What with?"

"Swords and spears, after quite a good little barrage of rifle-fire."

"Real hand-to-hand fighting, then?"

"Not very much. Scrub's men could shoot to hit. And I'd got some quite useful lads; and Scrub and I got off quite a number of rounds. And we didn't miss much."

"Did you actually fight anyone hand to hand yourself?" enquired John Desart.

"Oh, I don't know. I gave one lad a tap."

"Tell us."

"Oh, he was a priceless old bean, about six foot six, black as ebony, strong as Samson, and active as a cat . . . By Jove, he was a brave lad, too. All over the shop. What the best journalists call 'bore a charmed life,' too. O.C. storm-troops. After sprinting all round the ring, giving directions and heartening up his braves—not that they wanted it —he got off ten rounds from a damn great elephant-gun, and at the tenth, the whole congregation arose to its feet and we were for it."

"Rushed you, eh?"

"Somewhat."

"And this big black chap came for you, eh?"

"As it happened. I was just shooting frequent and free as well as looking all ways at once, as our little circle closed in, and suddenly this old lad was right on top of me as we all sprang to our feet to repel boarders . . . He'd got a thundering great curved sword, almost like the blade of a sickle set in a sword-handle, both edges sharp. As he landed off a rock in front of me he nearly reaped my head with his blooming sickle—horizontal cut, regular whistler. I ducked under it, and bayoneted him with my short rifle."

"What, had you a bayonet fixed?" asked the doctor.

"No, bayoneted him with a rifle, I said. Awful prod below the breast-bone, and as he doubled up I changed hands quick, slung the rifle up and conked him on the noddle . . . poor old lad . . . Hit him too hard, and he died. Brought the sword home with me as a souvenir of a good chap of whom I should have liked to see more . . . He ought to have been in the K.A.R. . . . Yes, it's a fine sword. They use them for hamstringing elephants. Do it on foot too. Curious weapon. No guard nor cross-piece. Just a small ebony handle . . . Yes— he died . . ."

"And then?" urged Major Fortescue.

"They wilted—what with our heavy steady fire, and seeing their C.-in-C. go down—drew off and stuck to the small-arm business for the rest of the day."

"All day?"

"Yes. They had to get to the water, you see."

"And that night?"

"Didn't do much. A bit weary, and their poor tongues hanging out. And when the sun rose upon the stricken field, lo, the two columns, of the K.A.R. were in position, having converged upon them with beautiful accuracy and timing."

"And then?"

"They got it in the neck."

"Old Scrub was a happy man that night, I'll bet," observed Major Fortescue.

"Well, that's just what he wasn't," said Colonel Mortimer. "What I was telling you, Tub," and again he eyed the Reverend Clarence Coxe with a look devoid of love or even esteem.

"He'd stopped a nasty one. Soft lead slug—in the left shoulder joint . . . And he had this awful trouble on his mind . . ."

"Yes, of course . . . sorry. The flow of your blooming eloquence had put Scrub's story clean out of my mind. Now tell us about that," requested Major Fortescue.

"Do," agreed John Desart. "And for once in your life, tell a tale properly."

"No, poor old Scrub's only happiness, once the fight was over, was because he knew he was going to die. I think perhaps he was happier than he'd been any night since I joined up with him . . . But he certainly wasn't *happy* . . . You remember what an awfully conscientious old bird he was at school, and how he used to take things to heart. Well, he hadn't changed a bit. Had the same old bouts of conscience and belly-ache. Cause and effect, I suppose, but I don't know which comes first—which is the *fons et origo mali.*"

"Most dyspeptics are conscientious," smiled the doctor.

"And most conscientious people are dyspeptic," observed Major Fortescue. "I am, myself. Sorry, Milly. Long John's fault."

"Well, that day I told you about, when I ran into Scrub, I saw that he'd got something pretty heavy on his mind. That down-in-the-mouth look he used to have, as a Prefect, at school, if he'd thought he'd given a juvenile criminal one too many, or beat him too hard . . . Only he'd got it really bad . . . Looked simply awful.

" 'What's up, Tat?' I said, when the camp had settled down for the night and we were having a pipe by the fire, that first night.

" 'Murder,' says he, in a deep sepulchral voice, and groans."

At the word *'murder,'* the Reverend Clarence Coxe sprang to his feet as though he had been stung, and his three friends, all looking uncomfortable, if not indeed somewhat guilty, avoided his eye.

" 'Well, they won't get you here, old son,' I said," continued Colonel Mortimer as though nothing had happened. " 'And the K.A.R. will neither arrest you, nor let you be arrested. So cheer up.'

" 'I'm not liable to arrest,' says Scrub. 'I wish I were. I wish I could be . . .' "

Colonel Mortimer, catching the doctor's eye, stopped in time to leave the words "tried and hanged" unuttered.

(Would Coxe never go?) . . . " 'If I didn't consider it a wrong and indecent thing to do, I'd shoot myself, ' " Scrub continued.

" 'Tell us, Scrub,' I said. 'Just in case I can be of any help.'

"He didn't tell me that night. Said he must think it over, some more . . . But he told me after the fight with the raiders. As I said, he knew he was dying, poor old chap . . ."

Colonel Mortimer fell silent, looked from the Doctor to Major Fortescue and glanced meaningly at the Reverend Clarence Coxe, who stood listening.

"Aren't you going for your usual morning walk, Coxe?" asked Major Fortescue.

"Yes," was the reply. "Time for my constitutional. Late, in fact. You've kept me here when I ought to have been taking the air, Milly," and the speaker giggled.

"Well, for God's sake take it now," begged Major Fortescue.

And, smiling wretchedly, the Reverend Clarence Coxe bade them be good boys and went away, followed by the gaze of three pairs of eyes whose glance bore no sign of affection, though much of pity and regret.

"*Now*, Milly, let's have it. What's this about poor dear old Scrub's death and the awful happening?" said John Desart, as with a sigh of relief, the three friends turned to each other again.

THE INNER BOOK

PART I

INTRODUCING COXE AND ALSO THE BOX

"Chi va piano va sano e va lontano."

PART I

Algernon Dashwood Coxe threw himself down on the large deep-cushioned settee in the sitting-room of Giovanna Blayton's flat, and shudderingly contemplated the box again, with unabated amazement and increasing horror. Also with a kind of protesting incredulity.

For, as he was reluctantly compelled to realize, it was the box of his dreadful dreams.

It was an Italian steel trunk, rather large, very strong indeed, and self-locking. Its two locks clicked and fastened themselves when the lid was closed. To open it, two different keys were required, though none was needed to fasten it.

No, there was no possible shadow of doubt. It was The Box. It was undeniably, though unbelievably, the authentic and identical box of his nightmares, those unspeakable agonies of mental torture that had so often caused him to keep himself awake, night after night, through very fear of sleep.

Algernon Dashwood Coxe, gazing at it with the uttermost repugnance and aversion, told himself that it was all that he was not.

For there was nothing Italianate, steely, large, or very strong, about Algernon, a pleasant-featured kindly-looking man with a clean-shaven whimsical mouth; large clear well-opened eyes of the kind termed dreamy, suggestive rather of thought than of action; a small delicately-formed nose; an even more delicate complexion; and a long and somewhat pointed chin.

Nor, indeed, did Algernon give the impression of being self-locking, or that two keys would be needed to open him.

Certainly Giovanna Blayton had never regarded him as having a locked mind.

On the contrary, she had considered him to be an extremely simple person, rather weak—indeed, where his mother was concerned, incredibly weak —kind, gentle, clever, honourable, utterly dear and unutterably lovable.

And here, in Giovanna's flat, sat Algernon Coxe, plunged in the depths of despair, his usually pleasant and kindly face a mask of misery and remorse, as he stared fascinated at the box.

Gazing until his eyes ached and the box seemed to dilate and contract, he realized that he must never see the thing again, and simultaneously knew that he must never let it out of his sight.

Out of his sight?

No, that was an exaggeration. He should have said out of his possession, out of his charge. He could place it in absolute safety under his hand, as it were, though not under his eye, and never see it again.

What to do with it? He must put it where he could feel that it was safe—absolutely safe.

And the best place would be in his own house. Only there would it be under his hand and yet not beneath his eye.

Yes. Somewhere in his own house. And in a room in which it would be not only safe, not only out of his sight, but where it would never be seen by anyone else.

The tank-room, of course.

That dark windowless room, right at the top of the house, which was half-filled by the great cistern, and in which was nothing else but a few derelict trunks, portmanteaux and anonymous rubbish.

Of course! Two or three old trunks. The box could stand up there in the darkest corner, with a trunk in front of it, another beside it, and one on top of it. He would lock the room and hide the key.

Safe, secret, forgotten. Yes, in course of time, forgotten surely.

Absolutely safe, for no one would ever enter the locked tank-room. Who should ever have any occasion to enter it? And even if they found the key and did so, what would they see by candle-light?

Two or three old trunks.

Of course, no one either would or could go into the tank-room.

Plumbers, if anything went wrong with the cistern, owing to burst water-pipes or other domestic catastrophe?

Well, he could go up with them and remain while they worked. He could keep his back to the corner in which lurked the box, and forget that it was there . . . forget what was in it.

There it would be absolutely safe.

Giovanna . . . Giovanna . . . Giovanna.

Algernon Coxe rose from the settee and, carefully avoiding the box, strode up and down the room, his pleasant and kindly face distorted, agonized, suggestive of that of a child about to cry.

Giovanna.

Oh God, how could he have done it?

Giovanna.

That vivid flower; that bright flame; that lovely thing, compact of colour, glow and glamour.

Giovanna.

Lying beside him on sun-kissed golden sands all a summer day.

Walking with him by enchanted seas . . . Dancing, light-prisoned in his arms, to elfin music

. . . Sitting beside him by fire-light on that—oh, Heaven—on that very settee.

And Algernon Coxe flung himself down on it, buried his face in it and wept.

For a time he lay thus, his body occasionally seized by a fit of trembling, occasionally shaken by an unconquerable emotion.

Suddenly he sprang to his feet, and stood listening.

Yes, someone was knocking at the front door of the flat. Should he answer the knock?

No. Let them hammer the door down. Yes, but suppose they did hammer the door down?

Another knock . . .

Oh, this was dreadful. They were knocking on his brain. He could bear it no longer.

As he crossed the room, Algernon Coxe wiped his eyes, ran his hands over his ruffled hair, pulled down his waistcoat, buttoned his coat, and endeavoured to compose his features.

The front door, immediately opposite that of the sitting-room, opened into a tiny hall. Standing in this he could see, vaguely outlined through the semi-opaque glass, the figure of a woman.

Who could she be? What could she want?

With a great effort of will, he forced himself to open the door and to appear normal.

"Oh, is Miss Blayton in, please?" said the woman.

Algernon Coxe stared at her.

A tall good-looking girl . . . Pity she dyed her hair . . . The moment one interfered with Nature's own colour-scheme one got a wrong effect . . . Nature's own tint was the only one that harmonized with the rest of the colouring . . . Not being Nature's, it obviously wasn't natural, and therefore didn't look natural . . . Giovanna would never dye her hair.

"Is Miss Blayton at home, please?" the girl repeated.

Rather a metallic voice . . . A pity people, especially women, did not understand the enormous importance of the voice. Nothing so revealing as the voice . . . Nothing so potent to affect the impression first produced . . . Giovanna's voice had been pure music.

"*Would* you kindly tell me whether Miss Blayton is at home, please?"

Algernon Coxe pulled himself together.

"Eh? Oh, yes, I beg your pardon. Giovanna is not here. No, she—er—has gone away—gone on a long journey."

"*Reely!*" said the girl. "That's strange! It was only two or three days ago that I saw her at the *Hors Concours*—the *Green Haddock*, you know— and she certainly said nothing about it to *me*."

"Well, she's gone," replied Algernon Coxe, and was aware that across his shoulder, the girl's eyes rested on the box.

"Where to?" asked the girl.

"I'm afraid I can't tell you," replied Algernon Coxe.

Still, eyeing the box, she observed, rather to herself than to him, as though musing aloud,

"H'm. You can't tell me? That might, or might not, be because you don't know."

Why did the girl wear a necklace of pearls which obviously had cost either five thousand pounds or five shillings? Giovanna never wore false pearls.

Why on earth did this quite pretty girl make that hideous scarlet mess beneath her nose. No human lips were ever that shape or that colour.

Fancy kissing that daub of paint. Revolting.

And probably she had a nice enough mouth of

her own. Not to be compared with Giovanna's, of course.

"Eh? I beg your pardon. I'm afraid I wasn't . ."

Good Heavens. The girl had turned on her heel and flounced off.

What had she been saying?

Closing the front door of the flat, Algernon Coxe returned to the sitting-room, shut the door behind him, and again flung himself down upon the settee.

Unconsciously, and following a bachelor habit, he put his feet up, and hastily, almost guiltily, put them down again when he realized he had put them on the box.

From the side-pocket of his coat he took his cigarette-case, opened it, saw, as he was about to take a cigarette, the photograph of Giovanna, hastily shut the case and returned it to his pocket.

She had given him that case at Polporth Cove in Cornwall. It was her first gift to him. She had taught him to smoke.

Polporth Cove . . .

Giovanna . . .

It had been on the very first day of his holiday in Cornwall that he had met Giovanna.

What a perfect morning, and what a perfect spot it had been.

Fit setting for what was to follow.

Glorious sunshine; a gentle breeze that brought the indescribable clean odours of sun-warmed seaweed; high cliffs surrounding the perfect tiny bay; great boulders studding a beach; immaculate yellow sand, which, twice each day, the maternal sea lovingly washed and adorned with shells and long ribbons of brightest green.

He had undressed behind a rock, put on his new bathing-suit and stepped forth to . . .

To encounter a mermaid?

Was it a mermaid?

No mermaid ever ran skipping to the sea in a scarlet bathing-suit, with a gay handkerchief round her head.

Nor did mermaids cry:

"Hullo, Merman! Come on!"

Nor did you seize their hands, run laughing into the water, and together plunge and swim.

A few minutes later, Algernon Dashwood Coxe and Giovanna Blayton were sitting on a ledge of rock, their feet dangling in the water, the sun warming their bodies, the glorious air exhilarating them; and each discovering the other.

"Down here for long?" asked Algernon Coxe.

"Live here," replied Giovanna, "except in winter. Daddy paints and I try to. He's James Augustus Blayton."

Algernon Coxe went through the motions of raising a non-existent hat and bowing low.

"By Jove," he said. "What a day!" and became subtle. "Does he bite much? I mean, do you think it would be possible for one to meet him? I mean, do you think you could present me to him?"

"Be easier if I knew your name," laughed the girl.

"Coxe. Algernon Dashwood Coxe. What's yours?"

"Same as Daddy's," the girl assured him.

"Then may I call you James Augustus?"

"I prefer Jo."

"Short for Joseph?" he asked.

"No, for Giovanna Giulia Francesca Bianca Orsola."

"Italian! . . . Wise to shorten it, I think. But I shall call you Giovanna. Jo isn't worthy. Giovanna is like you."

"How?"

"Absolutely lovely. Beautiful. Perfect."

"Tut. And again tut . . . How bold and bad is the Merman. You'll be a Forsaken Merman in a minute . . ."

"*Giovanna*," he murmured.

"Oh, *Algernon Dashwood*," she giggled, and then announced that she should call him Jimmy.

"Why?" he asked.

"Oh, Algernon Dashwood is too worthy," she replied. "Have you a fag in your pocket?"

"I haven't even a pocket, Giovanna. And what is a fag?"

"I have heard them called cigarettes by the precious," admitted Giovanna. "Are there any pockets in your clothes up there?"

"Lots."

"Cigarettes?"

"Alas! I don't smoke."

"Turn your face full toward me, Jimmy dear . . . In case I never see it again."

"You're going to see it again, all right, Giovanna."

"'Twill always interest me, James. That of a man who does not smoke! . . . Where did you contract the ghastly non-smoking vice?"

"Well, you see, my father doesn't, and of course my mother . . ."

"Hereditary, eh? Worst form of it, as no one knows better than I. Mother taught me to smoke . . . Heredity! . . . I inherited a terrible temper from Mother and a much worse one from Daddy. Sicilian temperament from one and artistic temperament from the other."

Algernon Coxe laughed.

"Sounds beautiful. Romantic . . . Black Hands . . . Camorra . . . Vendetta . . . Corsican Brothers . . ."

"It is comparatively rare for Sicilian girls to have Corsican brothers," murmured Giovanna. "I have none. Nor have I black hands."

"Brigands . . . Blood feuds . . . Vengeance . . . By Jove, you'd be a dangerous girl to offend! And anything you did, you'd do thoroughly. Are you very vengeful?"

"*Rather!* I should think so! Only yesterday I was annoyed, injured, insulted. I felt absolutely stung. But I had my revenge. I simply killed him. A wasp . . . Come on, let's swim. I'm tired of talking about me."

*　　*　　*　　*　　*

Algernon Coxe sprang to his feet, almost stumbling against the box. The telephone bell had brought him back to the present and to misery.

"Hullo!"

"Wracket, the butcher, speaking. For orders."

"For Miss Blayton? She's gone away."

"For long?"

"Yes, a long while."

"No use our ringing up for a week or two then."

"No. Nor for a month or two either . . ."

Algernon Coxe closed the conversation by hanging up the receiver.

Butcher!

He prowled aimlessly about the room, picking up and replacing small objects without seeing them.

He found himself staring at an enlarged snapshot of Giovanna and her father.

He had taken that photograph himself in the garden of Blayton's summer cottage at Polporth.

A bad man, Blayton, and over-prone to indulge and excuse, in the name of the Artistic Temperament, immorality, gross selfishness, drunkenness, laziness, and a sulky moodiness varied by spasms of uncontrolled temper.

There had been merry times in that household when "Mrs. Blayton" was alive!

Giulia Carlotta Bellinzoni *alias* Mrs. Blayton. Judging by his dozens of pictures of her, and also by Giovanna herself, she must have been a most lovely woman, or fiend.

Apparently she had been an unspoilt and untutored Sicilian peasant-girl when he first saw her and painted her in Italy among the alien vines.

Why couldn't the beast have left it at that, or left her alone?

He could hear Blayton's voice now.

"Gad! She was a lovely creature. Absolutely primitive. Pure Moorish, I should think. Proud as Lucifer. Uncivilized. Uneducated. Unspoilt. Absolute Nature. But I introduced her to Art.

"Had to make love to her though, before I could paint her as I wanted her. My word, I set a match to a powder-magazine when I did that. And it wasn't I who had to do the love-making then, by Jove!

"She was the perfect model! But of course you've seen her on canvas a score of times. But it wasn't only the face and figure. It was the fire. Mind you, I don't mind admitting that my *Sappho* is one of the great pictures of the world—and undoubtedly the greatest *Sappho*—because Giulia was my model. She *was* Sappho . . ."

And then the insufferable fellow would drain his glass, leer, and misquote:

> " 'Oh Isles of Greece, oh Isles of Greece,
> Where burning Sappho sighed and sung.' "

"Yes, I've been a lucky man, if there be such a thing as luck. Anyhow, the greatest painter of hot sun on honey sands by the wine-dark sea, the crumbling cliff, the cave, the grot, the very haunts of Sappho's self—met Sappho's own self and made her his model!

"Gad, those Sicilian days and nights! I took her to Taormina and painted her on the sands; in the sea; among the Greek and Roman ruins; on the cliff; everywhere. How she enriched my life, and how rich she made me . . .

"Then I took her to Naples and painted her in Pompeii as Aphrodite revisiting her ruined temple.

"But you know the picture, of course. America has it now . . . I must do another Aphrodite rising from the foam one of these days. I might do it down here . . . I would, if I still had Giulia . . . Must wait till Giovanna's a bit plumper . . .

"Gad, how those swine at Naples tried to *get* Giulia away from me . . . But not she! . . Some of them would have given her anything, but James Augustus Blayton had got her for nothing. She worshipped the ground I trod on. And she'd hold a pose until she fainted . . .

"I had her taught to read and write English, and she was quite useful looking after my accounts and things . . . Clever girl . . . Very useful. Hell of a temper though.

"And *love!* By Gad, she could love . . . Used to say, 'My lof for you—it is my life for me, yes,' and things like that. Used to make me laugh. Bit of a nuisance sometimes.

"Well! Poor Giulia! A shocking loss . . ."

Algernon Coxe had not cared to probe what might be an unhealed wound, nor to risk stirring poignant memories by asking Blayton how this irreparable loss had occurred. There had been no need.

"And simply never looked at another man," his host had continued. "No other man existed. I was her god, her idol, rather than her protector, her employer. And she—well—er, oh lovely, lovely, and as I say, the perfect model.

"A glorious, lithe, fierce panther of a girl, graceful, sinuous and strong in mind, body and soul—and a panther without a claw or a snarl, as far as *I* was concerned, though, as I say, she had the very devil's own temper.

"But, you know, the very cleverest of us don't know all there is to know about women.

"The lovely panther ceased to purr, and she produced the snarls and claws, all right, one day when I told her I didn't think I should paint her any more, or want her any longer.

"Some of the more jealous critics were beginning to hint that they and the public were getting a bit tired of James Augustus Blayton's eternal model as Sappho, Jael, Esther, Salome, Venus, The Gipsy, The Slave Girl, and so on.

"Gad, I shan't forget that morning. I'd just finished that glorious picture of her as Cleopatra; and when she really grasped that I was tired of her, both as a model and as a woman, she seized a palette-knife and tried to stab herself. Being rather annoyed, and thinking it was all bluff and bunkum, I just roared with laughter.

"It wasn't bluff though, b'gad. For after jabbing herself with the blunt palette-knife, she dashed off into the kitchen, just as she was.

"I called out to her to put her hat on, for modesty's sake, and cleaned my brushes.

"By and by, when I went into the kitchen, fully prepared to forgive her and tell her that, of course, I intended to do the handsome thing by her and the child, there she was with the carving-knife well shoved into her neck.

"Nice thing for me! Just think of it.

"I couldn't tell you what it cost me, one way and another, to prevent a scandal. She was game though, I will say . . . She told the doctor, an old friend of both of us—brought Giovanna into the world—that it was an accident . . . caught her foot and fell with the knife in her hand.

"Obvious lie.

"Everything possible was done for her, of course, and for a time it looked as though she'd pull through, but she developed pneumonia. Just didn't want to live, either. Luckily, Giovanna was at school, and I kept her there until she was old enough to be a companion to me . . .

"No . . . Poor Giovanna never had much of a mother, nor a mother's care and good influence . . . All she got from her was a devil of a temper and a queer box, an Italian contraption that Giulia set great store by. Said to have been specially made for a famous Sicilian brigand—a relation of hers . . . Lover, I dare say . . . I dunno . . . Always remained a regular peasant at heart, and kept her money and jewellery in the thing. Wouldn't trust any Bank, and actually made a will—leaving the box to Giovanna—on a leaf of the exercise-book in which she kept a record of the times I kissed her! Fact, she did!

" 'James kissed me so kindly last night,' sort of thing.

"Rummy woman . . . Would have faded early, though, and she was getting very boring . . ."

Yes, a nice man, Mr. James Augustus Blayton.

Poor little Giovanna! No wonder she had a queer temper and some queer ways.

What should she be but unbalanced and abnormal, this daughter of a primitive Sicilian peasant and such a man as Blayton, the artist?

What should she be but most utterly desirable, and lovable . . . most utterly detestable and hateful?

Hateful? Detestable?

Had he ever thought so before his mother had opened his eyes—had shown him how utterly hopelessly impossible was Giovanna?

Giovanna as wife of Algernon Dashwood Coxe!

It seemed that till then he had been able only to see her virtues. His mother was able only to see her vices.

Vices? Were cigarette-smoking, cocktail-drinking, card-playing for money, dancing at night-clubs, going to race-meetings, and such amusements of the modern girl, to be called *vices?*

Certainly it had given him just a faint sense of —not shock, not disillusionment—say surprise, incongruity, that first evening when he heard her say:

"Chuck me a fag, Daddy," saw her "field" it and light it from her pocket-lighter almost in one movement, and sit deeply inhaling tobacco-smoke with the greatest satisfaction and contentment.

He had hated to see the beastly smoke come curling like wraiths of poisonous serpents from her dainty nostrils; and when she lit cigarette after cigarette, each from the glowing stump of the last, he—well, he was sorry.

It seemed a desecration, a profanation.

Fancy the stench of nicotine from such a perfect mouth as that. Fancy love's first kiss tainted with that reek. And he noticed that the long and lovely fingers of that beautiful hand were yellow-stained.

But all that was forgotten, next morning, in the sheer distilled purity of the air and sunshine and sea, as they swam and rested and dived, and sat upon the warm sands.

The thought of that loveliness, which was but the setting for the jewel of Giovanna's own greater loveliness, made one's heart ache.

How nearly he had kissed her that second

morning as she mocked and teased him, and then put her hand in his.

Lovable?

Had any man loved any woman as he had loved Giovanna in those new-washed mornings of his new-found world?

And the day when he did kiss her, and, unbelievably, found his kiss returned, his embrace answered with an embrace as ardent as his own!

No, he must not think of that morning now. Better think of the evening and the hatefulness of James Augustus Blayton, who gave him the choice between a quarrel and a cocktail.

The man's contemptuous stare and insolent guffaw when he, Algernon Coxe, had simply and candidly told him that he had never tasted alcohol in his life.

"Good Gad! What do you drink then? *Milk?* What, aren't you *weaned* yet? Well . . . If you've never tasted alcohol yet, it's about time you did. For I can tell you one thing—no puling teetotaller is going to be the son-in-law of James Augustus Blayton . . . Are you a squittering vegetarian too?"

And Giovanna had laughed, in apparent sympathy and agreement with her father's point of view.

He had managed to swallow the beastly cocktail that Giovanna brought to him, bidding him drink to Happy Days, the brief toast unenthusiastically proposed by Blayton.

Yes, he had drunk one cocktail, and Giovanna had drunk three, and whether it was he or she who had been thereafter slightly intoxicated, he did not know.

What he did know, was that the evening was a disappointment, to say the least of it, and that he had almost hated the look of critical appraisement with which Giovanna had eyed him when he had absolutely, flatly, and finally, refused to drink wine, whisky or any other form of alcohol, at dinner.

What he had hated without qualification or any shadow of doubt, was Blayton's attitude.

"Do you propose to purchase your young man a piece of blue ribbon, or to teach him to take his liquor like a gentleman, Giovanna? . . . Or are you going to join the rot-gut swipes brigade yourself? . . . Believe me, my lad, the sooner you learn to smoke and drink like any other normal person, the sooner you'll have a chance of domestic peace. Domestic life's difficult enough, let me tell you, when there's a certain amount of compatibility of taste and temperament—but in a case like this . . . !" and so forth.

Giovanna had laughed, patted his shoulder, said:

"You mustn't take any notice of Daddy, dear," and, turning to her father, had added:

"Don't you worry. I'm going to take Jimmy in hand forthwith. His education is about to begin!"

No, of course, cocktail-drinking is not a vice. But three before her dinner, and then wine with dinner—a young girl . . . !

Nor is card-playing a vice, but did not the tiniest of clouds arise, a cloud no bigger than a man's hand, on that perfect morning of sun and sea, when, in reply to his loving question as to whether she were worried about anything, she had laughingly murmured something about having dropped more than she could afford, at poker, with some of Daddy's friends in Town.

"I'm afraid I haven't a poker face," she had laughed, and he had replied that he could bear that, in view of the fact that she had the very loveliest face that God had ever made to the better adorning and brightening of this world.

Nevertheless, he had experienced again that feeling of—not disillusion, not disappointment—perhaps discomfort, as he, probably quite errone-ously, visualized heavy-jowled, sensual-faced men round a green table, in a stifling room that stank of assorted alcohol and tobacco-smoke.

As he thought of the cigarette chain-smoking, of the cocktails, and of certain words and expres-sions that Giovanna had learned from her father and his friends, the cloud had spread and a chill had endeavoured to invade the happy warmth of Algernon's heart.

And then that other utterly beastly Cornish evening which he was practically accused of spoil-ing, when, after dinner, it was discovered not only that they could not make a four, but that thanks to his unbelievable ignorance of all card games, the party could not play cards at all.

At first they had affected to disbelieve him, had bade him come off it and cease pulling their legs. As soon as it dawned upon them that he was speaking the truth, they had become frankly in-sulting.

When, with one accord, they stared half-pityingly, half-accusingly, at Giovanna, she had frowned, smiled a little wryly, and remarked:

"Oh, well, it can't be helped! . . . We'll play roulette."

And when he had refused to play roulette for money, and she, shrugging her shoulders, had joined in the game—had the rift then appeared within the lute, the rift into which his mother had driven the shattering wedge?

But what, in God's name, after all, were these wretched trifles—a wisp of smoke; the compo-sition and flavour of a beverage; a method of passing an idle hour; a form of words—that they should sunder and break the hearts of a man and a woman?

Had he not so loved her that he loved the world and every man and woman in it, and God who made it?

And had not she—Heaven knew why—loved him as deeply and truly as he loved her?

Had she not, after crushing her lips to his, straining his body to hers, sworn that she would die if he ceased to love her?

Did she not refuse to say that she loved him because "love" was but a feeble and inadequate word for the worship, adoration, idolatry, the scorching passionate devotion, that filled her mind, body and soul, her days and nights, her life now and hereafter?

And yet, in spite of his love for her, her burning adoration of him, what else had they in common? Where would you find two people less suited than he and she for life together? . . . Their outlook on life, their tastes, standards, upbringing, heredity, environment.

Her home and his.

James Augustus Blayton and the Reverend Clarence Dashwood Coxe; and, Heaven above, her mother and *his*.

Yes, Miss Giulia Bellinzoni the artist's model and Mrs. Minerva Dashwood-Coxe of Melfont Parva Vicarage!

Incompatibility of temperament; utter unsuitability. Yes, but if Giovanna were incompatible and unsuitable for him, he was naturally and obviously as incompatible and unsuitable for Giovanna. God only knew what his attraction for her had ever been.

She had said it was his "differentness," his utter unlikeness to Boris Goudroff and the rest, the men, her father's friends, among whom she had grown up.

She had called him clean, straight, simple, dependable.

It had struck him as being really humorous—most painfully humorous—that anybody should call him, of all people, "dependable." It was just the very last thing in all the world that he was. Undeniably he was different from her other friends and, without being either a prig, a hypocrite, or a Pharisee, he could be quite content to remain different.

And yet it was this very "differentness" that had wrecked the barque of their happiness.

Could not he have made an attempt to become, outwardly at any rate, more like these people? Less rigid; less narrow; less—what? Let him be honest and say it—less everything that his parental training had made him.

Could not he have *made* himself a suitable mate for Giovanna? Was there, after all, any absolutely insurmountable obstacle in the path to their happiness?

There was. His mother.

Was there any real reason and cause why their wonderful love should have been poisoned and turned to hate?

His mother's interference.

§2

As long as he lived, he would never forget Giovanna's one and only visit to the Vicarage.

What a contrast between the two women, between her whom he worshipped and her whom he obeyed!

His mother, tall, stately, cool, the embodiment of British matronhood; a woman of great character; quiet, resolute, irresistible; a woman who throughout her life had never failed of her purpose; a woman who had had her way.

And what a way! Sane, sober, serious. The way of the true Christian woman ruling a Christian household—and parish—with dignity, power and strength.

Narrow and conventional?

Of course not, unless one would call a grand deep river conventional because, unlike the restless ever-rolling sea, it had banks and bonds and a fixed immutable course.

A great woman; a good woman; a wonderful mother who had taught him, watched him, and ruled him, from his birth; whom he had honoured, obeyed and *feared* from his birth.

And poor little Giovanna.

How the tiny child had seemed to shrink, to shrivel, overawed and overwhelmed by the mere majesty of his mother's presence.

Of course, it was but her nervous consciousness of this that had made her even more flippant than usual; had made her flippancy almost impudence and insolence—in his mother's eyes, at least.

How bewilderingly his fairy had become an imp; his lovely and original child had become a precocious brat; his "not impossible she" had become his mother's perfectly impossible daughter-in-law elect.

Why was it that Giovanna, the child of Nature by the sea in Cornwall, became a totally different Giovanna, only too evidently the child of James Augustus Blayton and Giulia Bellinzoni, by the side of his mother in Melfont Parva Vicarage?

Giovanna had seemed bent on making the very worst of herself, and certainly his mother had seemed bent on bringing out the worst that was in her.

When he had ventured afterwards to point this out to his mother, she had, with perfect truth, remarked that one could only bring out what was there.

Things had gone wrong from the first, beginning with his mother's long and searching look at Giovanna, which later the girl had referred to as a rude stare; and continuing with his mother's very naturally interested questioning, which Giovanna chose to consider an unwarrantable inquisition, and had answered accordingly.

For example, what on earth possessed Giovanna to reply:

"I was present at the wedding, but I really forget the name of the place," when Mrs. Dashwood-Coxe, in the course of conversation concerning a visit she had once paid to Sicily, enquired:

"I wonder whether your father and mother were married in that wonderful church at Monreale above Palermo? . . ."

That dreadful reply was really absolutely rude, and in the very worst taste, as well as being quite untrue, since, unfortunately, her father and mother had never been married at all.

And couldn't Giovanna have refrained from smoking, just for one week-end, instead of giving his mother cause to observe, with marked absence of criticism.

"Do you know, Miss Blayton, this is the very first time I have smelt tobacco-smoke in this drawing-room since I first entered the house, over twenty years ago."

"Do you dislike the smell?" asked Giovanna kindly.

"I loathe it," was the reply.

"All a matter of taste," observed Giovanna lightly. "I'll tell you a smell I simply can't bear—

that of a drawing-room that opens on to a damp and mouldy conservatory . . . Like a vault." And Giovanna artlessly eyed the door of the damp and mouldy conservatory on to which the drawing-room opened.

And again, when, at dinner, with a generous gesture in the direction of the jug of barley-water and the syphon of lemonade, the Reverend Clarence Coxe asked her what she would drink, need she have replied:

"May I have a whisky and soda, please?" and caused his mother to express regret at her unpreparedness, and to hope that Miss Blayton could manage without stimulants just for once.

His father, gazing at his plate, had maintained an eloquent silence.

Had his mother calmly and deliberately dissected Giovanna and laid her dismembered personality bare and quivering before him and his father?

Or had Giovanna deliberately, as he said, made the worst of herself?

Certainly she had made no effort to create a good impression.

Nor had his mother had it all her own way in the matter of unspoken criticism and unuttered comment.

What, for example, had Giovanna meant when she had asked with apparent innocence:

"Do you open many bazaars, Mrs. Dashwood-Coxe?"

Undoubtedly his mother had found more in the question than he himself had done, for she had afterwards alluded to it as a studied insult. When, with the intention of defending and exculpating the girl, he had asked Giovanna if she meant more than she said, and if so, what it was, Giovanna had smiled subtly, and replied:

"Dear Mamma opens a bazaar with massive and impressive dignity, every time she pours out tea . . . or sits down to table . . . or says 'How d'you do!' . . . When dear Mamma comes into the room one looks for the rest of the procession—and then one realizes that she is the procession, and the bazaar is now open."

Hurt and bewildered, he had asked Giovanna if she wished to insult his mother, and Giovanna, smiling her most Italian smile, had replied:

"No more than she wishes to insult me, Jimmy. Why should I, you funny boy?"

*   *   *   *   *

Algernon Coxe dreamed on: delved deeper and deeper into the past . . .

Could even the dullest masculine perception have failed to see that, in the drawing-room, after that painful dinner, the ladies were not peacefully enjoying the society each of the other?

With the utmost good breeding Mrs. Dash-wood-Coxe was now definitely probing into Gio-vanna's past, and Giovanna was answering her questions not only truthfully, but with truth adorned.

Fidgeting in his chair, while his silent father endlessly examined the toe of the boot of the crossed leg which he rhythmically swung up and down, he heard the question and answer which alternately angered him with each of the women whom he loved.

What possessed Giovanna to draw so sordid a picture of her past and present life, and so to stress the unorthodoxy and Bohemianism of her upbringing?

Only once had his father raised his eyes from that maddening swinging foot, to look him in the face, and that was when Giovanna confessed—nay boasted—that she had frequently sat for one or two of her father's more impecunious artist friends, notably as *The Syren of the Rocks*, in the picture of that name hung in the Royal Academy.

The Reverend Clarence Dashwood Coxe and Mrs. Dashwood-Coxe had seen that picture—before they had had time to look away.

The painful silence that followed the announcement was broken by the voice of Mrs. Dashwood-Coxe, a voice growing more and more hollow as the evening dragged out its interminable length.

"And who introduced my son to you, Miss Blayton?"

"Oh, we introduced ourselves—undressing on the beach at Polporth Cove—you know how one picks up a . . ."

A sinister sound interrupted the speaker. It was as though the Reverend Clarence had, by spontaneous combustion, exploded.

He rose from his chair, glanced at Giovanna, and, without a word, departed thence.

§3

That night, Algernon and Giovanna had had their first quarrel.

Miserably he had said good-night to his mother and Giovanna, and the gaze of his mother, as she coldly kissed his brow, had been one of pity mingled with reproach.

As he stood, pyjama-clad, gazing blankly at his reflection in the mirror, there had come a tapping, a gentle rapping, at his door. And to his surprise, Giovanna had entered. Giovanna, clad in a dressing-gown, of a type quite different from that worn by his mother.

Staring dumbly at this apparition, he heard it say:

"Jimmy dear, I want to go home after breakfast to-morrow, if I can't go before."

"What do you mean?"

"Well, what I really mean by those words, Jimmy, is that I want to go home after breakfast to-morrow, if I cannot go before."

"What do you suppose my mother will say?"

"That, dear Jimmy, I cannot tell you. But I know what she will think . . . And she'll open a bazaar, Jimmy. *Not* in aid of a fallen woman . . . She'll call a meeting, Jimmy. You'll be the meeting. And she'll take the chair. You'll take the carpet . . ."

And there was a little catch in Giovanna's voice as she went to put her arms round Jimmy's neck.

Jimmy drew back.

"Why do you want to behave as you have done? And what on earth do you want to come to my room for, now?" he blustered. "My mother is the best woman that ever lived."

"That's the trouble, Jimmy dear. I'm sure she is; quite the very best woman that ever lived—but I'm only honest. I have behaved naturally, and I have told the truth. Surely in such a house as this and in the presence of the best woman who ever lived, you wouldn't have me lie, or act a lie? And I have come to your room because you didn't come to mine and say 'Good-night' nicely and as though you loved me . . ."

"Come to your bedroom, Giovanna!"

"Yes, Jimmy dear. I am equally wicked and you equally good in a drawing-room, or a morning-room, or a library, or a bed-room or a dining-room, or a bath-room, or a box-room, or a conservatory, or up on the roof, Jimmy, with our feet in the water-cistern."

"Don't talk nonsense, Giovanna; and for Heaven's sake try to please my mother, and give her a better impression of yourself."

"A false impression, Jimmy?"

"Er—no—of course not. A good impression."

"But I'm not good, Jimmy. I smoke and drink and swear and gamble and sit for poor artists who can't afford a model; and I come into a good young man's room at night; and I'm absolutely honest and truthful and never to my knowledge did a mean or nasty thing in my life—and I'm not a damned superior, pompous, righteous, censorious, self-appointed judge of other people; an unchristian and . . ."

"Do you mean to say my mother is that?" he interrupted furiously.

"Oh, Jimmy! How could you say such a dreadful thing? . . ."

And then they had really quarrelled, and Algernon Coxe had been astonished at himself, astounded at the cruel and bitter things that he had heard himself saying.

At the height and the worst of this horrible business, Giovanna had burst into tears and sobbed:

"Oh, Jimmy, Jimmy, forgive me, forgive me, darling. It is absolutely my fault . . . *all* my fault," and again attempted to fling her arms about his neck.

For the second time the angry Algernon drew back, and held out an opposing hand.

Giovanna, flushing deeply, gave him a look that he remembered to this day, remembered now, sitting on this settee, and, turning from him, went quickly from the room.

Ere she closed the door, he heard his mother's voice and hers! They were speaking angrily—his mother's voice under better control than Giovanna's. Turning off the light he scrambled guiltily into bed—as from childhood he had done a thousand times at the sound of his mother's approach.

The door opened.

"You're not *in bed*, Algernon, are you?"

"Er—yes, Mother."

"*Oh! . . .*"

There had been no opposition to Giovanna's catching the first train after breakfast, a meal at which Mr. and Mrs. Dashwood-Coxe had found themselves unable to be present.

§4

But this would not do. He couldn't sit there all day long, staring at the box and raking up the past—on the very eve of his wedding-day.

How was he to get this great box away?

The best thing would be to go out and get a taxi, and simply give the man a hand with it down the stairs.

When they got to the house, he could suggest that, for a small consideration, the taxi-man should give him a hand with it, right up to the tank-room.

That would be the best way; in fact, the only way; unless he sent a carrier or a railway-van or something, to fetch and deliver it.

No, that would mean delay and risk.

Algernon Coxe rose to his feet, idly fingered an empty wine-glass that stood on the table, looked irresolutely about the room, picked up his hat, stick and gloves, and left the flat, to return, a few minutes later, with a burly gentleman arrayed, *inter alia*, in three overcoats and a yachting cap, the cracked peak of which obscured his left eye.

Between them, the two men carried the box

down to the taxi, and Algernon Coxe stood by and watched, with some anxiety and occasional adjurations, while the taxi-man secured it upon the luggage-rack behind the cab.

"Safe, Guv'nor? Ar! Not 'arf it ain't. That there box wouldn't fall off, not if I was to drive me keb till me whiskers grew long enough to 'ide the steerin' wheel from 'uman sight . . . Ar! Not till they fair got into the machinery. No, sir, you'll fall through the bottom of this 'ere keb before that there box falls off the back of it."

The taxi-man may, or may not, have been an optimist, but Algernon Coxe found the box still in position when he sprang from the cab, as it came to a standstill outside his house; and a minute later, he and the driver were carrying it up the four flights of stairs that ended at the small landing from which opened the tank-room door.

" 'Tain't 'arf 'eavy, Guv'nor," observed the taxi-man, whose sedentary life and profound belief in the nourishing, sustaining and curative properties of beer, tended to unfit him for strenuous effort.

"Well over a nundredweight, I should sye. What is it? Cloves?"

"*Cloves?*" panted Algernon.

"Yus, cloves what you wear. They comes 'eavy."

"Very heavy," agreed Algernon Coxe.

"Not as I minds what I does for a gent," continued the optimist, as Algernon Coxe opened the tank-room door.

"A gent what *is* a gent," he added, as his employer, having gently lowered his end of the box, felt in his pockets for money.

Completely satisfied of the perfect gentility of his fare, the taxi-man proclaimed and acknowledged it, while, with painful and stertorous strugglings, he made his devious and intricate way to the obscure hiding-place for its monetary evidence and expression—apparently a pocket on the inner side of his penultimate undervest.

Ere the front door clanged behind his helper, Algernon Coxe had dragged the box to the furthermost corner of this dark attic and hidden it as he had planned.

Nor was it until he had completed his task to his satisfaction, locked the tank-room door, pocketed the key, retired to his den, and wearily flung himself down in a big arm-chair, that he realized, with a feeling of the deepest annoyance and regret, that he had forgotten to lock the outer door of Giovanna's flat.

Anyone could walk in, merely by turning the handle of the front door.

He must go back.

It was with something of a shock that he found the door of the flat open, and heard sounds of movement in the kitchen.

As he stood, hesitant, in the sitting-room, a stout red-faced woman, clean and tidy, entered, determined of mien and somewhat aggressive.

"Who are you?" he asked.

"The same to you, sir, and many of them," was the reply. "Walking in without knock nor ring, nor by your leave . . . I do for Miss Blayton . . .

"Did you wish to see her?" she continued, without pausing for breath. "She's not at home. And surprised I was to find her out, and when I say find her out, I mean to find her not at home, when I come as usual to cook her dinner and to do for her . . .

"Can I give 'er any messidge, or are you well-beknownst and take a seat till she comes? I reckernize your face now, sir, from the photygrarf, or seeing you 'ere, but not knowing when or where Miss Blayton has gone, she not having said anything either way, I couldn't tell you, I'm shaw . . ."

"Miss Blayton has gone away," interrupted Algernon Coxe as the woman paused for breath.

"Ho? Meaning 'ow, sir?"

"Just what I say. She's gone away. But look here, do you mean to say you didn't know? . . . Didn't she tell you? . . . I've come to lock the place up . . . She's gone."

The woman stared open-eyed and open-mouthed, for the moment silenced by the shock of this announcement.

"My Gawd!" she whispered, and without apology, sat suddenly down upon a chair that stood conveniently close.

" 'Er box! . . . I see it was gone, d'reckly I went into 'er bedroom. I said to meself I says, 'Ullo,' I says, ''er trunk's gone,' and then thinks no more about it, bein' a bit be'ind-'and, and Brunt—'e's me 'usband—in 'ospital, and a dratted nuisance that *would* go and get run over just as 'e's got a job o' work, or more like a job o' work got 'im and 'e couldn't dodge it, as I told 'im to 'is face . . . And 'ow long's she gone for, sir? . . . Bit sudden, wasn't it?"

"Very sudden."

"And well you might say it, and me 'ere till eight o'clock last night and never a word said . . . Bit sudden and a bit secret, if you arst me."

"I didn't ask you," observed Algernon Coxe, "and I've come to lock the place up. Will you shut all the windows? Miss Blayton won't be back for—oh, months, perhaps."

The woman rose to her feet, dusted with her apron the seat of the chair on which she had sat, and heaved a deep sigh.

"Light come and light go," she muttered, "and

all the same a nundred years 'ence, please Gawd. Me old man out of one job and me out of another. Thank 'Eaven 'e's in 'ospital and best place for 'im. 'Arf a mind to git run over meself . . .

"And what about my money, sir?" she asked, turning suddenly upon Algernon Coxe. "Yerse, and me notice, too. Week's money come Saturday, and a week's money in loo o' notice, too, and fair's fair, and no gettin' away from it, law or no law."

"How much would that come to?" he asked.

"Two pun . . . hrrrmmph—ahem—er—*ten*, sir," was the reply.

"Two pounds ten? Right . . . Here you are," replied Algernon Coxe. "And here's another pound, since it is, as you say, rather sudden."

" 'Andsome said, sir, and 'andsome done, as the sayin' is, and no doubt Miss Blayton'll drop me a card when she comes back. As nice a young lady as ever I did for, though a rare one to flare out, if cause there was—or perhaps wasn't. . . . Yerse! Her and me was very congenital, as they say. . . . Very given to 'avin' 'er own way, and full o' maggots."

"*What?*" ejaculated Algernon Coxe.

"Full o' maggots, I said, sir. Always got some maggot in 'er 'ead, and nothink won't do, but what she must do it. Like this runnin' off now, and never an 'int to me by word o' mouth or scrape o' pen.

"Well, there it is—and then again it mayn't be, and me not knowin' you from Adam, not reely, nor Eve neither for the matter o' that, nor yet Pinch-Me as they say, and what proof? . . Ar! I s'pose you got the key?"

"Yes, I have the key and a limited stock of patience. Would you kindly close the windows and shut the doors and then I'll lock the front door," replied Algernon Coxe, producing a key.

A few minutes later Mrs. Brunt, still talking, preceded Algernon Coxe down the stairs that led to the front door of the flat vacated, for ever, by Giovanna Blayton.

THE INNER BOOK

PART II

THE LIFE AND ADVENTURES OF ALGERNON DASHWOOD COXE

PART II

CHAPTER I

On a day a dozen years previous to that bright May morning upon which he had welcomed his old friend Colonel "Milly" Mortimer on his return from his three years' big-game shooting-trip in Africa, Doctor John Desart bowed an aged roué from his consulting-room and, closing the door behind him, observed:

"Suffering from old brandy and the delusion that he suffers from delusions."

He then seated himself at his desk and glanced at the day's list lying thereon.

"Mrs. Dashwood-Coxe," he read, having crossed off the name of the aged roué.

Doctor Desart glanced at his desk clock.

"Good!" he soliloquized, "ahead of time. One need be when one has to cope with Minerva Dashwood-Coxe. What's the good of her bringing that poor boy to me again? . . . Expects me to undo, with one interview and a bottle of medicine, the harm she's been doing all day and every day, since he was born."

He touched the bell beside his desk and for the three minutes that elapsed ere the door opened and a smart parlourmaid announced: "Mrs. Dashwood-Coxe," John Desart looked back into the past.

Minerva . . . Minerva Coxe whom poor Scrub Tattinger had loved so passionately and devotedly . . . What a woman! . . Poor old Clarence Coxe. How she had taken him by the scruff of the neck and married him almost the very day he'd got the Melfont Parva living!

Serve old Clarence Coxe right, for being so weak. He had never even pretended to love her. As a boy he had undoubtedly hated her, especially when she boxed his ears and rode rough-shod over him, in all things. Poor old Poodle!

Jolly lucky escape for Scrub Tattinger, if he could only realize it.

Extraordinary woman . . . Really and truly conscientious—a walking conscience, in fact.

And yet she could do the most incredible things and reconcile her conscience with them.

Probably she did only what was right because whatever she did was right because she did it.

Any other woman, treating a man as Minerva had treated Scrub Tattinger, would be a shameless heartless jilt, a calculating self-seeking cheat.

But not so Minerva Coxe. She had been engaged to poor old Scrub when he transferred from his British Regiment to the King's African Rifles— as she had always known he was going to do.

She had promised to "wait for him," and Scrub was going to get a good station, and they were going to be married the next year, or, with luck, even sooner, if Scrub could afford it.

And then suddenly Minerva had "experienced a Call."

Also she had searched her heart and found that she had made a terrible mistake. Her love was really for the dear companion of her childhood's days, she said, the cousin with whom she had grown up; and the promptings, nay the imperious demands, of her heart were irresistibly strengthened by the dictates of her conscience which bade her remain, as it were, in the Church —a Vicar's daughter, a Vicar's wife.

Curiously enough, this had coincided with

Clarence's astonishing good luck, or rather his father's and his uncle's astonishing good "pull" influence—and Clarence's appointment to one of the best incumbencies in England. Lovely old Vicarage, lovely old village—and lovely old stipend.

And Minerva had done her duty.

Instead of wasting upon the desert air of Africa her great natural and trained gifts for parochial work, she had chosen the less spectacular, far more useful, and far more comfortable career of an English Vicar's wife.

Poor old Scrub had taken it hard, and Mortimer, in a furiously indignant letter to his old friend Long John, had said the woman ought to be scragged, as she'd spoilt the life of a fine soldier; and added that he hoped she'd spoil the life of a rotten parson.

Minerva Coxe! Now Mrs. Clarence Dashwood-Coxe, always spelt with a hyphen . . .

And this poor pitiable boy, Algernon, whose life she most certainly was spoiling without any doubt whatsoever, whether she spoilt Clarence's or not.

Minerva—Goddess of Wisdom! . . .

A tall woman, scarcely a head shorter than tall "Long John" Desart himself, a woman of imperious mien, erect carriage and commanding appearance, entered and advanced with outstretched hand and kindly, if slightly condescending, smile.

"Good-morning, Doctor," she said. "I've brought this tiresome boy of mine to see you again," and turning, indicated the somewhat shrinking, overshadowed and deprecatory figure of an overgrown weedy and pimply schoolboy of some fifteen years, upon whose weak and pleasant face was a look of puzzled consternation.

The boy's face lit up, beamed with intelligence and pleasure, seemed indeed to come to life, or at any rate to awaken, as Doctor Desart smiled down at him and shook hands.

"Well, Algernon, old chap," said the doctor. "What have you been up to now?"

Algernon Coxe looked up at the face of this wise man who was so understanding, so discerning and sympathetic.

It was one of the faces he liked, with its kindly twinkling eyes, humorous clean-shaven mouth, long sharp nose and big cheek-bones. One could talk to this chap and feel that one was understood.

Golly! What a lucky fellow his son must be . . . Fancy having a father like him. How immeasurably different from one's own bewhiskered stuffy and unfriendly father. Rotten job being the son of the Reverend Clarence Coxe, a parson who could no more speak without preaching than he could preach without speaking.

Wouldn't it be nice if Mother would go away and let him talk to the doctor himself. But, just the opposite would happen, as before.

Of course Mother knew best. And he couldn't possibly have come here, all across London from the hotel, without her.

"How are you getting on at school?" added Doctor Desart, dropping the boy's hand, and taking note of many things.

"Left," replied the boy, uttering his first word since entering the room. Hopeless to attempt to say more in Mother's presence.

"Ah, that's partly what I've come about," said Mrs. Dashwood-Coxe. "You will remember that when I came to see you before, Doctor, I had just withdrawn him from the Preparatory School to which I had sent him a few weeks earlier."

"Stag-beetles," murmured Doctor Desart cryptically, a far-away look in his eyes, and a sternly repressed smile twitching at his lips.

"Algernon, go and wait outside the door," said Mrs. Dashwood-Coxe.

"Perhaps you can find your way back to the waiting-room, old chap. Do you think you can?" asked the doctor.

"I don't know. I think . . . I . . . er . . ."

"Wait outside the door, Algernon," repeated Mrs. Coxe, and Algernon departed thence.

"Yes, exactly," continued the lady, the door being safely shut between Algernon and the horrid topic.

"I see you do remember, Doctor. I paid a surprise visit to that school, and found Algernon with a group of other boys watching two stag-beetles fight. I was horrified to think that a child of mine should join in such a brutal pastime. But what were my feelings when Algernon, whom till then I had considered not only a nice-minded, but an absolutely pure-minded child, calmly observed:

" 'They're just as jealous as they can stick. That's why they fight. They're stag-beetles and they both want the same doe-beetle. We've put her in the other box . . .'

"I took him back home with me that very day and I . . ."

"I remember," interrupted Doctor Desart, a little sadly. "And now?"

"And now I've had to take him away from Bull-borough," continued Mrs. Dashwood-Coxe.

"What is it this time, I wonder," mused the doctor, as he eyed his visitor. "Jealous Elephants?"

"I had a letter from him, and I went straight down and fetched him away by the next train."

"Got into trouble, had he?" asked the doctor, as Mrs. Dashwood-Coxe paused, and apparently pondered the depravity of modern youth.

"Not so much into trouble as into danger . . . Bad company. Pitch and defilement. He was being laughed at for being, I thank God, more innocent than his companions. They were all making fun of him and baiting him because he simply could not understand why they shrieked with laughter at a disgusting little poem, a Limerick I believe they call it, that one of them—the foul-minded little wretch—recited to them in the dormitory."

"Wonder which one that was," pondered the doctor.

"Was it a good . . . I mean, was it very bad?" he asked.

"I am not a judge of Limericks," replied Mrs. Dashwood-Coxe coldly. "But this was sufficiently coarse, vulgar and objectionable to make it my clear duty to go at once to the school. I interviewed both the House Master and the Head Master and brought Algernon home with me the same day."

"Did you give them the name of the boy who contributed the Limerick?"

"Certainly. And of those who shrieked with delighted comprehension and who proceeded to enlighten Algernon . . . *Enlighten* indeed. A nice school!"

"H'm! . . How did the authorities take it?" asked the doctor.

"To tell you the truth, doctor, I was surprised, pained and I may say shocked, at their attitude . . . That of the House Master was positively one of 'Boys will get hold of these things. The young beggars have a very acute if perverted sense of humour. This is really rather funny—and fairly harmless,' and to my utter consternation and surprise, the man actually laughed heartily as he read the poem in the letter I had had from Algernon. And if you can believe it, the Head Master said the boy had probably got it direct from his father, a well-known General whose name I will not mention, though it would serve him right."

"You haven't got the Limerick, I suppose?" asked Doctor Desart, not hopefully, of course.

"I destroyed it the moment I had shown it to the School authorities."

"And so you brought Algernon home again. And now you've brought him to me. What's wrong?"

"He just isn't well, Doctor. His appetite is extremely poor; he sleeps very badly and wakes up screaming and sweating from what he describes as most awful nightmares. Then he's so—I'm afraid that . . . lazy, is the plain fact of the matter. Absolutely lazy . . . idle . . . languid . . . I can't get him to take the slightest interest in anything, nor to do anything . . . He simply moons about, and whatever I set him to do, he does thoroughly badly, carelessly, and without any interest, or taking the slightest pains."

Doctor Desart studied the speaker's face, and his expression and nod were non-committal.

"And he is absolutely without initiative. He simply cannot and will not do a single thing unless I'm behind him or take him by the hand. . . . And he tells me lies!"

The doctor's face and nod changed, and distinctly committed him to acquiescence.

"Quite so," he said. "You spoke of nightmares. Does he dream much in the ordinary way, do you know?"

"I really couldn't say, Doctor. He doesn't tell me more than he can help. One has to dig things out of him . . . Oh yes, I remember, he certainly had one extremely nasty dream . . . In addition to his regular nightmare, that is."

"*Regular* nightmare?" commented Doctor Desart with raised eyebrows. "That's interesting and

very important. We'll come to that afterwards.
What was the nasty dream?"

"Oh, horrid. It upset him dreadfully. Made him
ill for days. I could see there was something on his
mind, and got it out of him. He actually dreamt
that he had killed me."

Doctor Desart inclined his head.

"Yes," he said, almost as though he had been
expecting something of the sort.

"Poor boy. A dreadful dream. He thought that I
was drinking deeply of a great cup of wine—he
described it as being like the chalice his father
uses—and he crept up behind me and poured a
deadly poison into it. I drank again and fell dead
at his feet. No wonder he's ill. Enough to make
him. In my opinion . . ."

Doctor Desart interrupted the torrent of Mrs.
Dashwood-Coxe's eloquence.

"The boy is not ill because he dreamed it," he
said. "He dreamed it because he's ill."

"And what do you suppose is the matter with
him, Doctor?"

"And now about this recurrent nightmare,"
continued the doctor, without answering the question. "What is it?"

"Oh, perfectly absurd! A lot of nonsense," expostulated Mrs. Dashwood-Coxe.

"Dreams are apt to be that," smiled the doctor.
"Or at any rate to appear so, until we understand
their symbolism. What does he dream?"

"Oh, something about a box," was the reply.
"He shrieks and screams and wakes up crying out
'The Box! The Box!' and when I go to him, all he
can say is that The Box is there again. Perfectly
absurd! As I tell him, suppose the box *is* there, it
can't do him any harm. The box won't bite him."

Doctor Desart sighed.

"He isn't in the box, I suppose," he asked . . .

"Claustrophobia?"

"No. He has never said so."

"Does he know what's in the box?"

"I really haven't asked him, Doctor. Is it of any importance?"

"It may be," was the reply. "Of the utmost vital importance."

"Oh well, you'd better question him about it yourself, hadn't you?"

"I'm going to," said Doctor Desart. "How long has he been having this particular box-nightmare?"

"Oh, all his life. Since he was old enough to know what a box is. Always been a most tiresome child at night . . . Bad dreams . . . Crying set-outs . . . Idiotic fancies . . . Afraid of the dark . . ."

"And he's getting no better, eh?" enquired the doctor.

"He's getting worse. Now what do you suppose is the matter with him?"

"Several things," replied the doctor, as he tapped his blotter with a pencil, and stared at the woman before him.

"Several things, arising out of one thing. In the first place he has a bad neurosis of some kind. He suffers from an inferiority-complex and he is a born and bred introvert. And last, but very far from least, he has quite definitely what is nowadays termed a mother-complex. You may remember that I diagnosed it and warned you when you brought him to me before."

Mrs. Dashwood-Coxe smiled tolerantly.

"Oh, that funny fashionable rubbish," she said. "You still use the new-fangled jargon, then? I suppose doctors, like other people, have to keep abreast of the fads of the times."

And Mrs. Dashwood-Coxe laughed quite kindly.

"Yes, yes," meekly admitted Doctor John

Desart, world-famed neurologist. "Still using the new-fangled jargon that Æsculapius used two or three thousand years ago. Same funny fashionable rubbish of γνωθη σεαυτον that appealed to him and Socrates and Plato and those other would-be-up-to-date chatterboxes . . ."

The doctor fell silent.

"Has he any pets?" he asked suddenly.

"No."

"Ever asked to be allowed to keep some?"

"Oh, he's always bothering me to let him have a dog."

"Oh, splendid," said John Desart quickly. "Get him one at once. Best thing in the world for . . ."

"I hate dogs," interrupted Mrs. Dashwood-Coxe. "Detest them. Nasty smelly things. I wouldn't have one about the house for anything. Fleas; bones; scratches on the doors and furniture. Lot of bother about feeding. Certainly not."

"Very useful in a country place . . . for protection . . . tramps . . . burglars . . ."

"Thank you, Doctor. I'm certainly competent to deal with either tramps or burglars if, and when, they come to my house."

And undoubtedly she was, John Desart admitted to himself, if somewhat grudgingly.

"Outdoors?" he suggested. "A kennel in the stable-yard. The dog never need come into the house. Let Algernon take it for a long run every day. Be his salvation. Self-expression: something to care for, and protect and love."

"I will not have a dog about the place, Doctor Desart. . . . And hasn't Algernon a mother to love?"

With this point John Desart did not deal.

"Well, now," he said. "What about a cat? Suppose he had a dear little fluffy kitten of his very own. He could lavish all his . . ."

"I object to cats as much as to dogs," was the cold reply. "A great nuisance. Smell; bring others; hideous noises in the night. No."

"A pair of rabbits, then?"

"Most certainly not."

"Well, one rabbit, then," suggested the doctor patiently, averting a mental eye from stag-beetles.

Mrs. Dashwood-Coxe declined to pursue the subject of pets, and indicated the fact by ignoring the doctor's further remarks on the subject.

"That's that, then," he said at length, and again paused as speculatively he eyed Minerva Coxe.

"Well now, what are we to do about it?" he continued. "You bring the boy to me. I tell you what's wrong and, as before, you've neither faith in my diagnosis nor intention of taking my advice. Merely a waste of my time and your money."

"What is your advice, Doctor?" the lady humoured him.

"Let him come into my nursing-home for a month or two and I'll guarantee that he makes a new adjustment to life . . . I'll promise to give him a new attitude . . . new values . . ."

Mrs. Dashwood-Coxe made a movement of her right hand as though brushing away cobwebs or flicking crumbs from the lap of her mind.

"What can you do there that I cannot do at home?" she asked with sweet reasonableness.

"Much," was the terse reply.

"As, for example?"

"In the first place keep him away from home and mother, and . . ."

"My dear Doctor Desart, would you kindly tell me what's wrong with his home and mother that he should be saved from them. Am I a particularly bad specimen of a mother?"

"Yes, about as bad a specimen as you'd find in a day's march," John Desart assured her, "for this boy, in his present condition, that is. It's exactly what he's suffering from. That and nothing else. A severe and prolonged attack of mother. An attack that has lasted for about fifteen years, save for those two brief periods of convalescence at school.

"And I tell you, Mrs. Dashwood-Coxe, it's death and damnation. It's red ruin, mind, body and soul, for that boy, if you won't let him have a mind of his own, a life of his own, a will of his own."

Mrs. Dashwood-Coxe rose to her feet. She had heard more than enough of the man's nonsense and of his rash and foolish words.

"Thank you, Doctor," she said. "I shall certainly not send him to your, or anybody else's, nursing-home."

"Well then, for God's sake, or rather for the boy's sake, send him back to school, if they'll take him.

"And if they won't, see if you can get him into another. Failing that, send him to Oxford or Cambridge at the very earliest date at which they'll take him, and, meanwhile, send him away from home somewhere . . . Anywhere . . . Let him visit . . . Send him for a voyage . . . Let him travel with a tutor, provided he's the right sort of person. I could get you the very man."

"Thank you, Doctor. Pray do not trouble further. Algernon will remain at home. I rather fancy that a boy's mother may possibly be as good for him as a hired stranger . . . I may perhaps consider the question of Oxford or Cambridge a few years hence. Good-morning."

"Well, if you bring him to me again before that time comes, I'll refrain from saying 'I told you so,' Mrs. Dashwood-Coxe."

"Can't you give him some medicine or suggest something sensible—er—I mean—er—something different?"

"Medicine's no earthly good," replied the doctor, "and I have suggested not merely something sensible, but the only thing sensible. And—might I have a few words with Algernon alone?"

"Alone, behind my back, do you mean? Whatever for?"

"Oh, young people often 'open up' better when they are not in the parental presence."

" 'Open up,' " said Mrs. Dashwood-Coxe, with mingled distaste and surprise. "I should be exceedingly sorry to think that Algernon had anything to say to you that I could not hear."

"No, no, of course he hasn't, and I assure you I've nothing to say to Algernon, either, that is unfitted for your ears."

"Very well then, Doctor, have him in and talk to him, by all means, in my presence."

John Desart sighed.

"I should like to ask him about that nightmare, anyhow," he said, and, going to the door of his consulting-room, he opened it and smilingly beckoned to the boy who stood without, dutifully awaiting the commands of his mother.

"Come and have a chat with me, Son," said the doctor; and taking young Algernon by the arm, he conducted him to the desk, seated himself, and, placing the boy with his back to his mother, strove to put him at his ease and get *en rapport*—in the circumstances an extremely difficult task.

A long chain of questions and answers followed, and soon the boy's face brightened, and a clear glimpse could be seen of what he might have been in different environment and with a normal up-bringing. John Desart sighed as he contemplated the changing face, and saw eager interest and intelligence take the place of apathy, dullness and hopeless misery.

"Never mind, old chap," he said at length. "We'll

soon get you all right, and make you want to play all the games there are, and read all the jolly books ever written . . . First of all, we're going to stop these wretched dreams that bother you . . . I want you to tell me all about this nightmare that you often get."

Algernon looked up quickly, fear in his eyes, and the doctor was aware of a mental shudder as the boy instinctively recoiled.

"*The Box!*" he whispered.

"Yes, tell me all about it."

"There's nothing to tell," was the reply. "It's simply there . . . And I nearly die of fright."

"Yes, but why? What happens?"

"Nothing. Nothing at all. It's simply there. It's awful."

"Are you afraid you're going to be shut up in it?"

"Oh, no . . . No . . ."

"Do you know what's in it?"

"No."

"Is it open or shut?"

"Oh, shut. Always shut. Tight."

"In the dream, are you afraid that it's going to spring open?"

"Oh, no . . . No . . ."

"I see. It's just a shut box that stays shut, and you don't know what's in it . . . But you're terrified by it."

"Terrified to death. I nearly die of funk. It's awful."

"There you are, Doctor," broke in Mrs. Dashwood-Coxe impatiently. "Just as I said. All a lot of nonsense. Perfectly absurd. A great boy like that . . ."

"How big is the box?" asked the doctor.

"Oh, big enough to get into."

"But you never dream that you've got to get

into it?"

"Oh, no . . . No."

"Have you ever seen a box like it?"

"Oh, no . . . No."

"I expect you have, if you could only remember.

"Now think. Have you ever been playing with other children—when you were a kid, I mean—and got into a big coffer? One of those things you sometimes see in the hall or in a corridor . . . big old boxes they keep for garden cushions and rugs, and that sort of thing."

"Oh, no . . . No."

"Never got into a big box in your life?"

"Never. Oh, no, never. No."

"Sure? Absolutely certain?"

"Perfectly certain."

"Well now, look here. You know that poem 'Ginevra'?"

The boy shook his head.

"Oh, come! I'm sure you must have read it or heard the story."

"No."

"Oh, but surely. About the girl, you know."

"What did she do, Sir?"

"Oh, think . . . You know what she did. Ginevra and the old oak chest."

"No. What did she do?"

"You really don't know . . . H'm . . . It isn't that then. I thought perhaps you'd read about Ginevra and got her on your young mind without knowing it.

"Well now, look here, old chap, believe me, that's a perfectly harmless ordinary box and contains nothing more terrible than pots of raspberry-jam and tins of sardines, potted-meat, biscuits . . . It's a tuck-box!"

And Doctor Desart laughingly clapped the boy upon the shoulder and gently shook him.

Algernon Coxe was not amused.

"Now, look here," continued the doctor. "When you go home I want you to write down all you know about this box. Just describe it to me and, if you can, draw a sketch of it. Then write at the bottom:

" *'It's an ordinary common box and couldn't possibly harm me or anybody else.'* Will you do that?"

"No," was the uncompromising reply. "I couldn't. Besides, it would be a lie . . . It *can* harm me, and it will . . . It will be the death of me."

"Algernon!" said his mother sharply. "You'll do exactly what Doctor Desart tells you."

"Yes, Mother," replied the boy and sighed heavily as Mrs. Dashwood-Coxe rose to conclude this unsatisfactory interview.

§2

On the following day Algernon Coxe fought with beasts at Ephesus, or rather at Melfont Parva; beasts incarnate and carnate; and, against all probability and his own expectation, displayed courage, moral and physical.

For he sat himself down and, albeit trembling and bathed in a cold perspiration, wrote a full account of his recurrent nightmare, and added a crude drawing of the box.

"Dear Doctor Desart," he wrote,—

"I'm awfully sorry. Mother says I am an abject coward, as well as a fool, and she's quite right, but it's awful when the box comes and my heart quite stops and then thumps like a fellow kicking on your door, and I tremble and sweat and want to shriek and scream the house down and to bunk for my life. But I can't make a sound and can't move. It is like I am bound hand and foot and gagged. And then there is a strangling round my neck, and then I fall and fall and fall for ever, and I rather think I faint.

"There isn't much I can tell you about the box, but it's always the same, and I should know it at once if I saw it anywhere. I jolly well hope I don't, though, for I think I should disgrace myself again in some way. Fall down dead, or run round yelling.

"It's a big box, like a trunk. With a heavy lid. It is made of steel and very strong, and it has two key-holes. It is big enough for me to get into, but, as I told you, I do not do so. It is always shut and locked. I do not try to open it, but I know it is locked. I have not the least idea what is in it, but it is something very terrible.

"You say it is a tuck-box and there is raspberry jam and sardines in it, but I am sorry to seem rude, Doctor, but it isn't. It is something too terrible for words. One thing I do know is that somehow it'll kill me. It is dreadful even to talk or write about it, and I feel ill and have that choking feeling round my neck while I do so.

"Here is the drawing. It is not good, as I can't draw much, but it shows you the shape and pre-portions.

"I am sorry I am such a fool and a coward, Doctor. Do try and cure me of it, if you can, but it is no good.

"Yours most respectfully,
"ALGERNON COXE."

Having completed his very painful task, the boy took the letter to his mother for approval or, more probably, for disapproval.

"Yes," said Mrs. Dashwood-Coxe when she had read this human document. "Yes, a nice letter for *my* son to have to write, isn't it? And can't you spell 'proportions' correctly yet? A nice confession of weakness and cowardice. Anyone would think you were some seven-year-old neurotic cottage-child, with neither education nor self-control . . . some wretched epileptic of tainted stock. Aren't you ashamed of yourself?"

"Yes, Mother, I am," truthfully answered Algernon Coxe, and departed to post his letter, deeply thankful that he had not been made to write it all again.

Turning from the pillar-box, near which stood a small knot of loutish youths, Algernon consulted his watch, and for a minute, gazing absent-mindedly at its face, hung in doubt.

What should he do? It was rotten at home and there was nothing to do. It was rotten out-of-doors and there was nowhere to go.

Returning his watch to his waistcoat pocket and thrusting his hands into those of his trousers, he slouched down the High Street of Melfont Parva, his eyes on the ground.

Dissatisfied, discontented, moody and miserable, he wandered aimlessly on, and found himself out in the open country. He climbed a stile, crossed a couple of fields, stood a while on the old Norman bridge that spans the Melfont Avon, and stared unseeingly at the deep and swirling water below.

Yes, if a chap jumped in there one night with a brick in each hand and a couple more in the side-pockets of his coat, his troubles would soon be over. No more nightmares and naggings and pi-jaws then. And he'd give no more trouble to his mother, either. But on the other hand, the doing of it would give her a frightful lot of trouble. There would be an inquest, and it would be in all the papers.

Absolutely rotten for his mother. A very cowardly thing to do, too.

But then, of course, he was a coward. His mother had always told him so, and there could be no doubt about it.

But it would also be a very ungentlemanly thing to do, and he hoped he was fairly gentlemanly, albeit a weakling and a coward.

One ought to face one's trouble and stick it out, not pity one's wretched self and try to dodge it by suicide.

And anyhow he was probably even too big a coward to do such a cowardly thing as commit suicide. He'd funk jumping into the water when it came to it, so that was that.

Perhaps he'd have the jolly luck to die young. If so, he'd cease being a trouble and a nuisance and an anxiety to his mother, without any of the beastliness of suicide.

Would she be sorry if he died? Why should anybody be sorry to see the last of such a mouldy specimen as himself? She'd be a bit sorry because that would be only decent, and because his mother was everything that was decent. Best mother anybody ever had, and really quite kind if only one gave her a chance by not being such a fool and a coward and giving her so much trouble.

She wouldn't punish him and pi-jaw him so much if she didn't love him and want to do the best for him.

All this nagging when you did wrong, and scolding and beating and being sent to your room on bread-and-water was all done for your good, and serve you jolly well right. As his mother so often said, 'Spare the rod and spoil the child', and it was because she loved him that she didn't intend him to be spoilt for the want of a few beatings —or a jolly lot of beatings, either.

Solomon said it too, and he was the wisest man

who ever lived. Golly, he must have been a busy man if he beat all his children himself.

Yes, it all proved how much his mother loved him.

But why did his father hate him so? From the first minute that he'd been old enough to know anything at all, he had known that his father really hated him. And undoubtedly he used to beat him because he enjoyed doing it, and not because he wanted to do him any good.

His father certainly beat him because he hated him, just as his mother beat him because she loved him.

He knew that perfectly well, because his father used to beat him when he was quite a tiny child— before he was old enough to do anything wrong. Father would do it when mother was away from home—but she had seen the marks one day, and asked him about it. He had tremblingly confessed that he had received a beating, and, curiously enough, his mother had not been angry with him.

She had sent him out into the garden and gone straight to father's study, and through the window of that room the sound of her voice had proceeded for quite a long time. It had almost sounded as though she were angry with father.

And he had never beaten him again from that day to this—but he had hated him all the more.

Of this Algernon was perfectly certain. One could always tell when people hated one—even from the way they looked at one, as well as from their manner, words and acts.

He could never remember his father speaking kindly to him, or ever giving him a caress. He did not believe that his father had ever kissed him. That was one good thing, anyhow.

Algernon yawned and stretched himself. Better

mouch home. Mother would want to know exactly where he'd been and what he'd been doing; and he couldn't very well say he'd been standing on the Avon Bridge and staring at the water. She'd want to know what he had been thinking about while he did so. It would be a bit difficult to explain.

As he turned from the parapet of the bridge to go back to the field-path, he saw approaching three of the youths who had been loafing at the corner when he posted his letter. Not village boys, but lads who strolled over from Bardsall on Saturdays and Sundays and very frequently on Mondays, too, especially in the season of bird-nesting, ripe-fruit-picking and other occasions when sleepy Melfont Parva offered attractions superior to those of the rather horrible town in which they worked, or evaded work.

Of a more sophisticated class, these, than the genuine country boys, inclined when in groups and bands to be a little truculent and dangerous, and known to local respectable youth as The Blags, The Cads, or That Lot from Bardsall; and many minor and some major offences were rightly or wrongly laid at their door.

Of this particular trio, one, the leader, was a rough-looking ragged fellow, some seventeen years of age; the others, smaller, dirtier and possibly more ragged, appeared to be a year or so younger.

"Please can you tell me the time?" whined the leader, halting in the narrow path immediately in front of Algernon, his two satellites closing in on either side.

"With pleasure," smiled the delighted Algernon courteously, and proudly drew from his waistcoat pocket the watch that his mother had given him on his recent birthday.

Algernon had looked forward with most pleasurable anticipation to the receipt of this long-promised watch. It would be lovely to possess such a thing, such a recognized attribute of adolescence, if not manhood.

It would be almost as good as having a pet, a thing that, alas, he had never been allowed to have, in spite of unconquerable yearnings. (Oh, if he could only have a dog, a cat, a rabbit, a white rat, or even a mouse of his very own.)

Because a watch is not like a dead thing. It goes, if it doesn't move about. If it can't talk, it can tell you the time, and you can undoubtedly listen to it. He could almost make a companion of a watch.

Of course, it was not to be compared with a dog or any nice warm responsive animal, but, as he might have known would be the case, things had not turned out as he expected. He had indeed received the watch on his birthday—a very nice silver one, with his name engraved on it, and the name of his mother, as well as a text and an adjuration.

Yes, on the cover was the inscription,

"To A. D. Coxe
From his Mother, Minerva Dashwood-Coxe."

Beneath this was an All-Seeing Eye and the text,

"Thou God Seest Me,"

the whole concluding with the urgent words, engraved in capital letters,

"TIME FLIES! BE PUNCTUAL!"

And after breakfast on this solemn day, the

watch had been presented to him; presented, indeed, rather than given, by his mother, with many well-chosen words. A brief kindly and helpful—sermon almost.

Algernon had stood with hand outstretched to receive the watch, and Mrs. Dashwood-Coxe had sat with hand outstretched holding the watch while she spoke. And ere all was said Algernon, clumsy, foolish and unworthy fellow, had allowed his tiring arm to sink to his side.

The gist of the little Address was that this Watch should be for ever a Token to him and also a kind of moral Goad as well as a concrete and constant Reminder that duty must be promptly done; that Punctuality is the Courtesy of Kings; and that Time, like an ever-rolling stream, bears all its sons away, it being notorious that they die forgotten, as a dream dies at the opening day.

And this to Algernon had seemed as a grain of comfort.

He would, his mother hoped, the Watch helping, never be late for a meal or indeed any other appointment; never miss a train; never be late in going to bed or rising from it.

He would, she hoped, wind it each night at nine o'clock, neither earlier nor later—each night for the next quarter of a century at least, perhaps half a century, or even more, for the life of a good watch carefully used and properly treated was almost endless.

By the time he had received the thing, had failed to express his gratitude with appropriate eloquence, facility and grace, and had retired with it to his bedroom, it was but a cold-faced unfriendly monitor instead of the beloved pet and companion that he had intended it to be. Ere long it became a thing of which to take such care that it was an anxiety and a nuisance—a ticking conscience; and, rather than friend, a treacherous foe that prevented all use of the former valuable excuse.

"I'm awfully sorry I'm late, Mother, but I didn't know the time."

Still it was very gratifying when, as did occasionally happen, people asked the time, and one had the pleasure and the pride of giving them the required information.

So Algernon readily drew forth his watch as the ragged youth whined,

"Please can you tell me the time?"

And the ragged youth promptly snatched it—the chain faithfully following, as it tore through the buttonhole of his waistcoat.

As he did so, the two smaller boys sprang upon Algernon, each swiftly seizing him by an arm.

Surprised almost beyond words, shocked to the depths of his soul at such rudeness, violence, treachery and ungentlemanly conduct, Algernon gasped in amazement.

What on earth should he do?

What would his mother have him do?

He knew perfectly well that she would never have him quarrel or fight. Why, it was one of the very bad sins, not nearly as terrible as that vague but deadly and awful thing called Sex, but still very bad.

Why, it was what Jesus Christ insisted on almost more strongly than anything.

Love one another. If a man smite you on the right cheek . . . Blessed are the meek . . . Love thy neighbour as thyself . . . Do unto others . . .

Yes, but this beastly boy had got his mother's watch, the watch he had been exhorted to cherish as the apple of his eye, to guard as his most precious and cherished possession, and to wind every night for fifty years.

What would his mother say if he let a boy come along and simply take it away from him?

Yes, and what would his mother say if, roughly and rudely and vulgarly, he fought and quarrelled and struggled with a Blag?

Think of his father's son doing such a thing.

Nice occupation for the son of Melfont Parva Vicarage.

"I say, you can't do that," he cried, as these thoughts flashed through his mind. "You can't take my . . ."

"Can't I? Watch me," was the reply, as the youth thrust his booty into his trousers' pocket.

"I say, that's mine."

"You're a liar. It's mine now," was the prompt debateable answer.

"It's stealing," expostulated Algernon. "You must give it back to me at once."

"*Shee*-urrupp," growled the boy. "Shut yer mouth before I do it for yer.

" 'Old 'im while I do a bunk," he bade his satellites, "and don' let 'im go till I'm on the road . . .

"On the road to Brickwell," he added, to make it clear to Algernon that it was not in Bardsall that he would be found by anyone so foolish as to pursue the matter further.

And turning, he shuffled off at a quick jog-trot.

Algernon's watch was going rapidly out of Algernon's life, and the realization promptly decided him as to the relative enormities of the sins of fighting and of being unfaithful to a trust. Either contained the sin of disobedience, so better to sin and regain the watch than to sin by losing it.

This point clearly grasped, Algernon most promptly lapsed from grace, and the gentle youth suffered a sea change into something wild and strange.

Undoubtedly there was some ancestral fighting strain in Algernon which even his mother's careful and excellent upbringing had failed to eradicate; for a strange Old Adam swiftly and suddenly arose within him from beneath *layer* upon layer of blanketing apathy, sluggishness, meek mildness and the more Christian virtues. His eyes blazed, his teeth clenched, and with a curiously swift plunge he flung himself forward between his restraining captors, violently withdrawing, as he did so, an arm from the clutch of each.

Algernon was free, furious, and futile, for, alas, he knew not the first elementary thing about self-defence, and even less about offence.

With tears of rage, indignation and excitement gathering in his eyes, he swung his open hand, somewhat in the manner of one who bowls a cricket ball, at the impish and ferocious face of one of the boys. To their great and equal and mutual surprise, a resounding slap was heard—and felt—and the boy staggered back, a hurt look upon his unpleasing face.

"Cor!" he gasped, in indignation, "Cop 'im, 'Ennery," and applied a ragged coat-sleeve to his nose as he dodged behind Algernon.

And then, by all the standards of well-bred and well-taught boys, Algernon fell from grace, for as 'Ennery protruded a curling tongue and two bony fists, Algernon kicked him well and truly in the stomach, as the other boy's hand grasped him by the collar from behind.

In extenuation, but not condonement, of this horrid deed, it may be pointed out that Algernon was extremely well bred in the belief that every sort and kind of fighting is sinful, beastly, utterly anathema, and that, as has been said, he was not well taught, nor taught at all, in the art of self-defence, much less in the honourable and sporting niceties of its practice.

Nay, he had been taught that even self-defence was wrong and that, smitten, rather than resent it, one should invite another smite.

And these facts did not so much cramp his style as bring it about that he had no style at all, but became a perfectly natural fighting animal, fighting perfectly naturally with what means and weapons Nature had provided. Hence the inexcusable kick.

'Ennery doubled up in horrid pain.

"Kill 'im, Arfur," he groaned as Algernon, swinging instantly about, instinctively clenched his right fist.

In this instance, instinct appeared inferior to reason or training, for Algernon's thumb was inside his closed fingers instead of reposing upon their knuckles.

Flinging his left arm as though in deep affection about his assailant's neck, Algernon, albeit receiving blows, bore the boy clumsily and heavily to the ground, and as he lay partly across him, thumped his nose repeatedly and most painfully with the under-side of his fist, exactly as though he was stabbing him with a dagger.

It was as if something long pent-up in Algernon now burst forth, and had its dreadful way; for, leaping up from the definitely defeated Arfur, he rushed at 'Ennery, flung this time both his arms about him, thrust his left leg behind him, tripped him, fell with him, arose, stamped upon 'Ennery's stomach, and then, safe from hampering pursuit, turned and flew, like arrow from the bow or bird from the twig, and swiftly chased the retreating bandit-in-chief.

"Hi!" he called as he ran panting. "Stop. Give me back my watch," and sped the faster.

The principal villain of the piece, glancing round at his pursuer, made swift appreciation of the situation; for here, untrammelled, came the owner, or late owner, of the watch; and there, in the further field, his faithless or crushed custodians supine sat.

What could have happened?

Bribery and corruption, or rude violence?

Henry and Arthur he would in either case eviscerate; but first he must perform the like office upon this yelping pup that dared vociferously assail him. That noisy mouth must be shut, or there'd be a reg'ler hue and cry.

Wheeling about, he mercifully, or astutely, gave the rash and foolish pursuer a chance.

"Shut it," he cried. " 'Op it. Bung off. I don't want nothink to do with you."

"Give me back my watch," shouted Algernon, slowing up.

"I 'aven't got yer watch. Why, I ain't even got one o' me own. You never 'ad a watch, and I ain't seen a watch, not since next week. Go away, I tell yer."

"Give me my watch," repeated Algernon, halting a few feet from the villain.

"I'll give yer a bash on the jaw," offered the villain. "That do instead?"

"Give me my watch," reiterated Algernon.

"Look 'ere, you're making yourself a nuisance. 'Oo d'yer think you're insultin'? You bleedin' little . . . You bung off, or I'll do yer in, ugly."

And with astonishing singleness of purpose, as well as of conversational topic, Algernon again cried,

"Give me back my watch."

It was too much; for neither by temperament nor training was the villain a patient person, nor one who suffered fools gladly.

With a quiet and sinister

"'*Ave* it, then," that had no allusion to the watch, he advanced upon Algernon, his right hand clenched and his left clutching.

Swiftly Algernon retreated.

He had not the slightest intention of doing battle, honourable or otherwise, with this big, grim, and dangerous-looking lout; but he was going to stick to him and follow him, yea, unto the world's end or the gates of Hell, and until he either died or recovered his mother's watch. . . .

The youth rushed and Algernon fled.

The youth resumed his swift passage to the road and Algernon pursued.

The youth turned about and, with a swift dash, almost captured his mosquito adversary. Algernon just escaped, saved principally by the villain's anxiety to quit the scene of his villainy and profitably to dispose of the proceeds thereof.

Arrived at the stile leading into the road, the thief climbed on to it, and from that vantage point hallooed and beckoned to his followers, now without marked speed or enthusiasm approaching along the foot-path.

Algernon hovered near, and Henry and Arthur drew nearer still.

In haste, yet hanging in doubt as to the reliability of his satellites the principal villain bawled instructions, bidding them seize, hamper, delay, intimidate or destroy Algernon what time he, their leader, fled to safety and emolument.

Great rewards should follow their obedience and success, hideous punishment their disobedience or failure.

Courageous, vengeful, and restored, Henry and Arthur converged upon Algernon as their leader leapt from the stile and ran down the road in the direction of distant Bardsall.

After him dashed Algernon, hotly pursued by Henry and Arthur.

"Cop 'old of 'im, 'Ennery," bawled Arthur, as the latter almost caught Algernon at the stile.

Over the obstacle went Algernon, and sprinted in the wake of the chief bandit, out-distancing his own pursuers as he ran.

Suddenly and swiftly the bandit wheeled about and, ripping out an ugly oath, rushed back at Algernon, now trapped between high-hedged steep banks, foes before him and behind.

The speed of his running brought Algernon almost into the arms of his chief opponent, and it was all he could do to check himself, halt, and back away from the big lout's quick *volte-face* and onslaught.

Back away he did, only to stumble and fall, half-sitting, on a low pile of stones left by road-menders; but instantly he arose, his right hand held back and downward, and, as he gained his balance, the hand flew forward violently.

Straight and true, a great stone crashed heavily into the face of the on-coming thief, who halted, sagged at the knees, and fell without a sound.

Henry and Arthur, as one man, came to a sudden standstill, stared in horror and fled incontinent.

From the trousers' pocket of his fallen foe, Algernon retrieved his watch and departed thence, his purpose achieved.

Algernon Coxe had dared to be like Daniel, had dared to stand alone, had dared to have a purpose firm and dared to make it known.

Positively, Algernon Coxe had had a purpose and had achieved it.

But what had he done?

He, Algernon Coxe, his mother's son, had been guilty of the enormity, the vulgarity, the degradation, the unchristian sin—of fighting.

He who knew perfectly well that not only in aggression but even in self-defence it is wrong to fight.

But really this had not been in self-defence. It had been in defence of his mother's watch.

Had it been any piece of personal and private property such as his pocket-knife, he would have let it go. Possibly his mother would take that into consideration when, in explanation of his torn collar and bruised face and cut lip, he made confession.

*   *   *   *   *

"What! What is this? What have you been doing, Algernon?" cried Mrs. Dashwood-Coxe on catching sight of what she could hardly believe to be her son.

"Fighting, Mother. I . . ."

"*What* did you say? Fighting? With whom?"

"Some Blags from Bardsall or somewhere. They . . ."

"Go at once to your room. I will come to you in an hour's time."

Mrs. Dashwood-Coxe always allowed an hour to elapse—whether that she might not strike in anger, or that the culprit might have an hour's anticipation of what he was about to receive, is not known.

Punctually at the expiration of an hour, as the cold unsympathetic face of his watch informed him, Algernon was punished with a conscientious care and skill, about which Doctor John Desart, a prejudiced person, might have found something almost sadistic. Nor did the plain facts with which he first tried to appease his mother avail him any more than the lies he assayed when the truth, as usual, failed to save him.

CHAPTER II

For the next three or four years, Algernon Dashwood Coxe, an only child, enjoyed, or endured, the concentrated blessings of his strong mother's watchful care and guidance.

If ever a youth was sheltered from wickedness and shielded from harm, it was he.

Of him, as of her husband, Mrs. Dashwood-Coxe could, and did, say that he had never caused her a moment's anxiety. This statement was true in a sense—the sense in which she used it, but it was not the truth, the whole truth and nothing but the truth, for although Algernon never intentionally caused her any anxiety, she did occasionally experience anxious moments when contemplating his appearance, health and habits.

His appearance certainly left something to be desired.

He held himself badly, slouched and shuffled.

He was prone to considerable untidiness as to hair, collar, tie and dress generally.

Though distinctly good-looking, he was apt to be pimply, pasty, dull-eyed and pale.

Only on those occasions when it occurred to his mother to suggest it, did he shave, with the result that his face was generally in a condition of callow fluffiness that added nothing to his attractiveness.

His health was really not very bad and was certainly not at all good. He complained, or rather he did not complain, of the violent headaches by which he was racked, and he complained but little of the frequent attacks of bilious misery which at this period darkened his life.

But so careful, probing and watchful a mother as his, could not fail at times to see that he was ill.

As to his habits, it may at once be stated that he had no bad ones and it may be added that he had few that were good.

He had not the habit of regular work, of regular exercise, or of regular reading. He had no hobby, no pursuit, no interest.

He mooned about, bored and depressed, and, generally speaking, did literally nothing when not accompanying his mother upon her various social, parochial, and domestic duties.

With her he drove about, making calls, visiting sick and aged parishioners, "paying the books" weekly at the shops, and with her he pottered harmlessly in the church, the churchyard and the Vicarage garden.

He made no friends of his own age, partly through lack of inclination, partly for want of opportunity, and largely because his mother had doubts of the suitability of most young people of his own sex, and graver doubts of the suitability of young people of the other.

One queer friend he had—an aged maiden lady, an aunt of his father's who, though not really insane, entertained the bitterest hatred of Mrs. Dashwood-Coxe.

Moreover she was a person of such deep cunning that she contrived to conceal this regrettable and indeed lamentable emotion with such success that its object was the last person to suspect it; and whenever Miss Smithers invited Algernon to visit her, as she frequently did, Mrs. Dashwood-Coxe was quite pleased for him to go.

What possible harm could come of his sojourning beneath the roof of an ancient gentlewoman, own aunt to the Rector of Melfont Parva, and who had in her service no hand-maiden whose years were less than sixty and whose morals less than perfect?

Between Algernon and this remarkable and eccentric old woman there were real affection and considerable understanding; and it came as a surprise to none when, at her death at the age of eighty-nine, she left him the house in London at which he had been so frequent and welcome a visitor, the whole of its contents, including the said aged and incorruptible hand-maidens, and her funded property producing the comfortable income of a little over a couple of thousand pounds a year.

It is distressing to have to relate that, when the Will was read, Miss Smithers' reputation suffered some eclipse (in the Melfont Parva Vicarage), by reason of the fact that she had caused therein to be set down the words:

"And I do hope that my said beloved great-nephew Algernon will with this money among other things purchase himself a pair of breeches and wear them like a man for up to this present day of writing the breeches in that house are worn by the wrong person whereof I name no names."

It was perhaps fortunate for Algernon that there were no other heirs presumptive to arise and contest the Will.

For, as the shocked Mrs. Dashwood-Coxe observed, the testator was obviously of unsound mind—a mind almost as unsound as was her counsel and advice.

It was perhaps as well for Mrs. Dashwood-Coxe's peace of mind that she did not fully grasp the seriousness of Miss Smithers' madness, and never heard a conversation that took place between her and Algernon on the occasion of their last meeting.

"And does your mother still take a cold bath every morning, a warm one before dinner, and a hot one when going to bed?"

"I think so, Auntie."

"And wash her hands about six times every hour?"

"I think so, Auntie."

"H'm. Quite like Lady Macbeth, eh? . . . Never addresses you as 'Spot' by any chance?"

"Good gracious, no, Auntie."

"Does she ever get any letters from Africa?"

"I don't know, Auntie."

"I thought perhaps you collect foreign stamps. But of course you wouldn't be allowed to waste your time so foolishly. . . . You neither waste nor spend time, do you, Algernon? Do you save time?"

"No, Auntie."

"Well, I hope to God I shall live till you grow up, and that I have my health and strength to show you how to waste and spend it both. . . ."

However, Miss Smithers' pious hope was frustrated, and she died without doing anything worse than leave Algernon her money.

§2

But this happened after Algernon's term at Oxford. Literally a term.

As Doctor Desart had anticipated, Mrs. Dashwood-Coxe brought her son to him again; and again the doctor gave her good advice, and forbore to say, "I told you so."

"Let's see. How old is he now?" mused John Desart, eyeing the sickly youth and pitying him profoundly.

"Eighteen and a half."

"Well then, I prescribe Oxford or Cambridge. Now look here, Mrs. Dashwood-Coxe. I am in a position to help you here, for, as it happens, Angus Taggart is a very old friend and patient of mine. . . . Will overwork himself. . . . As you may know, he's a prominent and influential Tutor at St. Just's.

"Now I'll write to him and pull a string or two. Let the boy go in October—and *let him alone*. Let him paddle his own canoe now. He's quite old enough to do so, and quite competent. I'll ask Angus Taggart to keep a special eye on him, and I'll tell the boy to go straight to him, at once, if he gets into any kind of trouble or difficulty. But he won't."

"But his health, Doctor, his health," interrupted the sceptical Mrs. Dashwood-Coxe.

"Exactly. Just the very reason why I want you to send him there," continued John Desart patiently. "He wants rousing, taking out of himself, waking up. You can't keep him tied to your apron-strings till he's bald, you know. He's got to go under his own power some day; steer his own boat. . . . What's to happen to him when you die?"

"I leave that in God's hands," replied the Vicar's wife, and there was a note of reproof in her voice as she eyed the doctor.

"Then why not leave a little more in God's hands?" enquired the doctor hardily. "Send the boy to Oxford, and leave his whole career in God's hands. God is just as competent while you're alive, you know. You need not wait until your death to 'leave him in God's hands.' Surely, with all the parental care, nurture and admonition that the boy's had, he can be trusted out of your sight?"

"It is not a case of trusting Algernon out of my sight, Doctor Desart. It is merely that I adhere to the not unreasonable belief that a boy's best friend is his mother, and that she is the person best fitted to understand him, to guide him . . ."

"But not to prevent him in all his doings, in the modern sense of 'prevent,' Mrs. Dashwood-Coxe," interrupted the doctor.

Algernon's mother rose to her feet, filled once again with a sense of annoyance and frustration.

However, Algernon should go to St. Just's, and then nobody could say she had not done every-thing possible, and taken Doctor Desart's advice.

A thoroughly irritating, aggravating and tar-some man, but the best doctor in Harley Street, or in England for the matter of that, and recom-mended to her by the Bishop himself. And was at school with Clarence.

"May I have a word with Algernon alone?" smiled John Desart wryly, as he touched his bell.

"I really fail to see any necessity for your talk-ing with Algernon behind my back, Doctor Desart. You have seen him and sounded him thoroughly, in my presence, and if there is anything more you want to say to him, send for him by all means. But really . . ."

"Good-bye, good-bye, my dear lady. And if you don't keep away from Oxford while Algernon's there, don't bring him to me any more. There'll be no need to do so, if you'll leave him alone."

*   *   *   *   *

Algernon Coxe went to Oxford and his mother—albeit she took him there, established him com-fortably according to her ideas, interviewed his Tutor, the Bursar, the Dean, the Warden, his scout and the hall-porter, and gave each of these personages and persons the benefit of her views and opinions—left him alone for a whole term.

This proved to be the happiest period, save one, of Algernon's life.

On the day that he came down from Oxford at

the end of term, his mother submitted him to a close inquisition, applying her relatively mild and gentle Third Degree, and decided, there and then, that to Oxford Algernon would not return.

For he admitted that young men there talked quite frequently and freely about—*Sex!*

It must undoubtedly have been a severe blow to the young man, and, not for the first time in his life, he came to the conclusion that he was a fool to tell his mother absolutely everything, and that it was about time he asserted himself and opposed his will to hers.

And, not for the first time in his life, Algernon discovered that it was vain to attempt to hide anything whatsoever from his mother, and puerile folly to suppose that he possessed a will that could for one moment withstand that of his strong-minded, determined and powerful mother.

As well might a frog oppose a steamroller.

And once more, Algernon settled down at home and, with the advantage of his father's library, made a desultory study of Theology in pursuance of a somewhat nebulous plan dependent on his mother's some day discovering a Theological College of suitable type and status. It is, of course, obvious and axiomatic, as she said, that human conduct, and indeed human nature, manifest themselves so differently in a Theological College, and render these latter so superior in every way to the mere lay and secular colleges of Oxford, Cambridge, and other Universities.

When not lying on his bed and reading theological or other works of fact and fiction, Algernon mooned miserably about the house and garden; accompanied his mother about her parochial and social occasions; and developed, at any rate, a praiseworthy deftness and aplomb in the drawing-room.

Few young laymen, indeed few curates, could compete with him in the nice conduct of a clouded cup or cake; in the swinging of a four-tiered cake-stand; in the carrying of three, or even four empty cups for replenishment; in the keeping of the ball of conversation rolling exactly where it should, along the lines indicated by his mother.

Yet, the more expert and efficient he became, and the more his mother praised him and pro-claimed her intention of making him her curate, the more did something good and fine in Algernon bid him rise up and hate himself, his life and his . . . Good God, no—not *his mother!*

No, no . . . a thousand times, no.

Not his mother, but his dependence on his mother, his position in this his home as his mother's tame house-trained cat.

And at length, just in time, and, as Algernon himself realized, only just in time, to save his soul alive, dear old Auntie Smithers died. Died, it seemed, that he might live.

For that smothered but smouldering spark of something good and fine—that glimmer of divine discontent that had made him ashamed of being what he was—burst into feeble but authentic flame, and Algernon, being then of age, of sound if warped mind, and fair if fluctuating health, did of his own effort and good courage, break away from maternal bondage and take flight to the house in Kensington that he had inherited complete.

And thither promptly his mother followed him.

Naturally and rightly, as every mother will agree, Mrs. Dashwood-Coxe declared that it was as much her duty as her joy to investigate; to inspect; to "go through" everything; to replenish; and above all to interview and examine the elderly housekeeper, cook, parlourmaid, housemaid and kitchen-maid; and to reassure herself that these were not five foolish virgins who would leave the lamps untrimmed and the beds unaired.

Having selected the room which was to be her own, and to be known thenceforth and for ever as Mother's Room, Mrs. Dashwood-Coxe settled down to this most congenial and useful work, and did it thoroughly.

Indeed, it was not until well-nigh three months had passed that she listened to the voice, growing ever more clamorous in her bosom, and telling her that her parish and her Clarence were both suffer-ing neglect—and possibly getting out of hand and into mischief.

CHAPTER III

It was, of course, with considerable and natural misgiving that Mrs. Dashwood-Coxe at length abandoned her offspring, not only to the ministrations of the five wise virgins, elderly and virtuous, each *senex et horrida*, but also to the temptations, innumerable as terrible, of life in what Mrs. Dashwood-Coxe termed the Modern Babylon.

It was with a sense of having done at any rate something, if not much, toward safeguarding her son, that she paid yet another visit to Doctor John Desart and asked him if he would be so good as periodically to interview Algernon and report to her upon his physical condition.

The doctor had acquiesced with some alacrity, but had again tarnished his own image in the mind of Mrs. Dashwood-Coxe by informing her that it was upon Algernon's mental condition that he would report, inasmuch as the greater contained the less.

"Mental condition, my good man?" had Mrs. Dashwood-Coxe exclaimed, startled from her best manners into her second best, by the doctor's phraseology and attitude.

"You talk as though the poor boy were an idiot."

"Oh, we're all a little insane on some points," replied John Desart. "Some of us more insane in fewer ways, and others of us less insane in more ways."

"My son *insane?*" cried Mrs. Dashwood-Coxe. "*My* son?"

"No, I didn't say he was insane, in the lay sense of the word," replied John Desart.

"But he has a long way to go before he has a sane, healthy, normal outlook on life. And now is his real chance to make a start; the start that was aborted at Preparatory School, Public School and the University . . . Once again, my dear Mrs. Dashwood-Coxe, I do beg of you, with all the earnestness and seriousness of which I am capable, to let him alone now, and give him a fair chance. *Let him alone.*"

"And now that he has this splendid and wonderful chance as you call it?" said Mrs. Dashwood-Coxe with some bitterness, "Now that he is safely beyond the dangerous and poisonous and destructive influence of his own mother, what special and particular advice do you propose to give him?"

"Oh, all sorts," smiled the doctor. "He has got to have a job, a game, a hobby, a circle of friends, and more especially and particularly—a . . ."

John Desart cut himself short. He must not go too fast with this woman, if her son were to be rescued from the results of her selfishness and possessiveness, and from her love of interfering, "bossing," arranging, and personally conducting the lives of other people.

"I expect he plays a great game of croquet, and a little pat-ball tennis," he continued. "I suppose it's too late for him to take up cricket, football, hockey, boxing . . ."

"*Boxing?*" interrupted Mrs. Dashwood-Coxe, and put a world of expression into the word.

"Well, fencing, then. Now that would be a splendid thing for him. Magnificent physical exercise, splendid for mental quickness, and as helpful in making a man of him as anything could possibly be."

Algernon with a sword in his hand!

"He can swim, Doctor," said Mrs. Dashwood-

Coxe, proudly and a little pathetically.

"Oh, splendid! . . . How did that happen?"

"An old bathing-woman taught him at Bognor. We used to go there every year. An excellent creature of irreproachable moral standards."

"The cold sea-water," murmured the doctor, reaching for pen and case-sheet, and as he wrote, added, "Nothing like it for the morals."

"How often do you want him to come to you, Doctor?"

"Just whenever he likes. As often as he likes. And once a week, whether he likes it or not."

"And you will communicate with me, at once, if there is anything you think I should know, or if he needs me?"

"I'll certainly write and let you know the moment I think he needs you," replied the doctor in a toneless voice, and added, as he eyed the arrogant face of his majestic visitor:

"Always provided that you do not assume that he needs you until I write and say so . . . Goodbye, Mrs. Dashwood-Coxe . . . Shall I write the prescription down?" he smiled.

"Write what prescription down, Doctor?"

" 'Leave him alone,' " and quickly John Desart opened the door.

§2

Algernon, as instructed by his mother, who wrote to him daily, made an appointment with Doctor Desart, thereafter visiting him weekly.

And John Desart did his able best to corrupt Algernon Dashwood Coxe and lead him from the straight and narrow path of virtuous idleness, innocuous worthlessness, false values, and microscopic futile ambitions.

Manfully he strove to enlarge the young man's

horizons, to broaden his mind, to stiffen his backbone, to instil into him a measure of self-reliance, independence and initiative.

In the good soil of Algernon's mind, he delved and sowed, and, for three months, he kept him from contact with his mother, and in as close contact as he could achieve with a circle of young people—including his own son and daughter—who were interested in art, the drama, literature, games, and life in general.

Algernon they at first found "sticky," priggish, pompous, ignorant and incredibly inept at games.

However, at the doctor's request, they regarded the attempt at Algernon's salvation as a good deed, though with little hope of ever really making him a "good scout."

"Long John, my lad," said Miss Jean Desart, aged nineteen, to her father, one morning at breakfast, after a few days' experience of the hapless and helpless young man, "Our Algernon is a sad piece of work. A Great Pure Earnest Prig. He really is God's Good Man."

"Oh, no. He is his mother's good man. So would you have been in his circumstances, my lass," replied the doctor. "Algernon's good stuff."

"It's been out in the rain all night then, I should think, for he's positively the wettest thing on dry land," replied the young lady. "But I love him dearly. He's so humble and sweet, really. And so genuinely a gentleman—a rare and refreshing old fruit, these days. . . . He tells me that he now has a great, yea, a consuming, ambition in life. . . . It is to grow daily more and more like *you*, John! I told him he might do worse—oh, a lot worse. . . ." And the young lady kissed her father lightly, *en passant*, upon what she called his bald spot and he the "double-crown" of his head.

Long John Desart's children were very kind to

their father, though firm, and considered that, on the whole, they had brought him up to be a credit to them.

§3

And at length the day arrived to which Doctor Desart had long looked forward—the day on which he felt he might, in fairness to an unknown woman, broach the subject which had for long been at the back of his mind, the subject of the beginning of the end of Algernon's long and tedious "cure."

"How old are you, by the way?" he asked him, at the conclusion of this momentous interview.

"Twenty-four," was the reply.

"Ever think about marriage?" enquired the doctor.

Algernon blushed.

"No," he said, and his nervous laugh was almost a giggle.

"Who'd marry *me?*" he asked deprecatingly.

"Well, hundreds of nice women would marry a couple of thousand a year and a comfortable house, Algernon, but we don't want one of that sort. We want somebody who'd marry Algernon for Algernon's sake, eh? Look here, my boy, you've got to fall in love."

"Yes, sir."

"And you've got to fall in love with a girl who'll fall in love with you."

"Yes, sir."

"And you've got to marry."

"Yes, sir."

"Oh, for God's sake, don't go on saying 'Yes, sir,'" snarled the doctor. "I'm not telling you to get your hair cut, or to take a taxi to Waterloo, am I?"

"No, sir."

"Wouldn't you *like* to fall in love with a nice girl

and marry her, and have her in your house for a companion? Someone to talk to and play with and squabble with; someone to work for, and think for, and take care of?"

"Yes, sir. But no-one would marry *me!*"

"Wouldn't you like to have a son to romp with, and cuddle and carry up to bed on your shoulder? Someone to plan for, and work for and live for?"

"Yes, sir. But no-one would marry me."

The doctor's hand closed upon a heavy jade paper-weight, as he looked at Algernon.

He sighed.

The best Harley Street physicians do not throw paper-weights at their patients. Not even jade ones.

"Now look here," he said. "New prescription. Fierce wolf named Algernon Coxe now roams about in well-cut sheep's clothing seeking whom he may devour. When he's found a tender lamb, he's to bring it to me for inspection."

"Who'd marry *me?*" said Algernon again.

"Any nice girl," replied John Desart encouragingly, and with a rather forced smile of bright optimism.

"And would it be quite fair to her?" asked Algernon. "Seeing that I'm such a . . . such a . . ."

"Most certainly," replied the doctor. "She'll see a good deal of you first, of course. Make up her mind, and accept you. Marry you with her eyes open—knowing all about you before she does so . . . Oh, trust me, my son; I'll tell her what sort of a dud and a scoundrel you are. She'll marry you all-right. Live happy ever afterwards, too."

"Jean's seen a good deal of me, sir," observed Algernon. "I think I know her better than any other girl. I've only met a few . . . She's a very nice girl . . . And she's always been very kind to me," he added meditatively.

"Perhaps she would marry me if I asked her," and he looked enquiringly at the doctor.

John Desart, distinguished, popular and famous physician, was not easily, or often, taken aback. He sat bolt upright in his chair, and stared hard at the apparently guileless face of the young man in front of him.

Was this a young fool, or a young knave?

Gradually his face softened, as a wry smile wreathed about his firm lips.

Hoist with his own petard!

Petard? But nothing had been further from his thoughts than "hoisting" anybody.

Surely there must be thousands of nice girls to whom marriage with Algernon Coxe would be a career?

A suitable career. Far better than wage-earning in some uncongenial and inappropriate capacity. Infinitely better than living and dying unfulfilled— just one more of the millions of "superfluous" women.

Nothing of a petard or bomb-shell about it at all . . . A thoroughly nice fellow without an atom of vice in his make-up.

He had almost said, "Not a redeeming vice in his character." . . . An excellent chap.

But Jean . . . His daughter Jean!

And what about somebody else's daughter Jean?

Well, that would be somebody else's lookout.

"No, Algernon," he said slowly and thoughtfully. "Not Jean. It wouldn't be suitable. Not quite the type for you. No. I shouldn't ask Jean."

"No, sir," said Algernon, obediently.

"No, my boy. You go off on this jaunt, as I advised. Have a month's absolute change and get all the fresh air, sunshine, sea-bathing, milk, cream, walking and sun-bathing that you can.

"Start from this Polporth Cove that Jean talks about, when you've had enough of it, and walk right round the coast of Cornwall. That would make a glorious holiday, and just what you want.

"Good-bye. Come and see me when you get back, and mind you're as hard as nails and as brown as a berry. Good-bye . . ."

§4

And so Algernon Coxe had gone to Polporth Cove, the place recommended to him by Doctor Desart's children, and had there met Giovanna Blayton, fallen desperately in love with her, as she had done with him, and had carried out Doctor Desart's latest prescription and found a wife—or rather, a lady most ready and willing to become his wife.

The weeks that Algernon Coxe spent at Polporth Cove with Giovanna Blayton, albeit not of wholly unclouded joy, were by far the happiest of his life, and the letters that he wrote on the subject of his engagement were positively lyrical. They showed forth, as did his whole demeanour, bearing and face, the great change wrought in him by the alchemy of love.

John Desart wrote that he was delighted beyond measure, and that Algernon was to bring his fiancée straight to Harley Street when they left Polporth Cove, that he might congratulate them both.

"If she's the right sort of girl, our Algernon is made," he said to his daughter Jean.

"Saved . . . Redeemed . . . And if she doesn't stand up to his mother, and tell her fairly plainly that now her day is over, so far as bossing the wretched Algernon is concerned, it won't be for want of my prompting."

"Long John, my treasure, the late Mr. Machiavelli has nothing on you," replied Miss Jean Desart. "But suppose she's the wrong sort of girl?"

"Then I shall tell Algernon not to marry her," was the reply.

"And he'll say 'Yes, Doctor,'" observed Miss Desart, "and start afresh . . . Daddy, why did you come between me and Algernon, my first, and probably last, suitor?"

"Because I want Algernon to marry a nice girl," was the doctor's reply.

Mrs. Dashwood-Coxe wrote that she was more astonished than she could say, at receiving Algernon's news, and, as words failed her, she would say nothing, except that the pictures painted by James Augustus Blayton, R.A., were not the kind of pictures that would be hung on the walls of Melfont Parva Vicarage, and that Algernon was to bring Miss Blayton to see her instantly—by the very next train, in fact.

Algernon replied that Miss Blayton was going to her flat in London shortly, as her father was going back to Italy, and that she would be delighted to come down to Melfont Parva at the very earliest opportunity.

Sensing a hint of disobedience, or rather a lack of instantaneousness in obedience, Mrs. Dashwood-Coxe frowned as she read her son's reply, and her compressed lips ruled a very straight line between her high-bridged nose and firm, handsome chin.

Engaged to be married was he? And without consulting his mother! Without a single word to his mother! Engaged to be married!

Perhaps.

CHAPTER IV

Algernon Coxe and Giovanna Blayton travelled to London together, and Algernon, having seen his fiancée to her flat, went to his house and thence promptly telephoned to Doctor Desart's secretary to make an appointment for the morrow.

It was his intention to get the doctor's endorsement and approval, both of his action and his Giovanna, and to go, armed with this endorsement and approval, to Melfont Parva Vicarage, straight from the doctor's house.

With Giovanna Blayton, John Desart was delighted, and declared that already he saw a far greater improvement in Algernon than was to be accounted for by fresh air, sunshine, sea-bathing and change. He was more alert, more animated, more purposeful, more disposed to have an opinion of his own, and to maintain it for a few seconds, if opposed.

After talking with the young people for a generous twenty minutes, he bade Algernon go and stand outside the door, as he had so often done before, or, if he preferred it, find his way back to the waiting-room, for he himself wanted to talk with Giovanna alone.

"Now, my dear," he said, as the door closed, "I've been trying to save this boy for nearly twenty years."

"Save him, Doctor? From what?"

"From his mother."

"A bad woman?"

"No, a good one. Blameless; virtuous beyond telling; but she very nearly succeeded in making an equally blameless and virtuous old woman out of Algernon.

"Painlessly extracted his will and replaced it by her own. Brought him up by hand . . . on pap . . . with a spoon . . . of which she kept tight hold. Poor boy was never allowed to have a thought or a wish or an idea of his own. I doubt if he was allowed to do up his own buttons until he was twenty-one. The woman seems to be thoroughly uncomfortable when the boy is out of her sight, and far from comfortable when he is in sight. . . . It would have been very bad indeed for a daughter, an only girl—but for a boy! . . . But poor Algernon has never been a boy—never had a chance. . . . But now he has one, at last.

"*You're* his chance. You can make a fine man and a splendid husband out of Algernon, but you've got to do a difficult thing. You've got to put his mother in her place and not take her place yourself. You understand?"

"No," said Giovanna, frankly.

The doctor eyed the very beautiful girl who sat in the low arm-chair before him, nervously buttoning and unbuttoning her glove. He saw not only beauty but strength, sensibility, passion and power expressed by the firm chin, the great eyes, the full lips, the nostrils, the forehead . . . Yes, this girl would do—if she'd play her part.

"Do you really love Algernon?" he asked, as he watched her, his head resting on his hand, his pencil gently tapping the blotter in front of him.

"Yes," replied Giovanna.

"Much?" asked the doctor, his keen strong face looking gentle, fatherly and kind, with the smile that Jean Desart adored.

"Much?" echoed Giovanna. "I absolutely worship him. He is far, far more to me than life. He is the dearest, gentlest, most unselfish and pathetic creature I have ever met. And if ever in this world there was a *gentleman,* with a truly gentle soul and nature. . . . Love him! Much?"

And the girl's expression and quiet laugh told the doctor more than her words.

He nodded his head and rose to his feet.

"Look here, my dear," he said. "What I meant was this. There's been nothing in the world wrong with Algernon but too much good mother. See that he doesn't have too much in the future. And don't you be a mother to him yourself. Be a wife, and make him be your husband, not your son.

"He'll never quarrel with his mother, and I don't want him to do so, but you must get him out from under her thumb. Don't spoil him. Make him spoil you—that will do him a lot of good. Don't think for him—make him think for himself and for you. You're a capable self-reliant girl with a will of your own. Hide it.

"Pretend to be a fluffy ass, and when you've decided that any course of action is the best one, lead Algernon to see that it is, and then encourage him to insist that it is. Make him think he's master in his own house, and a devil of a fellow at having his own way. See?"

The girl smiled.

"I think Algernon's perfect, Doctor," she said. "But I'm quite prepared to find his mother imperfect.

"And to find that she finds me something considerably worse than imperfect," she added. "Thank you so much, Doctor, for your kindness to Algernon."

"Well, now, it's up to you, my dear. You are to be his first wife and not his second mother, and if ever you come and tell me that Algernon occasionally beats you, I shall say '*Splendid!*'"

Giovanna Blayton rose to go, and, ignoring the hand extended by the bowing doctor, impulsively placed her hands upon his shoulders, raised herself on tiptoe and kissed him on the chin.

"Good Lord!" cried the startled doctor, and patted her heavily on the back as he opened the door.

<h2 style="text-align:center">§2</h2>

The visit to Melfont Parva Vicarage was not a success. It was, in fact, a complete, hopeless and utter failure, for Mrs. Dashwood-Coxe had intended it to be so, and Giovanna cared nothing, either way. Jimmy was going to have a wife, henceforth, instead of a mother, as that kind doctor had urged.

Giovanna's first and last meeting with Mrs. Dashwood-Coxe began coldly and ended distinctly hotly. It began at tea-time in a drawing-room in which one lady smelt tobacco-smoke with extreme distaste and the other smelt green-house with distaste as extreme.

It ended at midnight on a landing when one lady smelt vicious misconduct and the other smelt a pruriently putrid nasty mind.

It had lasted but from tea-time till breakfast instead of for the proposed week, and the young people, miserable, angry with each other and with themselves, returned to London, Giovanna to her flat and Algernon to his house, in a mutual spirit of coldness amounting almost to hostility.

<h2 style="text-align:center">§3</h2>

Mrs. Dashwood-Coxe frequently assured her husband, and indeed other people, that she was never one to interfere. With even greater emphasis than usual she re-affirmed this theory on the day of Giovanna's departure from Melfont Parva Vicarage.

120

"As you are well aware, Clarence," she said to her husband as they sat at their belated breakfast in the cheerful, sunny room, now purged and purified of Giovanna's cigarette-smoke and presence, "I am not one to interfere."

The Reverend Clarence gazed upon the face of his wife and there was a faint movement upon the surface of the black mass that was his moustache, beard and whiskers, a movement slightly suggestive of that of the corn-field which stirs at the whisper of the breeze unseen. Whether the movement indicated that the Reverend Clarence had smiled, grinned, sneered or snarled, none might know.

"I never interfere in other people's affairs, and I would be the last woman in the world to imagine anything so foolish as that a mother can choose a wife for her son . . . Marriages are made in Heaven."

The Reverend Clarence looked as though he might be thinking back, and estimating Heaven's responsibility in his own case.

"No," repeated Mrs. Dashwood-Coxe, "I never interfere . . ." and added a moment later:

"I would sooner see Algernon in his grave than married to that deplorable young . . . young . . . young . . ."

"Girl," suggested the Reverend Clarence.

"Sooner see him in his grave," re-affirmed his wife.

"One rarely does see people in their graves," mused the Vicar.

"An absolutely impossible person. Absolutely immoral or non-moral. Common and unclean . . . Night-clubs . . . Sitting in the nude for a gang of artists . . . Her face and figure portrayed and hanging in scores of public salons . . . shops . . . picture galleries . . . all over the place. The girl is cheap, second-hand, soiled goods . . . And if she thinks she is really going to marry my son, she never made a bigger mistake in all her mistaken life.

"I never interfere, as you know," she continued —and again it was as though a spirit moved upon the face of the whiskers, if not actually upon the face of the Reverend Clarence, which remained expressionless—"but this engagement must be broken off at once. It is unthinkable. She would drag him down. It is as much our duty to save him as it would be if he were drowning before our very eyes. And not only must he be saved, but *placed* in safety."

The Reverend Clarence again lifted his eyes from his plate and regarded the face of his wife and mistress—or, to avoid ambiguity—master.

"No mother should rush in where angels might fear to tread, and so far invade the privacy of her son's soul as to interfere . . . to say whom he shall, or shall not marry . . . actually to choose him a wife. But she can *guide* his choice . . . Oh, yes, she can guide his choice."

Beneath the screen and defence of his magnificent moustache and beard, the muscles of the face of the Reverend Clarence moved in some mysterious way his wonder to repress.

"Agatha Sharp," he commented, apparently to himself.

§4

Agatha Sharp was a born Disciple, and few leaders have had a more convinced, faithful or devoted disciple than had Mrs. Dashwood-Coxe in Agatha, from the time when this exceedingly wealthy orphan had, after a very tragic experience, decided that she did not like men and would never, never marry.

Agatha, beside being a born Disciple, was fast developing into a born virgin, or born old-maid; one of those good women whose sole interest in life is parochial, and who so frequently develop a passionate devotion for another woman.

The parish of St. Jude's provided her with work, and the church of St. Jude's with recreation —the mending of cassocks and hassocks, the arranging of flowers and other such useful and ornamental occupation, and Mrs. Dashwood-Coxe provided her with an outlet for her strong and repressed emotions and desires.

Agatha Sharp had recently taken a severely-furnished cottage-*de-luxe*, the garden of which adjoined that of the Vicarage. It was thus easy for her to pass from her actual to her spiritual home whenever her beloved and revered Mrs. Dash-wood-Coxe required her services, or her faithful Disciple imagined she might do so.

And on this same morning, Agatha Sharp did so pass from her garden to that of her adored friend and, a few minutes later, comfortably en-sconced in a wicker arm-chair upon the lawn, be-neath the great cedar of Lebanon, was hearing all about it: and not only all about it, but all about what Mrs. Dashwood-Coxe had thought about it, and had said about it to her husband, her son and the "young woman" herself.

Agatha Sharp was a good listener and enjoyed this signal mark of confidence. She became an even better listener, and enjoyed yet more deeply the confidence when it began slowly to dawn upon her not too perceptive mind that her mother-in-spirit was conceivably suggesting the possibility of desiring tentatively to visualize herself as Agatha's mother-in-law in the flesh.

Agatha was dumbfounded when this painfully

novel, rather terrible, scorchingly brilliant, idea shed its first ray upon the placid levels of her gentle mind; and when it rose full and clear above her mental horizon, suffusing with curious warmth and illuminating with strange new light her whole soul and being, she was inclined to be dazzled by it.

"But I don't want you to worry on my account, dearest Agatha," begged Mrs. Dashwood-Coxe, mistaking the source of her disciple's apparent emotion; "I can bear it, or rather I should say I will *not* bear it; I will not have it. As I said to his father at breakfast this morning, I would see my son in his grave rather than married to a girl who would dare to speak to me as she did, who would dare to indulge her filthy vices in my very house. Doubtless Algernon will be a little sore at first, a little annoyed and disappointed if his new toy is taken from him—for that's exactly what this girl is, a toy. She is a typical specimen of the toy-type, as distinct from the wife-type, and Algernon shall marry a *wife*."

And here the speaker placed her large and capable hand upon the small incapable one that rested on the arm of her chair.

"Since Algernon wishes to marry," she continued, "he shall do so. But though I was never one to interfere, neither am I the sort of mother that would sit idly by, and watch her only son rush headlong to destruction."

A pregnant silence ensued, a silence scarcely broken by the sound of Agatha's quickened breathing.

"Yes, destruction," affirmed Mrs. Dashwood-Coxe with explosive suddenness, "mind, body and soul."

"And pocket," she added, and sat grim-lipped gazing into space and the future—a future she would change in spite of Fate itself.

"Algernon cannot truly love a woman of that sort," said Agatha. "He is your son . . . Well bred . . . Brought up by you, at home, he must be fastidious . . . a gentleman . . . Surely he could only love a woman of his own class and kind . . . a lady, a gentlewoman . . ."

"*Love*, dear child?" was the indignant reply. "There's absolutely nothing whatsoever of *love* in this deplorable affair.

"A mere ephemeral infatuation, a disgraceful entanglement. Yes, infatuation is the kindest and most charitable word that one can possibly use . . . Love indeed! *Sex.*

"*Sex* and nothing else. Sickening and disgusting. Love? Faugh! A profanation of the word. When a man loves, he looks up, not down . . . We needs must love the highest when we see it, my dear Agatha."

Another pregnant silence.

"Agatha, my dear," repeated Mrs. Dashwood-Coxe, impressively. "We needs must love the highest when we see it," and again Mrs. Dashwood-Coxe pressed the girl's hand.

And as she turned her gentle eyes, large, placid and somewhat suggestive of the mild and kindly cow, to gaze upon the face of her second mother, Agatha all but gasped.

With opening lips—indeed with open mouth—she stared, half-comprehending, at her strong-minded friend.

"We needs must love the highest when we see it," said that lady for the third time, and gently and encouragingly patted the hand of Agatha as she spoke.

"The best way of driving something out, and keeping it out, is to put something else in its place," she continued, and enlarged upon her platitude.

"Perfect love casteth out fear and assuredly it casteth out infatuation . . ."

And for something less than a quarter of an hour, musing aloud, she harped upon her one-stringed theme.

Finally:

"No man who has had an upbringing such as that of my son could, when it came to the point in choosing a wife, hesitate for one second between an abandoned creature, such as that, and a pure sweet beautiful and well-born woman of his own class."

And Agatha felt the strong grip of Mrs. Dashwood-Coxe's hand clasping and squeezing her own with utmost significance.

Pausing for a moment in her monologue, Mrs. Dashwood-Coxe became aware that Agatha was speaking, or trying to speak.

"You were saying, dear?" she asked with the faint asperity that was apt to tinge her voice when she was interrupted in the midst, or indeed at the end, of a rounded period.

"Shall I tell you something?" whispered Agatha. "There's something I should like to tell you, dearest Mrs. Dashwood-Coxe. I think it would . . . it would . . . interest you a little."

"Yes, what is it, dear?" Mrs. Dashwood-Coxe humoured the girl.

"I'm so attracted to Algernon. When I first saw him, months ago, I thought what a nice man he looked, so different from that dreadful Delval who nearly ruined my life. I do like him very much."

"But you've never spoken to him, my dear. I didn't know you'd even seen him. He's been away nearly all the time, since you came to Melfont Parva."

"Oh, I've seen him twice—in Church. And once

he passed me in Love Lane and raised his hat and gave me such a pleasant smile. He had noticed me in the choir, I suppose, and remembered me. Meeting me suddenly, he must have thought he knew my face. Yes, such a pleasant smile . . . Such nice teeth . . . Do you know, Mrs. Dashwood-Coxe, I thought about him quite a lot afterwards."

Again the large strong hand patted the small weak one.

"And now to think that he has given his heart to this Scarlet Woman . . . Quite a blow."

And Agatha tittered self-consciously.

"Not given it, Agatha, lent it. Or scarcely that.

"Say rather, that the young woman, seeing it was ownerless, so to speak, had the brazen audacity and impudence to pick it up. No, not given it. Lent it, at the most . . . And believe me, it shall be returned . . . Returned undamaged . . . And quickly, too. I'll see to that. Oh, yes, trust me to see to that.

"Every young man passes through a phase of this sort—like measles and whooping-cough. *And,* as with these other infantile and puerile diseases, everything depends on the nursing, my dear Agatha. I will nurse him through this mental and moral disease as I've done through the physical ones."

Another of the pregnant silences that punctuated this portentous and fateful conversation.

"Now, suppose you come to dinner on—let us say Saturday week, dearest Agatha," said Mrs. Dashwood-Coxe at length. "Yes, and bring your songs and music. Algernon is very fond of music—devoted to it. He will accompany you."

And, turning, Mrs. Dashwood-Coxe took Agatha's face between her hands, and with deepest significance, kissed Agatha on the mouth.

"Oh, oh, *dearest* Mrs. Dashwood-Coxe," gasped

Agatha.

Algernon duly accompanied Agatha, though for a briefer space than his masterful mother *had* intended.

CHAPTER V

If no man can serve two masters, how many can serve two mistresses? Whatever their numbers, Algernon Coxe was not of them.

Bravely he tried, horribly he suffered, miserably he weakened and ignobly he failed.

"Give me a boy until he is seven years of age and I will make him mine for life," said the philosopher priest.

Mrs. Dashwood-Coxe had had Algernon for thrice that time and he was hers for life, her will was his will, her ways were his ways, and those who were not her people should not be his people.

Within the week, she followed him to London, installed herself in Mother's Room, and set to work—with all the strength of her strong will, all the power of her powerful character, and all the might of her mighty advantage as the mother whom he had never dared to disobey. Set herself to work to defeat Giovanna, to belittle her natural and acquired accomplishments, to blacken her character, and to befoul her image in the mind of her son.

Before long, home was an unhappy place where life was rendered unbearable by the presence of a cold, angry and reproachful mother who strove to tear him from his sweetheart and his refuge.

Giovanna's flat was gradually becoming an unhappy place where life was rendered unbearable by the presence of a cold, angry and reproachful sweetheart who strove to tear him from his mother.

In pursuance, to the best of her ability, of the policy and line of conduct advised by Doctor

Desart, Giovanna wrestled continuously with her lover's complex, his *idée fixe*, his terrible subjection to his mother's will and word.

To any other than a doctor or a loving woman, this subjection would have been ridiculous, childish, incredible, disgraceful.

To Giovanna it was pitiable, pathetic and terrible.

Within the space of a few weeks, almost the whole time of each of their daily meetings was devoted to arguments that degenerated into wranglings which ended with the *impasse:*

"I am your fiancée and shall soon be your wife. You chose me. You love me. Whom you marry is your business, not hers . . ."

"I am her son. I owe everything to her. I cannot disobey and defy her. I have never done such a thing in my life! . . . She is my mother. It would break her heart . . ."

Gradually Giovanna began to feel that her position was weakening, that she was slipping, and that Algernon was being drawn, as by this stronger magnet, back into the bondage of obedience to his mother.

Time after time, he had left her with a promise that he would "speak to his mother to-night," reaffirm the fact of his betrothal, definitely announce the date of his marriage, and firmly adhere to what he said.

Time after time, he had returned to her with the promise unfulfilled, and with the miserable confession that he had failed, for his mother had "refused to hear a word," and had flatly declined to consent to the marriage, either now, soon, later, or at any time whatsoever.

And gradually Giovanna began to feel that the time approached when she must stake everything on a single throw and say:

"Choose between your mother and me, once and for all. Choose now, or never come here again. Fix a date for our wedding or break off our engagement, and I will never see you any more."

But she was afraid.

If she could get Algernon to come and live in her flat for a few days; keep him right away from his mother; send, one day, for a priest, and say suddenly to Algernon:

"Let's be married now, here, at once," she would win.

As things were, she was afraid; for it was quite possible—nay, sometimes it seemed quite probable —that if compelled to choose, he would choose his mother.

When with Giovanna, he could be himself, have a soul of his own, and say "Yes, Giovanna." When with his mother, he could but be what his mother had made him, and say "No, Mother."

So Giovanna put off what might be the evil day, though feeling that the longer things went on as they were, the greater was the chance of the battle being won by the big battalions of Mrs. Dashwood-Coxe's power and opportunity.

Had she not quarter of a century's start, and had she not got Algernon there in the house all day and night, as against Giovanna's hour or two?

So Giovanna's simple mind and subtle brain turned to thoughts of stratagems and tricks. She pondered ways and means, and she considered schemes.

Since she had overcome Algernon's absurd scruples against visiting her at her flat—as all her other friends did—might she not take steps to bind herself to him in such a way that none but the meanest and vilest cur could, even for a moment, contemplate the severance of the bond?

That would defeat his abominable mother.

Since she gave Giovanna the credit for being a vicious hussy who had led Algernon astray, why not lead him "astray" to his salvation?

Would Doctor Desart approve of that?

She would go and ask him frankly, and whether he approved or not, she would do it if it were necessary; if it were her last hope and resource.

And suppose Algernon failed her then, and did break the bonds wherewith she had striven to bind him?

She would risk it, for his sake and her own happiness.

Meanwhile, what about jealousy—one of the strongest of all emotions and most potent of the springs of human action?

If Algernon could be made jealous, he might act.

Jealousy might prove stronger than this morbid filial love that kept him a supine slave devoid of will-power. But if real love, the love of a man for a maid had failed, could jealousy succeed?

It might.

Certainly the two together might triumph; love and jealousy against filial affection and dependence.

She would try it.

Yes, she would try the effect of jealousy first— and as Giovanna thought of jealousy, she thought by association of ideas, of Boris Goudroff, *the* Polish or Russian artist, and felt a little thrill as she did so, a sensation born of mixed feelings of disgust and admiration, fear and strong attraction.

She must take Algernon to that haunt of Boris and his kind, the *Hors Concours* night-club, known to its English habitués as *The Green Haddock.* Boris would attempt to make love to her, of course, and as a matter of course.

Thereafter Algernon should occasionally find him in the flat.

Yes, if a dose of jealousy were to be administered, Boris was most remarkably the appropriate and suitable instrument.

But she must be careful, very careful indeed—for while Boris was something of an unknown quantity, there was not much unknown about either the quantity or the quality of his strength, violence, savagery and colossal conceit and egoism —the last amounting practically to a mental disease.

Yes—this would crave wary walking; but Giovanna was prepared to run far greater risks than this, in order to save her lover and herself, to save her lover for herself.

Boris could take care of himself and look out for himself.

And when had Boris ever considered anybody, or spared anybody in pursuit of his own selfish ends, gratifications and pleasures?

She could manage Boris all right; and, surely, he grasped, by this time, the fact that not even his magnificent strength of body and mind, the power and force of his art, and his enormous vitality, violence, and general overwhelmingness, had availed to make her love him?

Had he been less egotistical, less selfish, less mean and vain and brutal and beastly . . . had there been no Algernon Coxe in this rather unsatisfactory world, Boris might have had his way.

Yes, she could manage Boris and make him "behave," even if she did appear to give him a little encouragement, and to lead him on, for a time.

In sheer gratitude alone, for the way in which she had helped him, he would forgive her if she raised him up a little and then cast him down; used him and made a convenience of him.

Had she not given him money, quite often, when he was literally starving; and, far more than that, had she not sat for him when he could not possibly afford a model; sat for him as Andromeda, and enabled him to paint the picture that had brought him some fame and some money?

Yes, Boris Goudroff should be useful to her now in return, whether he liked it or not.

§2

The *Hors Concours*, known to the nicer-minded of its English and American clientele as *The Green Haddock* and to its less nice-minded as something else, a night-club haunted by the same inevitable types as adorn other such sad places, was to some extent redeemed from the usual dead level of inane and dreary dullness, by the patronage of a curious clique of artists, art-students and those who serve the servants of the Arts.

Recognized artists and their easily-recognized models; art-students working (or not working) at the Slade, the Royal Academy Schools or the St. John's Wood School of Art; musicians, composers, a sculptor or two, professional dancers, chorus-girls, some actors and a few alleged actresses; queer specimens strayed, stolen or flung from the more orthodox ranks of their brethren, forgathered at *The Green Haddock* and with a certain liveliness, wit and intelligence, leavened the lump of heavy-eyed, weary pursuers of the pleasure that apparently they never overtook.

When not in Cornwall or Italy, James Augustus Blayton honoured this slightly murky pool of queer fish, and was the recognized *doyen* of its artistic clique.

Those there were, even here, who called him James Disgust-us Blayton, and either disliked or affected to dislike, the tone of his conversation, the savour of his jokes. And—when he had not only looked upon, but dined upon and supped upon, the wine when it is red—more particularly his conduct with, or toward, the ladies who accompanied him, accompanied his friends, or attended the Club unaccompanied.

Once or twice he had made even the management uneasy, and the management was a cosmopolitan rascal who had successively made Paris, Vienna and Berlin too hot for his comfort.

But since he had introduced Giovanna to the club, and fallen into the habit of bringing her there, Blayton had improved, and had earned credit for knowing where to draw the line in the presence of his daughter.

For this place—albeit she regarded it with no great liking or admiration—Giovanna had no very marked distaste, inasmuch as the men and women she encountered there were very much of the type she had always met in her father's house.

Of this set, all were very emancipated and modern; most of them quite harmless and well-meaning; a few of them intensely respectable citizens striving desperately to be raffish and unshockable; three or four were great souls encased in finer clay, pure and simple artists marked for success and fame in their own branch of art; or three were neither pure nor simple, nor were they artists, but just plain ordinary swine; and one or two were only redeemed from loathsomeness by a bright spark of the divine authentic fire of Genius.

Of these was Boris Goudroff, a gentleman of dubious nationality and Paris gutter birth, whose egotism enabled him firmly to believe and loudly to proclaim that anybody who supported him while he worked at his Art or rested and sought inspiration, was merely seizing the opportunity of a lifetime, and should be humbly grateful to Boris Goudroff for providing such an opportunity.

Boris found young women more receptive of this idea than other people, and more prone to recognize their opportunity of becoming benefactors, not merely of the noble Boris but of mankind in general and lovers of great Art in particular.

He, or rather she, who supported Boris while he painted a picture, or thought about painting one, deserved well, he said, of her generation and of generations yet unborn.

Yet, as a rule, his women supporters appeared to prefer that Boris should think well of them, and seemed singularly indifferent to the opinion of their generation, still less so to that of future ones.

But Boris did not think well of them, and did not for long conceal the fact.

He tolerated them as necessary evils, necessary only until the crassly stupid, blindly ignorant, and unbelievably soulless world awoke from its sottish slumber and realized Boris Goudroff—Boris Goudroff who should be hailed an Old Master while he was still alive—or rather as a Young Master greater than any of the Old.

He did not think well of them, because none of them was Giovanna Blayton; and he tolerated them as necessary evils because they were necessary to his existence and because they were in every way evil by comparison with the peerless Giovanna—who looked, as he often told her, like nothing but a *Picture by Boris Goudroff* come to life and escaped from its great gold frame or prison.

And a gold prison he would build for her when he was the most famous man alive, and as rich as he was famous; and, meanwhile, could she lend him a sovereign, for he never accepted anything less than gold.

§3

To *The Green Haddock*, one evening, Giovanna Blayton brought Algernon Coxe, in pursuance of her idea of trying to broaden his mind and make him more tolerant of those specimens of his fellow man and woman who differed in all respects from himself and his mother.

Also had she an eye to the inception and furtherance of her foolish plot for making Algernon jealous, and so adding the stings of the scorpions of jealousy to those of the whips of desire and of the urgings of love.

It had not been an easy matter to persuade him to accompany her to this delectable resort, and she had been compelled to ask him whether he supposed that a Club, honoured by her father and visited by herself, was likely to be so inferior a place as to be unworthy of a visit from the future son-in-law of the one and husband of the other.

"We won't go at all after we are married, Jimmy darling," she had smiled.

"Er—no . . . No . . . That is if we . . ." he had replied falteringly and stopped.

Giovanna had thought it wiser to refrain from making him complete his sentence.

Had he been going to say "That is if we—ever *do* marry?" or merely "That is if we—don't both like the place very much."

Certainly this poor pathetic Jimmy must be made jealous. He must be "bucked up," aroused and energized; must be given the courage of his conviction that Giovanna was his true love and soul-mate, whether the magic potion were jealousy or passion—or else his mother would win, and Jimmy would be lost indeed, and not only lost to Giovanna.

Poor darling weak Jimmy. How hard it was, and always would be, to avoid "mothering" him; and how slow and difficult a task to foster the growth of his dwarfed and stunted individuality, will and personality.

Algernon Coxe seated himself opposite to Giovanna at a little table beside the exiguous dancing-floor of the *Hors Concours*, and gazed around in wonder, if not alarm.

He found himself in a very large underground room, or hall, the walls of which were decorated with what are sometimes termed "conscientious nudes," but which had been rendered, by skilled hands, less conscientious and more conscious by casual adornment with here a garter, a sash, or a shoe, there a stocking, a hat, or what might be paradoxically termed a late-and-early garment of a date much more modern than that of its wearer.

From these curious and interesting mural decorations—frieze has perhaps too cold a suggestion to be appropriate—Jimmy's eye wandered to the long bar which occupied the whole of one end of the hall.

Here, dispensing little bread and much sack, was the fattest man on earth, who said that he confidently looked forward to being also the fattest angel in Heaven or elsewhere.

One of the many interesting sights of this place was that of the huge short-fingered hands of the fat man, manipulating bottles, pouring drinks and mixing cocktails with not only the air but the skill of a great conjurer and greater juggler.

This man or human mound, Jimmy, fascinated, watched a while, much as a rabbit whose safety is guaranteed by a lioness, might watch a boa-constrictor at his fell work.

At length his eye strayed from this wonder and

beheld others.

At a neighbouring table sat a sallow-faced blue-chinned individual, his head covered with a foreign-looking black felt hat which was not quite a sombrero, his neck swathed in a piece of black silk that was not quite a stock, his form enshrouded in a cloak that was not quite green with age, and his feet encased in cracked and lace-less patent shoes, whose pointed toes were not quite spikes.

With elbow on table and his head resting upon a rather grubby hand, he smoked curiously, and with a nice sense of technique appropriate to his general style and appearance; for while the little finger of the supporting hand closed his right nostril, he exhaled smoke through the left.

Pondering this phenomenon, Jimmy, ignorant of physiology, wondered whether this accomplished man would perhaps later close both nostrils and exhale the smoke from his ears.

The gentleman had a companion, but not company, for the lady who sat with him at table did, like himself, stare unmoving and unmoved, into the empty cup of coffee-grounds and cigarette-stubs that graced the table before her.

Silent, still, blank-faced and sunk in gloom, they sat and sat and presumably enjoyed themselves.

At the next table a party of four enjoyed themselves also; but in a different manner, with loud laughter, harsh or shrill, and great outcry.

The men were in evening-dress, the ladies almost in night-dress. One man was rubicund, fat, with huge prominent eyes, walrus moustache, and spreading ears exfoliating at right angles to the plane of his cheeks.

He did not look as though possessed of intelligence, but was evidently endowed with the kindred gift of a keen sense of humour, inasmuch as he positively howled with laughter at every single remark of every one of his companions.

Laughter so loud, so long—indeed so unbrokenly continuous, struck Algernon as something of which one might possibly grow weary as the hours dragged by; but he decided that, again, this might not be so, for one would probably become accustomed, immune, and unconscious, as of the plangent ticking of a raucous clock.

The other man was young, sly and sleek—sleek as a seal, and with a seal's large eyes and sharp intelligent look.

"Hair brushed back like a seal," mused Algernon. "Sharp white teeth like a seal. Would he snap and catch it if I threw him this piece of fish, I wonder? . . . The Walrus and the Seal . . . What a lot of people resemble animals! Which do I resemble? A rabbit, I suppose. And Giovanna a most lovely Persian kitten."

One of the partners of the Walrus and the Seal had caught sight of him and Giovanna and had drawn the attention of the party to them. Really they were unpardonably rude, for not only did they stare and snigger, but the other woman was distinctly heard to say:

"Oh, look what the cat's brought in. Jovanner's picked up the junest June Premier ever hatched in May," and the Seal to reply:

"No, that's not the *jeune premier*, it's the *ingénue* masquerading as one. Things are not always what they seem, and the cat did not fish it up from the bottom of the Well of Truth. More probably from some other kind."

Roars of laughter greeted this sally and mingled with that of the Walrus, which had never ceased.

To Algernon they were creatures as incomprehensible as they were objectionable, and he wondered that Giovanna should care to visit a place frequented by such people.

"Enjoying yourself, Jimmy darling?" she said at that moment.

"Oh, what else could one do in your company, Giovanna? . . . This is a queer place, isn't it?"

"We'll dance by and by, Jimmy."

"I still feel like an elephant when I try to dance, Giovanna," he demurred.

"Never mind, darling, you don't look in the least like an elephant . . . Dancing elephants are rather graceful, really."

What strange things Giovanna did say.

Hearing the sound of a violent smack and a loud squeal, Jimmy sprang round in time to realize that a gentleman, big, bald and bold, had smitten a lady's bare back with tremendous force, skill and resonance . . . but evidently his hand upon her was but in the way of kindness laid, for he shook and rolled with Bacchic laughter, and the lady's protest was more than half mechanical.

Doubtless he habitually did this when the spirit moved him, particularly cheap spirit in "double" measure.

Ere the surprised Algernon had time to turn away, the lady, a yellow-haired fat fairy, had caught his eye and, in exchange, poked out her tongue.

Algernon blushed and Giovanna laughed.

As he bent over his plate, in some confusion, he was almost knocked from his chair as a very small hairy old man, in faulty and maculate evening-dress, clasping a lady who might or might not have been his granddaughter, but who was much more than twice his size, fell, or was thrown by his partner, heavily against him.

"These hogs feedin' all over the dancin'-floor,"

growled the big girl and whirled her grandfather away.

As the couple gyrated, and over the head of her aged but active partner, she came face to face with the apologetic Algernon,

"Keep your dam' chair under proper control," she said, but softened her heavy curtness with a heavier wink.

Edging his chair a little farther from the undemarcated edge of the dancing-floor, Algernon came into slight but jarring contact with a lady sitting partly beside and partly behind him. She, an obvious French girl, with a fringe and at least one-of-everything direct from Paris, requested him with broadest Cockney accent, but the sweetest reasonableness, not to bloomin' well climb *all* over 'er—not until she'd finished her blinkin' supper any'ow, and she 'adn't so much as lapped 'er blighted gravy yet.

Her unnecessary petition was cut short by her partner, with the words:

"My lovely one, ma Diane de Poictiers, ma Ninon de L'Enclos, ma Louise de la Vallière, ma Rose du Barri, ma Mademoiselle de Maintenon et de Montespan as well, ma Gabrielle d'Estrée, ma Princess Lointain, for God's sake, shut your darling mouth, for you're only tolerable when silent and then you are adorable. If you utter another word I'll . . ."

Happily or unhappily, the threat was uttered in a lower voice and lost to all but she whom it did concern.

"That's Belwardine, the black-and-white man, and his famous Belle Babette from Brixton."

"He looks white enough," said Algernon, and Giovanna gazed upon him once again in wonder.

Jimmy really was too sweet for words and almost too good to be true.

"An artist, my precious," she said. "Draws with black ink on white paper. Hence the name. And the girl, Gertie Plumb, is his model. He illustrates 'Our Paris Letter' in the *Scream*. Gertie is his Parisienne and he's got the rest of Paris in his studio."

"How dreadfully tired these poor waiters look," said the kindly Algernon, observing a red-eyed pale-blue-faced vision of insomnia, who stood drooping near. "I'd like to send them *all to* Polporth Cove for a month."

"They'd die of boredom, darling, and the sunshine would kill them like germs. And how'd they earn the necessary for Mrs. Waiter AND all the little Waiters? . . . And anyhow they're doing it for money, aren't they?"

"Yes . . . But what are all the others doing it for?"

"Pleasure, Jimmy."

"They say the English take their pleasures sadly. Some of these people seem to take them like medicine—or poison."

"Shall we dance?" asked Giovanna.

"Might we wait until there's a little less of a squash?" asked Algernon.

"That would mean waiting till to-morrow, darling," replied Giovanna. "But we'll look out for a suitable opening for a young couple."

And Algernon looked out, but not with any marked symptoms of enthusiasm.

Most of the dancing couples were normal and typical night-club habitués, varying in demeanour, largely on the part of the women, from hopeless, joyless weariness and boredom, to that, largely on the part of the men, of determined and conscious hilarity.

Here and there among them were people whose weird freakishness of appearance and demeanour caused Algernon's wide eyes to open wider, and, concerning the *raison d'être* of some, he appealed to Giovanna for enlightenment.

"The man with side-whiskers, a fringe and sort of chignon, with the vast orange tie, or sash, round his neck, Jimmy? Oh, he—and anybody else like him, for that matter—is almost certainly either a failure in one of the Arts, or wishes to be mistaken for one."

"Wishes to be mistaken for a failure?"

"Yes, darling. Failure is the only true success."

"Eh?" said Jimmy, blankly.

"Paradox, darling. All great Truth is Paradox, and all great paradoxes true. If you can't sell a picture, it's complete and final proof that it is over the heads of the Philistines, or else a pearl cast before swine, or perhaps painted before the world is ready for it. It's always the world's fault if a book or picture or statue or opera or epic poem fails; never the fault of the thing itself."

"Oh," said Jimmy.

"The girl in the green sack, or rather half-sack —sounds like coals and coke, doesn't it—why, she 'made' *Purple Spots*."

"Oh? On what or whom?"

"*Purple Spots* is a book, darling. Lovely book. All spotty and purple."

"A failure?" asked Jimmy.

"Why, no, Jimmy. Nothing born in the purple can fail—'specially with spots on it. Oh, no, Melissa Proop isn't a failure, but, in spite of her success, her friends still love her and she is still welcome in the foulest circles."

"She's pretty, isn't she?" said Jimmy. "Sort of bloom on . . ."

"Yes," agreed Giovanna. "Sort of bloom on her like that on a grape or a peach—or the phosphorescence on rotten fish."

"Oh, Giovanna! Fish! . . ."

"Oh, Jimmy! . . . Nasty fishy muddy fish. Now she *would* carry all before her at Melfont Parva Vicarage.

"Carries a good deal before her, anywhere, innocent young thing," she added, and Jimmy changed the subject.

A large party entered the hall and proceeded to where three or four small tables had been joined together to form a large one.

"Oh, here's Daddy's band," said Giovanna. "I'll introduce you to some of them by and by. He sits at the head of the table and does Sir Oracle every Wednesday night when he's in town."

"By Jove! Who's the giant?" asked Jimmy.

"My most devoted admirer, darling, or should I say my late devoted admirer, now that you have come on the scene, Jimmy? He's your hated rival, darling."

"Do I hate him?" enquired Jimmy.

"He'll hate you, anyhow, my son," was the reply.

"He's Boris Goudroff, and a very coming man," she continued. "It would be a great investment to buy his pictures. He doesn't paint many, because he generally can't afford paints, brushes and canvas, much less models and a studio."

"What sort of pictures does he paint?" asked Jimmy, suppressing a yawn.

"Oh, corpses mostly—on battle-fields or gallows or mortuary slabs; maidens drowned in pools, and maidens who ought to be drowned in pools. He did a wonderful one of me as *Andromeda*."

Giovanna watched for a flush of anger or a look of disgust, chagrin or distaste, but failed to find on Algernon's placid face even so much as the faintest expression of annoyance.

"You know the story of Andromeda?" she

asked, a little sharply.

"Oh, rather. Chained to a rock. Perseus slew the sea monster."

"Let's dance," she said, and launched and steered her lover among the queer fish that darted, glided, rolled and gyrated in the somewhat turbulent waters of this cavern of *The Green Haddock.*

When, a few minutes later—Jimmy still carefully counting in time with the band—they passed the table reserved for the noisy party graced and ornamented by the presence of Boris Goudroff, a great arm shot out, and a huge hand, seizing Giovanna, pulled her and her partner, in a somewhat disorderly heap, down on to the wall-divan.

Scrambling to his feet, the indignant Algernon realized that it was the gigantic Boris Goudroff who had so unceremoniously gathered them unto himself.

"Soh, you pass me by, is it?" growled the artist. "Very nize. You could not see the leetle Boris, hein? Any peoples who cannot see ze leetle Boris, perhaps they feel him, hein? Perhaps he put his arm right round them and give them a hug that break both their leetle arms and all their leetle ribs—or perhaps he wring their leetle necks, hein? Now you dance with zis leetle Boris, and if you don' dance nize on your feet, he will dance with you sitting on his shoulder, hein?"

And springing to his feet, the giant literally whirled Giovanna from hers and plunged into the crowd.

Algernon remained seated on the plush divan. What extraordinary friends Giovanna had!

§4

As they came out into the street, and Algernon thankfully inhaled deep draughts of the clean sweet air, Boris Goudroff lifted up his mighty voice and bawled:

"Tahx-ee, Tahx-ee," in a sonorous and resounding bellow, and an answering hail from the near-by darkness preceded by a few seconds the arrival of a lurking taxi.

"I shall take you to home, Jo. Yes? Isn't it? No?" said Goudroff, opening the door of the taxi.

"Did you hear that, Jimmy?" smiled Giovanna. "Boris is offering to see me home."

"Oh, how awfully kind of him," replied Jimmy, cheerfully. "Er—if it isn't troubling him too much. I mean—er—if he's going in your direction."

Goudroff laughed loudly.

"I always goes in Jo's direction, isn't it, Jo? No?"

Giovanna stared at Algernon, her face hardening.

"Come along then, Boris," she said. "I'll give you a drink if you're good enough to deserve one . . . Good-night, Jimmy—or would you like to . . ."

"Oh, good-night, Giovanna, good-night. Thanks so much—er—I'll ring you up to-morrow."

"Good-night, Jimmy," said Giovanna, and got into the taxi, followed by Goudroff, who promptly put his arm about her waist and kissed her passionately.

"I said, if you were good enough, Boris," she protested, endeavouring to remove the huge arm that encircled her.

"What, like these silly swines call me Borris Goodenough," he replied, tightening his clasp. "I say 'I am not Borris Goodenough, nor Borris Goudenov, nor Borris Goudroff, you damnfool ignorance, but *Boreece Goudroff*,' isn't it? Yes. And who's this leetle dog you call Jeemy? I take hold of that leetle dog's leg and I take hold of his head— and then I pull. See which come off first. I zink I pull 'is 'ead off, yes. No?"

"I'm afraid Jimmy isn't as good at losing his head as all that, Boris," sighed Giovanna.

"What is it then that it is that this leetle Jeemy is?" enquired the Pole.

"Oh, various things. My future husband; an English gentleman; a clean, honest nice person, who wouldn't know a mean and dirty trick if he saw one. The kind of man that you could never even begin to understand, Boris."

"Soh? The leetle Jeemy is all such, is it? And what is poor Boris?"

"Among other things, a great artist," smiled Giovanna.

"Yes, yes, we know zat. Everybody except dam' pig-fools knows zat. What I say is, if ze nize pretty leetle Jeemy is fiancé, what is Boris?"

"Our friend," replied Giovanna.

"Oh, yes, Boris be friend of nize leetle fam'ly. Make what they call triangle, hein?" and the Franco-Polish gentleman roared with laughter and pressed his lips violently upon those of Giovanna, who struggled and fought with considerable skill but little success.

"No, I don't zink you marry zis Jeemy," Boris Goudroff continued, having reduced Giovanna to a state of limp quiescence.

"No, not yet, Jo. Not till I give the permission. I cannot marry you myself, because I haven't any money and because I haven't any dam'-foolishness to marry a woman. But nobody else isn't going to marry you, Jo. Not till Boris say it. I mean it—so be careful."

"Really?" replied Giovanna. "Very interesting! And how do you propose to prevent me from marrying Jimmy?"

"Oh, I tell ze pretty leetle Jeemy he must not. I tell him I smack him; then he be too frightened. I mean it, I say."

"Really, Boris, you positively are the most insufferably conceited creature outside a lunatic asylum. Do you really think that anything you said to Mr. Algernon Coxe would make the very slightest difference?"

"No? Well, I'll tell you what might make leetle difference. Suppose you disobey poor Boris and go to marry this Jeemy, and Boris come round to your flat the night before and say '*No.*' And tell you what I do to you and to him if you annoys me an' nuisance me by making me jealous. *No*, I say."

"And suppose I say '*Yes*,'" interrupted Giovanna.

"That is what I tell. You say '*Yes*' and Boris say '*No*,' Jo. You say '*Yes*' once more and then I jes' wring your leetle neck like *so* and do you up in parcel and post you to Jeemy with a note saying, 'If you *will* have my Jo, here she is,' hein?"

Giovanna yawned.

"I don't think I'll ask you in for a drink after all," she said as the cab stopped. "You've served my purpose, and you can go."

"Then I tink perhaps I ask myself in and I serve my purpose and then I go. No?"

Giovanna considered.

Her little scheme for making Jimmy jealous had not been a success. Should she abandon it and dismiss this impossible creature forthwith; have a final rupture, and make an end of their one-sided friendship?

Not yet, perhaps—not at once.

Jimmy might yet be stirred to feel jealousy, and roused to object, if he found Boris very much at home in her flat one evening. The moment he expostulated and said that Boris Goudroff was hardly a suitable friend, she would reply:

"Let's get married, Jimmy, and everything will

be different. Giovanna Blayton's acquaintances won't be Mrs. Jimmy's friends. I'll never see one of them again, especially this man Boris Goudroff. Let's get married, Jimmy, and I shall have some-one to look after me and keep me in order."

Yes, Boris Goudroff might yet be useful.

"Well, you may come in for a few minutes and have a drink, Boris, if you will behave yourself and go when I tell you," she said.

"Oh, yaas, I'm coming in all-right, Jo."

"Well, you won't have the chance much longer," said the girl . . . "I shall be leaving this flat, of course, when I marry . . . This'll be almost your last drink here, Boris."

Goudroff grinned.

"If you don't leave here till you marry, Leetle One, and don't marry till you leave here, Boris won't grumble you, hein? You are my girl Gio-vanna, and nobody isn't goin' to marry you—not even me," and the lips of the worthy Boris grinned widely.

Giovanna noted that his eyes did not smile in the least.

Turning, she led the way upstairs and un-locked the door of her flat.

*　　*　　*　　*　　*

"Time you were going, Boris. I'm tired."

"Tired? What's zat feel like? Zat why you are not nize to me to-night, No? All right, I go. I don't sit here and drink zis dam' nasty treacle, *crème de noyeau* and *crème de menthe*, an' look at a dam' nasty girl sitting on sofa any longer. Sooner drink crème de moo-cow and look at English big-tooth' spinster sitting on sofa in Royal Academy . . . Bah!"

Giovanna yawned.

"An' don't you play too much tricks wiz me, you Giovanna. You and your leetle Jeemy! I show you a something. And never say I didn't fair warned you. I bad enemy, see?"

"You're bad everything, Boris," replied Giovanna. "Rotten bad. Good-night."

And Boris Goudroff slouched out of the flat, banging doors behind him with shattering violence.

CHAPTER VI

When Algernon, returning from *The Green Haddock*, reached home in the small hours of the morning, he found with despondency and alarm that his mother was there, and waiting up for him.

Waiting "*up*," with a special peculiar intonation and a heavy emphasis upon the "up," was one of Mrs. Dashwood-Coxe's favourite expressions—one of her verbal specialities, conveying a world of reproach, accusation and disapproval.

She had arrived unexpectedly at the Kensington house, as was her wont, with the intention of remaining indefinitely, as was also her wont.

In a surprisingly short time she extracted from the reluctant Algernon a full account of all his doings since last she had seen him, and particularly of his admittedly deplorable activities of that evening.

If *The Green Haddock* and its habitués had seemed strange and undesirable in reality, how more than strange, how more than undesirable did they seem in the description.

If, on the homeward journey, Algernon had thought the place and people unpleasing and unprofitable, he now—as he falteringly described them in the cold and rarefied atmosphere of his mother's presence, and beneath the cold and penetrating judgment of her clear and steady eye—not merely thought, but knew, them to be worthless, raffish and disgusting.

And once again he saw Giovanna take the colour of her surroundings; beheld her with the pitiless criticism of his mother's all-seeing eye; compared her character and her life with those of his mother; and once again realized how truly right his mother was.

Not a word of condemnation or criticism was uttered by Mrs. Dashwood-Coxe, but every sentence of Algernon's replies to her questions resolved itself into a clear condemnation and a harsh criticism.

Mrs. Dashwood-Coxe was a very clever woman. Her son was not a clever man.

Often and often had he told his mother a lie. Never had he successfully deceived her and never, never had he disobeyed her command.

"My son," said Mrs. Dashwood-Coxe, when all had been confessed and the full and true account of the evening laid bare in all its hideousness.

"You must see for yourself that this cannot go on. Even if you were lost to all self-respect, all sense of duty to yourself, you have a duty to your father and, possibly, if I may suggest it, a duty to me, your mother.

"My dear boy, you must *see* that it can't go on. The moment you were away from me—as that Doctor Desart was so anxious for you to be—you at once got into trouble, fell from grace. To put it in the kindest and mildest way, you made a terrible mistake.

"Happily it is not too late to rectify it. You turned aside from the right path and took a false step. Thank God, you can withdraw. You can return to the right path, to the way of your mother's teaching . . .

"Algernon, *think*. Think of all you yourself have told me to-night; think of that girl's manners and conduct in my house; think of what she has done; what she has been; what she is; and ask yourself how you can persist in it."

"Mother, I have promised that I . . ." stammered

her wretched son.

"Algernon," Mrs. Dashwood-Coxe swept on, "if you are willing to break your mother's heart for this . . . this . . . I will not call her what she certainly is . . . If you are willing to bring your poor Father's grey hairs in sorrow to the grave, even so, think of yourself if you will not think of us.

"Algernon, to thine own self be true, and it follows as the night the day, thou canst not be untrue to your mother, your whole upbringing, your God . . .

Mrs. Dashwood-Coxe paused and fell silent, coldly and sorrowfully eyeing the unhappy Algernon.

"To think that you could ever come into your mother's presence straight from this girl's rooms— or room . . . How and where *does* she live, by the way?"

"She has a flat at 22, Blenheim Street, Marlborough Circus," replied Algernon, somewhat sulkily, and without looking at his mother as he spoke.

Had he been doing so, he would have observed a sudden and most remarkable change in the expression of her face.

Mrs. Dashwood-Coxe almost gasped.

"*What?*" she whispered, her face hardening, her eyes narrowing, a heavy frown contracting her brows.

It was as though her son had suddenly used foul and obscene language, or uttered some incredible insult.

"*What* did you say, Algernon?"

And one firm white hand rose from her lap to her breast.

"22, Blenheim Street, Marlborough Circus, is Giovanna's address. Quite a good road, and a very nice little flat . . . What's the matter, Mother?"

For, though her expression was inscrutable, her face had paled, and she was obviously under the influence of some powerful emotion. Was it anger, fear, indignation, horror, or a blending of them all?

Certainly he had, in some way, given his mother a terrible shock.

Was she really pale, or was it a trick of light and of his imagination?

No, she was white to the lips and staring at him and through him as though he were a ghost, or as though through him and behind him she could see a ghost.

Nor was Algernon's fancy far astray.

Minerva Coxe was seeing ghosts indeed. Ghosts of her youth, her innocence, her happiness . . . and of a man.

Seeing terribly the ghost of a man.

Algernon stared at his mother in surprise, the while his mother stared through him in horror and dismay.

"What is it, Mother? What is the matter? Are you ill?" he cried, conscience-stricken and alarmed.

Moistening dry grey lips, she asked in a low and toneless voice.

"Who told you that address?"

"What do you mean, Mother?"

"Where did you hear that address?"

"It's Giovanna's address. She lives there."

"How did she find it out?"

"What do you mean, Mother?"

"How did she find it out, I say? She must have known of it . . . But *how?*"

"I don't understand you, Mother."

"She must have heard of it. It is intentional. She went there deliberately and took you there.

Yes . . . yes . . . I see it. Deliberate and intentional. But how did she know of it? *How?*"

"What do you mean, Mother?"

"How long has the girl been there?"

"Oh, a long time . . . Two or three years."

"You mean that she took that flat and lived in it, before you knew her."

"Yes, Mother. Why?"

"You're perfectly sure? Absolutely certain that she took that flat and lived in it before she'd ever set eyes on you? Before she even knew of your existence?"

"Yes. Mother. Why?"

Mrs. Dashwood-Coxe appeared to be relieved by her son's assurance.

The colour slowly returned to her face, and there now appeared to be less of fear and anger, in her look, than of puzzlement and incredulity.

"22, Blenheim Street, Marlborough Circus," she said softly, wonderingly. "Is there a church almost opposite to the house, Algernon?"

"Yes, Mother. Why? Do you know the house?"

Mrs. Dashwood-Coxe's hand fell again to her lap and clasped the other, her knuckles showing white.

"It sounds vaguely familiar," she said. "It struck me that I'd heard it before. I rather fancy that, curiously enough, a friend of mine actually lived there . . . Or it may have been at some other house in the same road, or possibly it was Marlborough Crescent. And anyhow, it was years ago, long before you were born, so it's of no great interest."

Mrs. Dashwood-Coxe was herself again—or almost so.

Suddenly she rose to her feet.

"Come here, my boy," she continued, and placing her hands upon his shoulders, Mrs. Dashwood-Coxe fixed the deep gaze of her clear, hard eyes upon those of her son, and seemed to hold them while they endeavoured to evade.

"Algernon, you will not marry this girl," she said slowly. "You will break off all relation with her. You will never see her again nor answer any letter that she may write to you."

Algernon's eyes fell.

"Mother! I . . ."

"You will not defy your mother. You will not disobey her, you will not break her heart for the first loose-living woman that makes eyes at you."

"Mother, she's . . ."

"You will choose, Algernon. You will choose between her and your mother, *now*, and choose finally. *You will never again see your mother*, Alger-non, or else you will never see this . . . this . . . girl again."

"Mother, Giovanna is . . ."

"I will go and re-pack my suit-case now, Alger-non, walk to Waterloo, and sit in the waiting-room until the first train goes to Melfont Parva in the morning, unless you . . ."

"Mother, I . . ."

"Choose, Algernon."

"I must see her once if only to say good-bye."

"Very well, my son, you may see her once again —to say good-bye. And now I will say good-night.

"Sleep well, *for you have chosen wisely*."

And Mrs. Dashwood-Coxe kissed Algernon firmly on the brow.

§2

On the following morning Algernon by special request—conveyed with special intonation— accompanied his mother to Melfont Parva, and, with innate and trained suggestibility, soon came to see the truth of his mother's carefully unuttered suggestion of Agatha Sharp's infinite superiority to Giovanna Blayton.

Agatha practically lived at the Vicarage, and it was Algernon's privilege, each evening, after a day of easy and pleasant parochial activities, gentle tennis on the shady lawn, music in the cool drawing-room, and strolls about the moonlit garden, to escort Agatha to her door.

And so the days went by . . .

Receiving no letter from Giovanna, Algernon wrote none to her, and gradually the image of her dark beauty was somewhat obliterated or temporarily obscured by the blonde loveliness of Agatha.

Ere long, Algernon walked in a dream of fair women, and their twain images seemed to fuse, seemed to grow composite, to be superimposed the one upon the other.

And here and now, in the great peace of Melfont Parva, that of Agatha rather predominated.

Obviously and most essentially Agatha was a gentlewoman and had every one of the noble qualities that that fine word connotes.

And that Agatha was obviously and essentially a fool also, seemed a small matter. One does not desire brains in women or, to proceed from the undemonstrable general to the plain particular, Mrs. Dashwood-Coxe did not desire brains in a daughter-in-law, nor Algernon in a wife.

For, gently, warily, but inexorably, the strong hand of his mother guided Algernon's faltering footsteps along a peaceful easy path that led toward the point whence he should behold the dawn of a new, a higher and a better life—life with Agatha Sharp.

Gradually and slowly, as night changes to day, and as dawn imperceptibly grows and alters from black to grey and from grey to palest gold and faintest rose, so dawned upon the unshocked consciousness of Algernon, the perception that fates and forces outside himself, fates and forces too strong for him, were ordaining that he should engage himself to Agatha.

Clearly, his mother expected it.

Evening after evening, as she kissed him on the brow, Mrs. Dashwood-Coxe would ask, with raised eyebrows and expression faintly arch:

"Have you anything to tell me, Algernon?"

"Er—er, no; er—no, Mother."

"Not yet, my dear boy?"

"Er—no, Mother. What should there be?"

"Oh, come, come, you sly rogue. Do you think your own mother doesn't see what is going on?"

And when, from time to time, Algernon would suggest that he thought he would run up to town to-morrow for a day or two, his mother would negative the suggestion with some such reply as:

"Oh, not to-morrow, dear. We'll all three go up, a little later on. So much nicer for you. You'll love to take Agatha to some good Concerts."

And when his conscience pricked him, as it slightly did from time to time, Algernon would reflect that inasmuch as Giovanna had not written, she could not be suffering any feeling of neglect.

But Giovanna had written, urgent and despairing letters, and Mrs. Dashwood-Coxe, albeit an honourable and Christian woman, had considered it her duty to shield her son from the evil consequences of their receipt.

What Mrs. Dashwood-Coxe considered it her duty to do, that she invariably did; and anything that Mrs. Dashwood-Coxe desired to do, she invariably regarded as a duty.

So, increasingly conscious of his fate, the little victim played, and soon ceased to struggle against the ineluctable end.

§3

One evening, an evening of full moon, perfect as only an English evening can be, Algernon, a little troubled by his conscience, a little piqued by Giovanna's silence, more than a little desirous of love and understanding, greatly admiring Agatha's gentle beauty and most greatly yearning for finality, an end of mental struggle, stress and strain, suddenly and impulsively flung his arms about Agatha as she sat beside him in the shade of the great old cedar, and kissed her on the ear.

Agatha's arms stole about his neck and with a queer little half-sobbing catch of the breath, she returned his kiss in equal measure and upon his lips.

"*Agatha!*"

"*Algernon!*"

When they entered the drawing-room, there was no need for Mrs. Dashwood-Coxe to enquire whether Algernon had anything to tell her, and the good woman devoutly and humbly thanked God for all that *He* had done in achieving for her her heart's desire.

This was indeed an Answer to Prayer—prayer aided a little, perhaps, by the suppression of letters, the remorseless application of the power of suggestion, and the equally remorseless vilification of an innocent girl.

It was Mrs. Dashwood-Coxe's favourite dictum that Heaven helps those who help themselves, and surely Mrs. Dashwood-Coxe had helped herself industriously?

CHAPTER VII

"The highest and truest happiness lies in making others happy . . . You have made me very happy, Algernon," said Mrs. Dashwood-Coxe, as, seated on a sofa in the drawing-room of Algernon's town house, that determined and indomitable woman beamed upon her son and her daughter-in-law elect.

Though Algernon could find no flaw in this admirable argument, he failed to square practice with theory, for, in point of fact, far from enjoying the highest and truest happiness, he discovered himself to be profoundly miserable.

Loving Agatha, engaged to marry Agatha at a very early date, he longed for Giovanna; and daily the longing increased until it became an unbearable yearning that was rapidly crystallizing into a mad and reprehensible determination to go and kiss her instead of Agatha.

Her silence puzzled and worried him.

Twice and thrice he had attempted to telephone to her and had received no reply. Twice and thrice he had sat down to write to her and each time had torn the letter up, on reaching the sentence:

"I am now engaged to another woman."

It sounded absurdly as though he was providing Giovanna with a companion wife, as a kindly Mussalman might do, fearing lest Number One at times be lonely.

Besides, never having broken off his engagement to Giovanna, how could he be engaged to Agatha?

What *had* he done?

And once again, in a bath of cold perspiration

he realized that there he sat, Algernon Dashwood Coxe, in his own Kensington house, solemnly, seriously, and formally engaged to two women at once.

What had he done?

And what would Giovanna do?

Would she institute an action against him for Breach of Promise, bringing public disgrace and shame upon his mother, his father, Agatha and himself?

She might well do so.

What a terrible and ghastly thought.

What a cad and a cur he would look in the Law Courts. Fancy hearing all his letters read out in Court—his intimate private love-letters to Giovanna—punctuated by the loud guffaws of jeering apes.

From cold perspiration, Algernon went hot all over, at the thought of such a thing.

And this letter that he could not write. If he did succeed in composing it, and sent it to her, that would also be read out.

No, he must go and see her—not only because he yearned and burned to see her and touch her and hold her in his arms again, but because he could explain better, could make her understand how it came about, could beg her to forgive him—and could solemnly swear that not only did he love her just as much, but if such a thing were possible, far more than ever.

And also there was another thing—though no man retaining any shreds of decency and self-respect, any rags of honour to cover his weak baseness, must for a moment glance at it—Giovanna, simply refusing to accept the situation, refusing to hear a word about Agatha Sharp, *might* seize him and whirl him away . . . away from this terrible milieu of entanglements, compulsions, interference and misery.

But of course such a dream was absurd.

How could he possibly treat his mother so?

Or rather, how could he possibly treat Agatha so?

Dear, sweet, gentle, beautiful Agatha. How he hated her now that he had to marry her.

It was Giovanna he wanted. Giovanna—that bright flame.

Giovanna, who loved him and understood him. Giovanna, who would mother him and take responsibilities and who would never harry, interfere, compel and impose her will upon him.

Yes, Giovanna was a flame, a fire; and Agatha was tepid water—but the tepid water could not quench the fire in his heart.

He must go and see Giovanna.

§2

Algernon went.

Ensconced upon the big sofa, he found Boris Goudroff beside whom Giovanna had evidently been sitting.

"Good-evening," said Giovanna. "Kind of you to call."

"Soh!" exploded Goudroff, "it is our leetle Jeemy. Our nize pretty leetle Jeemy that has been hiding from us so long. Naughty boy, Jeemy. I sink I put you 'cross my knee. I sink I smack you, Jeemy, for making Giovanna unhappy; and then I say 'You go 'way, Jeemy, and don't you never come back no more. You make Giovanna unhappy and, much more worse, you make Boris Goudroff unhappy . . . So you go to 'ell.'"

Algernon Coxe had never really lacked physical courage. Completely ignoring the gigantic Goudroff, save for a quietly contemptuous glance, he asked Giovanna if he could see her alone, or whether, if the occasion were inconvenient, she would make an appointment for that purpose.

"Get out, Boris," said Giovanna, trying to suppress and hide the wild joy she felt, the surge of ecstatic happiness and gratitude to God. "You are *de trop*—now. Come in again to-morrow."

"Nozzing doing," replied Goudroff. "Why, you have not nearly enough kizz me, yet. You going to sit on my knee and kizz me some more and make lof to me," and he grinned malevolently at Algernon, displaying ripe red lips and great gleaming teeth through his black beard.

Algernon turned to the door that he had just closed, and opening it wide, stood waiting.

Giovanna faced the sprawling Franco-Russian-Pole, her mouth set and her eye glinting.

"Get out," she said again and pointed to the door. "You'll go now, or you'll never come back."

"All right. Kizz me again then, Joey, and I come again to-morrow for some more, hein?"

And beneath the disapproving eye of the disgusted Algernon, Giovanna kissed the Russian, clapped his big black felt hat upon his head, and hustled him from the flat—brushing her fingers thereafter as though removing pollution after contact with something unclean.

"And now, James?" she asked, closing the door of the room, and turning to Algernon, her face a clever mask of cool and disapproving ivory.

What followed was truly terrible to both these hapless people; and her lover's confession that he had actually engaged himself to another woman, without a word to his affianced bride, awakened, and turned to flame indeed, every drop of Neapolitan blood in Giovanna's body.

To Algernon, his beloved and beautiful Giovanna became a fiend incarnate, a she-devil, a vulgar and terrible woman who poured forth a deadly stream of vituperative insult, lashing him with scorching epithet and burning him with a scalding flow of dreadful invective, every sentence of which was rendered the more horrible by its ghastly and pitiable truth.

And it was doubtless the undeniable truth of the accusations and the insults that made Algernon do what in his whole lifetime he had rarely done—lose his temper and, with it, all self-control.

Before long, the two, furious, despairing; mad with rage, jealousy and sense of wrong; beside themselves with pain and grief and horror, were equally unbalanced and distraught; and, with accusation and insult, each lashing the other to greater rage . . . each hating the other beyond expression . . . each loving the other unbearably . . . each eager to wound, willing and able to strike.

"*You*, sitting there, pawing and kissing that filthy Russian beast, and inviting him here again to-morrow. Lying in his arms on that sofa; that foul mass of corruption and bestiality from your stinking night-club. You dissipated, flirting, depraved . . . Oh, *forgive* me, Giovanna darling."

"And you, you miserable, weak, backboneless jelly-fish. You poor feeble, witless, gutless mother's-darling. *You* should talk about Boris Goudroff. My God! He *is* a man, anyhow . . . One night you're here, engaged to me, going to marry me quite soon, and a few nights later you're engaged to another girl and going to marry her quite soon.

"You treacherous cur. Well, I pity the girl, you cowardly unreliable swindler; you miserable, priggish, worthless imitation. Get your loathsome mother to make you some little knickerbockers and buy you some little socks. And then, never you let go of her hand again—except for her to wipe your nose . . . Oh, Jimmy, Jimmy! Don't break my heart. You love *me*, you know you do! . . ."

And Giovanna flung herself down upon the sofa, her face buried in the cushions, her little body cruelly shaken from head to foot by rending sobs.

"Oh, Jimmy, Jimmy, how could you? How *could* you?"

"Oh, don't, Giovanna, don't . . . Oh, darling, don't cry like that . . . Yes! I'll give her up! *I'll give her up!*"

Giovanna sprang erect with blazing eyes and outstretched finger that almost touched his face.

"Give her up! You worm . . . You scrap of tissue-paper . . . Give her up? Yes, until you get home, and your mother lifts her little finger, and the girl grins at you. Give her up for how long? You *liar!* You poor weak, shifty cad! You creeping, crawling, sneaking jilt . . . Making love to two girls at once . . ."

"And what about you? What were you doing when I came in to-night? What about making love to two men at once? You deceitful disreputable . . ."

"What, *I? I* make love to a man? Oh, so you'd add the vilest insult to the foulest injury, would you? By God! You've done it to the wrong woman, Algernon Coxe. Don't you think you'll do this to me, and come off scot-free. If it's to be insults and injuries you'll find you're not the only one who can do a little in the injuring line. You are the most despicable and contemptible cad and cur and weakling that ever . . ."

And so it went on.

At last, unbearably hurt and insufferably insulted by the cruellest truths which were therefore the truest cruelties, Algernon sprang to his feet and strode to the door. Throwing it open and turning to shut it behind him, he looked at Giovanna, and for a second hung in doubt.

And his fate, his very life, and those of Giovanna Blayton, for a second hung in doubt also . . .

How could he leave her thus, weeping distraught and broken-hearted; he, the scoundrel who had broken her heart?

But she had said dreadful unforgivable things.

But they were true, and he undeniably was everything that she had called him.

He could not leave her thus, and if he did not escape now, he would have just such a scene with Agatha, equally wronged, insulted and broken-hearted.

And his mother! . . .

How could he face his mother if unable to tell her that he had broken with Giovanna, once and for all, and bidden her good-bye for ever?

He could not do it.

He must go.

Algernon Coxe turned upon his heel.

"*Jimmy! Jimmy!*" and, leaping from the couch, Giovanna rushed toward him.

"*Jimmy!*"

He turned again, and the girl threw herself into his arms—and the fate of these two was sealed.

For a minute they clung together, weeping, kissing, incoherent. Then drawing her lover back into the room, Giovanna closed and locked the door and led him to the sofa.

"Sit down, my darling," she said, and drew him down beside her.

"My darling, *my darling*, you can't leave me like this; and I cannot let you go . . . Oh Jimmy, forgive me and—*stay with me.*"

Stay with her!

Yes, he *must* stay a little longer with her, thought Jimmy.

Yes, now he must stay altogether, thought Giovanna, or she would lose him altogether.

He must not go back to that house, that horrible mother and that other woman who had taken him from her.

Now was the time to play her last card, the trump card that should win this dreadful game.

Giovanna played her last card and found herself a woman scorned.

Even she had under-estimated the strength of the inhibitions stamped and sealed in her lover's mind during its plastic and receptive years; even she had failed to realize that, to Algernon Coxe, even while madly and passionately in love, sex was the Terrible Thing, the physical manifestation of passion (ere blessed and sanctified by his Church) the true Sin Against the Holy Ghost; even she had not understood that from babyhood he had been seared, had been branded and had had burnt into him the belief that to "fall" as Adam fell was not only blackest Sin—but a thing utterly foul, horrible, degrading, dirty and beastly beyond description.

So Giovanna failed—and Minerva Coxe won.

Giovanna, temptress innocent and pure of heart, was spurned—and Hell had no fury like Giovanna scorned . . .

"*Go*, you hound," she gasped, and her Neapolitan mother—who slew herself because James Augustus Blayton wearied of her—would have recognized herself in her daughter. "Go before I kill you."

And she struck him in the face with all her

strength.

CHAPTER VIII

Mr. and Mrs. Algernon Coxe went for their honeymoon to Bournemouth.

In the mild air of England's most beautiful town, they mildly loved and lived and had their being—Agatha's a truly happy being, marred only by a strong suspicion that her *distrait* husband was sometimes thinking of That Other Woman; Algernon's a truly miserable being, brightened only by the hope that a measure of outward peace might now accrue to him.

"*'For men must kill the thing they love!'*" he would whisper to himself, and shudder.

One beautiful evening, as they sat upon a seat in the calm silence of the high East Cliff and gazed toward the distant Purbeck Hills and Old Harry Rocks across the bay, his arm stole about Agatha's waist as her beautiful head sank upon his shoulder.

"Isn't it utterly perfect," she whispered.

"Perfect, Giovanna," he replied, and they sprang apart as though stung.

"You *are* thinking of that horrible woman!" cried Agatha. "I knew it! I've said so a dozen times . . ."

She had, thought Algernon, and a dozen dozen.

"No, no, dearest Agatha," he reassured her.

"And I suppose that's why you call me 'Giovanna,'" snapped his mortified and unappeased wife. "Giovanna, indeed! Do you *want* to insult me, Algernon? . . . If you're always thinking of the wretched creature, why didn't you marry her?"

"Why indeed!" thought the profoundly unhappy

170

husband.

"I shall tell Mamma when she comes to-morrow," continued Agatha, who was beginning to exhibit signs that she might quite conceivably develop into a first-class nagger.

"Oh, don't tell Mother, dearest Agatha," pleaded Algernon. "It would make her awfully unhappy if she thought . . ."

"But it doesn't matter if I'm made awfully unhappy, I suppose; if *I* think . . ."

"Well, don't think it, darling, it's absurd."

"And it's not absurd, I suppose, for you to call me 'Giovanna.' But it's quite absurd for me to object to being called by another woman's name—and *such* a woman . . . Fancy a young wife, not a month married, being called by the name of another woman—a bad woman who was her husband's mistress!"

"*Agatha! . .*"

"Well, I'm glad you do remember my name, Algernon. On the whole, I prefer it to one that suggests barrel-organs and ice-cream . . . and vice."

Algernon sighed and held his peace—the beginnings of wisdom—and the little storm blew itself out.

§2

Mamma, installed in Mother's Room, was awaiting the happy couple, to welcome them on their arrival at the house wherein they were, she fervently hoped, to live long long happy years beneath her watchful guidance.

The faithful and ancient retainers, galvanized to new life, had the house in beautiful readiness and Mamma herself ordered the home-coming dinner, and, with her own firm capable hands, arranged the flowers with perfect precision if not perfect grace.

Warmly she kissed her devoted daughter-in-law with a—

"Welcome, dearest Agatha, to your home. May you never know a moment's unhappiness."

And kindly she kissed her son with a—

"Dear boy, I'm sure you're going to be so happy —now that you have been so sensible."

But upstairs in the bedroom, Mrs. Dashwood-Coxe learned from a tired and inclined-to-be-tearful Agatha that Algernon was still thinking of That Woman.

Mrs. Dashwood-Coxe pooh-poohed the idea that this was a matter of the slightest interest or moment.

"But of course, my dear," she said reassuringly, "it's only natural and inevitable that a man should sometimes think of the girl to whom he has been actually engaged. It would be a very extraordinary thing if he didn't. What he is saying to himself as he gazes at you is:

" 'Thank Heaven that I escaped that woman Giovanna.' And with the name on the tip of his tongue like that, he utters it.

"His very thought, his grateful thought, 'This is not that girl Giovanna' causes him to say the name that is in his mind, even though it be, as it undoubtedly now is, a name repugnant to him."

"Perhaps so . . . I hope so," replied Agatha, but with a shade more of doubt than of hope in her words.

And sufficient of doubt remained in the mind of Agatha—a mind neither deep nor broad, nor capable of large content—to make her incline to be a little watchful, faintly fearful, and slightly suspicious.

The unopened envelopes of Algernon's letters

were of deep, and faintly painful, interest; and so, very soon, were the letters they contained.

For, as she had to admit, Algernon concealed nothing, and left his letters, awaiting answer, lying for days at a time upon the beautiful old bureau that had belonged to the great-great-grandfather of the old old lady from whom Algernon had inherited it.

A most attractive and fascinating piece of furniture this, and one that obviously interested Agatha more than any other piece in the house.

It had large drawers and little drawers, large cupboards and little cupboards, horizontal pigeon-holes and perpendicular pigeon-holes and, alas, one or two locked drawers and locked cupboards.

Doubtless there were secret drawers and secret cupboards also; and a secret drawer was a thing that intrigued, fascinated and indeed almost obsessed Agatha.

For a secret drawer may contain a secret—souvenirs, photographs, love-tokens, or even secret letters secretly received from a discarded lover, or from a lover only apparently discarded.

And if there were not guilty love-letters of to-day, there might be a packet of less guilty love-letters of yesterday; and with such love-letters, a jealous wife might torture herself most exquisitely.

Moreover, having read them, she might torture and punish her husband. She might extract sentences, phrases, personal and particular expressions, terms of endearment and use them in bitter mockery and contempt.

One day Agatha's industry, patience and ingenuity were rewarded.

Pulling, one after the other, at each of the partitions between the pigeon-holes, she heard a sharp click. The back of the pigeon-hole flew open as the spring was released, and disclosed a little chamber, some six inches square. In this reposed, not an ancient will, a faded rose, a love-token trinket, not a packet of letters tied up with blue ribbon—but three modern and prosaic keys, the largest an obvious latch-key, the others apparent keys of drawers, boxes or trunks.

To the latch-key a common linen label was tied.

Why conceal keys?

One put certain keys in a safe place, of course, but why conceal them in a secret cavity?

A concealed latch-key! Intriguing and suspicious!

Agatha drew out the latch-key first, and with a cold pain at her heart, and a sensation of shock and of faintness, read the words:

Key of Giovanna's flat.

Oh! . . Oh! . . .

So the mild, amiable, and virtuous Algernon had the key of Giovanna's flat, had he? *Oh!* . . .

And Agatha sat staring at the horrible thing, her hand pressed against her heart.

And the two smaller keys? With what deception and wickedness were they connected?

And instantly Agatha thought of the big and heavy steel box that she had discovered in the locked-up tank-room when she and Algernon were making a thorough and complete tour of her new home.

She had had to get the key of that room from Algernon.

Yes, that box had two locks, she remembered, and the key-holes were more or less of the size that these keys would fit.

What was it Algernon had said when, at lunch one day, she had remarked:

"What is in the locked trunk in the tank-room,

dear? That big heavy one with the empty trunks beside and on top of it?"

So far as she could remember, he had said:

"Oh, odds and ends; books, bric-a-brac, pictures, that sort of thing."

Had he looked self-conscious and guilty as he answered the question? To the best of her recollection he had stammered and stuttered a little, but then Algernon was apt to do that at any time, if suddenly questioned.

Had she pursued the subject at all? Yes, she recalled saying:

"Why not have them out? Or are they just rubbish?"

And now she distinctly remembered his reply.

"Oh, they're not mine really . . . Let 'em alone . . . The box won't be there long."

And, supposing that he was minding the box for somebody, she had let the subject drop . . .

And now to see whether these two keys fitted the two locks of that same box, and, if so, to discover the reason for such secrecy as well as care, in their concealment.

Yes, this was not mere safe-keeping. It was *concealment.*

Why?

And straightway she went upstairs, got the key, entered the tank-room, always, for some reason, kept locked, and quickly discovered that the keys did indeed fit the key-holes as she had anticipated.

CHAPTER IX

Crossing the hall from the library to the drawing-room, Mrs. Dashwood-Coxe was startled by the sound of an appalling scream.

Shriek after shriek rang through the otherwise silent house.

There followed the sound of a heavy fall, and silence reigned once more.

With a little less than her usual majestic dignity, and at a little more than her accustomed unhasting speed, Mrs. Dashwood-Coxe almost hurried up the stairs.

Unguided by any sound, she entered each of the rooms above, and finally climbed to the highest floor where were the maids' bedrooms and the lumber-room, which, on account of its containing the great cistern, was known as the tank-room.

Seeing that the door of this room was open, a most unusual event—as her son had recently kept it locked and retained the key until Agatha had enquired why, and had asked for it—Mrs. Dashwood-Coxe entered the room and saw her daughter-in-law lying motionless upon her back before an open trunk, a big black box that she had hitherto never seen.

"Why, Agatha, my dear!" she said, and, as she bent over the prostrate girl, saw what the box contained—the most hideous, ghastly, and terrible sight that her eyes had ever beheld.

Mrs. Dashwood-Coxe neither screamed nor fainted, but slamming down the lid of the box, seized Agatha by the arm and dragged her unceremoniously from the room.

This done, she turned, shut the door, locked it,

176

removed the key, and stood eyeing the inanimate Agatha.

"*The servants!*" she whispered, and, dragging Agatha head foremost to the top of the stairs, put her strong arms about the girl's slight body, and partly carried, partly dragged, *her* to her own bedroom on the floor below.

Here, loosening the girl's clothing, spraying her with eau-de-cologne, placing cold wet handkerchiefs on her neck, forehead and wrists, applying smelling-salts to her nostrils, Mrs. Dashwood-Coxe soon restored her to consciousness.

Sitting up upon the bed, Agatha stared wildly round.

"*Oh! . . oh! . .* I dreamt . . ."

And then:

"*The corpse! The corpse!*" she shrieked. "*He's got that woman's body in the box! . . .*"

And uttered an insane scream . . .

"Hush, you fool . . . I mean, you foolish girl," said Mrs. Dashwood-Coxe, with angry urgency. "The servants! . . ."

And as Agatha commenced to scream again, she clapped her hand upon the open mouth, and forced Agatha back upon the pillow.

"Be quiet," she said, as though addressing a dog. "Be quiet, will you! Pull yourself together and be helpful. Control yourself . . . the servants . . . passers-by . . ."

Seizing Mrs. Dashwood-Coxe's wrist in both hands, Agatha tore the hand from her mouth.

"*Murder!*" she shrieked. "*Murder!* . . . Your son is a murderer, and you've married me to him. *I am married to a murderer.* He'll be hanged, and I shall be a murderer's widow. People will point at me . . ."

"*Quiet,* I tell you . . . If you make another sound, I'll . . . I'll . . . Let me think . . ."

177

If Mrs. Dashwood-Coxe had, like the rest of us, sinned the sins of pride, self-sufficiency, self-righteousness, arrogance and selfishness—she now suffered.

For here was she—God's Own Good Woman, Wife of the Rector of Melfont Parva, Model and Inspiration to the County, a Leading and a Shining Light unto all men, and particularly unto all women—in her son's house, with the murdered body of her son's lover, and with her son's wife shrieking, "*Your son is a murderer . . .*"

And, as she mentally staggered beneath the dreadful blow, she realized that she had brought her punishment upon herself, and that had she not schemed for her own ends, the murdered girl would be alive; and her son a happy man—instead of standing within the very shadow of the gallows.

As she had sinned, she suffered.

But Mrs. Dashwood-Coxe was not the woman meekly to accept punishment, to be shocked into submission to fate, nor to be crushed beneath a burden of sorrow, be it flung upon her never so suddenly.

'*My head is bloody but unbowed.*'

What to do?

Her son must be saved.

This screaming fool must be silenced.

Had the servants heard anything?

Was there already a crowd outside the house?

"Agatha," she said, as the girl struggled with her. "*Quiet!* . . . Listen . . . We must save Algernon."

"I won't be dragged into it! I *won't!*" cried the girl . . . "They'll bring me into it. They'll say I helped him do it. They'll say I knew the body was hidden here all the time."

"No, they won't. No, they won't," urged Mrs. Dashwood-Coxe. "Don't you see? *No one need ever know*. No one *does* know yet, but you and I . . . and Algernon."

"I won't be dragged into it, I tell you. I *won't*," cried the girl again. "It's what they call being accessory after the fact, and they might hang me, too. At best, they'd send me to prison for life . . . And you, too," she added. "Both of us dragged to gaol . . . To spend years in prison, through your precious son. It serves you right . . . marrying me to a murderer . . . I believe you knew all the time . . ."

"She's mad," said Mrs. Dashwood-Coxe.

And it was indeed obvious that the shock had completely unhinged Agatha's none too solid and stable intellect.

Thought after thought flashed through the mother's agonized but clear efficient mind.

Could she cajole this selfish noisy fool into silence about her appalling discovery?

No, this poor shallow soul had but the one thought—self-preservation.

And what about the girl's self-preservation from shame, disgrace, social ruin and the horrors of the public pillory of the press? But she'd fear even more the danger of being held, as she herself had said, accessory after the fact.

Could she bribe her?

How?

Could she give her an injection or a sleeping-draught? Keep her drugged and unconscious for days, somehow dispose of the box, and then persuade her that she had been ill, and that her memories of the corpse in the tank-room were but those of a hideous nightmare?

Hopeless . . .

The girl had had her eye on that box for some time, and she knew what she knew.

Could she somehow get the box away?

Algernon must do it: take it out of the house and bury it in the garden or leave it at the left-luggage office of some railway terminus for a start —and then declare the girl insane, swear there never had been any such box in the house.

Could she *kill* her here and now? And the strong white hands flexed and clenched.

The mind of Mrs. Dashwood-Coxe recoiled from that abyss, and for a moment, for the first time in her life, she was filled with a human sympathy for human sinners, and had a clear glimpse of the terrible compulsion under which some murders come to be committed.

Thus must poor Algernon have felt, ere driven to do this dreadful deed.

What could she do?

The question was answered and the matter taken from her hands forthwith, for, with a swift evasion, Agatha eluded her grasp, sprang from the bed, dodged, ducked beneath an outstretched arm, rushed from the room and, with a cry of—

"I *won't* be dragged into it," fled down the stairs screaming:

"*Help! Murder! Help!*" at the top of her voice.

Ere Mrs. Dashwood-Coxe could overtake her, the girl had gained the morning-room in which stood the telephone, and had slammed and locked the door.

A moment later she was ringing up the police.

CHAPTER X

The trial of Algernon Dashwood Coxe was held at the Central Criminal Court, Old Bailey, London, before Mr. Justice Jermyn; the Counsel for the Crown being Sir Henry Mackworth White and Mr. Eustace O'Gorman, instructed by the Director of Public Prosecutions; the Counsel for the prisoner being Sir Everard Witherby and Mr. Julius Warde, instructed by Mr. William Harringay; the indictment being: THE KING against Algernon Dashwood Coxe.

Presentment of the Grand Jury: Algernon Dashwood Coxe is charged with the following offence:

Statement of Offence: Murder.

Particulars of Offence: Algernon Dashwood Coxe on a date unknown in the County of Middlesex and within the jurisdiction of the Central Criminal Court murdered Giovanna Giulia Francesca Bianca Orsola Blayton.

The Clerk of the Court: "Algernon Dashwood Coxe, you are charged on indictment and also on an inquisition found against you by a Coroner's Jury that on a date unknown in this year you murdered Giovanna Giulia Francesca Bianca Orsola Blayton. Are you Guilty or Not Guilty?"

Prisoner: "Not Guilty."

A Jury was then sworn.

Algernon Coxe, looking and feeling dazed and incredulous, and with something of the air of an awakened somnambulist, gazed about him at the Court wherein he was to be tried for his life.

Wearily and almost stupidly he stared at the Judge, an imposing, stately, awe-inspiring, and indeed somewhat terrifying figure, with his grim austere face, an impression of bushy eyebrows, piercing grey eyes, prominent nose and thin-lipped straight mouth, framed between the great grey wig and red robe.

His life lay in the hands of this man.

Or did it lie in the hands of that oddly-assorted heterogeneous dozen of men and women in the Jury box?

He had heard their names read out, had heard their voices gabbling the oath, and watched them change by this strange metamorphosis from a group of commonplace men and women of like passions with him, into a hydra-headed Fate.

Was the Judge bound by what they said—merely a lever of the great legal machine which would be set in motion either to crush him to death in its grinding mills or to cast him forth into the pure air and sweet sunshine of life?

He believed that that was so.

If the Jury said he was guilty, the Judge must hang him, and if the Jury said he was not guilty, then the Judge must set him free.

Yes, but could not the Judge practically tell them whether they were to find him guilty or not guilty, and would not they be bound to obey him?

If so, that might be Law but it wasn't Justice. If he, Algernon Dashwood Coxe were on a Jury, and formed the opinion that the accused was innocent, he would not agree to finding him guilty if a hundred Judges so directed him a hundred times.

He studied the faces of the Jury.

He liked the look of the seaman-like Foreman, a brown-faced, blue-eyed man, who might have been an Admiral, intelligent, kindly, strong, a gentleman, one who very probably had sat on many a

Court Martial.

If he thought a man was innocent, he'd say so and stick to it in the face of any amount of direction by the Judge.

Next to him was a woman.

Was it a good thing—from the prisoner's point of view—to have women on Juries?

One could not generalize; one might, perhaps, expect a woman to be more averse from capital punishment than a man, and less disposed to have the death of a fellow-creature on her conscience.

Are not women the gentler sex—definitely softer, kinder, more forgiving than men? 'When pain and anguish wring the brow, a ministering angel thou' . . .

Yes, but what about 'the female of the species' being more vindictive than the male? And what about their notorious lack of logic, their action upon impulse, their substitution of intuition and instinct for pure reason?

That cut both ways, of course.

Any one of those four women would be just as likely to take the line of,

"Harmless-looking, pleasant-faced young man, of course he didn't do it. Don't care what they say," as she would be likely to take the line of,

"Poor young thing, cut off in her youth, poisoned and stuffed into a box and stuck up in an attic. Pretty girl, too. Of course he did it. Don't care what they say. Hang the wretch at once."

No, it wasn't theoretical generalities about the nature and character of women that were of interest, so much as practical particularities about these four women.

This one was a plain grey-haired tired-looking woman of about fifty-five, untidily and tastelessly dressed in an expensive way.

She looked as though she had a large family, a disappointing husband, some dogs, political or municipal interests, and a good platform manner. She, too, would make up her mind, whether logically or intuitively, and stick to her decision, though it were contrary to that of the remaining eleven.

On her left sat another woman, bronze-haired, scarlet-lipped, carefully made up, of much the same age and social status, but of different type; much smarter, harder, less intelligent, more opinionated, and extremely annoyed at finding herself where she was.

She looked as though she had no family, an absentee husband, a lap-dog, purely "society" interests, and a fondness for bridge, cigarettes, cocktails and scandal.

Algernon Coxe felt he was probably doing her an injustice in deciding that she was quite prepared to have him hanged at once, as the cause of her being in that stuffy and objectionable place.

Beside her sat a man who, from the first, had intended to sit beside her. Or was it that she had intended him to sit beside her? Birds of a feather.

These two would feel between themselves a bond of sympathy; fish out of water—the same water; a common suffering would make them kin.

He was speaking to her: she answering. Algernon Coxe imagined their conversation to be:

"Boring."

"Ghastly."

"How long will it last?"

"Oh, days."

"Hope they'll buck up about it."

"Not they. Law's delays."

"S'pose we can't 'record our vote' and go."

"No such luck."

The sort of people who'd hang a man to get

away to a bridge-party.

The fellow looked a typical club-window lounger —well-preserved; hair laid out to the best advantage, a little going a long way; clean shaven, monocled, full-lipped, pouchy-eyed.

Probably one might, without injustice, write him down as a soulless, selfish, sensual, *bon viveur.*

His neighbour was a fat man.

Simply a fat man, with a fat face consisting largely of fat cheeks; a round orb in the midst of which lurked two piggy eyes, one piggy nose and two fat lips that constantly moved in and out as their owner breathed.

Algernon Coxe, studying him, decided that his mind was as fat as his body and that he would wheeze

"Yussir" if the Foreman of the Jury asked him whether he thought the prisoner guilty, and wheeze

"Yussir" if the Foreman of the Jury asked him whether he thought the prisoner to be not guilty.

He would be all for 'armony, and agree with anybody about anythink. He wouldn't want to hang anybody, but the lor was the lor and the prisoner hadn't ought to of murdered the pore young thing, and whatever the Foreman of the Jury thought about it he was quite sure would be right, and he fully agreed.

Trial by one's peers!

Of what could this gross dull fellow be the judge, save of cheese, beer, steak, tripe, onions and shove-ha'penny?

Next to the man who looked both successful publican and jovial sinner sat a burly red-faced man with cropped grey hair, ragged grey moustache, rough heavy features and a look of resolution, directness and fearless honesty.

Carelessly dressed, ill-groomed, untidy and rugged-looking, he was indefinably a gentleman.

He would be patient, careful, slow, and, while fully admitting that he was stupid, demand to have everything clearly explained and then explained again. He would make up his mind slowly, almost reluctantly, and nothing on earth would avail to make him change it.

Behind these two women and four men sat another row consisting of two women and four men.

The first of these was a fair pretty woman of from thirty-five to forty, with a kindly, motherly, sensible face. Her large blue eyes looked gentle, pleasant, thoughtful, slightly wondering.

Algernon Coxe imagined her as happily married to a large affectionate man of wealth, position, and sporting proclivities. She would have two sons in the Sixth, or at the 'Varsity, and they would adore her and rag her unmercifully.

In her the quality of mercy would not be strained, but would drop as the gentle rain from Heaven upon the prisoner in the dock.

Next to her was the remaining woman. Indeed, she looked the prototype of the Remaining Woman. She might be anything between forty and fifty years of age, and her thin face expressed the unsocial attributes, bitterness, hardness and a weary scorn of things in general.

Algernon Coxe, studying her, gathered the impression of one who felt that the world had failed to appreciate her, had treated her ill.

Perhaps an unfortunate love affair?

He would not have been surprised to learn that she had been a militant suffragette who had much regretted the gaining of the franchise and the loss of excuse for further militancy; one who might have sat in great comfort at the feet of Miss Christabel Pankhurst.

As he watched her, she looked at him and, as their eyes met, the foolish idea came to him that this woman would willingly hang him because he was a man.

Beside this woman sat a tall old man, bald, clean-shaven save for a very tiny clipped moustache, bluish red cheeks and a prominent bluish red nose, in shape reminiscent of that of the Iron Duke. His myopic eyes, lack-lustre and suggestive of those of the tortoise, rested upon nothing with concentration, and betrayed no interest.

Upright, dapper and neat, he looked one of those self-respecting sterling, brainless people who daily do a foolish thing and never say a wise one.

The prisoner, whose life was in this man's hands, felt that at the end of the trial this worthy soul would still be wondering what it was all about, and would not be quite clear as to whether he had voted for death or deliverance.

Nay, it was entirely conceivable that, on returning to his home at Tooting, he would say to his plump and placid wife, the while she admitted that for once he had been somebody and done something:

"Upon me soul you couldn't tell which of 'em was which, bobbing up and down in that box and answering a lot of questions. I thought it was a red-headed fellow done it. He looked an artful member. I said to meself, 'That's the man,' I said, until I saw him get up and clear out of the Court . . ."

Trial by one's peers!

Beside this aged tortoise sat one whom Coxe's whimsical mind dubbed the aged hare, a loquacious, restless, self-important old man, much of whose extremely nasty face was fortunately hidden by a big dirty-white yellow-stained moustache and beard.

He evidently relished his position keenly and would talk of nothing but this trial and the great part he had played in it, for years to come.

His bored and weary family would have it for breakfast, dinner, tea and supper, until they knew it by heart; and his public-house acquaintances would have it with every glass he stood them, until the day came when not even his beer would wash it down their throats again.

And with every telling he would say:

"It is a terrible thing to have the life of a fellow-creature in your hands. But I did my duty. I did my duty."

Algernon Coxe hated the man fiercely—his smug, unctuous face, his watery eyes, his shabby-genteel get-up, between that of a cabman off duty and an extremely seedy something-in-the-city.

Ere looking at this fellow's neighbour, Coxe found himself imagining this man going, for the sake of an audience and a palaver, to the pastor of his chapel, and "unburdening his soul" as he would call it—telling him that he could not sleep at nights for thinking of the face of the man whom he had "hurled into eternity," or "cut off in the midst of his sins to stand before a Higher Tribunal."

Those were the kinds of expression he would use and enjoy, even as he was enjoying himself at this very moment. Loquacious, posturing humbug.

On the left of this person sat a long-lipped, big-chinned, middle-aged man in whose granite face gleamed a pair of the frostiest grey eyes. His hair was thin and sandy; his dress, neat and quiet, was bought for wear and not for show.

Sparing of gesture and miserly of speech, he either ignored the incessant chatter of the hoary hare or accorded him but almost imperceptible nods.

Solid, silent, slow and sure, he was, at a guess, a northerner, a successful manufacturer or man of business, retired from his bleak northern city. Possibly a Scots lawyer. Anyhow, a man with a mind of granite—a mind from which ideas would be hewn rather than moulded, decisions that would be as statues in stone and not shapes of jelly.

On his left sat another silent man—silent from very boredom and resentment. A young, clean-shaven man who looked too youthful to be sitting on a jury and too superior to all human emotion to find either pity for the prisoner or horror at the deed of which he was accused.

As he considered the young man's haughty supercilious and arrogant face, Algernon Coxe suddenly remembered the wise words spoken by a languid character in *Bleak House* to Lady Dedlock and the guests assembled in her drawing-room:

"Better hang wrong f'ler than no f'ler."

And those were the twelve "good men and true" who were to try him for his life.

A man was speaking. A cruel-looking, thin-lipped man with heavy black eyebrows that met above the great thin high-bridged nose.

A little of his jet-black hair showed beneath his wig. He looked like a raven, a hawk. A vulture? No, that was unfair. Rather an avenging angel, piti-less, ruthless—an angel of death.

This must be the Solicitor-General, Sir Henry Mackworth White, making his opening statement for the Crown.

"May it please your Lordship.

"Members of the Jury: Miss Giovanna Giulia

Francesca Bianca Orsola Blayton, the daughter of the famous artist, Mr. James Augustus Blayton, was a brilliantly gifted and talented young lady, who followed in her father's footsteps.

"For about half the year she dwelt in Cornwall beneath his roof at a place called Polporth Cove. Here, within the shelter of his parental care, and under the protection of his watchful and guiding love, she lived an idyllic life as a member of a charming and delightful colony of talented and cultured men and women, many of whose names, like that of her father, are household words, known, admired and respected wherever the English tongue is spoken.

"To this lovely peaceful and Paradisial spot, on the second of August last, came the accused.

"By the end of the month of August when the time arrived for him to return to his home in London, he was the affianced husband of the murdered girl, recognized and accepted as such, though with considerable reluctance, by her father, Mr. James Augustus Blayton, who frankly did not like him and made no secret of the fact.

"In London the accused wrote daily to Miss Blayton letters of perfervid love, letters glowing with the intense passion which, at this period, he undoubtedly felt for the unfortunate young girl so soon to meet, at his hands, her tragic end.

"As soon as Miss Blayton returned to the London flat that it was her habit to occupy while her father wintered abroad, the accused took her to visit his parents at Melfont Parva.

"But that visit was brief—brief; and for this poor girl, unhappy.

"Why?

"Because she was found unacceptable by the accused's parents.

"And again, why?

"Why should this girl, young, beautiful, talented, charming, innocent, with character above reproach, daughter of a man as respected as he is famous, why, I ask, should she prove unacceptable to the parents of this man, her fiancé?

"I will tell you, gentlemen of the Jury.

"It was because his parents had other views for him—other and more worldly, more materialistic views—and he was willing to accept them.

"You will learn that the comparatively penniless Miss Blayton had engaged herself to a man whose parents had already selected for him a wealthy wife.

"I do not say that anything had been definitely arranged, set down in black and white, openly talked about. I do not say that there was any actual engagement between the accused and this wealthy woman at the time when he met Miss Blayton.

"But I do say that it was the intention of his parents that he should marry her, and that his announcement of his engagement to Miss Blayton, his bringing Miss Blayton to their house, precipitated this intention.

"I do not say, for I do not know and have no means of knowing, how far the wealthy woman, then Miss Agatha Sharp, was aware of, and consenting to, this intention, this scheme, this plot. But what we do know is that, within the brief space of a few short weeks, the accused, who brought Miss Blayton to his parents' house as his fiancée, left his parents' house with Miss Agatha Sharp as his wife.

"From that same house, beneath the roof of which this poor murdered girl so recently slept and dreamed innocent dreams of happiness and joy, this man was married to another woman, a rich woman, a great friend of his mother—married to her by his own father, in his father's church.

"But meantime what had happened?

"The accused, at the suggestion of his mother, had broken off his engagement to Miss Blayton.

"For what reason? The basest of all reasons. Greed of gold.

"Deafened by the urgings and pleadings of his parents; blinded by the glitter of this gold; dumb before the hurt questioning and reproaches of the girl to whom he had solemnly plighted his troth, he did this mean and dastardly thing. He broke faith with the woman who adored him; he broke his word of honour and, gentlemen of the Jury, he broke a woman's heart.

"To marry money, he jilted this girl and showed himself the soulless, shameless cynic that he is.

"But, mark you, Miss Giovanna Blayton, young, innocent and simple though she was, could not be flung aside like a cast-off glove. She was a girl of spirit—and as the greatest of all poets has said, 'Hell hath no fury like a woman scorned.'

"Without for one moment suggesting that Miss Giovanna Blayton behaved like a fury, we may be fairly certain that this man had more than one extremely *mauvais quart d'heure.*

"There must have been scenes, reproaches, recriminations. Not the very sweetest and gentlest of women will accept the deadliest and cruellest of insults without a protest.

"A woman who did that would be something higher than an angel or lower than a worm, for even a worm will turn.

"Miss Blayton was neither; she was a woman, a sweet good gentlewoman, but she was a woman wronged, a woman scorned.

"And, mark this, gentlemen of the Jury, she was half Italian—and Italian blood is not sluggish in response to insult and injury. Nor need I tell you, men of the world, men of culture and education, that the Italians themselves have a proverb which is of peculiar and particular application in this case. As you will have guessed, the proverb to which I allude runs:

*'L'inglese italianato
E il diavolo incarnato.'*

"Precisely. An Italianate Englishman is a devil incarnate.

"Now, again without for one moment suggesting that Miss Blayton, an Italianate Englishwoman, was a devil incarnate, I do invite you still further to consider the effect, upon such a woman, of such treatment as she received at the hands of the prisoner in the dock.

"Imagine the reaction of such a nature as hers to such insolent cruelty, such barefaced impudent outrage, such insulting and disgracing injury.

"Is it not absolutely certain that when she recovered from the numbing shock of discovering that her lover was a perjured callous scoundrel, she would be filled with that anger and resentment which are the mother and the father of the desire for vengeance?

"It is as certain as that night will follow day.

"But if I use the word 'vengeance,' do not misunderstand me. Perhaps I should have said punishment, retaliation, compensation. Possibly these words convey my meaning better.

"She, a woman wronged, a woman scorned, were she English or Italian, or half English and half Italian, would, as Love—shocked, wounded, betrayed and slaughtered—died in her heart and its corpse putrified to hatred—she would, I say, give expression to that hatred.

"She would threaten.

"She would act.

"She might be content to invoke the social law that ostracizes the perpetrators of such crimes.

"On the other hand it is quite likely, nay more than likely, that she would feel it her duty to invoke the actual Law, the Law that so rightly and justly punishes, and severely punishes, all wilful and wicked breach of contract.

"Be that as it may. We do not know what she threatened, or what she purposed doing.

"What we do know, gentlemen of the Jury, is that she did not live to carry out her threat. She did not live to do what she had purposed.

"She was murdered, and her murdered body was found in a steel box, hidden—where?

"In the house of the accused."

The speaker paused dramatically, and pointed at Algernon Coxe toward whom the faces of the Jury were, with one accord, immediately turned and, with one or two exceptions, expressed a heavy and accusing disapproval combined with a morbid curiosity and strong distaste.

Algernon Coxe caught the eye of the Foreman of the Jury who, with pursed protruding lips and frowning brow, was looking at him as many a time he had probably looked at sailors brought up before him by the master-at-arms. He seemed to be weighing the accusation against the appearance of the accused, and to suspend judgment.

The tired-looking woman seated next to him seemed to be saying

"Is it possible?" as she scanned his face.

Her bronze-haired neighbour looked bored and disgusted with things in general and himself in particular, a look that was repeated on the face of the club-window lounger beside her.

The fat man stared as he would have stared at any other show. It would not be easy for his face to achieve any expression whatsoever, and if it did, it would surely be a long and difficult business to change it. But, on the whole, an acute observer might decide that the show at which the fat man now stared was a nasty one.

The burly red-faced man looked as though the story told by the prosecuting Counsel disgusted him, though he had not yet accepted it as true. Like the Foreman and the tired woman, he appeared to reserve judgment.

Looking along the second row of faces, Coxe saw, with a sense of unutterable gratitude, that the fair pretty woman was regarding him with a look that was definitely kindly and encouraging. Though she did not actually smile or endeavour to convey any kind of message, her face bore an unmistakable expression of

"I don't believe a word of it."

"I would like to kiss her shoes," thought Algernon Coxe.

The Remaining Woman, on the contrary, glared at him with a look of positive hatred and complete condemnation.

It seemed to Coxe that, in addition to morbid curiosity, disapproval and distaste, her face expressed a ghoulish gloating, a dreadful anticipatory joy. He fervently hoped that for his own sake and that of humanity in general, he misjudged this woman.

Her tortoise-like neighbour, the tall old man, was turning his noble nose and lack-lustre eyes toward the ceiling. His mouth was open. Doubtless also his mind, or the place where his mind should have been.

The bearded goat-faced ancient, whom Coxe had mentally called The Aged Hare, had, judging by his expression, already tried, condemned, hanged, drawn and quartered the prisoner.

He looked ferocious, triumphant, vengeful; and, beneath his tobacco-stained moustache and ragged beard, his lips worked and his jaws champed hungrily, as though he anticipated devouring as well as torturing and slaying the unspeakable villain who polluted the atmosphere that this bulwark of justice breathed.

Beside him, the long-lipped big-chinned man from the North stared impassive.

What he had heard had not given him a favourable, nor an unfavourable, impression. He bided his time.

The twelfth man deigned to turn his eyes upon Algernon Coxe. He gazed upon the prisoner in the dock as he would have gazed upon the maggot in the walnut. His face expressed contemptuous disgust. But this was of less interest inasmuch as his face had expressed contemptuous disgust before the trial began, and expressed it in equal measure whether turned upon the prisoner, the Jury, Counsel or the Judge.

Algernon Coxe looked up at the crowded gallery and saw much the same general expression upon the faces there.

A composite face, he felt, would have shown a gloating morbid curiosity, dislike and, on the whole, a condemnatory disapproval. He had a vision of an arena, a vast crowd—and thumbs turned down.

His eyes fell and for the first time he looked at his mother.

Large, upright, imposing, clad wholly in black, her sombre figure was a monument of grief, of pain personified.

Her face, terribly aged, bore an expression of sorrow and suffering bravely borne, of courage in the cruellest adversity. Her womanly brow consented to grief but conquered agony. Neither broken nor bowed, she showed the mettle of her pastures, the value of her faith, and the courage of her conviction that she would be justified thereof.

Beside her, her husband swung his foot and gazed at it and at nothing else.

Poor souls, how they must be suffering in this dull and dingy place, this ill-lit and ill-omened haunt of sorrow, sin and shame. Oh, how unutterably and vilely he had shown his immeasurable unworthiness of such parents . . .

What was the lawyer fellow saying? He had missed a lot of it.

"We thus have, gentlemen of the Jury, the prisoner's motive—if it were he who killed Giovanna Blayton—for this exceedingly deliberate cruel and callous murder. It was the desire to be rid of the obstacle in his path to wealth, and his added desire, nay urgent need, to be rid of a menace to his social security, his reputation and his good name . . .

"How many times he visited this unfortunate girl's flat we do not know. But what we do know is that *he was there on the day that she disappeared.*

"Witnesses will be called to prove that the accused, who appeared to be in a state of considerable agitation, came to the house at least twice on that day; that he called a taxi and removed the box in which her body was concealed, and took it to his own house.

"He then returned to the flat, dismissed the charwoman and locked the place up.

"While in the flat he informed at least three people that Miss Blayton had gone away—gone right away—gone away for a long time—and that he did not know when she would return.

"You will also hear the evidence of the Senior Pathologist to the Home Office, who made a postmortem examination of the body of the deceased and found not merely signs of poisoning, but absolute and incontestable proof that this poor girl had met her death by poisoning.

"Gentlemen of the Jury, Giovanna Blayton was poisoned by means of cyanide of potassium. Her body was found in the accused's house. He had every reason for wishing to get her out of his way. He is an amateur photographer who uses cyanide of potassium constantly and, as will be shown, a wine-glass bearing his fingerprints and those of the murdered girl, was found on the table in Giovanna Blayton's flat.

"The question probably at once arises in your minds as to how the accused, if he did murder her, induced his victim to take this poison.

"I will tell you something interesting—something that has a most sinister bearing upon this problem.

"Cyanide of potassium, also called hydrocyanic acid and, more familiarly, prussic acid, has an odour and a flavour of almonds.

"Now notice. On the sideboard in the dining-room of the flat stood two bottles of liqueur, one of them being that bright green concoction known as *Crême de Menthe* which has a strong flavour of peppermint, and the other being a cherry-coloured liqueur known as *Crême de Noyeau.*

"*Crême de Noyeau*, gentlemen of the Jury, has a strong odour and flavour of *almonds.*

"Can there be any doubt in the minds of reasonable men and women that the cyanide of potassium, with which deceased was poisoned, was administered in this liqueur, of which the odour and flavour are identical with those of the fatal drug?

"It would be the easiest thing in the world for the murderer to drop poison, whether from a phial or in tablet form, into the wine-glass from which his victim was about to drink.

"He would go to the sideboard, take out a couple of the smallest glasses there—wine-glasses —half fill each of them with the almond-flavoured liqueur and, while he stood between his victim and the glasses, he would poison one of them and take it to her.

"Or it may have been done when her back was turned. It would be only too easy to draw her attention to something in the street, to ask her to get a certain book, to suggest something which would cause her to go into the next room. Which of these things he did, we do not know.

"What we do know is that she drank the poisoned liqueur—quite probably at a draught.

"And this drug, as you are well aware, is of the most intensely poisonous type. One single drop of it, if swallowed, causes almost instantaneous death through stoppage of the heart.

"Gentlemen of the Jury, the prosecution alleges, and will proceed to prove, that the prisoner in the dock administered prussic acid to Giovanna Blayton, thrust her dead body into her own trunk, which stood empty in the bedroom, and removed it to his own house—obviously with a view to its final disposal at the earliest opportunity that presented itself.

"What other solution of the mystery is possible; what other theory tenable?

"In a statement to the police, the accused puts forward a tale which, were not the circumstances so tragic and so terrible, would be extremely amusing, so futile and so foolish is his story, so thin his explanation.

"According to this statement, he had not seen Miss Giovanna Blayton for some days before the date on which he removed the box containing her body from the flat.

"He fully admits, mark you, that there had been what he describes as terrible scenes between him and the girl whom he had so brutally and callously jilted.

"Had this poor girl been murdered by violence instead of by poisoning; had she been struck down by a blow delivered with some weapon of offence—such as a poker, or a heavy walking-stick, hastily snatched up in a fit of temper—there might possibly be the extenuating plea of sudden blind rage, the defence that there was not the slightest thought or intention of murder . . .

" 'I struck her—but I did not mean to hurt her, much less to kill her.' "

"Had the victim been shot or stabbed and the prisoner been in the habit of carrying pistol or knife, a plea in mitigation might still be put forward . . .

" 'We quarrelled. The quarrel became violent. We were both beside ourselves with rage and anger. I went mad. I didn't know what I was doing' . . .

"But can any such plea be put forward in the case of that most dreadful, most callous, most calculating form of crime—murder by poisoning?

"Here is premeditation in its most pronounced, its most vile, its most horrible and revolting manifestation—calculated, cold, and deliberate.

"In this country, happily, it is a rare thing for a man to carry a lethal weapon. Very few Englishmen go about with pistols in their hip-pockets or hidden knives in their belts. How many habitually carry poisons concealed about their person?

"I suggest to you, gentlemen of the Jury, that the accused went to the house of the deceased with a most deadly poison in his possession. He went, I say, with the fullest intention of committing murder, murder most foul, premeditated and arranged . . ."

Algernon Coxe was aware that he had yawned heavily and that at the very moment of his doing so, prosecuting Counsel had pointed at the prisoner, directing the eyes of the Jury from himself to the dock. He felt that the Jury as a body was most unfavourably impressed by his yawn, which they must consider to be either a lamentable exhibition of brutal indifference and callous levity, or else a piece of impudent bravado.

But how were they to know that he had not slept for three nights, that great bells were clanging in his head, that he wished he could fall into the sweet deep sleep of death, and that they were entirely welcome to hang him if they would only do so at once.

Let that grim Judge up there or that talking fellow who was earning his living by trying to weave a noose about a fellow-creature's neck, or any of those men and women of the Jury, have three consecutive sleepless nights—and see whether they would yawn when treacherous sleep at last approached.

Why is it that one can always sleep when one must not do so?

For weeks, now, he could sleep anywhen and anywhere, except at night and in bed and when he was alone in his cell. He could sleep here in the prisoner's dock, or in the room where the lawyers badgered him and people visited him . . .

. . . There was that police fellow again. What a thrice-told tale it all was.

Yet another policeman . . .

A heavy lethargy. Could one have been sleeping, bolt upright like this? Could one sleep with one's eyes wide open?

Presumably, for the policeman had vanished and a bald-headed fellow was talking about "the contents of the stomach" . . . "organs" . . . Beastly.

What a game it was! Catch-ball. Tossing the ball carefully to each other, to and fro. Those two understood each other, that prosecuting Counsel and this analyst . . .

Why, here was the taxi-driver. How incongruous he looked. He'd have been more comfortable if they'd fixed a driving-wheel on the edge of the witness-box and given him a seat behind it.

'Laughter in Court,' as the papers said.

"Ar, guv'nor. I said to 'im 'You'll fall through the bottom of this keb,' I said, 'before that there box'll fall off the back of it. Yer whiskers'll grow and cover the floor and go under the door, before that box'll fall off,' I said . . .

"Ar, that's right. Very particler 'e was about it bein' safe.

" 'Eavy! I should sye so . . .

"Ar, I did . . . Cloves, 'e *said* it was . . .

"Yus, right up to the top o' the 'ouse, 'im and me . . .

"Ar, that's right, sir. A very 'andsome tip indeed. A perfect gent . . . Intended to bribe me to keep me mouf shut? I wouldn't go so fur as to say *that*, I wouldn't . . . Yus—you might go fer to call it a most unusual 'andsome tip for liftin' a box upstairs . . ."

Algernon Coxe yawned again and with a shivering shudder, pulled himself together.

Who was this? He seemed to know the girl's face, but to save his life, he couldn't say when and where he had seen her. She seemed to remember well enough, however.

Oh, he had 'seemed thoroughly distraught' on this occasion, had he? 'Very strange indeed in his manner. Had not seemed to understand what she was saying to him. Had told her that Miss Blayton had gone away, gone extremely suddenly. Apparently he knew all this, though nobody else knew it, but hadn't the slightest idea where she'd gone or when she'd be returning' . . .

The girl seemed quite vindictive about it . . .

Who would they bring to attack him next?

At the end of this dreadful day, Algernon Coxe wondered whether he could really survive another such.

CHAPTER XI

The following night, Doctor John Desart, sitting solitary in his library, once again pondered the possibilities of saving Algernon Coxe. He would do his ultimate utmost best, short of perjury.

But of what real value would that best be, even under the wonderfully clever cross-examination of Sir Everard Witherby, the Counsel for the Defence?

What could Sir Everard Witherby bring out, except that Algernon had always been a youth of blameless life, a model of propriety and virtue? And that might not sound too well; might prejudice the jury against him. Quite as likely as not, some of them would say:

"Ah, yes, we know *that* sort . . . Still waters run deep . . . They're the worst of all when they do cut loose."

He had had a hope when this French Russian Pole or whatever he was, had appeared on the scene, but that had been quenched by Algernon's own voluntary statement that he himself had fetched the box from Giovanna's flat, and that Giovanna herself had written—in her own handwriting about which there could be no mistake—asking him to come for the box. And had sent him the keys of the box.

How very thin that story sounded.

It almost put the noose about the boy's neck, inasmuch as it put Boris Goudroff and everybody else clean out of court. If Algernon had himself brought the body to his house, who but Algernon would be the murderer?

And how could anybody but Algernon have

murdered Giovanna, *if* Giovanna had sent him that letter? If it had been typed, and the signature forged, it might have been part of an extremely clever ruse for shifting the blame from the shoulders of the real murderer on to those of an innocent man.

The doctor endeavoured to reconstruct the crime as, in those circumstances, it might have been perpetrated.

One. This Boris Goudroff, or some other ruffian, is murderously mad with jealousy because Giovanna has Algernon at her flat, and is going to marry him.

Two. The infuriated brute decides that if he cannot have Giovanna, nobody else shall; and, partly under the influence of that determination, partly in revenge upon both her and Algernon, considers ways and means of killing her without endangering his own unclean neck.

Three. Being a subtle-minded and scheming scoundrel, he hits upon what appears to him to be the magnificently brilliant idea of not only killing the girl, to punish both her and her lover, but of actually getting the lover himself hanged for the murder of his adored sweetheart!

Two birds with one stone.

How such a creature would smack his lips and rub his hands, over so absolutely priceless a consummation. Something like a really perfect revenge.

So what does he do?

He gets some cyanide of potassium from Paris or Soho or Jericho and has the minor, and—if less brilliant, still bright—idea of putting it into the almond-tasting liqueur which she is in the habit of drinking.

He then types a letter, as from Giovanna, asking Algernon to mind a trunk for her, and to come and fetch it from her flat on a certain day at a certain hour. He posts the two keys of the box at the same time.

On the previous night, he poisons Giovanna and puts her body into the box.

Algernon falls into the trap and, in all good faith, comes and fetches the box and keeps it in his lumber-room, there to remain until Giovanna asks him to return it to her.

Why not?

Perfectly simple.

But Algernon swears that the letter was written by Giovanna herself, from beginning to end; and that there could not be the faintest shadow of doubt as to its authenticity.

So that was that.

But then again, many and many an innocent fool has, in his fear of being punished for what he has not done, made *too* good a defence. And poor Algernon had had a wonderful training in making a good defence when accused of wrong-doing. It was indeed a marvel that his mother had not succeeded in making an arrant liar of him. It might be that in his fear and innocence he had over-done it and tried to prove too much.

There was that case, of course, of the man, who, accused of the murder of his sweetheart in Perth, swore—producing witnesses—that at the hour when the murder must have been committed, he was in Edinburgh. A perfect alibi, the best of all proofs of innocence, was to be his defence and salvation.

But unfortunately the alibi had failed, and all that he had really proved was that he, his brother, and a very old friend, were three perjurers together.

It being proved that he undeniably was in the neighbourhood of the girl's house in Perth on the day of the murder, he was found guilty and hanged. The real murderer confessed later, when dying.

Had the poor fool not attempted so good a defence, and shown himself a terrified and desperate perjurer, the Scots jury would have given the accused the benefit of the doubt that undeniably existed, and would have brought in a verdict of Not Proven.

Was it probable that Algernon was innocent, but had actually invented this story about a letter to strengthen his case?

It was certainly possible.

He might have been rung-up that night, and a voice, which he took to be Giovanna's, might have asked him to come for the box in the morning. He might have agreed and, in complete innocence, done exactly as he was asked.

But then again, how could Boris Goudroff, or any other man, simulate the voice of Giovanna Blayton sufficiently well to deceive Algernon who loved it and knew its every inflexion?

Goudroff might have had a female accomplice, of course. But was this going rather beyond the bounds of reasonable probability, if not possibility?

No. What is impossible in human nature? What wildest detective-thriller exceeded the improbabilities or impossibilities of the actual facts of real murders and other crimes?

And supposing Algernon had been deceived over the telephone, as was just possible, would he go and invent the whole story of receiving a letter?

It was quite possible. Anything was quite possible.

It's absurd to say that innocent people never look guilty—never blush and look unconvincing liars when speaking the simple truth. Poor Algernon, if innocent, might have felt that, the corpse being found in his house, things looked so black against him that he must bolster up the truth, add to the truth, and swear to something concrete and tangible—such as an actual letter.

Psychologically speaking, it was quite sound and sensible to assume that an innocent man, with no shred of evidence to help him, might well prefer to swear to a non-existent letter than to a real voice.

A letter is a concrete thing; to him it would be a symbol of solidity and reality.

And if, on the other hand, Algernon were guilty, as, one must admit, it certainly appeared, his defence was an ingenious one.

Very thin, but distinctly ingenious.

Far too ingenious, in fact, for poor Algernon Coxe.

And yet one never knew. If there were one thing in this world—except death and taxes—that was certain, it was the utter uncertainty of things. If there were one thing that a Harley Street neurologist really learned, it was to be surprised at nothing; to be surprised at no one.

But, if Doctor John Desart still had left any capacity for surprise; if ever in his life he were to say:

"Well, I *am* surprised," surely this was the occasion.

Gentle, simple, honest, lovable Algernon Dashwood Coxe being tried for his life as the murderer of Giovanna Blayton whom he loved!

The doctor sighed heavily, and sank deeper into his chair, his hand across his closed eyes.

What a world it was, with its sin and sorrow and suffering. And what an enormous amount of that sorrow and suffering was attributable to its sin. Nine-tenths of the people who came to him were ill by reason of their sins, or the sin and folly of their parents and ancestors.

What *was* sin?

Did an anthropomorphous Deity, inhabiting some distant and inaccessible Universe, make an arbitrary list of human activities and say:

"These are labelled '*Sins*'; do not do them? . . ."

'*The crimes of Clapham chaste in Martaban.*'

Sin a matter of latitude and longitude?

Sin a matter of bulk, wholesale or retail?

Praiseworthy, in time of war, to kill wholesale, with a machine-gun, men who have done you no harm; infamous in time of peace, to kill, with a pistol, the man who has done you the deadliest injury?

Could a man on a desert island sin? There was no-one against whom he could sin. Against God? Did an omnipotent, omniscient Deity really care what a poor human worm on a desert island said or thought about Him? If he said it he might not mean it, and if he thought it he couldn't help it . . .

The doctor's head nodded, for he was very tired. Pulling himself together, he sat upright and told himself to go to bed . . .

Sin? The world's problem, and akin to the problem of Pain. But the one is a variable and the other a constant . . .

Nevertheless, the fact remained that, whatever Sin may be, sorrow and suffering do inevitably follow it.

Where was the sin in this instance, assuming for the moment, that Algernon Coxe was innocent?

Undoubtedly in his overbearing, selfish, self-righteous mother's unwarrantable interference.

Not merely this last insufferable interference with her son's engagement to Giovanna, her presumptuous and impudent meddling in this case of natural selection; her insolent arrogant intrusion and intervention in a grown man's perfectly commendable and desirable love-affair . . . but her habitual relentless interference with the whole of his mind and thought and will; with his right, proper and natural doings throughout his whole life; his very personality, soul and self.

From his cradle she had dammed up, thwarted and repressed his life-force, his *élan vital*, his every effort and attempt at natural self-expression.

Algernon, as a child, would undoubtedly have been a splendid little chap if this abominable woman had let him alone and allowed him to be one—in spite of his being the son of Clarence Coxe.

But she, her husband's cousin, was a Coxe too, and she, good Lord! had energy, brains, determination and enterprise enough for half a dozen.

Why couldn't she have developed all of herself that was in Algernon, and have allowed him to grow up a man?

Anyone could see that he was a Coxe, but he wasn't a Clarence Coxe by any means.

It was she who ought to be in the dock, not Algernon.

It was her sin for which he was suffering. Who but she had made him the vacillating weakling that *would* give up his adored sweetheart because his mother told him to do so? And who but she had then come between them?

But for her, they would have been happily married by now. And Algernon's cure would have begun . . . Giovanna would have developed in him all the manhood, personality, enterprise and initiative that his own mother had thwarted and suppressed.

Sorrow and suffering following Sin. A pity that it wasn't invariably the sinner who got the suffering and the sorrow.

Not but what Minerva Coxe had now brought plenty of it on her own head. Still, it wasn't she who stood in the prisoner's dock. It was not for her that the door of the condemned cell stood open; not above her head that the hangman's rope dangled.

Yes, if Algernon Coxe were a murderer, the guilt was hers. And if he were innocent? . . . It was too appalling to contemplate.

John Desart arose, yawning, to go to bed.

The door of the room opened.

"A lady to see you, sir," said the parlourmaid.

"Well, she cannot see me at this time of night, as you know perfectly well, Matthews."

"Yes, sir, that's what I told her, sir, and she said she'd knock and ring and knock and ring until you did see her. She said she'd stay on the doorstep . . ."

"All night," said Mrs. Dashwood-Coxe over the maid's shoulder. "I knew perfectly well that you'd see me, Doctor. I followed her in."

"All right, Matthews," said the doctor, and the maid retired, closing the door behind Mrs. Dashwood-Coxe.

"Why didn't you telephone?" he continued, turning to his visitor. "In the circumstances, I should of course have seen you, at any time of the day or night . . ."

"I wasn't taking any chances. They'd have said you were out," replied Mrs. Dashwood-Coxe.

"Fresh developments since I saw you this morning?" enquired the doctor.

"No, but . . . I've come to ask a favour of you, Doctor . . . I know you'd do anything you could to help me."

"I would do anything I could to help Algernon,"

observed the doctor gravely.

"Then go into the witness-box and *swear he's insane;* swear that he has always been liable to do something abnormal, and has often had lapses of memory and of moral control . . . not responsible for his actions . . . homicidal maniac, if you like— but *save* him. Save us from the appalling, the unspeakable, disgrace of his being hanged . . .

"I could not bear it. It would kill me. Doctor, swear he's *insane*—always has been insane. You'll do that for me, won't you? You said you'd do anything you could . . ."

"And so I will, Mrs. Dashwood-Coxe," replied John Desart very gravely. "I will do any mortal thing that I can."

Mrs. Dashwood-Coxe threw out her arms, almost as though about to embrace John Desart.

"Oh, Doctor, God bless . . ."

"Anything that I can," repeated John Desart slowly, "but *that* I cannot do. I am not a liar and a perjurer. I cannot, and I will not, go into the witness-box and swear upon the Bible that your son is insane."

"You can! You *can!* You *must!*" cried the woman, as nearly distraught as it was in the nature of Minerva Coxe to be.

"Algernon is as sane as you or I," was the cold reply. "And I will not state that he is insane . . . neither in the witness-box on my Bible oath, nor in simple statement to your solicitor or anybody else."

"Doctor, Doctor, I will go on my knees to you! . . . Oh, save me, save me . . . You've always been fond of him . . . You've known him all his life . . . You grew up with his father . . . You were at school with his father.

"You *were* at school with his father," she repeated.

"Algernon is, was, and always has been, perfectly sane, Mrs. Dashwood-Coxe," replied John Desart.

"I know! I know! Of course he is. What else should the son of his parents be, but sane? . . . I'm asking you to *save* him . . . Have you never told a lie in your life, Doctor Desart? Of course you have. Even *I* have, myself. And if you could tell a lie over a small matter, cannot you tell one to save a life? To save the boy you're so fond of? To save me from a public disgrace and shame I shall never get over? To do a great right, cannot you do a little wrong?"

"A *little* wrong? Perjury? I hate to hear people talk about their conscience, Mrs. Dashwood-Coxe, but I must mention that I have one, both professional and private, in fact . . . I will not go into the witness-box and swear that Algernon is, or was, or ever has been, insane."

"You'd let this happen for the sake of your precious conscience, your professional conscience? You'd let my boy be hanged, and you'd bring me to the lowest depths of ignominy and shameful disgrace?"

" '*Magna est Veritas et praevalebit*,' " said John Desart. "Lies are not necessary for the salvation of the innocent."

"But he isn't innocent, Doctor! . . . How could he be—after a terrific quarrel, a fight in fact, and his scornful rejection of her lewd advances and vile temptations . . . Her murdered body actually concealed in his house . . . Don't let's beat about the bush . . . Of course he murdered her . . . It isn't for *us* to pretend to each other now, but to think how we can save him . . . And you can, at any rate, save him from being hanged. The shame and disgrace would be infinitely less if he were found 'insane and to be detained during the King's pleasure.'"

"You'd rather have him alive in Broadmoor Prison—as sane as you or I—and in fullest possession of all his faculties, would you? In prison *for life*, eh? With criminal lunatics?"

"Oh, yes, Doctor, a thousand times."

"Imprisoned for life—innocent—perfectly sane—with criminal *lunatics*, eh?"

"Surely anything is better than death on the scaffold? Doctor, I couldn't *bear* it."

"But you aren't asked to bear it. It's Algernon who . . ."

"The disgrace, I mean. I simply could not bear it . . . There is no real disgrace attaching to insanity. It is not a crime . . . Of course, a verdict of insanity, and life at Broadmoor, would be better than death on the scaffold."

"Have you obtained Algernon's views on that point?"

"No, but Algernon would do as . . ."

"Stop," interrupted the doctor, sternly.

"For God's sake, don't tell me *now* that Algernon will do as you tell him! Isn't the poor lad where he is at this moment, simply and solely through doing as you've told him, and through being brought up all his life to think what you think and say what you say, and to do what you want done?"

"Doctor Desart, you always were, and I suppose always will be, the most unfair, unjust and wrong-headed man alive. Hasn't everything that I've done, been for Algernon's good? Didn't he go astray the moment he left home and came to live in London—more or less in *your* charge? It's *you* who are responsible, *you* who are to blame."

Doctor Desart smiled a little wearily.

"Yes, you may smile, but facts are facts. The boy is to blame, of course, for giving way to temper and acting like a savage and a brute, but who led him into such courses? Who sent him to Polporth Cove? Who threw him in the way of this girl, and encouraged the intrigue? Who actually encouraged the girl herself to run after my son?"

Mrs. Dashwood-Coxe paused for breath, and Doctor Desart regarded her with renewed interest.

What a priceless psychological study this woman was . . .

"Yes," continued Mrs. Dashwood-Coxe, warming to her work, though still dignified and stately, if not calm.

"Yes, and who, in the very first instance, put into Algernon's head this idiotic and disgusting idea of finding a wife? A foolish and innocent boy like that—with a wife! Hadn't he a mother to look after him and manage his house? Why on earth should he be supposed to need a wife? It was you, and you alone, who put the notion into his head.

"And supposing for one moment that he had wanted a wife, who was the proper person to find one for him, you or I, his own mother?

"But for you, the idea of *women* would never have entered his innocent head. And now you actually have the incredible brazen impudence to blame me. *Me*, his mother, the one friend who tried to save him from the immoral adventuress with whom your wicked folly had saddled him! . . . You'd blame *me!* How like a *man*, isn't it? . . .

"And having brought the boy to the very foot of the gallows, and having tried to blame his mother for what you have done, you calmly refuse to lift a finger to help."

John Desart, making every allowance, merely sighed.

"Tell me of any conceivable thing that I can do, and I will do it," said he. "You may rule out perjury."

"Yes, I may rule out anything that would help me, may I not? Of course . . ."

Suddenly Mrs. Dashwood-Coxe fell silent. A vivid memory had been cast up from the depths of her subconscious mind.

She could see herself sitting face to face with this man, years ago, in this very house, just as she was doing now. She could hear her own voice saying in tones of expostulation:

"Mental condition, my good man? You talk as though the poor boy were an idiot."

And she could hear this man's reply, as plainly as though he were speaking now:

"Oh, we're all insane on some points."

Yes, and on that she had cried:

"My son *insane? My* son!"

And this so-called doctor had most certainly answered:

"He has a long way to go before he has a sane outlook on life."

As suddenly as she had fallen silent, Mrs. Dashwood-Coxe burst once more into speech.

"And where does the perjury come in, pray? Didn't you, in this very house, tell me, years ago, that the boy even then had a long way to go before he had a sane outlook on life?"

"Quite probably," replied John Desart. "It would most certainly have been true, anyhow."

"Very well, then . . ."

"But that," continued the doctor, "is a wholly different thing from being insane. Any person, for example, who is very ill from any disease whatsoever, has a long way to go before he has a sane outlook on life. The body must be healthy before the mind can be quite healthy. No one who is badly worried, fatigued, overwrought, anxious, frightened, ill, or upset in any way, has a normal outlook on life. Hence the great proportion of suicides, due solely to one of these causes. The suicide's outlook on life was abnormal and, had he not killed himself, he would have had a long way to go before he had a sane outlook on life."

"Yes, very well," agreed Mrs. Dashwood-Coxe. "Exactly. And what is the inevitable and unvarying verdict at the Coroner's inquest? 'Suicide while temporarily *insane.*'"

"The emphasis is on '*temporarily,*' Mrs. Dashwood-Coxe," pointed out the doctor.

"Well, then, was not Algernon temporarily insane?"

"All murderers are temporarily insane," answered the doctor. "Insane with rage; insane with jealousy, greed, revenge, fear, hatred, lust, or some such passion. It is clearly arguable that to be a murderer is to be temporarily insane. But it avails him nothing in a Court of Law. The view taken by the law—and very rightly—is that a man must curb and control the passions that lead to murder; not give way to them to the point of temporary insanity."

"To which of these passions do you suppose Algernon gave way, Doctor Desart?" asked Mrs. Dashwood-Coxe.

"If Algernon murdered Giovanna, I should say that he did it under the influence of mixed emotions, in which rage at her stinging scorn, and a despairing sense of his impotence, against *you* and the forces of circumstance and of life, predominated . . . Also jealousy . . . And an utterly unbearable hatred of himself and his conduct in jilting her . . . For, murderer or not, Algernon was a sensitive-minded honourable gentleman, and loathed himself for doing what you made him do to Giovanna—jilt her and break her heart.

"But he's not a murderer," he continued.

"Very well, then, save him," urged Mrs. Dashwood-Coxe again. "You believe he's innocent. Save him, then, I say. Swear that he was insane from childhood. You've been his doctor all his life. I've constantly had to bring him to you. Doesn't that show there was something wrong? Of course he was insane, and you know it. You've always disliked me and you feel that now's your chance to . . ."

"Hush," interrupted John Desart. "You don't mean it; so don't say it."

"Very well then, help me, I tell you. You've only to say that Algernon has been in your hands from babyhood and has never been normal. Of course he was insane. Insane from the time he could talk. Why—look at that absurd nightmare he has always had. I told you about it years and years ago. He screamed about that box from the time he could say the word 'box.'"

"Yes," agreed John Desart, "and that is the most amazing phenomenon that I've come across in all my personal experience and my reading and research. . . . It doesn't tally. . . . The symbolism doesn't apply. . . . He certainly had no signs whatever of claustrophobia. The box was a terror and horror to him from babyhood, but so far as I could see, it had no application, no significance. . . ."

"It was prophetic, of course—a warning," Mrs. Dashwood-Coxe informed him.

"Well, we psychologists don't regard dreams as prophetic, nor do we deal in supernatural 'warnings,'" replied the doctor.

"We regard dreams as cartoons, so to speak, sketched by the unconscious mind for the instruction and guidance of the conscious mind; the drawback being that, as a rule, the conscious mind is unaware of the fact, and would not have the vaguest idea of what the subconscious mind was driving at, if it were aware.

"And I cannot for the life of me, see what message Algernon's subconscious mind was trying to convey through the symbolism of a closed box of unknown contents. Nor can I see the faintest reason why the dream should take the form of a nightmare.

"I can understand some secretive, silent, powerfully self-repressed man dreaming about a closed box because his subconscious mind wished to deride and reprove him, and to point out to him that he was more like a walking coffer or coffin than a man. . . . It wouldn't be a nightmare though, and he wouldn't be likely to dream it more than once or twice. But there was nothing of the stern, silent, strong and secretive man about poor Algernon. He . . ."

"It was prophetic," asserted Mrs. Dashwood-Coxe again, "and it was a warning against Giovanna Blayton. It was her box, of course."

"Oh? And he dreamed about Giovanna Blayton's box twenty years before she came into his life, you think?" enquired the doctor, politely.

"Yes, it was a warning from God."

"It's an amazing, astounding and unique phenomenon, anyhow," said the doctor, "but how it was to help poor Algernon, one fails to see."

"And how *you* are going to help poor Algernon—and me—one fails to see, unless you'll do as I ask," said Mrs. Dashwood-Coxe.

"How you can refuse, how you can hesitate for one moment, I can't understand. The boy's life in the balance—and you pretend to be fond of him! And even if you really thought he was not insane, you can't be sure . . .

"And another thing. Have you forgotten that awful dream he had—the one in which he dreamed he had poisoned me? There you are again, you see. There it is, as plain as a pike-staff.

What was *that* but homicidal mania?"

"It was anything but homicidal mania," replied John Desart.

"And pray what was it, then?"

"Well, since you ask, it was a recognized and perfectly common phenomenon associated with what is termed a mother-complex."

Mrs. Dashwood-Coxe snorted.

"A mother-complex," repeated the doctor. "Your son's subconscious mind loathed and detested you."

"My son loathed and detested me!" said Mrs. Dashwood-Coxe, rising from her seat.

"I didn't say so," replied the doctor. "I said his subconscious mind. Had anybody asked Algernon, he would probably, in all good faith, have told them that he loved you most dearly; but his unconscious mind most certainly did not. Hence the dream—a wish-fulfilment dream."

Mrs. Dashwood-Coxe looked, for her, a little bewildered.

"I don't understand this 'subconscious mind' business," she said.

"Nor do I," replied Doctor Desart. "I wish I did."

"A farrago of nonsense!" Mrs. Dashwood-Coxe disposed of the subconscious mind.

"And it seems to me there's a great deal of what looks uncommonly like prevarication and evasion and excuse-making about this dragging in of this supposititious and nonsensical invention that you call the 'unconscious mind.' The plain fact remains that Algernon, who poisoned this girl, used to dream of poisoning his own mother. What's *that* but abnormal and insane? . . . Or am I to understand that you consider it a perfectly sane and normal thing, for only sons to contemplate poisoning their mothers?"

"It is a recognized and usual—and therefore

normal—feature in cases of a mother-complex or a father-complex," replied the doctor, "and means nothing more than that, subconsciously and quite unconsciously, the victim detests the person dreamed about. Many a boy who would unhesitatingly risk his life to save his father, whom he believes he loves, dreams that he has killed him. If he went mad, which means if his unconscious mind got control, he probably would kill him."

"You mean that Algernon would kill me, then?" pointed out Mrs. Dashwood-Coxe. "Well, what is that but homicidal mania?"

"As you are quite aware, Mrs. Dashwood-Coxe, I mean that *if* Algernon did go really mad, it's quite possible, indeed probable, that he might attempt to kill you."

"Then what are you boggling at?" asked the lady.

"And there's another fact to which I can swear in Court. Algernon once attacked, and nearly killed, a boy—with a stone. Flung it in his face as though he wanted to batter the poor child's brains out . . . Left him for dead, in the middle of the road—a terrible business. . . . I had just punished him severely for coming home filthy and dishevelled, with his collar and clothes torn nearly off his back—he admitted he had been fighting—when suddenly he said:

" 'Oh, Mother, that boy may be dead!'

"Imagine it . . .

"And then it transpired that he had left him lying there—to bleed to death—or to be run over—or—something.

"And pray what was that but homicidal mania . . . insanity . . . unbalanced abnormality? . . . And I tell you he'd forgotten all about it until he had been whipped—an hour or more after he had come home. . . .

"He is insane, I repeat—always has been—and subject to fits of violence accompanied by complete loss of memory and all knowledge of what he is doing.

"You know it, Doctor Desart, and I shall expect you to come into Court and testify, under cross-examination, that Algernon has always had homicidal tendencies—and would have killed his own mother. . . . If you don't do so, the world shall know that it was you who brought him to this pass and then would not lift a finger to save him. . . . For some reason you have always hated me, and you . . ."

Doctor Desart rose, rang the bell and opened the door of the room.

CHAPTER XII

Algernon Coxe looked round the Court.

Had he been here before, or was this the place he had been dreaming about? The people seemed wonderfully real. But so they did to Alice of course —until the whole pack of cards rose up in the air.

Here was one of them rising up anyway. What was he going to do?

Why it was that chap Witherby, Sir Everard Witherby, whom Harringay had said was the best man at the Bar in a doubtful case, and absolutely infallible in one so clear and simple as this.

This was one of the most curiously coherent and consecutive dreams that he had ever had. How naturally the fellow shuffled those papers, hitched up his gown, seized the lapels of his coat and turned that deceptively humorous and kindly face up to the Jury, that he might smile to them in his friendly and confiding way, putting himself *en rapport* with them, as one wise man of the world with a dozen others.

"May it please your Lordship.

"Members of the Jury, it would cause me unbounded surprise if I were to be informed that you were satisfied that the prosecution had made out a fair case that the unfortunate girl Giovanna Blayton had been poisoned by my client.

"It is, of course, not in dispute that her murdered body was found in a box, nor that the box was discovered by my client's wife in the attic of their house.

"When this shocking discovery was made—and nobody more shocked, horrified and surprised than my client—what did he do? Precisely what any one of you, gentlemen of the Jury, would have done if you had found yourself in similar tragic and distressing circumstances.

"He gave every assistance to the police and gave the fullest and clearest explanation of how the box came to be in his possession. Later on, you will hear from his own lips the interesting and dramatic story, a true story from real life—and remember, gentlemen of the Jury, that Truth is far, far stranger than Fiction—of how that box came to be where it was.

"What he cannot tell you—for he does not know —is how the body of the murdered girl came to be in this box or trunk.

"The facts of the case are these.

"My client, a man of blameless life and character, a well-known and widely-respected member of London society, the son of the Reverend Clarence Dashwood Coxe, Rector of the parish of Melfont Parva, proposed marriage to the deceased girl, and they became engaged.

"As has happened millions of times before in the history of the world, and will happen millions of times again, the young people discovered that they had made a mistake. They had been too precipitate. As they came to know each other better, certain incompatibilities of temperament discovered themselves.

"Their habits, ways of thought, outlook on life, were not in accord. They had had widely differing education, up-bringing, environment. It is enough to say that those of the deceased girl had been, as you will learn, markedly Bohemian. . . ."

Algernon Coxe frowned as he watched the speaker.

Of course this wasn't a dream. He was back in Court again, and if this man thought that he was going to whitewash him by tarring the memory of

Giovanna, he was mistaken. After all, they could only hang him if he did call out "That's a lie," in contradiction of any mis-statement concerning her. It had been his fault, and his alone.

What was the fellow saying?

"Now, gentlemen of the Jury and ladies of the Jury, there is not one of you but will agree with me that the solemnization of a marriage between two people who have not a taste in common, who see eye to eye on no point whatsoever, and who have already begun to quarrel, is ten times worse, nay ten-thousand times worse, than the cancellation of the engagement.

"I say, and I say it without fear of contradiction, that my client did a wise, sensible and right thing when he broke off this engagement, in order to save the girl and himself from a life of married unhappiness, a life of constant jarring, friction, strife, and misery.

"It was not an easy thing to do. It was his duty —to the girl as well as to himself. It was his duty, I repeat, and he did it.

"Of course the unthinking, the ignorant, the unintelligent and the *interested*, immediately cry out:

" 'Jilt! Philanderer! Rascal! Callous brute!'

"But you, ladies and gentlemen of the Jury, can estimate these parrot-cries and parrot-brains at their true worth, and can also appreciate at their true worth the courage and wisdom of my client in acting as he did.

"No moral coward he, to take the easy path and avoid the storm, the lightnings of natural indignation from the girl and her relations, the thunders of calumny from her family and friends.

"And storms there were, of course, as my client is the first to admit.

"Storms with a rain of tears, a hail of abuse,

cutting winds of scorn and reproach. . . . All very natural. Very customary. But, mark you, it was the storm before the calm. Yes, complete calm and acquiescence in the inevitable.

"And in the midst of this calm—the result either of a tardy realization of the obvious wisdom of the breaking of the engagement, *or*, gentlemen of the Jury, of the appearance on the scene of a more eligible suitor for her hand—in the midst of this calm, I say, my client receives from the girl, a letter.

"Now, gentlemen of the Jury, it is for you to realize that on this letter hangs the whole case for the defence.

"Had my client preserved that letter, there would have been no case whatsoever for the prosecution; and he, an innocent man, would not have found himself in the unfortunate position in which he stands before you to-day.

"But which of us is always wise?

"Which of us treasures and preserves every scrap of paper which might ever, possibly, or impossibly, be of any use or value?

"None of us.

"If we were to do that, we should each of us require a special building as big as a house, in which to hoard so vast an accumulation of rubbish.

"And again, ladies and gentlemen of the Jury, need I point out to you, men and women of the world, men and women of understanding and experience, that a man on the eve of his wedding is very much more than likely to destroy everything in the nature of love-letters—letters written to him by another woman.

"A man so foolish as to keep letters from a former fiancée would hardly expect, or deserve, the domestic peace that he would desire.

"Of course my client did not preserve this letter, nor any other letter, that he had received from Miss Blayton.

"Is it likely that he would?

"Would you, ladies and gentlemen?

"Would I?

"Would any sane and sensible person—particularly any person so conscientious, thoughtful, and considerate as my client has always shown himself to be?

"He did not keep it.

"Alas, that he did not!

"However, it being the last letter written to him by the woman he had loved, a letter received on the eve of the day before he was to be married, a letter that made an appeal to that kindness of heart upon which she knew she could rely—the letter, for these reasons made a quite indelible impression upon his memory.

"He read it through twice and thrice. He pondered its contents. He read it again.

"For long he sat in a state of indecision, torn between the very natural and laudable desire to do what the girl asked, and the equally natural and quite comprehensible feeling that it would be a most unwise step to take, a step that could lead to no good, nor to any real pleasure or happiness for the girl; and that it would be somewhat unfair to the lady he was to marry in two days' time.

"For in this letter, the girl asked him to visit her once more. . . .

"And thus, pondering the matter, weighing the pros and cons, reading and re-reading the letter, he came to know it practically by heart, before he came to a final decision and destroyed the document.

"Gentlemen of the Jury, my client will go into the witness-box and swear upon oath that he can remember practically every word of this letter, and, without notes, he will repeat it to you as he repeated it to his solicitor.

"Now, as you have already heard, the whole case rests upon the credibility of the existence and contents of this letter; and, in my mind, gentlemen of the Jury, there is no doubt whatsoever that when you have heard my client in the witness-box, you will be absolutely convinced that such a letter was received by him, and that its contents were what he states them to have been.

"They were as follows.

"The writer asked, as I have said, that my client should visit her once more at her flat where she would be awaiting him, at ten o'clock on the following evening, Thursday.

"She would wait for him until eleven.

"If, for any reason, he felt he must refuse, and so would not come, would he of his kindness do her the favour of taking charge of a box into which she was packing all her most valued and treasured personal possessions, as she was going abroad and did not want to store the box where its contents—especially the pictures and embroideries—might suffer from neglect and exposure to damp, or even to water, fire, or any other destructive agency.

"A friend of hers had had a most unfortunate experience through sending just such a trunk to a repository which was first burnt and then deluged with water.

"She was quite certain he would not refuse her this small favour and, in the event of her not seeing him on Thursday night, she would leave the box, packed, locked, and ready, in her sitting-room, to await removal.

"The front door of the flat would not be locked and the key of the door and the keys of the box would be on the mantelpiece of the sitting-room.

"Would he be so kind as to lock the flat up after him, and keep the three keys for her? She would not have dreamed of putting him to all this trouble but that her father had gone off to Italy as usual, and she had no other friend to whom she would care to entrust the box, or indeed, who had room to store it. As he was only too well aware, her friends were apt to be people of uncertain address and invisible means of support.

"And more to the same effect, as you will hear later.

"Now as you will remember, the prosecution affected to dismiss as a fabrication, my client's account of this letter—nay, his statement of its very existence.

"Why, in Heaven's name?

"What earthly reason is there to suppose that no such letter was written?

"My learned friend says that he does not believe in it.

"Well, I *do* believe in it.

"I most firmly believe that the deceased girl wrote and asked my client to come and see her, and if he were unable to do so, to come and fetch her box of personal treasures next morning.

"Why should she not do so? She was shutting up her flat. She had just been alarmed by the story of the burning of a repository, and she knew of no-one else to whom she would care to entrust this box, or indeed, who was in a position to store it for her.

"As you have learnt, both she and her father were birds of passage, and only had a *pied-à-terre* in Cornwall, a cottage which was shut up during the winter months. She could not send the trunk to this empty house, and if, indeed, she travelled all the way to Cornwall to deposit it in this place, it would prove but a damp and unsatisfactory resting-place for such things as pictures, beautifully bound books, silks and embroideries and so forth.

"There would also be the risk of fire and of burglary. I see no shadow of improbability about the story of this letter and its contents.

"I firmly believe that the unfortunate girl wrote this letter, and that she wrote it in good faith, fully intending to pack the box as she suggested.

"What happened after she wrote the letter we do not know.

"But what we do know is that the prosecution has produced no shadow of proof that my client has not spoken the truth, the whole truth and nothing but the truth.

"Now, on the contrary, ladies and gentlemen of the Jury, I am going to prove to you, to your complete satisfaction, that one half of my client's statement is true, and I invite you to say that, this being so, the other half is almost certainly true also.

"Where proofs do not exist, we have to take probabilities. And where one half of such a statement is proven true, you will agree with me as to the probability of the other half being true.

"Ladies and gentlemen of the Jury, the deceased girl *was* expecting a visit from my client at ten o'clock on that Thursday evening. As you will hear stated on oath, she dined with a man at a Soho restaurant and, after dinner, she declined his invitation to go on to the Shaftesbury Avenue night-club of which they were both habitués—a somewhat shady place of resort officially known as the *Hors Concours* Club, and to its patrons as *The Green Haddock*.

"And the reason that she gave, gentlemen of the Jury, was the fact that *she was expecting a visit from her former fiancé, Mr. Algernon Coxe, at ten o'clock that evening at her flat.*

"As you will also hear, the man accompanied her from the restaurant to her flat and stayed there until a quarter to ten.

"There is a church quite close to this flat, and the clock of this church chimes the quarter hours.

"As it struck the third quarter hour, the girl said to her companion,

" 'You must clear out now. I don't want Jimmy to find you here,' or words to that effect.

"And now, ladies and gentlemen of the Jury, I would draw your attention to another interesting point.

"My learned friend made much play with the fact that a liqueur known as *Crême de Noyeau* stood on the side-board in this girl's flat, and that this liqueur has a strong odour and flavour of almonds. Also that a wine-glass was found on the table, and on this wine-glass were the finger-marks of the dead girl and of my client.

"What he did not tell you was that another wine-glass was found on the mantelpiece, bearing the finger-marks of the dead girl and of the witness Boris Goudroff, the man with whom she had dined at the Soho restaurant, and with whom she had spent the evening up to a quarter to ten.

"This fact rather takes the wind out of the sails of my learned friend, unless indeed, we are to be left free to conclude that both these men poisoned the girl? And had there been half a dozen glasses, I suppose we might assume that there had been half a dozen poisoners at work?

"Now, in point of fact, my client, as I have already told you, did not go to the girl's flat that night at all.

"Whence then the finger-marks, alleged to be his, on the wine-glass?

"Ask yourselves, ladies and gentlemen.

"Is there one of you, is there anyone in this Court, who has never had occasion to say to a servant, a waiter, a companion on a picnic, to a charwoman:

" 'Look here, I say, this is a dirty glass,' or

" 'This glass has been put away dirty. It hasn't been washed since I don't know when.'

"What more likely, I ask you, than that in a flat of this description; a flat in which, to say the least of it, life was somewhat casual and Bohemian; a flat in which there was no neat-handed Phyllis in the shape of a severe and conscientious parlour-maid; a flat in which there was no regular maid at all, but wherein things were done haphazard and after-a-fashion by a rough-work charwoman—what more likely, I say, than that this glass, supposed to bear the finger-marks of my client, had been put away dirty, after being used by my client on some former occasion, and remained in that condition until it was again taken from the cupboard, either by the dead girl or the witness, Boris Goudroff.

"Yes, ladies and gentlemen of the Jury, *by Boris Goudroff.*

"For, as we shall presently prove to you, a most clear and distinct finger-print has been obtained from that *same* glass, a print of the thumb-mark of this same Boris Goudroff.

"Very well, it being made most abundantly clear that my client was expected by the murdered girl, the inevitable conclusion is that she had written a letter asking him to come to her flat at ten o'clock on the Thursday night, precisely as my client says.

"And the truth of this half of his statement being proved, he has every right to claim your acceptance of the other half.

"Similarly, your acceptance of his statement that he did not go to the flat at all, and the obvious explanation of the finding of his finger-marks upon the glass.

"But acute-minded, shrewd, and clear-headed men and women such as you, have naturally asked yourselves the question:

" 'If the accused did not visit the murdered girl's flat that Thursday evening, where *did* he go? Where was he from a quarter to ten (when Boris Goudroff—*perhaps*—left the flat) until he entered his own house and retired to bed at about midnight, as his housekeeper has testified?'

"Well, there again my client was unlucky, and there again the prosecution relies on purely circumstantial evidence—the most misleading, the most unreliable, the most dangerous form of evidence admissible.

"He simply went out for a walk.

"It was a fine clear night. He had been sleeping very badly for some weeks—as you may well imagine in view of the strain and worry of his recent breach with the dead girl—and, having a bad headache, he determined to try and walk it off, and to get so thoroughly tired that he would be sure of getting some sleep.

"He said to himself:

" 'I will walk straight on for an hour, and I will then turn about and walk back by the same route. Then I shall have walked for a couple of hours and done about eight miles. That ought to do the trick.'

"And I may tell you, ladies and gentlemen of the Jury, he had a further reason—one which you will appreciate. He did not wish to be at home if the telephone-bell rang. He did not wish to pick up the receiver and hear the voice of Giovanna Blayton asking him why he had not come to see her at her flat, and imploring him to do so.

"Which of us has not done something of the sort at some time in our lives? Was it a little piece of moral cowardice on his part? If so, let us hope that none of us is ever guilty of a greater act of moral cowardice.

"Let us also hope that none of us will ever be deterred from acting with delicacy, consideration, and true gentlemanly feeling, for fear that our motives may be misconstrued and ascribed to this so-called moral cowardice.

"Be that as it may, my client, in an honest, creditable, and, not only creditable, but credible, desire to spare this poor girl's feelings, left the house, went for a walk, absented himself from home, simply and solely in order that, whoever answered the telephone, if it rang, would immediately and truthfully reply that Mr. Algernon Coxe was out.

"Unfortunately, again, for this most unfortunate man, dogged throughout, as people often are, by a series of untoward events, a consistent run of ill luck—unfortunately again, I say, it cannot be established that the deceased did telephone to my client that night.

"She may have done so, of course, for how often does it not occur that in a by-no-means deserted and untenanted house, the telephone-bell rings and rings and rings, and remains unanswered?

"Maids and other domestics are, like the rest of us, but human; and how often have the words been uttered in the servants' hall, as well as in other parts of the house:

" 'There's that bell ringing again . . . Oh, *let* it ring! . . . I'm not going!'

"Or again, how often does it not happen that, in a house comparatively full of people, the telephone-bell rings, and is heard by no one.

"A closed and curtained door; or the accident of the three or four occupants of the house happening to be in different parts of it . . . Particularly so when the only occupants are servants . . . A couple of them have gone out into the garden for a breath of fresh air. One is upstairs turning down beds or drawing blinds, another has just stepped out for a moment to the pillar-box.

"Or again, all may be in the servants' hall or maids' sitting-room, and one of them may be making a great noise while filling a coal-scuttle or doing some such thing . . . A gramophone may be playing; an organ in the street.

"Of course that bell may have rung on the fatal night, and have remained unheard, even as it remained unanswered.

"And again, setting all these obvious probabilities aside, who is to say that the deceased did not telephone to my client at an hour later than that at which his servants habitually went to bed?

"As you will learn, it was quite an unusual event for any of them to retire at a later hour than ten o'clock.

"My client always dined at seven, and it was his habit to retire to his den and read for a couple of hours or so. At about a quarter to ten, the parlourmaid would bring a tray with a jug of barley-water or lemonade and a biscuit-bowl and any letters that might have come by the last post.

"She would then utter the unvarying formula:

" 'Everything is locked up, sir. Is there anything further you require, sir? Good-night sir,' and retire, and by ten o'clock or a few minutes after, the maids would be in bed and asleep.

"Who shall say that at any time from ten o'clock onward that telephone-bell did not ring, and that Miss Giovanna Blayton was not endeavouring to find out why her former fiancé had not acceded to her request, and to reproach him for not doing so.

"And, mark you, ladies and gentlemen of the Jury, had that bell been heard and answered, the maid who attended to it would now be in this Court to tell you how the deceased rang up my client herself, thus proving that he was not at her house.

"But it was not to be.

"And, again, my unfortunate client was not to have the good luck to encounter any friend or acquaintance as he walked abroad that night.

"Had he but looked in at a club, had he but made a call upon some late-sitting bachelor friend, or entered a tobacconist's shop or a hotel bar, he would not now be standing before you in that dock.

"You see, you understand, you realize and re-member, that it was not his custom to go out like this at night.

"He had no haunt, no place of call, no rendez-vous, no late-sitting bachelor friend upon whom it was his habit to thus drop in, late in the evening. It was entirely foreign to his habits and his tastes to go out at night, and it was only because this was a unique occasion, a uniquely painful occa-sion, that he went out—to escape the sound of that fateful bell—which thus went, alas, unheard.

"And so he met nobody; he saw nobody and nobody saw him.

"Is this strange? Let any one of us, let all of us, walk out from our respective houses at ten o'clock to-night, walk right away from our wonted neigh-bourhood for four miles or so, returning home at midnight, and see how many of us happen to meet a friend.

"One might do it a hundred times, and, at that hour of night and darkness, meet no one whom one knew.

"Is it remarkable that my client met no one and cannot actually prove that he was in the streets, and only in the streets, for the whole of the time between a quarter to ten, when he left the house, and midnight when he returned to it?

"But, equally, ladies and gentlemen of the Jury, my learned friend is unable to prove that my client was at the flat of the deceased girl that evening, and has made no attempt to do so.

"All that the prosecution can prove is the admitted and unconcealed fact that the body of the murdered girl was found in her own trunk in my client's house. It is for the prosecution to prove that my client had any faintest knowledge, suspicion, or idea, that this box contained her body— and this it most certainly cannot do.

"On the other hand, my client, who, as has been seen, gave the police every possible assistance the moment the shocking discovery was made, can give the clearest and simplest account of how this box with its—to him—unknown contents, came to be found concealed in his house . . ."

Again Algernon Coxe yawned heavily.

Was it possible the fellow was still talking? Good Heavens, couldn't these people take a gentleman's word for it that he had never murdered Giovanna; that he would never have injured a hair of her head? It was such a truly absurd idea.

Or *had* he murdered her and forgotten all about it?

Certainly there had been a most terrible row, a most shocking, unseemly, and degrading quarrel and he, who hated "scenes" more than anything on earth, had undeniably been protagonist in an incredibly dreadful scene.

And, undeniably, Giovanna had goaded him to

literal madness, and had herself gone uncontrollably raving mad when he, naturally and properly
shocked, had told her what he thought of her
conduct . . .

If that fellow would only sit down and be quiet
he could remember, perhaps.

How could one recall anything clearly and co-
herently while that voice boomed and droned and
exploded?

What would happen if the prisoner in the dock
suddenly screamed to his defending Counsel:

"Oh, for the love of God, sit down and let me
think . . . I want to remember?"

Much of what happened was fairly clear in his
mind, up to the point where he had sprung to his
feet in horror and shame, had rushed to the door,
and Giovanna had got there before him.

Standing with her back to it and her outstretched arm pointing a finger in his very face,
she had screamed:

"You beastly little Joseph. You nasty-minded,
smug hypocritical canting cur. *Love!* What do you
know of love, you psalm-smiting, Bible-punching
little reptile? You obscene little louse . . . I'd have
saved you and made you. Made a man of you, you
unclean rag. And you'd insult me so that . . . *Go,*
you hound—before I kill you. . . ."

Yes, he could remember that, all right.

But why remember it? Of what are our minds
composed that they should remember such things
so clearly, and fail to remember things of literally
vital importance.

What *had* happened after that?

If only that fellow would be quiet and let him
think.

But after all, what did it matter? What mat-
tered, now that Giovanna was dead?

Giovanna dead. Dead in his house. Dead in the

box.

That terrible Box that had dogged and haunted him from his earliest years; those nightmares; that Terror that so long had stalked by night.

The Terror had stalked him—and got him—as he had always known it would.

Well, and if it had got him, and he was put to death, what is death but peace, and what is peace but Heaven?

'At this stage of the proceedings the prisoner fainted in the dock and had to receive medical assistance' . . .

CHAPTER XIII

The Foreman of the Jury closed the door of the Jury-room and spoke at once.

What was wanted here was methodical procedure and firm, though tactful, discipline, if there were to be order instead of chaos, and business-like brevity instead of futile chatter and waste of time.

"Everything ship-shape and navy-fashion," was the motto of Captain Maxwell, R.N. (retired).

He did not know exactly what his powers were, but he was certainly going to exercise them as though they were plenary.

"Ladies and gentlemen," he began in a harsh and rasping voice. "Kindly answer to your names and sit down, in order, as I call them. It will be the order in which you sat in the Jury-box.

"Mrs. Melhuish."

The plain grey-haired gentlewoman, of about fifty-five, bowed, smiled, and seated herself. She looked, if possible, more tired than she had looked at the beginning of the trial.

"A good sort that. Sensible," said Captain Maxwell to himself, but only just to himself, for he was developing the bad habit of thinking aloud.

"Mrs. Balister Wynn."

The smart, dyed and painted person of the type, for some reason, termed "Society Woman" nodded and seated herself at the table beside Mrs. Melhuish. She looked, if possible, more bored than she had done at the beginning of the trial.

"For Heaven's sake, let's get it over," she murmured.

"Jumping Jezebel!" said Captain Maxwell,

almost soundlessly. "Soon squash her."

"Mr. Frankling Damier."

The man who vaguely reminded the Foreman of the late Mr. Oscar Wilde, whom he had once met, murmured:

"Present and correct," in a slightly mocking manner, and sat down.

"I see you're *present*, anyhow," replied Captain Maxwell, only partly to himself.

"Mr. William Snett."

The very fat man, who reminded Captain Maxwell of a certain ex-Sergeant-Major of Marines, and who now either owned or managed 'a nice little pub in Plymouth,' responded to his name with a wheezy—

"That's me, sir," and distrustfully lowered himself to the inadequate-looking chair.

"Thirty days double physical-drill, medicine-ball and round-the-deck running," frowned Captain Maxwell, as he glanced at the man.

"Mr. John Jackson."

The red-faced grey-haired man with a good rugged face, unadorned by a ragged grey moustache, nodded to the Foreman and took his seat.

Captain Maxwell liked the look of him.

"Sure, if slow," he murmured.

"Mrs. Everton."

At this juror, the Foreman took a good look, for, like most sailors, he had an eye for a pretty woman.

And she was a pretty woman, by Jove; just his sort. Big blue eyes, nice fair hair and complexion. Kind, gentle. Nice woman. Married. Blast the fellow.

"Miss Brighte."

Help! What a contrast! Bite you in the stomach if you contradicted her. Looked like a suffragette. Well, he'd stand no nonsense from her.

"Mr. Arlington."

"*Mr. Arlington!* . . . Sure your name is Arlington?" enquired Captain Maxwell, as the dapper tall elderly gentleman suddenly came to life and turned a Wellingtonian nose, rather than an enquiring eye, toward the Foreman.

"Er, yes," he said. "Yes, sir. My name is Arlington."

"Splendid," replied Captain Maxwell, quite audibly. "Keep it up," and he indicated a chair next to that occupied by Miss Brighte.

"Slow but not sure," he murmured.

"Mr. Punker."

The bearded old man, with unkempt hair, skipped forward, bowed low and washed his hands with invisible soap.

"I am Mr. Punker," he announced.

"Well, sit down, Mr. Punker, if you please," replied the Foreman, and added, but so inaudibly that only Mrs. Melhuish heard him:

"Wallah. Mr. Punkah-wallah. A Soapy Sam."

"Mr. Brown."

"Aye," said Mr. Brown, the hard-faced man of middle age, whose face, long-lipped, firm-mouthed and big-chinned, expressed obstinacy in every line.

"Slow and quite sure," observed Captain Maxwell.

"And Mr. Brabazon."

The languid youth drooped into a seat and sighed.

"I'd like to make you . . ." thought the Foreman, "*jump.*"

The last word he uttered aloud, and everybody not unnaturally did so.

His eleven colleagues being now seated, five on one side and six on the other of the long, narrow table, Captain Maxwell, standing, delivered a brief address.

"Ladies and gentlemen," said he, "we all want to get this most painful business finished as soon as possible.

"The first thing to do, is to find out whether there is any difference of opinion. If there is none, we shall be finished in a few minutes. I want those of you who have clearly and definitely made up your minds, one way or the other, to say so . . . No. Wait, please. We mustn't all speak at once.

"Will those who find the prisoner Guilty, beyond any shadow of doubt, please stand up."

Immediately five jurors rose to their feet.

Captain Maxwell sat down and wrote on the paper containing the list of names.

"Mrs. Balister Wynn," he said, and put a "G" opposite her name.

"Yes, certainly," said the smart woman whose paint-work, as Captain Maxwell termed it, was over-bright.

"Mr. Frankling Damier," murmured Captain Maxwell as, without replying to her remark, he glanced at the lady's neighbour.

"Guilty," said that gentleman. "Quite obviously."

The Foreman marked his list and looked at the third juror; and a close observer might have fancied he saw on his face an expression of fulfilled expectation as he said,

"Miss Brighte," and put a "G" opposite to her name.

"Of course the brute murdered her," snapped Miss Brighte, who trembled, apparently with irrepressible rage, and moistened dry lips.

"It is absolutely . . ."

"Mr. Punker," interrupted Captain Maxwell, and as Miss Brighte remained standing, motioned her to her chair with the curt remark:

"Presently, please."

"Yes, sir, I am Mr. Punker, sir," replied the hairy ancient. "I find the murderer thoroughly guilty."

Mrs. Melhuish, the juror nearest to Captain Maxwell, was seen to smile again at something the Foreman said to himself. It sounded like:

"The Guilty generally are thoroughly guilty, Mr. Punkah-wallah."

"And Mr. Brabazon," he added, again marking his list.

"Quite," murmured Mr. Brabazon and drooped deeper in his chair.

Captain Maxwell stood up again.

"That gives us five certainties . . . Now, I want those who feel absolutely clear and certain in their own minds that the prosecution has failed to prove the prisoner guilty . . . No. Please do *not* speak all at once. We shall all have our say afterwards, as we are not agreed . . . Will those who are quite sure that they wish to return a verdict of Not Guilty, stand up."

One juror arose.

"Mrs. Everton," smiled Captain Maxwell, and put "N.G." against the name of the pretty woman whose kind and gentle face expressed deep protest and commiseration.

"Oh, I'm sure he wouldn't do a thing like that," she said as she sat down again.

"Someone done it, any'ow," observed the fat man, and shook his head and cheeks and chins in approval of his own sapience.

Captain Maxwell eyed the fat man coldly, and the latter's head, at least, ceased to wag.

"Now," said the Foreman, "we have five clear verdicts of Guilty and one of Not Guilty . . . Five jurors besides myself have not expressed an opinion. They must decide one way or the other.

"After that, the minority must change its opinion and agree with the majority or else I must tell the Judge that we cannot agree."

"What happens then?" enquired Mr. Punker.

"We shall be kept here until we do agree, Mr. Wallah," replied the Foreman.

"What, all night?" queried Mr. Punker, in apparent alarm.

"Yes, and all day too, Mr. Wallah," answered the Foreman with apparent satisfaction.

"My name is Punker, sir, and not Waller, and I most certainly think . . ." began Mr. Punker, clearing his throat, but got no further, for the Foreman intimated that Mr. Punker's thoughts would be required of him later, and in due course.

"As I was saying," continued Captain Maxwell, "those who have not voted, must do so . . . I will ask those who have given their verdicts to favour us with their reasons for the conclusions to which they have come. That should help the undecided to make up their minds. When they have heard the others, they must decide one way or the other, and record their verdicts of 'Guilty' or 'Not Guilty.'"

"Mrs. Balister Wynn."

"I? Well, I mean to say . . . Don't see how there can be any two opinions about it. The gairl's body was found in his house. He'd had a frightful row with her, and he wanted her out of the way. Probably couldn't have married the other woman if there'd been any scandal . . . Breach of promise and all that . . . Shouldn't be surprised if the gairl was in trouble and all that."

"Ah!" exploded Mr. Punker. "*I* thought of that."

The Foreman looked at him.

"You would," he whispered.

"Nothing of the sort in the evidence," he continued aloud and brusquely, turning to Mrs. Balister Wynn.

"Not the sort of thing the prosecution would have omitted . . . Home Office Pathologist's autopsy . . ."

"Shouldn't be surprised, I say," reaffirmed that lady. "Anyhow, when you find a gairl's body in the house of the man who has a motive for murdering her, and only a silly cock-and-bull story to account for it, well, I mean to say, why waste time?"

And the lady shut her mouth with a snap, opened her handbag with another, and, producing a mirror, considered the effect of all this upon her complexion.

"Brass and paint-work," observed Captain Maxwell, looking at Mr. Frankling Damier.

"*What?* I beg your pardon?" enquired that gentleman.

"I asked you to be so good as to tell us why you have decided that the accused is guilty," replied the Foreman.

"W-e-e-l-l," said Mr. Frankling Damier, "I think Mrs. Balister Wynn has really said it all. Said the last word. Put the matter in a nut-shell and all that. Don't know that I've anything to add, you know."

"Well then, kindly repeat it all, since it's what you think; if you'll be so good, Mr. Wilde," said Captain Maxwell.

"My name's Frankling Damier," observed that gentleman.

"Quite so; we know it. I've got it down here," the Foreman assured him. "Yes, your name is Mr. Frankling Damier and you find the prisoner Guilty because . . . ?"

"W-e-e-l-l, as Mrs. Balister Wynn said, it's obvious, isn't it? He makes love to this gel. How far it goes, we don't know. Then he gets tired of her, and then along comes a gel with money and he jilts the first gel. She treats him to a scene, and

no doubt threatens him with all sorts of punishment and revenge. The gel disappears, and where
do you find her? In a box up in his attic, and the
feller can only spin a rumtifoo yarn about thinking
it was a box of clothes he fetched away . . . *Of
course* he did it. Don't see what there is to waste
time about."

"Smoke?" he added, drawing a gold diamond-
monogrammed cigarette-case from his pocket and
offering it to Mrs. Balister Wynn.

It was evident to all present that the time of Mr.
Frankling Damier, like that of Mrs. Balister Wynn,
was valuable.

Without awaiting the Foreman's invitation,
Miss Brighte sprang to her feet.

"Of course the brute's guilty," she said. "And
there are far too many of these brutal and dastardly murderers of innocent women undiscovered
and unpunished. What we want is not only women
Jurors, women Solicitors and women Barristers,
but women Judges. Yes, women on the Bench.
And when we have a woman Prime Minister, as
most certainly we shall, some day, we shall have
. . ."

"May we, before that happens, have your reasons for finding the prisoner guilty?" interrupted
the Foreman.

"My reasons? The same as any other sane person's reasons. Because it's perfectly obvious that
the man's guilty. If he weren't, why can't he
explain how the poor soul's body came to be in the
box?

"Why, it would have been a more convincing
tale if he'd tried to make out that that painter-
fellow murdered her, stuffed her body into the box,
and then forged a letter asking him to come and
fetch it. . . . How can anyone doubt for a moment
that this man Coxe is guilty, when he confesses

everything except the actual murder? . . .

"If the letter that he got from the poor soul was admittedly in her own writing, are we to be asked to suppose that the painter fellow Boris What's-his-name knew the contents of the letter, and thought it would be a bright idea to kill her and put her body in the box, so as to put the blame on to the other man? Is it likely?"

"Quite," murmured Mrs. Everton, ambiguously.

"Quite what?" snapped Miss Brighte.

"Quite likely," replied Mrs. Everton and apologized to the Foreman for interrupting.

The Foreman beamed his forgiveness.

"Rot and rubbish!" commented Miss Brighte. "I've never heard such nonsense in my life. You might as well say the Russian fellow and this man Coxe did it between them."

Miss Brighte wiped her lips and the Foreman hurriedly called upon the name of Mr. Punker, consulting, as he did so, his list to see that he had got the name correctly.

"Guilty, sir. I find this murderer entirely guilty," announced Mr. Punker, "and for the following reasons.

"He murdered his unfortunate fiancy because he had got tired of her and, mark you, that didn't happen until a richer woman came along. As the gentleman said in Court, blinded by wealth and deaf to her entreaties not to do such a thing, he poisoned her. He administered the fatal dose and then looked round for somewhere to dispose the body. And what did his eye fall upon? His fiancy's travelling-trunk and into this he disposed her.

"And what did he do then?

"Cool as you please, he calls a taxi, and her that should have entered his house a bride, enters it a corpse. What he intended doing with it, we don't know, but murderers are like that. They don't think till it's too late, and there's the body on their hands. Probably he reckoned to bury the poor girl in the cellar one night, like Crippen, or take the box to some big railway-station and leave it in the Left-Luggage Office, like that chap that murdered a woman in his office and went out and bought a second-hand trunk and put her in it and left her at Waterloo. What I say is . . ."

"Thank you," said the Foreman. "Mr. Brabazon."

Mr. Brabazon, lying back in his chair, his hands deep in the pockets of his plus-fours, sighed.

"He did it," he said wearily. "Because if he didn't, who did? Method of residuaries."

"Residuums," snapped Miss Brighte.

Mr. Brabazon regarded Miss Brighte long and thoughtfully and less as though she were the maggot in the walnut than as though she were half the maggot in the apple.

He then closed his eyes, bereft of speech.

Captain Maxwell did not close his eyes, though he narrowed them and looked as though he regretted that he, too, was, at that time and place, bereft of speech of the best naval brand.

"Now," he said, rising to his feet, "those who have definitely given their verdict as 'Guilty' have given us their reasons for doing so, and I hope this has been of some help to the undecided. I will now ask Mrs. Everton if she will be so kind as to favour us with her reasons for deciding that the prisoner is 'Not Guilty.'"

"Oh, I'm afraid I haven't anything worthy to be called reasons," replied the very pretty woman, flushing warmly.

"I just feel he isn't. He doesn't look like a murderer . . ." She halted, overcome with shyness and confusion.

"I believe very few murderers do, as a matter of fact," smiled Captain Maxwell encouragingly. "Fashions change so, you know. It's the same with burglars and prize-fighters. Most refined people nowadays."

Mrs. Everton laughed.

"Still," she said, "my intuition or instinct, or whatever one should call it, tells me he's innocent."

"Very safe guide in ordinary matters, I'm quite sure," said Captain Maxwell. "But I wonder if you could find any reasons for this intuition."

"Well," replied Mrs. Everton, "as I've already said, he doesn't look as though he could carry out a cold-blooded and deliberate murder, even if he wanted to. Nor does he look the sort of man who would want to.

"Secondly, I don't think the prosecution has shown sufficiently strong motive for a murder. I mean, you don't go and murder anybody because they've said they'll tell people you've jilted them, or because they are threatening you with a breach of promise action.

"Thirdly, I believe he was desperately in love with her the whole time . . ."

"Who has not often wished to kill a woman, even while he loved her?" asked Mr. Brabazon, the languid youth, sighing deeply, as in remorse for all those whom he had loved and killed.

"Fourthly, I don't think the man is any more of a fool than he is of a murderer," continued the pretty woman, "and if he had been going to kill this poor girl, surely he'd have thought of some better way of disposing of her body than taking it to his own house."

"Ar, that's right. . . . Stoopid. . . . Silly," nodded Mr. William Snett, and set his cheeks and chins a-tremble.

"Fact is," drawled Mr. Brabazon, "it's jolly hard to commit a murder decently. Most of these murderers are absolutely unfit to be murderers. Do the absurdest rotten things. No sense. No method. Haven't the vaguest idea how to do a decent murder. Just the sort of thing they *do* do—take the corpse home. Wonder he didn't take her home sitting on his knee, like a woman taking a kid to hospital. Rotten."

"Thank you so much," said Captain Maxwell. "But I was under the impression that you'd already favoured us. Most helpful and obliging, but . . ."

"Not at all, not at all," murmured Mr. Brabazon and, with long patience, closed his eyes once more.

"Then again everybody seems to think that his story of the letter that he received from her is absolutely false as well as feeble. . . . Well, I believe it," continued Mrs. Everton.

She stopped again, apparently overcome by shyness and the sound of her own voice.

"You don't," smiled Captain Maxwell, gently shaking his head. "I think you mean you'd *like* to believe it."

"Yes," she confessed. "That's the truth of it, I suppose. I'd like to believe it. Anyhow, I don't absolutely disbelieve it, and there's nothing actually impossible about it."

"But how? How do you mean?" asked the Foreman.

"Why, it's by no means impossible that she decided to do what thousands of other jilted and broken-hearted people have done—people who have been crossed in love—and made up her mind to travel for a time. Then, being a woman, she'd perhaps like to leave something in his charge, just to make him remember her, something he'd keep in the house and that would be a constant reminder of herself and their love. It might be petty, perhaps . . ."

"Very feminine," observed Mr. Brabazon in his sleep.

"Perhaps so," she continued, "but very natural in the circumstances . . . Such a girl as she was . . . Quite likely she'd want to do so—partly to annoy and trouble and punish him, no doubt, but much more as a reminder . . . Yes, I think it extremely probable she'd want him to have a souvenir—something to keep her memory green."

"What, her corpse?" asked Mr. Arlington, turning his commanding Wellingtonian nose and tortoise-eyes upon the speaker.

"Oh, don't be silly," said Mrs. Everton.

"Well, while she was writing this letter, and quite intending to get Mr. Coxe to come and fetch her box of treasures—silver, bric-a-brac, pictures, books—that horrid Russian, who sounds like Boris Goudenoff, strolled in . . . He's just the sort of man who'd read the letter over her shoulder . . . And I think she was just the sort of girl who'd read it out to him if he didn't, just to make him jealous. And it did make him jealous. And he . . ."

Mrs. Everton faltered.

"Better say it if you think it, Mrs. Everton," the Foreman encouraged her. "Privileged here, I suppose."

"Why, he murdered her, put her body in the box, posted the letter and just went away leaving the box for Mr. Coxe to fetch, next morning."

"*Blimey!*" ejaculated Mr. William Snett.

Whereafter complete silence fell upon the Jury-room, while all eyes regarded the confused and unhappy speaker.

"Oh, what have I said?" she continued. "I've accused another man of murder now . . . Still, he's a very nasty man, and appears to be a Bolshevist, too."

"And I'd kill every one of them," she added emphatically, "for what they did to that poor little prince and those harmless girls—the brute beasts."

"While freely admitting that I agree with you from the bottom of my soul, Mrs. Everton, it's my duty as Foreman of this . . ."

"Mena*jury*," said Mr. Brabazon.

". . . Jury to remind you that it is Algernon Coxe who is being tried and not the Bolsheviks— or Boris Goudroff . . . You'd find Coxe 'Not Guilty' because you think the girl may really have written that letter—but it's hardly likely that Boris Goudroff had cyanide of potassium handy in his pocket, just at the right moment."

"No, I suppose not," admitted Mrs. Everton.

"But it's possible," she added, "and he looks much more like a murderer, and seems a thoroughly nasty man."

"Yes, almost anything *is* possible," agreed Captain Maxwell, "but that fact tells as much against Algernon Coxe as against anybody else . . . And as for Boris Goudroff being a nasty-looking man— well, I mean to say——"

And Captain Maxwell accidentally looked at Mr. Punker—at the moment gazing at the ceiling as he explored a troublesome back tooth—and left his sentence incomplete.

"Anyhow," continued Mrs. Everton, "I've voted *Not Guilty* because, although things do look terribly black against the prisoner, I somehow don't feel that he committed the murder."

"We are much obliged to you for your exposition of your reasons, Mrs. Everton," said the Foreman, on the conclusion of that lady's remarks.

"And now I hope that the remaining jurors will

make up their minds as quickly as they can, and vote one way or the other. After that, the '*Guilties*' will have to try and convert the '*Non-Guilties*' or vice versa, so that we can do our duty and give a united verdict."

"Yes, and as soon as possible," observed Mrs. Balister Wynn, and,

"Quate so," concurred Mr. Frankling Damier.

"Now," continued the Foreman, "I'm going to ask Mrs. Melhuish, Mr. William Snett, Mr. John Jackson and Mr. McIntyre to be so good as to come to a decision, after asking, of course, for any further information that I can supply, or discussing any point which they may find a stumbling-block to a decision one way or the other.

"Mrs. Melhuish."

The grey-haired, plain, weary-looking woman who, though dressed without taste and with a general effect of untidiness, was unmistakably a gentlewoman, admitted that such intelligence as she had told her that the prisoner was guilty.

"In my heart of hearts," she said, "or rather in my brain of brains, such as it is, I find the verdict is *Guilty*, but I do so hate saying it . . . I don't think women should sit on juries . . ."

"Nonsense! Tripe!" snapped Miss Brighte.

". . . although I fully admit," continued Mrs. Melhuish, "that if women seek and demand equal rights with men, they should demand and receive equal duties. But even then, of course, they can't assume equal duties. They can't be soldiers and they certainly couldn't run battleships. But I'm wandering from the point."

"You are, Madam," the Foreman assured her, but quite kindly.

"Oh, well, I'm afraid I must vote *Guilty* then, but I shan't sleep quietly for months to come, and I'm afraid I shall see that poor young man's face as long as I live."

"And what about the poor murdered girl's face?" enquired Miss Brighte angrily.

"Yes, exactly," admitted Mrs. Melhuish. "It's because he murdered her that we are murdering him, and somehow I don't feel that two murders are better than one."

"Got to protect ourselves against such people, haven't we?" asked Mr. Punker.

"Oh, yes," again admitted Mrs. Melhuish. "I'm going to vote for your protection . . . I beg your pardon for saying that, but . . . Yes, Mr. Foreman, *Guilty*."

And taking a handkerchief from her bag, Mrs. Melhuish wiped her eyes, while the Foreman of the Jury placed a "G" against her name on his list.

"Thank you," he said. "You, at any rate, have the satisfaction of knowing that you've done your duty, however painful."

"Satisfaction!" said Mrs. Melhuish, dabbing her eyes. "Oh, don't . . ."

"Mr. William Snett," said the Foreman.

The fat man, who had been sitting bolt upright, arms akimbo, and fists, thumbs extended, planted firmly on his enormous thighs, turned his face toward the Foreman and peeped at him from the ambush of his fat.

"Well, Guv'nor," he said huskily. "I'm a kind-'earted man and I 'ope I'm a sportsman, neither of which wants to 'ang so much as a dawg, let alone an 'uman bean. Nice-lookin' young feller, too. Still, none the more and none the less, we can't 'ave people going about poisonin' people and stuffin' 'em in boxes and takin' 'em 'ome and puttin' 'em up in the attic like that . . .

"I 'ad a cosy little 'ouse up North with a good market-day trade with 'ot lunches. 'Eadquarters of the County Shove-'apenny League it was, and there used to be a dawg . . ."

"Guilty or Not Guilty?" interrupted the Foreman.

". . . as came regler with 'is master a farmer that fair took to me owin' to a pat on the 'ead and a biscuit and dawgs bein' understandin' animals, and what with one thing and another I bought 'im off the farmer. And wot did 'e turn out to be? A sheep-worrier! Couldn't keep 'im off it. Got shot twice 'e did. But would I 'ang that dawg? No."

"Guilty or Not Guilty?" interrupted the Foreman.

"Oh, guilty as you like, but I wouldn't 'ang 'im. I sold 'im. Sold 'im to an old girl as lived lonely, and said there was one thing about a dawg if 'e did bite the 'and that fed 'im and ate you out of 'ouse and 'ome, 'e didn't come 'ome drunk of a night, any'ow. So I sold 'im to 'er."

"To go on worrying and killing more sheep, I suppose," snarled Miss Brighte.

"Ar, that's right, Miss, but no business o' mine. Not when once I'd sold 'im. I didn't mind sellin' 'im, but 'ang 'im I wouldn't."

Captain Maxwell rose to his feet.

"Silence," he said sharply. "Stand up. Now then, do you find the prisoner *Guilty* or *Not Guilty?*"

"Me?" responded Mr. William Snett. "The prisoner? Oh, guilty," and distrustfully lowering himself back on to the inadequate chair, he blew into a red bandana handkerchief what appeared to be a few notes of the Last Post, to the strains of which the Foreman entered a "G" against the name of Mr. William Snett.

Captain Maxwell ran his eye round the company.

"Mr. John Jackson."

The burly grey-haired red-faced man with the

ill-kempt moustache and rough honest face, replied in the voice of a man of breeding, education
and culture:

"Well, Sir, I very greatly regret that it is not
open to us to find the excellent Scots verdict of
Not Proven. Had the body not been found in the
house of the accused, I'd rather have seen Goudroff in the dock and Coxe called by the defence
as a witness.

"But as it is, I am afraid I cannot accept
accused's story of a letter on the strength of which
he went to the girl's flat to bring away a heavy box
of odds and ends, and did so in good faith. He has
the key of the flat; he has the usual incentive and
desire to be rid of a troublesome mistress or fiancée; and—he has the body . . .

"Neither the defence nor anybody else suggests
that the murder may have been committed by a
third person, and if we have to admit that it was
committed by Goudroff or Coxe, the whole weight
of evidence and probability is in favour of Coxe
being the murderer.

"As has been pointed out, it's absurd to suggest
that Goudroff was in the habit of carrying about
with him a fatal dose of a deadly poison, and produced it and used it, on seeing a private letter
alleged to have been written by the deceased to the
accused.

"It's all too pat; too *à propos;* too utterly
improbable. I loathe to say so, but I feel that, as
it's useless to say *Not Proven,* I must say *Guilty,* for
I cannot conscientiously vote for turning him loose
on the world as an innocent man . . . *Guilty.*"

"Thank you, Mr. Jackson," said the Foreman
and entered a "G" against his name.

The clean-shaven middle-aged man who looked
like a successful Captain of Industry turned his
strong big-chinned face, with its long upper lip

and grim mouth, toward the Foreman and, in a quiet, rather musical, voice, with a marked but pleasing Scottish accent, stated that he had not yet made up his mind.

"I incline to haud that it isna proven upon him," he said. "Things look black . . . aye . . . and they found yon puir lassie's body in his hoose.

"W-e-e-l, ye'd find whisky in ma hoose—but I didna put it there and I do not drink it, for I'm a teetotaller.

"On the ither hand, the man who had the corrpse is the man wi' maist reason to wish the lassie a corrpse. Moreover, she's killed wi' a poison wi' which he's known to be fameeliar and to keep in his possession. An' I canna say his story o' yon letter sounds like gospel truth. It didna ring true in ma ears as I heard it.

"And on the ither hand, as the leddy says"— and he bowed in the direction of Mrs. Everton— "he doesna look a murderer nor sic a fule as to take the lassie's deid body home for his wife to find it. Nor do I haud that the prosecution could show a strong enough incentive for sich a dastardly cruel fule murder . . . No, ma mind isna made up, and I willna say *Guilty* nor *Not Guilty* until it is."

"Not if we sit here for a week, I suppose," drawled Mr. Brabazon.

"Nor yet if ye sit here for a month, ma mannie," was the reply.

"Thank you, Mr. McIntyre," said the Foreman.

"Well, ladies and gentlemen," he continued, rising to his feet, "of the eleven of you, nine have found the prisoner 'Guilty,' one of you has found him 'Not Guilty,' and one has not yet made up his mind. . . . A very heavy majority in favour of 'Guilty.' . . .

"Now I propose that for half an hour we just

relax and become informal. Any of the majority who think they have reasons and arguments which they could usefully suggest to Mr. McIntyre or Mrs. Everton might do so.

"As all the other ladies have voted 'Guilty,' they might perhaps talk to Mrs. Everton, and I would respectfully propose that they don't all do so at the same time.

"Perhaps Mr. Jackson would have a chat with Mr. McIntyre, since he also was for some time undecided, but has now made up his mind quite definitely.

"Please don't think I want to bring any sort of pressure on the minority party, but I want Mr. McIntyre to make his decision and Mrs. Everton either to stick to hers, if she feels she must, or to come into line with the rest of us, if she feels she should."

There was a general pushing-back of chairs, a producing of cigarette-cases and pipes and a babel of conversation.

Miss Brighte and Mrs. Balister Wynn bore swiftly down upon Mrs. Everton, and the one endeavoured to convert her by shouting in her left ear while the other did so by shouting in her right.

Mrs. Melhuish held a watching brief for Justice by adding her voice whenever those of the others made a rare simultaneous pause. But as she never got beyond the words:

"And, of course, you must see, dear," the ends of Justice were not greatly furthered.

Mr. Jackson, offering Mr. McIntyre his cigar-case, enquired whether they should have a smoke and a chat together.

"Oh, aye," said Mr. McIntyre, accepting both suggestions.

Mr. Punker, eyeing the cigar-case, hardily drew up his chair and endeavoured to favour both gentlemen with his views, opinions, and exhortations.

Mr. Frankling Damier joined the ladies.

Mr. Arlington concentrated upon a crack in the ceiling.

Mr. Brabazon slept, and the Foreman of the Jury, from beneath the hand that shaded his eyes, regarded the animated and charming face of Mrs. Everton.

*   *   *   *   *

Suddenly Mr. McIntyre rose to his feet and began to pace the Jury-room from end to end, entirely ignoring the remarks of any who addressed him.

Anon Mrs. Melhuish came round to where the Foreman sat patient at the head of the table.

"I think we've convinced Mrs. Everton," she said. "Her last remark was 'Well, I suppose you're right, but it's dreadful to have to condemn the poor fellow.' So no doubt she'll vote *Guilty* when you ask for final decisions."

"Thank you," replied the Foreman. "Isn't there a proverb to the effect that, 'Convince a woman against her will; And the more you convince her— she'll think so still'?

"However, we've got to give a unanimous verdict."

Babel continued, many talking and few listening.

As suddenly as he had arisen from his chair and begun pacing the floor, Mr. McIntyre halted and turned to the Foreman.

"Yon mon's guilty," he said. " '*Guilty's*' ma vairdict."

The Foreman rapped loudly upon the table.

"Kindly take your places, ladies and gentlemen. We have now ten verdicts of *Guilty* . . . Mrs. Everton, are you still strong in your belief that the prisoner is not guilty?"

"No, I'm sorry to say I'm not, Mr. Foreman," replied the lady addressed.

"For two reasons . . . One is that it seems to me that if you all think he's guilty you're probably right, and it's presumptuous of me to think I know better than everybody else . . .

"The other is, I've come to the conclusion that the wish has been father to the thought, and I've wished to find him innocent rather than thought that he was so. . . . So I've changed my decision."

And she, too, produced a handkerchief and dried a welling tear.

"Guilty," she added with a little snuffle.

The Foreman wished that he could go and console her, take her hand, pat her back, put his arm round her waist, draw her head on to his broad shoulder and say:

"There, there, my dear. It's a shame, but . . ."

"Hrrrmph," he barked loudly, and Mrs. Everton jumped. "Thank you, my—er—thank you, Mrs.—er . . . You are now all of one mind and unanimously return a verdict of *Guilty*."

"And you, Sir?" cried Mr. Punker avidly. "Don't you think he's as guilty—as guilty—as—Socrates himself? . . ."

"Wot did 'e do? Poison somebody, too?" asked Mr. Snett.

"No, Sir, he was himself poisoned," replied Mr. Punker weightily. "Poisoned by the Law—for corrupting the Maid of Athens. . . . Don't you think this Coxe is entirely guilty, Mr. Foreman?"

"I? Well, I haven't made up my mind," replied the Foreman of the Jury. "I'm absolutely undecided at present. . . ."

CHAPTER XIV

Up from the horrible subterranean depths and out into the dock, the prisoner, Algernon Dashwood Coxe, was brought back to hear the verdict of the Jury and the sentence of the Judge; either to hear the Foreman of the Jury say "Not Guilty," and the Judge say "You are discharged and leave this Court without a stain on your character"; or to hear the dread word "Guilty," and the voice of the Judge condemning him to death.

Anxiously, with agonized face and unconsciously imploring eyes, he scanned the faces of the Jury.

From that of the Foreman he could gather nothing. To the prisoner he looked as he supposed he must have done on the bridge of his ship, strong, assured, serene, and impassive.

The tired grey-haired untidy woman, seated next to the Foreman, gazed across at the prisoner as though searching his face once again, to reassure herself, and there to find confirmation of the conclusion to which she had come.

Her bright and bronze-haired neighbour was repairing her countenance and endeavouring to counteract the ravages of thought and emotion, if any, incidental to her labours in the cause of Justice.

Her neighbour, the club-window lounger, consulting his watch, was apparently suggesting some superior diversion, as soon as the Court should rise and the pestilent fellow in the dock be consigned to an awful death or restored to the bosom of his family.

The fat man was staring with concentration.

Evidently the show interested him even more now than it had done before.

Was it because he was gazing upon one whom he had helped to save from a ghastly fate, or was the fat brute merely gazing his morbid fill at a living corpse, a man who would go from that dock by a dreadful Via Dolorosa to the scaffold?

The man on his left, he of the ruddy countenance, grey hair and ragged moustache, looked toward him not at all. He stared at his finger-nails and looked gravely troubled.

Was this because he had acquiesced in the killing of a fellow-creature, or because, having refused to do so, he was troubled in mind, and still uncertain of the wisdom and justice of his decision?

The nice pretty woman at the end of the back row was furtively applying her handkerchief to her eyes.

Of course it must be a very painful and trying ordeal for a woman like that. Ha, ha, yes, a "trying" ordeal indeed. Damn them all, how dared they sit in judgment on him! Who were they to presume that they could assess, estimate, or understand, another person's temptations, frailties, and feelings?

Understand?

"Tout comprendre, c'est tout pardonner."

Yes, perhaps they would understand and pardon.

She would pardon whether she understood or not. If he lived, he would seek her out and ask her to give sittings to the greatest portrait-painter in the world, that he might possess a perpetual reminder and presentation of her sweet and gentle kindly face.

Those tears might well be of thankfulness that she had been able to save him, or they might just be tears induced by weariness and emotion after such a unique and painful experience.

The woman beside her stared at him gloatingly, triumphantly, but she had done that throughout the trial, apparently just for the pleasure of seeing a man in so distressing and humiliating a situation.

The somnolent old tortoise on her left still looked as though he wondered what it was all about, and why the man in the dock was still there. It would be interesting, most painfully interesting, to put him through a searching examination and discover just how much, if anything, he had really understood.

The Aged Hare beside him, exchanging with the tortoise the respective roles of the creatures in the fable, was still as active as ever, and as distant from any thoughts of slumber.

The long-lipped Scot had evidently made up his long-lipped mind and closed it for ever on that subject.

But his face was utterly inscrutable.

Inwardly he might be rejoicing wildly at having saved the life of an innocent man, or he might be grieving deeply at the terribly painful necessity of condemning one whom he considered to be guilty —but of outward sign of any feeling whatsoever, there was none.

Upon the face of the languid youth there almost appeared to be an expression of something other than boredom, possibly a faint gleam of pleasure at the thought that this dud show was about to end.

What had been his verdict? "Better hang wrong f'ler than no f'ler?"

Anyhow, they'd have to be unanimous, and it was unthinkable that the Foreman of the Jury, the nice woman next to him, the ruddy-faced man, and the kind pretty woman, would ever vote for the death of the unfortunate fellow-sinner whose life was in their hands.

No, the Jury would not find him guilty.

Algernon Coxe looked at the Judge.

Supposing for one foolish moment that that collection of decent kindly men and women in the Jury-box did find him guilty, which was really quite unthinkable, would that old man sitting up there in his red robe, his ermine, and his wig, sentence him to death? His face was stern and somewhat hard and cold, but that was probably merely a professional mask behind which lurked the real man, just, kindly, and merciful.

Oh, merciful Judge . . .

The quality of mercy is not strained . . . It is twice blest. It blesseth him who gives and him who takes.

What a beatified life this Judge must enjoy, participating in the fruits of the twice-blest mercy he dispensed.

The quality of mercy is not strained.

Was he saying it aloud? If so, they would think he must be mad . . . Mad! . . They would never hang a man who was mad, would they? No, he couldn't have been repeating that beautiful line aloud, or one of these warder-fellows would have told him to shut up. And the few people who were not staring at him already would have turned round and looked at him at once.

How could those fashionably-dressed women— ladies they would call themselves, of course— there in the gallery, sit and gloat over his shame and suffering?

Of course to them it was not so much a gallery in a Court of Law as a gallery in the Theatre of Life, and from it they were watching a play that was real—a wonderfully-acted play, absolutely true to life in its stark realism.

Probably the part of the prisoner would be better acted on the stage, and the actor be much more convincing than Algernon Coxe; for he was quite a poor sort of prisoner, with nothing dramatic or interesting about him.

Just merely a perfectly ordinary person, fetched in out of the street as it were, and with neither aptitude nor training for the part of hero, or rather villain, that he had to play . . . A person wholly devoid of attraction, save for the fact that he had committed a murder, or at any rate was accused of having committed one.

Quite a poor actor, and yet the audience in the gallery stared at him apparently enthralled; silent and motionless, as though he were another Henry Irving.

Now, if they'd only look at the Judge, one could understand it. On the stage of what theatre would they see the part of Judge better acted?

Or at those bewigged lawyers. What living actors could better play the parts of prosecuting Counsel, Counsel for the defence and Junior Counsel, than those able men with their papers and their whisperings, their hitchings-up of their gowns, their two-handed grasp of their lapels— why, there was one of them who had tipped his wig awry to scratch his head with the end of a pencil. Now what actor would have thought of that?

And the Jury, too. Could any dozen trained professional actors give a more convincing presentation of a casual collection of ill-assorted men and women gathered together to form a jury? It was really splendidly done.

But then, of course, for the matter of that, those men and women up in the gallery were really playing their parts splendidly. Not Beerbohm Tree himself could have trained a stage-crowd to behave more naturally and realistically; to wear a more enthralled thrilled look, a more avid gloating expression.

Had they no shame, no sense of decency whatsoever? Every single one of those staring men was a cad, be he who he might, and every one of those gloating women was a female cad. If they weren't, they wouldn't be there. They'd have some decent job to do in life, instead of crowding into this gloomy stuffy shabby hole to watch a fellow-creature suffer.

Supposing he had murdered Giovanna Blayton and was to be hanged for it, what business was it of theirs, and what right had they to treat his agony as a show and spectacle, staged for their amusement?

Talk of the decadent Romans with their cries of *Panem et circenses do* and *Christiani ad leones*! What had two thousand years of civilization and Christianity done for this foul type, with "*Thumbs down*" stamped upon its sensual face?

Why didn't something happen? How long had he been here?

Algernon Coxe glanced at his wrist-watch. Apparently for a few seconds, as the minute hand had not moved perceptibly.

With a painful effort he glanced at his mother. God, what she must be suffering, poor soul! And how bravely she was bearing it. Erect as ever. Dignified, impressive, imposing as she had always been. A creature of a regal and commanding spirit.

What a woman!

And what a son for such a woman!

Had he hurt her, when she visited him last night, by his self-centred lack of appreciation, his failure to rise to the heights on which she moved, his inability to entertain and express the feelings appropriate to the occasion? He could have bitten his tongue out afterwards when he remembered his doltish and selfish reply to her brave yet humble words:

"It is my punishment, Algernon. I have said '*Thy Will be done*,' but I have been too determined that *my* will should be done. I have meant for the best, but I have not paused sufficiently to be sure that my will and God's Will were one. I have sinned and this is my punishment—my heavy punishment."

And what had he answered to this humble, brave, and noble admission?

"It seems to me it's *my* punishment, Mother."

What a currish, caddish, observation.

But then, of course, he had been in prison a long time and what with confinement, anxiety, mental strain and insomnia, he had not been himself.

And there was Agatha looking more like a miserable ghost than ever.

A very different woman from his mother.

Like himself, a weaker vessel altogether.

Would he ever know whether Agatha believed, or did not believe, that he had murdered Giovanna Blayton?

The truth of the matter was that Agatha was of a thoroughly jealous nature. She had hated Giovanna, or rather she had abhorred, loathed and detested the *fact* of Giovanna Blayton.

She hated her for loving him, and probably hated him for loving, or having loved, Giovanna.

And oh, how the poor suffering creature must be loathing this dreadful business; the awful publicity, the shame, the disgrace. She must hate him for that, if not for the other. And of course, so good a woman as she was, must abhor him for murdering Giovanna as well as for loving her, if she believed that he had murdered her.

Did he kill Giovanna?

He was really beginning to forget.

That fellow down there with the thin lips and heavy black eyebrows above his thin high-bridged nose, had practically proved it beyond the shadow of a doubt.

But on the other hand the man with the chubby kindly face and misleading expression of jovial geniality, had almost persuaded him that he was innocent.

But had he persuaded that dozen of men and women in the Jury-box?

Well, one would soon know—and they looked a decent set of people.

And the Judge must certainly be kinder than he appeared.

And there is a merciful beneficent God of Love watching over us . . . And the quality of mercy is not strained.

How long had he been back in Court? He glanced at his wrist-watch. Still for only a few seconds, apparently, as, again, the minute hand of his watch had not moved perceptibly.

What was that man saying? Who was he? The Clerk of the Court.

"Members of the Jury, have you agreed upon your verdict?"

The Foreman of the Jury was answering:

"We have."

"Do you find the prisoner, Algernon Dashwood Coxe, *Guilty* or *Not Guilty* of the murder of Giovanna Giulia Francesca Bianca Orsola Blayton?"

"Guilty of wilful murder."

Algernon Coxe seized the rail of the dock in front of him and summoned all his manhood to prevent himself from fainting again.

Through a bluish mist he peered at the Clerk of the Court.

"You say that he is *Guilty* and that that is the verdict of you all?"

The man was now looking at, and speaking to, him. Through the bluish darkness that was thickening about him, he could just see the man's face and, through the sound like the rushing of waters, he could just hear his voice.

"Algernon Dashwood Coxe, you stand convicted of murder. Have you anything to say why the Court should not give you judgment of death according to law?"

Anything to say? Of course he had, but he could not say it. He was going blind; he was deaf, and his dry tongue clave to the roof of his mouth.

But of course the Judge would now intervene and tell them that, all formalities having been completed, the prisoner would be recommended for mercy, reprieved, and soon set free without a stain on his character.

He looked at the Judge and found the Judge regarding him with a heavy sad severity.

He was speaking.

"Algernon Dashwood Coxe, the Jury have found you guilty of wilful murder. It is my duty to pass sentence according to law. The sentence of the Court upon you is that you be taken from this place to a lawful prison and there hanged by the neck until you are dead."

Algernon Coxe, finding that his knees were giving way, pressed them hard against the front of the dock. He could see nothing.

But ought not the Judge now to ask:

"Algernon Dashwood Coxe, have you anything to say in stay of execution?"

Why did he not do so?

Algernon Coxe tried to speak, although he could not see.

He heard another sound that broke the deathly stillness of the Court, the sound of someone falling heavily to the ground.

He strove to see—that he might know whether it were his mother or his wife who had fallen.

The warders led him from the dock.

THE OUTER BOOK

IS HERE CONTINUED, BEING

PART II

SERVING AS AN EPILOGUE

EPILOGUE

And as the door of the lounge of the Pelham Club closed behind the bent and slouching form of the Reverend Clarence Coxe, Colonel Milly Mortimer turned again to Major Fortescue and Doctor John Desart, and told them the astounding story of the confession and death of their boyhood's friend, Scrub Tattinger.

After the fight with the Abyssinian, Arab, and Soudanese outlaws—slave traders, elephant-poachers, raiders, cattle-thieves and murderous brigands, whom they had held up at the water-hole, while the pursuing columns of the King's African Rifles converged upon them, Colonel Mortimer counted the costs of the action.

He found that they were quite certain to include the life of Colonel Tattinger, with whom he had been at Prep. School and Public School, and with whom he had served in the British Army and the King's African Rifles.

There was practically no hope for a man whose left shoulder was literally shattered by the great slug of soft lead, probably split-nosed, flattened, or cupped, which, entering, had made a small hole, had mushroomed on the bone and, leaving, had torn a hole the size of a saucer.

Lacking all medical care and appliances, medicine, proper food and skilled nursing, there was absolutely no hope for a man whose condition would be critical even if he could be placed immediately in a fully-equipped hospital.

The loss of blood had been tremendous, fever was bound to follow, and the wound would become gangrenous. But death, due to weakness and shock, would probably precede that.

Colonel Tattinger, who had seen so many men die in similar condition, was under no illusion as to his chances; and, what added to Colonel Mortimer's fear and anxiety, was the fact that his friend seemed not only to believe that he would die, but definitely to desire to do so.

Something of a doctor, from the circumstances of a life of African active service, wherein accidents, injuries from wild beasts and men, wounds, disease and death, were matters of almost daily experience, Colonel Mortimer knew that the will-to-live is the finest medicine and curative force, and a willingness-to-die the most fatal handicap.

In his experience, it was invariably the white man who, while conscious, put up a brave fight, however serious his wounds or illness; and the fatalistic Mussalman, Arab or Negro, who said "Kismet" and consented to death while conquering agony.

Yet here was his friend, the bravest of the brave, and typical fighting soldier, not only refusing to fight his old foe, Death, once again, but welcoming the ancient enemy with open arms.

"You'll pull through all right, Scrub," he said. "We'll get you down to Loiyan on a stretcher, and there'll be all sorts of good things there—chloroform, antiseptic stuff and lint and bandages, if not an assistant-surgeon . . . The flying columns are travelling quick and light, and haven't got a thing with 'em . . . They've all gone on after a party of the raiders who got away . . . Buck up, old chap, and take a hold. There's bound to be somebody at Marsabit if not at Loiyan, and we'll have him up as quick as a camel can go."

"No good, old chap," whispered Colonel Tattinger. "Number's up, this time . . . and I wouldn't have it otherwise. If the Havash hadn't shot me, I should probably have shot myself. I've been trying to—and trying not to—since I read that paper. It had been at the bottom of my chop-box, under some tins, for months before I saw it. I only read it on the day you joined me . . ."

"What paper?" asked Colonel Mortimer.

"Newspaper . . . *Sunday News of the Day* . . . Had an account of Algernon Coxe's trial for the murder of that girl."

"Yes, wasn't that a ghastly business? . . . Unbelievable! . . . But I don't want you to talk now. I want you to sleep. Achmet Ali is bringing some hot soup, and I'm going to put this spot of brandy in it. And I've got two tablets of morphia, thank God. A nurse gave me a tube with twelve in it, over fifteen years ago. Two left."

"Good," whispered Scrub Tattinger. "Wish it was two hundred. But I've got to tell you something first, Milly, in case I don't wake up again. And there's something I want you to do for me— something you *must* do."

"Of course I will," said Colonel Mortimer, "but you tell me all about it when you've slept."

"I'll tell you now, while I can," was the reply, "and I won't touch a thing until I've said it. I must sign a statement, too . . . You may be able to see what ought to be done . . ."

"But what can be done now, when it's all too late?" asked Mortimer.

"I'll tell you . . . Let me finish, and promise that you'll do what you can . . . That you'll do whatever you think best . . . Do *something* . . . And then you can give me whatever you like. Only let me sleep, and, for God's sake, don't let me wake again."

"Get it off your chest, then, Scrub, only be quick. I want to get you under the morphia and down to Loiyan at the earliest possible moment."

"Yes, it won't take me long, and I must tell you while I've got the strength and my mind is quite clear.

"It's like this, Milly. You know the state I was in when I had to go home on sick leave, and they invalided me out of the King's African Rifles and out of the Army altogether . . . What with the blood-poisoning I got from that lion's scratches, and the general thin time I'd had that year, one way and another, with black-water fever, dysentery and malaria, I wasn't quite myself.

"Mind you, I don't want to make excuses . . . It's more an explanation than an excuse; but facts are facts and there it is. I was not myself.

"And I hadn't been home long, and was just beginning to crawl about once more, when down I went again, with a most pernicious go of 'flu. Talk about our tropical diseases! They are little rays of sunshine compared with 'flu.

"And yet they seem to think nothing much of it at home, though compared with the rest, it's David to Saul, for slaying its tens of thousands . . .

"But I'm wandering . . ."

"Yes, I'll shout for that soup and you have the morphia and a nice sleep now, Scrub," interrupted his friend.

"Lord, how miserable I was!" continued Colonel Tattinger, "and how I loathed London. Couldn't keep warm, except by huddling over a roaring fire all day, and going to bed with two hot-water bottles at night.

"At last I got so perfectly putrid, mind, body and soul, that I thought I should go off my head and put an end to myself, if I didn't get better . . .

"Then old Long John Desart had a brain-wave, and gave me some real sound advice—saved my life.

" 'Look here, Scrub,' he said, 'about nine-tenths

of this is mental, you know. Active service has unfitted you for the dangers and horrors of London.
Get you back to the peace and quiet of Darkest
Africa, my lad. What you want is sunshine and
fresh air, and the life to which you are accustomed. Go back and get up to a high and dry part,
and take it easy for a bit among the lions and the
elephants. You'll die of hump and misery and
nothing else, if you moon about at a loose end in
this fog and cold and damp.'

"By Jove, I felt a new man at once. The very
idea of going back acted like a tonic, and almost a
cure. It had actually never really entered my thick
skull that one could retire from the Service without retiring from Africa. Well, off I went at once
and booked my passage straight away; then home
I toddled to my little flat and started packing my
simple and threadbare kit . . . the 'short and simple flannels of the poor' . . .

"How I enjoyed doing it, though I was so weak
and shaky that I felt I really must have a good
whisky and soda or a good cry, every half-hour;
and I can tell you I fairly counted the minutes until my ship sailed; and you can bet it was the very
first ship that was going as far as Aden. It sailed
from Liverpool, and I had to go up by train.

"Like yourself, I loathe being bothered with
luggage when I'm travelling, so I sent all my stuff
in advance, and had absolutely nothing to take
with me, as is my custom. All I had to do was to
hop on to a 'bus which, passing the door of my
flat, went straight to Euston.

"And here's a strange thing, Milly. I had actually rung my bell and told the ex-valet chap, who
runs the house, to call me a taxi, and then I remembered this 'bus and cancelled the order. Why
waste ten bob when you're a seedy, needy pen-
sioner? . . And if I'd taken that taxi, I shouldn't be

lying here telling you this now . . .

"Well, well . . . It being a fine night, I went up on top of the 'bus—which I had all to myself—and began to feel that I was something faintly resembling a man again.

"By and by, the 'bus drew up to the side of the road and stopped; and the driver got down and shoved his head into the bonnet.

"When the conductor joined him, I called out to know whether we were likely to be held up for long, as I had a train to catch. The driver replied that five minutes would do it, for he 'knew exactly what was wrong with the innards of the old gal.'

"D'you know, Milly, I actually stood up, with the idea of going and having a look, as I know something about motor-engines; but, feeling tired and weak, I didn't do it.

"And there again—had I done so, I shouldn't be dying here now, and telling you this.

"I sat down, and, looking idly round, realized that I was in the street in which I had had a little flat when I was staying in London before going to Africa for the very first time.

"And not only that, but the 'bus, curiously enough, had pulled up outside the house.

"Once more, if the 'bus hadn't done that, I shouldn't be telling you this. If it had only gone on a few yards further or stopped a few seconds earlier . . .

"There I sat, looking at the windows of what was once my sitting-room, and thinking what a queer thing it was that the 'bus should have stopped just at that spot.

"Yes, that was the place all right, and absolutely unchanged in all those years.

"By Jove, it brought back memories, watching the windows at which I had so often sat and looked out, with *Her* beside me.

"Memories . . . And a pain in the heart . . . And I prayed for the dam' 'bus to go on. I turned my eyes away and forced myself to think of the future instead of the past.

"I thought of the merry rocks of Aden, 'like a burnt-out Barrack stove,' and of landing at Kilindini; trolleying along the white coral road to the Mombasa club; lying and looking out of the window of the Uganda Railway train and seeing a real live beast again; going to the Nairobi club and hearing the news . . . getting my safari together . . . wondering how the Wa-kamba were shaping as askaris . . .

"I was just speculating whether good old Achmet Ali would take on one more trek with me, when the light suddenly came on, in the room a few yards from where I sat.

"It was my old sitting-room, and a pretty girl had switched on the light.

"Do you know, the furniture in that room was, so far as I could see, absolutely unchanged. Certainly the arrangement was the same; and there, in the place where it used to be, was what looked like the identical big sofa on which I and the sweetest and loveliest . . .

"Well, it all looked the same, anyhow. And I watched the girl as she moved about my old room. And if the sight of the outside of the place had brought back painful memories, you can imagine what it was like to see that unchanged interior, with the same clock that *She* had stopped on that last night 'because it was ticking our last moments away too fast.'

"The very table at which we had had our last dinner; that settee; those arm-chairs . . .

"My God, it was awful.

"But do you think I could look away? I simply could not. And I couldn't move to leave the 'bus. I wanted to, Milly, but I couldn't.

"Aren't we punished in queer ways? Don't tell me there are such things as chance, accidents, coincidence . . . I was brought there to get my punishment and I got it.

"That very room where she and I . . .

"So I sat and watched this young girl as she moved about the room. An extraordinarily pretty girl but, I thanked Heaven, a complete contrast with my . . . my . . .

"As I watched, this girl went to the side-board and poured out a glass of wine, or something.

"Then she went and stood beside a big open box that I had noticed directly she switched the light on. It looked like a black steel uniform-case, only bigger.

"I wasn't in the least interested in her and in what she was doing, for it was of another woman that I was thinking.

"I was seeing that room as I had seen it so many years ago, and seeing quite a different person in it with me . . .

"My gaze was just following the girl idly and subconsciously until, suddenly, she did a most extraordinary thing which promptly brought me back to the present, and caused me literally to sit up and take notice.

"Standing beside this box, she dropped something from her left hand into this glass of wine, or whatever it was, and then held it up to the light as though watching something dissolve in it. Her hand was perfectly steady, and the expression on her face calm and normal, though perhaps a little tense.

"Then she smiled, as though at some thought, raised it higher, and her lips moved as though giving a toast.

"Then she drank it off at a single draught and

put the glass down on the table beside her.

"And then it was that I got the surprise, for she immediately stepped into the box, crouched down, reached up her hand, and pulled the lid forward.

"It shut with a heavy clang and a click which I most distinctly heard through the open window.

" 'Good Lord!' I said, 'that's a rum go,' and at that very moment the 'bus started forward, and was soon at top speed.

"Now, as I've told you, Milly, I was weak in body and mind, tired, stupid and feeble. If I'd been in normal health, I should certainly have hopped off that 'bus, whether I lost my train or not, got into that house somehow, and satisfied myself as to what the game was.

"But I wasn't myself and I didn't do it.

"Oh, God! Why didn't I?

" 'Of course,' I told myself, 'it's a music-hall artiste practising some trick stunt . . . Vanishing lady act, or some conjuring business . . . Or it's just a lass having a lark with her young man, or her sister or mother or father or somebody. They'll come into the room in a second or two and she'll bob up and say "*Bo*." '

"I vacillated; I hung in doubt; and I realized what a dam' fool I should look if I barged in there and found the lass sitting on the sofa with her lover . . .

"And every minute the 'bus was taking me farther and farther away; and I had my train to catch.

"If I missed it, I missed my boat, and I felt I could not go back and face another week or fortnight of London. And all my kit had gone on. I'd got nothing but what I stood up in.

"So I went on.

"And I am a murderer."

"But, my dear chap," soothed Colonel Mortimer. "Suppose you had gone in, the moment you saw the box shut; you couldn't have done anything. As I remember the case, it was a self-locking steel trunk. And besides, you remember, the keys were not there. You couldn't have done anything. She'd taken cyanide of potassium, and would have been dead in half a minute. You couldn't possibly have saved her."

"No, but *I could have saved my son*," was the reply.

"Your *son?*" ejaculated Colonel Mortimer, and then decided that his friend's mind was going already. This was delirium.

"Yes, my son," repeated Colonel Tattinger, clearly and calmly. "My son."

A brief silence.

"My son, whom I have never seen . . . My son, whose death is at my door . . . Her son and mine . . .

"God, how she must have suffered!

"It's a cruel punishment, Milly. Even if we sinned, did we deserve this? It's too much; too *awful*. And if she sinned, is the punishment proportionate; reasonable? . . .

"To think that I could have saved our innocent boy, by getting off that 'bus!

"Could have saved his life, and could have saved Minerva from such cruel agony and suffering as few women have had to bear.

"Milly, you must let her know that the boy was innocent, for it will be some comfort, some alleviation . . .

"Or will it? . . . Won't that make it even worse—the knowledge that he died innocent, and that he suffered that torturing sense of injustice in addition to imprisonment, disgrace and death?

"Think of what that boy went through—

innocent. Hanged for the murder of a girl who committed suicide! . . .

"The she-devil! . . .

"Will it help poor Minerva to know that he was innocent, or will it add to her agony, if that were possible?

"I leave it to you, Milly. Tell her or not, as you think best—but think a lot before you decide.

"But don't, *don't* let her know that it was I who could have saved the boy . . . her boy . . . our boy.

"But I suppose she'd have to know. It will be in the papers when you see the Home Secretary, and put things in train for clearing 'Algernon Coxe's' name and memory. That must be done for Clarence Coxe's sake, as well as for Minerva's and Algernon's.

"Not that Algernon cares now, poor boy . . . He knows . . . he knows . . .

"Milly, how shall I face my son to-night?"

Colonel Mortimer took his friend's hand and could not speak.

"My boy . . . whom I murdered . . ."

Colonel Mortimer swallowed hard, and pulled himself together.

"You're imagining things, old chap," he whispered. "Algernon Coxe . . ."

"*My son;* Milly. I'm going to tell you everything because I'm dying, and it's got to be told. Though I don't think I could have told it to anyone but you. You're safe, Milly. Always were one of the best; good sound solid chap. Not like me. You wouldn't have been weak, and let her have her way. Yes, I can tell you, Milly, and you'll know what to do.

"It's a cruel legacy to leave you, but what can I do? His memory must be cleared. I'll tell you.

"And she'll forgive me for telling you, when she learns that our boy was innocent. But then she'll know it was I who could have saved him . . . Well, she must if she must; and I must bear that, too . . . We shall all three meet where everything's forgiven.

"I loved her when I was a school-boy, and I hated poor Clarence Coxe because he lived in the same house and saw so much more of her than I did.

"I don't think she loved me then, nor for a long time afterwards.

"She used to tell me to wait till I was a man, whenever I proposed to her, as I did every time I saw her when I was on leave from Sandhurst and from my Regiment. She would say jokingly that perhaps she'd marry me as soon as I was a Captain, and perhaps she'd marry Clarence as soon as he was a Vicar . . . whichever of us got it first.

"I simply pestered her, and I think she began to think more of me when I was a Lieutenant, and less of an unlicked cub.

"Of course, I spent all my leaves at home, and as you know our houses were almost adjacent . . . She seemed to like me better each time that she . . .

"Then, when I suddenly got a letter ordering me to report to the Colonial Office for early embarkation for East Africa and the King's African Rifles Minerva gave way.

"She seemed to fall in love with me at last, and all of a sudden.

"I was going to be a Captain in no time, and get a decent station like Mombasa or Nairobi or Zanzibar; and she was coming out to wonderful Africa. Such a marvellous change for her, from humdrum Millham, where she'd lived all her life. She seemed quite carried away by the idea, and I was in the seventh heaven. We both were. We lived in an absolute delirium of joy; a whirl of excitement and glow and glamour and love . . .

"Minerva, of whom I had always thought as being a little cold—if she had a fault at all—turned from iceberg to volcano, and I—I was *weak*, Milly, I was weak.

"It's I who should have been hanged . . . Hanging's too good for me.

"When the time came for me to go to London, she insisted on coming too, and I was weak, Milly, as I've said. And you know how strong Minerva is . . . A will as strong as mine was feeble . . .

"Minerva always had her way, and she had it then. I doubt if any man—or woman either—ever successfully opposed Minerva.

"Don't think I'm putting the blame on her, Milly. God forbid. The fault was wholly and entirely mine, for I should have been strong. It was my fault—my crime.

"And why should Minerva pay the penalty? Why should she be punished for my weakness and my wickedness?

"She simply told her people that she was going to London to stay with a friend—and it was true. Minerva always told the truth. *I was the friend* . . .

"You know the letter that cut my life in halves —the letter that came that day at Kinguna, when you and I were together."

Colonel Mortimer did, indeed, remember it, and how it had turned a happy, bright and cheerful youth into a bitter joyless and unhappy man, apparently of middle-age and little interest in life.

"In that letter Minerva told me that she was going to marry Clarence, and to marry him at once, in desperate haste, and for the best of good reasons. There was no time to come to Africa and track me down at the back of beyond where, perhaps, a letter could only reach me by runner, after weeks or months of travel from Nairobi. She could not and would not face the almost certain discovery.

"Fear of scandal was stronger than love of worthless Scrub Tattinger."

Silence.

"Mind you, she did love me. She loved me passionately, but . . ."

"She loved herself better," growled Colonel Mortimer.

"Not at all. Nothing of the sort. Don't say that, Milly. We're told that perfect love casteth out fear. Well, in this case, fear cast out love. Naturally enough, too. Think of the position—and such a woman as Minerva—looked up to and admired by everybody as the model of English womanhood that she was—and is.

"It served me right. I should have been strong. If I had been, she would never have married Clarence Coxe, and my son would never have come to this dreadful end.

" 'The mills of God grind slowly, but they grind exceeding small.'

"Why couldn't I have got off that 'bus, and again why couldn't I have read an account of the trial in time to have cabled to the Home Secretary and have saved his life?

"It's something, I suppose, that I read about it before I died and can clear the boy's memory, and give her what comfort there is in knowing him to have been innocent.

"But there again, as I said before, would it be a comfort or one more stab at her poor heart, to know that the boy suffered unjustly?

"I'll tell you what, Milly. Tell the whole truth to Long John Desart. He is one of the most understanding and wisest men alive. Tell him everything, and you and he agree as to what will be the best thing to do. Decide whether to tell her that the boy was innocent, and don't spare my memory

. . . No, on second thoughts, don't spare me. Don't spare my memory in clearing my son's.

"And suppose you and Long John can't see eye to eye, call in Tubby Fortescue. He's known all of us all our lives . . . And nobody on earth—but Clarence Coxe, who must always have known it—will ever know that 'Algernon Coxe' was my son, except you, John, and Tubby . . . And Minerva need not know that you know . . .

"I'm going a bit faint, Milly . . .

"Her letter to me is in an oil-skin cover, in that little flat tin box that's got my money and papers in it . . . It proves that Algernon is my son, if ever the question should arise—which it won't—not while Minerva's alive, anyhow.

"Now write the truth down briefly, Milly, and I'll sign it before you give me the morphia. Be quick, old chap. I keep getting a bit faint."

Colonel Tattinger died that night.

II

Doctor John Desart was shown into the dining-room of the Melfont Parva Vicarage.

To him entered Mrs. Dashwood-Coxe, stately, impressive, in deepest mourning still.

"This is an intrusion, Doctor Desart," she said, as he rose to greet her, "and I wonder at your . . . your temerity, your insistence; I had almost said insolence. After my writing and wiring that you would *not* be welcome here . . . I do not ask you to sit down, nor can I offer you any hospitality."

"No, Mrs. Dashwood-Coxe, nor would it be acceptable. I have come in absolute sincerity and honesty, in the belief that I can serve you . . . give you a little comfort . . . peace of mind."

"*You!*" cried Mrs. Dashwood-Coxe with something as nearly approaching a bitter sneer as so well-bred and good a woman could achieve.

"*You!* You who could have saved me untold suffering by a word when I begged you, almost on my knees, to swear that, although poor Algernon was a murderer, he was not a conscious, intentional, and responsible one."

"He was not a murderer at all. He was absolutely innocent. He *did* receive that letter. It was written by Giovanna Blayton before she committed suicide," replied the doctor.

"Rubbish! Of *course* Algernon did it. And of course you could have saved him."

"Once again, Mrs. Dashwood-Coxe, had I been a perjured liar and unworthy of the public position that I hold, my false testimony and lying witness would *not* have saved Algernon . . . A hundred people knew he was as sane as you or I—his maids, Giovanna's father, the taxi-man, the char-woman, the girl at the flat, and, of course, his wife, Agatha.

"I've come to tell you that Algernon was innocent, and to prove it. If you prefer to hear the story standing, it will not take very long, but I beg of you to sit down."

Mrs. Dashwood-Coxe drew herself a little more erect.

The doctor bowed.

"Very well," he said.

"In the first place, then, Algernon's father is dead," continued John Desart.

"Clarence *dead?*" cried Mrs. Dashwood-Coxe, startled and incredulous. "He left here, in the best of health, only yesterday."

"I said the boy's *father*," replied John Desart. "He is dead."

"They say that specialists get the diseases in which they specialize," she said, staring at him with hard glittering eyes.

"Meaning that I am mad?" asked Doctor Desart.

"Obviously quite mad," was the toneless reply.

"Richard Tattinger is dead," said John Desart. "He died in Colonel Mortimer's arms, and, with his last breath, told him a terrible tale. Listen and I will tell it to you.

"I will then give you two documents, one signed by Richard Tattinger and one, a letter written to him by you."

Unflinching and unfaltering, Mrs. Dashwood-Coxe heard John Desart to the end.

When he had finished, she bowed her head in pious resignation.

"Thy Will be done," she whispered.

And,

"But oh God, grant me the strength to bear

this, my burden, *for Thou hast been pleased to afflict me and to try my faith* almost beyond my strength."

John Desart, for the last time, gazed upon her in sheer amazement.

TWO FEET FROM HEAVEN

CONTENTS

ISABEL
AGAIN

EXCUSE

Three enormous elephants were playing together near the edge of an extremely steep slope. Suddenly, two of them butted the third with such violence that he fell over the edge, and rolled headlong down the precipitous hill-side. Crashing through the undergrowth, and knocking down trees, his vast body continued its swift career until brought to a stand-still by a great rock. Staggering to his feet, the dazed and bewildered elephant, gazing about him in search of the adversary, espied a mouse.

"You are very *very* tiny," he roared at her.

"Yes," sighed the mouse. "You see, I have not been too well, just lately."

PART I

A GIRL AND TWO MEN

CHAPTER 1

The kneeling girl sat back on her heels and stared uncomprehendingly round the room—a neat clean bed-sitting-room-kitchen, in a horrible tenement house in one of those slums that are of little ornament and less credit to the capital of the world's greatest Empire.

As though drawn by a terrible fascination or some irresistible force, her gaze returned to the dead man lying on the floor beside her; and then, with an almost conscious effort, to the man sitting with his back toward her in the ancient mahogany and horse-hair armless arm-chair, designed in Victorian days for the comfortable accommodation of crinoline-wearing ladies.

He was trembling like a leaf, shaking uncontrollably from head to foot as though with unbearable cold, or the rigor of incipient fever. His face buried in his hands, his body bowed almost to his knees, he seemed to be about to burst into tears; to faint; to collapse upon the floor.

No help from that quarter. Rather, must she help him. She must take charge of the situation; she must *do* something—and do it soon.

But not for a minute. She must pull herself together; realise what had happened; set her wits to work; and make a plan.

Yes, in a minute. . . .

It had all been so sudden; and she herself had been so near to death.

Five minutes ago she had been alone in this room, this very room that she had had cleaned, white-washed, papered, and floored with linoleum —not a bug in the place, nor a louse neither, perhaps not so much as a flea—and had been as happy as any woman in the world.

Happy, because it was her wedding-night.

Happy was not a big enough word for it. She had been beside herself with happiness and joy and thankfulness.

Her wedding-night—and, kind God, look at it now!

Perhaps it was her punishment because it was to have been her wedding-night without any wedding. Not but what he had offered to marry her; had asked her, and begged her, to marry him.

But she had refused. She was not going to marry him and be a burden; a mill-stone round his neck, as they say.

Why should he marry a flower-girl? He, who had seen better days, and would see better still. Why, he might have been a gentleman in an office, a gentleman in a shop—and a good shop, too. He might have been a real actor, or anything. She could tell by the way he spoke when he forgot to talk Cockney. She could tell by his hands, and by his face. She could tell, best of all, by the way he was always so polite to her; so kind; never a rough word—the sort of man who would not black his wife's eye once, from year's end to year's end.

No, it would not have been right to marry him—not until she saw how things went. But he wanted someone to look after him. God, *how* he did! And this was the only way in which she could look after him properly.

She had lived with him, in his room, all those weeks when he had been so terribly ill and nearly died.

Her wedding-night; and five minutes ago the room had been like Heaven—nearly everything in it brand-new. Pretty paper on the dresser and the shelves; mugs and jugs hanging on the hooks; a

nice piece of oil-cloth on the table. Fairly ran-
sacked the Sixpenny Bazaar she had, to have
everything nice. Ever so nice! A good second-hand
chair each; everything lovely; and, although she
said it herself, she had done wonders with a pot of
blue paint; touched up the mantel-piece, the iron
bed, the window-sill, the floorboards round the
linoleum, the skirting, and the dirty old door, too.
. . .

Five minutes ago she had gone to the cupboard
to get out the things for—not exactly the wedding-
feast. A nice tin of salmon, a new loaf, real butter,
a couple of ounces of the tea he liked; and the
wedding-cake—a pretty bright yellow with cherries
in it, and a lump of peel on the top, a whole pound
of it.

And, as she stood looking at all these good
things, the door had opened, her heart had
jumped for joy, and she had whirled round with
her arms thrown out . . . to see the dreadful
grinning face of that dirty brute now lying there
. . . dead.

Dead.

He had killed him.

And he would swing for it, unless she could
think of a plan; for he had hit him on the back of
the head, and she knew quite well that if you
came up behind anybody and coshed them, it was
murder. Whereas, if you went for them face to
face, it was only self-defence. Soapy-the-Slipe had
told her that if a house-holder shot a burglar in
the back, it was manslaughter, if not murder. And
being a burglar himself, Soapy ought to know.

It was not fair, it was not right, that anybody
should swing for this low brute; swing for having
killed him. Anybody who did him in ought to get
something out of the poor-box.

Did not everybody—except the police—know

that the beast was a murderer himself, as well as a ponce and a cosh-bully? Everyone, except the dicks, knew who had done it when Lotte Klaus was found murdered in her room, and when Olga Dobroff was taken out of the Canal, and when Steffi Linden's body was found in the empty shop.

No doubt he had an alibi all right, but each of the girls had something too—and that was a thumb-mark bruise under the ear on the right side of the neck. That was how he killed people, according to Liz—and she ought to know, as he had done it to her and she had passed right out. Either he did not want to kill her, or somebody came along, just as he grabbed her by the throat and pressed with his thumb under her right ear. Awful it was, she said. Felt herself fainting. Perhaps it was because the blood could not flow up into her head?

That was at least three girls that he had killed; and now he was killed himself.

And they would hang the man who had killed him—killed him to save her life; for undoubtedly the brute-beast had been killing her in the same way, and not just giving her a fright, just hurting her. No. He had had it in for her ever since she had refused to pay him "rent" for her flower-pitch; refused to go and live with him; refused to have anything to do with him.

And now she must do her best for the man who had saved her; the man who had been willing to marry her; the man whom she loved a thousand times better than anything in the world, and ten thousand times better than she loved herself.

Mastering an almost unconquerable repugnance, she knelt up, bent forward, and touched the hand of the man who lay on his back beside the bed.

Not cold yet. No, it would not be—in so short a

time. But he was dead all right. Of that she felt convinced; but she must make absolutely certain.

No pulse at the wrist. . . . Could she bring herself to put her hand in under his shirt and feel if his heart was still beating?

It was not.

Shuddering, but with a sick and dogged determination, she touched the glazed and staring eyes, bent, and put her ear against the ugly gaping mouth; rose to her feet, went and unhooked the small cheap mirror from the wall, and held it to the lips and nostrils. There was no dimming of the mirror's surface. The brute was dead.

Rising and replacing the mirror, she turned and looked at the back of the bowed figure in the chair. He must go, the sooner the better, and the further the better. He *must* go, and she must somehow persuade him to do so. The Police . . .

He must pull himself together first, though; for he could not go out like that. Took things too hard; all nerves he was. If ever there was a man who needed looking after . . .

Crossing to where the man sat with his back to the corpse, his face still buried in his trembling hands, she knelt beside him and put her arm about the shoulders that shook like those of a sobbing child.

"There! . . . There! . . . There! . . ." she said, as though he were a small boy, and she his mother. "There! . . . There! . . . It will be all right . . . It will be all right," she murmured, as she stroked his hair, and gently patted his shoulder. "It will be all right, my dear. . . . You haven't hurt him, really. Just knocked him out; and serve him right."

Putting his arms about her, the man drew her to him in a close embrace.

God, how he trembles and shakes, thought the woman. I can't let him go out like this. . . . But I must. He *must* go; and he must not be seen. . . .

"Listen, love," she said softly, as she stroked his cheek and held his head tightly to her breast. "You did what was right, and you served him right. There is nothing to be upset about, like this; but you mustn't be here when he comes round. He doesn't know who hit him, see? He won't know what happened, for he never saw you. But if you are here when he comes to—he'll kill you. Not now, p'raps, because he won't be feeling too good; but he'll lay for you—him *and* his gang. . . . They're dreadful men; lowest of the low. Race-course gang, they are. Call themselves The Slashers. They carry razor-blades fastened to little sticks, and they'd slash your face to pieces. That man they call Dinty M'Ginty—they cut his mouth up to his ear both sides, because they thought he'd squealed to the p'lice. . . . You must go before he sees you."

The man tried to speak, but achieved only an inarticulate sound.

"You *must* go," said the girl. "You will, won't you? To please me? . . . Think what it would mean to me if they coshed you one night, or cut your face to ribbons."

The girl thought rapidly, calmly and clearly.

Not only must he go, but he must not be seen leaving her room or leaving the house. Suppose he ran right into a p'liceman, and the busy noticed how strange he looked, white and trembling and wild-eyed. If a flattie stopped him and spoke to him, he would go all to pieces—and tell him every-thing. And even if he did not meet a p'liceman—and there were always a lot too many of them about that district—he might meet some man or woman on the stairs who would notice him and remember the time. There were always a lot too many people on those stairs, coming and going, not to mention kids, sharp-eyed as anybody.

And it would not do to wait until it was quite dark and there were fewer people about. The dead man might very well have one or two of his pals waiting for him at the street corner, or in the "Red Lion." Sort of man who would bring two or three along with him—so that they could swear he was never out of their sight, not once the whole evening. She could almost hear him saying to them,

"I'm jest goin' in 'ere a minute. 'Ang around 'arf a mo' and I'll be with yer. Then we'll go in the 'Red Lion' five minutes earlier than wot we did go in, see?"

And then, but for her man, whom she was awaiting, just happening to come in the nick of time, he would have killed her in a couple of minutes, rejoined his friends, and set up a dozen alibis.

He must go directly this awful trembling stopped, and he must . . . An idea! She wasn't over-bright, God knew, but this was a thought. He must shove on her old skirt, put her big shawl round his shoulders and half over his face, and pull her felt hat down over his hair. Good job the old hat was like a pudding-basin, anyway. . . . And what about his trousers showing under the bottom of the skirt, and making him look a figure of fun? He would have to tuck them in his socks like chaps do on bicycles. Lucky he was a small man, had small feet, and was toff enough to wear socks—black ones, too.

Another idea! Dreadful. She had nearly forgotten it. The poker!

The p'lice were awful nowadays, according to the Sunday papers, the way they could find out things with spy-glasses and chemist-stuff. They could tell in a minute who had had hold of what. The moment the head flattie got hold of that poker he could tell whose hand had held the small end, and whose head had been hit by the knob. It was like magic.

Finger-prints—and they would know just whose.

Why, once they got the idea in their heads that there had been somebody else here in the room, besides herself and the dead man, they would soon find out who it was. Just by examining anything he had touched—the door-handle, chair-back, the oil-cloth on the table where he had rested his hand, the poker . . . And they would start with that at once. They would say,

"Yes, that is what he did it with. Now we'll soon know who it was."

Suppose she washed it? No good. You could not fool them. The only thing to do was to get rid of it. He must take it with him. She would wrap it up in a sheet of the news-paper that she had used to cover the cupboard floor. He would have to get rid of it—chuck it off London Bridge or something.

That was better. He was not shaking and trembling quite so badly now. It was as though he had been shivering cold, frozen nearly to death, and the heat of her body pressed against him had warmed him through.

"Listen, dear, you *must* go . . ." she said again. "He's coming round."

She turned her head and looked over his shoulder.

"He's breathing better now, and he's beginning to move," she said. "Oh, he mustn't see you; he mustn't. What would happen to me if they killed you? What should I do? Look, I'm going to get my other skirt and my shawl and hat from the cupboard, and you must put them on. Then, if any of his gang are about, they won't know you. They'll think it's a woman. . . . They'll think it's me. . . .

"Now, I'm going to fold the bottoms of your trousers across and pin them and push them just inside the tops of your socks. You must keep the shawl well up to the hat at the back, up round your neck, and over your mouth. Hunch your shoulders; make yourself look small; and take short steps."

Yes, that looked all right. No p'liceman would give him a second glance as he hurried by in the dusk; and it was getting foggy too, thank God.

She had pushed the table toward the bed, so that the corpse would be concealed from the man when he rose to his feet. But the precaution was unnecessary, as he kept his back turned to it, and carefully refrained from a single glance in that direction.

"There," said the girl. "That's good. That's fine. Keep the poker like that, under the shawl and under your arm. Point it downward, so . . .

"And you understand, don't you? Straight from here to the Canal; down the steps to the towing-path; under the bridge; and then chuck the whole lot in the water. Wrap up the hat and the coat and poker in the shawl and throw it in, in one bundle. Better still, kneel down and hold it under the water until it's soaked, and sinks. Mind there's nobody about, though. And if a busy or a dick or anybody did see you, and said *''Ere wot's the gime?'* you just laugh and say *'Runnin' away from me mother-in-law!'* See?"

Talking volubly; stroking and touching the man continually, as she spoke; the girl tried to smile.

"It's nothing, dear love. Don't be so upset. What right has he got to come up here and try to kill me? Why shouldn't you hit him? You did the proper thing, like any man would. There's nothing to be upset about.

"Only him and his gang mustn't know," she added. (In other words, the police mustn't know—not when you've killed a man from behind.

Two men and a girl in a room, and one of them killed from behind. Just plain murder, they would say).

The man, still shaken by the violence of his emotions—of rage, hatred, fear, and jealousy—put his hand upon the girl's shoulder as though to steady himself, to prevent himself from falling should his trembling legs give way beneath him.

"Understand it all? Remember it all?" smiled the girl as she gazed beseechingly into his hunted, haunted, frightened eyes.

"Yes . . . Yes . . . Yes . . ." he said hoarsely. "I understand. . . . What *have* I done . . . ? What *have* I done . . . ?"

"You've done what was right, love—and they'll pay you out for it if they know. Those Slashers, I mean. . . .

"Now, when you've got rid of those things in the Canal, where are you going?"

"I don't know . . . I don't know . . ."

"Well, I'll tell you. You are going to the station for Brighton; and that's where you are going next —Brighton. . . . It's a lovely place, and there's millions of people; and it's far, far away. I went there once. Brighton. They'd never find you among all those people. And I'll write to you there at the Post Office, like my father wrote to me, when I went there. I'll just write and tell you that, when he came round, he never knew what hit him. I'll tell him it was a great big strong man who lives here in the next room—champion boxer—and he says he'll knock his block off if ever he comes round here again. Something like that, see?"

"He's . . . recovering . . . coming round . . . getting better? . . ." mumbled the man, but he did not glance toward where the corpse lay, part-concealed by the table.

"Yes, dear. . . . Yes. . . . You *must* go now," urged the girl. "Before he sits up and sees you. He's a killer; and so are all his gang—and it's the very worst in the whole East End. . . . Now, you must open the door quickly and slip out, and I'll keep out of sight."

"But what about you?" asked the man, as he turned to go. "What about when he . . ."

"I shall be all right," the girl assured him. "I'll tell him that unless he clears off quick, I'll fetch a copper and give him in charge. I'll do it, too. . . . Walking into people's rooms and wringing their necks for nothing."

"Are you sure he . . . ?"

"He'll be only too glad to get away," interrupted the girl. "After a biff on the napper like that he'll want to get away and lie down—not in a p'lice-cell, either. No. Now *go*, love. *Go.*

"Kiss me good-bye," she added, as the man extended a still shaking hand to open the door.

And, as she threw her arms about his neck, he kissed her as a child kisses its mother, in farewell, rather than as a lover who is parting from his bride.

He is still dazed, thought the girl. Hardly knows where he is or what he is doing.

Was it safe to send him out like that?

No—nor to let him stay any longer. She must think and plan and act; and he must be getting further and further away while she did so.

"Now, go," she said, firmly and finally, as she fought to control the working of her lips and quivering chin, and to hold back the unshed tears a moment longer. "Straight to the station; take the first train to Brighton; get a kip somewhere for the night; and go to the Post Office for my letter to-morrow."

"The big one, the General Post Office," muttered the man. "Yes, I'll do as you say, and I'll write."

"Yes, yes, love. But don't put your name or any address. Just in case. That race-gang goes to Brighton. Now, *quick*, he's sitting up!"

Swiftly turning to the door, the man hurried from the room.

Well, that was that. . . .

He ought to be safe enough if he did as she had told him.

Now, to think hard for herself.

How long would it take him to get to the High-way, by way of the Canal? Give him twenty minutes; and if he got a bus at once, as he ought, he would be at the big Station—she had forgotten its name—in, say, about half an hour more.

How long would he have to wait for a train to Brighton? Not long, at this time of day. Lots of people went down in the evening—worked in London and slept in Brighton, so she had heard. Some people had the luck. Suppose he had to wait an hour. How long would the journey take? An hour and a half, perhaps.

Why, if nothing went wrong, he should be safe in Brighton within three hours; and safe he would be, surely.

Right. Now, the next thing. She had either heard, or read in the Sunday paper, that not only could the p'lice tell who had handled things—like that awful poker—but that they could tell just how long a stiff had been a stiff. A p'lice-surgeon could kneel down beside the body, give it a prod or two, and say "*Been dead three hours*"—or three days, or whatever it might be. No good telling any lies about that. Then how should she account for the time between the murder and her telling the p'lice? She could say she was too frightened to do anything; she could say she passed out; she could say she had gone balmy and did not know where she was or what she was doing. . . .

Yes, and not so silly a tale either, for that is how *he* had been from the moment he had hit the brute and knocked him out. Gone clean off his rocker. Dotty. Just as though he was drunk.

Dropping into the chair in which the man had sat, she pressed her clean white apron to her streaming eyes. She ought never to have sent him out like that. Not alone. She ought to have gone with him.

Bosh! That would have doubled and trebled the chance of his being caught. A dead man found in her room and a p'lice-hunt for her and the man seen going out of the house with her. Besides, she must be going balmy herself to think like that. Talking about going with him when her whole plan depended on her stopping here. Still, he ought not to be alone. He was not fit to look after himself, even before this happened. Perhaps that was partly why she loved him so, because he needed her— needed someone, anyhow—to look after him. Like a child he was.

And, Christ, how she loved him! . . . It *hurt.* . . .

And how it was going to hurt until he came back to her. But when would that be? *How could that be*, if she were to save him—really save him, once and for all? She was a fool to kid herself. She would never, never. . . .

And, as the man had done in that same chair, she bowed her head in despair, covered her face with her now creased and crumpled apron, and trembled from head to foot while she sobbed aloud, giving way to grief, horror, pain, and cruel disappointment.

But this would not do. This was not getting her anywhere. This was not helping him.

But what could she do—except wait? Wait until he was safe.

What could she do while she waited? She could not sit there for hours with that—that *Thing*—lying there so still and silent on the other side of the table. . . .

Suppose it got up, and with dead sightless eyes and cold out-stretched hands, came toward her, and seized her by the throat—again. . . .

Bosh! The beast was dead—and a good job too, except for the danger in which its death had put her man; the wreck and ruin that it had made of her life.

Her wedding-night!

Now, then, enough of that. Light the lamp, pull down the blind, lock the door, and write to him. And she must do it right too; make it sound true; or else he would come rushing back by the very first train—come back as fast as he possibly could. That is what he would do if, for one moment, it entered his head that he had *killed* him—and left her to it.

Having got a penny bottle of ink and a rusty-nibbed pen from the top shelf of the cupboard, she took a piece of ruled paper from the table drawer, drew up a small kitchen chair to the table, and, after a hasty and horrified glance at the dead body lying within a yard of her chair, wrote,

Dearest Love,
You will be glad to hear that all is well. The patient got better very soon. Just after you went. I gave him a glass of water, and he pushed off a bit

shaky on his feet. He had something to say, but I told him that if he ever came back he'd get a worse illness than that, see? And a couple of doctors he would not like. He won't come back. He's had enough, and he doesn't know what happened. But he'll guess. I mean he'll suspect like—that it was you; so you must keep away for the present. Wait until him and his gang are in prison, as they are bound to be before long. You must not come back until I write and ask you to. Please don't, darling love. I beg you not to. It might get me into bad trouble with him and his gang, too. If he thought it was all a put up job, and you waiting there to cosh him. We'll go to some other part of London later on, when I write and tell you. Do take care of yourself, darling love, and don't worry and make yourself ill again. I promised to let you know if I get any trouble from them. But I shan't. I am going to the police about him. That's the real truth; as true as I sit here writing to you now. I am going to the police and he will never bother me again, so don't worry.

Good-bye for the present, darling love. Hoping this finds you as it now leaves me at present. Always your most loving,

You Know Who.

Now she must find the envelope that she put somewhere when she moved in. Yes—under the news-paper, when she lined the dresser drawer; and she had a stamp in the back of her Bible, a bit dirty and old-fashioned looking, but it was all right.

Should she go out and post the letter now? No. It might do him harm in some way. Anybody who might have seen him go out of her room—and thought it was she—might be suspicious if they now saw her coming out—without having returned, so to speak. If she posted it early in the morning, when she would have to go out to do what she had to do, he would get it to-morrow all right. She had heard that trains run all day long to Brighton, every hour almost.

Besides, if she went out of the room now, she would never be able to come back into it. Not alone. She could stay in the room with . . . It . . . but once she went out, she would have to stay out. If she opened that door and came back into the room, she would expect to see It standing waiting for her. Or, perhaps, It would be sitting in that very chair where he had sat. Funny—she could stay with It all night, so long as she could keep her eye on It and know that It did not move. But she could not go away and come back again.

No—it would be all right so long as she sat and watched It. Knew where It was and what It was doing. . . . Doing nothing, of course. . . . But she could not so much as turn her back on It now.

So all night long the girl sat and watched the body of the murdered man; sat wide-eyed, and watched. She did not sleep, nor close her eyes, but for long periods of time sat in a kind of waking dream that was neither coma nor stupor, but a subjective state which was at once super-passivity and absence of mind, as distinguished from lack of consciousness.

Between these timeless stretches of Time she returned to a state of terrified awakenings. . . .

How could it be? How could God have allowed it to come about, that she—who had never wished anyone any harm, much less done them any, and had always striven to be respectable and to do what is right—should be sitting here, with the body of a murdered man, in what was almost a strange room. For she had only taken it a week ago and had never slept in it.

But she was to have slept in it to-night, her wedding-night.

And now, look at it. . . .

Well, life was like that. For the poor, anyhow. You spend your savings on getting everything nice. You get everything right to start a life that is to be as happy as the day is long, and buy your wedding bed and paint it up all beautiful, and before ever you can use it, a man is killed on it, and your lover is on the run, hiding from the p'lice—the very night that was to be his wedding-night.

Silly fool to have supposed that she was going to be happy!

Yet how happy she had been cutting out that pink paper with the scallopped edge, and fitting it to the mantel-piece and the dresser and the shelves; choosing that lovely bit of yellow and red and blue and green carpet; screwing those hooks into the shelf for the tea-cups; buying things at the Sixpenny Bazaar. Why, if she had been going to be married in two churches and a chapel, with a satin dress and a cab to go to the station, for the honeymoon, she could not have had a nicer home to come back to.

With an effort, the girl withdrew her fascinated and horrified stare from the corpse, and glanced round the room. Lovely. And clean as a new pin.

It was too bad. . . .

Dawn.

Rising stiffly from the chair she pulled up the blind.

Now God give her strength, courage and sharp wits, for she must go to the p'lice. He must be safe in Brighton by now and there was nothing in the room to show that he had ever been there. No tobacco knocked out from a pipe; no cigarette ends; nothing. And she had remembered to tuck his cap into the side pocket of his coat, under the shawl.

How ghastly It looked in the pale early light.

No, she could never have come back here alone with That waiting for her.

As she opened the door, the girl took one last lingering look round the room that was to have been her peaceful, beautiful, happy home with the man she loved better than life itself.

"Good-bye," she whispered; and, with tears running down her face, slowly descended the common stair of the common lodging-house.

Out in the street she looked from left to right. No-one. There never was a copper if you did want one. Better go up to the High Street.

A few minutes later, shortly after passing a pillar-box and posting the precious letter, as she turned a corner, she almost ran into a figure in blue.

"Excuse me, Sir," she said, "but I've . . ."

Pretty girl. Nice and clean-looking. Nice hands and face. Ever so nice. Been crying.

"Now, are you out a bit too late, or up a bit too early?" asked P.C. Brock, a kindly man, with genial pleasantry. "If you've been up all night it's time you went to bed. And if you just got up, remember it's the early worm gets caught by the bird. Eh?"

Poor girl looked as though she was in rare trouble of some sort. Didn't seem to hear what he was saying to her.

"Excuse me, Sir," she repeated, "but I've . . ."

"You've what? Lost yourself? Well, come along and we'll find you."

She could not say it.

She must say it.

"I've committed a murder," she blurted out.

"Have you now!"

P.C. Brock hooked his thumbs into his belt and, rocking himself gently to and fro from heel to toe, eyed the girl with increased interest.

"Before breakfast and all, eh?"

Murder. Looked more like the sort that gets murdered—in this part of the world; unless she had been and chucked her baby off the bridge. Might be that, of course, poor lass. If so, what did she want to come and tell *him* about it for?

"Early in the morning to be pulling policemen's legs, isn't it?" he smiled.

"It's the truth. I've killed a man."

And if she had, it was ten to one that it served the blighter right. One of those wife-beating husbands.

"Killed a man, have you? Well, well, well! And what did you want to do that for? Didn't you like him so much?

"Or you been dreaming?" he added more sharply.

"Will you come along with me, please?" replied the girl.

"Well, that's generally what *I* say, but without the 'please'. Come along with you? Where to?"

"My room. It's in Lugg's Tenements, Lugg Lane. The body is there."

"Sure?"

"Yes. I hit him on the head, from behind."

"Sure he's dead?"

"Quite sure."

What was the game? Something new, if they were going to play the cosh-moll trick on a Member of the Force. It could not be that. She did not look that sort, either. Neither did she look the sort to give her husband a dot on the dome that would put him out for keeps. Still, you never knew; and if you did you were generally wrong. Better go along and look into it, anyway, if only to see what the game was.

"All right. Come along, then," he said. "But don't forget it's an Offence."

"*Murder?*" whispered the girl.

"No. Making up a cock-and-bull story to waste my time and fetch me off me beat. That's an Offence."

"It's not a cock-and-bull story. It's the truth."

"Ho! And was he your husband?"

"No, he wasn't."

"Your young man, then?"

"No. He was a low . . . beast."

"And so you up and killed him, eh?"

"Yes."

"Well, well, well! Think of that now!"

A pack o' lies, of course, but what *was* the game? Very interesting, anyhow.

"Down here," said the girl.

"Yes, I know Lugg Lane. Nice place," said the policeman. "And you live in Lugg's Tenements? 'Nother nice place. . . . What do you do for a living?"

"Flowers."

"Where's your pitch?"

"Corner of Prince Albert Road and Kensington High Street—until he drove me off it."

"Ho! One of those, was he? Collected rent without owning property, eh?

"What was he doing in your room this time in the morning?" asked P.C. Brock.

The girl made no reply.

"Did you lock the door of your room as you came out?" asked the policeman a little later.

"No."

"Then I shouldn't be surprised if the corpse hasn't got up and gone away, should you?"

" Very surprised," said the white-faced girl,

through trembling lips that she struggled to keep controlled and taut.

"I tell you he's dead," she said again.

"Any blood about?"

"Yes."

"How did you kill him?"

"I told you. Hit him on the back of the head."

"Pity you done that. At the back, I mean. . . . What did you hit him with?"

The girl made no reply, and, a minute later, turned into the ever-open door of the filthy little entrance-hall from which the stone stairs climbed steeply to the floors above. Preceding the constable, the girl led the way to her room, opened the door, and stood aside for him to enter.

"Well?" yawned P.C. Brock. "What you done with him? In the cupboard or up the chimbley?"

"The other side of the table, down by the bed," whispered the girl.

Passing between the table and fire-place in the direction of the bed, the policeman saw the body of the murdered man.

The corpse lay flat on its back, face upwards.

" *'Streuth!*" murmured P.C. Brock, and emitted a brief low whistle of surprise.

For surprised he was; indeed, amazed. Not that he should have found a man murdered, and murdered in this particular way, in this particular house and slum, but that such a girl with such a face should have done it.

If ever he had seen a low-type street-walking cosh-moll in his life—and he reckoned he had seen a few—this was not one. Neat, tidy, clean, quiet, nicely-spoken, and with a face as sweet and gentle as his own wife's.

Well, well! There it was, and you never knew—with women. No doubt the bloke deserved it. One of those lousy swine that lived on girls, like as not.

A dirty ponce that had got what was coming to him.

Yes, and what was coming to this nice quiet pretty girl? What the hell did she want to go and give herself up for, instead of having a run for her money and, perhaps, getting away with it? What did she want to pick on *him* for, to arrest her? . . . Pity. . . . Rotten job. . . . Still, there it was. Duty is —duty.

"Shall I go and fetch another p'liceman?" asked the girl, ignorant of procedure and fearing that she might be left alone—alone in the room that was to have been her Earthly Paradise.

"No," replied P.C. Brock sharply. "You stay where you are; and don't touch nothing.

"Lock that door and give me the key," he added. ". . . Right."

Going to the window at the foot of the bed, he opened it to its full extent and leaned out.

No-one about. There soon would be, though. If not, he would knock up somebody in the house here, and scribble a note to be taken to the Police Station. They would not dare to refuse, or destroy a note, though they would not take a verbal message.

A man turned the corner by the "Red Lion" and approached on the other side of the street.

"Hi!" called P.C. Brock, and, as the man looked up, said,

"Tell the first policeman you see to come to Lugg's Tenements, Lugg Lane, and if you don't see one, cut up to the Highway and find one."

The man's answer, as he took to his heels, was brief, profane, and insulting.

"Right! I'll be seeing yer!" shouted P.C. Brock, as the man ran off; and his tone did not seem to promise that it would be a wholly social occasion.

Turning back into the room, he addressed the

girl.

"Know anybody in this tenement?" he asked.

"No. Nobody. But I'll go to the Station for you, if you like."

"No. You'll stay here and keep me company—in case I get lonely," replied the policeman in a firm but kindly manner. "Who lives across the landing?"

"I don't know."

"Well, we'll find out. . . . Now, don't you try to get away from this room. I shall keep me eye on this door."

"Don't leave me alone here!" cried the girl.

"All right. Stand in the doorway, if you like. But don't try any tricks, or you'll be sorry."

"Oh, talk sense," begged the girl. "Should I have gone out and given myself up, and brought you here, if I had wanted to get away?"

"No. Not as you were feeling then. But women change their minds sometimes. So I've been told. Right. You stand there, where I can see you, if you don't want to be left alone. But don't you take one step towards them stairs."

Having crossed the landing, he stood sideways and knocked at the opposite door. Receiving no response he knocked again, louder. A minute later the door was opened by a bare-footed woman wearing a skirt and shawl.

"My Gord!" she whispered on realising that her early morning caller was a policeman. " 'E ain't in trouble again, is 'e?"

"Don't know," replied the policeman. "Is there a man here?"

"No, there ain't. Me and me daughter are . . ."

"Sure you are! But I want someone to nip round to the Station for me."

"Well, me daughter's in bed and I'm . . . I know! Young Tommy 'Icks, Number Seventeen. 'E'd go

323

fast enough. That, or any other mischief, the young . . .”

“Well, you go and get him for me.”

“Well, I . . .”

“Yes, I know you do. Now, hurry up, Mother; and I’ll be waiting in there. Go and get him and bring him here.

“ ‘*Blige a policeman*’,” he added, “like the song says, and live happy ever after. Hurry up, Mother.”

He again crossed the landing to where the white-faced girl waited in the open door.

“Cor!” ejaculated the woman, as she caught sight of her. “The trouble is *there*, eh? Me and me daughter see ’er go out last night, all ’uddled up and ’*idin’ ’er* face; and I passes the remark to me daughter then and there . . .”

“Pass the remark to Thomas Hicks,” interrupted P.C. Brock. “You can say all that later.”

“I’ll be seeing yer,” he added, as he closed the door. It was, apparently, a favourite locution of this intelligent young policeman.

Poor girl looked like death. Rough luck.

“Sorry to keep you waiting, miss,” he said, as he again went to the window, and neither of them seemed to see anything strange in the apology.

He bent out over the window-sill, and looked up and down the street. Suddenly, he whipped out his whistle, blew a short sharp blast on it, and waved a beckoning hand imperiously.

A square-shouldered, square-faced, square-toed man who, in his neat quiet mufti looked rather more noticeably like a policeman than he would have done in constable’s uniform, hurried diagonally across the road.

“Good luck, mate!” said P.C. Brock, as the man came within hearing. “Right on the spot and on time. As always. . . . Get in touch with the Station quick. Got a stiff up here. Murdered. Statement, anyway."

"Police-Surgeon?" asked the man tersely.

"Yes. Not that he can do much. Bloke's dead all right. Coshed."

"Right. I'll ring the Station and then come back."

§2

"How long has he been dead?" asked Detective-Inspector Sindall quietly of the Police-Surgeon.

"Oh, hours. All night, pretty well. A good six to eight hours. More, perhaps."

"Somewhere between seven and ten last night, then?"

"That's about it."

"And cause of death that clout on the head, eh?"

"Certainly enough to have caused death, any-how. Base of the skull fractured. Badly depressed fracture, too."

"Usual 'blunt instrument'?" asked the Inspec-tor. "Yes. Black-jack; butt-end of a flat-iron; or the kitchen poker."

"Well, that's all, I think," said the Police Sur-geon a little later. "I'll send the ambulance along."

"Now, Miss," said Detective-Inspector Sindall, turning to the girl, who stood white-faced, silent, and motionless in the furthest corner of the room. "It was you who brought the Police-Constable here, wasn't it?"

"Yes, Sir."

"You find the body?"

"No, Sir."

"You told the Police-Constable that you had killed the man, didn't you?"

"Yes, Sir. I want to tell you all that . . ."

"Yes. Wait a minute. It's my duty to warn you that anything you say now, may be used as evidence at the—er—inquest. Or trial. You want to make a full statement?"

"Yes, Sir. I do, please."

"Well, if you come along to the Station with me, I'll write it all down. Then I'll read it over to you. Or you can read it yourself, of course. And then sign it."

"Yes, Sir. Thank you. I'm quite ready."

"Well, I'm not. Not quite. Just one or two things to attend to, before we go along. Let's see. . . . You told the Police-Constable that you had killed deceased yourself, didn't you?"

"Yes, Sir. He was . . ."

"Wait a minute, now. All in good time. Just answer one or two questions. You can say all you want to say afterwards. Before we go, just tell me how you killed him, and what with."

"I hit him on the back of the head."

"That's right. You—or somebody else—certainly did. Now, if you are speaking the truth, tell me this. What did you hit him with?"

That was what had been puzzling the keen-eyed and quick-witted officer. Where was the weapon of offence, invariably known as 'a blunt instrument,' though why it should not be a sharp one, the Lord only knew, for you could hit a man as well with the one as with the other. Now, if they said blunt-ended, perhaps . . .

"Well?" he prompted, as the girl made no answer. "What did you do it with—and what did you then do *with it?*" he asked again, speaking in a quiet, friendly, and almost fatherly manner.

The girl compressed her lips and shook her head. Shook her head and, with the knuckle of a quick fore-finger, prevented a tear from trickling down her face.

"Now, now. Don't take on. Sit down a minute," said the detective. "I'm not cross-examining you, so to speak, you know. And you aren't bound to say anything at all. Not at present. But I thought that as you say you killed the man, you wouldn't mind telling me what you did it with—and where it is."

Again the girl shook her head, and seemed to swallow a lump in her throat.

"Well, as you like, my dear. But if I owned up and said I'd killed somebody, I wouldn't mind saying what I'd done it with. Still . . ."

Queer. Very puzzling. Just like a woman. Go the whole hog—except the last bristle of his tail.

Going to the door, he opened it on the broad back of P.C. Brock, who was just informing a wide-eyed and wide-mouthed group that the charge for admiring him would be one penny, if they did not . . .

"Brock," said Detective-Inspector Sindall, "get down into the yard at the back of this house and search for a hammer, club, cosh, poker, flat-iron, or any other 'instrument', blunt *or* sharp. And if it's got any blood or hair on it, so much the better. Tell Dickson down at the entrance to do the same along the street. Though there isn't much chance there.

"Now," he said, closing the door, and looking at the girl, who seemed as though she were about to faint. "If you won't help us along with the little matter of what you used, will you tell us what you did with it? I can quite understand that you don't like to say *club*" (no tremor or other re-action), "*hammer*" (no look or sign), "*heavy mantel-piece ornament*" (no, that didn't ring the bell), "*flat-iron*" (no facial or other response), "*black-jack, cosh*" (no; very self-controlled or else it wasn't either of them), "*poker . . .*"

Ah! Her eyes moved sharply toward the fire-place. One of her hands jerked slightly. Yes; and, by gad, there was a faint faint flush on her face. That was it.

"Now, I don't want to bother you with a lot of questions, and you're going to tell us all about it at the Station, I know, but just one more before we stroll along."

And then, after a brief pregnant and uncomfortable silence, the sudden sharp question:

"*Where's your poker?*"

"Never had one," whispered the girl.

"What did you poke the fire with, then?"

"It was never poked."

"What a funny fire!"

"It was never lit till to-night."

"Oh? . . . Oh, I see. Only just moved in here?"

"It was the first fire I had."

"And deceased? Mustn't mind my asking—but did you bring him here?"

"No."

"Had he ever been here before?"

"No."

"How did he come to be up here, then?"

"He's followed me in the street before now. He must have found out which was my room, seen me come up, and waited till I was in the room."

"And then?"

"He attacked me."

"And you picked up the poker and . . ."

"I've told you—I never *had* a poker."

"Well—whatever it was. You picked it up and hit him with it?"

"Yes."

"And he had his back to you when you hit him?"

"Yes."

"And how did that happen?"

"He was . . . He was . . . He was going out of the room."

"I see," said Detective-Inspector Sindall, departing from the truth. "And you won't tell me what it *was* that was lying handy, and that you picked up to hit him with?"

"No."

"Nor what you did with it afterwards? . . . Well, well. We'll be getting along. After you've had some breakfast you'll feel better, and I expect you'll want to tell us all about it, eh?"

But at the Station it was decided that the girl did not so much want to tell them all about it, as to tell them her version of it—and that only partial; since, for some strange and puzzling reason, she refused to say what instrument she had used to kill the man whom she admitted, nay, professed and claimed, to have killed single-handed.

PART II

THE VICAR OF LITTLE PUDDING AND JACINTHA HIS WIFE

CHAPTER 1

There are, in the south of England, three villages rejoicing in the sprightly and stimulating name of Wallop, and respectively known as Upper Wallop, Middle Wallop and Nether Wallop. Facetious wayfarers, motorists, cyclists and hikers, wax hilarious over the names, and are apt to threaten each other with a middle wallop, if not indeed with a nether one. I mention these authentic names in extenuation of that of our own very real village, Little Pudding, which causes the same kind of amusement to similar humorous transients. But in their tedious jests they do but show their ignorance, for we are not rightly pronounced Pudding as in suet, batter or Xmas, but Pŭdding to rhyme with scudding or budding. Little *Pŭdding*, then, please, a village that has hardly changed a stone since Norman times or a red brick since those of the early Tudors. It is, moreover, as lovely, peaceful and sequestered as any in England. This is due to the facts that we are miles from the railway and that we have nothing to attract what we call "They sharry-bangers—the incomen toads."

We have only a perfect Norman Church; a village street of half-timbered cottages; and some scattered houses, Elizabethan and earlier, in several of which live the descendants of the original owners. We have never, thank God, been discovered, advertised and exploited; we are not self-consciously picturesque; we have no antique tea-shoppe and lack even a ye olde petrol pumpe. Our inn is an inn and not a gimcrack hotel with fake attractions; not pseuder Tudor nor psuedo Tudoh,

333

but the very unchanged building in which yeomen and bowmen have drunk their honest brown ale, generation after generation and century after century, since it was first built in the days of Edward the Third.

And, talking of yeomen and bowmen, we have in the church a wonderful old muniment-chest, and in that muniment-chest is a sheep-skin parchment bearing the names of the yeomen and bowmen who went from our village to Crecy. Among them are Dickon Hogben, Richard Iggulden, Thomas Woodman, Henry Wayland, Geoffrey Bowyer, Johan Thane and William Wright.

On our beautiful War Memorial, given by Sir Giles Herriott of Herriott Hall, are the names of the yeomen and riflemen who went to the Great War, five hundred years later, and who never returned. Among them are those of Richard Hogben, Richard Iggulden, George Woodman, Henry and Thomas Wayland, Stephen Wright and John Thane. The men of Crecy were equipped and led by a Sir Giles Herriott. Our present Sir Giles went to France in 1914, and his son is there now, as I write. So are the sons of the other men who fought there a quarter of a century ago; and on our next War Memorial there will still be some of those same names that are writ on the muster-roll of Crecy.

So we have continuity at Little Pudding and roots deep in the ancient heart of this our England.

Has a life-time in this peaceful, lovely place made me a historical artist; or is it that, being a natural painter and lover of History, I see it and its past as one and indivisible, and love it almost as I love Life and Beauty?

And of all that is beautiful and interesting in this place, I find Jacintha Neystoke most beauti-

ful, and her husband Richard Neystoke most interesting. No, that is hardly correct, because I
admire Jacintha so greatly that she interests me
more than any other human being does; but
Richard Neystoke is the most interesting, puzzling
and intriguing man I have ever met.

It was very early in our acquaintance that he
first puzzled and intrigued me—and that was
many years ago.

It really was a rather curious episode, and it is
one that I have never forgotten.

I thought at first, or, let me say, I pretended to
think, that I had received the highest and most
genuine compliment that ever painter received
upon this earth, not excluding him to whom the
birds of the air paid the remarkable compliment of
trying to eat the painted fruit from his canvas.

My picture was *The Trial of Joan of Arc*, not
unknown to fame, as it was generally said to be
the picture of the year at the Royal Academy—to
which Neystoke and his wife had been unable to
go. Thus it came about that I was able to give
them a very private view of the picture when it
came back to my study for a while, before going to
its long home in the Tate Gallery.

As it happened, Neystoke saw it first and alone
—fortunately, perhaps. The light being good, I was
working in my studio when the Vicar walked in, as
I had invited him to do, whenever he felt he
wanted to see me, and the parlour-maid said I was
"busy." If I really did not wish to be disturbed, by
anyone at all, the maid would say I was "engaged."

In his nice shy and charming way, he asked if
he might watch me painting for a little while, as,
though no artist himself, he was deeply interested
in pictures, and the technique of painting.

By and by, after I had finished what I was
doing, and he had told me about some little

parochial business, I asked him whether he would like to see *The Trial of Joan of Arc.* He professed to be delighted at the opportunity of seeing here, in the very room in which it had been painted, what he was pleased to call my great and famous picture.

I drew aside the curtain that covered it, let up the sun-excluding blind that screened the east window, placed a chair for him, returned to my work, and left him to it.

There followed a long silence . . .

Suddenly, I heard a sound so unexpected, strange, and—I had almost said alarming—that I turned sharply round to where the Vicar sat.

"Oh, *God!*" he groaned softly to himself, and, as though forgetting my presence, forgetting everything but the pictured scene, buried his face in his hands as if to shut it from his sight.

I stared in amazement, and realised that he was trembling; shaking, indeed, from head to foot.

"Oh, *God!*" he groaned again, like a man in agony; like a man who had suffered a dreadful shock, if not a mortal wound.

Well, this was very remarkable, to say the least of it. I had not realised that the picture, though admittedly tragic and powerful, was as powerful as all that.

The art critics who infest the Academy and enrich the public press with their doubtless valuable opinions, had used both these adjectives quite freely; had professed to find it heart-searching and of terrible appeal; they had said that no-one could gaze upon it unmoved, or fail to be haunted by the face of Joan or by those of her cruel, remorseless and fanatical judges. But I had not read or heard of anyone being so uncontrollably affected as the Vicar apparently was; I had received no tidings of tears, groans, or rigors of tremblings.

Undoubtedly people had stood before the picture and for very long periods, and, moreover, with rapt expressions upon their faces. But there are people who keep a rapt expression in stock for the sort of pictures that are said by the critics to merit it, just as they keep for annual use a curious jargon of technical art-terms, unknown for the most part to the humble individuals who paint the pictures.

Rapt, yes; genuinely, perhaps, now and again; but groans, tremblings and appeals to the Deity, no!

And yet this amazing performance on the part of the Vicar was only the overture, for, before my astounded and incredulous eyes, his body bowed more and more, his head sank lower and lower, until he finally slumped altogether, collapsed, and slid sideways from the chair.

"Well, well!" I thought again, really for a moment too astounded to move. "That's what I call a true compliment!"

For, though you may turn on a rapt expression to order, you cannot turn on a faint, and pass out on the floor—not convincingly, with your face as white as a sheet and with every appearance of being a perfectly good corpse.

For a fraction of a second, I almost persuaded myself, as I say, that here was the ultimate compliment, the greatest that could be paid by man to mortal man. Something far more gratifying than the envious praise of fellow-artists; than the squeals of the self-invited at the private view; the gaping crowds day after day while the picture was on show, and, finally, the purchase for the Nation.

A highly intelligent person of fine taste and discrimination had come, had seen, and had been conquered to the ultimate extreme of being bowled clean over, literally knocked off his perch, conceivably struck dead!

Literally a case of 'See Marindin's picture and die'.

Could it possibly be that to this man the scene was so clear, the atmosphere so real, the protagonists so alive, and the Immortal Heroine herself so actual, that he had identified himself with her to the extent of himself suffering her sufferings, and really fainting as, in point of fact, the Martyred Maid herself did, at one point of her incredibly brutal trial?

I suppose it was really only a matter of a second or so before I lifted poor little Neystoke up, laid him on the divan, and sprinkled some water from a flower-vase on his waxen white face. I was just contemplating the sacrilege of wrestling with his dog-collar, the fastening of which was, presumably, at the back of his neck, when he opened his eyes and boyishly enquired as to what was up?

I told him that my conceit of myself was undoubtedly up; and, as far as I knew, he was the only person who had been what my cook calls struck all of a heap, by the sight of one of my pictures.

Declining brandy in favour of a glass of water, he sat up, pulled himself together, and began to look a bit better as the colour returned to his face.

"Have you been over-doing the fasting?" I asked.

Of course, I knew perfectly well that my picture had had nothing to do with this all-too-timely attack, but I noticed that, nevertheless, he took one swift glance at it, and visibly shuddered, before he replied.

"No," he said.

"I only fast before Communion Service," he

added.

Then, after an uncomfortable silence, he shot at me the question which, I think, he had been trying to refrain from asking.

"*Who?*" he said, suddenly and urgently. "*Who is she?* I mean *where* did you see her?"

"Who?" I asked. "See whom? Joan, do you mean?"

"Yes. Yes. The woman. Yes, Joan of Arc. She's . . . I know her . . . Did she sit for you?"

Well, well, well, I thought again. Here's a rum start, as cook also says. And I told him exactly how and where and when I came to get that face of all faces for my Joan. . . . A case of murder. . . .

That ideal face, born and fashioned—and tortured—for me; or, rather, for posterity. The face that I hope, and sometimes believe, will be honoured and admired five hundred years hence—when I am a very Old Master. A face that may be as famous and far-known as that of Mona Lisa herself.

It was, indeed, a strange business, and I thought of little else for a very long time.

"There is more in this than meets the eye," said I to myself in my wisdom.

And there was certainly more in it than met the ear also, for he never said one word in explanation and enlightenment; and I, of course, refrained from questioning him.

Well, Richard Neystoke is our Vicar, then, and no parish ever had a better one; absolutely first-class; gifted; conscientious to a fault; and as kind, courteous and helpful to the humblest old villager as to Sir Giles or Lady Herriott themselves. A gentleman, in fact, and the right man in the right place; for our people are still clearly and sharply divided into the ancient classes of gentle and simple, though our simple are mostly very gentle folk and our gentle apt to be quite simple persons.

But of Richard Neystoke more anon.

Concerning Jacintha, his wife, I will only say that she is a fascinating woman, witty, spirited, courageous, quick, tolerant and kind. It is my ambition to paint her as Mary, Queen of Scots (for I am still an artist[13] of sorts) but have not yet got her to sit for me. She would be the perfect model for a portrait of that lovely and unhappy lady; and until she will consent, my best picture remains unpainted—*The Happy Days of Mary, Queen of Scots*. I would do a self-portrait in the background, a faithful gentleman of her Court, I think. Yes, I would paint myself there behind her and so stand for ever, Jacintha's friend and servant. Not Darnley. Not Rizzio. Not Bothwell. Just an innominate lover who stood and waited—in hope that he might serve. For I have waited for some years now; and have at last been granted the reward of an opportunity to do her a service that she over-values far beyond its meed.

But it is Richard Neystoke's story that is of interest, for Jacintha, happily, has none. None beyond a tale of quiet domesticity and routine simple life, her troubles only those caused by the curious state of her husband's mental and physical health.

Being an artist with a love of portrait-painting, I am, of course, a physiognomist. I study faces professionally, apart from my agreement with

---

[13] Denzil Marindin, b. 1895, d.   . Painter of historical scenes and portraits. His most famous picture, *The Trial of Joan of Arc*, was bought by the Trustees of the Chantrey Bequest. The Liverpool Corporation bought his *Execution of Montrose*, Birmingham his *Henry VIII and Cardinal Wolsey*. Had five pictures of historical scenes hung in the Royal Academy; and his portraits of William III and Mary, of de Ruyter and of Van Tromp went to America. Stubborn opponent of impressionism, cubism, dadaism, surrealism and all new modern trends in art.

Pope's belief that the proper study of Mankind is Man; and I glance at every new face I meet, to see whether it exhibits anything of interest, shows any sign of originality, difference from the mass, something that makes it paintable. (I looked for years, and in vain, for my Joan of Arc, and found her at last in the prisoner's dock of a Criminal Court of Justice.)

Richard Neystoke's face interested me when I first saw him in the pulpit here, and mainly because of its contradictions, its strength and weakness, its pride and humility, its asceticism and sensuality, and because of the repressed fanaticism that it indicated. The face, thought I, of a man possessed of a dual personality.

It interested me yet more when I came to know him well and to see him almost daily, because gradually I realised that it was the haunted face of a frightened man. Fear lurked behind the kind smiling eyes and occasionally it peeped out. From the time when, not long after his arrival here, he spent that hour with me in my studio, I began to see that he was living under a great strain; was bearing some burden that was almost too heavy for his strength; and that anxiety and apprehension were his familiar companions. Never did he seem able to relax, and even in what should have been his hours of ease, he was tense; his hands were always clenched or grasping each other so tightly that his knuckles showed white and hard.

From that day, soon after Neystoke's first coming, I used to talk about him to my old friend Dr. Bennett, who was just as deeply interested in him—or rather in his curious nervous condition—as I was myself, but in a different way.

To Bennett he was a study in pathology, to me in humanity.

Later, at Jacintha's earnest request, I persuaded him to consult Bennett professionally, and thereafter Bennett would not discuss him at all, though formerly he did so quite freely. Whether this was because Neystoke was now his patient, and the health of his patients was not a subject concerning which the punctilious doctor cared to talk; or whether he had learnt something about Neystoke which was entirely confidential, I do not know. Anyway, Bennett became very guarded and uncommunicative, indeed secretive, when I mentioned the Vicar's name—and that made me wonder and speculate the more.

After I had known Neystoke for a year or so, and we had got on very friendly terms, I asked him to sit to me for his portrait. I wanted his face badly, for an historical composition that I had in mind, a three-figure Borgia picture, the brother and sister and an anxious frightened man who was in their power, and who feared that the foot of a fourth person, showing beneath the edge of a curtain, was that of an assassin. A chance for some lovely colours and psychological portraiture —and Neystoke's face for that of the frightened man.

I was amazed at the vehemence with which Neystoke refused to let me paint his portrait, even before I had said a word about the historical picture. He looked positively alarmed at the suggestion. It was not a question of bashful and retiring modesty; of being too busy; of objecting to acting as a model for me, or anything of that sort. It was sheer fright; and though I laughed at myself as a fool for thinking such a thing, I knew it with complete certainty.

Then came the curious and very revealing episode of the police visitation, which confirmed my persistent belief as to fear being at the root of Neystoke's nervous condition; gave me new and startling grounds for much wider speculation; and made him even more interesting than before.

I would have given a great deal to have felt justified in asking Jacintha some questions, but I refrained. I decided that I would wait and hope; wait and hope that she might come and confide in me and ask for my help.

I should like, here and now, to make it quite clear that my interest in Neystoke is wholly friendly; that there is absolutely nothing of vulgar curiosity in it; and that, whatever else I may be, I am no busy-body, gossip or Paul Pry. It is merely that I am deeply interested in him. I like and admire him exceedingly; I more than like and admire Jacintha; and I would have done anything to help him in any way I could—for his own sake as well as hers.

The curious police episode happened in my own house. Jacintha had gone away for a week, to visit her mother, who was ill, and to look after her father until she recovered; and I had invited Neystoke and Dr. Bennett, our mutual friend, to a quiet bachelor dinner. We had all three been at the same University and the same kind of school; we all knew and enjoyed a glass of good wine, a good cigar and good conversation; I have an excellent cook and a first-class parlour-maid—and my little dinners are usually pretty successful.

This one was not. We had scarcely begun when the maid came in and murmured quietly that Sergeant Hollis and a constable were at the front door and wanted to know whether the Vicar was here, and, if so, whether the Sergeant could speak to him. I asked my guests to excuse me and went out to interview Sergeant Hollis, whom I knew to be an officious and fussy sort of ass, though thoroughly well-meaning; and to see whether it was really necessary for the Vicar to be disturbed during dinner. As I expected, it was not urgent or important in the least; just some nonsense about a cow that had strayed from the paddock into the Vicarage kitchen-garden through a gate not intended for the use of cows, and carelessly left open. Sergeant Hollis and the Constable, passing by, had been in time to avert the impending tragedy, as the cow began her evening with a fat lettuce.

It was like Sergeant Hollis to go up to the house with news of his good deed for the day, and then, learning that the Vicar was dining with me, to track him down.

No bushels for the Sergeant's light.

Having thanked him curtly and said I'd warn the Vicar about the gate, I returned to the dining-room and facetiously played the fool.

"*It has come!*" I groaned. "*The police are at the door!*"

"Run you down at last, have they?" enquired Bennett, as I glanced from him to Neystoke.

"No. *It's the Vicar they want!*" I replied, and realised, while I spoke, that he was sitting as though petrified, his soup-spoon poised half-way to his mouth, which was open. It was still broad day-light at seven-thirty that bright June evening, and I saw his face turn pale, grow pinched and old, without any shadow of doubt. No, it was upon him that the shadow fell, the shadow of Fear. Almost of Death itself, I thought.

Bennett laughed suddenly.

"All up, Vicar!" he laughed. "Will you go quietly?" And then, dropping his table-napkin, he looked away and bent down slowly to pick it up.

"Awfully sorry," I continued hastily. "Nothing wrong at the Vicarage. Sergeant Hollis is a pudding headed wind-bag. . . . Cow in the kitchen-garden and a lettuce in the cow. Hollis had to come and say he had effected her arrest. He would."

"You should have given him half-a-crown and a nice thistle," observed Bennett, coming up to the perpendicular and looking not at the Vicar but at his own plate.

Neystoke pulled himself together, sighed deeply, said he must thank Sergeant Hollis; and the episode, which had lasted half a minute, ended as I sat down in my chair.

But in that half-minute I had seen a man thoroughly frightened; seen him receive a great shock; fall into a pit of terror; and look as though about to faint. There was no possibility of doubt that the words *'The police have come'*, had caused him to start suddenly; and the sentence *'It's the Vicar they want'*, had been as a death-sentence, dealing him a blow from which he only recovered as I explained the reason for their visit.

What was one to make of a thing like that?

Nothing—for as I have said—Neystoke was a splendid chap; a scholar and a gentleman; a model Vicar, and a powerful influence for good.

Very funny though—and I wondered what Bennett would say about it when next we met. Bennett said exactly nothing about it, which was precisely what I expected him to say.

Perhaps he hadn't noticed anything?

Very unlikely, for Bennett is wonderfully clever at noticing, as any good doctor must be, of course. Anyway, we never referred to the incident, but though we said nothing, we thought the more. I certainly did, my very great interest in Richard Neystoke became yet greater, and I cultivated our friendship carefully. I saw a great deal of him— and of Jacintha—and we spent many afternoons in each other's gardens and dined together frequently.

Jacintha is the perfect hostess and Richard tried hard to be the perfect host. He only failed through his curious and incurable attacks of absent-mindedness, and his habit of creeping quietly out of the room every few minutes. Before his guests had been there long, he would fall into a reverie—a sort of brown study—and forget them completely. His mind and thoughts would be obviously elsewhere; he would look as though sunk in grief, sorrow and regret; his face would wear its drawn, anxious and worried expression; and in his eyes I would see the look that I knew to be one of fear and apprehension, the look that I had so plainly and unmistakably seen on the night that the police had interrupted our dinner. Then he would go away for a while, even if we were at table.

And always when I alone, or I and other guests, were present, Jacintha, bravely and admirably playing her part as hostess, watched him anxiously, watched and waited for this failure of attention; this abandoning of his guests; this lapse, and sinking into forgetfulness of the present; and would do her best to recall and rally him, rouse him, and take him out of himself, as they say.

It must not be supposed that there was anything of boredom in this distrait condition, anything of weariness in well-doing on the social plane; for Richard Neystoke was the soul of hospitality, loved entertaining, and was at once too fine a spirit for boredom and too genuine a gentleman willingly to fail in the nicest courtesy and consideration to his guest or to his host.

But there it was—the memory, fear, remorse, or some other painful pre-occupation that haunted his mind, shadowed his life, and increasingly affected his health and happiness.

Worse still, from my point of view, it affected Jacintha's peace and happiness of mind.

Then came the dramatic day when it was made patent even to the bluntest and dullest clod in his congregation that there was something radically wrong with the Vicar; and to Jacintha, to Bennett, and to me, that the time had come for something to be done about it, something really definite.

It was an ordinary Sunday morning, and as the Vicar ascended the pulpit steps, I was, instead of considering my latter end, contemplating that of the painted stone effigy of sixteenth-century Sir Giles Herriott, as he knelt on his tomb with his back toward me, a wife on either side of him, and the six daughters of the one on his left, and the six sons of the other on his right. How, I pondered for the hundredth time, could he have had six daughters, ranging from twenty years of age to two, by Lady Jane; and six sons, ranging from twenty years of age to two, by Lady Mary; especially as, in effigy, he was a black-bearded gentleman of about forty summers, Lady Jane a likely lass of about thirty, and Lady Mary another of about the same age? Had he kept two homes and gone hawking? . . .

And suddenly I switched my mind from these unworthy and undesirable Sunday morning reflections and looked up at the Vicar as he rose from his knees, moved the Bible or his sermon-notes to one side of the cushioned ledge before him, gazed round the church and, in a clear, strong voice, gave out the text on which he proposed to preach.

Possibly with the thought of World Crises in his mind, he had taken for his text, that Sunday, the admonition 'Thou shalt not kill.' He glanced, as usual, at Jacintha, looked straight at me, gazed round once more at the full church, cried almost like a prophet of old, *'Thou shalt not kill . . .'* and, after a brief dramatic pause, groaned audibly, staggered back, collapsed, fell, and rolled down the pulpit steps into the aisle.

Jacintha and I reached him first, with Dr. Bennett a good second. I thought at first that he was dead, heart-failure or something of that sort; but a few minutes after we had carried him into the vestry he revived and, as soon as he realised what had happened and could speak, was most contritely apologetic for the trouble and disturbance he had caused.

It was about the most dramatic thing I had ever seen; and, so strangely and uncontrollably does the mind work—my mind, at any rate—that I could not help connecting this with the occasion of the police visit. I knew it was idiotic and I instantly rejected it, but the thought persisted in my mind that there was some connection with the text and the attack in the pulpit.

'Thou shalt not kill.'

§2

Next morning while I was working in my studio —which was once a byre—the door opened and in walked Jacintha.

"Good morning, Denzil," she said, "I have come . . ."

"I thought it was the sun," I interrupted. "But it is you; and you have come to say you are going to sit for me as Mary, Queen of Scots."

"I have come for advice and help, because you are my friend and a very wise gui . . ."

"You have been going to the films, Jacintha. I don't like the expression 'wise guy'."

"I was going to say wise guide and philosopher."

"I have to be *wise* and philosophical when you are around, Jacintha."

"It is about Richard," she said.

I had to give up pretending to be cheerful and facetious. She was obviously upset.

"Come over to the house," I said, "and we will get comfortable in the study. What about a pot of my best China tea? I prescribe it."

"Oh, don't stop your work. Couldn't you carry on while I talk?"

"I don't want to 'carry on' with you, Jacintha. And there is no comfortable chair here for you. Worse still, there is none for me. Come along."

"Now then," said I, a few minutes later, as I gave her what my cook always describes as 'a nigh sot cupper tea' "you are worried about Richard . . . He ought to go away, you know."

"Yes, that is what Dr. Bennett says; and he is going to get in touch with a nerve-man whom he says is a wizard. A Dr. Fieldwicke."

"Oh, yes, I know the name. About the best nerve-specialist alienist and psychologist we have got."

So Bennett was going on those lines, was he? Quite right too; and if anything could be done for the health of Richard Neystoke's body, or the healing of his mind, Fieldwicke was the man to do it.

"Oh, that's very reassuring," I said.

Poor Jacintha fell silent and sat for a minute, gazing at me, her really very lovely face marred by a look of worry and anxiety. Now, could she have kept that expression and pose while I painted her as . . . I had the grace to be ashamed.

"I will go up to London with him if Bennett can't," I said.

"Would you, Denzil? I should be so grateful. As a matter of fact, Richard does not want to go at all; and absolutely refuses to go with Dr. Bennett or with me. I believe he'd let you take him, for I equally firmly refuse to let him go alone."

"Well, Bennett can write to Fieldwicke and I will take him. I am perfectly certain Fieldwicke will soon put him right. Bennett says the Vicar is absolutely sound and healthy, physically speaking. I mean there is nothing organically wrong. It's all purely functional, and simple to cure."

Jacintha was not listening to my unconvincing attempt at consolation.

"Denzil," she interrupted, "there is something I have not told Dr. Bennett. . . . I don't know whether I ought to do so, although it is for Richard's own good. He hates me talking about him to the doctor. It is very distasteful to me to go against his wishes. But—you know what I mean."

"Yes, my dear, I do; and I think you ought to tell Dr. Bennett absolutely anything and everything that might help him, so that he can tell Fieldwicke. We laymen really have no idea of how important the least thing may be if it is at all symptomatic."

"Well, it is this," she said. "During the last few months he has developed an extraordinary habit; and it is growing more frequent. You know the Vicarage well, of course."

"Lord, yes, Jacintha. Stayed there as a kid, long before you were born."

"Well," she continued, "you know that little bathroom that opens off his dressing-room?"

"Yes, tiny place. I remember his predecessor turning it into a bathroom. Made an item of interest to the village gossips for a year."

"Well, as you know then, there is absolutely nothing in that room but the bath and the heated towel-rail. Not even a wash-hand basin. . . . But he goes and locks himself in there a dozen times a day."

"Doesn't sound very alarming to me," I ventured cheerfully. "Not smoking on the sly? Or got a bottle of whisky there, has he? No, there isn't even a cupboard."

"It isn't a joke Denzil. It isn't a bit funny. As I said, it is getting more frequent. Twenty times in the day, he goes there and locks himself in . . . He will often do it just when he ought to be setting out for a meeting or a service or something . . . Just when we are sitting down to dinner . . . Sometimes even in the middle of a meal . . . He will get up in the night and go and turn the water on. Even if we have got people in the house, he will get up and go off in that direction. If I stop him, or call him back, he is obviously quite upset."

In one way this did not sound very serious, and yet, in another way, it did. At any rate, it looked as though it might be a symptom of something serious. I pondered for a moment and then gave what I felt to be the best advice.

"You must tell Bennett. I am perfectly certain it would convey something to Fieldwicke," I said. And then I suddenly remembered a little incident which occurred at that same bachelor dinner-party which the police had interrupted. Neystoke, while Jackson was clearing the table for nuts and wine, had murmured an apology and asked if he might run upstairs to the bathroom for a moment. As there was to be a finger-bowl by his plate in a minute, and he knew there was a wash-hand basin in the cloakroom by the front-door, I thought it curious that he should go upstairs. He did, however, and I heard the bathroom taps running.

He was away from table nearly ten minutes, and although I had thought it queer at the time, I had forgotten all about it.

§3

Next Sunday the Vicar was at Church as usual, and preached the sermon. As he went up into the pulpit I was anxious and uncomfortable, wondering whether he would give out the same text; and whether he would have another attack or seizure if he did so. I was afraid to look at him and equally afraid to look at Jacintha—who must have been even more anxious and uncomfortable than I was. I kept my eyes on the grim Herriott lying on his tomb with his crossed feet resting on a dog, to show that he was a Crusader; and tried to fix my thoughts on what exactly I would like to do to the execrable human louse who had scratched his abominable name on the Crusader's shield. . . .

It was not until the Vicar was well under way that I switched my mind from these charitable thoughts and looked up at him.

Although obviously nerve-ridden, ill, and suffering from strain, he preached his sermon manfully, but he did not preach on the Sixth Commandment.

He took for his text 'Suffer little children to come unto Me' . . .

They came all right, half a million of them, that week, from London; and we got our full share.

The detachment that arrived at Little Pudding came from some of the worst slums in London, and were pitiful to see—although before they had been with us a week I do not know whom I pitied the most—them or their hosts.

Until he simply had to give up and go, the Vicar was wonderful with them, and became their hero, for he could speak their language, and understood their needs, wants and tastes. He was to their parents as a brother.

I knew he had been a slum-parson or something of the sort, before he married Jacintha; but even so, I was surprised to hear him arguing, protesting or admonishing in slum idiom and accent barely comprehensible; or conducting a band of beer-buoyant costers and donahs from the 'Red Lion' to the station—one with them and of them in everything but dress.

He was perfectly splendid and my respect for him increased yet further.

§4

One afternoon, shortly before it became obvious that I must take Richard Neystoke up to Town and deliver him to the great nerve-specialist, I strolled down to the Church to give Jacintha a hand with something or other—Harvest Festival if I remember rightly—and came upon three boys seated on a tomb with their heads together and, by their appearance, plotting mischief.

"Hullo," said I, "who are you?"

They had not heard my approach across the grass and started up, obviously prepared to duck, dodge and run. Seeing that I was not a policeman and apparently harmless, they stood their ground, while the one who was evidently the leader replied:

"Me? I'm Itler."

"Oh, yes?" said I. "And the others?"

"That's Sloppy the Gob,"—indicating a similar boy—"and that's Chimp Chopps," was the prompt reply—if I had got the remarkable names aright.

The speaker interested me immediately. Had I been painting a picture of Fagin and his young gentlemen, this boy would have made an excellent Charlie Bates or Artful Dodger; for the face was old beyond its years, the mouth hard, firm and compressed; the cheek-bones high, and the general expression one of alert cunning. Yet the eyes were attractive; well-set, well-opened and genuinely blue—a much rarer phenomenon than is generally supposed. The lashes were long and the eyebrows arched and well-marked; though between them, unfortunately, was the deep frown-mark that generally indicates suffering or bad temper.

Yes, the face interested me, at sight. And, particularly about the eyes, it reminded me of another face; though whose I could not remember.

Sloppy the Gob, however, did not look interesting, and would have been more attractive had he not been suffering from impetigo, under-nourishment, the deplorable garments of a much larger person, and the lack of a handkerchief. His face, his whole body cried *'J'accuse!'* He was a living reproach to Society. Very moving. Probably he had been weaned on gin and fed on crusts. For England, his England, who can find six million a day for War (and very, very rightly), could not find sixpence a day to give him milk from a free dairy in the slum in which he had been bred. Much less could his England, who can buy a thousand million pounds worth of battle-ships, battle-planes, and war material, buy that same slum and abolish it.

But she really ought, perhaps, to do a little more for these slum children, who do so much for her when their time comes; if only that she may provide them with stronger and better bodies against that day of battle.

They will find the spirit, all right, if England, their England, will find them, at any rate, enough food to nourish their bodies while they are babies.

Chimp Chopps, too, would have been more attractive had he not squinted ferociously, with an amazing obliquity; had ears less like those of a bat; a bridge to his nose; a chin; and a mouth that remained closed.

I produced three pennies, bade them invest them well, and not squander them in riotous living; and forgot all about them as I entered the Church and saw Jacintha.

But I was reminded of Itler that very night, for he came into an extraordinarily interesting dream in which I saw not only him, but someone whom I had forgotten and had not seen for—oh, fifteen years or so.

§5

It was one of those weird dreams that one never forgets, and was the more memorable by reason of its being—what dreams so rarely are—quite funny.

I dreamed that I was lying asleep in my bed, as indeed I was; and that quite suddenly, I awoke and sat up in that bed, awakened by a feeling that I had visitors.

I found that indeed I had; and that they were an Angel and a house-fly.

Now, however rare, as visitors to one's bedroom, Angels may be, house-flies are not uncommon. But this particular house-fly was most uncommon, inasmuch as he was of the same size as the Angel! Nor could I be sure in my dream as to whether the Angel was as small as the fly, or the fly as big as the Angel.

Anyhow, there they were, and made to the same scale and proportion.

On either side of my bed was an oblong tomb of the size of the Herriott tomb in the Church. On the left-hand one stood the fly, and as he nicely filled the flat top of the tomb, he must, I now perceived,

be about the size of a well-nourished hippopota-
mus.

On the right-hand side was an exactly similar
tomb, on which stood the Angel, now more than
life-size, cold, marmorean and ultra-angelic.

As I gazed, in some concern, not to say per-
turbation, from the Angel to the house-fly, that
abnormal insect, lowering its head and raising its
body to an angle of some sixty degrees, stood up
on its hands, so to speak, after the manner of
leisurely, cogitant house-flies, and, with its hind-
legs, brushed, preened and smoothed its wings.
One has often seen a fly act thus. But rarely has a
similar sequel been witnessed; for, coming down
to the horizontal position again, the fly, glancing
across at the Angel, observed provocatively:

"And that's more than *you* could do!"

I felt that the statement was justified but
uncalled-for, and could not imagine the Angel
accepting the challenge.

As I watched the cold, beautiful figure to see
how the fly's remark would be received, if it were
not very properly ignored, I was thrilled to realise
that the marble Angel did, in the Galatea fashion
and tradition, come to life. Came to life and smiled
at me; and the face, warm, bright and instinct
with intelligence and emotion, was that of my
long-lost and long longed-for Joan of Arc. It was
the face that I had last seen fifteen years ago; that
of the girl who had stood in the prisoner's dock at
the Old Bailey, on trial for her life on the charge of
murder.

I knew her instantly, for I had sketched her
face in court a thousand times. From those
sketches and from memory I had painted her as
the central figure of my picture, *The Trial of Joan*

of Arc.[14]

It is amazing how happy one can be in a dream. In fact, I am not sure that one's most purely happy moments do not come in dreams, as well as those of most profound terror, horror and fear.

While I sat and gazed at the girl, I felt happy and joyous to the point of exaltation. Somehow, I felt that all was now well with her, and that she herself was, in some way and for some reason, quite happy also. I remember that I wondered whether this were because she actually was now what is called an Angel; and now knew, after a tragic life, the happiness of the peace that passeth all understanding. . . .

"*H'm!*" said the fly; and, glancing at it, I saw that its triangular face was that of the boy who had called himself Itler.

Then I knew of whom the lad reminded me; or, rather, of whose eyes his had reminded me. They were exactly like the anxious eyes of my Joan of Arc; and I speak as a portrait-painting physiognomist.

Had Itler been the woman's son they could not have been more like hers.

Looking back again, to study those blue, long-lashed eyes, with their finely-marked, distinctive eyebrows, reminding one of 'the mournful-browed Œnone', I saw that the living, breathing, smiling girl was fading; not changing back into the cold permanence of marble, but dissolving, wraith-like, into nothingness.

"*Wait!*" I cried. "*Stop!* . . . I must paint you from life. Paint you this time as *La Pucelle of Domremy*, as Joan, before she became Joan of Arc, in the days when first she heard the Voices . . ."

---

[14] Now in the Tate Gallery.

I woke to find myself crying:

"Wait! Wait! I must paint you again! This time from life."

"*Life*," said I to myself, as I lay back to ponder the intriguing dream that had taken me back to those hectic days of some fifteen years ago.

CHAPTER 2

Had it not come on to rain as I walked down that somewhat squalid London street, it is quite possible that I should not have painted my really extremely popular picture, *The Trial of Joan of Arc.* I forbear to shudder at the thought of what a loss the world would have sustained.

I had gone up to town to see the charming old scoundrel who keeps a junk-shop in that street, and who drops me a post-card whenever he thinks he has got something that I ought to see.

He has a pitying tolerant affection for me, as might a mother have for her idiot child, because I am that phenomenon, unique in his experience, an honest man. He does not know the phrase 'quixotically altruistic', but that is how he regards me when I tell him that 'an 'ole tin 'at', priced to me at ''arf a thick-un', is a Spanish peaked-morion, for which I could probably get twenty-five pounds, and for which I should be entirely willing to give him ten. More than once he has offered me a 'dirty 'ole picshur, cheap at a nicker' for which I have been—in common honesty—compelled to offer him twenty pounds, and tell him it is well worth fifty; to me, at any rate.

It was through discussing with him the probable value and reasonable price of a really fine print, that I was caught without an umbrella or an over-coat in the rain, and brought briefly into the life and orbit of my Joan of Arc.

Curious that a post-card from that dirty, ignorant and stupid old junk-dealer should have brought me to London that day, and that my examination of his stuff should have kept me until the right moment.

But of course it was fated and decreed.

For, as the rain fell suddenly and heavily, I glanced up and saw a black board on which were painted the words *Coroner's Court.*

Well, a Coroner's Court would provide as good shelter as a King's; and my sadly limited knowledge of civic lore would be enlarged if I attended for a brief space. Hastily, I turned into a short passage, hurried down it, entered a door-way and found myself in a big room that seemed part dissenting-chapel and part school-room.

On a dais in front of the high leaded windows, the school-master or preacher or Coroner sat behind a great desk. On his right, in a couple of long pews, sat the choir or the Jury. On his left was what might have been the lectern, and was the witness-box.

Before and below him was the nave in which sat, not precisely the worshippers, but a reasonably reverent congregation.

Before and below the Coroner also sat some sort of court functionary, clerk, beadle, or tip-staff, whose face I immediately coveted for my portrait-gallery—the rogues'-gallery department. I would have paid quite a lot to have secured the man as a model, had I been painting *The Trial of Lady Lisle.* He was the perfect Judge Jeffries and a most evil-looking brute.

That was well worth coming in for, thought I, as I studied the inflamed, insolent and brutal face of this Coroner's Officer, this last of the Bow Street Runners, or whatever he was.

The Coroner did not interest me at all; just an ordinary, middle-aged, donnish person; fussy, querulous, self-important and very efficient.

I should have liked to paint the Jury then and there, exactly as they were, dull, dreary, shabby creatures; unintelligent, uninterested and bored. They all seemed to have bilious eyes, leaden complexions, amorphous noses, straggling moustaches and what are, I believe, called quiffs. I should have called the picture *The Jury. Trial by my Peers!*

I suppose they were very small shop-keepers of the neighbourhood; but there was not one of them who appeared to have, in the words of the late Prime Minister of England, the intelligence to run a whelk-barrow.

Gazing upon those twelve doubtless good men and true, I felt that Trial by Jury might be an extremely dangerous and undesirable process.

But I could not paint them—gild their dull horizons nor cast perfume upon their . . . What *was* the perfume? Carbolic acid, barely triumphant over crude humanity. Horrible. I would arise, go forth and see if it were still raining, and whether there was a chance of getting a taxi.

I was about to rise from my hard and narrow seat when Judge Jeffries arose and shouted,

"*Emrith!*"

I had not been paying much attention to the doubtless interesting proceedings, but I suddenly became as alertly attentive as ever I had been in my life; for, on that strange cry of '*Emrith*', there stepped into the witness-box, from a bench on which she must have been sitting, unnoticed by me, *the owner of the face for which I had been looking for months, for years.* . . . My Joan of Arc!

"Is your name Emma Heath?" asked the Coroner.

"Yes, Sir."

The woman of the name of Emma Heath took a greasy Bible from the loathsome Jeffries and gabbled the oath that would turn any mis-statement into criminal perjury.

She was young. She was lovely. Not as loveliness is known to the admirer of the chocolate-box beauty and the tooth-flashing, goggle-eyed, boneless-faced female whose pink-and-whiteness is supposed to make magazine advertisements attractive and alluring.

She was lovely because her features were perfect.

Her face was carved in ivory; and its expression was at once gentle and strong; exalted and tragic. The truly beautiful eyes were sad; the mouth both sweet and firm; the brow noble; the cheek-bones well-marked but not too high.

She *was* Joan of Arc—as I saw her in my rare moments of inspiration, vision and understanding.

She was Joan of Arc at the time of her trial. Joan, after suffering hardship; disappointment; the cruelty of brutal men; failure; treachery; and dreadful, tragic loss.

Oh, to have her, with the right dress and background, posed as I would have her, for the Trial at Rouen, before those brutal judges who condemned her to the stake.

On the other hand, although she was deplorably dressed in shawl, apron and ragged skirt, with a felt cloche hat like an inverted pudding-basin covering most of her beautiful hair, she was in a way on trial. She was standing there before a Court; and the face of the villainous beadle would do admirably as that of one of the judges.

Yes, I must get her as my model, at all costs. Doubtless she would sit to me if I paid her more than she could otherwise earn; and once she understood that there was nothing in the least undesirable or improper about my proposal. I could hire or borrow a studio in London if it should prove impossible to get her to come down to my own, which I should have preferred. Perhaps

Mrs. Bennett could help me.

Anyway, there was my Joan of Arc, and, having found her, I was not going to lose her. With her as my model and inspiration, I would paint a great and glorious picture. Paint a noble picture; live to see it famous; and know that my name would live to be that of an Old Master!

Having studied her face with the utmost intentness, I began to sketch it, and then to rough in the kind of dress that would be worthy of the face, and appropriate to the scene and setting.

How was Joan dressed at the Trial? Presumably still as a man. Doublet and hose. Half-armour? Probably not. A helmet? No, bare-headed. But I should not sacrifice colour, beauty, drama, anything at all, on the narrow altar of absolute historical accuracy. Nothing absolutely inaccurate, of course; but my Joan of Arc should . . .

Hullo! What was that! . . . *She had killed a man?* . . .

Utterly absurd and impossible; and, if she had, it served him damned-well right. It was the most absolute nonsense! But why was she admitting it; confessing it with complete frankness?

Even the Jury forgot the coppers it might be losing by neglect of its shops; woke up; came to life; and positively took an interest in what was going on.

I most sincerely wished that I too had been paying attention to what was going on here, instead of letting my mind dwell on that other trial, five centuries ago, while I sketched the woman who, to me, was Joan of Arc herself. So far as I had been aware of what had been happening, I had imagined that this girl was giving evidence as a witness in the case of some deceased coster-monger.

What was it that the Coroner had just said?

"But you struck him on the back of the head. How do you explain that, if it was done in self-defence?"

"Well, Sir, he must have turned his back for a moment," replied the girl, reasonably and helpfully.

"He certainly must. You attacked him while his back was turned to you, and yet you say that you struck him in self-defence?"

"That's right, Sir."

"Now, according to the medical evidence, the bones of the deceased's skull were fractured by a heavy blow, dealt with some blunt instrument. Unfortunately—both for the deceased and whomsoever struck that blow—the bones of that skull were unusually thin. But that is not all. It was not the only blow. In fact, there were several blows—many—dealt on the man's back and shoulders."

The Coroner took his eyes from the white face of the girl and consulted the papers on his desk.

"In the Police Surgeon's own words, '*Repeated heavy blows were rained upon deceased, as shown by bruises upon his neck, shoulders and back.*' All struck from behind, you notice," he said, glancing at the Jury. "One very heavy, fatal blow on the back of the head, and a number of sharp blows on the upper part of the body."

And then, turning to the girl again, he eyed her long and thoughtfully.

"Do you say you struck all those blows—at a person whose back was obviously turned to you—in self-defence?"

"That's right, Sir," replied the girl; and she spoke with conviction, as though ready—if not actually anxious—to promote the ends of Justice at any cost.

It was absurd, of course. Surely anybody, even

the elderly case-hardened Coroner, could see that that face was not the face of a murderess; could see that that girl had not the physique of a man-killer.

How I wished I had come in at the beginning of the inquest and had paid more attention to what was going on.

Apparently there had been no witnesses, and the only evidence had been that of the girl herself. Surely she should be properly represented, especially as she seemed to be cheerfully and foolishly making the worst of her case.

And then I was comforted to remember and realise that this was not a trial but an inquiry, the object of which was to discover how the deceased had come by his death. The girl was not in the prisoner's dock, of course; she was merely contributing what information she could towards the answering of that question and the elucidation of any mystery there might be.

True; but the police were handling the case and, in the event of the jury returning a verdict of murder against 'some person or persons unknown', it would be the immediate duty of the police to discover the murderer; and it was painfully clear that they would not have far to look.

It seemed that the corpse on which the inquest was being held, was that of a man that had been found in the room rented and inhabited by Emma Heath; and that she confessed, indeed claimed, to have killed the man—but in self-defence. That much I had gathered almost subconsciously while I studied and sketched her face. . . .

There was a deadly silence in the Coroner's Court. Literally deadly. And as the Coroner, still eyeing, indeed studying, the girl, said again,

"You say you killed the deceased yourself; alone; without assistance. You say you killed him in self-defence. . . . And the man was killed from behind,"

"That's right, Sir," replied the girl once again.

And as I watched with the utmost intentness, studying every shadow of expression, however slight, on her calm and almost smiling countenance, I wondered greatly; and I was thankful for the curious chance or kindly fate that had directed my hesitating footsteps into that dingy court. For, surely, scarcely anywhere else in the world could I have found a face so apt and perfect for my requirements; so calm; so strong; so uplifted; so inspired. That was the word—*inspired*. Just as Joan must herself have been. It was the face of Joan successful, fulfilled, ecstatic and triumphant. Consenting to death. It was the face of Joan of Arc at her trial saying to her God, '*I thank Thee;*' saying to herself, '*I have done that which I had to do;*' saying to her judges, '*Little men, now do your worst.*'

Almost without closing my eyes I could see this girl clad as Joan may have been. Manacled, perhaps. Facing not a coroner and twelve petty tradesmen, but a be-furred, ermined and cowled bench of lay and ecclesiastical judges; and gazing calmly, not upon a dingy sordid Coroner's court-room, but upon a stone-flagged, groined and pillared vault or hall of Rouen Castle.

She must sit for me.

I would immortalise her, and, incidentally myself.

She was Joan of Arc reincarnated.

But even if I got her to a studio, even to my own at home, could I recapture that look, that uplifted expression as of the inspired soul, willingly, if not gladly, contemplating martyrdom? Yes, perhaps I could if, while she posed, I talked to her about this horrible inquest, re-calling to her mind the feelings and emotions that she was now experiencing.

Anyway, there was the face and I must paint it; and I must get her out of this.

The intelligent jury empanelled by Mr. Harrington, the Coroner, returned a verdict of *Wilful Murder* against Emma Heath; and she was arrested and committed for trial at the Old Bailey.

§2

Well, so was I. Committed for trial as to whether I had the sufficient pity, ability, self-determination and self-interest to get her off. If money and brains could do it—my money and a better man's brains—it should be done.

The terrible situation in which that lonely, friendless girl now stood, appalled me and appealed too, to anything of decency and chivalry that may be somewhere concealed in my nature. For I felt in my bones, I knew in my inmost consciousness, that that girl never killed a man, whether in self-defence or not.

As a man and as an artist I must do my best for her.

I had been guided to the feet of a living Joan of Arc, and I must not lose her for want of any effort that I could make.

I owed it to my art; to myself; to her; to the public; to posterity. . . .

My normal and artistic consciousness both awake and aflame, I hurried straight from the Coroner's Court to Lincoln's Inn to see my admired and faithful friend—who is also my solicitor—a tough, tenacious Yorkshireman, a very fine lawyer and, curiously enough, Hillman, Jackson, Jackson, Walters and Scrope.

"Look here, Thomas," said I, "an embattled, or rather, empanelled band of brainless brutes has just condemned Joan of Arc to death."

Thomas eyed me calmly, with his considering, judgmatic gaze.

"Evidently you read the *Morning Record*," he observed. "The news is stale by about five hundred years."

"Listen, Thomas," said I. "A reincarnation of Joan of Arc, answering to the name of Emma Heath, was to-day arrested and committed for trial at the Old Bailey on the charge of Wilful Murder. She is absolutely innocent."

"How do you know?"

"I don't know, but she is; and if one British Jury can bring in a verdict of Wilful Murder in this case, another might; and in that event, she'd be hanged."

"Not necessarily," replied Thomas calmly. "Might get off with a life-sentence. Sure to, if there were a recommendation to mercy. Be out in twenty years or so."

"And a fat lot of good she'd be to me as Joan of Arc then, wouldn't she? Besides, that is not the point. She is as innocent of this murder as you are; and has led a far more innocent life—on general principles."

"Then she certainly ought to be saved. What do you want me to do?"

"Brief the best man in England. The two best; the three best; and get her off."

Thomas regarded me pityingly; a look with which I am all too familiar when I take my bright ideas to him.

"How would you like Sir Edward Marshall, Sir Henry Curtis and Oliver Roland for a start? Cost you about what you've got."

"The best will have to be good enough. Get the best. Get to work; and get this girl acquitted."

§3

After fourteen or fifteen years, I do not remember the details of the trial of Emma Heath very clearly, though parts of it, little incidents, sentences from Counsels' speeches, sharp phrases, stand out with the utmost clearness.

The girl's face, of course.

And in the gloom of that horrible Criminal Court of the Old Bailey, her white face seemed to shine as with the illumination of an inner light. More than ever was she, to me, Joan of Arc, arraigned for crime, and not only proud of what she had done, *but grateful that she had been allowed to do it*, nay, chosen as the instrument to do it.

I do not mean that she said as much in words, but it was in her look, her bearing.

This time, while I sketched, I paid more attention to what was going on, and got a fairly clear idea of the case.

According to Sir Hector Withers, for the prosecution, no-one, save the girl in the dock, knew what happened in her room that night. There were no witnesses of the actual murder, and, apart from her full confession, it was only upon circumstantial evidence that the case could be decided.

I hated the fellow from the moment he stood up and began to speak. A great black, white-headed eagle. I hated that predatory eagle or, rather, vulture; that cruel man whose delightful business it was to put a hempen rope about the white neck of the girl in the dock; a girl to me, and surely, to any clear-sighted and understanding person, utterly incapable—*utterly* incapable, mentally, morally and physically—of committing a murder.

Unfolding the case, he described how the girl had accosted a police-constable just after dawn, told him that she had killed a man in her room, and that she wished to give herself up. Going with her to her room in the slum tenement in which she dwelt, the policeman had found the body of a man who had evidently been killed. There was no possibility of suicide, death having been caused by a heavy blow, struck with a blunt instrument upon the back of the head.

Had the girl not made full and free confession—as the Jury had heard—to the committing of this murder, the police would have had some slight difficulty in accounting for the motive for this crime, and in satisfactorily clearing up one or two minor details.

For example, the weapon or instrument used. The prisoner declined to give information on this subject; but, as the Jury would hear, she had been seen coming out of her room—wearing hat and shawl—at about eight o'clock in the evening. It was probable, indeed fairly certain, that, hidden beneath her shawl, she carried the aforesaid blunt instrument, and somehow disposed of it.

A woman and her daughter—neighbours of the prisoner—standing at the door of their room, which was on the same landing as that occupied by the prisoner, were able to swear to the time being towards eight o'clock; for another neighbour, living on the floor above, had just come down the common staircase and, in passing, had asked the time.

"Now," said learned Counsel for the prosecution, eager and anxious for the triumph of the Crown, and the hanging of the girl whose face was a certificate of innocence, "now, Members of the Jury, mark this. The accused spoke to the policeman who was passing this tenement, at five o'clock in the morning and, as the Police Surgeon will tell you, the murdered man had then been dead for about twelve hours. That, I submit, explains why no weapon of offence—no 'blunt instrument' wherewith a man could be struck upon the head with such violence that he was killed—was found in the woman's room."

I think those were his exact words, but for some reason I know that the following were—for they are indelibly engraved on the tablets of my memory. Speaking slowly and with the utmost impressiveness, the vulture said,

"Here is a clear case of homicide; and, in this country, although every accused person is presumed to be innocent until proved to be guilty, it must be remembered that every homicide is presumed to be murder until the contrary is clearly established—and indisputably proved. In view of her confession and in the said absence of any circumstances whatsoever which might point to it being something else, you must—for it is your duty—presume this case to be one of murder, and find this woman guilty of murder."

It was a long speech and in its cold, logical and remorseless marshalling of facts, terribly convincing and prejudicial to the mind of any hearer.

Nevertheless, I hoped, and at moments believed, that the Jury must realise that, save for the girl's own confession, the Prosecution had had a very difficult task.

There were few witnesses, and their testimony uninteresting. The policeman to whom the girl had made her first confession, and who had found the body in her room. The woman and her daughter who had avidly testified that they had seen 'Emrith' come out of the fatal room at ten o'clock, holding her shawl up to her face, her hands and arms and anything that she might have been carrying, concealed beneath it.

Of the dead man nothing appeared to be known. If he had had any friends they had not come forward, and the police had been unable to establish his identity or to discover anything about him.

By the time the case for the Crown was set forth, I was anxious. I was more than anxious—I was cold with fear.

And there in the dock, in no-wise anxious, and completely free from fear, stood the girl—in the very shadow of the gallows.

She puzzled me more than anyone or anything has ever done in all my life—until I met Richard Neystoke.

What on earth made her persist in her confession and plea of 'Guilty.' Obviously it was the Prosecution's trump-card; and without it, they would, I felt sure, have lost. Had I been a member of that Jury—even though unbiased by the girl's look of innocence—I should have said 'Not Proven.' By no means proven. No motive; no weapon; nothing but the fact of a man's dead body having been found in her room. A pretty damning fact, of course, but . . . And then that awful, idiotic, fantastic confession.

§4

But there was nothing cold or incisive about Sir Edward Marshall. His method was the very opposite of that of Prosecuting Counsel. Obviously, or, rather, apparently, he was seething with rage; or, rather, burning with a fierce and noble flame of indignation and resentment against the injustice of the false accusation.

He had already exhibited these symptoms while Counsel for the Crown was addressing the Court.

Twice when Sir Hector Withers was speaking he had sprung up and protested. Once when, as I thought, most unwarrantably, insolently and improperly, Withers had referred to the Prisoner as "a woman of a certain class." Up sprang Marshall with almost a shout, certainly a cry, of indignation.

"*M'Lud!* I protest! With all submission, I protest most strongly. My learned friend has not the right or justification for using that opprobrious term, and . . ."

The Judge, apparently waking from profound slumber, interrupted him, and to me it was as though a graven image came to life and spoke.

"I heard no opprobrious term," he whispered in a perfectly audible voice—in an amazingly audible voice. "We all belong to our respective classes."

"With submission, m'Lud," murmured Marshall with a glance at the Jury and an eloquent shrug of his shoulders.

And again, soon after, he sprang to his feet with loud, hurt indignation in his voice when Withers, once more, as I thought, most unjustly and improperly said:

"What was in the mind of this woman when she took the deceased home to her room—that room from which he never emerged alive—we do not know."

"*M'Lud!*" came the cry, wrung from the outraged soul of that great advocate and actor. "*M'Lud!* I protest again! This is beyond all right and reason! . . ."

The old parrot, on its perch above, came again to life, opened a wise eye and murmured to itself, to God, to the circumambient air and, possibly, to Sir Edward Marshall:

"Allow me to be judge of that."

"To insinuate, m'Lud; to imply; openly to say,

that this young innocent girl who earned her living in the light of day and the public market-place by selling flowers, *took* the deceased—who may or may not have been murdered, whether in that room or elsewhere—*took* him to her room is, with all submission to your Lordship, *abominable!* I . . ."

"Sit down," whispered the parrot, quite unruffled and quite equal to coping with the histrionics of Sir Edward Marshall.

And then, turning his eyes, but not his bewigged head, in the direction of Prosecuting Counsel, said,

"There is no evidence that the accused took, led or invited the deceased to her room."

And after a deferential bow and a 'With submission, m'Lud,' the great river of Prosecuting Counsel's eloquence had flowed on.

In comparison with it, that of Sir Edward Marshall was a stream of boiling lava.

Never in the whole of his long experience; never in his life; had he known, or heard of, so flimsy a case as that made out by the Crown. Personally, he would have been ashamed to the depths of his soul to have had any hand in the bringing of such an indictment—so poor and flimsy a mass of 'evidence'—to use a term of which it was unworthy. There *was* no evidence! Why! The Prosecution had not even attempted to show a motive. It had been wholly unable to produce the weapon with which the alleged assault had been made. They had not had the slightest success—however unceasing and unscrupulous their efforts—in blackening the character of the accused.

Let the Jury look at her; let them try to imagine that fragile girl making a ferocious attack upon a burly ruffian and killing him with her hands!

Nor had the Prosecution been able to produce

one solitary witness whose evidence was of the slightest value to them or which could do the faintest injury to the fair fame, character and conduct of his innocent client. Let the Jury but *look* at her!

The Jury looked; as indeed did everyone else in that great Criminal Court of Justice; and, had they seen what I saw, they had beheld a girl incapable of crime of any sort; a girl without any feeling of shame, horror or fear, at finding herself in the terrible position in which she stood. Nay, more; a girl who was fortified and sustained by some inner feeling akin to satisfaction, and gratitude to Fate.

And let it not be thought for one moment that there was anything most faintly suggestive of impudence and brazenness in her bearing; nor that her manner even remotely suggested that she belonged to that pitiful class that loves notoriety, and would rather be brought into the lime-light by the committing of a dreadful crime, than remain obscure. No-one could possibly have looked less conceited or impudent; for she was not even self-conscious.

I do not actually say that she looked happy, but she looked—what shall I say—*fulfilled;* content; unashamed, because she had nothing of which to be ashamed. She was calm; unafraid; and resigned.

Even now, I have failed to describe her look and bearing satisfactorily, for she did not look resigned so much as readily acquiescent, willing to pay the great price for a great gain; for a great achievement and success. So must Joan of Arc have looked, facing her judges with the knowledge that nothing that they could do could possibly undo what she had done. She had saved France! She had saved her King! And now she was prepared to die for France and for her King!

What had this girl saved, and for what or whom was she now happily prepared to die?

I would have given a year of my life—years of my life—to have been allowed to set up my easel and canvas there and then, and paint the face of this girl, who, to me, *was*, as I say, Joan of Arc reincarnate.

As brave; as serene; as pure; as innocent; the essential martyr of a burning faith; and noble. . . .

Then, turning to the Jury, Marshall fairly overwhelmed them with a flood of burning eloquence, tearing to tatters the speech of Prosecuting Counsel. And so he came to the one damning and apparently irrefutable fact of the girl's own plea of '*Guilty*', and her statement and confession made to the police.

Fixing his glowing, penetrating, almost hypnotic eyes upon each member of the Jury in turn, he congratulated himself that, in this case, he was blessed in having to address twelve people of obviously high intelligence, sensibility and sense. People of their knowledge, experience, wide reading and understanding, would instantly *see* how probable it was—how almost inevitable—that a young girl, such as they were about to rescue from the terrible situation in which a cruel and adverse fate had placed her, might well go temporarily insane on entering her room and finding there a blood-bespattered corpse.

"Picture that dreadful room!" he cried. "Picture that dreadful scene which met the poor child's eyes as she struck a match and lit a candle or lamp. . . . Her heart would almost cease to beat! She would faint; probably fall headlong to the ground and lie senseless, still as that corpse which lay within a few feet of her. When she recovered consciousness, perhaps in darkness, she would not dare to move. It was a situation terrible enough to turn her brain; to drive her permanently insane. Probably, as a result of where she was, of how close she lay to that dreadful Thing, she fainted again. Is it any wonder that, when able to move, she staggered to her feet and fled from that terrible room; cried incoherently to the first person whom she met—a policeman, as it happened—that she had committed a murder? . . . Why, it is a phenomenon not only well-known, but extremely familiar, to neurologists, nerve-specialists and psychologists, this impulse to confess something—some act, some crime—that the patient has not committed and is quite incapable of committing. I withdraw the word confess because in such a case it is not a confession, it is a mis-statement made under a misapprehension. And the Police should withdraw—just as you yourselves will mentally withdraw in your own minds— that incoherent statement made by a poor distraught girl at a time when her mind was unbalanced, unhinged by horror and by shock.

"Need I tell you, Members of the Jury, that a murder is scarcely ever committed without one or two, or sometimes a dozen, 'confessions' being made by people who are totally innocent of the crime? The Police know it well, and there is no police official, no member of the Criminal Investigation Department, who would dare to deny it.

" 'Yes,' you may say though, being people of acute intelligence, 'but is the accused in such mental condition *now*? Was she distraught, her mind unhinged with horror when she pleaded *Guilty*, to this preposterous charge?'

"The question is well asked and there are two answers.

"The first is, '*Yes, perhaps so. Indeed, very likely.*' For there is such a thing as delayed shock.

There is such a state as protracted numbness caused by shock. Though the body may recover and the mind be otherwise normal, hallucination may persist. Although that poor girl standing there, awaiting release by your sympathetic understanding and verdict of '*Not Guilty*', may appear to behave in a perfectly normal manner, one department of her mind may still be abnormal, damaged, deranged. And the result of that injury which affects her memory is that she is still under the impression that she killed the man whom she found in her room. For remember—and I most solemnly charge you to remember—that the Prosecution has not brought forward one shred of evidence to prove, to indicate, to suggest, that she ever saw that man alive.

"And the second answer to that question; why did she plead guilty? It is an alternative which may well be considered by anyone whose mind is not too crassly stupid, too grossly ignorant, too besottedly prejudiced to accept the theory—in truth, the simple truth—that she cannot remember what *did* happen before she fainted. . . . Think of the horrid sight that confronted her there in her humble room. . . . And if there be such a stupid person in this Court, I offer him this alternative suggestion, and it does her infinite credit: having once said she was guilty—she sticks to it!

"She says, 'My mind is blank as regards memory of what happened after I opened my door. I know that some time later, minutes or hours, I realised that I was lying on the floor and that near me was a dead body; blood; the murdered man; and my one impulse was to get away—go to get help—and that to the first person I met, I said I had murdered a man.'

"When more coherent, she elaborated the statement; told the Police—and, mind you, Members of the Jury, I don't *say* that the Police prompted her —told the Police that she must have killed this man in self-defence!"

Sir Edward Marshall turned from the Jury and, with an appealing gesture of outflung arm, bade them look once again at this alleged murderess who had violently and brutally attacked a burly ruffian and battered him to death.

"I ask you, Gentlemen! I ask you!" he said, and his wise, pitying, kindly smile and a slow, grave shake of his noble head, should, I thought, have carried conviction to a heart of stone and a brain of wood. I wondered that the Jury did not rise as one man and request that the case might be stopped.

Now it was as good as won, surely, thought I, until I realised that, argue as he might, ridicule the Prosecution as he could, appeal to the common-sense of the Jury as he did, he had refrained from putting his innocent client in the witness-box. And that always looks bad.

The Judge and any thoughtful member of the Jury must conclude that when Defending Counsel feels that he cannot safely do that, he must be afraid that the accused will either say too much or give the wrong answers.

Why he did not do it I knew only too well, for Thomas had told me, before the trial began, that the girl was being extremely difficult. Sir Edward Marshall and his junior had had a long interview with her in a special room in the prison in which she was detained while awaiting trial. And Marshall had admitted to Thomas that he was puzzled, bothered and rather anxious. For the girl insisted that she was guilty, and he had found it impossible to persuade her to plead otherwise.

The story that she told Marshall, and that he repeated to Thomas, was that the man—a stranger to her—walked into her room while she was sitting there, locked the door, accused her of queering his pitch—presumably the pitch on which she sold flowers—and attacked her.

Suddenly, someone tried the door, or knocked on it, the man turned his back to her and took a step towards the door; instantly she picked up a weapon and struck him on the back of the head with all her strength. He fell to the floor, and she struck him again and again. She then collapsed and fainted. When she came to, she dared not move but stayed there until day-light, until full dawn perhaps. When the sun rose and there was sufficient light for her to see that the man was still there and obviously dead, she went out and told the policeman what she had done.

Of course he could not put her in the witness box, if she were going to insist that she killed the man.

If only the fatal injuries had been in front. If only she had struck him as he first approached her, or as he turned back from the door towards which he had taken a step.

As it was, there was the body of a murdered man, killed from behind, and a woman who confessed to having killed him.

As for her story of the man having attacked her and she having killed him in self-defence, what evidence was there of its truth? None. For as the Surgeon forthwith ascertained at the request of the Police, she bore not the slightest mark of any injury whatsoever. There was no bruise upon her face, arms or shoulders; no wound or scratch; she could point to no damage to her eyes or her nose or her mouth. Her clothing was not torn. Her hair was not disturbed.

On the other hand, the alleged assailant was literally battered to death; and, once again, attacked from behind.

No, as told by Emma Heath, it was a thin story, though when re-told by Sir Edward Marshall, a convincing one; a pitiful story of touching and powerful appeal.

His peroration was magnificent and as he sat down, obviously moved by his own eloquence, if not by real feelings of indignation against false accusation and pity for injured innocence, I felt that even the ranks of Tuscany could scarce forbear to cheer.

In his summing up, the somnolent-looking Judge showed that he had followed every word with the utmost attention, and that from beginning to end he had missed no single point. And the most biased person could not deny that he was absolutely fair. But on the whole, I felt that his judgment went against her. At times I could have stood up and cheered; at others my heart sank within me; and, by the time he had concluded, I felt apprehensive.

What seemed to weigh with him heavily was the fact that she had been seen to go out from her room in hat and shawl, obviously concealing something beneath the latter.

"Why," asked the Judge, "should she have gone out into the street at that time and made no attempt to get help for the injured man? Why have made no confession then to the first policeman whom she met? Or, if she failed to find one, why not have gone to the nearest police-station?

"One of the strangest features about this extremely puzzling case is the accused's conduct at this point. To my mind there can be no doubt that she went to dispose of the weapon alluded to by the medical witness as 'a blunt instrument'.

"Why, you must ask yourselves, did she wait

for many hours before summoning help, in spite of the fact that she was able to go out into the street and, in some way, dispose of part of the evidence of the deed. That, you have to consider in conjunction with the fact that the man was attacked from behind. . . .

"As you have noted—in this curious case, so singularly devoid of evidence—no motive has been produced; no finger-prints have been found, save those of the accused; no suggestion of robbery has been brought forward in support or contradiction of accused's story; and on her statement and confession alone, which she reiterates and re-affirms, the whole case rests. . . . She says she killed this man; she says she did it in self-defence; she went out and disposed of the weapon; she called in none of her neighbours and apparently spoke to no-one at all; she waited all night and then called a policeman.

"If you think that, in spite of her plea of self-defence, the established facts point to murder, it is your duty to find the accused *Guilty*. If, on the other hand, there is any doubt in your mind, the prisoner is entitled to the benefit of that doubt. . . ."

I do not pretend for one moment that that is in any way a verbatim account of what the Judge said, for I was paying far more attention to the girl than to him. I was studying her face much too intently to follow carefully what he was saying; but that was the gist of it, and, as his quiet, patient, monotonous voice flowed on, I felt that the tide was also flowing—against the girl whom I had done my best to save.

And it seemed to me—in fact, I was certain of it—that as the Judge's summing-up seemed to go against her, the look of—what shall I say—

acquiescence, satisfied resignation, happy martyrdom that ennobled, almost glorified, her pale, fine
face . . . increased. Definitely, to my mind, that
look of satisfaction increased. She looked faintly
disappointed when the Judge dwelt upon the fact
that, but for her plea of *Guilty*, and the insistence
of the fact that she and she alone had committed
the murder, there was little evidence against her.

Did she want to be found guilty? Be condemned to some such appalling sentence as penal
servitude for life? Did she want to be hanged?

There was something behind all this. Couldn't
Sir Edward Marshall see that there was? But if he
could and did, what point would there be in
proclaiming the fact; drawing the attention of
those wooden-faced, dull-eyed Jurymen to the
amazing phenomenon.

The Judge concluded his summing-up and
bade the Jury do their duty. The Court emptied
and what must surely be to any accused person
the worst time of the whole trial, began.

What must her feelings have been as she sat in
that cell below the Court? I could only judge by my
own. Suppose they did find her *Guilty?* Suppose
she were condemned to death? It was a possibility,
if not a probability, too awful for contemplation,
and I hoped that the thought of my contemplated
picture played by now a very small part in my
great anxiety and deep concern.

But on one thing I was determined. I would
immortalise her; and, if I never saw her again, her
face should be that of my Joan of Arc. I could
paint it from memory and from my sketches almost as well as I could if she actually sat for me;
and I should be inspired. The central figure would
be *real*, and in her face the dullest and stupidest
should find what even they could read. Because
for me this had been the Trial of Joan of Arc; the

trial of an innocent; of one who, for some reason, was willing if not anxious, to be found *Guilty;* to be condemned; to be a martyr.

Why? Absolutely unfathomable.

It was entirely beyond my understanding then and it is beyond it now. Why did that girl wish to be found *Guilty*, or, at any rate, firmly refuse to plead '*Not Guilty*', and to withdraw her confession? It was not as though some husband, lover, brother, or any other was to be shielded and saved.

Innocent women have offered their lives for guilty men for love and in the noblest spirit of self-sacrifice and altruism. But there was no suggestion here of a fellow-criminal. No-one to be shielded. Neither the Prosecution nor the Defence had suggested anything of the sort. Nor had fingerprints on any object indicated the presence of any third party.

It was insoluble.

And yet I knew, as well as I have ever known anything in my life, that there was a mystery here. That, in spite of a Coroner's Inquest and an Old Bailey Trial, we had seen and heard nothing of the real truth.

Why was this girl consenting to death but conquering agony?

I don't know how long I sat in that agony of suspense, doubt and puzzlement.

There was a stir in the grim and grimy Court Room as the Jury filed back into their box; the Judge returned to his high place; and the girl—white-faced, calm, confident and almost smiling—came up the steps into the glass-sided dock, accompanied by two wardresses.

I could scarcely breathe. . . .

The voices of the Clerk of the Court and the Foreman of the Jury broke the tense silence of the Court.

The Jury found the Prisoner guilty of manslaughter and the Judge condemned her to three years' penal servitude.

I think the sentence shocked everyone in the Court except the girl herself. I cannot say that she actually smiled, but there was a suggestion of the dawn of a smile upon her face, and a look, not of satisfaction or pleasure, but of unregretting acquiescence. That, perhaps, is the best description I can give of that beautiful, proud and almost saintly face.

I never saw her again, but should you care to see her as I did in those final minutes, go and look at my picture, *The Trial of Joan of Arc.*

PART III

ITLER IN ARCADY

CHAPTER 1

On a flat-topped tomb in the ancient church-yard of Pudding St. Phillip, sat the biggish boy or smallish youth whose eyes and heart-shaped face had reminded Mr. Denzil Marindin of the girl who had, all unknown to herself, been the model for his famous picture, *The Trial of Joan of Arc.*

Perhaps only an artist, one who had made so prolonged and careful a study of the face in question, would have seen any point of resemblance between the rather hard, rather cunning countenance of the boy, with its high cheek-bones and grim set mouth, and the face of the woman, rapt, ecstatic and withdrawn; the resemblance between the gutter-snipe and the saint.

Gazing round the green and mossy church-yard and out across its low wall to the lovely vale upon which the hand of autumn lay as yet but lightly, the slum-bred boy wondered how much longer he could bear it. In his own vernacular, 'Ow the 'ell 'e could stick the gawd-forsaken 'ole another dy wivout goin' bugs? (The last word had no entomological significance, but to anyone who knew anything, who was a regular attendant of the sixpenny cinema, it simply meant batty, nuts, crackers or loco). Wot the 'ell did the people *do?* Where did they *go*—specially at nighttime? . . . 'Im for 'ome.

The sound of a low whistle roused him from despondent dreams of the better life and Billiter's Rents. Good. Here was the Gob and Chimp.

With striking symptoms of extreme caution, two members of the Blackand Gang crept round the corner of the Church and, dodging from tomb-stone to tomb-stone, approached their local and temporary leader.

"Wot 'o! Itler," cried the larger of the two. " 'Ow yer goin' on?"

"I ain't. I'm goin' orf," was the reply. And, with complete change of voice, added in a high falsetto: "Aime gowing 'ome to lunch."

"*Lunch*, blimey!" he continued in more natural manner. "That's wot they calls it!"

" 'Sright," agreed the Gob, "and they calls supper 'dinner'. And if you calls the dorg a bloody old flea-farm, they ses '*O! 'Ush!*"

"Ar," agreed Chimp. "Yer spends 'arf yer time 'ushing and the other 'arf wondering wot yer better 'adn't sy next. 'Streuth!"

The boys fell silent, contemplating the misery of their lot and the horrors of War thus far revealed unto them.

"Jer get to that plice?" inquired Itler, breaking the brooding silence.

"Yus," replied the Gob. "There ain't no-one there. We goes from door to door asking 'Chink Gotti livin' 'ere?' and they wags their silly 'eads and looks like we're talking Yiddish or somethink."

"S'pose we can't find none of the rest of the gang, lets us three go 'ome alone," suggested the Gob.

"When we can't stick it any longer," replied Itler. And rising to his feet, added cryptically: "It's de oily woim dat gits coit by de boid. . . . Me belly tinks me troat's cut. . . . *Lunch!*" He spat contemptuously and then cried: "Come on!"

§2

Itler's real name was a mystery, even to himself. His mother called him Dick or Dickie, but this could hardly be termed his Christian name, inasmuch as he had never been christened. When asked as to his surname, his mother said it was Garden, but as she had never married a single one of all her friends, Itler could have had no legal claim to it.

Should any inquisitive person—such as a police-officer, a London County Council school-attendance officer, an inspector of the Society for the Prevention of Cruelty to Children, a slum-parson or some lady or gentleman warrior of the Salvation Army—press the boy closely on the subject, he would admit, to one, that his name was Gusty Ponker; to another, that it was Thomas Tiddler; to a third that it was Oratio Nelson, John Ripper, Sweeny Todd, or Alexander Sloper. (Why the 'Ell couldn't they look after their own perishin' names—and scribble 'em on an ensanguined wall?)

The name of Itler, by which he was honourably known to all his friends and acquaintances, had been given to him in a moment of exasperation, and perhaps rueful admiration, by Chink Gotti, captain and leader of the Blackand Gang of Billiter's Rents. Chink Gotti's own name was a curious one and a synthetic, as his father was a Chinese gentleman of no fixed abode that was known to the police, and of no visible means of support—or only very briefly visible, as slipped in secrecy, darkness and a tiny white packet, from one grimy hand to another. But on the proceeds of this un-ostentatious work, he had set up house-keeping in a Limehouse cellar with Bianca Gotti, the organ-grinder's daughter, and begotten a son who was given his mother's name and his father's nick-name. . . .

It was something a little self-assertive, trucu-lent, forceful, rebellious and quarrelsome about the newly-joined member, something different,

brainy, resourceful and resolute, that had caused
Chink, one day, to enquire of this bloke Garden as
to who he thought he was—Itler or the Lor'mare o'
Lunnon? Thereafter, when the fellow cast ridicule
and contempt upon his leader's schemes and proposals, Chink Gotti would address him scathingly
as Young Itler; and, for years before the out-break
of Hitler's War, it was as 'Itler' that Garden was
known. That Chink should have been well aware
of the attributes of Herr Hitler thus early and
accurately, was due to the fact that the elderly
fence, for whom Chink worked, was also a Hyde
Park orator ('Nothink like lettin' the perlice see
plenty *of* yer and know all *about* yer') and a pot-
house politician whose objection to Dictators of
every kind was strong. He was by conviction a
Communist and by nature an Anti-everything.

So to Chink Gotti it seemed good that the ikey,
uppish and cocky-chopped boy should be given an
opprobrious nick-name that summed up both the
deficiencies and self-sufficiencies of his undesirable character.

The Blackand Gang of which Itler was a prominent and, by the rank-and-file, highly approved
member was not, up to the glorious year of grace
1939, a very desperate or dangerous one.

Certainly not in the neighbourhood of Billiter's
Rents where, under the wise guidance of Chink
Gotti, it confined its activities to what he called
small-time rackets and knocking down ginger—the
former producing such insignificant spoils as are
the fruits (literally) of barrow-snatching—apples,
oranges, bananas, and so forth; the latter providing merely light amusement and diversion.

On the other hand, when time and opportunity
were ripe and Chink Gotti announced that business was even more important than pleasure, the

activities of the Blackand Gang were frequently
such as would lead them from the paths of wickedness to Borstal or into an Approved School, had
they been caught red-handed by the police.

However, inasmuch as only one of them, he
known as the Gob, had ever been apprehended
(and, being at that time of the tender age of six,
had stoutly refused to squeal), depredation, deeds
of profitable mischief and plain, undeniable thefts
and house-breaking, if not burglaries, had never
been traced to the Blackand Gang of Billiter's
Rents.

Thus it was that Chink Gotti and his followers
were merely and tolerantly known to their own
local police as Young Devils and not—what under
less sagacious leadership, they might have been—
as Habitual Juvenile Criminals.

But cunning and artful as Chink Gotti, constantly advised by his friend and patron, the
fence, Uncle Joe Schinkler, might be in his leadership of the Blackand Gang, there could be no
doubt that many of his fine schemes were greatly
improved by Itler's suggestions, when they were
not so derided by that upstart as to be altogether
abandoned. Well might Chink feel that there
would have to be a show-down before long; in fact,
a purge of the Gang. For there was undeniably
another party arising and growing fast.

However, Chink being older, bigger and far
stronger physically, if not mentally, morally and
spiritually, than Itler, there was at present no
question as to leadership, no cause for fear, and
no hurry.

So the Gang flourished in raucous, bickering
harmony, obeyed its leader implicitly, studied
gangster films assiduously, perfected its technique, and improved its knowledge of the language
believed to be spoken in the Bowery, East Side

slums, Chicago dives and the Palatial Apartments of the Gangster Barons.

To such rare females of the species as, with Chink Gotti's approval, were upon occasion allowed 'to run with the Gang', they alluded as their gun-molls.

And week by week and month by month, Itler's influence, power and position in the gang had steadily increased until Chink began to feel by no means sure that a beating-up and expulsion from the Gang would prove the perfect solution that he had imagined. He could beat him up all right and he could kick him out all right, but suppose the whole bloomin' gang followed him?

Not so bloomin' easy.

What Itler needed was to be taken for a ride and bumped off. Only there was nothing to take him in, nor to bump him with. He'd have to be content with a damn good 'iding and like it. . . .

Itler! Sneerin', cocky, stuck-up, ikey, bloody-well-pleased-with-'imself young burgher.

Chink Gotti 'ud *show* 'im. . . . War to the knife. . . . *Itler!*

Then came a greater war, the dispersal of the Blackand Gang and the arrival in Little Pudding of Itler and his colleagues the Gob and the Chimp.

§3

In the lives of the Reverend Richard Neystoke and Jacintha, his wife, Itler was a disturbing element. By the boy, both were determined to do their very best. They were earnestly anxious that he should be happy and should get nothing but good, and enormous good, from his sojourn in the country. They would consider that they had failed miserably and disgracefully if he did not go back at the end of the war, physically, mentally, and morally the better for his stay in the infinitely more wholesome surroundings and conditions that, happily, they were able to provide for him.

That they had set themselves no easy task was obvious quite early, for not only did the boy evince stout and determined objection and opposition to all the processes of improvement, but he had also a strange and marked psychological effect upon the Vicar, a phenomenon that puzzled Mrs. Neystoke exceedingly.

There could be no doubt about it, that when the boy was present, the Vicar was extremely nervous, uncomfortable and ill—the Vicar, beloved by every one of the villagers, old or young, and who was as much at home with the village children, hobbledehoys, girls, old women and old men, as he was with his friends, Dr. Bennett, Denzil Marindin, the Herriotts or herself! No, having studied and watched her husband for years, with care and insight, she could not deny or doubt that his health had been markedly worse since the boy came into the house. It was most queer, and she felt she must talk it over with Denzil, that amazingly understanding creature.

What made it stranger was that she was quite sure that Richard liked the boy as much as did she herself. He was amazing, shocking and pitiful; he was—at times—delightful, or rather, his attitude to life, his views and opinions were a source of delight; and, so far as she herself was concerned, she would have been extremely sorry had he run away.

Nor would this regret have been solely due to a sense of failure. What she could not understand was the boy's reaction to life at the Vicarage; for he made no pretence of preferring it, or any aspect of it, to the life from which the activities of his noble name-sake had caused his expulsion. He made no secret of the fact that he looked forward to returning to that life, and cared not how soon that return might be.

This shows that of Itler it was not true, as yet at any rate, that he needs must love the highest when he saw it, for he could *not* enjoy the admirable comforts and amenities, not to say luxuries, of the Vicarage. And at first sight this might well seem strange, for Itler had come thither from one of the smallest rooms, in one of the ugliest slums, in one of the poorest spots in darkest London.

It might have been expected that he would have been delighted with such a bed as he had never seen before, nor ever imagined in a vision of fair beds, with its soft pillows, white sheets and flowered eider-down.

But no.

In it, Itler felt trapped, smothered, cribbed, cabined and confined, especially between the time when kind Mrs. Neystoke tucked him up and that when he had contrived to struggle free again. To one who had always slept, pillowless and uncovered, with nothing between him and the aged and rotten planks of the floor, save a reasonable layer of sacking and amorphous female garments, this bed was very strange, very uncomfortable, unwholesome and unnatural.

However, he could always 'op out of it and doss down in a corner, arising, as was his wont, before day-break and making his silent way from the house. (The Vicar never knew exactly how he did this, for the doors were always locked and bolted on the inside, as usual, when the maids came downstairs.)

One would have supposed that Itler would have appreciated and enjoyed the attractions of the maids' bathroom, placed freely at his disposal nightly.

But when it was made clear to him that not only was the diurnal hot bath permitted but enjoined, Itler was perturbed and, in a curious way, offended. In mild and reasonable manner he had asked the Reverend Richard Neystoke whether he thought that he was cooty, crummy, or, perhaps, dirty?

Smiling pleasantly, the Vicar had replied:

"Not unduly. Not more than was to be expected."

"Right," replied Itler and enquired patiently whether the Vicar regarded him as a bloody goldfish?

"Come! Come!" expostulated the Vicar. "That sort of language won't do! There must be no talk of—er—bloody goldfish in this house."

"Well, a bloody 'addock, then?"

And the Vicar and Itler were patently at cross purposes.

After an attempt at forcible scouring during which Itler exhibited remarkable strength of body, fluency and scope of invective, and a wily slipperiness not wholly accounted for by soap, an armistice was called, and a treaty was arranged.

Itler, on the one hand, undertaking and contracting to 'barth 'is 'ole pink perishin' purple body' from top to toe (though that was not *exactly* how Itler phrased it) every Wednesday and Saturday night; provided that, otherwise, and at all other times, the Vicar and Missus would *Let him Be*; passin' no remarks about 'is neck, 'is ears, 'is 'ands nor 'is 'ead.

Mrs. Neystoke, tactlessly enquiring—when grudgingly she agreed to the terms of the treaty—as to the frequency and method of Itler's previous bathing arrangements, learned that there was no frequency and less method.

In fact, he was not in the habit of bathing.

"Had he never had a bath in the whole of his life?" enquired Mrs. Neystoke.

"Well," Itler had considered, "depends on wot yer calls a barf. I went baving once with the Black-and Gang in the canal down 'Orseferry Bridge way. Only once though. Young Spottydog 'Arris went and got drownded under a barge, pore little sod. I goes in an' tries to lug 'im out, an' got me 'ead stuck in black mud! . . . No more bavin' fer me."

"Have you ever seen a bathroom before?" enquired Mrs. Neystoke.

Cor! Yus. 'Corse 'e 'ad. There was one in Billi-ter's Rents. Ol' Grinanbearit, the Eyetalian organ-grinder, kept three monkeys in it, under some chicken-wire. Let 'em out on 'ire. . . . Seen a bath in a empty 'ouse too, where the Blackand Gang camped for a week. Posh it was. They kep' their fire in it. Laid a stick across the top and dangled a tin can of water over it, cookin' spadgers and such.

"And it didn't occur to you to have a bath in it?" enquired Jacintha Neystoke, with the smile that Itler loved.

Naow! . . . It was a copper wot occurred to 'em. He pinched Smoky Doolan and Smoky was birched. . . .

Anyway, it was agreed that Itler would well and truly bathe, with hot water and soap, twice a week, provided that otherwise he was not beggared about by nobody.

And the Reverend Richard Neystoke and Jacintha, his wife, undertook on their side, not to beggar Itler about in the matter of ablution.

One would have supposed again, that Itler would have had no fault to find with the food, table-appointments and *modus operandi* of dining at the Vicarage.

Yet Itler did object, and very strongly; most especially on the last of these counts.

For he had, for some fourteen of his sixteen years, been in the habit of sitting down on a door-step to eat; of eating without use of any implement, save his nimble fingers; and of dispensing with any form of plate, save perchance upon occasion, the greasy and disintegrating piece of newspaper supplied by the fish-and-chips merchant.

However, these were Lucullan feasts costing two-pence a time, and only procurable when the Blackand Gang was in funds. . . .

Patiently, Jacintha Neystoke endeavoured to teach Itler the right and proper use of knife, fork and spoon. But he never really took to these hindrances to eating.

Nevertheless, he obliged; he humoured Jacintha, within reason, and only once had 'words' with her on the subject.

This was when, trying him beyond his strength, she proposed to make Itler eat quivering jelly with a small fork.

Itler rebelled. It wasn't sense. Not when he'd got a damn great spoon alongside the fork. . . . What was the spoon *for*, anyway?

"Oh, but everyone eats jelly with a fork," said Jacintha.

"Well, 'ere's one as don't," countered Itler, and took up the spoon.

"An' 'e don't," added Itler, "becos 'e ain't a bl——"

"*Eh?*" cried the Vicar sharply.

"Ain't a blue-be'inded boundin' baboon. . . .

"Like I see at the Zoo," he added, lest he be not understood.

No, definitely, Itler did not like sitting on a chair, facing an array of china and cutlery, the use of which made him nervous and clumsy, to eat food such as never before in his life had he encountered.

He did not like egg and bacon. And ow the 'ell was 'e to get the drippy yellow stuff into 'is mouth if 'e mustn't use the blade of 'is knife, or mop it up with a lump of bread?

Innocently, one day he asked the Vicar if he'd ever tried swillin' vinegar wiv a fish-'ook. The Vicar had not.

"*Naow!*" commented Itler darkly, as he regarded the silly fork and the unmanageable contents of his plate.

Abandoning the dining-uplift struggle, with a curiously disappointing sense of defeat, the Vicar and his wife relegated Itler to the kitchen, that he might take his meals in peace and comfort with the maids.

And easy thence was Itler's descent to ground-level, for ingeniously he set himself to render his table companionship undesirable, until Cook roundly told him that if he couldn't behave, he could take it on the mat.

So Itler took it on the mat, in his hands, the mat being by the back-door. On the step he ate in the desired peace and comfort; and thus everyone was happy, including the Vicar and his wife, who never knew of the arrangement. For, as Cook remarked on the subject, what the eye don't see the heart don't grieve for, since ignorance is bliss and least said is soonest mended.

§4

And, now, as has already been stated, Itler was going back to the Vicarage for lunch.

Lunch! Why couldn't they talk English and call dinner, dinner. That's what it was, wasn't it? And if anybody was lucky enough to get a bite of scoff at night-time before he went to bed, that was supper, wasn't it? . . .

As he passed under the viaduct which crosses the road a quarter of a mile beyond the High Street of Little Pudding, Itler's eye fell upon a huge advertisement, the corner of which flapped in the breeze. On this corner was printed, in large capitals, the address of the Covent Garden firm responsible for this wayside ornament. And inasmuch as Covent Garden is in the West Central district of London, the final hieroglyphics of the legend were W.C. 2.

Noting this fact and that the thick, heavy paper on which the letters were printed was detached from the board, Itler stopped, frowned, considered for a moment. Then over his face spread the very charming smile that displayed his excellent teeth, lit up his clear blue eyes, and gave his hard young countenance so desirably different an expression.

Very carefully, and not at all in the manner of one committing an act of idle wanton mischief, Itler tore off the part of the corner of the poster that bore the bold black letters, W.C. 2.

This piece of paper, some nine inches square, he forbore to fold. Laying it carefully upon his flat stomach, he slipped the lower edge beneath the top of his trousers, placed his braces across the left and right-hand sides respectively, and buttoned over it the painfully immaculate and respectable jacket with which Mrs. Neystoke had so kindly provided him.

A little later, by devious ways, he arrived at the Vicarage kitchen door, and, carefully scouting, made his way thence to his bedroom.

Removing the, for some reason carefully treasured, W.C. 2 from its hiding-place, he deposited it in the wash-stand drawer.

After lunching in comfort, peace and privacy, on the kitchen doorstep, he again crept upstairs and, knowing that Cook would for some little while longer be busy about the ingestion and digestion of 'lunch', he raided her room and borrowed her ink-bottle and pen; also her scissors.

With those and W.C. 2. he spent an engrossed and happy hour in adding an undeniably neat, convincing 'd' just above and to the right of, the figure 2; in trimming the thick paper to a straight-edged oblong; and in embellishing its sides with a nice black border.

Having finished this work to his satisfaction, Itler reconnoitred, and, finding the coast clear, he returned Cook's ink-bottle, pen and scissors to the place whence he had borrowed them. He then interested himself in the contents of every box, drawer and cupboard in the room, until, hearing Cook wheezily approaching, he went to earth beneath her bed, swiftly and silently as does the fox pursued.

The next day was, as he knew, to be the occasion of the Little Pudding Autumn Flower Show, an event of such local importance, an annual fixture so long and seriously anticipated, a social occasion of such desirability that, War or no War, it had not been postponed. Were not the Little Pudding chrysanthemums famous throughout the County?

The flower show was held in a big marquee pitched in the paddock which adjoined the Vicar's garden and was separated from it by a holly hedge. In this hedge was a gate giving direct and easy access to the kitchen-garden and Vicarage back premises. . . .

At the height of the proceedings, a boy might have been seen to lurk warily near the gate, on the Vicarage side of it. When anyone approached, he took his station behind it as one prepared to open it and extend a ready welcome. On the other side of the gate, facing the crowded field, hung a neat, printed notice.

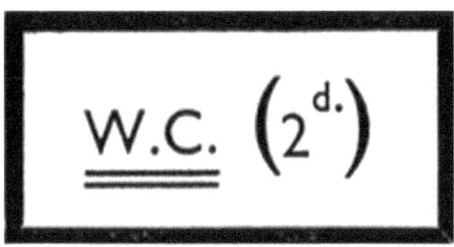

Many thought it very considerate of the Vicar, a nice gentleman who thought of *everything.* Some there were who felt that the Vicar might have waived the small charge.

A few captious individuals took the view that the presence of the boy was superfluous. . . . Personally conducted, so to speak! . . . A collecting box beneath the notice would surely have been sufficient?

Some were definitely surprised; some amused, some a little shocked; some, in sore need, very grateful.

In fact, the little matter formed a topic of discussion in Little Pudding long after Itler had expended the forty-four coppers with which his foresight had provided him.

Here again, perhaps, Cook's aphorism was applicable, and the Vicar's ignorance bliss—especially as he was already very worried and really seriously ill.

PART IV

RICHARD NEYSTOKE REMEMBERS

CHAPTER 1

Dr. Vincent Fieldwicke looked up from the letter he was reading, and covertly studied the face, hands, posture and dress of his new patient, as the latter stared idly out of the window. A very good face of its kind, average perhaps, but fairly high average; sufficient forehead; eyes well opened and well apart; nose thin and bridged; chin adequate, certainly not retreating; and mouth sensitive, with lips neither of mean and bitter thinness nor of sensual thickness.

Yes, quite a good face, the upper half very intelligent if not highly intellectual; the lower half non-vicious if not strong. He'd have a look at the ears and palate in a minute. No very interesting problem here. Probably an easy matter to get at his trouble and put him right. No organic disease, according to this letter from Dr. Bennett, but very ill, with the typical somatic evidences of mental conflict. . . .

Keyed up. Highly strung. Very taut indeed; and at the same time languid and weary. Hands tightly clenched; foot jerking continually . . .

Dr. Fieldwicke returned to the letter.

. . . And so I think he's definitely a case for you, for while there is absolutely nothing organic, he is undeniably ill and getting worse. Usual symptoms —insomnia, acute gastric disturbance, extreme lassitude and inability to concentrate, neuralgic pains, fainting fits and so forth. Apparently no medical history, and, so far as one can tell, a blameless record.

He is, by the way, a very fine man, very popular

*in the parish, and I've never heard a breath of
scandal of any sort.*

*Well, I think that is all I can tell you and it's
probably all you'll want to know from me. Of
course, I shall be only too delighted to answer any
questions, if you care to write or ring me up. Or I'd
come and see you, as I am very fond of Richard
Neystoke, for he's a really good chap.*

*By the way, I've had the greatest difficulty in
persuading him to come to you, and only contrived
it by assuring him that you were his one hope and
last chance—which I believe to be the case. Anyway, I can't do anything for him, although I've done
my best. . . .*

Again, Dr. Fieldwicke glanced from the letter to
the Reverend Richard Neystoke, who sighed deeply, took out his handkerchief and mopped his forehead, although the morning was a cold one, and
the room not overheated.

A clergyman. Kittle cattle! The most difficult
class of patient, averse from subjecting themselves
to close inquisition. Very natural too, for they were
more accustomed to questioning than to being
questioned, to hearing confession rather than to
making it.

Richard Neystoke turned to glance at a picture
on the wall. (Yes, that lure generally fetched the
patient who sat waiting in that chair, and caused
him to turn his face at the desired angle.) Dr.
Fieldwicke studied the head, now exactly in
profile. Quite a good back to it; quite a good space
of brain-pan between the ear and the top of the
head; ear very well-set, convoluted and lobed; not
much bone and corner to the jaw; but the *tout
ensemble* adequate and satisfactory. No help so
far.

The Reverend Richard Neystoke turned from

the picture and met the gaze of the famous neurologist.

Dr. Fieldwicke smiled.

"Well, Mr. Neystoke," said he, "I've read Dr. Bennett's letter and I'm going to read it again, before asking you one or two questions. You're not in a hurry, are you?"

"No, Sir," replied Richard Neystoke, "thank you. I'm not such a fool."

And while the great man re-read the letter, Neystoke in turn studied the doctor's face.

Powerful and intellectual. It was partly that combination that gave it its most unusual and arresting quality. A face as strong and forceful as that, might easily be brutal and arrogant, hard and cruel. A face as extremely intelligent and intellectual as that, might easily be weak and gentle, feeble and vague. But here the domed head and lofty forehead were accompanied by the jutting chin, the jaw of strength, and the straight, firm-lipped mouth of relentless resolution.

A powerful face, granite-hewn, and across it the rare smile played like a gleam of sunlight. And the eyes, thought Richard Neystoke, seemed to look through one. They seemed to read one like a book. Difficult eyes to meet unless one were speaking the truth . . . the truth . . . the truth . . . the truth. . . . Richard Neystoke stirred uneasily in his chair, and the doctor, without looking up from the letter, made note of the sudden movement.

He'd follow that train of thought in a moment. For not only could the great alienist, unlike most people, follow his own trains of thought to their logical conclusion, but he could follow those of other people. He could also make those other people follow them, and very frequently, to a conclusion which surprised, shocked or shamed them. Sometimes it was to a conclusion from which the unwilling follower shied away, or vehemently denied in terror.

Dr. Fieldwicke laid the letter on his desk and suddenly raised those penetrating, compelling, almost hypnotic eyes to those of his patient, whom he found to be regarding him with a look of awed respect, not to say fear.

That was as it should be. First something of awe, not unmixed with fear; then hope and trust; and, finally, personal liking combined with complete faith.

This type of man would probably begin by hating him, though he might not admit it, even to himself.

"How do you get on with your wife, Mr. Neystoke?" he asked, fixing his patient with a probing stare, and the somewhat school-masterish look which said:

"Tell the truth and tell it quickly."

Richard Neystoke realised that he must do so; but that although it was all very well to give prompt and honest answer to this curious question, what would he do later, when this nerve-specialist wizard began to dig and to delve, as he would, in dangerous ground. How could he bear it when that thrusting, questing spade drew close to the deeply buried . . . coffin . . . which contained the skeleton?

He couldn't. He would be utterly unable to bear it at all. He had told Bennett that he didn't want to come to this man.

Besides, it was absurd. How could he help him, much less cure him, by relentless prying into his past and discovering what he had done?

Surely he himself knew best about that?

It was all a lot of mumbo-jumbo. He should never have listened to Jacintha nor allowed Denzil Marindin to bring him here.

And yet Bennett had said that this man was his one hope and this was his last chance; and Bennett was a sound doctor. There was no doubt about that.

The distinguished and highly successful neurologist took note of the hesitation. What was the real reason for the man's inhibition? Lack of concentration, or a subconscious defence against the question? Was this the trouble? Probably one of the greatest of all causes of the illnesses based on maladjustment.

"My wife?" replied Neystoke, a faint note of resentment in his tone. "How do I get on with her? Why, splendidly. Splendidly. Best of friends."

"Ah. Any children?"

"*A* daughter."

"Age?"

"Fourteen."

"And you are devoted to her, I expect?"

"Devoted. Absolutely."

"So that you live a perfectly normal married life with your wife; and have no domestic trouble whatever?"

"Yes. None."

Well that might or might not be true, although doubtless this patient thought it was.

Mrs. Neystoke would have to come and see him later on, and he'd form his own opinion after a talk with her. Quite possibly the whole family life was a sham and a lie, bravely bolstered up by an honourable gentleman and gentlewoman.

"Splendid," he commented. "Not every man is as fortunate in his home life."

There was a brief silence while Neystoke watched the psychologist with anxious eyes.

"Tell me," said the doctor suddenly, as he again fixed a probing stare upon his patient's face, "when did you first realise that you hated your father?"

"I . . . My father? Hated him?"

"Yes."

"But Doctor . . . My father was one of the most upright and noble-minded men who ever lived. He was Dean of . . ."

"Yes. Yes. But that hardly answers my question."

"Hate him?" murmured Neystoke.

"I want you to think it over," said the doctor, "and with complete mental honesty and detachment. No sentimentality and no self-deception."

Richard Neystoke's eyes fell before the steady gaze of the stronger and wiser man.

"And your mother? I feel sure you loved her very deeply," suggested Dr. Fieldwicke.

"Devotedly. She was a saint. I worshipped her."

"I am sure you did," smiled the doctor.

"And you took all your troubles to her. And put them in her lap. And left them there, so to speak, didn't you?"

"Exactly. That was just the relationship between my mother and myself. Always."

"And when you were in any scrape, or when danger threatened, it was to her you went."

"Invariably."

"Yes. But not to your father. It never entered your head to take your troubles to him, did it?"

"Well, he was a very busy man and . . ."

"Too busy to hear a small confession, or an appeal for help, from his son?"

"You were afraid of him, of course," he added.

Neystoke made no reply. What was the point of this stupid inquisition into his relations with his father. He resented it very strongly.

"He had time to thrash you occasionally, I expect?" said Fieldwicke.

"He did his duty in that respect," answered

Neystoke, his voice and manner almost sulky.

"I wonder if you yourself regarded it as an important part of his duty at the time?"

"I didn't like getting a beating, naturally. But I have the sense now to realise that my father was following Solomon's injunction against sparing the rod and spoiling the child."

"*Have* you?" replied Fieldwicke, in a manner that Neystoke found unpleasant. "Well, I want you to consider that point very carefully. Give a good deal of thought to the question as to whether your father didn't spoil both."

"I certainly wasn't a spoilt child," observed Neystoke, in some mental confusion.

"No. But you may have been a spoiled one," was the reply. "And what's more, you may be suffering from it now."

"You don't believe in corporal punishment then, Doctor?"

"I won't commit myself to a sweeping generalisation, but I most certainly do not approve of corporal punishment for a sensitive child," was the reply.

"No. Nor for a dog," he added, in a voice that was almost a growl.

"I have the greatest respect for my father's memory," observed Neystoke defensively.

"I'm sure you have. You keep the fifth commandment as strictly as all the rest. But it is not your father's memory that we are concerned with now. It's your present condition, and I want you to consider with absolute honesty, the subject of your attitude to your father when you were a child."

"Certainly, Doctor. But I can assure you now, immediately, that . . ."

"Well, don't," interrupted Fieldwicke. "Assure me a month hence, or when I ask you again . . .

"Right. Now then," continued the doctor, "please tell me frankly and fully about any anxiety, worry, care, trouble, of which you are *consciously* aware. And tell me that as freely and fully as you would tell a physician or surgeon about any bodily trouble that drove you to consult him. You must keep nothing back, if I am to help you."

"But I have no such anxieties, Doctor. I am perfectly happy except for this wretched physical illness and . . ."

Dr. Fieldwicke cut short his patient's protestation. "Any financial trouble? Are you in debt at all?" he asked.

The Reverend Richard Neystoke laughed derisively at such an idea.

"Nothing of the sort," he said shortly.

"Not worried by any friction with a churchwarden or prominent member of your congregation?"

"No, Doctor. We're quite a happy family."

"Good. Now tell me this. What do you *fear?*"

"*Fear?* I? . . . Nothing, Doctor."

"You're to be congratulated. Most people have fears and phobias of some kind. If it's only that of illness, accident or old age. . . . No fears at all, eh?

"Now I'm going to ask you a question that you'll like even less than some of the others. Are you being—in any shape, or form or method, by any sort or kind of person, directly or indirectly—blackmailed?"

"Most certainly not."

"Now I'm going to ask you one last question that your *conscious* mind can answer me, and then we'll talk about the immediate future. How do you stand with regard to your Faith. Your Faith in God, your Church, and the Doctrine that you teach."

"Solid as a rock. My Faith is perfect and it is whole. Paradoxically I may say that I do not believe. I do not *believe* because I *know*. Why, without my Faith I should be nothing. I should be lost. I should commit . . ."

"Splendid again! Once more you're to be congratulated," interrupted Dr. Fieldwicke, in his most matter-of-fact voice. "Well, then, it sums up to this. That your home-life is perfect. You loved your father and worshipped your mother. You have no anxieties, worries or troubles of which you are conscious. You stand in fear of no-one and nothing. And the Faith in which you live—and by which you have your living—is perfect.

"Now, Mr. Neystoke. You either cannot or will not tell me the cause of the mental sickness which in turn is the cause of your bodily sickness. But if you care to put yourself in my hands, give me the requisite time, and especially if you will be absolutely frank, honest and truthful with me, *I'll* tell *you* what it is. And when I have discovered it, and we've dug it up out of your subconscious mind, where it's festering like an abscess, your mind will be healed and your body too, in consequence."

Richard Neystoke looked up from the carpet upon the pattern of which he had been brooding moodily.

"You can cure me, Doctor? Make me well again, so that I can enjoy life—enjoy my work, my hobbies, my leisure; be myself and carry on my . . ."

"Yes," replied the specialist. "I believe so. Certainly I can do you a great deal of good.

"Always provided," he added, "that there is complete accord between us and you are helpful. *The truth* . . ."

Richard Neystoke glanced down again.

". . . the whole truth and nothing but the truth, in answer to the questions that I shall ask you—however painful, repugnant or apparently offensive they may be.

"And now, will you come into my nursing-home or travel up and down to see me on alternate days, for however long may be necessary?"

"Which do you advise?" asked Neystoke meekly. "I'd do anything . . . anything . . . to get well again, and shake off this terrible . . ."

"The nursing-home, most strongly. For there you'll get help of various kinds, constantly, from my partner, colleagues and nurses—all specialists in their respective departments."

"I'll come," replied Neystoke impulsively. "When? How soon can I?"

"Now, if you like," smiled Dr. Fieldwicke, and the smile was warm and kindly. "You can go straight down there to-day if you like. And your wife could send your things over to-morrow perhaps. How would that suit you?"

"I'll go straight from here. My friend, who is waiting, will take me," replied Neystoke, and smiled for the first time that day.

"Right. I'll ring the Matron up. I just want a few particulars first," and the doctor took a case-sheet from a drawer in his desk.

CHAPTER 2

Marstone Park, as Dr. Fieldwicke's widely known nursing-home is called, is beautifully situated in surroundings as peaceful as they are lovely. Any soul-sick, mind-tortured patient who sojourns there for a time, must inevitably benefit, apart from the sustenance, help and healing provided by the staff of highly-trained experts who minister to them.

It must not be supposed, however, that this great old house, that stands by the sea in the midst of its green-swarded park-land, is a private lunatic asylum, or anything like it.

Neither by the Doctor's wish nor by the law of the land can a certifiable lunatic be admitted to enjoyment of its amenities for the healing of mind and soul and body. Nor, if any unhappy patient who was a border-line case, crossed the margin that separates the sane from the insane, could treatment at Marstone Park be continued. The Doctor, admitting failure, would ask the unfortunate sufferer's relatives to have him certified and removed to the appropriate place.

No, the people who, on their doctor's advice, and with the concurrence of the founder and proprietor of Marstone Park Nursing Home, are able to go there, are as sane as the rest of us. But their minds, though sane in the ordinary acceptance of the word, are 'insane' in the sense of being unhealthy; and inevitably their unhealthy minds have more or less severely affected the health of their bodies. Nor must it be supposed that the word 'unhealthy' used in this sense means what it does in the ordinary acceptance and use, as when we say of a man—a writer of books perchance—that he has a thoroughly unhealthy mind. In point of fact, such a man's mind may be perfectly healthy, though his taste be bad, his moral standards base, and his attitude to life deplorable.

No, at Marstone Park a mind is regarded as unhealthy when it is not at peace; when there is conflict within; and the state of mental stress and strain and disharmony affects the physical health.

So Richard Neystoke found himself in the society of people as normal as himself. Some more ill than he, some less; some very attractive, some most interesting; some the reverse. Not a few were slightly eccentric; some excitable; some lethargic. In fact, a microcosm of the world of men and women, a diversity of creatures with nothing in common but suffering.

On arriving at the house, after the long drive from London in his friend's car, the latter part through charming country-side, Richard Neystoke had been impressed and delighted, first by the huge old house, in its peaceful and lovely setting; secondly by its austerely luxurious and comfortable interior; and thirdly by the kindness and friendliness of his reception.

He 'took to' the Matron at once; indeed, as he cheerfully and humorously wrote that night to his wife, it was a case of love at first sight. It was, fortunately for him, a case of mutual liking, approval and attraction. Intuitive and sensitive, he knew within the first five minutes that here was someone who would understand him, sympathise with him, and give him help. He hoped that he would see much of her, and that her title of Matron did not imply that her work was wholly or mainly on the domestic side.

In point of fact, Sister Grey was a nurse of wide experience and very marked ability, who was called Matron by direction of Dr. Fieldwicke in order that she might have equal authority in both the administration and the nursing branches of his big establishment.

It was his humour, when introducing her to patients or their relatives, as, 'Sister Grey our Matron; my right hand, who also knoweth everything that my left hand doeth and is apt to prevent it in some of its doings . . .' to add, 'She is Marstone Park really, you know.'

Woman residents of Marstone Park were wont to wonder why the Doctor did not marry her. Stupid men-folk to whom they made this remark were apt to reply that it might be because he didn't want to, and conceivably because she didn't.

Nevertheless, not one, nor two, nor a mere half-dozen of the Doctor's staff and the Doctor's patients had fallen in love with her and begged her to give to the one, the love and care, the kindness, help and healing, that she gave to the many.

For Elspeth Grey was a remarkable woman, in that her twenty years of life in sick-room, hospital and nursing-home had left her face unlined, her brown hair untouched with silver, and her manner as gentle, easy and unassertive as though she had never suffered, seen suffering, nor held strong and arbitrary power and command. Great strength behind great gentleness, high humour hidden by fine seriousness, lofty and rigid standards accompanied by wide tolerance, gave her face the expression which was the best feature of its undeniable beauty.

In spite of hard and exacting work, of hours both long and late, and of great and grave responsibility, Sister Grey, even in her severe uniform, looked much younger than her forty years.

"Ah, Mr. Neystoke," she said as she advanced to meet him. "We've been expecting you. The Doctor rang up and told me you were coming. You'd like to come straight to your room, wouldn't you? . . . Then perhaps you'd come and have tea in the drawing-room, and I'll introduce you to one or two men whom you might think interesting."

Richard Neystoke found his room delightful; neither big nor small, neither over-furnished nor bare, and offering a delightful if not magnificent view across terraced lawns to the sea.

"Oh, how very nice," he said appreciatively. "I'm sure I shall be most comfortable here."

"I'm sure you will," Sister Grey agreed with him, her warm and kindly smile an assurance in itself.

"Now I want you to do exactly what you like," she added. "Either go to bed at once, and stay there until the Doctor visits you to-morrow; or have tea in that arm-chair by the window; or come down and have tea with us in the drawing-room."

"Oh, I'd so much rather stay here, if I may. I don't want to go to bed yet, but . . ."

"I quite understand. You shall have tea up here in peace. And then I'll send Nurse Weston to talk to you. She'll be your special nurse. I do hope you'll like her. But I'm sure you will. Everybody does. And I want you to feel you can talk to her quite freely. It will help you—and us—tremendously if you can come to accept her as a real and valuable friend."

"Thank you. I'm sure that . . ." replied Richard Neystoke, somewhat doubtfully.

"And I want you to remember this," added Sister Grey, as he broke off, "that whatever you say to her *in confidence* will not be repeated. You may rest assured that if you say to Nurse Weston *'Please do not tell anybody what I have just said,'* she would not dream of doing so. She would repeat it neither to me nor to the Doctor, nor to anyone else."

When Sister Grey went out of the room, Richard Neystoke already felt a little better. Also that the room was not as bright as it had been.

CHAPTER 3

For the first fortnight of his new and strange life at Marstone Park, Richard Neystoke was profoundly miserable. His daily interviews with one or other of the two principal psycho-therapists, Dr. Fieldwicke and his partner Dr. Stortford, were painful, repugnant and humiliating. He feared and hated them.

The questions that the doctors asked seemed to aim at stripping layer after layer of protective and defensive covering until his very soul was laid bare, which was precisely what they did aim at; although what Neystoke called his Soul, the doctors called his Subconscious Mind. It was a mental third-degree, applied for his benefit and ultimate cure, intended to discover the cause of the conflict of which his mind was the battleground and his health the casualty. And he bore it badly, this probing, searching, relentless questioning that dug and delved into his past life, from earliest childhood up to the time when his illness began; into his sex life, his school and college life, his professional and family life. At the end of the week he felt that he could bear it no longer, and but for the comforting advice of the Matron, and the fear of what Jacintha, Dr. Bennett, and his friend Marindin would say, he would have fled.

"Don't be silly," urged the Matron, Elspeth Grey, "and don't be weak and cowardly. . . . Stick it out. Face it as you would an operation. It *is* an operation, and a painful one; but what does that matter, if it leads to a cure—as it will. Of course it will, if you co-operate with the doctors."

"I feel worse than I did when I came," replied

422

Neystoke.

"And you'll soon feel worse than you do now," was the reply. "But there are people here who feel far worse than you do, Mr. Neystoke—or ever did."

He hated it when she talked like that. (Another thing to hate about the beastly place!) But he did not hate *her*. Very far from it; and he wanted to stand well with her, be worthy in her sight, impress her favourably, and win her sympathy.

And the beastly place was extraordinarily comfortable and well-managed. Nor were his days anything but restful, easy and pleasant, save for the infernal inquisition that got ever nearer and nearer to his secret.

And what was the use of their digging and delving in his Unconscious Mind when the whole terrible trouble was there in his consciousness; there always, day and night, in his thoughts and his dreams. He had been a fool to come. It was a waste of time, and it was extra and unnecessary suffering and cruelty. He knew what was on his *conscience*—and he'd take good care that they never knew it. It would have been far better for him to remain at home, as he had repeatedly told Bennett and Jacintha and Denzil Marindin too. A silly waste of his money, his time, and his little store of nervous strength—this fighting to protect his secret; fighting the very people he should be helping; struggling to keep hidden what he should be striving to lay bare. . . . But Sister Grey might help him perhaps . . . a little . . . when she knew him better. He had felt that she might be able to help him, the moment he had looked at her.

If only he could go to her, as a child to its mother, and tell her everything. . . .

Each morning he arose, at leisure, after a dainty early-tea in bed; went into the nice little "communicating" dressing-room; shaved and dressed without haste; descended to the sunny cheerful breakfast-room for an excellent meal of eggs-and-bacon and coffee; went for a stroll in the grounds after he had glanced at the paper, during a digestive rest in a deep arm-chair in the hall; and then, in fear and trembling, went to the quiet cosy consulting-room for his interview with Dr. Fieldwicke or Dr. Stortford, according to the day.

For Dr. Fieldwicke spent alternate days in Harley Street and Marstone Park, his work at the latter place being supplemented by his partner during his absence.

Of the two doctors, Richard Neystoke preferred the junior partner, chiefly by reason of the fact that he seemed the less dangerous, the less likely to trip him up, trap him and make him betray himself. And yet, in another way, interviews with him were more unpleasant, for Stortford was a convinced and bigoted Freudian, while Fieldwicke followed Jung of the broader and more comprehensive theory of the cause and cure of those diseases which are inflicted on the body by the mind.

It was Stortford who delved into the soil and sub-soil of the field of Neystoke's sex-experience, Fieldwicke who put him on the rack of inquiry into other phases and chapters of his life-history. And from the interviews he would emerge trembling, sweating, feeling ill to the depths of his soul and the extremities of his body. He would then go and lie down on his bed, and Nurse Weston would come and minister to him with both mental and medical comfort and cheer. After a talk with her and the taking of a sedative, he would gradually feel better and she would leave him to have a nap or to read a book.

At one o'clock, he would go down to lunch; and,

forgetting his troubles, his physical aches and pains, enjoy the bright and cheerful conversation of the nurses and of those of his fellow-patients well enough to be downstairs, and willing enough to enter into the corporate and communal life of the house.

Richard Neystoke soon discovered that, even among these, there were many patients who suffered as much as he did, and made no moan.

After lunch, he would sit awhile in the hall, the great conservatory or 'winter-garden,' the library, or out on the terrace, and then go for a walk with Nurse Weston, who, he realised, was an adept at conducting the conversation into the channel that she desired. And this channel invariably led round to himself; his doings; his tastes, hobbies, work, opinions, likes and dislikes; his experiences and the general history of his life. She did not question him, orally examine him, and (in his own words) 'grill' him as the doctors did; but with a skill that he could more easily admire than evade, she made him talk about himself.

Most of us find ourselves pleasant subjects of conversation and Nurse Weston learned a great deal about Richard Neystoke. This, as in duty bound, she duly reported to Dr. Stortford at her daily interview with him, an interview held for this purpose.

After the walk came tea in the drawing-room and the opportunity of conversation with the lady-patients, most of whom were not much in evidence until this hour of the day. The evening, until dinner, was spent at billiards or cards, in reading or conversation, in letter-writing or the pursuit of such time-killing devices as picture-puzzle arranging, patience-playing, and particularly any form of work that patients could be induced to undertake.

It was a leading article of faith at Marstone

Park that Occupation is Salvation and one of the most important duties of the nurses was to find something for every patient to do. If he were not bed-ridden, he must have a job and a hobby; something suitable to his years, abilities and gifts must be found to employ such of his time as was not devoted to out-door exercise or games and to indoor reading and diversions, such as bridge and billiards. There must be no vacuous idling, no brooding upon real or imaginary woes and illnesses.

Richard Neystoke, who played neither cards nor billiards, but was a great reader, was set a course of study for his early-evening occupation, the reading of a subject of which he was ignorant, and the following of which would give him plenty of mental exercise and something to think about—especially in relation to himself. At present he was wrestling with a deep and difficult subject, set forth by a very learned psychologist in a fat tome entitled 'The Unconscious Mind.' For relief, if not recreation, he was provided with a somewhat lighter book entitled 'Dream Symbolism and the Subconscious.' He found the going heavy and the reading grim.

At seven he would return to his room and dress for dinner. This was another delightful meal, well cooked and served, again rendered cheerful and bright by the efforts of the nurses who sat among the patients and worked hard to turn what might have been a depressing and dismal function into an excellent imitation of a social occasion.

After dinner, music in the drawing-room, conversation, reading, billiards, cards and similar mild diversions until time for an early retirement to bed, all patients being encouraged to be there by ten o'clock. Few needed much encouragement, sleep being their haven and their heaven, their release from thought and from suffering. No patient retired earlier than Richard Neystoke, for it was when he had gone to bed that Sister Grey, on her rounds, came and talked to him, providing the one bright spot in his unhappy day, and almost invariably giving him the comfort that he needed and the sympathy for which he yearned.

For in spite of her occasional bracing brusqueness and her quick efficient squashing of self-pity, she was truly sympathetic with what she realised to be his very genuine suffering, his exhausting mental conflict, and his resultant physical illness. Sister Grey knew, no-one better, that the agony of tortured and torturing nerves is far greater than that of physical wounds; and that, even in a war-time hospital, there may be unwounded men more truly pitiable than those who are suffering bodily injuries from shot and shell. She knew that no-one can hurt us as we can hurt ourselves, that no injuries are as great as those that are self-inflicted, and that the tortures inflicted upon our bodies by our minds are the worst that we can suffer.

§2

Of his companions in misfortune, Neystoke soon found one or two interesting, agreeable and amusing; some dull, unattractive and depressing; one, at least, alarming; others pleasant enough but self-centred and concerned solely with their own symptoms and sufferings. Some were pathetic, some wholly admirable, some detestable; but all were more or less sick in mind and body.

One who intrigued Neystoke from the first was Mr. Fothering, a sprightly gentleman of middle-age; a barrister, wealthy, widely-travelled and experienced; a charming and polished citizen of the

world. Beyond looking somewhat worn and hag-
gard, he appeared to be in good health, played
eighteen holes of golf without undue fatigue, and
seemed to enjoy life as much as most healthy people do. It was shoes that troubled him, as—breaking the rules of the establishment, which forbade
the subject of their symptoms in conversation between patients—he confided to Neystoke during
the course of a pleasant afternoon walk. Shoes.
They wouldn't behave, and they *would* obtrude
themselves upon his night thoughts. He had, as
he explained, a stout brown pair for walking, a
thin brown pair for indoors, a similar couple of
pairs in black for use when he was not wearing his
grey flannels, his patent-leather shoes for use with
dinner-kit, his indoor house-shoes, bedroom
slippers, and bathroom slippers. Fortunately, he
had not brought his riding-boots, for they were the
worst of the lot and incited the others.

"*Incite* the others?" asked Richard Neystoke in
great agony of mind, for the subject of shoes was
nearly as distasteful and painful to him as that of
bare feet. He faced the horror bravely however, for
Fothering was obviously talking seriously and indeed earnestly. "Incite them to what?"

"I'll tell you," continued Fothering. "When I go
to bed, I take off my dress-shoes and put them
beside the others, which stand in a row along the
wall, toes outward. That's all right. Then I finish
undressing and get into bed, and perhaps read a
bit before I put out the light. Then, at the first
yawn, down goes the book, I switch off the bed-
side lamp and settle down to sleep. To sleep? Not a
bit of it! Those damned shoes start at once. First
of all, I can't be sure whether I put the dress pair
with their heels to the wall, as the rest are. I tell
myself that it is absurd, for of course, I must have
done so. But it's no good. I have to turn on the

light and get up to make sure. . . . It's all right of course, they are pointing toes-outward like the rest, and I get back into bed and settle down, quite re-assured. But not for long. In a minute or two I am wondering whether I did not pick them up— and put them down again the wrong way round. I have to make sure, of course. Yes, naturally, I must make quite certain. I find it's all right again. I hadn't moved them. This time I am careful not to touch them, and then I know I can't have changed their position. Then I return to bed, put out the light, and settle down again. To sleep? No fear. No such luck. No. In about a couple of minutes I begin to get an uncomfortable feeling, which soon grows into a firm conviction, that the whole lot of them are wrong. They ought not to be pointing out into the room like that. They ought to have their faces to the wall. I don't know the reason, but I do know the *fact*, and that it is a vitally important one. So up I get again and turn them all round . . . Then perhaps I can get a little peace and go to sleep, you'd think. You might well think so, but you'd be wrong. The damned things start whispering to each other. I can never quite catch what they say, but it is something about me, I know. They couldn't and wouldn't do me any harm, of course, but they are disagreeable and discontented. They don't know what they *do* want. . . . So I put on the light again, get up and re-arrange them in a line instead of a row, with their sides along the wall instead of their heels or toes. It may work, or it may not; and even if I get to sleep, I wake up and wonder whether I dreamed it all, and feel that I must get up and make sure.

"One night I got so angry with them that I took the whole lot out in the corridor and arranged them against the wall there. That taught them a lesson. But they won in the end, for I simply had to go and fetch them in again, towards morning, after they had kept me awake all night.

"One time, I just stood them in the middle of the floor, in a row, near my bed, where I could see them, and be quite sure they were all in order. . . . They simply stared me out, with all their eyes. Five pairs of eyes to each shoe! I couldn't stand it, of course, and soon had to put them back against the wall—when they started their old tricks at once.

" 'What tricks?' Why, making me wonder, as soon as the light was out, as to whether they were all pointing the right way, of course. Kept me awake till morning."

"I wonder the Doctor doesn't give you a sleeping-draught," said Richard Neystoke, feeling, as he spoke, that he ought not to be discussing with Mr. Fothering his symptoms and treatment.

"Oh, he did, at first; just so that I could get some rest and recover a measure of health; for the continual broken nights and almost complete lack of sleep are killing me. Insomnia is hell, you know; worse than any other trouble you can have. . . . Yes, the Doctor has some fine stuff for making you sleep. Did me a lot of good when I first came. But now I've got to cope with the shoes myself, until he can find out the real cause of their extraordinary conduct. Then I shall be quite well again."

"Do they ever trouble you in the day-time?" asked the deeply interested Neystoke. "Now *my* feet simply . . ."

"Good Heavens, no!" scoffed Mr. Fothering, interrupting. "Who on earth would be such a fool as to take any notice of a row of shoes—except to see that they were properly cleaned and ready for wear?" and he laughed, so scornfully that Neystoke felt quite ashamed of his foolish question.

That night, when Sister Grey came for her usual talk with him—a talk of which the subject-matter was more carefully selected, arranged and guided, than he ever realised—he ventured to ask her a question that was troubling his mind.

"Forgive me for asking, Sister," he said, "but is Mr. Fothering mad?"

"No more mad than you or I," was the answer, given in the firm and quiet voice that he so greatly liked to hear. "He is perfectly sane in the ordinary sense of the word.

"Like everyone else here," she added. "And don't forget that you must not ask me questions about the other patients, for I shall no more discuss them with you than I would discuss you with them. Now tell me what you have been doing to-day, besides going for a walk with Mr. Fothering."

"Oh, nothing much. I read some of 'Thus spake Zarathrusta,' and I had a delightful stroll with Nurse Weston this morning, and . . ."

"And gave her the slip, didn't you?" smiled Sister Grey. "And found your way down to the beach?"

"How did you know that?" asked Neystoke in considerable surprise; for, having abandoned and eluded Nurse Weston when she went into the lodge at the southern entrance to the Park, he was quite unjustifiably certain that no-one had seen him go off or could have known where he went. . . . Who had been spying upon him? It was really intolerable, outrageous, and he'd . . .

"How did you know?" he repeated as Sister Grey smiled at him as does a wise mother at a foolish child.

"Sand on your shoes," she said, "between the welts of the soles and the uppers. Do you confess —both the evasion and the escape to the sea?"

Richard Neystoke smiled ruefully. How they watched one! Spied on one.

"You are all too clever for me," he said. "And you know too much."

"That is what we are here for," replied Sister Grey. "Of course we are cleverer than you, in our own special department, or how could we help you? And we don't know too much, because it is impossible for us to know too much—about your thoughts and your doings. And your motives for your doings. . . .

"Tell me," she continued, leaning back in her chair and eyeing Neystoke thoughtfully, searchingly and yet very kindly. "If I ask you a question or two about it, will you tell me, and answer me with the absolute truth and the whole of the truth? And if you see what my questions are aimed at finding out, will you volunteer the information if the questions don't elicit it?"

"I will, Sister," replied Neystoke. "I'll help you to the utmost of my power. I should be a fool to do otherwise.

"Besides," he added, with the shy smile that made his face so boyish and pleasing, "I'd do *anything* for you."

"Good," observed Elspeth Grey abruptly. "Tell me this, then. Why did you bolt as soon as Nurse Weston's back was turned, causing her a great deal of unnecessary anxiety and bother, searching high and low for you? She had to report you missing—and she got into trouble for dereliction of duty. Why did you run away? Do you dislike her?"

"Dislike her!" exclaimed Neystoke, sitting suddenly upright in his bed. "Why! No. Nothing of the sort. I love her."

"Well," observed Sister Grey drily, "we are commanded to love one another, so you are quite in order. But why do you dissemble your love to the extent of both giving her a lot of trouble and getting her *into* trouble?"

"I'm really and truly most awfully sorry," admitted Neystoke contritely. "I never thought of that aspect of my escapade. All I wanted was to get away by myself."

"Simply because you wanted to be alone? . . . You are going to tell me the absolute truth, as you promised, aren't you?"

"Yes, er—yes. Of course, Sister. I did want to be alone—er—just then, and as we were in that part of the Park."

"Oh, it wasn't an attack of nerves and a longing for complete solitude? . . . *'That part of the Park,'* you said. Why that particular part?"

"Near the sea," replied Neystoke, and the watchful eyes noted that a look expressive of unwillingness, not to say sulkiness, passed over the ingenuous face of the Reverend Richard Neystoke. It now looked rather like that of a nice child being defensive lest it be trapped into admission of sin. What a dear he was, really; and how cruel one would have to be in order to be kind. If she knew anything of the awful devastations of mental conflict, this poor man was going to suffer badly before he was healed; and with a pain and misery far greater than he was suffering now. A pity there is no anæsthetic for use in mental surgery.

"You wanted to get to the sea," she said reflectively. "And you didn't want Nurse Weston to accompany you. You wanted to go quite alone. Wasn't that it?"

"Well . . . yes. Yes, I suppose I did," admitted Neystoke.

"Obviously you did. You know quite well that you did," observed Sister Grey somewhat severely and reprovingly.

"Yes," replied the wretched man, with an

obvious physical wriggle, symptomatic of his little mental squirm.

"Why? Did you want to bathe? Did you feel that you simply must undress, rush into the sea and let it wash right over your head—that sort of feeling?"

If he could and would admit that this really was the case, she would have done a splendidly useful piece of work this evening.

"Oh, no! Not at all. I do assure you, Sister, that I had no intention of undressing and bathing. I hadn't the very slightest desire to—er—bathe."

She was a little disappointed, but too well accustomed to such experience to realise it. Ninety-nine out of every hundred lines of investigation led nowhere. . . . So it was not a case of a subconscious urge to rush into the sea and symbolically wash all sins away—or some particular sin?

"You felt you must go down to the sea—but not to bathe. Did you by any chance want to *hide* something—in the sand? Or throw it as far out into the water as you possibly could?" she asked. He would not be the first patient at Marstone Park who was affected with an unconquerable urge to find a hiding-place for something—something quite subjective and intangible—and who prowled about like a mother cat seeking a safe refuge for the kitten she carried in her mouth, or a dog with a bone that he must completely conceal from every prying eye.

"Hide something? In the sand? Really no, Sister. I do assure you that such a thought never entered my mind," replied Neystoke with obvious truthfulness.

"Then did you want to go alone in order to search for something that the tide might have brought in and left behind? Do you do that? I mean, do you sometimes feel you must go to a beach and search?"

"No. Nothing of the sort, Sister."

"Have you ever had any painful experience by the sea, or by the water's edge anywhere, at any time? Ever been nearly drowned, seen anyone drowned when you were a child, or lost any dear friend through drowning?"

"No. Never anything of the sort. I love the sea and have only the happiest experiences and remembrances of it. Truly."

"Very well. Now will you tell me something, voluntarily, and without need for any more of these impertinent questions of mine. Just tell me the truth as to why you wanted to get down to the beach alone."

"I just . . . felt that . . . I wanted to," was the hesitating reply. "I didn't want Nurse Weston to watch me, there, and see what I did."

"Why—what *did* you do?" asked Elspeth Grey quickly.

"Nothing, Sister. Nothing. Really I didn't."

The Matron sighed.

"Good-night, Mr. Neystoke," she said. "Sleep well . . ."

Richard Neystoke turned his face to the wall and almost wept.

In the night, unable to sleep, he arose and put his three pairs of shoes and his slippers into the ward-robe and locked the door. He would not admit such a thing, even to himself, no, not for a moment, but he had rather fancied that he could hear them whispering to each other about him. And he had to admit that, naturally, they must absolutely hate to be put upon *his* feet, of all people's. He hadn't thought of that before.

§3

Then there was Miss Lottie Lasbury, a gentle, charming and delightful woman of about thirty summers, who looked so frail, fragile and ill. She was sweet and it was very nice and agreeable to have a talk with her, for she was really intelligent and well-read. But, sooner or later, and generally much sooner, she would make a most terrible grimace at you. Most rude, insulting and offensive. It was as though a devil suddenly peeped out from her eyes and then contorted her face, making her poke out her tongue at you, screw up her shapely little nose, stretch her mouth widely and squint with a loathsome leer.

Really *very* trying, especially the first time it happened. And Richard Neystoke felt quite sure that it wasn't a rictus of the muscles, a nervous spasm that suddenly twisted and marred her face, or a contortion that was the involuntary expression of sudden and unbearable pain. No, it was intentional, though the knowledge that she did it, and had to do it, was a terrible cross almost too heavy to be borne; and she was at Marstone Park in the hope of being cured. All this was confirmed by Nurse Weston who spoke in defence of the poor lady when Neystoke complained of this abominable way in which she had insulted him when he offered to help her wind her skein of wool. Thereafter he sought her society in deep sympathy and pity, until, one day, he caught himself in the very act of doing it to the house-keeper, a woman whom he disliked. . . .

Colonel Lethwell, a powerful and brawny man, in the prime of life, was another most agreeable companion, who had been to most places and done most things. To talk with him was a delight and an education, but to walk with him was a risk of grave embarrassment. For suddenly the Colonel would sit down upon the ground and declare that nothing on this earth or in Heaven above would induce him to get up again. He was sure that he would turn giddy if he did, and that his brain would go into a spin, dive and crash to everlasting smash, ruin and damnation.

There was nothing for it but to abandon him and go for some kind of vehicle for his removal; and he had been brought back from his walks on trucks, wheel-barrows, farm-carts, delivery vans, and the casual passing motor-cars of the kind-hearted. But he must be lifted into, or on to, the vehicle, for arise of his own volition he would not. A fine soldier, husband, father and gentleman, likewise as sane as the Doctor himself, Richard Neystoke liked him very much indeed, but had to give up going for walks with him, or even for little strolls about the grounds, for fear he also be constrained to sit suddenly down, and stay down, lest he too should turn giddy, his brain go into a spin, dive and crash to everlasting smash, ruin and damnation.

But there were plenty of other down-stair patients to talk with, though almost all were either terribly depressed or listless, obviously unhappy, sick, anxious and suffering.

Young Johnny Milterby was one of the most attractive persons you could meet, until he proved to be a truly phenomenal liar and quite unable to visit a fellow-patient in his room without surreptitiously taking away some souvenir of his call, preferably money. Indeed, the belief grew in Neystoke's mind that on several occasions Johnny visited his room in its occupant's absence; for it was hardly likely that the gold pencil his wife had given him, his silver matchbox, his pocket-knife and three silk handkerchiefs could all have fallen out of his pockets when he was walking abroad. He felt it his duty, both to himself and the house-maid, to mention the matter to the Matron and to state plainly, that though he could prove nothing as to the cause of the disappearance of some of his small portable property, he had definitely missed things, on at least three occasions, after visits from Johnny.

He was amazed when she replied that, if he gave her a list of the things he had lost, she would see that they were all returned to him; also when she stated that Johnny was no more a criminal thief than Neystoke himself was. For Johnny never spent the money that he stole, never smoked the cigarettes or cigars, never used the ties or hand-kerchiefs, never sold or otherwise parted with the gold and silver articles that he stole, but merely put them on the table or mantelpiece in his room, for anyone to see, remove and return to their owners. . . . Her great fear was lest someone, righteously indignant, should curse Johnny for a filthy thief and, very naturally, threaten to prose-cute him; as this would probably cause him to run away—and it would only be a matter of days before he was in prison.

Thereafter when Neystoke missed anything, he went straight along to Johnny's room, and Johnny instantly returned it—not with shame and contri-tion, but in the spirit of one who has found your dog, wandering and lost, and has kindly taken it home and cared for it until claimed by the owner. He was always very glad to be able to find, among his large collection of odds and ends, anything that Neystoke had lost, and to be able to restore it to its rightful proprietor. . . .

"Yes. The boy's a bloody jackdaw," declared

Colonel Lethwell when Neystoke mentioned his curious experiences with Johnny.

"Exactly," agreed Neystoke, "a bl . . . er . . . yes, a young jackdaw and quite as blameless and innocent. . . ."

§4

But, oh, thought he, as he sat alone in his room, that evening of the fourteenth day of his 'cure,' if only he, the wretched Richard Neystoke, could say the same of himself; could only know himself to be as blameless and innocent as a bird, even a thieving jackdaw.

For daily they were getting nearer, digging and delving deeper and deeper toward the spot where he had buried the evidences of his awful deed; the thoughts and memories of an unforgettable and unforgivable act. Why, he himself never so much as walked in his day-dreams and reveries, his thoughts and memories, anywhere near that terrible spot. Much less did he ever, even in his worst moments, deliberately take a spade and mentally dig there. But these men and women, these doctors and nurses, walked straight to the place and dug like . . . like . . . terriers; like navvies, with picks and shovels; nay, worse, like detectives and policemen 'acting on information received', and were excavating a great hole where they expected to find . . . to find . . . What?

He could not say the word. Yes, better say it. He'd be saying it for them soon if he were not wary, watchful, ever on the alert and the defensive. They were digging and delving and in the right place, the place where they expected to find —*evidence*—of a great crime.

And then? When they had succeeded in uncovering it? Would they give him away? Give him up?

Send for the police and hand him over to them?
. . . This man is a criminal. He came as a patient,
because his sense of guilt was weighing him down,
crushing him and making him ill. It had at last
grown insupportable and he broke up. Under our
questioning he gave in, collapsed, and confessed.
Take him away . . . ?

But wouldn't anything he said here be private
and confidential, and treated with the utmost
respect, secrecy and privilege? . . . The seal of the
confessional . . . 'Should a doctor tell . . .'?

Of course a doctor should not tell anything that
he learned from a patient in such a manner. It
would be the grossest breach of personal confidence. It would be sheer treachery. But, even so, if
they did not send for the police and denounce
him, they'd turn him out of the place at once,
naturally. And what should he tell Dr. Bennett
when he asked why he had returned home so
soon? What should he tell Jacintha? What explanation could he give to Denzil Marindin who had
finally persuaded him to go to Fieldwicke, and had
brought him here in his car?

And what would Dr. Fieldwicke tell Bennett
when the latter asked him, as he was bound to do,
about the patient whom he had sent him.

And, possibly worst of all, what would Elspeth
Grey say to him? It did not bear thinking about.
He could imagine her look of hurt and shocked
surprise on finding that the Reverend Richard
Neystoke, to whom she had been so kind, was a
criminal, a man who had committed one of the
most base and dreadful of all crimes.

Richard Neystoke groaned aloud.

No, the first fortnight of his stay at Marstone
Hall was not, on the whole, a very happy one.

But for Sister Grey, he would have run away

that very night.

CHAPTER 4

There was a quiet tap at the door and, in answer to Neystoke's call, Sister Grey entered the room. To Neystoke's impressionable and imaginative mind, the room seemed the lighter and brighter for her coming, almost as though the sun had shone in at the window.

It may be, thought he, the dazzling whiteness of her uniform, the almost luminous pallor of her face, the brightness of her clear eyes and the sheen of her hair. . . . But I think it is her personal aura. It may, of course, be my imagination, but there must be something very wonderful about her to stimulate my imagination to such an extent that I . . .

"Well?" smiled the Matron, interrupting the train of his thought. "Do I alarm you as much as all that?"

"No. I wouldn't say that 'alarm' is the first and chief emotion which you arouse, even in my undoubtedly timid mind," replied Neystoke gravely. "Why? Do I look frightened?"

"Yes, you did. Your mouth positively dropping open, like a caught-out school-boy. Guilty, you know. I rather expected you to say that, whatever it was, you weren't doing it!"

The Matron, watching Neystoke's face, noted the change of expression, the passing of a shadow as it were, across his face as she said the word 'guilty' . . . What less guilty creature ever harboured something that it considered a guilty secret, poor dear?

"How did you sleep last night? Did you dream at all?"

"Oh, I didn't have a very good night. I never do. Dream? Yes. One of a peculiar idiocy."

"Do tell me all you can remember of it," begged the Matron.

"Really, it was too stupidly childish for words."

"That doesn't matter. Its silliness has no relation to its importance," was the reply.

"Well, wait until you hear it—and I shall be glad if you will tell me how such a conglomeration of fantastic lunacy can be important."

"I will tell you before you tell me the dream. You know, quite as well as I can tell you, that the health of the mind and body are interdependent. If you are frightened, anxious or worried, the health of your body is quickly and badly affected. Fright can actually cause death, as you know. In the same way, if your liver is out of order, if you've got indigestion or tooth-ache, your mind can't be calm and clear, and your judgment balanced. One can do a good deal for certain unhealthy conditions of the body by the use of medicine. Specifics; like quinine for malaria, for example. And one can do a good deal for certain unhealthy conditions of the mind by allaying fears and removing the causes of anxieties and worries. All that is very elementary, of course, and a child can understand it."

"Even I could," agreed the Vicar of Little Pudding.

"Splendid. For a long time now, the best doctors have been increasingly inclined to approach the problems of a big group of bodily illnesses from the angle of the mind, realising that medicine is utterly useless, and surgery worse than useless, when the physical illness is caused by the mental state; and of recent years, they have gone still further and have studied the effect upon the body of what they call the Unconscious Mind, now generally termed the Subconscious."

"What is the Subconscious?" asked Neystoke, as the Matron paused for breath and to see how he was bearing up, beneath all this eloquence.

"I wish I could tell you. I daresay Dr. Fieldwicke wishes he could tell you, in a sentence. He has told it in about one hundred and fifty thousand words, and I want you to read his book very carefully. . . .

"I suppose one could best sum it up by saying that the Unconscious or Subconscious is that part of the mind that can't think or determine. It is with our Conscious Mind that we think and reflect and make decisions. You know in ordinary conversation you say 'I don't do it consciously'. No, when that happens, you do it absentmindedly or subconsciously. The Conscious Mind wasn't doing its job, and left the matter to the subconscious. Anyone who did that regularly would be insane. A good simile can be got from the idea of a ship. The captain on the bridge is the Conscious Mind and directs the ship of the individual across the sea of life. The ship goes exactly where he steers it, and he is responsible for its going there. But down below, and knowing nothing of where the ship is going, is the chief engineer, without whom the ship can't move at all. The chief engineer represents the Subconscious Mind. Those two men are equally valuable, important and essential to the functioning of the ship."

"How right you are!" smiled Richard Neystoke. "I never heard such wisdom! No, never!"

"Now you are going to hear some more. Not only are the captain and the chief engineer essential to the functioning of the ship, but their *agreement* is absolutely essential. They have got to work together, by the bridge telephone and voice-pipe. The captain tells the chief engineer to increase or decrease speed, and the chief engineer can tell the captain. . . ."

"Not by the bridge telephone or voice-pipe," objected Richard Neystoke. "He couldn't back-answer."

"Well, perhaps you know more about ships than I do," smiled Elspeth Grey, "but conceivably he could send a messenger, couldn't he? Or even go himself and tell the captain that too much coal is being consumed or even that the engines absolutely must be stopped for a little while because . . ."

"Someone's baby has fallen down a ventilator and the mother wants it back," interrupted Neystoke.

"Quite so. Or the bearings have seized."

"What do they seize?" asked Neystoke. "I've often wondered."

"The cranks, I expect."

"Serve 'em right. I've always hated cranks."

"So do I," agreed the Matron. "What I was leading up to, was this. . . . Are you paying attention?"

"Yes, Matron; of course I am. But I want you to go on leading up, and never getting there."

"I am being serious, Mr. Neystoke."

"I know. I love it when you are serious. You look . . ."

"I am rather a busy . . . body."

"No, don't say that. You . . ."

"I'll tell you something, Mr. Neystoke. You are getting very much better, and I hope you realise it. Most excellent. Now listen to me. I was talking about the captain and the engineer . . ."

"Awfully nice fellows, but couldn't we talk about . . ."

"Yes, some other time. They are awfully nice fellows, as you say, but suppose they had a tremendous row . . ."

"Tut!" ejaculated Richard Neystoke.

445

"Had a tremendous row, and both downed tools. Captain flung his sextant on the deck and jumped on it; while the engineer threw his best and biggest spanner in to the—er—works."

"Poor old ship," murmured Neystoke.

"*Exactly*," said the Matron, with emphasis. "Poor old ship indeed! That's just what you are—a poor old ship; your captain and your chief engineer quarrelling. In other words, your Conscious and Subconscious are at variance."

"Sad, sad, sad," murmured Neystoke. "What are we going to do about it?"

"Listen. I'm trying to tell you."

"I could listen all day."

"Five minutes will be enough. As I was saying, what I want you to grasp is this. You, yourself, said just now that the chief engineer can't back-answer to the captain when he rings the bridge telegraph or shouts something rude down the voice-pipe. And that's just the point. Your subconscious mind can't talk freely and easily to your conscious mind. I think you suggested that the chief engineer would have to send a messenger up to the bridge or go himself, if there were something urgent that he must say to the captain. Similarly, with the Subconscious Mind; it has to send a message as best it can, or go itself—take charge so to speak. . . . And the only way in which the Subconscious Mind can send its messages is through *dreams*."

"I rise to remark that they are extraordinarily silly messages," observed Richard Neystoke.

"And I rise to reply that they are only silly to silly people who won't try to understand them, or lack the intelligence to do so," replied the Matron.

"Oh," observed Neystoke. "And what about when the engineer himself goes up to the bridge—in other words when the Subconscious Mind takes charge of the situation and . . ."

"Stop! You've said it!" interrupted Elspeth Grey. "When the Subconscious Mind brings the message itself, and takes charge of the situation, to use your own words, *it is* in charge of the situation and *of you* . . . And then you are a lunatic, Mr. Neystoke."

"I am, am I?"

"Yes. A lunatic is simply a person who is 'in the grip of the unconscious'; a ship in sole charge of the engineer—who knows nothing whatsoever of navigation, and could no more bring the ship to port than he could fly."

" '*In the Grip of the Unconscious*' ", murmured Neystoke, savouring the phrase. "Sounds like the title of a book. Sub-title: '*or Off to the Looney-bin.*' "

"Yes, just that," agreed Elspeth Grey, very seriously.

"And I should have to leave here, shouldn't I, Sister?"

"You would. And you will," she added, her face set in its severest lines, "unless you will let us all help you; and begin by telling us what you dream."

"The captain listens to the engineer down in the engine-room. Lets him send his messages, eh?" smiled Neystoke.

"Yes. It is the most important—the most utterly urgent—thing you have to do; essential; *vital.*"

"By the way, why should the troublesome fellow want to send messages up to the bridge at all?"

"Because there is something dreadfully wrong in the engine-room, and if it isn't seen to, the engines may stop altogether."

"Boiler burst and ship blow up," said Neystoke, with an air of exaggerated gloom.

"Yes. And I've seen so many people 'blow up', that I can't regard it as amusing. . . . You want to get better, don't you?"

"Not too quickly, Sister."

The Matron made a small sound expressive of annoyance, and glanced at her wrist-watch.

"Yes, Matron," Neystoke hastened to reassure her. "I want to get well this very minute."

"Very well. Please realise that you can't dream anything so fantastic, impossible and absurd that it doesn't convey something to the specialist who has made a study of dream-symbolism and of the dreamer. Although there are millions of different dreams, there are really only a few dream-symbols; and dreams can be classified accordingly. It is by the symbols used by your Unconscious that the doctor can understand what the Unconscious is trying to tell you."

"What is a dream, Sister?" asked Neystoke, interrupting with only apparent irrelevance.

"A dream," replied the Matron, "is a picture—a cartoon—drawn by the Unconscious Mind for the consideration of the Conscious Mind. The Unconscious Mind expects the Conscious Mind to understand it, and to act accordingly."

"And suppose the Conscious Mind can't understand it?"

"Then it must find one that can; someone like Dr. Fieldwicke or Dr. Stortford."

"H'm, yes. One can understand something going wrong in a ship's engine-room and the engineer wanting permission to stop the engines, draw the fires, slow down the revolutions, let off steam, or play the fiddle; but what is it that goes wrong in the Unconscious Mind so that it has to draw these funny cartoons as—er—picture-messages for the Conscious Mind to understand and act upon?"

"Oh, all sorts of things. One must not pursue a simile too far; But if some foreign body had got into the engines, it would have to be got out before they could run smoothly again. It would be a bad thing if everything that wasn't wanted on the decks, for example, was thrown down into the engine-room, as if it were a lumber-room rather than an engine-room. All sorts of things might get into the engines."

"Dead cats, beer bottles, superfluous old maids, all sorts of things," agreed Neystoke. "Do a lot of harm."

"Yes, quite. Well, we have a common phrase: 'Put it right out of your mind; forget it;' haven't we? We all of us tend to thrust undesirable thoughts, undesirable memories, out of our minds, out of our conscious minds that is, and we thrust them into the Unconscious. That is what we do when we say: 'We won't think about it any more; we'll forget it.'"

Elspeth Grey noted that Richard Neystoke was now entirely serious. The smiling levity of his face and manner completely changed; his gaze grew watchful and attentive . . . concentrated.

"Now, up to a point, that's all right, but only up to a point. The engineer draws the line somewhere; the dead cats, for example, that you suggested . . . And there are certain things that the Subconscious won't meekly accept. It draws the line; it revolts—like the engineer; it wants a word with the captain; and it sends messages. It sends the ideograph or picture-cartoon that we call a dream."

"What sort of things trouble the Unconscious, then?" asked Neystoke.

"Why, the very things that we don't like to think about; that we thrust away, because they worry us; frighten us; accuse us; cause us shame, and other unpleasant feelings. We thrust them down into the depths of forgetfulness. But what we call forgetfulness, is only another word for the

Subconscious Mind and the Subconscious Mind is like the elephant—it never forgets. Everything you have ever known, seen, heard, thought, read or experienced is there in your subconscious mind; and everything that was in the subconscious mind of your father, of your mother, of your grandparents, of all your ancestors, is there; and that is why, in dreams and delirium, you remember things you never knew. You may talk a language that you have never learnt; never heard, even."

"Is that why blameless maiden ladies sometimes shock the surgeon and nurses by using language, when under an anæsthetic?" asked Neystoke.

"Yes, the language or phraseology of some Georgian or other ancestor is there, in the poor lady's Unconscious; and is released because the Unconscious is temporarily in charge."

"All most interesting," murmured Neystoke.

"Yes. One of the most absorbingly interesting subjects of study—the Unconscious Mind; and even more important than interesting."

"What does it do besides invent silly dreams and annoy you?"

"Well, it does everything that your Conscious Mind doesn't do. Looks after the running of your respiration, circulation, digestion and the working of the involuntary muscles. Runs the ship, in fact, as we said. . . . And all so silently and efficiently and intelligently, until you go and upset it: and then it complains; and if its complaint doesn't receive attention, it gets obtrusive and finally dangerous, and *then* . . ."

"You are going to frighten me, Sister."

"I want to. I want you to be absolutely terrified —of neglecting your dreams."

" '*The gypsy warned me*'," hummed Richard Neystoke.

"Well, don't say she didn't, when it's too late. *Now*—did you dream last night?"

Neystoke grinned.

"Yes. Anything less portentous or more idiotic you couldn't possibly imagine."

"No? Are you sure? Suppose you tell me and let me judge of that, eh?"

"Well, if you can make anything—what's the word the Doctor's so fond of—significant—out of riding to hounds on a tea-kettle and wearing bed-room-slippers, you ought to be Court Astrologer to the Shah of Persia. There ought to be a Delphic Oracle and you——"

"Yes, and you ought to know by now, that there are *'more things in heaven and earth'*, and that ignorance is not always bliss. Now, then, you were out hunting in this dream?"

"I was. Not the Quorn or the Pytchley, but our own perfectly good little Hunt."

"And you were riding a tea-kettle?"

"I was. And wearing my bedroom-slippers. They were . . ."

Abruptly he stopped, and, from the depth of her experience, Elspeth Grey knew that he had suddenly come upon a snag; that he had been going to say something which must not be said.

"Yes? They were?" she prompted.

"Well, they were on my feet."

"Yes? What else were they?"

"Oh, they were two in number."

"Ah, well!" she sighed. "Go on."

"That's really about all, except that the tea-kettle wasn't a very good goer. Radiator not exactly boiling, you know."

"You mean you lagged behind the rest of the Hunt?"

"Well, who wouldn't, in the circumstances? You can't expect . . ."

"How were you dressed—except for the slippers, concerning which, you are not telling me the truth, the whole truth and nothing but the truth?"

"Now, look here, Sister, who's telling this dream? You or I? They are my slippers, aren't they?"

"How were you dressed?"

"In what is beautifully termed 'full canonicals'. Now, what do you think of that for a cartoon, devised by my Unconscious for the enlightenment of my Conscious Mind? Is it, or is it not, a farrago of puerile idiocy?"

"Do you mean to say that it conveys nothing to you at all, Mr. Neystoke?"

"Nothing whatever, Miss Grey," replied Neystoke, mocking her voice and precise diction—in an entirely inoffensive manner.

"I think perhaps you had better call me . . ."

"Elspeth? How nice!"

" 'Matron', I was going to say. And I think you have wasted enough of my time, this morning," she said, rising.

"Ha! So you can't interpret the dream, or, rather, make sense of utter nonsense?"

Elspeth Grey sat down again.

"I don't think you are really as stupid . . ."

"As I look?"

"Yes, and as you pretend. Listen, and don't interrupt. I don't know whether you are really fond of riding to hounds, but your Subconscious doesn't like your doing it. Perhaps you do it to get in contact with a set of your parishioners whom you might not otherwise meet, and of whom you might not otherwise see much? . . . Do you like riding to hounds?"

"Sister! Don't let it go any further; I hate it! Horses terrify me; and they always have. I never know which end is more dangerous. Horses think

I am a fool, and I think horses are beasts; and we're both right."

"Well, whether you are telling the truth or not, your Subconscious loathes the idea of your riding to hounds; and it tells you so in that dream, by making you look as ridiculous as a parson could well be—dressed up in clerical garb *and* bedroom-slippers, *and* sitting on a tea-kettle . . ."

"Why a tea-kettle, Elsp—er—Miss—er—Matron?"

"Another interesting gibe, I think. Tea-kettles, tea-pots, and tea-cups are all in a clergyman's line of business. Five-barred gates, bulfinches and pink coats are not."

" '*Get thee to a nunnery*'; get thee to a bun-fight, eh?"

"Exactly. And you couldn't keep up with the hounds?"

"No. We pounded along, miserably behind."

"In fact, you weren't keeping up with the hunting set of your parishioners?"

"Far from it."

"No. And your Subconscious was drawing your attention to the fact; telling you that that wasn't the way to keep up with the sporting-set. I am not going to express an opinion of my own about blood sports, but I think your Subconscious takes the view that your joining those people in what might conceivably be termed their unedifying and un-profitable pastime . . ."

Richard Neystoke bowed his head in his hands in facetious manner . . .

"Spare me, Sister," he said.

"Don't interrupt."

"You would never have finished that sentence. You were getting all tied-up, het-up, and . . ."

"And what have you not told me about the slippers?"

"Why, Sister; my wife gave them to me. Part of

a Christmas present. She can't buy me gaudy ties, handkerchiefs and socks, you know. Parsons are so limited in their little fallals, doodahs, dinguses and whatnots; so she let herself go—in bedroom-slippers."

"And they were gaudy, were they?"

"Yes."

"What colour?" she asked sharply.

Again, the expressive face that she was watching so intently, changed, hardened, grew pinched and perceptibly paler.

"What colour?" she repeated. "Morocco slippers? *Red?*"

"Yes, Sister," said Neystoke, waiting a second before replying.

"Red," she said. "Crimson? Scarlet?"

"Yes. Yes." And volubly he explained. "So inconsistent with clerical dress; so absurd. . . ."

"H'm. Yes. In fact, the whole dream was absurd and you, a figure of fun as a hunting man, guyed unmercifully by your Unconscious. Very absurd. . . . And the absurdest thing of all," she added, "is the fact that you won't tell me more about the slippers."

"Sister, I . . . What more is there to tell you? I . . ."

"All right. Another time, perhaps. But although you haven't told me everything about the dream, don't you think that my interpretation of it is right? Don't you feel that your Subconscious is saying: *'Don't be such an ass; the hunting-field is not the place for a parson, and least of all, for you.'* . . . It shows you making your cloth ridiculous and it's telling you what you already know—and prefer to forget and ignore. Think it over and decide whether I'm right or wrong. I may be wrong. One has to know a great deal about the dreamer and every detail of the dream, before one can interpret it accurately—and I don't know much about you, Mr. Neystoke. And I don't think you are being quite open and ingenuous about all the details of the dream. . . . Now, I really must go."

"Wouldn't you stay if I thought up another dream?"

"No; and don't be tiresome. You are not here to 'think up' dreams, but to help us to help you—and we can't do that until we know what your Subconscious is driving at. So please try to remember what you dream, and tell us the truth about it. Do remember that though what I've said of the psychology and significance of dreams is crude and amateurish and inaccurate, the essential fact remains that your dreams are of the utmost importance."

"Why, of course, Sister. Are we not such stuff as dreams are made of?" said Neystoke, as he rose to open the door.

"Well, more dreams and less stuff," smiled Elspeth Grey. "Good-bye for the present."

The Matron would have been painfully interested, could she have seen her patient's smiling face change to a mask of misery and pain; seen him cross the room, cast himself upon his knees by the bed, bury his face in his hands, and groan:

"O, God. . . . O, God! . . . Help me . . . Pity me, forgive me, and help me. . . . But they will find me out. . . . *My sin will find me out.* . . ."

CHAPTER 5

Richard Neystoke was aroused from unhappy reverie by the entry of Nurse Weston, bearing the dainty tray of morning tea and toast.

"Well? How did you sleep?" she asked, giving him her pleasant, friendly smile.

"Oh, fair to moderate, thank you, Nurse. No complaints," replied Neystoke, pale and weary-looking. His head ached badly and he felt as though he would like to stay in bed—for the rest of his life.

"Any dreams?" asked Nurse Weston.

Any dreams! What was his sleep but a long horror of dreams?

Feet . . . Feet . . . Feet . . .

"Oh; nothing of any interest," he replied.

"But you must let the Doctor judge of that, Mr. Neystoke. I do hope you will. You really must. You *will* tell him all about them, every detail that you can remember, won't you? You don't know how important it is. . . . It's your Unconscious trying to tell you what is wrong. Once we know *that*, we can get to work to put it right, and then *you'll* get right. Get quite well again."

All very well for Nurse Weston to talk, but how could he tell Stortford about these dreams—always about feet, generally his own, but sometimes . . . *hers*. They would drive him mad. He was getting so conscious of his feet that he was beginning to think of them as he walked, and that caused him to stumble. And it tired him so terribly to watch them; be aware of them; make sure that they were going where they should; behaving quite normally and looking quite normal too—especially

456

as to colour. Not red. Last night again. Three dreams, each about feet: and that mocking *punning* that was so often a feature of these idiotic but sinister nightmares.

He had dreamed that he was toiling, with infinite difficulty and weariness, up a steep and difficult path that led, he knew, to the Gates of Heaven. Through the dreadful gloom of a dreary minatory landscape, pursued by some undefined but awful Fear, he climbed, fighting for breath and aching with pain. . . . At last he reached the plateau and beheld a wall of immeasurable height in which were gates of gold. As he drew near, more in terror than in hope, he was aware of a shining Presence that waited before the Gates of Heaven; and he was aware that he stood, a humble suppliant, before St. Peter. Before he could kneel or speak, the Keeper of the Gate glanced at him, pointed at his feet, and turned away. Looking down, he was aware that his feet were splashed with red. But he sprang eagerly forward, almost reached the door, shaped like the eye of a needle, that gave access through one of the great gates, when a loud and terrible voice cried:

'*Two Feet from Heaven*,' and he sank, fainting, to the ground, knowing in his agony of mind and body that he could never approach nearer to the Gate, never come within two feet of it.

Feet . . . Feet . . . Feet. . . . There was *blood* upon his feet.

He had awakened from his uneasy sleep, sweating, dry-mouthed and afraid, afraid to the depths of his soul.

Sister Grey had come in later, talked to him as only she could talk to him, and given him a tablet.

He had dreamed again—of feet.

He was in a great Cathedral officiating or

assisting at some important ceremony of most solemn and most sacred significance. Chanting a hymn, the choir headed a procession of superior beneficed clergy and high Cathedral officials in surplice and cassock, stole and academic hood; some, at the end of the procession, in episcopal robe and mitre. And among them, in a gap that left him very noticeable, prominent and exposed, he walked, correctly dressed for this most solemn occasion, but he was trembling and afraid of he knew not what. And suddenly, he was aware that his shoes were of leather that was scarlet as a soldier's coat, scarlet as—Sin. Then a great voice reverberated through the long-drawn aisle and fretted vault, beginning:

'Though *thy* sins be as scarlet . . .' and all men knew that the words applied to him, referred to him; and all eyes turned toward him and gazed at his feet, the most conspicuous object in the Cathedral . . . in the World . . . in the Universe.

Again he awoke, bathed in sweat and shaking with fear, only to fall asleep again and to dream that he was back in his own church, sitting in his accustomed seat near the altar.

The church was empty and there was no light, although he was aware of his surroundings. He knelt to pray. Light came, and grew slowly. It emanated with a kind of phosphorescent glow from a block of marble, the pediment of a statue, a pediment on which there was some small object, disproportionately small in fact, and not a statue. He could not see distinctly, but the light was increasing and he was aware that this tomb or statue-base was something new in the church of which he knew every stone, every beam, every little jewel of window-glass, every inch of flagged floor and of walls and roof. Something new and— strange. The light grew brighter and he saw that what the flat top of the tomb or pediment bore, was but two fragments of a statue, the feet of a statue, and they were a woman's feet. As he stared, again in fear and horror, the feet became recognisable, familiar, feet that he had seen a thousand times. . . . He knew them as he did his own; he knew the shoes that they wore. He had once tried to put them on his own feet, for his own were small, even for a rather small man. He was looking at *her*—but nothing of her was visible but her feet—feet that he had praised and loved.

Suddenly letters of brass, that turned to letters of fire, burned brightly on the side of the pediment; and he read with feelings which were a strange mixture of pain, fear, horror, grief and a repulsion that was almost disgust:

These are two feet—from Heaven.

When he awoke he found that he was weeping.

Yes—it was easy for Sister Grey to talk, but how could he tell those dreams, with their dreadful insistence on the subject of feet, an insistence that was driving him insane, and their dreadful punning on the word 'feet'; telling him that he must live and die outside any earthly or heavenly Heaven, and only two feet from it. . . . Insisting that *hers* were two feet from Heaven itself, as indeed he knew they were, in spite of the fact that he hated to think about her—hated it so greatly that almost he hated her, hated her even as he hated himself.

Of course Stortford would very soon find out all about her, if he told him about those dreams, about her, and why he left her—and before long everything would come out.

Yes! He *had* been a fool to come here, not only wasting his time and his money, but inflicting extra suffering upon himself unnecessarily, as well as running into great danger of discovery and the exposure of his terrible secret. For them to say that they could cure him, if he would help them to find out what was troubling him, was like telling a man you could cure his head-ache if he'd agree to your cutting his head off.

He had been a fool to come here—and if he had never done so, he would never have met Elspeth Grey!

CHAPTER 6

IT was the busy custom of Drs. Fieldwicke and Stortford to lunch together at Marstone Park upon alternate days, and discuss the progress of their patients; Dr. Stortford reporting matters of note to the senior partner, and making proposals and suggestions in the light thereof.

"And what d'you make of the Reverend Richard Neystoke now?" asked Dr. Fieldwicke, one day in the second week of that patient's sojourn in the nursing-home. "Personally I'm inclined to like him very much, and to feel rather sorry for him. . . . Got anything, yet?"

"No-o-o . . . No," replied Stortford slowly and thoughtfully, as he deposited his cigarette-ash in his coffee-saucer. "He has defeated me so far, though I fancy I may be on a scent that will lead somewhere. . . . But that he's thoroughly on the defensive, I feel certain. He'd give anything to be cured, except the one thing—the price he'll have to pay—confession of something or other."

"Like that, is it? You think he's really conscious of what it is that's causing the neurosis?" asked Fieldwicke.

"I am pretty sure of it. But I think there's considerable subconscious trouble too. If he'd confide in Sister Grey, if not in Nurse Weston or me, and get the conscious part of it adjusted, I think we'd soon find what's festering in his subconscious mind. Something pretty serious, I should say."

"Dreams at all interesting?"

"Only as being good stock stuff. Tremendous mother-complex. Loathed and feared his father, and has made his Old Testament God in his father's image. Strong inferiority-complex. And he's up against his job, and doesn't know it. . . . Dreamed the other night that he was conducting a funeral in Westminster Abbey and that with surplice, cassock and stole he was wearing very bright red boots and a cocked-hat with plumes!"

"Pretty indicative," smiled Fieldwicke.

"Yes. Another night he dreamed he was preaching from his own pulpit and was suddenly aware that his voice was making no sound at all. He had been struck dumb. And when he went to flee from the pulpit, he found that he had no trousers nor boots. He prayed that his bright red socks might be spared unto him, but, no, they too vanished and he was barefooted."

"Ah! Bare-footed. Did that strike him as particularly bad?" asked Dr. Fieldwicke.

"Yes. I asked him that, and he said it seemed an appalling thought that the congregation should see his bare feet."

"Very interesting—and helpful," mused Fieldwicke. "You'll follow that line up, eh? . . . I suppose it is the feet-of-clay-exposed-to-the-world idea again?"

"Probably—but I'm not sure. He professes to be thoroughly happy and comfortable in his job. Won't confess to any dissatisfaction with his work as Vicar of Wakefield, or wherever it is."

"Quite pleased with himself, eh?"

"Say 'satisfied'. Without smugness or conceit. Simply says that everything is all right there, and that he doesn't worry about his work in the least."

"Nevertheless, it looks as though he'll have to change his job if he wants to save himself alive," mused the Doctor. "The subconscious is never wrong. And what else is that cocked-hat-with-canonical-dress but ridicule on the part of the Unconscious?"

"A clear case. Also a nice inferiority-complex exposure, in the no trousers and bare feet dream," agreed Stortford.

"Yes. Unless, as I say, there is something very special about the bare feet. That certainly will be worth following up. . . . And what about the bright red boots and then the bright red socks. One would have expected him to dream that he found himself in the pulpit wearing nothing but his little short under-vest, if his unconscious was going to treat him to a straight-forward inferiority dream. . . . Bare feet . . . And the congregation mustn't see them . . ." mused the Doctor. "I think you've got something there."

The two psychologists sat in thought concerning their interesting patient.

"There was a point about the funeral dream that interested me," said Stortford suddenly. "Without any particular reason or object, I happened to ask him, after he had finished describing the dream, whether he knew who it was he was burying. To my surprise and considerable interest, he was quite taken aback by the question. Not exactly upset or alarmed, but confused and bothered. He declared that he did not know who was in the coffin, but he was a second or two late in answering. He hesitated quite definitely. Now that's queer—because obviously he either knew or did not know—and there was no need for him to stop to think about it. Very well; if he did not know, there wasn't the slightest reason for hesitating—therefore he did know."

"And denied it," said the Doctor.

"Knew, and denied that he knew," affirmed Stortford. "And that is very interesting and may be important."

"Yes . . . I don't see how we can connect it up with the bare-feet dream, do you?"

"No. Not yet," mused Stortford.

"I like him very much indeed," he added. "So does Matron—and that speaks well for him."

"Has she any ideas about his trouble yet, or hasn't he loosened-up to her either?"

"Told her nothing, so far. But she thinks she has found something. Won't say anything until she is sure. Cautious lass. Sure but slow."

"Well," said Dr. Fieldwicke, rising and extinguishing his cigarette, "I must be going. . . . If, later, you really feel that Neystoke has defeated you, I'll . . ."

"Oh, no, no," replied Stortford hastily, "I only meant—so far. I'm going to cut his life up into a series of parts, make him do his utmost to re-live them in memory, and then tell me the salient facts that he has recaptured from each. . . . I may get fresh clues and new lines, if not something solid."

"Right. I'll give you another week with him, for that," agreed the Doctor.

CHAPTER 7

Elspeth Grey, briefly resting, sat and sipped her tea before the fire in her cosy and tastefully-furnished sitting-room, thinking over the problem of the most interesting of all her patients. Most interesting, because most appealing and most attractive? Perhaps. Certainly, apart from the absorbing question of his illness and its cause, he was a most likeable person; so considerate, so grateful for any help one could give him; and, in spite of his own misery and suffering, so unselfishly anxious to help any other sufferer in any way that was possible. He could and did help others far more than he could help himself.

She would have to break down that stubborn resistance somehow or other. Nor had she any doubt as to her ability to do it, provided he could stay the course, would stand the mental torture, and not run away, his cure uncompleted and his last state worse than his first.

There was undoubtedly a secret; something that he was hiding and would do his utmost to hide; and that something was what was killing him. How many years had he spent in trying to thrust it from his mind, out of sight, recognition and knowledge, deep down into his unconscious, there to fester and to poison the well-spring and source of mental and physical health, the source of life itself?

If only he would fully and truthfully describe his dreams and . . .

A knock came at the door and Nurse Weston entered, radiant and excited.

"Got something for you, Matron!" she said,

almost before she had closed the door. "Mr. Neystoke. Really useful, I do believe!"

Elspeth Grey was aware, with a sense almost of shock, if not shame, that her heart sank slightly, that she was ever so faintly hurt, ever such a trifle disappointed that Richard Neystoke should have consistently refused her his confidence—and given it to Nurse Weston. Very promptly and firmly she crushed the miserable seedlings of such unworthy feelings, and smiled brightly at her excellent and enthusiastic co-adjutor in difficult good works.

"Splendid, my dear," she said. "I *am* glad. Well done. . . . Has he told you what it really is that . . ."

"Oh, no, Matron," replied Nurse Weston. "Not a word out of him. Not even about a dream. But I know why he goes down to the beach alone, when he can, and why he is *always* dashing into the bathroom."

The expression on the Matron's face was very rewarding, as well as her quiet:

"Good for you, Nurse. The Doctor will thank you for that, if . . ."

"Oh, there's no doubt," Nurse Weston assured her. "I got the idea from the fact that there was sand *inside* his socks one day, and grains at the bottom of his bed—coupled with the other fact that when he rushes off to the bathroom he does *not* wash his hands there, although he uses the soap and a towel!"

"Good work. . . . How do you know?" asked Elspeth Grey.

"Traps," was the reply. "Three times running; and then—the keyhole!"

"My dear!" smiled the Matron.

"Yes. On Saturday, I saw him go into the bath-room and waited till he came out. Exactly nine minutes. The bath-water ran for three minutes. I went in as soon as he was round the corner, and noticed that the wash-hand basin was dry, the bath wet, the soap wet, and a small towel wet. He had not had time for a bath, and he had not washed his hands in the basin. Why run bath-water to wash his hands? . . . I dried the basin thoroughly, dried the bath, got a new piece of soap and two clean, dry towels, one small and one very large. Then I locked the door and went and paid him a visit, staying about a quarter of an hour, talking about interesting and significant dreams of which I had been told by various patients. As I went out again, I said I'd like him to come for a walk with me at three o'clock. Then I hung about at the corner of the corridor, with one eye on his door. Sure enough, out he came at about ten to three, dressed to go out, but still wearing his bed-room slippers. I hurried along and unlocked the bathroom door. . . . When he came out a few minutes later, the basin was as dry as a bone, the bath wet, the soap wet, and the small towel wet. . . . Suddenly I saw it, and it was the slippers that gave me the clue! Although I was sure, I checked-up again and got the same results. Basin not used; small towel only used—and no time for a bath, anyway. *Then* I used the key-hole, the very next time.

"Sand inside his socks and traces in the bed, that Monday when he had gone straight to bed after coming in from his walk. After lunch to-day, I told him I shouldn't be able to go for our afternoon stroll and suggested that he should take a long walk by himself, right round the grounds, and then have a good rest and tea in his room. Ten minutes after he set off, I took the direct path to the beach and there he was. And what do you think he was doing? *Paddling!* Or rather, standing in the water with his feet and ankles covered. . . ."

"Oh!" whispered Elspeth Grey softly. "I see now."

"Yes," continued Nurse Weston eagerly. "There's no possibility of doubt. He bathes his feet a dozen times a day; a score of times; oftener, if you count his morning and evening bath and his paddling in the sea. . . . Significant and symbolical, I should say."

"Most," agreed the Matron. "Really sound work, Lilian. You must tell the Doctor at to-morrow's interview. He'll give you a very good mark indeed. It may prove most helpful. Invaluable, probably. Perhaps lead to complete success. Clear the whole trouble up. Well done, you."

"Thank you, Matron," beamed Nurse Weston. "Shall I say anything to Mr. Neystoke about it? Let him know that I am perfectly well aware that he spends half his time in washing his immaculately beautiful feet?"

Elspeth Grey considered, or appeared to consider, this question for a long minute.

"No," she said at length. "Tell the Doctor all about it, but say nothing to Mr. Neystoke. A very great deal may depend on how, and when, he is accused of the—cleanly habit. If his guard is down and it is done suddenly at the right moment, he may say something illuminating; give himself— and his secret—away, before he has time to think. Anyway, the knowledge that Mr. Neystoke has this habit should certainly give the Doctor the key to the mystery which the poor man is making of some incident of his past. It ought to be the beginning of the end of his trouble. . . . Well done, Lilian."

CHAPTER 8

Richard Neystoke got into bed, switched off his bed-side light and settled down to an earnest and honest endeavour to *remember*, in accordance with Dr. Stortford's urgent exhortation. Before going to sleep, he must do his utmost to re-call what he could of the events of his childhood up to the time of his going to Prep-School. He was to try to discover what were his very earliest recollections of all.

This preliminary remembrance-task, covering the period of the first seven years of his life, was simple and unobjectionable enough. He could be absolutely open and frank about it, and tell Stortford everything. It would be the later periods that would be difficult—and one would be impossible. He would have to select, when he came to that part; to edit, to skirt round; perhaps he would have to prevaricate, even to lie . . .

Then what on earth was the good of his being here—in this place where they pried, searched, analysed and pursued one's secret shrinking thoughts as they drew back, shrank away, took cover, or fled? Fled in terror, pursued by the Truth, by the Hound of Heaven.

Yes, the Hound of Heaven would catch him yet; and then what would he do, what would become of him; of his fair fame, dignity and position; of his wife and daughter? . . . He must protect himself against Stortford. When it came to *the* period, he would refuse to remember; he would close his mind to all recollections; and what he had buried so deeply, once and for all, in his mind, he would keep buried. If he would *not* remember it, they couldn't remember it for him; could not dig it up and expose it to the light of . . . truth. No, he'd just forget what was better forgotten; refuse to answer; lie, deny, baffle him and escape his nets of questioning.

But to-night it was all right; he could remember to the very best of his ability; and to-morrow he could remember without inhibition, and pour it forth to Stortford without fear or concealment of anything at all. Any question could be answered immediately and with perfect candour.

And now to close his eyes, relax, compose himself and throw his mind back to his third birthday and to earlier days if possible.

§2

I am three years old to-day, he thought, and everybody is especially kind and good to me. Even my father smiles with a bright flash of white teeth shining between his moustache and beard. His lips show red too, and I hate them. Yes, that's the truth, the simple fact of the matter; I realise it, for I am afraid he will kiss me. He does so occasionally, when Mother is present, but never when he and I are alone together; and I dislike it intensely. I loathe it. Why? Partly because his mouth always smells of smoked cigar-stumps, which is the most dreadful smell on earth; or of wine or whisky, which also are horrible smells. Partly because I think of the Wolf who *was* Red-Riding-Hood's Grandmother and said: 'All the better to eat you with.' I *know* that some-day I shall be forced to say: 'What big teeth you have, Papa,' and what will happen then?

He kisses me, and I very nearly say it. What a terrible thing if I had actually done so! Imagine being eaten on one's third birthday. . . . Mother took me up on to her lap and we hugged and hugged each other; and then she gave me a wonderful and beautiful ball. Later in the day it rolled away from me and went down some sort of drain, and I suffered my first great grief. I can remember the pain, horror and shock of that bereavement, with the utmost distinctness, to this very day. I can see the ball rolling; its colours, bright in the sunlight, giving me immense delight; and then that sudden and shattering eclipse. I can also remember the sympathy of Jane, a maid whom I loved, and her promise that she would recover the ball if she had to have the drain up to do it. I did not believe her, but I loved her the more. My father's attitude was not one of sym- pathy but of contempt for me, a cry-baby. Mother comforted me to the best of her ability, but I do not recollect that I ever had another such brilliant, faery ball. It was almost worth the loss, though, to sit on her lap, dissolved in tears, but with a mel- ancholy pleasant sense of a bereavement that had called forth such a demonstration of her love, sympathy and understanding.

Can I recover anything earlier than those mem- ories of my third birthday? No. . . . Yes. I can. It is more like seeing a picture in which I appear, than remembering events. I can see a fair-haired child sitting in a large and gaudily-painted wheel- barrow precariously conducted down a garden path by a boy whose ambition is greater than his strength and skill. There is a sudden lurch and the fair-haired child is flung out on to a low rockery edging a fish-pond. The wheel-barrow over-turns completely and covers him. That is the picture and I am the child in the barrow; but I cannot remember any pain or anything else about the affair, except sitting later in my Mother's lap while she hugs me to her, rocks herself to and fro, and, as the tears run down her cheeks, repeatedly cries: *'He might have been killed! He might have been drowned!'*

Curiously enough, I do not see this in a picture as I see the wheel-barrow incident, but actually remember it.

I was only two years old then, though I may have been nearly three. Stortford is welcome to all that.

What else is there in my third year? Nothing in particular, except the great love I had for my mother and that she had for me. I remember the agony I suffered, one night, when she did not come home at dinner-time. She and my father had gone to London, and had missed their return train. When she did not come to say good-night to me, and I learned that she had not returned, I burst into tears and refused to be comforted, for I knew that she was dead. Something terrible had happened. I should never see her again, and I wanted to die. I cannot recollect that I was in the slightest degree interested in the fate of my father. . . .

In my fourth year I fell in love—and this indisputable fact may interest these psychologists who persecute me so . . .

I am four, and I am in love with a wonderful little human doll who lives near us, and to whose party I have come. I have never felt like this before. I know that it is a new, beautiful and poignant sensation, although I do not know those words. I do not want to sit beside her, put my arm about her, or kiss her, as I do my mother, but only to look at her. And I want to give her something, anything, everything I possess. I try to think of some gift that might be acceptable to her. I would even give her the long-lost faery ball if it came back to me.

When the time came for me to go home, and I had to say good-bye to her, I felt myself going hot and then cold all over, and as though I should suffocate. I am quite certain that my heart per-formed physical as well as amorous, or rather spiritual, antics for I felt as though I should die—a passing faintness, of course. And I was dumb, bringing Jane, who was in charge of me, to shame, and causing her some annoyance.

'Such a stupid bad-behaved boy. Have enough to say for yourself as a rule. Where's your man-ners?'

That night I lay awake to think of her. All next day I thought of her and longed to see her again. Indisputably it was a case of love at four years old. I loved her, and was in love with her—as truly, as identically as was ever any adult in love. She became an obsession, and I thought of little else. I pondered ways of introducing her name when I talked with Mother or Jane, and once at least, I undertook, alone, the long and difficult journey to her house and back, that I might perchance get a glimpse of her at a window or in her garden. I did not venture to call at the house, of course, being for some reason terribly afraid lest I should betray myself, and my state of mind be discovered. That would be appalling. It did not bear contemplation. Why, people might laugh at me, or, far worse, say something slighting about Her. How long my passion lasted, I do not know, but it must have been of some months' duration, for it began at Christmas time and it was not until the approach of August and my departure to the sea-side that I summed up courage to tell Mother that I should so like to see Claire Bell again.

Mother was all acquiescence at once, declared that she was delighted to think that I had a 'little friend,' and promised to ask her to tea next week.

Claire came. After conquering our shyness we got on splendidly. I showed her all my toys and then took her out into the garden to give her a swing. . . . I was in an ecstasy of worship. . . . When she got off the swing, she put her arms about my neck, kissed me on the lips, and killed my first love-affair dead.

She had spoilt everything. I could not explain it . . . I could only know it. When Mother promised that Claire should come again, I told her that I didn't want to see Claire Bell any more. When, after the holidays, I was invited to go to tea with Claire, I flatly and firmly refused to go. My first sudden *revulsion*, and flight from what I no longer liked.

My first fugue, as they call it here.

Doubtless this will interest Stortford—and shed some brilliant or baleful light upon my complex character or the nature of my mysterious 'Unconscious' of which they talk so much. . . .

That happened in my fourth year. What can I remember of my fifth?

But Richard Neystoke recalled but little of the events of that year of his life, for at this point in his researches he fell asleep.

CHAPTER 9

So it was the period of his life which was spent at Prep-School that he had to resurrect to-night, was it? The years from seven to fourteen, during which he grew from childhood to boyhood. Well, that was sufficiently safe ground. He'd have no need to shy away, like a frightened horse, from anything that he did, or that happened to him, then. Nor would Stortford be able to dig anything up. Anything that would be embarrassing, much less terrifying, that is; for he'd inevitably get something or other out of the soil of his mind, however unpromising that soil might be.

An unpleasant expression, come to think of it, for soil was an ambiguous word. The soil of his mind. The filthy soil that was his mind. . . . Was his mind soiled? Soiled beyond all cleansing? . . . Repentance, forgiveness of sins, absolution, as *soil*ment. . . .

He had repented. God knew he had repented. Or had he only regretted and mistaken regret and remorse for repentance? Certainly he had never confessed. Except to God, of course, and what was the point in doing that, since God knew already. . . . *Thou God seest me.* God saw him do it. So where was the sense in kneeling down and describing what he had done? And not only did God know that he did it; but, being omniscient, had known that he was going to do it—and had not prevented him. From the beginning of Time, which had no beginning, God, who had no beginning, knew that he would do that deed. Therefore it was ordained, and he *had* to do it. If he, Richard Neystoke, had had any choice in the matter, there would have been a doubt as to whether he would do it or not—right up to the moment of his doing or not doing it—and God would not have known which it was to be. God himself would not have known what was going to happen—which was absurd. God *knew*—and Richard Neystoke *had* to commit the crime. Then why should God punish him thus? Why make his life a hell of mental and physical suffering? Was God just? Was there even any God at all? . . .

But this would not do. He had been told to dig into his boyhood's memories and see what he could find that might be helpful to Dr. Stortford in discovering the cause of the complex or neurosis or whatever they called it, that was making him so ill.

Well—he wouldn't find it there. Nor during his Public School years, nor at Oxford. It was hidden in the story of the next phase of his life. And he'd keep it hidden too. If they couldn't do anything for him without his giving his great secret away, he would have to go without. He had been a fool to come, but he hadn't really understood what it meant. Yet he'd never have met Sister Grey. . . . Though perhaps the less he dwelt on that aspect of the subject the better.

But, again, this would not do. He'd be asleep before he had recalled anything from his Prep-School days.

I am seven and have just arrived at Merrivale School, he thought. I am heart-broken and in the depths of grief and despair at being separated from my mother. If I could possibly find my way home I would run away, in spite of what my father might say or do, just to see Mother again, feel her arms about me, kiss her and hug her with all my strength.

How *could* she have done it? How *could* she have borne to send me away from her, and not see me again for months? It was Father's doing, of course. I know, not only because it is just what he would do, but because I heard Mother talking to him about me, and caught her words 'educated at home'; 'have a good tutor'; 'much too delicate to go yet'; 'more sensitive than other boys'; and similar good reasons for not parting with me. The only gleam of comfort in the blackness of my wretchedness is the thought that I shall not see Father while I am here.

But gradually I find that school is not such a bad place, after all; that the Head-master's wife is very kind indeed, and that the Matron is very friendly and motherly; that the Head is not as fierce as he looks; that the Masters are quite all right and that many of the chaps are quite decent. . . . I get through the first term fairly well, though I am not very much good at games. The bigger boys are apt to be a little scornful of me, but I make friends with a few of the younger ones.

How clearly I remember the end of the first term and my return home. I am almost insane with excitement and joy. And my first sight of Mother! It *hurts* me that I cannot give greater expression to my love than by kissing and hugging her. I want to bury myself alive in her when she puts her arms about me.

Father was pleasant and friendly at first, but in a day or two began to find fault with me. He would mock the way in which I spoke to Mother and be unpleasant and sarcastic. . . .

All too soon I am back again at school, and this term, something happens that may interest Stortford. I fall in love again. Not this time with a girl, but with another boy, one Harry Johnson, and it is not merely a case of liking and friendship. I feel towards him as I felt towards Claire Bell. My heart beats perceptibly quicker when he comes into the room, and my breathing is affected.

He was not in my class, so I did not see very much of him, but I made opportunities of meeting him when I could, and of being near him. At night, I lay awake and thought about him, imagined him speaking to me, pictured myself daring to ask him to be my friend. I think I should have trembled from head to foot, and have been unable to say a word, if he had come up to me and said something nice and friendly.

I tried to tell Mother all about him when I wrote my weekly letter home, and I pretended that we were really friends, sat beside each other at table, and walked together when we went out in a 'crocodile' or for a sweat-run. I described things as I should have loved them to be, instead of as they were. One day I had a bright idea. I would give him a present.

I saved hard and accumulated a shilling. What should I buy him? It was a great problem, and exercised my mind for days. Perhaps I had better speak to him, and, when I knew him better, I should be able to find out what he would like. I might have more money by then, too.

And all this time I am really practising self-denial that I may save the more. I delight in going without sweets, ginger-beer, buns and oranges, for I feel I am doing something for him. I experience real pleasure in this mild mortification of the flesh; but I hope that some day he will know, and will admire me the more and love me even better. . . .

One day I find I am standing beside him on the touch-line as we watch a first-eleven match and scream our shrill encouragement to the heroes who are upholding the honour of Merrivale. I suppose the excitement gives me confidence and courage, for suddenly I throw off my normal shyness and diffidence, slip my hand under his arm and say,

"Johnson . . . Will you be my friend? . . . I do love—I mean like—you so."

Johnson stares at me amazed, incredulous, and for the moment, dumb. Then he realises that he is not dreaming and has heard aright. He recovers the power of speech—and uses it.

"What *beastly* cheek!" he cries. "A kid like *you!* Friends with *me?* I've got a friend; two friends; ten friends so sucks to you, young Neystoke. . . . Beetle off—and don't speak to me again, or I'll . . . *Shoot!* Wilson! *Shoot! . . . Goal! Hooray . . .*"

Amidst the cheering, I creep away and manage to reach the empty dressing-room before anyone speaks to me and makes me burst into tears. For many days thereafter I know what real suffering is. But, being still a child, my mind is resilient and I recover before the end of term.

By the time I have got home to Mother, I feel that I *hate* Johnson.

My second revulsion and flight. Fugue.

But that was, nevertheless, a case of pure un-adulterated love. It was neither friendship, liking, affection, nor anything of the sort. It was sexual love, without the faintest trace of sex-feeling or conscious sex urge or desire, of course. All I wanted was to love him, serve him in any way I could, give him anything I had. I wanted to see him, be near him, listen to him and admire him; be allowed to love him; and, oh, how I wanted him to love me.

Since Dr. Stortford is of the Freudian school and refers every possible human motive, act, thought and deed ultimately to the sex-impulse, he's welcome to make what he can of that episode. Personally, I like Jung's theory best and I shall . . .

shall . . . what?

    Richard Neystoke yawned again and fell asleep.

CHAPTER 10

And to-night I am to review my Public School days and make a note of every salient event that I can recall, thought Neystoke, as wearily he laid him down to rest, some twenty-four hours later.

It had been rather a bad day, on the whole. Dr. Stortford had upset him with his grilling questioning and had forced him, once or twice, to prevaricate. No—to tell down-right lies; and he hated doing that. But there were some things about which one could not tell the truth. Might as well walk into a Police-station, give oneself up, and have done with it.

Yet what was the good of his remaining on here if he did not play the game? They had invented it, and if you played it with them properly, they could cure you; end the conflict that was tearing you to pieces; and give you the rest, for need of which you were sick—sick unto death almost.

Well—he couldn't do it. Not beyond a certain point. But being the wizard psychologists that they were, perhaps that could enable him to make a new adjustment to life without his having to confess his secret to them? Besides, they always talked about this Unconscious Mind and how your physical and mental health completely depend upon it. If it is dissatisfied with what you are doing; if you have thrust some dark secret, some piece of ugly knowledge, some evil or terrible experience, deep down into it, in order that you may forget, then that secret, evil knowledge, or terrible experience will fester there, they said— poisoning the wells and springs of Life; and the Unconscious will revolt, will strive to get rid of it, will worry and gnaw and assail your conscious mind and body until it *does* get relief and satisfaction. It *will* have light let into the dark recesses where the secret hides—the Light of Truth.

According to Stortford the troubled Unconscious must have its air and light just as human beings, animals, birds, trees and grass must have the physical air and the light of day. The voice of the troubled Unconscious must be heard and obeyed, or you will be ill, you will go mad, you will die. . . . But my dreadful secret is in my *conscious* mind. I know what I have done. I remember it daily; and nightly I think of it. I dream of it. How then can it be 'buried in the Unconscious', and how can the Unconscious be so troubled and diseased as to make my mind and body sick?

No. There is no health in me and none to be obtained here, since the Unconscious is their sole field of operation.

But I must go through with it now—and I may get help of some kind from someone, somehow. Perhaps Sister Grey . . . ?

But I have to recall the years I spent at my Public School, and tell Stortford anything that I can remember which might be of the slightest psychological significance, interest and importance.

I am at School, he thought, the great and famous School of which I am justly proud and shamefully unworthy. But although I was there for quite four years I really remember very little of the details of my life as a Public School boy. Perhaps because I was quite happy and because I led an undistinguished and uneventful life, being neither near the top nor the bottom of the class and examination-lists. I never won a prize nor earned a thrashing. Or, rather, I never got one.

Once the grief, misery and pain of again parting

with Mother was over, I took to the routine like a
duck to water, and, but for the separation from
her, liked life at school almost as well as that at
home. I was away from Father and able to bear
absence from Mother far better than I could at
Prep-School, being older, tougher and more self-
sufficient.

No. I can remember nothing of any importance.
Life at that school seems to have been uneventful,
peaceful and happy, and to have passed with
extraordinary rapidity.

Perhaps the most important memory, from
Stortford's point of view, is that of my great friendship with Arthur Dellingham, and the trouble that
old Jemmings made for us. He was a beast, and
not even a just beast; one of those men who are
better fitted for anything other than school-
mastering, and take to it because they are fit for
nothing else. He must have hated boys and hated
his job, for he was a picture of dyspeptic and
disagreeable misery, and lived in a perpetual state
of resentment. The only pleasure that he seemed
to get out of life was convicting boys of sin and
getting them into trouble. I don't say he was an
actual and practising sadist, but I do say that the
infliction of punishment gave him pleasure; and
when he couldn't inflict it personally, he loved to
procure it. I never knew an Englishman so filled
with *schadenfreud.*

Arthur Dellingham was a very much older and
bigger boy than I, and we were mutually attracted.
I liked him enormously, and the more I saw of
Arthur the fonder I became of him. I did not love
him in the way in which I had loved Claire Bell
and Harry Johnson; but as I would have loved an
elder brother.

It would have filled me with happiness if Arthur
could have come home with me and lived at our

house. I should have greatly desired it, and rejoiced exceedingly. . . .

But thinking it over, I believe that Arthur loved me as I had loved Harry Johnson, for he lost no opportunity of speaking to me, being in my company, and arranging future meetings and walks. At a Public School, it is not altogether easy for a big boy to be a great deal with a small one, but Arthur and I contrived to meet very frequently —or rather, he contrived it. And apparently he had the same urge to give me things, that I had when I was in love with Johnson, for he treated me most generously at the tuck-shop. Poor Arthur was terribly jealous too, and hated to see me talking or walking with anyone else.

Now, in what way was his very real love for me 'unhealthy', to use the term approved by the Jemmings of this world? In what way was my affection for him unhealthy? I am perfectly certain that Arthur was all the better and the finer for an emotion that was objective and that made him generous and self-denying and protective and self-forgetful. What higher, nobler and better human manifestation, act, attitude or spiritual occupation can there be than loving? God is Love—which means that Good is Love and that Love is Good.

Enter the beastly Jemmings, treading with miry, clumsy cloven-hoof, upon what was delicate and beautiful beyond his earthly understanding.

One Sunday afternoon Arthur and I go for a long walk, find a green and pleasant field, and sit down in the shade of a mighty elm that grows up through a high, thin hedge. Presently, I lie back and stare up into the great tree's green canopy and Arthur leans upon his elbow and talks. I can remember much of it now, for a little later there was reason to do so.

"Golly! I shall hate leaving, next year," says

Arthur, bringing me back to earth. "Hate even to think of it."

"Why?" I ask, hoping that I already know the answer.

"Why? Leaving *you*, of course," he replies. "You know that. I can't bear to think that you may come and lie down, perhaps, under this very tree, with some other chap. Someone I hate, I expect. I hate him in advance, anyhow. . . . Lord! I shall miss you, Rickie. . . . You'll faithfully promise to come and stay with us, every hols, after I have left, won't you?"

"Of course," I promise earnestly, and with every intention of keeping my promise, for except for Mother, Arthur is the only person of whom I am truly fond and to whom I can talk quite freely and naturally, without any fear of being ridiculed.

"Good," says poor old Arthur, and adds, "I am most frightfully fond of you, Rickie. . . . I think I love you more than I have ever loved anybody. *Anybody*—including my people. And as for girls . . . !"

Poor funny old Arthur; a most unusual boy.

By and by he adds: "I wish you loved me as much as I love you, Rickie. . . ."

"*Oh, you do, do you!* . . ." replied the voice of Jemmings from beyond the hedge. "Very interesting. . . . Dellingham and Neystoke, both of Stanwick's House, I think. . . . Go back to school at once and tell your House-master that I sent you. . . . I'll tell him *why* myself."

We sprang up and stared in amazement at the hedge. There, peering, and parting the leaves and branches, was the man whom every boy in the School disliked and whom those of his own House hated. Miserably we made our way back, our hearts full of resentment, anger and a sense of injustice. What had we done to have our afternoon spoilt and to be reported by the loathsome Jemmings? Arthur seemed to me to be in an unwarrantable state of anxiety and fright.

"He'll go to the Head," he prophesied miserably. "I swear I'll commit suicide and leave a stiff note for the Coroner, if the Head believes Jemmings, and I have got you into trouble. I shall be sacked, of course, but he might sack you as well as me. . . . I'll tell him that I'll *do* it too, if he punishes you. . . . The chaps ought to boo that beast Jemmings out of the place. If they all did it, all the time, he'd have to go. Perhaps the Head'll believe us though. Unless Jemmings lies like a . . . like a . . . like the lying swine he is. . . ."

"But why should the Head do anything to us at all?" I asked in great puzzlement. "We weren't out of bounds or trespassing or anything. There's no rule against our going for a Sunday afternoon walk together, is there? . . . What's the row about?"

"Oh, a sneaking beast like Jemmings can always work up a row about two chaps chumming, if they are of different ages and sizes," replied Dellingham.

"What on earth has their age and size to do with it?" I asked, bewildered. "If it's all right when they are of the same age and size, why shouldn't they be special friends if . . ."

"Oh, you'll find out fast enough," replied Arthur unhappily. "It's a foul shame. . . . I'd sooner have quarrelled with you for keeps, than have got you into a row, Rickie. Specially a filthy row like this. I never thought . . . I swear I'll tell the Head that everybody in the School knows Jemmings is a beast, and only happy when he is getting someone into a row. . . ."

He fell miserably silent, and strode along so fast that I could scarcely keep up with him.

"Think of our maters . . ." he said, as we came in sight of School, and it seemed to me that Arthur thought of others far more than of himself, although he believed he was in danger of disgrace, a flogging, or expulsion, and probably of all three.

"Well! We'll speak the truth," he said as we parted, "and if Jemmings doesn't, I'll call him a damned liar in front of the Head. May as well be bunked for something as for nothing."

Personally, I was more perturbed and puzzled than apprehensive and frightened as Arthur seemed to be; and, as I entered Stanwick House, it struck me that it might be a very sound plan to go straight to the Under House-master, whom I greatly liked and respected, and tell him absolutely all about it. We had broken no rule of which I knew, and it might possibly help Arthur if I could get Mr. Spens to help. He'd believe me all right, and if he told our House-master and he believed too, he might speak to the Head. I had an idea, too, that he wouldn't be frightfully pleased at what Jemmings had done.

Spens eyed me queerly when I had finished telling him, and asked me a number of questions of which I did not see the point. He then took me to the House-master's study and left me outside the door while he went in and talked with Mr. Watkins. By and by, he came and called me into the room, and I had to stand in front of the well-known desk, behind which Watkins always sat entrenched when he interviewed boys who were in any sort of trouble. He too stared at me as though he had never seen me before, and asked me questions about my friendship with Arthur.

"Now, then," said he, when he had finished, "tell me exactly and absolutely truthfully, everything that you and Dellingham said and did while you were lying under the tree."

I did so, to the best of my ability, remembering as much as I could of our conversation.

"Have you really told me everything you said, and that Dellingham said?" he asked, when I had finished; and I assured him that I honestly thought I had told him all that we had talked about, and practically every remark that we had made.

"And now tell me exactly what you *did*; and look me straight in the face while you tell it?" he said, very seriously indeed.

"We did nothing, except lie there," I assured him. "I didn't even throw a stone or pluck a blade of grass."

"And Dellingham? What did he do, besides talking to you?" he asked.

"Nothing, Sir," I replied. "Nothing at all . . . Oh, yes, he did. He took a knife out of his pocket, opened it and kept throwing it down, point first, so that it stuck in the ground."

"Oh, he did, did he?" observed Mr. Watkins, and I thought there was a faint smile under his moustache. "And did Mr. Jemmings catch him red-handed in that nefarious proceeding?"

"Yes, Sir. The knife was sticking in the ground when he spoke through the hedge," I admitted.

"Ah! The knife was sticking in the ground, was it?" he said, and, as he rose to his feet, added, "Who knows what injury the careless knife of the reckless Dellingham may have done to the grass-roots of that field? . . . You may go."

As I scuttled from the room and held the door open for a moment, I heard him say to Spens:

"And who knows what harm our vigilant moralist Jemmings may have done, in an even more valuable field? . . . I think I'll see the Head at once and try to obstruct the course of—er—injustice. . . ."

Next morning I was sent to the Headmaster's study, my heart in my boots, and terrified almost to speechlessness by fear of I knew not what. There were Jemmings, Watkins and Dellingham, the last red-eyed but looking pale as Death and wan as a ghost, evidently terrified too. Also completely bewildered, I thought.

The Head questioned me about the events of the previous afternoon; and then, as Mr. Watkins had done, bade me fully and faithfully describe all that happened. Conquering my terror as well as I could, I complied to the best of my ability.

When I had finished, the Jovian-fronted majestic Head eyed me long and thoughtfully, and then asked me a final question which I thought a strange one.

"Has Dellingham ever behaved in any way improperly to you?" he asked, and confronting that stupendously great and awe-inspiring man, I for one could not have told a lie, had my need been utterly desperate. As it was, I could reply with the utmost candour.

"No, Sir! He has always been most kind and friendly and affectionate to me, and I am very fond of him indeed."

Did I see a twitch beneath the all-concealing beard and moustache, and something almost like a twinkle in the piercing eyes? From me he looked at Dellingham, who faced him bravely and did not hang his head.

"Your House-master gives you an excellent character," he said slowly. "I believe what you have said. You may go."

Then turning to me, he said:

"You too. I do not believe that you did any damage to that field. You may go." And as we turned thankfully away, he spoke to our accuser in a far less kindly tone, and he spoke in French!

"*Trop de zêle, Monsieur Jemmings,*" said he.

That was the last I heard of the matter, for neither Watkins nor Spens ever referred to it. Nor did Dellingham on the few occasions when we met again. Few, alas, for though he was as friendly as ever, I was tired of him and avoided him. Soon I positively disliked him, and I fear that I showed it.

Another case of my innate fickleness, instability and changefulness. . . . Revulsion, in fact. . . .

I very soon forgot all about him, I must admit.

That is the school-memory that stands out most clearly from the haze of those four happy years, and if it interests Stortford, he is welcome to it.

Another thing that happened one hols might be worth telling, though. One never knows what may be 'significant' and important in the sight of these psychologists. To me, anyhow, it is both significant and symptomatic—of my weakness and lack of self-control.

Also of something slightly abnormal in me. . . .

My Uncle, whom I infinitely preferred to my Father, and who was, I think, quite fond of me, had given me a gun on my fifteenth birthday, a single-barrelled, twenty-four bore, hammerless ejector. Quite a nice little weapon—almost too good for a boy, in fact, especially for one who wasn't really keen on shooting.

"Single-barrel—to teach you to aim straight and not rely on a second chance, Son," he said. "Now remember! A gun is always loaded, and no-one but a criminal lunatic ever points a gun at another person. And when not being aimed, a gun should point at the sky as it rests on your shoulder, or at the ground as it lies in the crook of your arm. . . . And only a particular and special kind of fool ever shoves through a hedge with a gun in his hand. . . . A gun dangerous? Of course it is. So is a razor, not to mention a decayed tooth or a chill on the liver. All Life is dangerous—from crossing the street to eating oysters. You've got to learn to face danger and cope with it. Now you use that gun properly these holidays, and I'll give you a sovereign. If you shoot yourself, I'll take it away from you."

I carefully obeyed him, and treated the gun as though it were alive, malicious, and anxious to get me into trouble, if not to destroy me. I used it once —only, and killed one thing with it; but that was enough. It was a young rabbit, and I shot it *sitting*, miserable young criminal that I was, and so utterly unworthy to be the nephew of that fine sportsman, my Uncle!

I think my real reason for this cold-blooded murder was that I might not have to return to the house and confront him empty-handed, after a day on the rough-shooting land that he rented.

But what makes the incident so memorable to me, and perhaps 'significant' to Stortford, was my curious re-action, my amazing conduct after I had fired that fatal charge of number-fives.

The rabbit jumped, kicked, fell over on its side and lay struggling as though in a fit of convulsions. It must be suffering horribly, I thought; and I felt awful. I must put it out of its misery as quickly as possible. Rushing to where it lay kicking, I banged it on the head with my gun-butt— and then again—and again. But even when it lay still, I could not stop. I was at once horrified, angry, disgusted, frightened, remorseful, and terribly *excited*. I hated fiercely, madly, the creature I had killed. I went on banging and bashing and hammering the pitiful corpse, until it was barely identifiable as that of a rabbit at all. . . . Suddenly I stopped, ran away, and was very sick. After that I lay down, shaken and trembling, and began to weep.

I have never shot bird or beast since. I never fired the gun again (nor did I find a place in my Uncle's will, although supposed to be his favourite!).

Another *revulsion*, flight, 'fugue', and another example of my curious instability of mind and character.

It was a curious experience and as unpleasant as surprising. I have only experienced anything like those emotions on one other occasion, and then they were entirely similar but vastly magnified—the same horrible sort of seizure, to call it that, but a thousand times worse. Of that I will not think. Not to-night, anyhow. And though I will tell Stortford about the rabbit and the effect that my killing it had upon my mind and body, I will not tell him or anyone else, about the other affair. Nor even to dear Elspeth Grey, as I like to call her in my thoughts. . . . Why should I? . . .

I think that is about the only other event of the slightest interest. Stortford told me particularly to remember my experiences with girls during these impressionable, formative years, and exactly to record my attitude toward them. That is soon done. No experiences—and no attitude other than complete indifference.

The only 'woman in my life' was Mother, and I loved her completely, took all my troubles to her, consulted her before ever doing anything, and was never away from her for longer than was necessary. And thinking of her reminds me of my Father and of one other matter that might interest Stortford, though it falls into neither of the two school periods.

During the holidays that intervened between leaving Prep-School and going on to my Public School, I grievously offended him by accidentally

setting fire to his study, and telling him a thump-
ing lie about it; and, in my utter terror, sticking to
it desperately. In the first place, I had no business
to go into the room at all, for it was strictly out of
bounds for everybody in the house. Having gone in
there to borrow a book which he hated lending, I
had no business to strike matches instead of turning on the electric lights, which I feared to do lest
the brilliance betray me, in the dusky twilight,
through the, as yet uncurtained, windows. I suppose I dropped a still glowing match or match-
head into the waste-paper basket, but anyhow,
not long after I had crept out of the room, carefully
shutting the door behind me, there was a smell of
smoke in the house, and the study was found to
be on fire—curtains, chair, desk and the old painted wainscoting being well alight. . . .

It is the effect of the thrashing that is of possible interest. It hurt me immeasurably, and, in
my agony, I howled without shame or restraint.

I believe I have a fine capacity for physical pain
and suffering, due perhaps to a highly-strung and
supersensitive nervous system. I also have a very
thin skin—and my Father had a very strong arm
and a most supple riding-switch. I was very sore
for many days and, in a way, I have been sore ever
since. That it did me harm, I am perfectly certain,
if only because it taught me Fear, the very worst of
all possible lessons that can be taught to any
human being. I don't, of course, mean any special
and proper fear, as in the sense of the burnt child
dreading the fire, but Fear in the absolute. There
is no more deadly, devitalising, destructive mi-
crobe that can assail and poison the human mind
and body. I would never even teach a child to 'fear
God'. Teach it to love God, trust God, obey God,
thank God, worship God, but never teach it to *fear*
God, or anyone or anything else.

Why cannot we teach Love, and labour unceasingly to eradicate Fear? Why cannot we follow Christ's Gospel of Love, if we pretend to call ourselves Christians, and leave primitive Arabic tribal superstitions alone? And what lowest of low and ignorant priests or pastors ever preaches *fear* of Christ? What professing Christian ever takes up the attitude of,

"Look out, Christ is listening! He'll take a most horrible revenge on us. I am terrified to death of Him!"

And yet we still allow little children to be taught fear of 'God' and spread before their innocent eyes the choice ingenuities of Hell-fire and Eternal Damnation.

Fear! What have I done! What have I done—under its influence? . . . But my thoughts are wandering from those earlier memories.

Well, my Father struck a most cruel blow at my trust, admiration, filial sentiment and confidence in him, by what seemed to me at the time as a savage, cruel and brutal assault upon me. If my own Father could do this—what would strangers do to me? What would the World do to me when I went out into it, naked and defenceless? I could not have Mother with me always. . . .

Yes, it may interest Stortford to know how that cruel thrashing affected me in a hundred ways—one of which was to make me almost consciously hate my own father—whom I had always feared.

If I could only tell Stortford the truth, I feel sure he would connect the flogging that taught me Fear and the strange rabbit-pulping incident, with the deed that darkened my life, ruined my health, and wrecked my peace of mind.

Well, one's thoughts wander and one's memory is treacherous, one's memories are elusive and . . . Wonder if I shall sleep to-night. One thing—if I lie awake long enough, I shall see Sister Grey look in, on her night rounds. Worth the loss of a night's sleep. . . .

This insomnia is the devil, and if . . .

Richard Neystoke yawned and fell asleep.

CHAPTER 11

And to-night I have to recall everything that I can of the three years I spent at Oxford, thought Richard Neystoke, as he got into bed the following evening, especially anything whatsoever in the nature of sex experiences.

It will be a pleasant task, for they were undoubtedly the three happiest years of my life, and I would give anything to be allowed to have them over again. But if Stortford thinks he's going to get any lurid sex-stuff out of that period, he is mistaken, for I went up to Oxford innocent and I came down innocent. What is called a virgin youth, I believe. I heard plenty of sex-talk—far too much, in fact—and I joined in it; but I did not find the subject of absorbing interest. Some men seemed to think of nothing else; I thought of almost everything else.

It wasn't that I was by any means feeble, unhealthy and lacking in virility. On the contrary, I was strong, vigorous and robust. But I was extremely fastidious and, thanks to my Mother's influence and teaching, had attained a high degree of, shall I say refinement and good taste, apart from any question of conscience. And she had given me a tremendous respect, indeed a veneration, for all woman-kind. Moreover, in the Oxford of my day, there were no temptations. It was a sequestered, monastic and celibate life that we led, and any man who wanted to transgress had to go elsewhere and seek the means and opportunity. Some boasted that they did—there was indeed a London train unfavourably known as the Flying Fornicator—but I found their tales of amorous adventure rather revolting, and was not in the slightest degree tempted to join in this, to me, incomprehensible form of 'pleasure'.

No, nothing for Stortford's Freudian researches to discover, no neurosis based on my sex-repression or upon remorse for sex-indulgence. Not during the Oxford phase of my life, anyway.

Oxford. . . . I am again at Oxford, the wonder city 'of dreaming spires and prayers in stone', the medieval gem that its criminally careless guardians allowed an ambitious inventor to turn into a busy, crowded and noisy manufacturing town. . . .

I have just come up, on a lovely October day of pale sunshine that turns the old grey walls of the Colleges into honey-coloured Parian marble, and fills their gardens with Autumn's lovely tints of gold and red and bronze. I walk in a dream of joy from my sitting-room into my bedroom and back, viewing for the hundredth time my new domain, my very own place apart, where I can do exactly as I please. I am my own master, in my own rooms, with my own furniture—my time my own, my comings and goings my own unfettered acts.

I am almost reconciled to the parting from my Mother. I realise that I can now express my own individuality and self, be myself, and live my own life without interference from my Father. I sit down in my own deep arm-chair, beside my own merrily-burning coal fire and look round the ancient room. Generation after generation of students have lived in it for over four hundred years! To think of the men it has known, the scenes it has witnessed, the changes of dress and manners and habits that it has survived. Why, its first inhabitants must have come to Oxford in part-armour, and wearing swords. Courtiers of King Charles the First have eaten and drunk at the old table; and have gazed from those mullioned leaded windows, leaned out and called to friends passing along that ancient street, in cloak and sword, plumed hat and big-spurred boots. . . .

I am filled with a subdued yet glowing happiness, am all churned-up within, and far too excited to sit still for long. I must do something. I'll write and tell Mother all about it. But I cannot even sit still to do that. I must go out and see the High again, the Corn, and the Broad, and the little narrow aged lanes between the Colleges.

I race down the stair-case, across the quad, through the lodge, and out into the wonderful world of Oxford, and indulge in a small orgy of spending in the lovely tobacconists, book-shops, picture and furniture showrooms, haberdashers, and all those terribly attractive shops, whose keepers, in those days at any rate, positively blushed with embarrassment when the ignorant "fresher" offered cash payment for goods purchased.

Money! Away with it! And perish the thought of it, between gentlemen and old-established Oxford tradesmen who had probably had the honour of serving one's father and grandfather unto the third and fourth generation, if not the thirteenth and fourteenth. I return to my rooms—*my* rooms —for I want to see them again and savour my freedom anew, my pride of possession and my sense of safety and security. A retreat of my very own, in which I can, when I wish, be as private, secluded and alone, as an oyster in his shell.

I loudly and bravely bawl the name of my 'scout'—my very own man-servant—and when he comes with his obsequious, yet nice confidential-servant sort of manner, I bid him bring me the biggest and most sumptuous tea that he can encompass and produce. And soon I am again sitting in front of my own fire, and beside me on the hearth-rug is a tea-tray on which are tea and cake and scones and bread-and-butter, while in the fender is a sizable dish, beneath whose domed cover lurks a noble pile of buttered toast. . . .

That night I dine in Hall, and at the freshers' table meet my contemporaries, make tentative acquaintanceships; and eye with reverence the second-year men at other tables; with awe the third-year men, ancients and giants that are a race apart. The Dons at the High Table which stretches across the top end of the Hall at right-angles to the undergraduates' tables, are, at present, beyond one's ken and comprehension, above and beyond reverence and awe. One has no more feelings toward them than toward Martians or Monarchs. . . .

And, after Hall, back to my rooms—*my* rooms—accompanied by a new acquaintance, the man who had sat on my right at dinner. He was also the man who was to be the means of inspiring me with the highest and noblest aspirations, and of bringing me to the situation in which I committed the crime which I can never expiate—and the memory of which is slowly and remorselessly *destroying* me, bringing my life to ruin and my soul to damnation. . . .

Cecil Desarum. . . .

The fine flower of our civilisation; the most sterling, upright and honourable man I ever met; unselfishness incarnate; a truly great and noble spirit; a gentleman and a noble man, whose ancestors had doubtless been noblemen as the name de Sarum implies—it was in an evil hour for me that I met him and fell beneath his spell.

When I am feeling my general worthlessness most acutely, and suffering most painfully from the inferiority complex, as Stortford calls what I had imagined to be my humility and self-deprecating modesty, I take pride and reassurance in the thought that Cecil Desarum took to me from the very first; sought me out and cultivated me; slowly, but surely, grew closer and closer to me; and, before long, not only honoured me with his friendship, but became my most special and particular friend.

He did me a world of good, even in one term, broadened my out-look, deepened the current of my thoughts, and gave me a purpose in life.

He was not religious, though he became a priest. He was something infinitely better—he was good; and he was utterly unselfish. It was his theory that there is only one great sin, the father of all other sins, which are dependent upon it and ancillary to it—Selfishness. If only Everyman would be unselfish, sin would disappear from the world, and the millennium would have come and we should have Heaven upon earth.

When he became a priest he preached the gospel of Unselfishness and nothing else; the gospel that can be offered to Roman Catholic, Protestant, Non-conformist, Mussulman, Buddhist, Hindu, Confucian, Taoist, Shintoist, Agnostic, Atheist, or any other. Christ's own Gospel of 'Do as you would be done by', the undenominational, unritualistic, unfettered and universal Gospel of 'Love God with all thy strength and love thy neighbour as thyself.' Or, as Desarum with that lovely saving salty humour of his would say,

'Love the beggar as much as you can; and even if you can't and don't love him, treat him as though you did.'

That was Desarum's guiding light and he followed it unswervingly—followed it into the darkest of the slums that ornament the bright city of London; and there lived and worked until he died of living and working for the dirty, diseased, down-

trodden and dreadful neighbour whom he honestly and truly did try to love as himself. As himself?
He loved his neighbour far more than he did himself, for Cecil Desarum did not love himself at all.

Why did he love me especially? I was not a
pious youth. I was not religious. I was not in the
least inclined toward good works and the society
of the righteous. I went to church from habit, and
because I had to do so; but I had never experienced the slightest spiritual benefit from the
process. I was taught by my Mother to say my
prayers, and I repeated the same two stock
prayers nightly and mechanically under her
supervision. But I had never *prayed* in my life,
and would as soon have thought of taking my
troubles to God as I would have thought of taking
them to my Father. So far as I could gather, God
was an irascible and rather vengeful old gentleman of the strangest predilections. And I did not
in the least admire or like the God of Wrath who
emerged from the welter and confusion of teach-
ings concerning Him, that I received in church,
from Sermon and First Lesson and in my enforced
study of the Old Testament. . . .

So it was on that first evening at Oxford that I
first met and liked Desarum who became my close
friend and remained my best and dearest friend
until I fled and hid from him, fearing the level gaze
of his clear and searching eye.

We sat in our arm-chairs that evening, drank
our coffee, smoked our manly straight-grained
pipes, and talked far into the night, chiefly about
ourselves, our hopes, our aims and our ambitions.
Not that I then had anything that could be called a
fixed ambition or a firm purpose, as Cecil had. He
was going to be a missionary—to the heathen
English of the slums; preaching, chiefly by

example, the Gospel of Unselfishness, of Kindness and of Help—and not the ignoble self-help of Samuel Smiles and his great Victorian kin. He did not express his intention in these words, of course, but merely said that he was going to be a slum parson and work among the poor as one of themselves, leading the same life of poverty, hunger, dirt, and squalor that they did. How else should one know of their struggles, hardships and temptations; their handicaps, their real lives and their moral and spiritual needs?

I rose just a little above my own level that night, as I sat and communed with the best and finest mind that hitherto, mine had ever encountered.

Thereafter I saw Desarum daily, and we talked for hours as we walked out into the country, sat over tea, or foregathered in his room or mine after Hall. Halcyon days of unalloyed bliss, the best and highest as well as the happiest of my life. It was all so pleasant and so peaceful that term slipped by at an incredible speed; and so uneventful that I can remember but little save that lovely sense of peace, happiness, security and freedom.

My scout would call me at seven, and, dragging from beneath my bed the spartan hip-bath, would pour into it two cans of cold water, place a jug of tepid shaving-water on the dressing-table and depart. I would bathe and dress quickly and find an ever-recurrent joy in going into my sitting-room and seeing the blazing fire roaring up the chimney, the room tidy and inviting, the windows open to the morning air; and hearing the song of the birds in the College garden. Then perfunctory and compulsory Chapel and a stroll round quad and garden, and back to a noble breakfast with a worthy appetite.

After breakfast, the best pipe of the day, sweet, soothing, digestive; and then, gay, eupeptic, debonair and carefree, a gentle walk in cap and gown, with note-books beneath one arm, to whatever lecture my time-table might indicate.

From that lecture to another, in some other College again, and, that rite performed, a gentle saunter round the shops of the Turl, the Broad, the Corn, and the High, and so to 'battels', lunch in my own room. Sunshine on old oak and white linen and on silver tankard full of nut-brown ale; a fairly frugal meal as custom decreed, because the afternoon would be devoted to more or less violent exercise; the second pipe of the day, with a book in the deep arm-chair and, at two o'clock, Cecil's welcome entrance and some such proposal as,

"What about Woodstock to-day? Fourteen miles altogether. Two hours to get there, half an hour for tea at the Bear, and two hours back. Be in comfortable time for Hall."

And for those light-footed hours we would talk unceasingly. Good talk too, thanks to Cecil whose mind was as keen and fine as it was clear and strong. After Hall, a pipe and then a couple of hours of work upon to-morrow's classics, or at the essay to be read to my tutor; and at about ten or so, a knock at my door and Desarum for another talk; and so to bed, at mid-night or later.

On Sunday mornings we would go to the University Church of St. Mary to hear a Bampton Lecture or a sermon by the Vice-Chancellor or some other distinguished Don or visiting divine. In the afternoon a long walk as usual, and, in the evening, a visit to the terrifically 'high' Church of St. Barnabas, to enjoy the singing, the incense, the living warmth of the ritual, and the fine preaching of the almost Roman Catholic vicar.

What wonder that I can remember so little

detail when the whole is a glowing mass of
memories, inextricably commingled, of a uniformly
jocund period, a joyous monotony of happiness
and peace?

I had no triumphs and scored no successes. I
neither played games nor read for Honours. I just
wilfully and wantonly enjoyed the glorious life of
ease and freedom with which my fortunate fate
had provided me. But though I studied little, I
read a good deal and learned a tremendous lot—
much of it from a better source than books. I
learned from my fellows, men from every part of
the British Isles, the Empire, America and Europe;
and my mind was polished by constant contact
with the varied minds of others; broadened and
deepened by reception of their widely differing
ideas; strengthened by exercise in the mental gym-
nastics, to participation in which their arguments
invited it. I learned more and better from listening
to my contemporaries in formal debate, in hearing
their reading of papers on every subject under the
sun, and in taking part in endless conversation
and argument in their rooms and mine, than I did
from all the lectures and annotated text-books
prescribed for the advancement of my learning by
those set in academic authority over me.

And I learnt much, and won vast entertainment
and amusement from, my fairly successful and
prominent membership of the Oxford University
Dramatic Society.

And most of all I learned from Cecil Desarum,
his splendid and powerful influence the greatest of
the blessings with which glorious Oxford so generously endowed me.

(And yet I am here, O God! Here in this resort
of wrecks and failures; here hiding from *myself*
and from Thee!)

What can I remember from those old, most

happy, far-off things and battels long ago, that I can offer to Stortford to-morrow?

Well, there's the Affair of the Photographer's Assistant. And, of course, the business of my Getting Religion, if that is what it was. Anyhow, it is a vulgar and ugly phrase to use concerning the renaissance of a soul and the endowment of a mind with a high and noble purpose.

About the Photographer's Assistant . . .

One term, I attended lectures regularly at Magdalen, from twelve to one, and so passed daily the shop of a well-known photographer, one of whose staff, an extremely pretty girl, was evidently in the habit of emerging from the studio soon after one o'clock, presumably in search of lunch. The first time I saw her, I noticed the beauty and delicacy of her refined and rather ethereal face; with its flawless complexion; straight nose; cupid's-bow lips above a good chin; and bright well-opened eyes beneath straight brows. Perhaps I did not notice all this the first time I saw her, but by the third time I had seen her, I knew this and more. I knew that her beautiful head was well set on her white and shapely neck; that her hair was silky and of the colour of honey; that her big eyes were grey as well as kind and gentle; that her hands and feet were small; and that she carried herself extremely well. By the end of the week I was carefully timing myself to meet her, and faintly regretting that on Sunday I should not see her.

One day, in the following week, failing to meet her, I stood and gazed at the assorted photographs that adorned the window, until she came out of the shop. I fancied that she looked quickly at me, and that a faint flush warmed her fair and delicate skin.

At the end of a fortnight, I was lying awake thinking of her and wondering how I could possibly see more of her; for even these swift, brief, daily glimpses were precious to me—as we went our ways like ships that pass in the day and may not speak to each other in passing.

What would happen if I did speak? And what could I say? An undergraduate at Oxford cannot accost a shop-girl, even though the shop be called a studio, and talk and walk with her in the street —or, rather, he could not do so in those days. It may be different now, of course. There was one thing I could do though—I could smile at her, and if she smiled back, I could thereafter bow and raise my mortar-board, as though she were a lady of my proper and regular acquaintance.

A day or two later, her eyes met mine as I approached, and I gave her a broad and beaming smile, a most unmistakable grin of greeting and friendship. To my delight, she returned my smile in the most delightful and natural manner, with a flash of perfect teeth. Indeed, it was a perfect smile and my fastidiousness could find no fault in it. Next day as I smiled, I raised my cap and bowed as though we had been introduced and knew each other. She returned my smile and bow charmingly and with a natural ease and grace. Not only was she lovely, nicely dressed and dainty, but she had poise.

Again we passed, smiled and exchanged friend-ly inclinations of the head, and, as I lay awake that night, I admitted that I was in love. . . . In love with a shop-girl! . . . And whether it be significant and important to Stortford or not, it is important to me that this thought, as it phrased itself in my mind, and in those ugly slighting words, completely changed my whole social out-look and my attitude to my fellow-men!

'In love with a *shop-girl*!' And why should not a lazy, self-indulgent undergraduate, who had never done an honest day's work in his life, or a useful deed, consider it an unbecoming, derogatory and unworthy thing that he should have fallen in love with a girl who worked for her living, and had the ability and energy to do so? Was work, then, a disgraceful and defiling thing? Was a shop a shameful milieu for the exercise of what wage-earning capacity one had? How was a shop-girl necessarily less admirable and respect-worthy than a chorus-girl, a Society-girl, or any other kind of girl? . . .

Here, aided by love, was the leaven of Desarum's precept at work already, the theory and teaching of his practical Christianity that regarded all men and women as equal in the sight of God.

Yet it was Desarum who blighted my budding romance and put an end to my first adult love-affair before it had well begun. For I was so much in love, so obsessed, that I simply must tell some-one about it, and naturally Desarum was the one I must tell. The moment I had told him, he re-acted strongly and took a firm line at once. There was no sympathy, congratulation, deep interest, or any-thing of the sort. No fuel for the ardent flames of love; but a prompt and heavy douche of cold water.

"Rotten!" he said. "You can't and you shan't have an affair with an Oxford shop-girl, for several reasons—none of which is that she is a shop-girl, though one of them is that this is Oxford. You haven't come here to moon and spoon; but to pre-pare yourself to do something useful in life, some-thing for your fellow man, as you haven't got to devote your time to earning your own living . . . What? '*I don't know what love is.*' Anyway, it isn't much if it's concerned only with externals. How can you be in love with a person to whom you have never spoken and of whom you know nothing? She may have a perfectly vacant mind and a worthless character, for all you know. Obviously it's just pure physical attraction—and you can take the 'pure' both ways; for I give you credit for having the best intentions, as well as the silliest . . . Suppose you did get to know her—what do you propose to do? Meet her at night and loaf around the streets with her until you are progged[15]—and incidentally let her in for quite a bit of no-good, as a danger to innocent undergraduates? It's just a damned silly attack of calf-love, like measles or chicken-pox, and I'm ashamed of you . . . Don't go past Plimpton's any more—at lunch-time, or I've done with you."

I proclaimed the innocence and beauty of my love for this beautiful girl, and spoke of natural selection, love at first sight, and the inevitability of physical attraction preceding that based on mental and spiritual affinity, community of tastes and standards. How could these be discovered until the attraction of externals had led to association?

Desarum eyed me thoughtfully.

"You do honestly believe that this is genuine love, the real thing, permanent and indestructible?" he asked.

"I do," I replied stoutly, feeling like Dante affirming his undying worship of Beatrice.

"Right, then," was the prompt reply. "I won't say you must wait until you go down, and are no longer an Oxford undergraduate under discipline and tutelage, before speaking to her. But I do say that you must wait a year. I'm a great believer in the one-year test of a man's staying-power. If you'll keep right away from her till this time next year, and are then still in love with her, I'll call on

---

[15] Challenged by the Proctor, the University censor of morals, who is, incidentally, policeman, judge, jury, prosecutor and executioner in one.

her employer, make her acquaintance, introduce you to her, and get my people to invite you both to our place for the Christmas vac. How's that?"

And of course Cecil had his way with me. I avoided the shop; I crept about miserably, sighing like a furnace; I wrote poetry; I read all the Great Love Stories of the past; I began to enjoy my melancholy, and treasure my broken heart; and at the end of term I parted from Cecil as from one whom I wholly and nobly forgave for a great wrong that, with the best intentions, he had done me.

When I got home I told Mother all about it, as I told her everything; and before the end of the vac realised that I loved her better than all the pretty shop-girls in the world.

Desarum and I never referred to the matter again, nor did I ever again see my loved-and-lost-one. I never even knew her name; but to this day I can see the lovely friendly smile she gave me. Kind smiles from strangers are rare in civilised countries.

Well, I can also tell Stortford, with absolute truth, that throughout the period that I was in love, I never had a single carnal thought. It was a pure flame of altruistic feeling, ethereal and sublime—in the sense of the word 'sublimation', of which they are so fond here. . . . I never for one second wanted anything from her, wanted to get, to gain, to take. So far as I thought beyond the morrow and the ineffable joy of merely seeing her, I wanted to *give;* to give anything; everything; myself, and all that myself could offer, could bring, could make, and could be. . . .

But here was my fatal instability and changeability again; my incurable tendency to sudden *finishing*, to *revulsion* and *fugue*.

What else was it that I remembered just now? . . .

Oh, yes! My sudden conversion, from a state of spiritual laziness and stagnation, to one of tremendous vitality and enthusiasm—a conversion indeed, a transfiguration. It was almost as sudden and great a change as that wrought in Saul of Tarsus at Damascus. . . . Was it too sudden and too great to be lasting and fruitful? No. It did bear fruit—some of it the bitter fruit I eat in misery today. But though it was fruitful, it was not lasting —not permanent. One of those violent fires that do soon burn themselves out. But not very soon and not vainly, I think. Had it not been for my sudden and awful fall from grace, it might have burnt with the steady flame and ever-glowing heat of that great fire of crusading fighting faith that illuminated Desarum and gave warmth to all who came near it. It did not last—but in all humility I do not think that I am infirm of purpose, weak, and lacking in resolution and tenacity. If it were a case of 'unstable as water thou shalt not excel', Desarum would never have been my friend. I cling to that as a drowning man to a spar—the fact that I suited and satisfied Desarum, as constant companion, confidant and friend—and it helps me to keep my head above the waters of despair. . . . I was once worthy of Desarum's friendship and he enjoyed my society.

It was a sermon—no, an address—that converted me from passivity and negative virtue to a most active and positive yearning to do something fine and useful; something not only and merely unselfish and self-denying, but practically and solidly helpful to others.

A friend of Cecil's, a man of means and family who might have become a Bishop but for his higher and nobler ambition to be a successful 'slum parson' had come to Oxford to address the members of his old College on the subject of the

East End Mission, to the upkeep of which they modestly subscribed, and in which they took a tepid interest. It was the occasion of the annual treat which he gave a select band of his slum parishioners, a visit to Oxford, a day in the country combined with a picnic in punts on the river, and a general fresh-air 'do'. A few undergraduates who were going to be parsons or missionaries would help with the punting and feeding of the strange flock, mingling and communing with the poor creatures as freely and easily as might pheasants with hedgehogs or canaries with sewer-rats. Desarum did the organising at the Oxford end, and met Vibart-Stourton and his band of slum men, women and children at the station.

I, of course, wanted to help him, and joined in the fray, the orgy of desperate entertainment of the almost unentertainable, whose ideas of a good time inclined more toward rivers of beer than to living streams of waters, and even to those of the Thames.

And on the next day, Sunday, Vibart-Stourton preached in the morning at St. Barnabas Church, and in the evening at that of St. Philip and St. James. In the afternoon he addressed all undergraduates who cared to come, in the Hall of his College.

With Desarum I attended the service at St. Barnabas, and nothing on earth would have kept me from going to the afternoon address or the evening service at the Church irreverently known as Phil-and-Jim. . . .

I went to bed that night a different man. I may say that I went to bed a man who had, until that day, been a boy. My whole life was changed. I was thenceforth, I felt, dedicated, consecrated, not consciously to the service of God, so much as to that of Man, my fellow-man and my fellow Englishman.

What Vibart-Stourton told his hearers in those two sermons, and in the more intimate and personal address to the undergraduates, shamed me, hurt me, inspired me, filled me high with the spirit of service and sacrifice. It was at once a most heart-searching and pitiful appeal, and a scathing, scalding indictment. An indictment not only of slum-property owners, of all exploiters of the poor, of soulless Councils and Boards and Institutions, but of Parliament and of the People. It was nothing less than a True Bill brought against the People of England—that they should tolerate this monstrous thing, this shameful and disgraceful infamy.

There was no hint of politics in sermon or address; no taint of Communism; no plea based upon Socialism; no appeal to religion of any kind; but a calm, cool statement of the conditions under which life was lived by English men and women— and worse, by English children—in the foul slums that lie within a stone's throw of the richest and most luxurious houses, churches, squares, shops, and streets in England or the whole world.

Vibart-Stourton spent the Monday in Oxford; dined with our Dons; and, after Hall, came to Desarum's room; and I had the privilege and honour of hearing those two talk from nine till mid-night. I was thrilled and enthralled, and I dedicated myself, there and then, to the service of the slum-dwellers of the East End of London. I swore to myself, and I promised Vibart-Stourton and Desarum, that I would live the life of those poor people, be one of them and devote my life to working with them and for them. For a year I would earn my living in a real slum, taking no advantage of my gifts of fortune—not even of my superior education —so that I might really know what they had to contend with, what were their greatest needs, what their cruellest hardships, and, in the light of that knowledge, what was the best, truest and greatest help that could be given them.

"And then?" asked Vibart-Stourton, smiling kindly, as I declared my determination to devote my life and my income to the same work to which he had devoted his.

"When I have lived wholly and entirely with them, and as one of them, for a full year, I shall decide upon what is the best thing for me to do. I might go on living with them and helping individual cases of special hardship—children, cripples, incurables, widows, sick—or I might try to get elected to Parliament for some slum constituency. Failing that, I might tour the country, lecturing on slum life and trying to rouse the national conscience. I might write articles in the popular press, pamphlets, books. I might take Holy Orders and become a slum-parson, and, after working in my parish all the week, go and preach, in fashionable churches, to the wealthy, and raise funds, interest influential people, and . . ."

"And all that," laughed Desarum, beaming warm approval. "That's the stuff, Rickie. But do your year first. Survive that undaunted, and with your young enthusiasm undimmed, before you decide about taking Holy Orders and becoming a slum parson. I'm not sure that it isn't more of a handicap than anything else. The real slum-bird is an extremely shy bird; very prejudiced and suspicious where the clergy are concerned."

"Yes, unfortunately," agreed Vibart-Stourton. "Except for those that try to exploit them; professional cadgers who regard the 'Oly Joes as easy prey and fair game. It takes priest or parson a very very long time indeed to establish himself in the slums as an accepted and acceptable friend, who is there to help anybody and everybody in any and every way, materially as well as spiritually. No, I am afraid the black coat and dog-collar, or cassock and biretta are, as Desarum says, a handicap. . . . A great one; almost fatal to real success, in some cases. There *are* examples of course, splendid and noble ones, of brilliant achievement; but they have been in spite of the cloth; at first, at any rate. The dress sets the man apart, and, nine times out of ten, he remains—apart. When it is realised (if it ever is) that he means well and does well, the kindest comment that you hear is just that. Sort of:

' 'E ain't bad for a 'Oly Joe. 'E means orl-right an' 'e don't do no 'arm. . . . But what do 'e know abaht anythink? Nothink. 'Is belly's filled for 'im and someone pays 'is rent. Never out o' work because 'e don't do none. . . . Talk to *us* abaht the Lovin' 'Eavenly Father and Gentle Jesus wot looks after the spadgers! Don't look after *us* between 'Em, much, do they? . . . Ar, well! 'Oly Joe's orl-right—only 'e don't know nothink and 'e knows that wrong.'

"There is," he went on, "and there inevitably must be, an insurmountable wall between the average uniformed clergyman and the slum-dwellers among whom he tries to work. However genuine, self-sacrificing, hard-working and truly philanthropic he may be, there is a great gulf that he cannot cross. Not in those trousers, collar and hat. Nor with that accent. To the most tolerant, the most grateful, of those hungry, dirty, hand-to-mouth, almost-homeless slum-dwellers, there is a suggestion, however unconscious, of 'the butterfly upon the road'."

He eyed me kindly for a moment as he knocked out his pipe.

"And don't think that, however good and strong

your will may be, you can just walk into the slums and *be* a slum-dweller, be one with them and of them. Not a bit of it. You'd be viewed with the utmost suspicion, dislike, distrust and enmity. You'd probably have to clear out again, pretty soon and pretty quickly."

"Why suspicion?" I asked. "Suspicion of being what?"

"A copper's nark," was the prompt reply. "They'd be perfectly certain that you were either a spying stool-pigeon of the police, or else an actual plain-clothes man himself. . . . Anyway, you'd be something objectionable and dangerous, or you wouldn't be there—with your superior accent, your better clothes, your lily-white hands and your invisible but obvious means of support."

"But one would dress the part, of course, live as they did, get a job of some kind, locally; and try to talk as they do," I said.

Vibart-Stourton laughed pleasantly.

"My dear chap," he said, "you'd have a better chance of persuading the French that you are a born-and-bred Parisian, if you went straight to Paris now, and lived in the Rue Cherche Midi. It's a difficult language to learn, genuine Cockney; and not an easy accent to catch, either. A case in point—George Bernard Shaw, that self-proclaimed omniscient, pretends that he knows the particular dialect of the East End of London. In point of fact, he showed his special ignorance instead—by making Eliza Doolittle the Dustman's Daughter, say, in her native accents wild, *'Not bloody likely!'* in the dreadfully daring phrase that shocked, delighted and stimulated the theatre-goers of the Naughty Nineties. . . . Brave Bernard! . . . And yet, until he wrote it and an actress mouthed it, such a phrase was never heard on land or sea, in slum or fo'c'sle, from Cockney soldier, sailor, coster, 'bus-driver, bargee or dustman. Never. *Never once* in all the history of Whitechapel or Seven Dials, Hoxton or Bethnal Green."

"What would be the correct phrase?" I asked, smiling at the fervour of the genuine virtuoso.

"Why, Eliza Doolittle or any other Cockney, male or female, wishing emphatically to deny probability, invariably says: '*No bloody fear!*' Invariably. And if you used the famous Shavian phrase in slum-conversation, you would immediately stamp yourself as a fraud. In that particular, I mean. . . .

"No. It's no *facilis descensus*, going down into the slums," he continued. "To live as a native, I mean. About as difficult as doing that in Mecca."

"Can't it be done, then?" I asked, my young enthusiasm somewhat damped, for I had sworn to myself, before God, in the House of God, that I would be an English missionary to those English, and live with them, among them, of them—and for them.

"Yes. By the right man," replied Vibart-Stourton, after a brief, reflective silence. "By the right man, with the right spirit *and* the right—er—guts. Resolution, fortitude, determination, pluck and patience. Give me a chap with those and I don't care what his religious views are. Nor whether he has any."

"And what is the right way, for the right man?" asked Desarum softly, and I knew that he too was going to do his best to find out whether he were the right man or not.

"Step by step—downwards," was the prompt reply. "Apprenticeship in a very poor suburb. Daily visits of reconnaissance, scouting, observation, into the slum country. Careful study of the vowel sounds, of the idioms, manners, customs, and particularly such Rites as the offering and accepting of a drink. Learning not to say 'Thank-you', not to say 'Please', or 'Excuse me', and not be rude, by the near-slums' exacting standards; to say '*Giss a light Maite*', instead of 'Might I borrow a match from you', and '*Gurn a-wy*', instead of 'I think you are mistaken' . . ."

"Graduate, district by district, in fact," said Desarum.

"Yes. Street by street, almost—until you have at last promoted yourself from Deptford to Lime-house by way of Bermondsey, Rotherhithe and Southwark, or Wapping, Shadwell and Barking. . . . Done gradually and by steady descent, you might in time almost get down to the real criminal quarters—and consort, on equal terms, with bur-glars, pick-pockets, thieves, racketeers, coiners, wide-boys, molls and prostitutes, publicans and sinners. . . .

"As Christ did," he added. "But what you really want, I take it, is to get among the honest English poor, who work cruelly hard for a pitiful wage, with everything against them, from the cradle—they never had—to the grave that is their only hope of rest and surcease from misery and pain."

"That's what I want," I said. "To live in those slums with those people, until I know so much about them, and am so really one of them, that I can speak *as* one of them—whether in the Press, the Pulpit, or the House of Commons. . . ."

Vibart-Stourton eyed me straitly for a space, considering, speculating, and then the charming friendly smile illuminated his austere face.

"Good," he said. "And I pray there's depth of earth."

In me, he meant, of course; hoped that the good seed of his talk had fallen on soil that was not of the wayside, not stony, not thorny, not fallen where the birds of worldly air would devour it up. And again I swore to myself that I would see to it that the seed should bring forth fruit a hundredfold. I would devote my life, my all, my *self* to this work, and become such a man as Vibart-Stourton himself, a man really worthy of the friendship of Desarum.

"Well, good-bye for the present," said Vibart-Stourton, later, as he rose to go. "Come and see me in London, and I'll take you to Toynbee Hall for Canon Barnett's blessing, and to meet the men who are working there. You must have long talks with all of them. They'll be of the utmost help to you—before you start. But not after you have taken the plunge. Not in the novitiate year, that I prescribe and that you promise to undergo. You must paddle your own canoe then. One whole year in the real slums, as a slum-dweller, earning your own living there—and no palliatives. No more holiday, relaxation, relief or change than they themselves can get. . . . You can go hop-picking with them and take Bank Holidays as they do, but nothing more. . . . No better room, bed, washing-and-bathing facilities, sanitation, clothes, boots or income than the average slum-dweller has. No comforts in the cupboard—box of cigars, cigarettes or good Christian tobacco. No bottle of good whisky, or any medicines they can't get. Nothing whatever that they haven't got. . . . No sneaking off home, or to a West End Hotel or service-flat for a rest, a breath of fresh air, some decent food and drink, and a good wallow among the flesh-pots. . . . Even so, you are a thousand times better off than they are, because you know you *can* leave it all, and eventually will leave it all; and because you have mental resources that they have not—and the inner light and warmth of your enthusiasm, your purpose, your mission and crusade;

your Gospel—The Gospel of Unselfishness. And before you leave the mean suburbs for the real slums, see whether you can pass yourself off on Father O'Reilly as a genuine coster-monger. Or come and try to take me in. . . . Think you'll stick it? Good. . . . God help you. You'll need it. Good-bye. . . .

Yes. That is how Vibart-Stourton talked to me that evening towards the end of my last term at Oxford; and added the last fuel to the flames of the fire that Desarum's talk and example had kindled in my youthful breast.

Well, let Stortford make what he can of my Oxford memories. Nothing very lurid there. Nothing fine and Freudian for him to seize upon and drag forth into the light of day, to be aired and sublimated.

Sublime enough, I should think, an ardent, selfless desire to serve one's fellow-men, less fortunately situated than oneself.

Service . . . Unselfishness . . .

Was my fall and the ruin of my happiness, my work, my character, due to Selfishness, which, according to Desarum is the one great Sin and father of all sins? . . . I don't know. . . .

I suppose so. Yes. Jealousy must be based on love of self, fundamentally. Was I selfish in what I did on Miranda Burbidge's account? Yes. I was angry; savagely, insanely angry; mad with rage. But was it not I myself who was outraged, and on my own account—because she was mine? . . . Should I have been enraged to the point of insanity if she had been a stranger to me? . . . No . . . Self! Self! Self! But Miranda was . . .

Richard Neystoke, with a conscious effort, switched the current of his thoughts to other matters.

Sister Grey. Elspeth Grey. Elspeth. Would she come in to see him before he fell asleep.

Sister Elspeth Grey . . . Lady Jane Grey . . . Janey Grey . . . Miranda Burbidge . . . Had he been selfish in leaving . . .

He shot up in bed.

Selfish! He had been the most selfish, mean, cowardly . . . No—he could not bear to think of it. He must thrust it back into the shadows; thrust it deep, deep down; thrust it from him altogether, *always.* It was this wretched place, with its horrible digging and delving; its enforced self-examinations; its probing, questioning, searching; its eternal introspection that was upsetting him, troubling him, making him feel worse than ever. They were making him afraid; afraid of what he might do, say, confess. They were making a nervous wreck of him. They were stripping him bare. He had been a fool, a thousand times a fool, to listen to Denzil Marindin, Jacintha and Bennett . . . Stortford or Fieldwicke would get it out of him. Or, one of these days, he'd confess all to Sister Elspeth Grey. To Elspeth. What would she do? Turn from him in horror? And what would he do then? Put an end to it all, probably, for he could not bear it much longer. No longer, in fact, if Elspeth turned against him. In whom was there help if not in her.

In the Lord my God is help and salvation.

But God knew already—and in Him was there no help, for there had been no answer to prayer. Had he not prayed daily and nightly for forgiveness and help? Had he not entered the Church, God's own Holy Church, as a servant of God and devoted his whole life to the service of God?

Who could, who would, help the wretched Richard Neystoke in his dreadful agony.

Who could? . . . Who would? . . .

As though in answer, the door opened silently and Sister Grey, on her nightly round, entered the room like a ghost, the light from a tiny torch shining on the carpet at her feet.

"Sister!" whispered Neystoke.

"Hullo! Not asleep yet?" was the scarcely audible reply.

"I was just thinking about you," said Neystoke, and switched on the bed-side light.

"Thinking you'd like to tell me what it is that's troubling you?" asked Sister Grey, as she seated herself in his chair.

"No. Thinking that I would *not* like to do so—and fearing that some-day, I might—*malgré moi* . . ."

"Oh! Don't be so silly, Mr. Neystoke. What *is* the good of coming here to be helped, to be cured, if you won't help us to do it. Make yourself the chief obstacle, in fact. The only obstacle. . . . You are ill because you are hiding something. Hiding it from the doctors and worse still, from *yourself*. . . . That's the real tragedy."

"But how do you know?" he asked.

"Because you are so ill. So ill—without any sort or kind of organic disease. You'd be in perfect health—if your mind weren't ill, full of conflict instead of harmony. . . . Having watched you and talked to you—as we all have—the doctors are certain of it. And they can do nothing for you—no-one can do anything for you, unless you'll first do something for yourself, set your own conscious mind at rest. Unburden it. Stop trying to climb the terribly steep hill of Life with a burden too heavy for your strength. Then help the doctors, in every way, to get at what is troubling your unconscious mind. For you can't defeat *that* in the awful struggle that your life has become. The Unconscious always wins, you know. . . ."

"And then?" smiled Neystoke, watching her face and delighting in the thought that all this earnestness and vehemence was for him, for his welfare.

"Despair . . . Madness . . . Death," replied Sister Grey uncompromising, and the smile died from Richard Neystoke's face. "Please, *please*, let us help you. Don't go away from here as ill as you came, and with no chance of recovery.

"Now," she continued, "tell me what drives you to do this *bathing of your feet* twenty times a day. *Why do you do it?*"

Neystoke leaned his head upon his arms that rested upon his raised knees, the better to hide his face.

Oh, God! What was this? At last . . . At last . . .

Should he, could he, make a clean breast of it; tell her everything. She'd tell the doctors—and they'd tell the police. But if she gave her word to respect his confidence? She would tell no one then —not even Fieldwicke. And if he did confess, how could he ever look her in the face again. Yet it would be easy to tell her. It was an impasse, a strange paradox, that he would sooner tell her than anybody—and that she was the last person whom he would wish to know of it.

"Not now," he groaned. "There is nothing to tell you. Give me a little longer. . . . Will you stay till I go to sleep?"

"Yes."

Richard Neystoke looked up and smiled at Elspeth Grey.

"I should be cheating. Please go back to bed yourself," he said. "I shouldn't sleep while you are here."

"I'll stay till morning, if you'll tell me all about it," was the reply. "Get it all up and out, and I'll guarantee that you'll find that it isn't so dreadful after all. Not nearly as bad as you think. . . . And even if it is, you'll feel better. At once. And before you go you'll feel quite well—and be well too. . . . You've got two troubles. One needs lancing, opening and draining. You know that yourself and only you can perform the operation. You *must* talk about whatever it is instead of for ever thinking about it and turning it over in your mind. The other needs—discovering and digging up and ex-posing to the air and sun-light of realisation and recognition. . . .

"But I've told you all this a dozen times," she sighed wearily, "and you'll neither help yourself nor help others to help you. You're wasting your time here and wasting ours as well."

"Sister! . . . I . . . I . . . Not yet. Not now. I *can't*. Perhaps I shall be able to tell you when . . . Would you be bound to tell the Doctor if . . ." Neystoke raised his head and looked Sister Grey in the face, and her heart ached for the white-lipped, suffering man; for a soul in agony.

Rising to her feet, she approached the bed.

"Listen," she said. "If you told me something in strict confidence and I gave you my promise not to repeat it and not to reveal what I had thus learnt, I would as soon have my tongue cut out as betray your confidence. . . . Sounds dramatic and porten-tous—but that's the plain fact of it."

Richard Neystoke reached out and took Elspeth Grey's hand.

"Sister," he said, "I am a . . . I am a . . . I can't . . . I'll tell you another time . . . In confidence . . . I am going mad, I think. I must try to . . . Oh, if I could only die and . . ."

Though able always to appear poised, detached and calm, a wide and deep experience of suffering had not blunted Elspeth Grey's sensibilities and great gift of sympathy. Far from being rendered callous or indifferent, she was continually selfremonstrant on the score of her lack of real detachment, her necessity to suffer with the sufferer, her inability to achieve a cool aloofness.

For this man; so gentle, kind and lovable; so obviously harmless, unselfish and good-hearted, she felt a great, a deep sympathy and a strong attraction. . . . Help him—save him—she must.

"Don't talk nonsense," she said sharply, withdrawing the hand to which he clung. "Don't be selfish, weak and silly. You'll be pitying yourself instead of helping yourself, next. . . . Now, lie down and I'll go and get you a sleeping-draught and we'll have a talk to-morrow. You'll speak to me really freely and openly, I am sure, and you'll help Dr. Stortford, won't you?"

She could see that a tremendous struggle was agitating the unfortunate man, that he was torn and tortured . . .

"*Please*," he groaned, suddenly. "A secret . . . in confidence . . . Sister . . . I must tell someone or go mad. I must tell you . . . Not another living soul . . . You wouldn't betray me. *I am a murderer . . .*"

Elspeth Grey stroked the bowed head that again rested on the drawn-up knees. Poor, poor, distraught and suffering creature. What agony of mind! . . .

"Is that all?" she said. "There are lots of worse sins than murder. I daresay it was quite . . . defensible. Commendable even. There are lots of people who ought to be murdered. You shall tell me all about it, another time. Now lie down and try to sleep. I am going to get you something . . ."

When Sister Grey returned Richard Neystoke was asleep. Before switching off the shaded light, she studied the pale, thin face of the patient concerning whom she thought frequently and long. Did it look less drawn and lined already, calmer, more peaceful? Was the burden less already; lighter and more bearable even, for those few words of confession? Would he regret and retract; or give in now, tell her the whole story, ease his conscience and find peace at last? . . .

It would be a wonderful thing if she could bring him peace, almost the greatest gift that one human being could give to another. Poor soul! . . . Poor dear! . . . As if *he* had ever done anything of which he had real need to be ashamed.

CHAPTER 12

And to-night he wants me to think back over the years that elapsed between my leaving Oxford and taking Holy Orders, does he, thought Richard Neystoke as he turned out his bed-side light and composed himself for sleep, the following night. To think most carefully and remember every salient and significant event, especially those of my sex-life during that period, eh?

I wonder what he would say and do if I obeyed him literally; told him all about Miranda Burbidge; all about that vile brute who terrified me so; told him everything that I did and suffered during that terrible time. . . . I couldn't even tell Elspeth Grey the whole of it.

Was I a fool to confess to her last night? No. It did me more good than anything has done ever since that dreadful night. Not only the act and fact of telling her, but the way in which she took it. A bald, crude confession of the fact that I am a murderer, without one word of explanation, palliation or excuse! . . . And she took it as calmly as though I had said 'I am a vegetarian'! . . . A wonderful woman, as wise and strong and understanding as she is lovely. And one feels that one is absolutely safe with her; one's secret as sacred as with a priest in the confessional.

I wonder how much I could tell her without making her despise and dislike me. Condemnation I must expect and shall receive; but I couldn't bear her hatred and contempt. One scarcely thinks of her as capable of such feelings for a patient—indeed for anyone—but she has never met a murderer before. . . . And yet she received my announcement without an apparent shadow of surprise, much less shock, horror or repulsion. Probably she did not believe me. Thought I was indulging in a little childish exhibitionism.

How much dare I tell her? How much Stortford? Nothing to him. Nothing whatever. I will tell her all I can—and the relief will be unspeakable. There would be no further relief, no benefit of any sort, no point, in telling it again to Stortford. . . .

Try to remember it all again? No need to try! I won't even think about it. . . . Too painful. . . . My mind always shies away from it—like a horse that will not approach and pass something terrifying. It *is* terrifying. I cannot bear to go over it all again in detail and in cold blood.

But perhaps I had better try to do it. Then I can select what is fit for Elspeth Grey's ears. I won't tell her any lies, but I cannot tell her the whole truth. I won't put my conduct in a favourable light, white-wash myself, or make excuses—but I must not, I cannot, and I will not, forfeit her good opinion of me, her liking for me. And I know—and thank God for it—that she has formed a good opinion of me and does like me.

Besides, if I force myself to go over it all just once, I shall be fore-armed against Stortford's digging and delving; his devilishly clever and artful questioning. I'll be honest with myself for once, absolutely honest—whatever I may be with him, and however economical of the truth I may be with Elspeth.

I have left Oxford, with the deepest regret; and, in the true missionary spirit, genuine and ingenuous, have begun my apprenticeship to work in the slums, my novitiate, as a modern working, if not begging, friar of orders grey and purpose high and firm, dedicated and devoted to work among the poorest poor; to the study of the conditions under which they live; and to the doing of what it may be in my power to do with speech and pen, with example, with money, and with untiring work, to ameliorate, in however little degree, their hard and cruel lot; unfair, unjust and unworthy of their England.

I am a lodger and referred to as 'the lodger', and I am hating it very much indeed.

I don't think I could ever go fishing again. My sympathies with the fish out of water would be too strong. I think I should feel more at home if I were in a foreign country. More allowances would be made for my peculiarities, and there would be room for understandable misunderstandings ascribed to mutual misapprehension of a foreign language. So it is that Englishmen feel at first in America, the very community of language making the difference of attitude, outlook and habit, the more marked.

I have a small bedroom to myself, but must take my meals with the family; my hostess having something else to do than to wait upon me. The lodger—in this part of London—is not a pampered person and, until house-trained, must walk warily. I make terrible mistakes at first, and fall between two stools of opinion, my host regarding me as a social climber—a fool pretending to be better than he is; my hostess, on the other hand, with truer insight, putting me down as a falling star or rocket, who has seen better days. Both are suspicious of me and, for opposite reasons, contemptuous.

Far more contemptuous than either is their daughter, a girl of about eighteen, who, for some reason—doubtless a very good one—dislikes me intensely; regards me as an almost inexpressibly poor creature; and loses no opportunity of snubbing and humiliating me. She is not cruel to be kind, but cruel to be as cruel as she possibly can, and I learn a lot from her. . . .

She improved my manners enormously, and but for her I should have had to remain in Golden Row longer than I did. Whenever she mocked me in a high falsetto sneer, I knew I had said the wrong thing, or the right thing in the wrong way, and studied to improve. I have quite forgotten her name, which seems ungrateful, but I have not forgotten the tone of her reply when, at my first meal with that happy family, I began some modest request with the foolish words: 'Might I trouble you' for whatever it was.

Her elder brother, only faintly hostile and less contemptuous, regarded me with considerable amusement.

Of the two young children, I liked the small, stolid boy and took good care that he should like me. I bought him body and soul, with copper coins and copper-sulphate sweets. At least, I imagine that was the main ingredient, judging by their colour, of those appalling 'drops'. Quite a sinisterly appropriate term I thought.

The little girl, a precocious, wizened, elfin creature, I could not love or like, alas. She remains the only lady whom I have ever really hated. But from her, too, I learned, among other things, what the rest of the family really thought of me. It gave her pleasure to tell me, and gave me pain to listen to the language in which she told it. However, she did but quote.

I forget exactly how long I stayed with Mr. and Mrs. Nimmo, but it was long enough for me to fit myself for my first downward step and to appear less of a *lusus naturae* to my next hosts.

Not only did my accent, idiom and knowledge of Public-House and other Rites vastly improve, but my personal appearance and wardrobe. My hair was properly cut; my cap was worn at the correct angle over one eye; my neckerchief properly adjusted; and my suit—impeccably cut—soiled and creased. I had the right kind of boots and a heavy leather belt; I could say 'rahnd the 'ouses' as to the manner and neighbourhood born.

I had amazing good luck—if there be such a thing as luck—in finding the next lodging on my downward path to the true slums.

The first had been easy enough. I had merely selected a mean and poverty-stricken street in an extremely poor suburb, and walked along it until I saw one of the usual cards: Bed and Breakfast: Bedroom to Let: Lodgings for Single Man.

My next step was in search of something much lower than this level of respectability.

Getting off my bus, I walked until I was lost in a maze of narrow streets, courts and alleys, which lay to the north of a broad and busy main thoroughfare.

It was the sort of neighbourhood of which I was in search. What had I better do? Should I ask a policeman? On the whole, perhaps, better not. Partly because I must now cultivate the proper attitude towards the police, as though they were my natural enemies; and partly because it might be a mistake to draw the attention of the police towards myself. I was a fraud, and though exposure would not lead to punishment, it would to failure. Furthermore, there was no policeman in sight.

The nearest Public House? No, I felt sure that would be the wrong move.

At the corner of the street where I stood in doubt, was a small shop over the door of which was the name 'Odger', and above the window, the remarkable legend, 'Oil and Italian Warehousemen'.

How Odger could be either Oil or Italian, or indeed Warehousemen, I could not understand, and obtained no enlightenment when, on entering, I beheld a very large and very white woman behind the counter.

Forbearing to ask whether she were Oil, Italian, Warehousemen and Odger, I glanced round for something to buy. The stock was of a bewildering variety, an *'embarras de richesse'*, including neatly tied bundles of firewood stacked against the counter; an open barrel of treacle, on the surface of which was a rich and varied crust of sawdust, flies, dirt, a large feather and what might, or might not have been, a mouse; some rashers of what I felt sure was bacon; numerous tins of coruscating brightness, containing salmon; boxes of eggs, non-committally labelled 'eggs', without comment; and on the shelves behind the counter, an array of boxes, packets, pots and jars, of contents unspecified.

There were undoubtedly rats and mice also, though probably not for sale.

I have a highly developed olfactory sense, which is sometimes a blessing and often a curse.

Undoubtedly, the shop sold cheese, though none was visible. Certainly paraffin; and something that had a peculiarly vicious and penetrating odour that competed with considerable success with the cheese and paraffin. What was it? Kippers, red-herrings or some such weary fish, awaiting release?

"Wotcher want?" enquired Odger, the Oil and Italian Warehousemen, suddenly.

"Pink gol'fish," I replied promptly.

Reaching to the shelf behind her, the large white woman took down a tin of salmon, and I was amazed to note that upon the hands which appeared from under her shawl, were black kid gloves, aged, ill-fitting, but authentic.

> *Oh, fat white woman, whom nobody loves,*
> *Why do you serve in your shop in gloves?*

thought I, misquoting the remarkable original.

Were they the last vestiges of mourning? Or had she just had a manicure and was taking care of her hands?

However, I had not come into the shop to speculate thus idly—nor indeed, to speculate at all. The purchase was an act of propitiation, and the excuse for converse and inquiry.

"Where can a bloke get a good kip rahnd 'ere, Missus?" I asked, as I felt for my money.

"For the night or the week, or wot?" enquired Mrs. Odger.

Having heard what I had to say, she eyed me thoughtfully for a while, enquired as to whether I could pay in advance, and then admitted that she had got a back room on the floor above the shop, that she would be willing to let to a respectable single man. . . .

We came to terms, and my search was ended almost before it began.

Later, Mrs. Odger admitted that she took to me on sight; decided to trust her instinct; and took a big risk.

That it was a risk was obvious, for she was elderly, an invalid, and lived alone in the house—a house in which there was a constant and terrible temptation, 'the takings' sometimes amounting to pretty well a pound's worth of coppers and small silver!

Mrs. Odger lived in the room behind the shop. Above the shop was her parlour—a nightmare of pink vases, crimson plush, and ferocious oleographs. The other room was mine.

It was typical of the kind of inconvenience to which the poor have to submit, that there was no access to the upper floor, save by way of the shop and the inner room which was Mrs. Odger's boudoir and also bedroom, dining-room, sitting-room, kitchen, scullery, and, presumably, bathroom.

My bedroom was the size of this scene of all Mrs. Odger's domestic activities, but it seemed larger as it was more mercifully furnished.

From another point of view, merciful was not the *mot juste*, as the bed was a marvel of discomfort; the chair, a danger to life; and the enamelled washing-set, chipped, rusty and leaky.

Definitely, this marked quite a step down in the social scale, but to me it was preferable because of a greater privacy. What meals I had indoors, I had alone, and my room was never invaded for any purpose whatsoever. In fact, it needed only a chair —a practicable chair—to be a real bed-sitting-room. But a more depressing room, with a more hideous outlook, I never beheld.

Well, it was the sort of room in which this sort of people lived, and I must live in it if I wished to know exactly how they lived and what effect such living had upon their minds and souls and bodies.

Perhaps, in one way it was worse for me than for them, as the contrast between this life and my way of living at home and at Oxford was so great.

On the other hand, as Vibart-Stourton had said, I was infinitely better off, because I knew that it was only temporary and that I could at any time escape.

Mrs. Odger, at first dull, stupid, resentful, as well as malodorous, pudding-faced and repellent, turned slowly but surely into an admired and valued friend, if not exactly a fairy god-mother.

Although unable to 'do for me' by reason—as

she pointed out—of the stairs and her spasms, she gave me good and motherly advice and a midday meal at a price which I am sure left her no profit.

Poor dear, she was troubled not only with a bad heart—in a purely physical sense; by legs, in a sense not defined; a bad husband, a bad son (both in prison) and a bad landlord, but also with a bad phobia.

She was not so much afraid, as absolutely certain, that, sooner or later—probably sooner—she would be 'done in' for her money and her stock; as aged lonely shop-keepers not infrequently are.

I think that the impulse which moved her to accept me as lodger was that of a gambler. If I were a good 'un, as instinct told her, she'd be safe from murder as long as I was her lodger. If, upon the other hand, I were a wrong 'un, well then the sooner the better, and get it over.

I learned a lot concerning the attitude to life, the views and philosophy, of the honest poor, from Mrs. Odger. And I like to think that I was able to do something for her too.

Curiously enough, what I learned about shop-keeping through giving her a hand during the Saturday night rush—when there might be two women and a child in the shop at once—stood me in good stead later, and enabled me to get a job when in sore need of one.

It was pitiable to see the poor soul, blue-faced from a heart-attack, panting for breath, and moving painfully on legs that could scarcely support her, trying to get from her bed in the back-room to the shop, rather than disappoint a customer and forgo a transaction in which the profit might, or might not, be as much as a farthing.

To me, the business was a little difficult at first, because much of it was done without weights and measures; some customers should be given credit and others should be given nothing save abuse.

I well remember my first customer, a gaunt angel-child of some seven or eight summers, who looked as though they had all been winters, and who planked a handle-less teacup on the counter, demanded a pennorth of jam, a nayporth of tea, a pennorth of marge, a nayporth of sugar, and a rasher—the said rasher not to be transparent and to contain some traces of lean.

"What kind of jam?" I asked, in my innocence and bewilderment. What *kind* of jam? The jam yer eats, of course. What did I think it was for? To put in yer 'air? And I realised that to the child and, indeed, to Mrs. Odger, jam was *jam;* and if you found an apple pip in it or a plum-stone, a strawberry leaf or a raspberry pip, you could christen it accordingly if you wanted to.

How was I to know what amount of jam constituted a pennorth? I must "smack a dollop in the cup. She'd brought one, 'adn't she? 'Ow much? Table-spoonful. There's a wooden one in the jar."

Curious what things one forgets and what one remembers.

Most distinctly I can see myself transferring a large spoonful of the jam from the seven-pound jar into the cup; see the face of my first customer; and hear the one word of comment when, looking into the cup, she estimated the amount of the cochineal conserve. To this day I don't know whether that one exclamatory word expressed pleased or shocked surprise; anguish; contempt; protest; or self-congratulation. For the one word uttered by the angel-child was:

"*Christ!*" . . .

Before I had been with Mrs. Odger long, I had become her prop and stay; her right-hand man, accountant, stock-taker and occasional salesman.

I put up the shutters at night; I swept out the shop at dawn; washed the counter; dusted the rashers; banged the kippers together as one does books; removed the top dressing from the treacle; put the retrieved conglomerate in a zinc pail, and marked it down in price. (It *was* a mouse, whose appealing hand I had seen above the dark Lethean surface; and there were cockroaches and spare-parts of other insects too.)

In doing these things, I helped Mrs. Odger and I greatly helped to forward my own purpose, for I got to know the people of the neighbourhood; learned much about them and their ways; learned their language, and took on a protective lack of colouring.

In the day-time I looked for work, occasionally found it, and learned my own value—or rather, lack of value—in the local labour market.

I got a job in a wood-cutting establishment that lived under one of an endless row of boarded-up railway arches, and lost it through stupidity and clumsiness. I cut to waste; I cut myself; my employer cut my wages and, after a fortnight, cut his losses.

I also got a job at pushing and minding. Pushing a barrow and minding it while the owner went into houses to haggle over the purchase of rags, bottles and bones. This was only a temporary job, lasting while the ol'-clo' man was too ill and too weak to push and to shout his war-cry as well as to haggle.

The courage and tenacity of that sick and suffering old man was something at which to wonder; and to cause a sense of shame. . . .

What I very soon learned was that it was useless for me to try to live the life of the slum dweller if I were to use my educational advantages for obtaining work. The unskilled man and woman fighting for life, struggling for food and shelter, on the verge of destitution, has not had two thousand pounds worth of school education; has not been to a Public School, nor to a University. And I was going to know very little of their struggles for work and of their chances of employment if I were going to use my educational advantages easily to obtain comparatively well-paid clerical work.

For exactly how long Mrs. Odger and I lived in virtue, I cannot remember to-night; but I know that the time came, all too soon, when I felt that I must take another downward step. I had learned just about all that this neighbourhood had to teach me, and must dawdle no longer in idle luxury—for comparative luxury it was.

Why, there was a gas-ring in my room, and though it was a dirty stuffy hole, there was still a lot of paper on the walls and practically all the glass in the window.

Moreover, it was a dwelling to which I was to look back with fond and loving regret, for there wasn't an insect in that room, save for the fleas and flies; large, lethargic flies, bloated upon feasts of bacon, cheese, kipper, the anonymous jam, and other comestibles.

I admit that the fleas troubled me at first, and I used to pursue and kill them vindictively. But the day came—and still more the night—when I regarded fleas as harmless, friendly fellows, happy and hearty, and, beyond the occasional need for a scratch, quite negligible.

Compared with lice and still more with bugs, they were almost lovable, and, moreover, showed excellent sport. I know no better fun—to one addicted to blood sports and bored almost to suicide in a terrible room he cannot leave—than a rousing good hunt o'er the hills and dales of a stripped bed—a covert that is always a certain

draw—after an active flea of good will, high courage, and low cunning. Like the fox, he positively
loves being hunted; and, unlike the fox, he can
jump a thousand times his own height.

Well do I remember one who showed such
splendid sport, giving me a good twenty minutes'
run, that when I had captured him, I let him live
to hop another day. I opened the glass of a large
tin watch that I wore, inserted him through the
crack, shut down the glass, and gloated upon him
until night, when I released him.

I think that I must have been rather near the
end of my tether just then. I had not read a book,
nor spoken to an intelligent human being for
weeks and weeks.

Where was it that I went when I left Mrs.
Odger? Was it to Bonn Alley? It must have been,
because it was from one of our customers that I
heard of the desirable vacancy for a reasonably
single young man.

Bonn Alley was very nearly authentic slum, but
not quite. For though not snobbish there, as we
were in Mrs. Odger's neighbourhood, we had our
pride, and I don't think that any room in the whole
length and breadth of that exclusive street housed
more than one family.

The fact that practically every room did house a
family, varying from two to about ten in number,
made me something of an aristocrat and a marked
man, inasmuch as I had a whole room entirely to
myself.

In Bonn Alley I was not nearly so happy as I
had been with Mrs. Odger. And strange as it may
be, it is a fact that when the time came for me to
leave her, I realised that I had been comparatively
happy; and hated going. I had got quite fond of
Mrs. Odger; a sentiment that was reciprocated, for
she not only wept but positively sobbed, as the

final moment approached. One of the few women to whom I have ever given cause to cry.

Also, one of the few women whom I have ever kissed, for kiss her I did—closing my eyes and holding my breath—and it should be counted unto me for righteousness as a good and brave deed, if it were the only one I ever did.

Faithfully I promised to come and see her at least once a week—a promise I kept until she died. This, the poor dear soul did a few weeks later, all alone; and I hope it was some satisfaction to her to think that she had cheated the unknown villains whom she had so long expected to come and do her in.

If I had served what I thought was a difficult apprenticeship in Golden Row and in Mrs. Odger's shop, I now began to serve a far more arduous and unpleasant time as a journeyman slum-dweller in Bonn Alley.

Here I met my first Bug. I met a family of Bugs, a tribe of Bugs, a nation of Bugs, and in the end they defeated me. I became bug-conscious, bug-ridden—mentally speaking, and got a bug-complex.

From those flat ferocious insects I learned hate, loathing. Never before and never since have I so hated, loathed, abhorred any living creature—always excepting, of course, the man whom I . . .

No, I won't think of him. . . . Think of that. . . . Not now, anyhow. Not while . . . I won't think of him at all, for I never think of him . . . think of *that*. . . .

They can't make me speak of it; confess it. . . .

Having been introduced by Mrs. Odger's customer to the loathsome little man who collected the rents of the house (in which I believe there were twelve rooms housing eleven families and myself), I took the room and then proceeded to

furnish it; again, with the help and advice of this
same customer, Mrs. Billing, a very nice charwoman.

This was an interesting and intricate process
which made me proprietor of a rickety iron bedstead, on which the sagging, rusty laths supported
a rather dreadful mattress, stuffed with what the
second-hand furniture dealer described as "best
quality flock, strite from the bloomin' sheep"; (why
not call it flock of sheep then?); a straw-stuffed
bolster; a thing that had begun life as a cushion;
and a couple of brown blankets. Also a table, a
chair and a washing-stand, all rickety; a kettle,
saucepan and frying-pan, all second-hand; an
irreducible minimum of crockery; and the wooden
part of a lady's hand-mirror which still contained
some of the mirror.

There were many more things which I should
have liked, but I had to play my part carefully,
thoroughly, and to the life; and not spend more
than a pound on furnishing my new room.

I had to do this because, from the level of Bonn
Alley and downwards, rooms are not let furnished.
This is because a tenant would either use as
firewood such of the furniture as was combustible;
and, sooner or later, would, one night, silently and
alone, depart with the rest—a process known as
shooting the moon.

One also does it with one's own furniture—in
avoidance of payment of arrears of rent.

On my first night in Bonn Alley, although lying
upon my own bed, guaranteed of unsullied mate-
rials and immaculate history, I awoke burning and
itching as though from contact with the shirt of
Nessus.

I thought at first that I must be ill; must have
contracted some terrible disease which first man-
ifests itself by high temperature and burning

itching skin.

Then something dropped on my face and I almost shrieked, for I have a more than feminine nervous re-action to things that drop on my face and crawl, in the night.

There is no instantaneous switching on of lights in the slums; there are no bed-side tables with books and a convenient drawer. Beside my uneasy couch, there was a cane-chair, a candle and a box of matches.

By the time I had got a light I was almost frantic with horror, and at the end of an hour's sanguinary conflict, I think I was almost hysterical with loathing, wrath, and disgust.

Yes, I was certainly getting near the slums now, and experiencing what must be one of their main delights. Could I ever conquer this feeling of apparently unconquerable repulsion and sick disgust? I *must* do so.

Meanwhile, it was legitimate to attempt any and every means of self-defence.

From the conduct of my wily, resourceful and remorseless foes, I gathered that light would be my best weapon. Like other evil things, from light they fled. Could I but instal half-a-dozen sixty-watt electric light bulbs, I might be safe, and free to sleep in peace. But as the nearest electric cable was miles away, the thought was vain. Nor could I ring my bed about with a hundred burning candles.

I must take advice on the subject. But probably the first person to whom I said:

"How do you prevent bugs?" would reply,

"You don't."

What should I do if the only alternative was to get used to them? I supposed that it could be done. Had I not read that, in India, good men of the Jain sect give such insects as fleas, lice and bugs a treat on certain feast-days? (Their own or those of the insects?) But even that was different from making life one perpetual feast-day for the little creatures. Even St. Francis would draw the line there, one imagines.

Having slain every insect that could not escape me, I again lay down to rest. I must have been very tired, too, for I fell asleep.

But not for long.

I think that room must have been empty for some time—and also the bugs. I think, too, that those that had escaped and gone home had unselfishly spread the news far and wide, for the second assault was made in even greater numbers.

This time I supplemented superior strength with strategy, and endeavoured to cut off the enemy's retreat before attacking him. In vain. He was more clever than I, and had many lines of retreat.

Down from the ceiling; up through cracks between the rotten and ancient boards; in under the wainscoting; through holes in the plaster, the hordes escaped, and all I could do was to slay. . . .

By the morning I was not precisely a nervous wreck, but definitely not In Tune with the Infinite; and at the risk of drawing attention to myself, as an objectionable person who had ideas above his station, I sought out, in the distant High Street, a painter-and-paper-hanger and explained to him my curious requirements.

I wanted my room papered, first with brown paper and then with the thickest and toughest paper that he had; and when I said room, I meant room —walls, floor and ceiling—though the floor paper was to be different, a kind of tar-paper, tough and enduring.

I certainly surprised the proprietor of this one-man business, but as I agreed to pay a substantial deposit in advance, and he was only too thankful to have a job, he came and got to work at once, did it quickly and well, and, as I requested, did not say nothink to nobody.

For two nights I slept at the Hammersmith Rowton House, and had excellent cubicle-accommodation at a charge, if I remember rightly, of fourpence a night, and the use of a large cooking-range in the basement.

My first night at home, after the papering, was by no means peaceful, but I think that my assailants were stragglers who had taken refuge in cracks and crannies of my furniture, instead of accompanying the main army to its base.

I developed a technique of which speed was the essence. Swift procuring of light, throwing off of bedclothes and a snatching of opportunity.

In the end I won an incomplete victory, both over the insects and over my super-sensitive fastidiousness. I reached a point where a bug or two was neither here nor there—though greatly I would have preferred them to be there rather than here. But I could never bring myself to regard them as I did the flea, that care-free, happy fellow —a great bounder, of course, but not a loathsome stinking sneak.

Later on, when I earned my living "barking on the tober", I became friendly with the proprietor, trainer and exhibitor of a troupe of performing fleas, and asked him, one day, whether it would be possible to train bugs. As his sole reply was a prompt and far-flung expectoration, I gathered that he regarded the bug much as I myself did.

Anyhow, one thing that disgusting parasite did, was to deepen my sympathy with the slum-dweller, and to increase my understanding of that prolonged process of irritation, discomfort and bitter misery that is his life.

Another thing that made existence in Bonn Alley less happy than it had been in Golden Row and at Mrs. Odger's, was noise.

The Alley was never quiet, and most of the noise was made by children. They almost made me hate them, with their constant din, raucous and shrill, pitched on a note of infinite irritation. They quarrelled perpetually and unceasingly; and, although the Alley was only a few feet wide, they always addressed each other at the tops of their voices and called to each other at the full strength of their lungs.

This puzzled me; for surely it is easier to talk than to shout, and surely they badly needed all the muscular and nervous energy they got from the bread-and-lard which was, apparently, their sole diet.

Nor was it that they had to shout in competition with the noises of traffic, for Bonn Alley has none, there being a row of iron posts at either end.

The noise was worst before nine in the morning, between twelve and two, and again from four-thirty almost to mid-night. But during the hours that some, at any rate, of these children were presumably at school, I was usually out in search of work, so did not benefit from the oasis of silence, save on those days when, giving way to the claims of the weary body, I stayed at home.

And, besides the noise made by the children, there was generally some kind of row, racket or rumpus going on in the house or close to it. There were frequent and noisy quarrels between the ladies, who dressed with a curious monotony, almost a uniform, in a man's cloth cap, a torn and dirty blouse, a lop-sided skirt and an apron of sacking.

Sometimes they fought, and then I was constrained to sit with my hands pressed over my ears, and to subscribe to the theory that the female of the species is more deadly than the male.

There were other constant noises, some vocational. I believe a cobbler hammered just above me; somebody below worked a sewing-machine at most hours of the day and night; babies wailed; and people would argue or converse interminably on the stairs outside my door.

Another curse was the Smell. I never got used to it and it took me by the throat afresh, every time I entered the house. It was compounded of many elements, but the senior partner, dominating all the rest, came from our Insanitary Inconvenience.

Although as a Christian I should not do so, I still wish ill and evil to those who had a vested interest in that worst and vilest ingredient in the Smell. Ill and evil to the scoundrel who planned the horrible death-trap; to the knave who jerry-built it; and to the criminal who made money by taking a high rent for our wretched rooms and doing nothing whatsoever to render our Insanitary Inconvenience less of a horror and a menace.

How little I thought when I entered into possession of that horrible room at Mrs. Odger's, that, from my next abode, I should look back to it as to a haven of peace and comfort, bordering on luxury.

If this were not a real slum, how much worse would my last state be? I put the thought away, and plunged, so far as was permitted, into the social life of Bonn Alley.

I wanted to know everyone in the house; everyone in the street; how they lived; what they did; what they lacked; what they wanted (which is not always the same thing); and what could be done for them by a Society anxious to do its best to help them.

It was not an easy task to get to know my fellow-lodgers and my neighbours. Far more difficult than it is to make friends and acquaintances in the superior social circles of a cathedral City, for example. There is no calling in the Bonn Alleys of East London. Not, at least, with paste-board and ceremony; though there is plenty of calling, with abuse, from windows.

It is difficult, because the manners and customs, habits and ways of the denizens of those streets are as "different" as those of any Central African or Central Asian tribe, and the stranger is viewed with as great suspicion and distrust.

It is only in the Public Houses that, with offers of beer, one can make advances, and then it must be done carefully and in the right manner.

Even the children are suspicious, and to give a strange child a half-penny, a toy or a bag of sweets is an act liable to lay one open to the gravest suspicion.

One has to tread warily and do kindnesses not only by stealth but with the worst possible grace and grudging churlishness. To offer to turn the mangle for an under-nourished consumptive woman, who was coughing her soul out as she earned her daily pence, was to make an improper overture, and to run the risk of assault from the husband or son whom she supported. I speak with the knowledge of experience.

But for the Public Houses, their only and essential Clubs, I do not know how I should ever have got on friendly terms with these exclusive people.

I am, perhaps, almost unique in that I drank my way to grace.

I must not, moreover, forget the help I got from Dipper the Dope. I believe his name really was

Dipper, but whether he obtained his soubriquet by actually selling or taking some kind of narcotic drug, I don't know. He certainly sold none in Bonn Alley, but he may very well have earned his living by that foul means in the West End.

I do not want to judge, much less condemn, anybody; to no-one do I, or will I, say 'I am holier than thou'; but I am free to confess that Dipper the Dope was a very bad little man indeed. A panderer to the vices and a parasite upon the vicious.

His most respectable occupation was that of corner-bookie; and in pursuit of this profession and his clients, he went from door to door, which is to say, from room to room.

He was the most unplaceable person I have ever met, for he could talk like a curate—and not the stage caricature of a curate, either; like a bargee; like a Billingsgate porter; like an instructor to a thieves'-kitchen school. He spoke French with what seemed to me to be a good accent, and was well-educated. I welcomed his visits and, to encourage him, did business to the extent of such investments as "Sixpence each way on Pink Eye for the Three-thirty".

He had an amazing flow of conversation and a fund of stories; he was sharp-eyed, observant and clever; and early he penetrated my disguise.

One day he suddenly ceased speaking to me as one coster-monger to another, and spoke in what was either genuine, or excellent imitation of, what is known as the Oxford Accent. It was rather sudden and rather alarming.

"Gawdstreuth! Wotta bleedin' row them perishin' young barstards maike! Carn't hear yerself think, can yer? What I would say, dear boy, is that those fellers, Herod and Pharaoh, weren't properly appreciated. We could do with the pair of them down here . . . Ever hear the real truth of what passed between Pharaoh and his daughter? No?

> *Pharaoh's daughter, bathing,*
> *Found Moses by the Nile:*
> *Thought she'd take him home to father*
> *And keep him for a while.*

> *But when Pharaoh heard the story,*
> *He said "That's a likely tale!*
> *Just about as probable*
> *As Jonah and the Whale."*

No, I hadn't heard that one. Was it in the Apocrypha?

Yes, it was. Came just after the revised version of Jehu, the Exceeder of Speeds.

What was that one?

Oh, didn't I know it?

> *Now Jehu had a chariot*
> *Of ninety-five horse-power,*
> *And buzzed it round Jerusalem*
> *At eighty miles an hour.*
> *But he had to throttle down a bit*
> *When he got into Jezreel,*
> *For little bits of Jezebel*
> Would *catch up in his wheel.*

Curious I hadn't come across that, he mused.

Had I heard the one about the Bishop and the Barmaid? No? And didn't want to? Well, now, what about a bit of business? Was there anything I specially fancied for Newbury to-morrow?

There wasn't; but if he'd give me a list of runners, I'd close my eyes and pick one with the point of a pin, unless it so happened that among them was a horse the second letter of whose name was R: either of these methods being rather better than that of making a close study of form, and betting on probabilities.

I would then invest the sum of half-a-crown with him, provided that he would meet me on Saturday night at "The Marquis of Granby", and do what he could to introduce me to such of my neighbours as might then and there be present.

"Cully," said Dipper the Dope, extending his right hand, "put it there—with five bob in it—and I'm your friend. I've been in trouble myself; known times when the thump of the rozzer's hoof was the foot-step of Fate. . . . And if it should be a case of a quick-change and a quiet get-away; or of the planting of some bright rocks[16] behind a good 'fence', I'm your man."

I thanked Dipper the Dope and assured him that, at the moment, I went in no fear of the police, nor in search of the receiver of stolen goods.

"Bit of a penman?" he asked.

"I can sign my name," I said.

"It's signing other people's that brings the profit and the trouble, isn't it? Get Honours at your University? No? Ah, well, Honours are not without profit save in their own country so long as you can wield a pen neatly—in someone else's cheque-book. Now suppose I could find you one or two nice clean cheques? No? . . . Well, can you pass a bit of snide?"

"No," I said. "I'm on the level and I'm going straight."

Dipper the Dope winked and lapsed into the local vernacular.

"Give a pore bloke a chawnst, guv'ner," he mocked. "I'm tryin' to hearn a *honest* livin'. Me 'ands is clean."

---

[16] Diamonds.

The remark must have been metaphorical, but the acting was extremely good—the whining cringing pick-pocket to the policeman.

Dipper the Dope may have been a bad man, but he was as good as his word, and was, socially, very helpful. He vastly improved my Public House technique and knowledge of etiquette. He taught me how and what to offer a lady, and to judge the age at which it were better to suggest a Dog's-nose, a Mother's-Ruin or a Port-and-lemon. That was in the genuine Public House, of course. In the dirty beer-shop it was beer and more beer; stout and more stout; gin-an-'ot upon occasion. For a man to call for fancy drinks was also to call undesirable attention to himself as a flash swanker, a foreign body and, probably, a nark or even a dick.
. . .

I think that the lesson that I learnt most thoroughly in Bonn Alley was the bitter cruelty that illness is to the poor.

For the pain and misery of illness, of which we complain, is the least part of it to them. They care little for the physical suffering and bear it stoically. The real awfulness of illness lies in the fact that it means the ruin of these people who live upon the verge of ruin; it means the loss of a job; the loss of the daily poor earnings; and that means the loss of not only the food that nourishes you, but the roof that shelters you, the bed on which you lie, the "sticks" of furniture that you have painfully gathered together, and all but the irreducible minimum of clothes that you wear.

And they are so prone and exposed to illness, with their under-nourished bodies; the insanitary conditions of their lives; their lack of change of clothing when wet through; the cold they endure in winter; the moral and physical ignorance and dirt in which they live; and their pathetic belief in the sustaining and invigorating qualities of beer and gin for themselves and their babies.

Introduced, guaranteed and sponsored by Dipper the Dope, I got to know several families who lived in Bonn Alley and the neighbourhood, and had rather a success with middle-aged and elderly ladies, charwomen, door-to-door pedlars, costers and stall-keepers.

It was rather a *succés d'estime* than a *succés fou*, for I made poor headway with the men-folk. Rightly and justly they regarded me either with definite dislike or contemptuous tolerance, and drank my beer condescendingly.

In that milieu, in that stark mart of male capacities, strength, and fighting-power, I was their inferior, and they knew it as well as I did. Undeniably they were stouter, stronger, braver men than I; more enduring, more undaunted, and far better equipped to wring a livelihood from the arid or muddy stones of that cruel market-place.

I came to have a great respect for those unskilled labourers, living hungrily on the fringe of the casual-workers' market; unorganised part-time dockers, coster-mongers, market-porters, odd-job seekers and snatchers, who would regard municipal dustmen as aristocrats, made men, dwellers upon velvet.

I respected them more than I liked them, for they were suspicious, touchy and difficult people, who were not at any pains to oil the machinery of social intercourse with insincere, if pleasing, words and graces.

I learnt their way of life; learnt what life meant to them; and I unsuccessfully competed with them for their jobs.

A very few I was able to help without "flashing

the rhino", and rousing suspicion that I was a fraud and the spy of such natural enemies as the police, landlords, and those Municipal Authorities who existed to harass and annoy, to persecute and prosecute.

Why was it that I left Bonn Alley when I did?

Was it because . . . ?

No. I remember. Love and War; Venus and Mars.

I unintentionally found favour in the sight of a young coster-girl and extreme disfavour in the sight of a middle-aged but powerful and truculent coster who was not her husband.

Frankly, I fled: but to be quite fair to myself, it was more from the lady than from her protector—rather a misleading allocution, in view of the fact that nobody on this earth ever had less need of protection than Sally Draper.

I don't think I should have had the courage to be so cowardly as to run away from Sam Porler, but I had the cowardice, and to spare, to flee before the fair and brazen face of Sally.

Yes, it was on the night when she sat beside me in "The Marquis of Granby", full of stout and gin and love, her arm about me, that she uttered the promise that to-morrow she would move in with all she possessed and abide with me; and that I got me to a monastery, fled to a Rowton House.

It was while I was staying at the Rowton House and exploring the adjacent truly-genuine slums, that the Hand of Fate or the Finger of God—doubtless the same thing—directed my steps, one night, to the place known locally as Dahn-the-Gaffs.

This was a bright spot in the encircling gloom—at night, at any rate, for it was then filled with light, music, joy and laughter.

What if the light were that of naphtha flares; the music the brassy blare from a steam round-about; the joy but fleeting, floating upon a tide of alcohol; the laughter raucous and shrill?

No matter. Here *were* the things most missing, most lacking, in that dreadful neighbourhood; the things, the want of which was part of the cause of the prevalent ill-health of mind and body and soul.

Light, music, joy and laughter.

It was through my apparently accidental stumble on Dahn-the-Gaffs that I came to dwell in the real slums, to know some splendid people, to love a noble and beautiful woman, and to do the dreadful deed that ruined my work, darkened my life and brought me here.

Here, where I have found Elspeth Grey.

"Dahn-the-Gaffs" was the widely known name of the very poorest and lowliest form of circus. I imagine it was the mere residue of the actual, humble circus that toured England in the spring, summer and autumn months.

On a very foul and muddy acre of ground, entirely surrounded by tenement houses, was a small and ragged 'big-top'; a boxing-booth; a side-show tent in which were exhibited a Fat Lady, a 'real mermaid', which was, I believe, the stuffed skin of a manatee or sea-cow; two "full-grown" Central African pigmies, who were, in private life, George and Maria Wilks, aged ten years and born and bred in Whitechapel; a Wild Man and Woman of Borneo, of the same name, and their reputed parents; a Bearded Lady, whose beard was affixed nightly; a Zulu chief who was a Jamaican Negro, one of the nicest men I ever knew; and a few other wonders.

There were also some swing-boats, a steam round-about, and, against the walls of three sides of the square, some gaudily-painted caravans, in two or three of which lived the proprietor and some of the principal members of the circus.

Among these was a fairy of uncertain age but most undeniable agility who rode the faithful old "resin-back" and jumped through hoops; a pair of equally passé acrobats, who were also fair jugglers; and a strong man, who lifted iron or iron-looking weights on which were inscribed figures of astronomical dimensions. . . .

This Elysium lay immediately behind the thronged and brightly lit High Street, the entrance being by a short passage between a greengrocer's and a butcher's.

Entrance to the ground was free, but outside the 'big-top' was a platform on which, between their acts, paraded almost the entire company, while a man, known as 'the barker', extolled the merits of the show and poured scorn upon such mean people as entered the fair ground, saw all that they could for nothing, and departed leaving not a penny piece behind them.

I estimated that the barker's scorn should have affected seventy-five per cent of the visitors to the ground; but it failed to do so, their withers being obviously unwrung.

It was a marvel to me that the nightly takings of the circus should have been sufficient to pay the rent of the ground, the cost of lighting, and to feed the animals and artists who performed there.

Perhaps the takings were not sufficient unto this last.

Anyhow, it was, as I have said, a place of light and life and laughter, tremendously attractive by comparison with the dark, dull, sordid slums in which its patrons lived.

Certainly it attracted me, accustomed though I was to a superior form and level of entertainment.

The effort to make out a two-hour show in the

'big-top' thrice nightly, was pathetic; and no artists on the grandest stage or in the most magnificent circus in the world ever worked harder, or made a braver struggle for success.

The weary woman, in her jaded, tawdry finery, on the under-fed horse; the juggler-acrobats, in their dirty, oft-mended fleshings; the poor, desperately facetious and hilarious clowns; and then—The Play!

Actually, those brave creatures, with no stage, backdrop, foot-lights, wings or curtain, gave a *play*, in the ring (after the circus show—when that performance was concluded because it could be spun out no longer), and that is a difficult and rather dreadful thing to have to do.

I know; for I, God forgive me, acted in some of those plays, as well as "barking on the tober"!

How on earth did such a thing come to pass?

I remember. Of course! On the third occasion of my visit to the place, a big man lurched heavily against me, almost knocking me down. It was in the passage between the shops, rather dark, and I thought at first that it was a wanton assault, and then that the man must be drunk. As I staggered back against the wall, he reeled and would have fallen, but for the support of a girl who had her right arm around his waist, and his left arm across her shoulders.

The man groaned and then said:

"Hold up, old horse," as he made an effort to pull himself together.

"He's ill," said the girl. "Do help me."

Of course I did my utmost.

"We'll get a taxi," I said.

"Yes," said the girl bitterly, "or a golden chariot."

And I realised, once again, what a lot I had to learn, and what a long way I had to go before I should be at home in my part.

Between us, we got the man into a neigh-bouring Public House, and I got him some brandy which soon, if temporarily, revived him.

In the brightly lit bar, I saw that the man was elderly, clean-shaven and handsome, with a fine head of well-kept hair. His neat blue suit was old, shiny and frayed at cuff and trouser; his boots were split; he had neither collar nor shirt, but about his throat he wore, with an air, a table-napkin folded like a stock.

I thought I had seen him somewhere before, but differently dressed.

His speech and accent were those of an educat-ed man, and I guessed, correctly as it proved, that he was an old actor.

When I had time to take note of the girl, I saw that she was young and pretty, with that frail pale prettiness by no means uncommon in the slums of London; that she was dressed like the other girls of the neighbourhood; but that this did not pre-vent her from differing from them in some indefin-able way. Even her fringe failed to make her look common, but rather gave her head the appearance of that of a medieval page-boy.

Her superior appearance and speech were ac-counted for by the fact that she was the man's daughter—and he, as I learned later, was quite definitely a Shakespearean scholar. Perhaps I should be speaking more exactly if I said that he knew the more popular of Shakespeare Plays com-pletely and entirely by heart, and had made a close study of the rest, memorizing long speeches which many highly-educated people have not even read.

This man was a living example of the truth that Shakespeare in himself, and alone, is a liberal education; for he had had no schooling and was, beyond his Shakespearean knowledge, ignorant and uneducated.

But he was a born trouper, the son of barn-storming troupers; and the highest peak of his frustrated career of hard work and semi-starvation had been when he was "with" Henry Irving! Undoubtedly, there had been a few nights—whose glory compensated for a life-time of disappoint-ment, failure and misery—when he had trodden the boards of the Lyceum Theatre, making the most of an understudy's opportunity in some small part in *Henry VIII;* and again, in *King Lear,* in 1892 or 1893.

And now he earned a few shillings weekly as a "barker on the tober" (the attraction-shouter on the platform outside the circus big-top), and actor in the incredible plays given in the ring, after the circus.

His daughter shared his bed-sitting-room, and had a small bedroom of her own on the same floor, in the rabbit-warren of a house in which they lived near Dahn-the-Gaffs. . . .

That night I helped to get him home, for he was obviously very ill; fetched a doctor; got a prescrip-tion made up; and was rewarded with the poor fellow's job!

True to the brave standards and slogan of the genuine trouper, his one thought—even while, white-lipped and blue-faced, he fought for breath —was: "*The Show must go on*".

From the way in which he said it, the poor old man might have been sustaining the title-role in *Hamlet* or *Macbeth* at a West End theatre! And it was for his sake, and not my own, that in a mo-ment of mad inspiration I offered to go to the Boss at Dahn-the-Gaffs and propose myself as substi-tute barker, and as understudy—in some part so small that I could rehearse it before night.

Perhaps what I learned at the O.U.D.S. was the most useful of all my Oxford studies?

I found the Boss to be a large and terrifying man, with husky voice, protuberant eyes, purple face, enormous fists, a most daunting manner, and a really kind heart.

It was a cause of some pride and satisfaction to me that, having heard what I had to say, he looked me up and down, expectorated with virtuoso skill, and huskily growled:

"*You?* Barker on the tober? A gutter-snipe tough like you? Act in the big-top? Go and look at yerself! You ain't got the ejucation for a start! . . . Nor the brass an' style . . . Not you! . . .

" 'Ere! Get up there and bark at me," he added, pointing to the small platform at the rear of his own caravan.

Mounting the steps, filled with high ambition and a burning desire to keep Horatio Burbidge's job open for him, I took a deep breath, put on an exaggerated Oxford accent, and poured forth a torrent of balderdash concerning the Pigmies of Central Africa; the Wild Man and Woman of Borneo; the Mermaid who had sat and combed her silken tresses upon the rock in the wine-dark Ionian sea that laved the golden shores of the Cyclades . . .

"*Gorblimey!*" murmured the Boss, as I paused for breath. "Yer *wasted* 'ere!"

Eyeing me thoughtfully as I descended to his level, he asked.

"Wot's the gime? On the run? . . . Well, don't matter to me. Right, yer 'ired—same wages as Burbidge. Can yer scrap?"

"No," I said." Why?"

"Well, I coulder put yer on me string in there." And he jerked a large thumb in the direction of the boxing-booth, where surely the world's six most hard-working men nightly challenged all comers and boxed three rounds with anybody, from semi-professional heavy-weights to hungry coster-lad novices.

Later I was to wish to God that I had studied that art in the Oxford Gymnasium, in the days when I affected to be an aesthete, to scorn an athlete, and to despise the rugger-roughs and the boxing-toughs. . . .

The Boss then took me to another caravan and called from his breakfast the protean person who, among many things, was ring-master, stage-manager, and leading-man of the acting troupe or cast.

Some of this gentleman's breakfast was still with him, for, from an over-full mouth, and between gulping swallows, he inquired as to 'oo the 'ell I was and wot I knew abaht it.

"Ho!" laughed the Boss. "Wait til yer 'ear the perisher spout! 'E's a bloody marvel!"

And that night I did make my debut as a professional actor.

Behind the back of the leading-man, what time he waved a rusty rapier and declaimed, I inserted Poison in the Cup.

The cup was a pint pot; the poison was a lump of washing-soda. And when, on my offering it to Sir Hantonio, he tasted something wrong—as well he might—and observed,

'Villun, thou 'ast brought a dirty mug!' I forbore to laugh.

My job at Dahn-the-Gaffs was a wonderful experience; it brightened my life; helped me enormously; gave me a sound and solid foot-hold in the slums; and brought me into contact with delightful people, as well as with the general public.

I only made one enemy, and that, unfortunately, was the wife of the Boss, with whom I began badly, through failing to curb an incurable or, rather, then uncured, flippancy.

She had a young son, Hildebrand; a younger daughter, Hildegarde; and consulted me as to a third and similar name, should she happily be blessed with a third and similar offspring.

Instead of taking this as a kindly tribute to my knowledge of high-falutin' stage names, I thoughtlessly said I considered that Hildebrand, Hildegarde and Hildebuggins would make a nice set.

I was a fool and rather a cad.

However, I made amends, if not my peace, with the lady, by producing all the rarest and most chaste names of which I could think, such as Aphasia, Coryza, Sprue, Dengue and similar unusual names which might appeal to one tired of Tom, Dick and Harry; Maria, Lizzie and Sal.

And, remembering this trifle, I also remember how amazed and interested I was to learn that the name of the old actor's daughter was Miranda. Presumably, he was learning *The Tempest*, by heart, at the time of her birth, and saw himself understudying a more successful actor in the part of Prospero. Anyway, the name of that bred-and-born slum-girl was Miranda Burbidge!

Not only did my fortuitous, if not fortunate, meeting with this strange old Thespian provide me with what I so badly wanted, a job in the slums, but also with lodging; for reduction in his almost irreducible circumstances compelled him to give up his bed-sitting-room and take his daughter's smaller and cheaper little bedroom. The girl insisted on this and shared a room with an older girl, Liz Bennie, whom she helped in her business of buying flowers before dawn at Covent Garden, and selling them at a street corner in Bayswater.

I at once took Burbidge's room, and was soundly and plausibly established in a genuine slum; in a house in which I was under no suspicion of being a fraud; and in an open and above-board job which was my *raison d'être*, and showed all men how I earned my living.

This was splendid, and I settled down to study slum life as might an exploring anthropologist study the manners and customs, habits and ways, history and ethnology of a strange, difficult and somewhat savage tribe.

As a matter of fact, I was much happier here than I had been in Golden Row, Mrs. Odger's shop, or Bonn Alley, in spite of the definitely lower, filthier, poorer and even more sordid way of life. This was because I had company, acquaintances, indeed, I may say friends. Not the sort of friends that I should, at one time, have chosen in conditions of free selection, but they were really just as interesting; quite as worthwhile; and, in some cases, much more admirable than some of the people whom I had known at Oxford and in my former walk of life.

I shall never forget my Three Old Men.

They were as fine in their way as any three old men to be found in the Classics, in the Bible, in historical or modern literature. Three great "characters"—and good characters, too.

First there was old Burbidge himself. Simple, vain, and filled with the spirit of the true artist; who worshipped his daughter, behaved with the utmost unselfishness towards her, and regretted far beyond any personal failure, loss and deprivation, the fact that he had been unable to provide her with a better kind of life.

"But mind you, Richard," he would say to me, "I have taught her not only to read and to write and to talk well, but to read Shakespeare and like it. You try her, sometime. Make any quotation you like and see if she doesn't cap it. Anything from

Twelfth Night to *Love's Labour's Lost*. She's a good girl, too; good as gold. If only I could have given her a chance in life!" And he would literally wipe away a genuine tear, for he made no secret of the fact that he was a person of sensibility as well as sentiment.

Then there was his crony, a circus friend and colleague, whom he had known for many years, Tom Brickett, an ex-professional pugilist who, even yet, though close on sixty, was not the least considerable member of the Boss's string of Let-em-all-come Boxers who nightly paraded outside their booth, and challenged the world.

Undoubtedly, this old man could still hurt. What was doubtful, was whether anyone could hurt him; for if, during the last and third round of the third house of the evening, he were feeling a little tired, he would lower his guard and request his opponent to 'it 'im 'ard.

"*Do* 'it me," he would say. "I'm 'arf asleep."

I believe he was the very last of the genuine old bare-fist prize-fighters. He told me how, as a young-man, he was one of the seconds to Jem Smith (I think it was), the last Englishman publicly to fight in bare-fisted battle.

If I remember rightly, he said that the fight took place in France, on an island in the Seine, a whole boat-load of British "sportsmen" having accompanied the two pugilists beyond the reach of the long arm of the British Law.

Tom Brickett, survivor of a thousand fights, who was nothing more nor less than a fighting machine or a fighting animal, was one of the kindest and gentlest creatures I have ever met. A nice, friendly, lovable old man, who never said a nasty thing or did a mean one. He was, in short, a gentleman; and he had the greatest admiration and affection for his old friend Burbidge, whom he regarded as a ruddy-well perishin' marvel of en-lightenment and erudition.

And so he was perishing, poor chap; for he was dying of consumption.

Burbidge used no 'language' that was not Shakespearean, though even thus handicapped, he could be quite effective in commination and condemnation. He had quite a pretty wit too, and inasmuch as old Tom Brickett invariably alluded to himself as a pore ole Bloody Duck, Burbidge would, in polite, if not reproving paraphrase, ad-dress him as his Ruddy Sheldrake (which is, I believe, a bird of the duck family, enriched with red hair on the head—or, perhaps I should say, feathers).

And the third of this charming trio was Ole Bill Munry, the fish-hawker. Again, as simple and kindly a man as ever lived; truthful, honest and generous to a fault.

The Ruddy Sheldrake always addressed him as Stinker—he also being truthful to a fault—for Ole Bill Munry did indeed smell appallingly, with an ancient and fish-like smell that, when he sat near my fire—which I am happy to say he often did—became almost unbearable.

I don't imagine that Bill ever washed. This, and the fact that he lived in such intimate association with fish, handling them at Billingsgate, pushing them on his barrow, carrying them on his head, holding them out in one hand and smacking them with the other, while earnestly extolling their charms and virtues, had so impregnated him and his clothing that he was more fish-like than any fish that ever rendered up its perfume in the sun-shine on a barrow.

It must not be thought that Bill was dirty in his habits or careless of his appearance. His thin hair was always well-brushed, and if there were fish-scales upon it, there was also oil of some kind, applied for appearance sake—cod-liver oil, perhaps. Nor did he fail in the evenings to knot a white kerchief about his brawny neck, to polish his boots, and to button up his thick reefer jacket. This, I think, had once been blue and nautical, but was now, in front at anyrate, black, hard and shiny as a beetle's wing. By day, and about his lawful vocations, he wore it open, or slung empty-sleeved across his broad thick shoulders; for evening wear he buttoned it up, and always looked trim and neat.

The company of these Three Old Men gave me pleasure and profit, whether about the fire in the room that had been Burbidge's or in the bar of 'The Black Boy', where I stood them as much beer as they would accept, and as was consistent with my position.

As the days and weeks passed, it became—to my very deep regret—more and more evident that poor Burbidge would never return to work.

Waylaying the doctor, I asked him what was wrong.

"Everything," snapped the doctor.

"And when do you think he will be able to go out again?" I asked.

"Never," was the prompt reply.

And then, inasmuch as I cared nothing at all what the doctor thought of me, as he neither was nor pretended to be, a slum-dweller, I assumed the alleged Oxford accent and a euphemistic, not to say affected, style, and observed.

"Look here, my friend, inasmuch as I'm paying your bill and am deeply interested in Mr. Burbidge, will you have the goodness to give me a brief prognostication as to the immediate future of his health?"

The busy young doctor stared, grinned and

changed his manner as much as I had done mine.

"Well," said he, "there's marked cardiac fibrillation, mitral murmur, and indications of aneurism of the aorta; there is also considerable pulmonary congestion and, of course, an advanced tubercular condition of . . ."

"Thank you," I interrupted. "How long?"

"A few days." And he bustled off about his errands of mercy, his abrupt manner doubtless covering a kind heart.

When I told the Boss that it was highly improbable that Burbidge would ever return to be a barker on the tober, he promptly changed my temporary status to a permanent one, and started, forthwith, to exploit my limited abilities.

So pleased was he with my barking gifts that he found new jobs for me in that capacity, one of which was a special bark for the Fat Lady, now promoted to the status of a special feature and to a tent of her own.

I thought-up a highly eulogistic and stimulating spiel which, while attracting the public, gave her no offence. Hitherto, she had had a great grievance in this matter, for the blurb—so to speak—written out by the Boss had, paradoxically, treated her with levity, included all sorts of fantastic dimensions, and wholly untrue estimates as to her appetite and powers of absorption. One alleged item of her supper being a pail of stout, the pail itself being exhibited on the platform, as evidence and proof.

Instead of inviting the public to walk up and see the revolting human hog who weighed fifty stone, had a one hundred and twenty inch waist, and broke any ordinary human chair upon which she sat, I described her as one of England's truly great women; defied any lady in the crowd to produce as proportionately small a foot as hers; and

concluded with a statement concerning her—
which was for once the truth—that she had a
lovely complexion and beautiful hair.

The Boss added a feature to this—a statement
to the effect that for the sum of one penny, she
would impart to any lady the secret of her beauty,
and invaluable tips on the care of the complexion
and on general beauty-culture for women.

The 'secrets' were printed on a hand-bill and, at
a penny each, must have shown a profit of about
ninety-nine per cent.

I also removed from the former spiel an
invitation which I thought offensive. For in the
original draft appeared the words: *'Walk up! Walk
up! Walk up and see the fattest woman on earth!
There is no deception, ladies and gentlemen, so
don't be satisfied with seeing her. Any gentleman
who likes, can come up on the platform and pinch
her—not 'ard—and in a proper manner.'*

I am bound to admit, to the credit of the roughs
and toughs of Dahn-the-Gaffs, that, so far as I
knew, advantage was never taken of the invitation.

I had a few words with the Boss over this
addition, but stuck to my point and, for that and
my glowing eulogy, earned the Fat Lady's gratitude
and favourable opinion.

So favourable indeed, did this become, that she
made me a firm offer of marriage. It is not given to
every man to be able to make such a boast, and to
but few, to receive so kindly and complimentary
an overture from a lady whose name he doesn't
know.

Poor dear, what a hellish life! . . . But I felt I
could not join mine to it, and I declined on the
grounds of total unworthiness. Nevertheless, it
was a great satisfaction to me to know that she
was made a prouder and happier woman by becoming a separate side-show all to herself.

But life is full of equal and opposite re-actions that ensue upon our actions, and as I could not get the Boss to entertain the idea of similarly promoting William Wilks, the Wild Man of Borneo, the latter became an even Wilder Man, and unreasonably threatened me with a thick ear.

It must have been about this time that I became acquainted with grief in a new insect guise.

I became lousy, in spite of frequent and regular ablutions, and reasonable care of my hair. To this day I am not quite certain whether the bug or the louse is my private enemy number one. Probably that is the insect of the moment, and, when dealing with the bug, he holds pride of place; when dealing with the louse, he is the greater.

Nor, at the time, was I quite certain whether the bug or the louse was the host of the typhoid bacillus. Anyway, both were hosts in themselves, and in their numbers, 'and I learnt about slum-life from them.'

I think I got my—one can hardly say baptism—of lice from the idiotic uniform with which the Boss provided me, as Burbidge's clothes were much too large.

Apparently the proper garb in which to bark, is a cross between an old-fashioned town-crier or beadle and that of a hunting squire or John Bull of the eighteenth century.

But why do I remember all these trifling events about people, and decline to remember Miranda— resolutely put her out of my mind, and refuse to think of her?

It is a curious thing, because Miranda turned those sordid, grey and dreadful slums into—what at the time seemed—crystal shining ways of Paradise, and, as I climbed the foul stone steps that led up to the floor on which we lived, I was climbing up the golden stair to my heaven upon earth.

I fell in love with Miranda as I had with Claire Bell, with Johnson, and with the photographer's assistant at Oxford. I loved her as I did those three people, with a very pure and beautiful love that was quite selfless and unselfish.

And I loved her, in part, as I had done my mother.

Looking back, it seems strange that a man brought up as I had been—at Public School and Varsity—should have fallen in love with what was, after all, a slum girl, scarcely distinguishable from the coster girls, factory girls and street hawkers. I say scarcely distinguishable, but that applies only to the casual eye, lacking in understanding and perception. To me, she was wholly different from the ordinary slum girl, even in speech and externals.

But I don't think that is as relevant as the fact that I had myself become, to some extent, a slum girl's equal. I had already lived long enough with those brave, pitiable people to readjust my standards; to overthrow mental false gods and half gods; to know that worth makes the man; and to prefer grimy gold to shining brass.

It would have been quite impossible for me to fall in love with Miranda when I left Oxford; and the fact that I could now do so, showed what a lot I had learnt, and how tremendously my taste, judgment and standards had improved; my knowledge and understanding increased.

For Miranda was a fine woman—kind, unselfish and brave. She laughed at nobody and with everyone—and few of her betters would have found her life a laughing matter. She loved her father as he did her, and nursed him devotedly—and her house-work, cooking and nursing were done after a long, hard and very tiring day's labour.

I must admit that I always found Dickens' story of Little Nell and her Grandfather (The Old Curiosity Shop?) to possess an emetic quality; but the tale of Miranda's care of her father, the way she worked for them both, nursed him, provided food and kept the home together, would not make a nauseating tale of sentimental slop. An epic rather.

In point of fact, it was terribly difficult for me to give financial help. What I could give was always regarded as a loan and, sooner or later, was repaid.

I think, perhaps, that speaking impartially and without bias, Miranda was the finest person I ever met.

Naturally I thought so when I was in love with her, but I think so still, for she was devotion and unselfishness incarnate, and while endowed with great virtues, was wholly free from petty vices.

And one could talk to her; for she was neither dumb, nor ignorant, nor shy. Poor Burbidge had taught her to recite almost every long speech in Shakespeare, trained her voice and accent, and given her a good vocabulary. Imagine what a companion I found her; actually *there* in that dark plague-spot; actually a pretty and attractive girl, with whom one could talk!

I suppose I was still sufficient of a fool and snob, ass and cad, to have felt uncomfortable if I had walked with her down the right side of Bond Street on a sunny June morning; taken her to visit my stuffy friends; or strolled with her in the Paddock at Ascot. I suppose the contrast between her style of dress and that of girls more fortunately placed, would have been too much for my miserable susceptibilities.

And yet one might walk the streets of Mayfair, or visit any Royal Enclosure very frequently, without meeting many women who were Miranda's superior in the things that matter. And had she been dressed as a "lady", she would have looked—as well as played—the part.

I soon began to visit Burbidge's room daily, and to spend more and more time there. Not wholly hypocritically, I told myself, moreover, when here was a job to my hand, a piece of the sort of work that I had come to the slums to do; for if I spent the day with Burbidge, talking and reading to him, while his daughter was at work, I was well employed.

I was also well rewarded by Miranda's gratitude.

But in time it became rather difficult for me to explain how I could spend so much of so many days with the sick man, and still earn enough to lend money, as well as to pay my rent and feed myself.

Feed myself! Shall I ever forget that food? For I kept strictly to the slum standards and limitations.

Breakfast—tea, bread and margarine. Dinner—pease-pudding and faggots. Tea—no such meal. Supper—bread and margarine, and the mouse-haunted cheese.

One dined out (at mid-day), of course; and occasionally supplemented pease-pudding and faggots with a slice of dog's-body, a suet pudding ameliorated by an occasional raisin.

One soon got to know the best of the hash-joints, where, in an atmosphere of steam, stench of boiling cabbage, and other culinary smells that came from dirty oil stoves, one endeavoured to enjoy the *plat du jour*, which might be a variation of the pease-pudding and faggots, such as a kind of Irish-stew of anonymous ingredients; hard, heavy dumplings in a thin gravy with some fat and cabbage; or—in times of affluence—pig's-trotters; a basin of stewed eels, or a portion of a comestible that I should like to have seen in the making, and known as brawn. So far as one could tell, it consisted of small cubes of pork fat embedded in a gelatinous substance indistinguishable from house-decorators' size.

On feast days and social occasions, such as when Miranda let me take her out to dinner (midday), or, better still, to supper, one could call for and obtain delicacies such as pinkish-greenish slices of ham; corned-beef that seemed more corn than beef; soused herrings; and such dainty sweet-meats as treacle-pudding or very tough enduring pastry endowed with the sort of jam that I had first met at Mrs. Odger's shop.

Of course there was always fried fish and chips, but my high rebellious stomach was generally defeated by the smell thereof, which one met at a hundred yards' distance. And one cannot, without comment—even in a free democracy—enter a restaurant holding one's nose, and continue so to hold it while one eats.

To take Miranda out was my reward for looking after her father during the day, and no fortunate youth ever got greater pleasure from taking a lovely debutante to a dinner-and-show in the most gilded halls of virtue on the highest and most social plane.

I loved walking and talking with Miranda, and doing things that brought a smile of happiness to her pale face and brilliant eyes; but opportunities were not numerous. She had a good deal to do when she got home from work, and I had my barking and Thespian duties between seven and eleven in the evening.

But there were Sundays and Bank Holidays; I
came to know the value of the Sabbath and the
glory of the Bank Holiday when I lived the life of
the slums.

Looking back, I realise that that phase of my
slum existence was relatively brief, for poor Burbidge must have died within a few weeks of my
first meeting him. And it was not until it was over,
that I knew how amazingly happy I had been,
there in that ghastly human rabbit-warren of a
house, with its row and stench, its fleas, bugs and
lice. Eating that horrible food, tramping the streets
in search of experience, barking on the tober, and
acting in the big-top at night, I was happier than I
had ever been before, or have ever been since,
until the coming of that brute they called Tich . . .

No, I won't think of him . . .

I won't remember that . . .

We were coming out from Dahn-the-Gaffs after
the last performance. Old Tom Brickett was walking in front with Burbidge, Bill Munry, and a lady-
friend of Bill's; Miranda just behind, and I over-
taking her.

Suddenly, a lout who was shuffling along,
shoulders hunched, hands in pockets, and cap
over one eye, seized her arm and growled in a
husky voice something like,

"Ho! You, is it? Gotcher! Nah, wot abaht it?"

Miranda turned to me, looking frightened, and I
said the appropriate thing as I gave the fellow a
shove.

In a moment he turned into a dynamic ferocity,
and I was as a babe in his hands. It was most
humiliating, for the ruffian—although he was no
bigger than I—was twice as strong, hit me as he
pleased, and then, seizing me by the throat,
almost shook my head off. I would have given

anything, including my immortal soul, to have been one of those despised athletes, craggy-faced and broken-nosed, who boxed for Oxford; for when it comes to the stark encounters with Life, especially in the slums, the pansier graces are at a discount.

Just as the brute ceased trying to shake my head from my body, only to grab me by the ears and knock my head against the wall, I was aware that the aged Tom Brickett had stepped up beside us. He did not raise mighty fists and aim a pile-driving blow at the face of my adversary, but there was a deft, quiet and intimate movement of one of his hands, which did not rise above his waist; and my assailant grunted, doubled-up, sagged and collapsed. To me, it looked like a conjuring trick; to the other man it must have looked like sudden death.

"Lookin' for trouble?" asked Tom, with an air of quiet surprise. "*Do* get up," he begged reasonably, as the man made no reply.

When he did get up, Tom made his little movement again, and with the same remarkable result.

"Yer got to mind yer manners, mate," he observed, turning away.

A few minutes later, as we sat having our evening quick-one-and-the-other-half in the bar of 'The Black Boy', I asked Tom what exactly he had done to the man, and whether he had really hurt him.

"Why, you see wot I done," replied Tom. "Hurt 'im? No! Why, I only gave 'im a short arm jab in the right spot. 'Oo is 'e? Wot started it?"

"It was through me," said Miranda. "He's a horrible low beast. Pretends that Lizzie Bennie and I pinched his flower-pitch while he was away from it—on tramp, or in prison more likely. He knocked her tray of violets over and upset our basket.

There was a crowd round by the time a policeman came along, and he cleared off. Liz says he's a dip—a pick-pocket—they call 'Tich', and a proper swine."

"I shall 'ave to 'it 'im one day," observed Tom Brickett.

Yes, that was the first time I saw that appalling creature, with his horrible white face, brightly red-rimmed watery eyes, long rubbery nose, loose blubbery mouth, and appalling strength.

There was something utterly evil and animal about him—ape-like, with the intelligence, morals and manners of an ape, and an ape's incredible strength.

Miranda must have known how utterly humiliated, degraded and miserable I felt; but when I parted from her at her door that night, she thanked me without apparent irony, for looking after her, standing up for her as she called it! But for Tom Brickett, I should still have been lying down, rather than standing up for her. But it was I and not he, who got the thanks.

How very like a woman. . . .

I asked her, next day, whether it was likely that she and her partner would be molested again on their pitch, by this man, and was mightily relieved when she said it was unlikely, as they were going to move from Bayswater to a corner in Oxford Street, where they thought the police would allow them to set up a very small stall, and there were no previous claims.

I never got as far as association with the Wide Boys, but I learnt that the lowest type of that sub-human animal ran a racket which took the form of going, singly or in gangs, and imposing a levy on such people as flower-girls, aged beggars, old women pedlars, decrepit street-musicians, and blind or maimed stall-holders who were not on their list of subscribers. People of the type of Bill Munry they would carefully avoid.

Knowing what I did of the lives of these poorest of poor people, my blood boiled at the thought of there being creatures so foul, mean and base, that, rather than work for themselves, they would prey upon them. . . .

I had almost forgotten this very painful incident, when one day Miranda told me that she had seen the man whom her friend Liz referred to as "Tich", and that he had followed her home. He had not molested her in any way, nor spoken to her, but she was quite sure that his object had been to find out where she lived.

I had some idea of offering to go with her to Covent Garden and thence to her pitch, spending the day there—helpfully, if possible—and escorting her home at night; but quickly realised that this was just plain silly. I had not come to the slums to spend my days selling flowers in Oxford Street, nor to be a slum-girl's protector, however platonic.

Nor would such a proceeding be comprehensible in this milieu. The position would be misunderstood, and Miranda's 'friends' would be loud in comment. Already, they undoubtedly resented her quite unconscious superiority, and the fact that she was inclined to keep herself *to* herself.

If I behaved like that, they would soon be alluding to her as a cosh-moll—which is a lady who takes up with a gentleman who carries a cosh, which is called a life-preserver because it doesn't always fail—when properly applied—to preserve the life of the victim. The lady's work in the matter is to decoy other gentlemen within the orbit of the gentleman who carries the cosh. Unconsciously they come, and unconscious they remain.

Those were the reasons I gave myself for

abstaining from an offer to protect Miranda, the real reason being that as a protector, I was completely worthless.

This pale-faced, sickly-looking shambling ape was a better man than I, worth about three of me in fact, on the physical plane.

What I could do and did do, was to go for a stroll along Gidding's Row and up Silver Street and along Mortimer's Rents toward the High Street, and meet Miranda returning from her work.

But on one of these evening strolls before going to the tober, I almost ran into the man known as "Tich", on turning a corner. He attacked me immediately and with a promise of my complete evisceration.

Precisely what happened, I don't know; but I contrived to refrain from flight, from kicking, and from biting. But I did butt, and felt no shame; though why this should be a less dishonourable mode of warfare, I do not know. I also clung to him with an ivy-like tenacity—believing it to be good strategy inasmuch as the closer I was to him, the less could he hit me; and this was certainly true. While I hung about him and impeded the movement of his arms, I must, in the sight of any true sportsman, have given a puerile, feeble, ineffectual and generally disgraceful exhibition.

I did not suffer much, save from the truly horrible odour that emanated from "Tich", until he contrived to get both my wrists in the grasp of one of his remarkably powerful hands. He then took me by the throat and pressed on the right side of my neck with his thumb. In a surprisingly short space of time I felt horribly ill, my sight failed completely, and I fainted.

"Tich" must have been interrupted soon thereafter, for, when I recovered consciousness, I found a policeman bending over me, and soon realised that I had not been very badly kicked.

I suppose that policeman saved my life, thereby compensating to some extent for what others of his kind have caused me to suffer in apprehension and terror.

So I am remembering the appalling "Tich" after all! But how could it be otherwise, since but for him . . .

How did the end come about? How did the circumstances arise, that led to the end of it all? . . .

First of all, I lost my job at Dahn-the-Gaffs, or, rather, the job lost me, for the Circus went on tour, and I declined the firm offer to accompany it as barker and as juvenile lead in 'The Corsican Brothers', 'Maria Martin', 'The Shaugraun' and other plays to be given by the circus repertory-company in a real tent of their own, with a stage, foot-lights and curtain.

But for my dedication to the slums, I should have accepted this offer, and looked forward to enormous fun.

No! I must not lie to myself, even if I do to other people. No offer in the world would have induced me to leave Miranda then. . . .

Soon after that, Horatio Burbidge died; Miranda was broken-hearted; and turned more and more to me for sympathy, comfort and help.

Partly in the real goodness of his heart, and partly because he was finding that work tired him more and more, old Bill Munry gave me a job and, for a time, I was his roarer and barrow-pusher. To this day I am not really fond of fish, and am unduly susceptible to relaxed and husky throat. Nevertheless, I was very glad of the job, for it gave me again my necessary *raison d'être* in the slums, and gave me a better insight into the hardships, difficulties and trials of the coster's life.

I knew how it must feel to speculate one's capital in a perishable commodity, carry or push it for miles and miles, shouting the while at the top of one's voice and with the full strength of one's lungs; and at night, probably crawl wearily home and put the valuable residue, together with one's hopes of profit, beneath one's bed. . . .

I had cause to marvel at old Bill's strength and endurance, for, in addition to his far-flung day-round with the barrow, he had an evening-round in a different locality, with a basket. This, with its load of shellfish, he balanced on his head and, having reached the suburb in which he was known, walked slowly along the pavement bawling,

"F-i-i-i—*ny*sters!"

For, strange to relate, he actually had quite a sale for supper-time oysters in that neighbour-hood, at one-and-sixpence a dozen. He also carried cockles and mussels and, occasionally, a lobster or crab.

I walked this round with him, adding my tuneful cry to his on the other side of the street, taking the orders that were given, the proffered dish and the money, and then running across to Bill for the required sea-food.

Believe it or not, I did this round alone on several occasions when Bill had what he called a bit of a bleedin' sniffle, and a doctor would probably have called a sharp go of influenza with a temperature of one-hundred-and-three.

One comforting feature of those illnesses was the fact that Bill could always treat them himself with beer—that wonderful food, drink, medicine, solace, anodyne and nepenthe of the dweller in slums.

It was from Bill Munry that I learnt something

of the homely slighted coster's trade, and of the sociological problems of the coster's difficult and exacting profession.

"It's the flatties that's the curse. . . . They got their job to do, I s'pose, but Gawd knows why," he would say. "Why the 'ell can't the Lord Chief Nibs of the Police or the Lor' Mayor o' Lunnon say whether costers is right or wrong? . . . Damn well shoot the poor burghers—or let 'em alone. Wot's the good o' muckin' 'em abaht; movin' 'em on; tellin' 'em they're causin' an obstruction when there ain't nothink to obstruct, and they bin there on that pitch fer 'undreds o' years? Jer know wot the result is, boy? All the youngsters as had oughter be costers like their fathers, is all turnin' boxers or burglars—or joinin' the Wide Boys. Nothink else forrit. They got the guts fer both the decent trades, and if they fails to make a do of it as boxers, they turns to burglars. That's wot the busies are doin' fer costers."

And indeed, it seemed to me a most idiotic lack of system and consistency, and an undeniable pestering and persecution of costers who were breaking no law, doing no harm, and serving a very useful purpose for the community of the poor. I have a shrewd suspicion that that was their offence—injuring the vested interests of shop-keepers by under-selling them—to the public benefit.

It was while I was working for and with Bill, reeking of fish, and in deep sympathy with Jonah, that Miranda and I—chaperoned by Bill—had our wonderful Bank Holiday on Hampstead Heath.

Let no-one sneer at 'Arry and 'Arriet at 'Appy 'Ampstead, until he has lived their life, earned that day as they do, looked forward to it, and saved for it as they have.

I thoroughly enjoyed it; Miranda loved it; and

so did Bill—up to the last happy moment when he
could eat no more, could even drink no more, and
fell peacefully asleep beneath a bush. But that
was not until we had had all the fun of the fair—
swing-boats, round-abouts, coconut-shies, shoot-
ing-galleries, and all the rest.

And having disposed Bill to sleep, with his coat
beneath his head and his neckerchief over his
face, Miranda and I wandered off far-away.

Miranda told me later that that was the very
happiest day of all her life, and that if she was
never to know happiness again, she didn't care.

Miranda had a very sweet and kindly nature,
was generosity personified, and loved to give. She
was one of those women to whom loving is giving;
and I was wholly unworthy of the love that she
gave me.

We got home the next morning. Bill the next
afternoon.

The events of that day of our happy holiday on
Hampstead Heath marked the beginning of a new
era in the relationship between Miranda and myself.

Suddenly, overnight—that very wonderful and
lovely night—we came very close together, mentally and spiritually. To me, it was a wholly new experience, this relationship, and so it was, I think,
to Miranda. Something unique in both our lives.

We talked together more freely and intimately;
she opened out, as it were, to me and to my
friendship and love as does a flower to the sun. I
quickly came to know a far more interesting, attractive, and delightful Miranda; and to realise
that she was by far the most charming, desirable,
and lovable woman I had ever met in all my life.

It really amazed me that her mind should be able to interest mine. The surprise was not due to the fact that my mind was in any way superior to hers, but to our so different standards of education and experience; our so widely divergent heredity, back-ground, and past environment.

Hers was a fresh, intelligent, and enquiring mind; she could, and did, think; and now that her shyness had worn off, she could and did, talk— and in a very pleasing and interesting manner.

But there is no perfection in this world, and the imperfection in our mental relationship was the immense divergence between my sense of humour and hers.

Miranda was by no means humourless, but she could see nothing in the slightest degree funny in what struck me as truly and extremely funny. On the other hand, she could laugh heartily, and with obvious enjoyment, at situations in which I was wholly unable to detect the faintest element of humour.

She could, for example, study and enjoy allegedly "comic" papers which were, to me, nothing but contemptible conglomerations of pointless banality, fatuity, and boredom.

Or, when we had opportunity and means to visit the cinema, she would thoroughly enjoy professedly comic films which merely left me wearily aghast at the depths to which human vacuity and stupidity could sink. Sheerly dreadful rubbish, in an hour of which there was not, to me, the slightest occasion for the ghost of a smile.

No, I could not endure what Miranda could genuinely enjoy, in the matter of humorous mental provender.

On the other hand, neither could she find amusement in what delighted me. Time after time, I tried to make her laugh at what I thought were really good jokes, samples of true humour, and really funny situations.

I was bitterly disappointed for example, not in her, but in the profound difference between her sense of humour and mine, when I failed to get even a perfunctory smile from her in the matter of Sir Edmund Gosse's poetic house-maid.

I had been trying to discover whether she had any liking and feeling for verse—outside the Shakespearean knowledge imparted by her father —and she had just then mentioned, with pardonable pride, the fact that a distant relation of hers was in good service.

The juxtaposition had reminded me of the famous poetess.

"There is a very clever and well-known man who writes books, and about books," said I. "And he had a house-maid who used to think about things—as you do, Miranda. She used to write poetry, too. One day, she asked him if he would be so kind as to tell her whether the moon turned round and round, as the earth does. When he said "No, it does not", she remarked that, in that case, nobody had ever seen the other side of the moon. Never. Ever. It seemed to strike her as a strange and remarkable thing; a great thought. For, after she had left, Mrs. Gosse found in her room a piece of paper on which she had written a short poem about it.

> "O moon, lovely moon, with thy beautiful
>   face,
> Careering all over the boundairies of space,
> Whenever I see thee, I think in my mind,
> Shall I ever, O, ever, behold thy behind?"

Miranda did not smile. Miranda flushed very faintly, and changed the subject.

The fact that I assured her that this was not a story, but absolute historical truth, seemed to make the matter rather worse.

Time after time, I tried her with really witty, really funny, smoking-room stories which are also told in the drawing-room, even the best drawing-rooms, but not one of them evoked a smile; my cleverly developed and dramatic climax would produce either a blank *Oh?*, or a puzzled *Why?* in place of the laughter for which I had hoped.

It was the same with the "silly" story. To her, it was just silly and in no-wise amusing.

When, sitting with her, her father, Bill Munry, and other friends, I told her of the Man Who must have been Mad, she looked at me as though she thought *I* was; or, possibly, was adversely affected by my mild potations of stout-and-bitter.

"It was a Bar just like this, Miranda," said I confidentially. "It was a barman just like George; and a man leant against the bar, just like old Tom Brickett, there. Only those two in the Bar. Tom Brickett and the barman. Suddenly, a man rushed in and asked for a large glass of port. Quick! Directly he got it, he drank off the port, and then bit out great pieces of the top of the glass! When he put it down and rushed out again, there was nothing left but the foot and the stem and the thick bottom part of the glass! The barman went quite white in the face, and when he could speak, he cried to the other man,

'Good Lord above us! Did you see that? He must be *mad! . . . Mad!*'

'Yes,' agreed the man who was leaning against the bar. 'He *must* be mad. He's left the best part of it!'"

Not a smile. Only a wondering look, as in consideration of my mental condition.

No, we had no common ground there, and I realised that it was a very great pity.

It is a wonderful and binding thing between two people that they should unite and fight for something; perhaps even more so, that they should work together for something; but, possibly, the most wonderful, the most important, is that they should laugh together at something. And at the same something.

Dear Miranda! If only we could always, or only occasionally, or even just once, have really laughed ourselves helpless at the same thing, our lives might . . .

But I want to remember, not to speculate on might-have-beens. . . .

What happened next?

My illness.

I got up one morning—or endeavoured to get up—feeling terrible. I had been rather off-colour for a fortnight, but that morning I realised that I was really ill. I had to get back to bed; and there I lay staring at the cracked and filthy ceiling of that horrible room, realising just how the poor feel when illness overtakes them.

Were I one of them now, I thought, I should lose my job, my weekly shillings; my money would soon be gone; there would not even be half a stale loaf, a piece of soap-like cheese, or a mildewed half-tin of condensed milk in my cupboard. My rent would soon be overdue, and the landlord's agent—the hyena's jackal—would bid me pay up or 'op it. The sale of everything I owned in the room, save, perhaps, my bed, might keep that foul ceiling over my head for another week, and then . . .

What does happen to them then? The river-police can tell of a certain number; and anyone who cares to walk the Embankment at night can tell of scores of others—scores representing hundreds—sleeping in doorways, under arches, squandering a cadged penny at the night coffee-stall, or, after a lucky touch, fourpence on the luxury of a doss-house kip.

Bill Munry came in, that day, to see why I had not reported for duty; and, finding me very ill, showed his sympathy in a practical manner—not with flowers and grapes—but with a jug of beer and a shilling. Had I drunk the beer, the results would have been disastrous.

In the evening he brought me a meal cooked by himself—a kipper, inserted head-first into a jug which was then filled with boiling water. To show my grateful appreciation, I endeavoured to eat it—and the results *were* disastrous.

I more or less passed out thereafter, and only remember a nightmare of dreadful head-ache, a feeling of indescribable horrible illness, and of imminent dissolution. I awoke briefly from this horror to find Miranda laying a cool wet handkerchief on my forehead.

She installed herself in my room and nursed me, for I had typhoid fever.

By the time I was able to crawl about again, I not only loved Miranda as a lover, but as my mother—a case of what the people here would call 'transference', I suppose. I loved her, worshipped her almost, with a grateful adoration but little this side of idolatry.

And all the time that I was ill she somehow managed financially, for I was too weak, too often delirious, too often in a coma-like sleep, to think about money or anything else but suffering and Miranda.

At times, I was so weak, so near to death, that miserable tears of self-pity ran down my face when she went out of the room.

I can really remember little of that dreadful time, but I know that Miranda saved my life, and to do it must have gone very short of food and sleep. You who have nursed a sick man who is too weak to turn over in bed or to raise a hand, imagine nursing him in a small hot room, in a filthy stinking slum; a room that contains practically nothing but a rusty and most ill-equipped bedstead, a table, chair and wash-stand! She must have spent several nights, at the crisis, sleeping on the floor.

Still, Miranda pulled me through, and I got well enough to crawl out and sun myself on the canal towing-path—a lovely place, lacking nothing in coal-dust, soot, mud, rusty corrugated-iron, and triple-distilled extract of utterest ugliness.

And then? . . .

Then, one night, Miranda came round to see me, and I noticed how worn she had grown, and that she was even paler than usual. She had been crying—a most unusual thing for Miranda. At first she denied this, and that she was deeply troubled, but later admitted that the trouble was the sub-human "Tich". Even so, she was reticent, but begged me to promise that, if ever we met him when we were together, I would run away! It made me writhe with shame.

Before she went—leaving me feeling as though a light had gone out—she said,

"Look here, Richard, you want someone to look after you—all the time, I mean. You're not strong enough to scratch for yourself yet. Let me come and do for you. I can work for us both, until you are stronger. You oughtn't to live alone.

"You haven't the sense," she added, smiling.

Suddenly, the thought entered my mind—why

not ask Miranda to marry me? Make a real gesture to Life! A real symbol of my true and lasting dedication to the slums, or, rather, to the work of ameliorating the lot of the slum-dweller.

Even though I did not propose to live the whole of my life in the slums, and intended to return— more or less—to my own walk of life, and enter Parliament, journalism, pulpit or platform, and from there to try to arouse the national con- science, I could take such a woman as Miranda with me—without making her unhappy, I mean. She was so adaptable that only a change of dress and coiffure would be necessary as protective col- ouring among the women with whom she would then associate. For though she could, and did, talk the language of the slums, she could also talk as her father did, and as he had taught her.

Impulsive ever, I proposed to her then and there, as she sat on the side of my rickety, rusty bed.

Tears came into her eyes, and she put her arms about my neck.

"You don't want to marry me, Richard," she whispered.

"That's just what I do want, Miranda," I said, wondering whether it were the truth.

"I mean you don't need to, don't have to. All I want is to look after you. I'd slave for you, dear. I'd do *anything* for you."

"Well, marry me, then, Miranda," I said, and pressed my lips to hers.

For I did love her; I loved her then, with all my heart and soul, desperately, and I wanted her more than anything else on earth.

"No," she said, "I won't be a mill-stone round your neck. I won't let you marry me, dear, but . . . but . . . I'll be a good wife to you. Look, let's go right away from this part, to where nobody knows us, and where that beast won't look for me. I'll get another pitch right off the old beat—out Kensington way, or somewhere. I'll find a nice room and we'll furnish it, and you mustn't try to work until you're strong again. Why, you're a bag of bones, Richard! . . . We shall make do, and you'll soon find another job. The best of the flower-season is coming on, and I shall make more on my own than I did in co with Liz."

"You and Liz parted brass rags?" I asked.

"Yes, Liz has done a scarper. Wind-up properly. That 'Tich'! Said he'd have ten shillings a week from her, or do her in. Filthy little ponce!"

"What about going to the police?" I suggested.

"*Police!*" said Miranda, and left it at that.

It made me see red that this foul parasite could terrify decent, honest, hard-working girls, and leave them no choice but to abandon their arrangements and desert the pitch where they had a little business-connection.

"I'll . . ." I began, clenching my ineffectual fists.

"No, you won't, Richard," interrupted Miranda, putting her hand over my mouth. "You'll keep out of his way. He's a devil and a brute-beast, and as strong in his hands and arms as two men. He's a strangler! Liz says it's well known that he strangled one girl who kept him. He's dangerous. That's why I want to get right away from this part."

And Miranda found what she considered a good room in a gaunt and hideous tenement-house, and furnished it.

Proudly but shyly she boasted that she was quite well-off. Poor father had left her money that he had scraped together and put by for her, and she had saved quite a bit. She had got four pounds seventeen shillings and sixpence, and owed nobody a penny!

I too, professed to be in funds, having received a windfall from that extremely well-known—if mythical—slum-creation, Rich Uncle Bert.

Between us, we had ten pounds, a more than adequate capital for furnishing a home and starting life.

Had I any moral scruples about thus going to live with Miranda?

None whatever.

I knew it would make her life infinitely happier; or, rather, would change it from a dull loneliness, little removed from misery, into radiant happiness.

I don't think I was wholly selfish, but, of course, I realised that it would make an incredible difference to my life in the slums. Also, I had some vague hope and intention of marrying her sooner or later, when I felt that I had really learnt all there was to know of the needs of these poor people, and the time had come to go away and put that knowledge to profitable use. I felt sure that, rather than part from me and see me go away into a different life, she would marry me and go with me.

When thoughts of what Vibart-Stourton and Desarum would say, if they knew that I was 'living in sin'—as the smug phrase goes—with a slum girl, I just put such thoughts away; thrust them out of my mind. Were they their brother's keeper? They were not the keepers of my conscience, anyway.

So Miranda furnished the room, and, poor dear, even obtained a window-box for its beautification. For Miranda had ideas; she had taste and discrimination. Her father had not steeped her mind in Shakespeare, all those years, for nothing.

It was Miranda's whim and humour, her very

understandable fancy, that I should not see the room until it was finished; that I should not set foot in it until the day that we "moved in". She was to "have everything lovely", everything ready—food in the house, a fire in the grate, and be there—waiting for me.

When she got home from her work, she was to dress up in her best and, at seven o'clock in the evening, I was to open the door and walk in.

It was to be beautiful. To her, the wonderful and glorious beginning to a life of romance . . .

Romance in the slums!

It was pathetic, and it was devilishly cruel. How can Fate—how can God—allow such things?

On the night before, I went home with Miranda, that I might know my way to our room; and at the door of that room I left her with lingering, impassioned kisses. She had work to do there—final touches to put to our room, before I joined her there on the morrow.

I spent the next day in a state of excited happiness—a condition of exaltation—filled not only with joy and longing and thankfulness, but with an earnest determination to let nothing but good and happiness come of our union. Whatever happened, I would never, by word or deed, give Miranda cause to regret that she had met me, that she had loved me, that she had offered to lay her life and work and devotion on the altar of my welfare. So often she had said to me,

"How *different* you are, Richard! Quite unlike any man I have ever met. I didn't know there was anyone so kind, so gentle, and so—what shall I say—thoughtful and considerate; and you are so polite to me. . . . It is so nice to be really loved."

She had said this again, the night of the Bank Holiday, and had added,

"There's a mystery about you, Richard. You're

like the Fairy Prince in the stories—I believe you've been a bank-clerk or a gentleman in a shop."

"I have been in a shop, Miranda," I admitted, thinking of Mrs. Odger's.

"I knew there was something different. I thought that perhaps you'd been an actor." And after a long silence,

"You're not in trouble, are you, Richard?"—and I knew what 'in trouble' means in the slums— "Because if ever you were, you'd tell me and let me help, wouldn't you?"

"And you'd meet me at the gates of the stone jug when I came out of stir, eh?" I laughed.

"Yes, Richard. And I'd work for you and look after you for the rest of your life if you wanted me to. . . ."

And now I was going to look after Miranda for the rest of her life. I would make her happy, and it seemed to me that if I made one slum-dweller— only *one* slum-dweller—happy for life, some good would have ensued from my descent into the abyss.

The next evening . . .

No . . . No . . . I won't remember it . . . I won't think of it . . . I *can't!*

God help me . . .

The next evening, having attired myself carefully, I made my way to my new home.

Going up the long flights of stone steps that served the floors and innumerable rooms of that rabbit-warren of a tenement, my heart beat fast, and not only by reason of my climbing the steps— the golden stair that led to my earthly paradise.

Trembling, I threw open our door—hearing as I did so a dreadful sound that seemed to make my swiftly-beating heart stand still.

There were two people in the bright clean-looking room—two people over by the bed. One was the man "Tich". He had Miranda by the throat, and he was holding her down across the bed, strangling her and growling in his throat as he did so.

With a dreadful sick feeling of horror, fear and shame, I knew that he was ten times stronger than I.

And suddenly, I went mad with a berserk rage, and was as one of those Malays who run amok.

Between the door and the bed was the fireplace, and standing leaning against the side of the grate was a short, thick, and heavy poker. Snatching it up as I dashed across the room I seized it by the pointed end, whirled it above my head, and brought the heavy knob down on the back of the strangler's head.

It was a hard blow, and I saw the blood well out as the man's head dropped forward, and his body relaxed. I realised that I had stunned him—and then, at the sight of blood, I became completely insane, and behaved exactly as I did when I shot the rabbit.

As he slumped to the floor, I struck him again and again and again with all my strength, not on the head, but on the shoulders and back . . .

I came to my senses to find Miranda hanging on to my right arm, and endeavouring to get between me and my enemy, and to thrust me back.

"*Don't! . . . Don't! . . . Don't! . . .*" she cried, in a hoarse, screaming whisper. "You'll kill him! They'd call it murder if he died!"

And, as I stood trembling and looking down upon the unconscious ruffian, I suffered the same re-action as I had done on the only other occasion when I had shed blood. I was shaken with violent spasms of sobbing and was violently sick.

I crouched, trembling, in the arm-chair that was to have been mine, my face in my hands, to shut out the dreadful sight that I felt I must not see again, if I were to return to sanity. If I looked again, I should leap up and rush from the room, rush down the stairs and out into the street, *screaming that I had shed blood; had hit a man on the head* . . .

Meantime, Miranda—with what seemed to me incredible courage, and with a calmness and coolness that I could even then admire, but could not imitate—got cold water and a handkerchief, and did everything that should be done for the man—who, a few minutes before, had attacked her and endeavoured to strangle her.

As I sat there, helpless and useless, my head in my hands, sick and faint, horrified and frightened to the depths of my soul, I heard her say,

"He's stunned. . . . He's quite unconscious, Richard. No need to fetch a doctor though—besides . . . if . . ." she faltered and stopped.

I knew what she meant. If a doctor were brought, he would find me and her and an injured man, and a heavy, blood-stained poker lying on the floor beside his damaged head.

Nevertheless, the only credit that I can take to myself for the part I played that night, is for having the sufficient humanity and decency to get to my feet, and, averting my eyes, go to open the door with the intention of going to get a doctor.

What I had done had been done in a fit of utter madness, and, whatever it might be in Law, was not wanton and brutal assault; but if, in cowardly fear of arrest and trial, I allowed the man to suffer unnecessarily—that would be disgraceful.

But Miranda was across the room before I was, and locked the door, snatched the key and put it in her pocket.

"You can't! You mustn't!" she whispered. "He's only stunned! A doctor could do nothing else for him; and he'd send for the police. Sit down in the chair."

She turned it with its back to the unconscious man, and I sat down, for my knees were giving way, and I felt that I should faint.

"If he doesn't soon come round, I'll get a doctor," she promised. "But he will. He's strong—and tough."

"But he may be badly hurt—since he is actually stunned," I said.

"Then he'll come round," replied Miranda. "And when he does, *I'll* go for a doctor, not you. You must get away. If you're gone before the doctor comes, they'll never know who did it. You can get a train and go right away to that big town in the south of England. Brighton it is . . . No-one knows you here, Richard . . .

"Did anyone see you come up the stairs?" she asked.

"I didn't meet anybody," I said.

"Well then, look, you need not come into it at all. He did not see you, and will never know it was you. If he sees you when he comes round—he'll never rest until he has got his own back. He and his gang will *murder* you! Or he and his gang will slash your face with razors. Blind you with them perhaps. They *do* such things as that."

She threw herself down beside me, clasped me to her and drew my head down upon her shoulder, as though I was a child. Strive as I might to control myself, I was shaken by spasms of trembling, and by rending sobs that shook me from head to foot—a kind of fit. And Miranda, almost nursing me, became as my mother. I clung to her mentally, spiritually and literally.

"You must *go*—at once," she kept saying. "*You*

must go—before he sees you."

And this was our wedding evening.

Her arms about my neck, mine about her body, we clung and kissed and wept in a wild and mad ecstasy of horror and fear—the unconscious man there, behind us, a few feet away.

To each of us it was an incredible nightmare, an utter impossibility, a hideous, devilish spell, woven about us by Fate, as a spider weaves its dreadful bonds about a fly. That such a thing should happen to us in our new home—on our wedding night.

But it was a nightmare from which we must awake, a spell that must be broken—for it was too utterly and entirely impossible to be true.

And as we lay in the chair, each striving—as it were—to protect the other, to help the other, save each other from great evil and terrible danger, we listened; listened continually for the faintest sound.

The day died and shadows entered the room, and I grew more and more afraid.

For a brief period I must have been unconscious; I must have fainted, for it could not be that I slept.

Suddenly, Miranda sat up, and I could scarcely see her white face.

"Listen, Richard," she said. "Do you love me?"

"You know that I love you, Miranda, more than I have loved anyone or anything in all my life."

"Will you do something for me?"

"I'll do *anything* for you, anything you ask."

She kissed me on the lips.

"I know you will. This is what I want you to do. Wait until it's quite dark and then go. In case anyone who knows him should see you go out of the room, or meet you on the stairs, I want you to wear my hat and shawl and skirt. Just in case any of his gang are down there waiting for him. I'm going to wrap the poker up in a sheet of news-paper . . ."

I shuddered uncontrollably at the thought of touching it.

". . . and you must hide it under the shawl and get rid of it as soon as you can. The knob's too big for you to poke it down a drain, but you can throw it in the canal."

And for the first time that evening she wept.

"But, Miranda!" I began. "My dear, I . . ."

"Don't talk, Richard. Don't interrupt me. I must think of everything, and keep it all clear in my mind. You *must* get away, and no-one must see you go. It'll make everything so much easier for me and safer too—if he never finds out who did it."

"But," I began again, "but suppose he has to be taken to hospital—and some innocent man should be accused of attacking him and bashing him on the head, like that?"

"Well, then you could come forward and say how it happened, but it won't. It *won't* happen— no-one will be taken up. You get away and leave it to me. I'll drag him outside on to the landing; and then fetch the doctor. I'll say I heard a noise outside my door, and went out—that I thought he must have fallen down the stairs—that perhaps he was drunk, or, perhaps, one of another gang coshed him."

And then I think I must have fainted again, for there is a period of which I remember nothing. But, on waking up from a sort of coma, or recover-ing consciousness from a faint, I found myself deadly cold and trembling from head to foot. I must have made some movement, for Miranda knelt down beside me, and took my face between her hands. There was a little light in the room now —from a street lamp—and I could just see her.

"Richard," she said, "you must go. There is no-one about on the stairs, nor down in the alley. Slip these clothes on—and get rid of them as soon as you can, when no-one will see you—just in case you meet any of his gang coming up, or anyone notices you as you go out into the street . . . Don't let's say a long good-bye . . . Go quickly, Richard."

I went.

Yes, I let her persuade me and urge me—and I went. Did I pretend to myself that my going would help her? Would be better and safer for her, and make things easier for her, as she said?

How could I tell all this to Stortford? How could I tell Elspeth Grey? What excuse could I offer?

None—for I can offer none to myself even.

Explanation there is, but it's no excuse. I was in such a condition of nerves, such a state of horror and terror, that I barely knew where I was, what I was doing, and what had happened.

I knew that there was some Thing, some immeasurable and indescribable Awfulness from which I must escape. In plain truth, my mind was completely unhinged; it was numbed, and moribund, and inoperative. I was not responsible for my actions.

I can best describe the situation when, at last I rose to my feet, by saying that Miranda's mind was in charge of my body, and it obeyed her will.

It was she, rather than I, who arranged the skirt and shawl and hat that she produced; she who tucked my trouser-ends into my socks; she who wrapped the poker in news-paper and bade me be sure to keep it beneath the shawl.

"Don't write to me, Richard," she said. "Not for a while—not for some time. Then just let me know where you are, and how you are . . . And whether you still love me. Now go. Go quickly, and go as far from here as you can."

And my body obeyed her will.

As I opened the door and stepped out on to the landing, I almost shrank back again, for the door opposite was open and two women were lounging in the doorway. Without speaking, I hurried down the stairs and out into the darkness.

Which way must I go?

Miranda had said something about a canal. Yes, I remembered passing some steps which led to a sort of wharf by a timber-yard.

And I retraced the steps by which I had come earlier that evening—or years before, or aeons, or in another existence.

Fortunately for my peace of mind, the long street was dark and quiet. One side of it being bounded by a high wall and a series of lofty ware-houses. It must have been to the right, and between just such warehouses, that I had caught a glimpse of the black, oily water.

By and by, in the light of a lamp, I saw the opening between a warehouse and a wall; just behind it a short, dirty, flight of steps leading down to the canal. With a feeling of unutterable relief, and thankfulness, I struggled out of the skirt, wrapped it round the poker, rolled that bundle and the hat in the shawl, and thrust it into the water.

My mind must have begun to function again, for I remember holding the bundle under the water, that it might soak and quickly sink. This I did crouching in terror lest someone should emerge from under the neighbouring arch that carried the road across the canal. I had been afraid to venture into its darkness, for, even where I was, I could only just distinguish the edge of the canal bank.

Into a side pocket of my coat, Miranda had thrust my folded cap; this I now put on my head and pulled well down over my eyes, and hurried away from that horrible place, wondering whether the bundle—weighted with the heavy poker— would remain for ever at the bottom of the canal.

As I passed a brightly-lighted shop, I noticed that my trousers were still tucked into my socks; and this gave me a shock. Bending down to adjust them, I received a ten times more terrible shock and a fright—from which I have not recovered to this day.

On both my boots was a stain—a dark splash, and smear and stain, that in parts, gleamed dully in the bright light. I almost fainted—for there was *blood* on both my boots.

In the middle of the toe-cap of one of them was a round splash, a great drop, the size of a florin . . . I touched it with my finger—it *was* blood.

As I straightened my body, I staggered and almost fell. Supposing anyone came out of the shop and saw me, with my white face, my blood-stained boots and hand? Was there blood on my clothes? Was I splashed with blood from head to foot? What could I do?

If a policeman had turned the corner at that moment, I should have gone up to him and said,

"Look at my boots! Look at my feet! Look at my hand! It is the blood of my fellow man! I struck him on the head! It cries for vengeance! I am just as brutal and savage as he. I have met violence with violence and have shed human blood. I who came to the slums to spread the Gospel of . . ."

But when the shop door opened, with a loud ping of the bell, I turned and fled, back to that horrible spot where I had sunk the blood-stained poker; for I must wash the blood from my feet.

I have been washing blood-stains from my feet ever since; from that day to this. I walk in blood; I look behind me to see the blood-stained prints which I must leave where'er I go.

And once again I fled, this time leaving foot-prints on the pavement, foot-prints that I saw as I passed beneath a lamp-post. The foul water of that canal, or the blood of my fellow man?

As though running would enable me to escape from my own foot-prints!

I ran, realising—but not caring—that a running man is even more noticeable than one who walks with his trousers tucked into his socks.

Far more by chance than sense of direction, I reached the High Street, and soon after, jumped on to a bus that was going in a westerly direction.

I remember wondering what I had better say when the conductor came up the stairs and asked for my fare. "As far as you are going" would, perhaps, be best.

That would be all very well, but where was I going?

Miranda had spoken of the South.

What did it matter where I went, so long as it was about as far from London as I could get?

Did the conductor look at me curiously?

No, of course not. Why should he? There was no blood on my face, surely? And I had washed it from my feet.

Would all men look at me curiously, henceforth?

Fearing the conductor's eye, I got off the bus when it stopped in a thronged and brightly lit thoroughfare. I feared and hated my fellow man, but only in a crowd could I feel safe.

Where should I go?

A policeman loomed up, gigantic, and I cringed,

recovered myself, and dashed into the midst of the traffic.

A paper-boy ran by, with a bundle beneath his arm and a placard dangling in front of him.

Man attacked in a slum tenement.—Was that the evening's news?

No, not yet. And I must not buy a paper.

I had read of a man who had committed a murder, and who first drew attention to himself by the manner in which he rushed into a news-agent's, snatched up a paper and scanned the headlines.

No, I must not be seen staring at a news-paper with burning, anxious, horrified eyes in a white and anxious face, for I felt like a murderer myself.

Suppose I read that some wretch, some creature known to be an enemy of the injured man, had been arrested, and was on trial and in danger of prison! Or that the police were already looking for *me!*

I jumped on to another bus which was standing by the curb, and sat with my cap pulled down almost to my nose, and with my hand across my mouth. I was trembling from head to foot; and my feet in my sodden boots, were numbed and dead. I might have been a murderer, instead of a man who had brutally struck another and knocked him unconscious, so criminal and hunted did I feel. Of what was I afraid—the Slasher Gang or the Police, and the Law? . . . It was of *myself*, of my conscience that I was afraid.

I was fleeing from *myself.*

The bus stopped. What was this? London Bridge? Where could I go from here?

Why, to Brighton! As Miranda had said. That was a big place, and I could lose myself among the tens of thousands of people that thronged it. I would hide there, for as long as I dared, and then I would go on tramp.

Suddenly, my heart sank to an even lower depth of fear and misery.

Money!

How was I to get to Brighton? How live there, until I could write to my Bank and get a remittance? And would that be safe? Suppose I gave my Bank Manager an address, and there were a hue and cry in the papers—my name and description. Would he go to the police?

Instinctively searching my pockets, to see whether I had enough for my fare, I found that, in the side pocket of my coat, were some pound notes. Miranda, thinking of everything, must have put them there, as she knelt beside my chair.

When these were gone, I would write to my Bank, giving Brighton General Post Office, *poste restante*, as my address, and asking the Manager to send me fifty one-pound notes. Directly I had got the money, I could take train to Birmingham, and from there, go to Cardiff; and from Cardiff to Liverpool, and there I could either live in the slums, or go on tramp, or take a ship to America.

Even being quite honest with myself, I remember but little of the days and weeks that followed. I lived through days and weeks and months of dreadful fear, and almost every night I had a hideous nightmare.

One, the worst of all, was recurrent; and in it, I dreamed that I had committed murder. I lived through every detail of the last day and night in the condemned cell. I heard the feet of the men who came to lead me from the cell to the gallows-shed; I was pinioned; and I walked behind the chaplain along the corridor, across the yard, up some steps, and on to the scaffold in an out-building; from a beam dangled a noosed rope; I was made to stand with my feet within a chalked circle where two hinged flaps met; the rope was placed about my neck; a bag-like cap was drawn over my head; and, after an eternity of indescribable agony, I fell to a hideous awakening.

In another dreadful dream, I was fleeing, leaden-footed, my boots splashed brilliantly with blood, and all who saw me pointed at them, and joined in the chase.

In another, I attended the funeral of the man whom I dreamed I had murdered; and I knew that, as they lowered the coffin into the grave, the lid would open and the corpse arise, seize my blood-stained feet, and drag me down, living, into the grave.

And, awake, I live in a dream of self-disgust and shame that *this* should be the outcome of my mission to the slums. Violence . . . Assault . . . Brutality . . . Returning Evil for Evil . . .

How did I live through that period of misery, remorse and terror?

I tramped; I travelled by train; I lurked in slum lodging-houses; and often I slept in the open.

And though I watched continuously the placards outside the news-paper shops, I saw nothing on them to alarm me, and I never bought a paper.

I had a weak, foolish and cowardly feeling that so long as I knew nothing, I was in less danger of arrest for brutal assault and attempted homicide.

Should some hoarse-voiced ruffian have run up bawling, ' 'Orrible Murder! Attacked Man now Dead!' and bearing a placard on which was written 'Man Injured in London Slum dies in Hospital!' I should have had to buy a paper and draw attention to myself by my demeanour. I should have read my own name and description in print, and, perhaps, seen a dreadful portrait of myself; I might have read that the police had a clue to the whereabouts of the wanted ruffian, who had been reported by lodging-house keepers and others, as having been seen in Brighton and elsewhere. . . .

Now, let me be honest with myself, since I am forcing myself to remember so much.

Was the inhibition, which prevented me from buying a paper, the base and cowardly fear that I should read that an innocent man had been arrested? And that I must, therefore, immediately go to the police, and make a statement and confession, and give myself up?

I would give anything, *anything*, to be absolutely sure that I should have done so. That even I would not have allowed an innocent man to go through the ordeal of an Old Bailey trial, much less to have suffered punishment for my act.

I cannot be sure. I *can't*.

I was in such a state of horror, self-loathing, and mental incoherence, that there is no telling what I might have done.

I think, as a matter of fact, that I was, for quite a long period after my assault on the man "Tich", in a condition indistinguishable from madness. The realisation of what my body had done, had given my mind so appalling a shock, that I was very much in the same condition as is a shell-shocked soldier; a condition of hysteria—in the medical sense of the word—of paralysing self-horror, anxiety and neurosis.

It must have been that which caused me to lie shuddering, trembling, sweating, crying, and, at times, screaming, in an ecstasy of uncontrollable self-hatred and grief.

In one spike—as they call the casual wards—I had a fit, and I think that even the rough, weary, broken-down occupants of that horrible room were sorry for me.

Why could I not have died?

604

No wonder I have become a psychiatric problem, who, even now, has very marked symptoms—
and no disease.

Can they help me here?

I believe Elspeth Grey can help me.

I think it was tramping saved me then—the
open-air life and regular monotony of healthy exercise.

By the time my fifty pounds had gone, I had
neither heard nor read one word concerning the
assault.

I decided that I would move gradually up the
social scale until, well-dressed, well-groomed and
well-spoken, I could return to my proper station
and walk of life.

I was beginning to feel safer, and realised that I
should be safer still in my proper sphere than in
that of the tramp, the slum-dweller, doss-house
kipper, and outcast.

Yes, I had better return to my own way of life;
far better do that than walk the highways and by-
ways or the slums, in fear of every policeman, in
fear that every burly man who looked at me and
addressed me might be a plain-clothes officer.

And, one day, quite suddenly, I realised that I
had done with the slums *for ever*, and that no
power on earth would induce me to enter a slum
again, or willingly speak to a slum-dweller.

My last and greatest *revulsion*.

I had done my best there—and failed; failed
shamefully and disgracefully; I was utterly unfitted for such work; I was too highly-strung; too
emotional and too impulsive; and, alas, God help
and forgive me, there was no depth of earth in me.

Why should I ask for forgiveness—for that?
Could I supply the good deep earth? Had I

arranged for its depth? Was it my fault that it was shallow—that I am shallow, as I know I am? Or did the hand of the potter . . .

No . . . No . . .

Where am I? What am I? What becomes of me —if I lose my faith in God?

Oh, it is hard to understand. It is hard, when intelligence revolts, for Faith to remain placid, calm and clear.

It was with a tremendous sense of relief, release and a fleeting glimpse of happiness, that I admitted and declared my apostasy. I was free—I had escaped from the slums, from the pit; and the gates of Hell should not prevail. No more slums, and no more slum-dwellers—*and that included Miranda Burbidge.*

Revulsion! . . .

My love for her was absolutely dead. It had died that awful night; died as suddenly as had my love for Claire Bell, for Harry Johnson, and for the girl whose name I never knew—the photographer's assistant at Oxford. I could not think of Miranda Burbidge without seeing that unconscious man with the bloody head; without seeing myself as the hunted assailant, who fled from that appalling room to wash his blood-stained feet in the foul black waters of the canal.

I had finished with it all, and I had finished with *her*—and I prayed to God that I might never see her again.

But I was ashamed. I had the grace to be bitterly ashamed. For though my connection with her led to my becoming a ruffian who appealed to brute force, it was not her fault. Of course it was not. She was entirely blameless. But the fact remained that she was inextricably associated with the horror that cut my life in halves, and laid the second half in the blackened ruin of failure.

Yes, I was, and am to this day, ashamed that my love for her died so suddenly and so completely.

'Unstable as water thou shalt not excel.'

But who, or what, made me unstable? Upbringing, heredity, environment, I suppose. And, if so, was I responsible for my heredity, environment, and upbringing?

No, I told myself, I was not.

Nor was I to blame because I could think of Miranda Burbidge with nothing but horror and repulsion; could not think of her in any other setting than of that blood-stained room.

Thus I excused myself—and returned to my home and my former way of life.

But the Hound of Heaven pursued me, and before it, my spirit fled in shame and fear, as my body had fled from London and along the roads and rail-roads of England.

For a man may escape from all else—but from himself he cannot escape.

Escape . . . Flight . . . Fugue . . .

And ever with blood-stained feet that nothing can cleanse. Not all the waters in the rough rude sea could wash the blood-stains from such a ruffian's feet.

What did I do next? . . .

I forget. I honestly do forget.

After a period, brief or long, in which I endeavoured to imagine a sort of Paradise Regained, I went to see a very wise man—whom I had always admired, respected and feared more than I liked him—my Mother's brother, a dignitary of the Church, and Dean of St. Botolph's.

My real motive in going to him was partly to find the answer to many questions, partly in the hope of finding a sort of refuge and sanctuary, and largely because I was toying with the idea of entering the Church.

At first, of course, I rejected the idea as a kind of impudence amounting to blasphemy.

How could I, a hopeless failure, who shed the blood of his fellow-man, an unbalanced violent criminal who left red foot-prints in his wake, foot-prints of blood-stained feet, dare to dream of such a thing? Who was I to set myself up as a light and a beacon to guide the feet—feet unstained by blood—of other and better men, into the way of Peace? Let me first find peace myself, and that, of course, was my real motive—my yearning to find peace, forgiveness, and safety. Above all, the safety of the protection of Mother Church. Safety not so much for, as *from* myself and my uncontrolled passions.

The phrase and idea '*Mother Church*' attracted me enormously . . .

My Uncle not only welcomed me—as warmly as it was in his dour and undemonstrative nature to do—but he welcomed the idea of my taking Holy Orders. He thought I had seen the Light, heard the Call, become a serious young man at last, and shown my first signs of wisdom.

He recommended a Theological College, arranged everything for me, and, later, used his influence on my behalf, getting me my first curacy with an old friend of his—later to become my father-in-law; and, after I was married, obtaining for me the incumbency of Little Pudding . . .

One of the first questions I asked him—as we were taking coffee after our very first dinner together, I believe—was whether he remembered a case of brutal assault in the East End some months ago, when a man of the hawker or coster-monger class had been found badly injured in a woman's room, if I remembered rightly . . . What was the woman's name? . . . Oh, yes, same name as the famous Shakespearean actor, Richard Bur-bidge—and I was, indeed, a cunning actor myself, as I casually asked the question. How I dared, I don't know.

I suppose it was because the very last thing in the world that would occur to my Uncle was that I could possibly have anything to do with such an ugly business.

"No," he said. "No, I don't remember any such case, and I certainly haven't seen the name Bur-bidge lately. Why do you ask?"

"I remember thinking that it was a curious name for a slum woman to have . . . Miranda Bur-bidge, that was the name, Miranda."

"Yes, unusual name," agreed my Uncle. "Did she commit the assault? Was she the woman in whose room the injured man was found?" he asked idly, as he cracked a walnut.

"I . . . didn't follow the case," I replied. "It seemed rather a mysterious business—that and the unusual name made me remember it. I didn't see a paper for a day or two afterwards, and I've wondered once or twice since, whether the assail-ant was caught."

"Don't know. Don't remember it at all," said my Uncle. "Yes, unusual name—nearly as unusual as Badalia Herodsfoot of slum fame."

And several times later, to the right sort of people, and on the right occasion, I asked the same question.

"Do you remember a case of a man being found in a woman's room in Bethnal Green, with his head almost battered in? The woman had a most curious and unusual name—for a slum woman; I was trying to remember it the other day."

And always the same answer,

"No, I don't remember the case. Why? What happened? Was it very interesting?"

And I would explain that I had just read in some paper, somewhere, sometime or other, something about such a case, and I'd wondered if they had caught the attacker. It was really the woman's name that had interested me; it was such an unusual one—for a coster-girl, that is to say.

And never did I find anyone who had any recollection whatsoever, of any such name or any such case. Apparently, no such case ever came into court, no such savage assault had ever been committed.

But that did not remove the blood from my feet.

Unexpectedly, I enjoyed my year at the Theological College, in spite of the fact that it was so different from Oxford. It gave me a haven of refuge, and a fleeting sense of safety.

When I was ordained, I did my very utmost to repent of all my sins, including that one which I regarded as my greatest sin of all. I strove to obtain forgiveness, and to feel that I had made my peace with God.

For a time, I enjoyed a sense of comfort, security, and peace. But only for a time.

Never, never, shall I forget the feeling of utter dismay, the bitter disappointment that quickly turned to horror, the trembling fear that smote me one day, as I stood in the Church, about to kneel and pray before the altar. For, glancing down, I saw that my feet were shining brightly, *shining with a deep red glow.*

I stared in amazement, and then fell to my knees, buried my face in my hands and sobbed aloud with mingled relief and hysterical fright, as I realised that the sun shining through the red cloak of St. Martin, in the East window, cast the lurid light that encarnadined my feet.

But after the first shock of relief at finding that I had not gone mad, that I was not dreaming dreams and seeing visions, as I stood upon the steps before the altar, and thought some dreadful miracle had taken place, turning my feet to the colour of blood—the thought struck me,

"What an appalling omen!"

God, Thou seest me! In Thine own House, before Thine own Altar, I receive a sign—a sign that I am to be despised and rejected of men and of God. I, who went to save and help and guide and improve the slum-dwellers—and soon proved myself as bad as any of them, and set them a vile example of brutality and violence. *I*, the apostle of the Gospel of Love, Unselfishness, Kindness and Peace.

"Love thy neighbour as thyself."

I think my real suffering, my real punishment, only began then.

It was the thought, the feeling, the fear, that God and Mother Church had refused me and cast me out, that made me (subconsciously, at first, at any rate) turn to Jacintha, my Vicar's daughter; made me see in her another and a different refuge —an earthly and more kindly mother.

A more lovable woman never lived, and I really did love her. I love her still—of course I love her— but I was never *in* love with her. And although Jacintha is an admirable mother in every way, she could not and did not fulfil the role for which I cast her.

Of course I had no right to erect a mother-pedestal, and set her upon it. Far, far less any right to blame her because I thought she failed as Woman-in-the-Mother aspect.

There is something of the mother in all women; much of the mother in most women; some women are Mother Incarnate; and most women mother all they love. Such women mother their own grandfathers; mother strange mangy dogs; and they mother their lovers and their husbands as they mother their own children.

So Jacintha failed me.

No. No. What a coward and cad I am! Far, far more likely is it that I failed Jacintha.

What I should have said, was that Jacintha failed to live up to my entirely erroneous conception of her; failed to be the entirely imaginary person that I wished her to be.

What right had I to make an image in my own heart—an image of the perfect and protecting *mother*—marry that image, and then complain because it was not Jacintha?

And so that refuge failed me, and I walked alone on blood-stained feet—a whited sepulchre, blood-stained in a white surplice. . . .

Then came the worst day of all my life—worse, even, than that on which I did the dreadful deed— the day on which I saw Miranda's portrait in Marindin's studio, and learned that I was worse than a failure; worse than a renegade from my chosen life-work in the slums; worse than a violent-tempered brute . . .

That I was, in fact, a murderer.

What I suffered on that day, and what I have suffered on every dreadful day that has dawned between then and now, no-one will ever know. No-one could imagine.

I, a beneficed clergyman, a man sanctified and elect, the Vicar to whom other men look up—*a murderer!*

A criminal who should be in gaol, and who, had he been caught and brought to trial, might well have met a shameful death upon the gallows.

It was as though I began upon that day to die—and have been dying ever since.

If my self-reproach was great and agonising before, what has it been since? I know not how I have carried on my life from day to day; faced my fellow-men; prayed before the altar of my church; gone up into my pulpit and preached.

I, a murderer.

A criminal with the brand of Cain upon his brow; the blood of his fellow-man upon his head—and literally upon his hands and feet.

No wonder that I am doomed and damned to all eternity.

Never, as in my dream, to approach closer than within two feet of Heaven.

God help me and forgive me . . . And let me die . . .

There is no health in me, and I am here.

And I have met Elspeth Grey.

I love her—I love her because she is the Mother Incarnate, the woman who could understand, forgive, comfort, and heal.

§2

Richard Neystoke sat up in bed, turned on his reading-lamp, and looked at his wrist-watch.

Three o'clock.

Hours of misery and suffering before the dawn came.

Joy cometh in the morning—to some people, he

thought. A wretched hour, three o'clock; too late and too early.

She would have made her rounds and gone to bed by now, and it would be four hours before she might, perhaps, come in to see him on her way down-stairs.

It was just possible that if he left his light on she might pass by, see that it was burning, and come in.

If she came to-night, he would tell her every-thing; he would humble and abase himself to the lowest depths, and throw himself on her mercy. She would pity him—and pity is akin to love.

If Elspeth Grey should ever love him as he loved her, it would be . . . salvation; it would be such a . . . compensation—for everything he had suffered. It would have been worth the suffering, the enduring of the merciless buffeting of the storm, to come, at last, to such a haven.

It would give him a sense, not only of peace, but of absolution, assoilment; it would be a sign— a sign that at last he was forgiven.

He would leave it to Fate.

If she came to-night, he would tell her every-thing, and he would tell her that she could end the bitter suffering of all those years. She could make him whole; she could heal him—and to heal is to give health.

Yes, he would leave the light burning until the sun rose—if she did not come before. By day-light, he could tell her nothing; but if she came before then, he would make full and complete confession . . .

A mother-confessor and a heart-broken peni-tent.

He would tell her everything—but he would say nothing about Miranda.

A few minutes later the door opened, and Elspeth Grey entered.

"Not asleep yet?" she asked, with deep concern in her voice. "Haven't you slept at all?"

"No. And I shan't sleep again until I've told you —everything."

Elspeth Grey drew a small chair up to the side of the bed, and took the hot hand out-stretched to her.

"Tell me," she said.

And Richard Neystoke told her everything, except about Miranda.

CHAPTER 13

"Well, I suppose he may as well go home now," said Dr. Stortford to the Matron. "I'll make my report to the Chief, and I think he'll agree that we've done all we can for him. He ought to get better now, I think; get well, *if* he has told you everything."

"Yes, if," replied Elspeth Grey. "I fancy there were reservations."

"Yes, and he has not been extraordinarily helpful in the matter of his Unconscious. I should not be surprised if there is still something there."

"He says he feels really better," mused Elspeth Grey. "The usual sense of tremendous relief and release. Cured or not, I am sure you've done him a world of good."

"*You*, you mean," smiled Stortford. "He has appointed you his mother, and he'd like to . . ."

"He'd like to get well and get home," interrupted Elspeth Grey. "And I hope the Chief will let him go, though I shall be sorry," she added truthfully. "I shall miss him."

"Yes. About the most interesting case we've had," said Stortford, though it was not entirely as a case that Elspeth Grey was thinking of Richard Neystoke.

"Pretty bad break, I suppose, to affect him so seriously," continued the doctor.

"Yes."

"Police business?"

"Yes. He thinks so, anyway."

"Quite safe now, I suppose?"

"Yes."

"And you've promised not to talk about it?"

"Yes."

"Especially not to tell me or the Chief?"

"Yes."

"Well, I'll tell you, and you need neither affirm nor contradict," smiled Stortford. "He committed a murder. Probably in a state of violent fear, and found himself in that position which our ill-defined and idiotic murder-law calls 'Guilty but insane', because the victim—of the Law that is, the murderer—is neither guilty nor insane; not guilty of wilful and premeditated murder, nor insane. . . . It was a man he murdered, and he did it crudely and clumsily—a bluggy business—and then put his foot in it. Both feet. In the pool of blood, I mean; and left foot-prints behind him as he walked away. That's clear enough from his dreams, and his mental re-actions. Why, the other day, in our word-capping game, he trumped my 'poker' with 'skull', and a week later, my 'blow' with 'head'. And that's not all, and it's not the worst part. I'm not certain even now, whether he has managed to shove this said 'worst part' deep down into his Unconscious; or whether it still floats around and bobs up into the day-light. The murder may have been, and probably was, entirely excusable—if not laudable. But he let somebody in; a woman, I think; and left her to hold the baby, so to speak. And though he won't admit it, he wishes she were dead, and hopes she is. He attends her funeral frequently in his dreams. Knows who is in the coffin, and won't say; hopes the corpse won't either. . . . Yes, he's a murderer all-right, and behaved very badly about it. Treated somebody worse than he did the victim," and Dr. Stortford gazed triumphantly and enquiringly at Elspeth Grey.

"Just fancy!" said she, non-committally.

Stortford uttered the short sharp bark which

was his form of laughter, and which generally signified that he was not amused.

"Yes, and fact too," he said. "A murderer and a responsibility-dodger; and still one of the very nicest chaps you'd meet in a life-time. Probably lived an absolutely blameless life before and after —model husband, model father, model friend, model vicar. Let us hope he doesn't fall into the clutches of our delightful criminal law and punishment-system," he added. "For they'd certainly hang him. And if I went into the witness-box and told them that he was probably less of a murderer than I am, prosecuting and defending counsels, the jury, and the judge himself—especially the judge himself—they'd want to shove me in the dock with him. . . . Well! Well! . . . Good work, Sister."

After a long and rather harrowing interview with Dr. Fieldwicke, in which he received the finest of good advice, some painful admonitions, and a definite accusation of disingenuousness, Richard Neystoke was told that he might as well return home; and that, if he did as the doctor advised, he would probably find himself in very much better health—for a time, at any rate.

And was he cured, he asked?

No, definitely not; and the fault was largely, if not entirely, his own. Few people could speak more plainly, and to the point, than Dr. Fieldwicke.

Richard Neystoke's interview with Elspeth Grey that night was also long, and more than painful, being one of the most poignant hours of a life already too full of them.

The last thing he said, as she finally withdrew her hands from his, and turned to depart, was,

"I must see you again . . . I shall come back . . . I must . . ."

As she opened the door, Elspeth Grey turned, and gazed with a long level look.

"Don't!" she said. "You must not! I beg and pray that you will never . . ." and hurriedly she closed the door, lest her strength should fail and she should break down and turn back.

In the morning, Richard Neystoke's friend arrived to take him home in his car.

CHAPTER 14

On arrival at the vicarage, the Reverend Richard Neystoke realised how much he loved his home, his daughter, and his Jacintha.

Jacintha also realised that something more than his home-coming made Richard so unusually affectionate and demonstrative. As women will, on such occasions, she decided that he had met someone very nice at the Nursing Home, and privately wondered whether it would be a fellow-patient, or a member of the staff. Probably the latter, as ladies sojourning in Nursing Homes for the mentally disturbed, were not, she imagined, apt to be of the disturbing kind.

Would it have been his nurse?

"What sort of a nurse did you have, dear?" she asked.

"Oh, such a nice girl—Nurse Weston. Charming, and so friendly and helpful. I shall miss her frightfully."

"And the Sister?"

"Oh . . . very competent. Sisterish, you know."

So it was the Sister.

Jacintha was glad that Richard had not brought her a present, or she would have been really concerned—for him, of course.

She did so hate him to be hurt; and a woman like that might very well hurt him. She would not understand him as well as his Jacintha.

"Poor Richard," she sighed.

Of course he would never, never do anything rash. Nothing that would cause him to forfeit the approval and respect of his congregation—not to mention those of his wife. He would never run off with someone else, however bored he might be. But in making a fine and final renunciation, he'd certainly suffer, even if the woman were ever so careful and wise and gentle.

Poor dear Richard.

But if Richard found the dear old home just the same, and the dear old Jacintha just the same, and the dear young Rosemary just the same, and the dear old parish and his dear old friends quite unchanged, he noticed a remarkable difference in the boy whom his friends were wont to address as Itler.

Evidently Rosemary had taken him in hand, and to some purpose. He was a different creature. Far less hang-dog, furtive and resentful; far more cheerful, smiling and friendly. Apparently he had learnt to laugh, too.

According to Jacintha, Rosemary was the cause of the change. She had treated him just as she did a stray mangy dog, a homeless hungry cat, or a broken-winged young rook, such as she had found in the spinney.

Itler was a stranger, and she had taken him in —into her orbit, interest, life, and capacious young heart.

Having made him her willing and obedient slave, by treating him as a fellow-tough, she had not only taken him fishing, and taught him stump cricket, but she had, upon occasion, bade him abandon his doorstep and join her at school-room tea.

To this, Itler had raised no objection, whatso-ever. On the contrary. And he had endeavoured, as far as in him lay, to comport himself in seemly manner and with inoffensive manners. This he did more readily and successfully because Rosemary never rebuked nor corrected him; never bade him

eat "properly", nor refrain from licking his fingers
(" 'Ow else clean them? On the blinkin' table-cloth?
Or wash them in the tea-cup?"); never bade him
not to fill his mouth too full (" 'Ow could yer, so
long as yer could 'old it?"); nor requested him to
desist from talking with his mouth full ("If yer
could talk, it wasn't full, was it?").

When he unfortunately dropped a spot of jam
upon the cloth, and very neatly and successfully
removed it with the tip of his tongue, she made no
comment; and Itler was grateful.

He showed his gratitude by endeavouring to
imitate Rosemary's table-manners—not that these
were fantastically elegant—and anxiously to prevent himself in all his doings in this difficult business of assimilation.

Fideliter didicisse artes emollit mores.

And, gradually, under the influence of precept,
example, and yearning to please, Itler did faithfully study the arts of gracious living, to the improvement and easement of his ways, manners
and customs.

To the slum-bred and wizened boy, something
was happening, something that happens even to
other boys who are not slum-bred nor wizened,
and who are more accustomed to meeting delightful long-legged coltish girls; to boys less accustomed to regarding such girls as something wonderful—if not superhuman and apparently straight
from that curious hinterland of reality known to
the more articulate as fairyland.

PART V

ITLER OUT OF ARCADY

CHAPTER 1

Itler was beginning to revise his opinion as to the demerits of the rural life. He had found a new and a great interest. This was provided by the sayings and doings, and the extremely lovable and attractive person and personality of Rosemary Neystoke, newly returned home from a visit to her grandparents.

Rosemary, at the age of fourteen, was fond of animals; fond of novelty and novelties; free from conventional inhibitions; frank, fearless, and ever seeking a new thing.

To her, Itler was a strange animal; definitely a novelty; certainly a new 'thing'; and obviously full of possibilities.

He could spit to a remarkable distance, and in a most curiously effortless manner—no splutter about it, whatever; just a neat, quiet, and accurate ejection.

He could also whistle in a variety of most attractive ways; placing his curving thumb and index finger in his mouth, he could whistle shrill as the curlew on the hill, producing an ear-piercing sound that an agitated steam-engine might envy. Also, placing the tip of his tongue against the roof of his mouth, he could utter most charming notes, a sort of whistling recitative which, while a genuine honest-to-God whistle, did convey the sense and meaning of words. He could imitate song-birds too, which was curious, inasmuch as until coming to Little Pudding, the only birds that, to his knowledge, he had ever seen, were sparrows and an occasional pigeon—neither kind notable for sweet variety of song. Now he imitated, distinguishably, a thrush and a black-bird, and was practising to emulate the nightin-gale.

"Turnin' into a perishin' canary, ain't I?" he would say to Rosemary.

"Yes, just like a blinkin' canary," Rosemary would agree.

Then, too, he had wonderful tales to tell of life in the great Wicked City. Tales, that, to the country mouse, were bizarre, absorbingly interesting, and almost incredible.

Just fancy being free to come and go as one would! Free to stay out until mid-night, or not to go home until morning; free to go with one's chosen friends and camp out in an empty house, cooking spadgers on a pocket-knife over a gas jet, or a pigeon over a fire lighted in a bath; to hold high revelry and feasting on the proceeds of raids; free to conduct guerrilla warfare with policemen and with other robber bands, and to live like Arabs—street-arabs.

Then, too, he undoubtedly knew wonderful words, exclamations, locutions, of the most re-markable and satisfying kind. Golly! Fancy letting some of them off in the hearing of Miss Struthers. Give her a free perm.

And he could climb like a cat, run like a hare, jump like a flea, and fight like a fiend. She'd seen him have two fights. Lovely!

But there was one thing he couldn't do, and that she could do pretty well. He couldn't ride. She was teaching him, and putting him through it, too. Bare-back and snaffle; stripped saddle and snaf-fle; stripped saddle, no reins, and arms folded; the same with jumps; and then—proper riding.

Perhaps, when Daddy came back, he'd let her keep Itler as her own private groom. He could keep behind her until they'd got well away, and he could ride her second horse when she hunted.

Meanwhile, having Itler meant something to do —and someone to do it with—in stuffy Little Pudding.

She had had serious thoughts of joining the Blackand Gang at Itler's kindly invitation, and accompanying them on reconnaissance, scouting, or even foraging expeditions on reasonably distant towns and villages. But having seen his lieutenants, Messrs Gob and Chimp, she somehow felt that, even in her oldest and dirtiest jersey and jodhpurs, she might be too conspicuous a member of the gang.

And this, inevitably, led to trouble for Itler. As has happened before in the history, both of leaders and of ordinary men, the intrusion of women was the beginning of wisdom—and trouble.

There was a division of loyalties, and also, bitter ill-feeling. Gob and Chimp took it badly, and though they knew not Browning and 'Just for a handful of silver he left us; just for a riband to stick in his coat', they spread the news, in sorrow and in anger, that Itler had took up with a moll. The Gob, indeed, was wont to use a term heard in kennels.

"Divided loyalties", is, in point of fact, a misnomer; for Itler, however lost to sense of right and wrong (as distinguished by his betters), however steeped in vice and villainy, was richly endowed with two virtues which some people consider to be the first and foremost, the finest of all—courage and loyalty.

He had the cold, hammered courage of the underdog; and with it, the loyalty of the one-man dog —to the man who is his true and only god.

To the Band, to his friends, his fellows, and his beliefs, he was as loyal as hilt to blade; and neither bribe nor threat, neither fear nor love itself, would ever have made him disloyal, made him, as he would say in his strange synthesis of Cockney-Chicago dialect, "squeal". And, by squeal, he meant not only accuse and betray, but abandon and desert.

But, strike him perishin' pink, he could learn to ride a norse when he was given the chance, couldn't he? He could take time off from the Gang to improve himself as a leader, couldn't he? Wait till Chink Gotti saw him on a norse!

§2

In the fullness of time it came to pass that Chink Gotti did see Itler on a norse.

From a conveniently hidden spot in the shrubbery, Chink watched the equestrian antics of the abominably swollen-headed upstart lieutenant of the Blackand Gang. His mouth set in a bitter and contemptuous sneer.

The muckin' little barstard! Runnin' abaht with a fancy moll, and puttin' on swank! He, Chink Gotti, would push the perisher's chest in for 'im. . . .

And, when Rosemary had trotted away on her fifteen-hand hunter, Chink emitted a low and peculiar whistle, to which Itler responded as does a well-trained dog to his master.

" 'I got a norse! I got a norse! I got a norse!' " quoted Chink, bitter with contempt and disgust, as Itler joined him.

"Yus! And I got a nass!" replied Itler, stroking and patting Chink in a manner that failed to soothe his savage breast.

Anger and offended dignity almost moved the leader of the Blackand Gang to strike his insolent subordinate. Almost, but not quite; for such was not Chink's way. He had other, better and safer methods than corporal punishment when desiring to retaliate.

"One o' these days, I'll cut yer liver out and strew yer arahnd, all over the bleedin' shop," said he.

"Not to-day, though," replied Itler brightly. "Wotcher come 'ere for?"

"See you, *and* give you orders. . . . Know Corkey the Coke?"

Itler's heart seemed to flutter slightly, and sink a little. He did know Corkey the Coke, and he feared him very much indeed. For Corkey the Coke was really bad. Dangerous, 'e was; wot 'e said went; and 'e said a lot and said it nasty. Chink Gotti was a perishin' pink-eyed fool to have any truck with Corkey the Coke. No good ever came of that—except to Corkey—and that "good" generally landed 'im in stir.

" 'Ow did 'e come down 'ere? You bring 'im?" he asked.

" 'Ow did 'e come down 'ere? 'Ow d'yer think? On 'is 'ands and knees, or shufflin' on 'is fanny? Me bring 'im? Naow! Wot yer talkin' abaht, young Itler?"

Young Itler was talking about one of the very widest of the Wide Boys, a young gentleman said to hail from Cork and to be addicted to the ped-dling of coke—which is cocaine—and hence the soubriquet.

And in denying that he had brought him to Little Pudding, and the parts adjacent, Chink was over-modest. For there could be no doubt that there was a connection between Corkey's arrival and an interesting and curious letter which Chink had written to his dear old friend and kind patron, Mr. Joe Schinkler.

It might seem an unwise proceeding for Chink to write, on the subject of Corkey and his activities, to Mr. Schinkler, but even in the practically impossible event of the letter being tampered with, its contents were vague to the point of incomprehensibility. . . .

Read Sob,

Howyer blowin? Me 2. Prospex also. Guys got dough. Spoc dusty in the dome. Nix on the big gaff. Some snappers and dirty diddlers. Young Itler with olijo. Good fag to wercs. Dame got big rocks. Oyster pips like nuts. Itler lamps. Big Peter in grubjoint. Cokey brings pint of soup. Edisni boj. Creepers. Hoppin this finds you in the pink as it now leaves me.

Your ever lovin little granddaughter,

Jooby.

Over this letter old Mr. Joe Schinkler had smiled happily.

"Goot poy!" he murmured, and read the letter again, translating it swiftly.

Dear Master,

How is your health? I trust that it is as good as is mine own. The prospects of business are also good. There are wealthy people here. The local and yokel police are, as you might suppose, quite unintelligent. The Manor House to which I referred, is uninteresting—from your point of view. Large and unfriendly dogs roam the grounds at night, and the doors and windows are fitted with burglar-alarms. Our young friend Itler resides at the Vicarage, and the said Vicarage would be an excellent gaff to screw—in other words, desirable residence to burgle. The Vicar's lady is the possessor of very fine diamonds, and has pearls the size of walnuts. Our friend Itler has seen and described them to me. There is a large safe in the dining-room. I suggest

that Corkey the Coke brings nitro-glycerine. It would be an inside job. There are ladders available. Sincerely hoping that you are as well as I am,
Your loving grand-daughter,
Jooby.

"Goot poy! Goot poy! Clever poy!" smiled Mr. Joe Schinkler, gently rubbing his hands together. "An inside job, eh? Little Itler goes down and unbolts the back-door, eh? And if he has not done his job all-right when they come, they can put a ladder up to his window. But he'll do it. He'll do it all-right, when Corkey the Coke has had a word with him. Yes, he too will be a goot and clever poy when Corkey has said him some words!"

And old Mr. Schinkler had written a note to his grand-daughter, saying that her little friend, Bessie Coker, would be coming to pay her a visit quite soon, and would like to bring home some nice lettuces and a rabbit.

Chink Gotti having retrieved the letter from the Post Office at Swintonford, which was quite a long walk from the village of Beeston, where Chink was sojourning, had lost no time in coming to instruct Itler in the part that he was to take in the nice game that his leader, Chink Gotti—and his patron and exemplar, Corkey the Coke, and their old friend, Mr. Joe Schinkler—proposed to play in the sleepy village of Little Pudding.

It was a very small part indeed, and Itler need not make no song and dance about it. All 'e got to do on the first of the month—and 'e can't forget that date—was to go down, when the servants and family had gone to bed, and unbolt and unlock the scullery door. Yus, that there one where Itler sat on his fanny and scoffed 'is grub. That was all 'e got to do. And, by Gord, 'e 'adn't better make no mistake about it, or Corkey the Coke would be at

631

'is window in 'arf once, and get into the 'ouse that
way. And if Corkey was put to that trouble, 'e'd
'urt Itler—and 'urt 'im ugly. . . .

And wot did Corkey the Coke want at the Vicarage? Itler had inquired miserably.

Want? Wot did 'e *want?* Wanted to see if they'd
forgotten to put the cat out, and 'ad given the
canary 'is beer. Wot did Itler *think* Corkey'd want?
To arsk the Vicker if 'e'd said 'is prayers? Anyway,
it wasn't nothink to do with young Itler, wot 'e
wanted. All Itler 'ad got to do, was wot 'e, Chink
Gotti, Leader of the Blackand Gang, told 'im to do,
and that was to unlock and unbolt the back-door,
go back to 'is bed, and know nothink about it.

And wot was Chink Gotti, the perishin' Leader
of the perishin' Blackand Gang, goin' to do?

No concern of young Itler's.

Right, then. Wot Itler did or did not do, was no
concern of Chink Gotti's, and Itler wasn't goin' to
open no doors—not for nobody.

Well, if nosey-parker Itler must know, Chink
Gotti's job was to 'elp Corkey the Coke knock off
the fast car outer ole Mrs. D'Evereux' garage, and
drive away the jalopy wot Corkey come down from
London in. Useful, important man, Chink Gotti
was. Goin' to join Corkey's own gang, by-and-by—
the Wide Boys—and young Itler better be wide
that night too, wide awake, and leave that door
unfastened. Then 'e could go to sleep till Kingdom
Come.

That young moll gotta bicycle, 'adn't she?

Itler stiffened, and the look he gave his chief
was not respectful. Wot about it?

One could use it. Chink reckoned 'e would
knock it off to-morrow.

"Anyway, wot I was goin' to say was, you get a
noil-can and oil that lock and bolt, see?"

"And you go and oil yer . . . brains!" snarled

Itler. And the adjectives he used to qualify the noun are not to be found in the medical text-books.

§ 3

And thus the boy known to his mother as Richard Garden, and to his friends as Young Itler, was placed upon the horns of a dilemma, and faced with his first great moral difficulty and problem.

To squeal, or not to squeal?

The whole of his slum-training, nurture, precept, and admonition, said: *No*, of course he couldn't squeal. What remained of self-respect, if a person sank to that awful depth? He was yellow; he was a scab; he was beneath the contempt of the honest man, and even further beneath that of the dishonest man.

On the other hand, was he to help in the robbery of Rosemary's house? Take part in the theft of her mother's jewels? Equally: *No.*

Without ever having heard the phrase "divided loyalties", even if he had heard the word loyalty itself, he knew that he was now faced with the problem of divided loyalties, and the question of to whom his loyalty was due.

At first sight, to the Band, of course. To the band of brethren of which he was the lieutenant. To Chink Gotti, the chosen and recognised leader to whom he had voluntarily sworn loyalty—though not again, in those terms and words. He had his duty to the Blackand Gang and its Leader.

And what about his duty to the people who had been so kind to him? What about gratitude? Love and gratitude? Though these terms were not in his vocabulary, the sentiments that they expressed were very definitely in his spirit. He loved the

wonderful little girl who had given him glimpses of
new worlds and he was deeply grateful to her, to
her mother, and to her father.

Then, of course, there was the question of what
Corkey the Coke would do to him, if he failed him.
Corkey would think as much of strangling him
with a cord, tying a brick to the end of it, and
shoving him into the canal on a foggy night, as he
would of doing the same for a perishin' kitten.
However, that aspect of the matter could be put
aside.

The point was, should he go and tell the police
all about it; should he tell 'Oly Joe about it?
Should he tell Rosemary and leave it to her; or
should he keep his head shut?

Shut, of course.

He could not, and he would not, squeal. And
that point could be set aside, also.

Now, then, should he unfasten the back-door
for Corkey the Coke that night? No. Damned if he
would. He'd no more do that than he'd squeal.
And that point could be set aside.

Thus, there remained the difficult question as
to whether he should do anything at all in the
matter.

And, after long cogitation and considerable
nail-biting—a bad habit prohibited by Rosemary,
and into which he again now fell—he decided that
he would do nothing. He would not help; he would
not squeal; and he would not hinder.

But wasn't this again, a dirty dog's do? To
stand aside and see his benefactors robbed without a word of warning?

Oh, 'Ell! . . .

Better wait till the night, and see what happened—one thing that wouldn't happen being
their finding the back-door unlocked and unbolt-
ed.

§4

Corkey the Coke was not a violent man. He had never killed anybody roughly, noisily, nor in messy fashion. He never swore, blustered, nor threatened, but occasionally gave sinisterly quiet promises, and kept them.

" 'E 'asn't unfastened the door," he whispered to Chink Gotti. "I can't open it. . . . I can open '*im*, though, one fine night," he added softly. "Come and get the creeper."

A few minutes later, the top of the ladder came to rest beneath the window-sill of the room in which Itler slept. This, too, was closed and fastened. But that was not a matter of any importance.

Taking from his pocket the kind of tool-knife which is, in itself, "circumstantial evidence", Corkey opened a long thin blade, inserted it between the sashes of the upper and lower windows, pushed back the catch, raised the lower window, and stepped into the room.

Switching on his little electric torch, he saw that the bed was empty. He also found that the door was locked, and the key, still in the lock, was on the other side of the door.

Corkey the Coke smiled instead of swearing, as he recognised the cleverness of this move. A lock in which the key rests cannot be picked.

However, there are other ways. From a bag which hung across his shoulders like a satchel, Corkey took a blunt-nosed long-handled pair of pliers, with them seized the slightly protruding end of the key, and, with a powerful grip and wrench, turned it round and unlocked the door.

At the very moment that he did so, the young gentleman whom most particularly he desired to interview opened the front-door of the house and was welcomed with a brilliant beam of light which dazzled his eyes.

"Safe in the arms of a policeman!" he observed with cockney coolness and humour.

"Too right," agreed Sergeant Hollis, gripping him firmly with his great hand.

For the 'dusty domed' local yokel police were on to Corkey the Coke from the moment that Chink Gotti had obligingly helped him to knock off Mrs. D'Evereux's fine fast car.

When a London gentleman turns up in a battered flivver, changes its number-plate, hides it, and borrows another car, the matter becomes of interest to those whose business it is to be interested in such doings.

Sergeant Hollis was ambitious and smart; so was Constable Hogben, waiting round at the back until such moment as the sound of his superior's whistle let him know that the time had come to seize the culprit *in flagrante delicto.* The place to nab the blighter was inside, and get a good solid burglary case, and no nonsense about "loitering with intent".

Had Sergeant Hollis been even smarter than he was, he would have seized Itler by his head and clamped that fine large hand over the boy's face, so that he would then have been dumb. For, even as Corkey the Coke opened the bedroom door, he heard a whistle that told him all he needed to know.

Unlike Corkey the Bad Man, Sergeant Hollis the good man did swear, but too late—for a whistle cannot be recalled. It can be repeated though, and, with a swift movement, and with all his strength, Sergeant Hollis blew a long and loud blast on the instrument provided for that purpose.

"Yer would, would yer, yer little barstard!" he

growled, as he flung Itler from him, dashed into the hall and up the stairs.

Coolly, calmly, and almost slowly, Corkey the Coke closed the bedroom door, locked it on the inside, and stepped lightly across to the window.

Yes, there was the other flattie at the bottom of the ladder. Where was Chink Gotti? The little yellow swine must have done a scarper without giving him a warning. It must have been young Itler who had whistled in the house. Had he just gone down to open the back-door? If so, why had he locked the bedroom door? Attend to that later, for the fool flattie was actually coming up the ladder. Splendid. Half-way up would do nicely.

And when Constable Hogben was almost half-way up the ladder, Corkey jumped straight on to him.

Landing at the bottom of the ladder with the unfortunate constable beneath him, Corkey laughed, sprang to his feet, dashed into the shadows of the shrubbery and disappeared.

By the time Sergeant Hollis had broken down the bedroom door and descended the ladder, Corkey had reached his hidden car, started up the engine, and was well away.

He reflected that, though he was not an unkind man, and never rough or cruel, he would, at some future ineluctable date, take young Itler by his left ear, and Chink Gotti by his right ear, and hammer their heads together until their brains were well and truly mingled. For once, he *would* be messy.

Meanwhile, Itler's first and natural thought and impulse was immediate and distant flight.

But, no. On second thoughts, why should 'e? 'E 'adn't done nothink. 'E'd opened no door. On the contrary, 'e'd locked one, and closed and fastened the window, too. 'E'd done 'is duty by Rosemary and her home and family.

On the other hand, 'e 'adn't squealed. On the contrary, when, in the very 'ands of the police, 'e'd given a warning whistle that to any criminal slum-dweller or Wide Boy could mean but the one thing.

Well, whatever happened, there'd been no burglary, anyway. But wouldn't it be just 'is perishin' luck if both sides turned on 'im? The family and the police because 'e 'adn't squealed. Corkey and Chink Gotti because 'e 'adn't opened the door.

Anyway, 'e wasn't one to bunk, on either account. After all, what each side grumbled about, the other side should praise 'im for, *surely?* Just 'is rotten luck that the cops had butted in, and that 'e'd come out of the front-door just at the wrong minute.

Wot 'e bin goin' to do was to make an 'ell of a bang with the front-door to frighten Corkey and Chink, and then, go round to the shrubbery at the back and make a noise like a police whistle. This 'e 'ad started to do directly 'e'd 'eard the ladder scrape 'is window-sill. 'Ow was 'e to know the cops were there?

And cripes! That was a nasty thought! 'Ow'd 'e ever persuade Corkey and Chink that it wasn't 'im 'oo'd tipped-off the Cops?

Well, 'e wasn't goin' to bunk. 'E'd tell Rosemary as much as 'e could without splittin' on Corkey and Chink, and she'd 'ave to believe 'im. She would believe 'im, of course.

No, 'e wouldn't do a scarper until Rosemary rounded on 'im, and that would be never.

'Ow explain to the cops and 'Oly Joe why 'e was goin' out of the 'ouse at that time of night, if 'e didn't know nothink about no burglary? Well, 'e'd tell the truth again—the truth they were so bloomin' fond of—and say 'e often got up and went out and mucked about in the middle of the night.

Wot else was there to do in a perishin' 'ole like Little Puddin'?

Boy, like Man, proposes, and a not-always-kindly Fate, disposes.

CHAPTER 2

"Now, then, Master Richard Garden, me lad," said Sergeant Hollis, and produced his note-book and a portentous frown. "Now, then, I want all the facts outer you.

"So spill the beans and come clean," he added, giving his pencil an emollient lick.

"Wot about?" asked Itler, glancing round the austere library and moistening dry lips. 'Ere was a gripin' drammer of Real Life in the Under-world—the Tough Guy and the Smart Aleck Cop.

Sergeant Hollis eyed the boy long and searchingly.

"Ever 'eard of the birch?" he enquired conversationally.

"No," replied Itler. "Ever 'eard of a cop gettin' a walk-out powder through threatenin' hinnocent people and gettin' statements from them under false pretences and brutal . . ."

"That'll be enough outer you, me lad. I'll do the questioning," interrupted Sergeant Hollis. "Do you know a man named Corkey the Coke?"

"Lor' Mayor o' Lunnon, ain't 'e?" enquired Itler. "Yus. Not to say *know* 'im, that is."

Sergeant Hollis glanced at the Vicar as one who needs sympathy.

"No, he ain't the Lor' Mayor o' Lunnon," he said patiently.

"My mistake," admitted Itler. "Would 'e be 'Ome Secretary?"

"Wot? The gentleman that sends young criminals to Borstal or prison?" enquired the Sergeant. "No, Corkey the Coke ain't 'Ome Secretary, but the 'Ome Secretary might sign something for *'im* some day.

"Now, then," he snapped, with a change of voice. "When did you last see . . ."

"Me aunt?" asked Itler.

". . . the man known as Corkey the Coke?"

Itler obviously racked his memory.

"Last Lor' Mayor's Show day."

Sergeant Hollis closed his note-book with a snap, rose suddenly to his feet, and stepped toward Itler in an undeniably menacing manner. A large and heavy hand rose swiftly—and scratched its owner's head.

"Would you like to come down to the Station with me, all nice and quiet? Have a little talk with me in a cell there, instead of 'ere?" he enquired.

"Wot's the charge?" asked Itler.

"Look 'ere, son, you're in an awkward spot, and if you've got the sense of a louse, you can get out of it. . . . If not, you know wot the charge'll be, all-right. It was an inside job, and *you* was on the inside."

"Was that where you copped me?" enquired Itler.

"We'll come to that, later," replied the Sergeant. "Like you'll come to Borstal or Wormwood Scrubs.

"Now, then. You been seen about 'ere with an older lad . . ."

"Do you mean the Vicker?"

". . . an older lad they call Chink. When did you see 'im last?"

"About a minute ago," replied Itler. " 'E went past the window."

" 'E did, did 'e?"

"Well, I may've been mistook. Wot's 'e like?"

"Now, look 'ere. Just to oblige the Vicar, I'll give you another chance. . . . You ever 'ad a word with a lad who's been to an approved school? Ever 'ad a talk with a boy who's been birched?"

"No. 'Ave you? I don't ersociate with that sort," replied Itler.

The Sergeant eyed Itler long and thoughtfully. His head may have itched again, for he scratched it; but undeniably his fingers did.

"I wish you was my own boy—just for five minutes," he said, and there was a note of earnestness, if not of paternal affection, in his voice.

"Wot 'ave I done to deserve that?" enquired Itler.

The Sergeant reverted to the cold and formal manner of officialdom.

"As I said, I'll give you a last chance, young Richard Garden. If you tell me, fully and truthfully, all about this affair—'oo it was put you up to opening the front-door; where the man they call Corkey the Coke 'as got a 'ide-out; where the boy they call Chink is; and 'oo was going to fence the sparklers, it just may be—just *may* be, I say—that I'll do as 'Is Reverence says, and leave you 'ere in 'is 'ands—until you're wanted for evidence, that is.

"Now, then. Wot do you know about Corkey the Coke?"

"I know 'e ain't Lor' Mayor o' Lunnon," admitted Itler promptly.

"Nothing else?"

"Nothink. If 'e ain't Lor' Mayor o' Lunnon, I don't know nothink about 'im. Just my mistook."

"Ho! And wot's the surname of the boy the others call Chink?"

"Featherstonehaugh," replied Itler. That was a fine name he had once seen over a shop and greatly admired.

"Ho! It is, is it? And was it '*im* got you into all this mess? Going to get you a birching—and land you in quod?"

"Not while there's police to protect me, I 'ope," replied Itler.

"Now, then. I'm going to write something in this 'ere book," announced the Sergeant.

"You can draw somethink, too, if you like," replied Itler.

"I'm going to write your answer to this question, so be careful wot you say, for it'll be used in evidence against you.

"Did you open the front-door of this 'ouse to admit anybody on the night of the first?"

"No. Write it down, and there ain't any *k* in it."

"Do you know the names of either of the two people 'oo made burglarious entry on the night of the first?"

"Yus. You told me them. Write all that."

"Do you refuse to give any information about wot 'appened on the night of the first?"

"No."

"Good. Seen sense at last, 'ave you? About time, too! Now, then. Out with it, and don't talk too fast."

Itler folded his arms across his meagre chest.

"On the night of the first prox.," he began, in a toneless and monotonous recitative, "I was awakened at or about two a.m. in the morning by a sound outside the 'ouse. It seemed to come from beneath my window. 'Wot the 'ell was that?' said I, feelin' nervous and alarmed. I listened 'ard. It came again. It was our old tom-cat! 'Pore feller', thinks I, ''e wants to come in.' . . . Gettin' outer bed, I dressed 'astily, went down stairs, opened the front-door, and, be'old, it wasn't the cat tryin' to get in, but a damn great copper! Wot '*is* business mighta been at that time of night . . ."

Sergeant Hollis rose to his feet.

"I'll settle *your* business later, me lad," he said, quietly. "When you'll 'ave plenty of time to think up more funny things to say to the next policeman that arrests you."

"Aw! I don't need no time for that," replied Itler.

§2

"Well, Sir, if you'll undertake to see 'e don't run away, I'll leave 'im 'ere with you; but suppose we make an arrest, we'll want 'im," said the Sergeant to the Reverend Richard Neystoke.

"He won't run away," the Vicar assured him. "I've talked the matter over with my wife, who, by the way, still believes in the boy. And I've sent for his mother; she may be able to influence him to tell all he knows.

"Mind you," he added, "I don't want him to get into serious trouble. And, if you don't catch the burglars, I'm not going to prosecute him, or anything like that. We've no proof, you know."

Sergeant Hollis smiled and shook his head sadly.

"Proof, Sir? 'Im undoing the front-door, while they comes in through 'is bedroom window!"

"Yes. But why do that?"

"A get-away, Sir. Any burglar with the sense of a lou . . . any burglar who knows 'is job, I mean, thinks of the way out, as well as the way in. Might not be able to use it, of course, but it doubles 'is chances of escape, if 'e's disturbed. In at the front-door and out at the back, or versey the vicer.

"Yerce," he added, "plain enough. This young rogue Richard Garden lets them in when they taps at 'is window, and goes straight down and opens the front-door for them to escape by. If I 'adn't pinched 'im, 'is job woulder been to go back and watch from the window and give 'em a whistle—*which 'e did*—if anybody come along."

The Vicar sighed.

"Looks like it, and you know best, Sergeant. The boy swears that he didn't admit them, and that he was just going out for a walk."

"Sure," smiled Sergeant Hollis. "At two o'clock in the morning!"

"Well, he clings to the story," continued the Vicar, "and I must confess that my wife believes him absolutely."

"Ar! The ladies!" said the Sergeant kindly. "Well, Sir, we'll do wot we can, and no doubt, we'll nab 'em. Nothing's missing, luckily."

"No," he added to himself, as he went down the drive. "But that young devil they call Itler will be missing before long, I'll lay, if they don't watch it.

"Probably lead us to 'em, though, by bunkin' back to London," he reflected, brightening up.

PART VI

THE VICAR FEELS BETTER

CHAPTER 1

The train wandered gently into Swintonford Station, came wearily to a stop, and sighed deeply.

A neatly-dressed woman, who looked about forty-five years of age, but who was not as old as she looked by some ten years, straightened her battered black straw hat, drew her shawl closer about her shoulders, smoothed down her clean white apron, picked up her basket from the seat, opened the door of the carriage, and stepped down to the empty sun-drenched platform.

"How can I get from here to Little Pudding?" she asked of the bucolic porter.

"Walk," succinctly replied the man, observing that she was of his own class.

"Thank you," replied the woman politely. "Could you tell me how far it is?"

"Three good long miles," replied the man.

"Thank you," said the woman, and walked out of the station.

Three miles, and no breakfast! Well, not to say breakfast. A cup of the tea she had made last night.

Perhaps she'd better do as Tom always said (and did)—"When in doubt, have a Dog's-nose." Not that she held with going into public-houses at this time in the morning, but—three miles!

Yes. Seeing as it was a bit of a holiday like, and there was all that way to go, and her feet not as good as they had been, perhaps a pint of stout and six pennorth o' gin would . . . Yes, of course they would . . . What time did they open here? Same time as in London, no doubt.

When the woman emerged from the small pot-house known as the Railway Hotel, she undoubtedly felt better, warmed and stimulated—what her late father was wont to call 'a better and a wider man'.

. . . Nice and filling, a good Dog's-nose; cheered you up a lot.

What sort of scrape could young Dick have been getting into? He was a good boy, even if he were a bit mischievous, and a good boy to his old woman, as he called her. It could not be anything serious. He'd been knocking off a few apples, or something. Perhaps he'd been pinching a few flowers out of front-gardens, and selling them to their owners at the door.

On the other hand, they would hardly have sent for her if it had not been something rather bad. Wouldn't be a police job, surely? Never been in police trouble yet, even if he had been born in prison, poor little chap.

It was a shame.

He'd been a better son to her than she'd been a mother to him. Been fair dragged up, he had, running the streets night and day, and in bad company, too. But what more could she do for him when he was a kid, than get him food and some rags of clothes, and keep some kind of a roof over his head—when to do that, she'd had to get up and go out at four o'clock in the morning, to be at Covent Garden in time; and was out all day till it was dark? How could she see that he went to school? And how could she look after him properly when he turned thirteen, and began to scratch for himself?

But it wouldn't be police trouble—not for young Dickie, even if he did belong to a "gang" of other boys.

God grant it wasn't the police, for she never

wanted to be spoken to by a policeman again, as long as she lived; and if they took poor Dickie and shut him up—as they had done her—she'd go mad. *She* knew what it was. It would be the death of her.

Too fond of making jobs, the police were, as Bill always said. They had got to earn their living, like other people—but a little chap like Dickie! Couldn't they just warm his young ear, and let him go?

Oh, well! It was no good meeting trouble halfway. Perhaps there wasn't any trouble at all. And if there was any, she'd just get him away and hide him—unless the police had got him already.

But of course they hadn't.

What a long way three miles was. . . .

Denzil Marindin, in the act of cutting his morning rosebud from his favourite bush in the garden, glanced up as a woman passed the entrance gate of the little drive.

A stranger. The poor woman looked tired. Walked with a list to port. What would that be? Accustomed to carrying the weight of a basket on her left shoulder and right hip? Mother of one of the evacuees?

What a foul word. Surely it was London that was evacuated—not the children? The Government were the evacuators (and evacuants!), London the evacuated, and, also, if a word had to be coined and used, the children were evacuments. Horrible! Nearly as bad as that vile locution 'issued with'. An Army crime against the English language. And yet an officer, presumably an educated man, will say 'Has this man been issued with new boots?' The proper reply would be 'How can you issue *anything?* Certainly not a man, with or without boots?' As bad as those careless people

who say they are disinterested, when they mean
that they are uninterested.

Suppose painters painted as carelessly as some
writers wrote, then—er——

"Eh? I beg your pardon?"

The woman had stopped by the gate and was
speaking to him.

Going towards her, that she might not have to
shout,

"I am afraid I didn't hear what you said," he
repeated.

"Excuse me, Sir. I was asking whether you
could direct me to where the reverend gentleman
lives . . . The Vicarage, that is. My boy's staying
there."

What a nice voice and diction she had. It hardly
went with her appearance . . . dreadful hat . . . old
shawl . . . apron . . . and deplorable shoes. . . .
Very clean and neat though.

"Yes. Straight on. You go under the bridge, and
it's on the left. It's the only house, and it stands
alone—you can't miss it."

"Thank you very much indeed, Sir."

Now that was an interesting face, very interesting. Lovely eyes. Probably a great deal younger
than she looked. Aged terribly quickly, those very
poor working women. Horizontal brow lines, eye
wrinkles, nose-to-mouth lines far too deep for the
age of the eyes. Very nice smile. Rather wonderful
eyes—reminded him of somebody.

"Have you come down from London?" he asked,
as she turned away.

"Yes, Sir. And walked over from Swintonford.
To see my boy."

"Have you been down here before?"

"No, Sir. Never."

"Oh, I thought, perhaps, you had. I'd an idea
I'd seen you somewhere before."

"No, Sir. Good morning."

Gentleman a bit too friendly?

"I could have sworn I'd seen that face before", thought Denzil Marindin, as he turned to go back to the house.

And he would have been right, for he had seen it fifteen years before—in the prisoner's dock in the Old Bailey. But it might have been nearer fifty for the amount of likeness between that girl and this woman who had spent years in prison, and even longer years in fighting alone the battle of life in the slums, for the maintenance of her child and herself.

§2

The door of Richard Neystoke's study opened quietly, and Walson, his impeccable parlour-maid, appeared.

"There is a person wishes to see you, Sir," she said. "Name of Garden."

"Oh, yes. Thank you. That boy's mother. Show her in . . . I don't want to be disturbed while she's here, but you might send someone to find the boy and tell him to wait outside till I send for him."

"Very good, Sir."

As the door closed, the Reverend Richard Neystoke placed a chair in front of his desk, and seated himself in his own comfortable one behind it. Thus did he interview parishioners and others upon the more serious occasions, when it was his duty to be admonitory; to speak straitly to sinners for their good; and to make it clear that, however velvet the glove, the hand of the Vicar could be of iron until repentance was professed and reform promised.

A difficult case this, and rendered no easier by

Jacintha's attitude. Nor by Rosemary's, as far as that went—and it was apt to go a good long way, these days, in the Neystoke household. A young woman of increasing inclination to the loud and clear expression of strong views. Always knew what she wanted, and had no hesitation in making those wants known. Jacintha was not firm enough with her.

And she knew what she wanted in this case. She wanted Itler to be allowed to go, and the sooner the better, and to go scot-free. When asked whether she strongly disapproved or not, of his base ungrateful conduct, she had replied that the thought of it made her sick on the carpet. Nevertheless, she did not want him punished, because she had taught him to ride.

When her father had mildly observed that he did not very clearly see the connection, Rosemary had replied that neither did she, but the fact remained. Anyway, Father was *not* to have him sent to prison; not to have him punished in any way—if only because he did not know any better. But he was to be sent away at once.

Jacintha's line had been different. She had, in the face of reason, common sense, and all probability, refused to believe that the boy had had anything whatever to do with the burglary.

"I didn't ask him a lot of silly questions about what had happened, that night," she had said. "I merely told him that I was going to believe him if he told me that he had not admitted the burglars, or helped them in any way. And that was what he *did* tell me; and he looked me straight in the face. *And* he was speaking the truth. . . . If you get him birched, sent to a reformatory, or punished in any way for this, I'll . . . I'll never forgive you, Richard."

And then she had given him one of her enigmatic lovely smiles as she added,

"And if you just hand him over to his mother, and let him go, I'll forgive you everything."

"What have you to forgive *me*, my love?" Richard Neystoke had asked.

"Surely you know that better than I do!" she had replied.

A most intriguing dear, who kept one guessing. Guessing rather uncomfortably sometimes.

Perhaps it would be wiser to do as she and Rosemary wished. Peace in the home. And as no harm had been done, there was no great reason to feel vindictive. But, of course, it was utter and absolute nonsense for Jacintha to talk about the boy being innocent. Sort of line a woman *would* take—with her instinct, intuition, and what-not, instead of being guided by masculine common sense.

Well, he would see what the mother had to say, when, perhaps, he could be magnanimous.

The maid opened the door.

"Mrs. Garden, Sir," she said, and Itler's mother entered Richard Neystoke's library.

Very respectable-looking working woman. He knew the type well, alas. The sort of woman who . . . What an unpleasant aroma of alcohol. It was a long time since he had . . .

"*Richard!!*"

The blood drained from Richard Neystoke's face, leaving it as white as that of a corpse. His knees trembled and gave way. He sank down in his chair. "*Miranda!*" he whispered.

No . . . No . . . No . . . Great merciful God, *no!* . . .

That was her voice . . . That was her face . . . This was the woman who . . .

"Excuse me, Sir," she murmured, and also sank on to a chair.

"*Miranda!*" he said again. "It can't be that you are . . ."

"*Richard!*" murmured the woman, with white lips. "I never thought . . . I never dreamed that . . ."

Hadn't she? Hadn't she? Hadn't she come to blackmail him? . . . No. That wasn't fair. He had written to her and asked her to come . . . Mrs. Garden . . . Nevertheless, it might be a put-up job. She had probably brought the husband with her—a piece of moral "moll-coshing".

But, no. He must be fair. She had never known that the name of the Vicar of Little Pudding was Neystoke; and Miranda Burbidge had not been the sort of woman who would do such a thing as attempt blackmail. But that was fifteen years ago.

A pulse hammered heavily in his temples, and an idiotic line kept repeating itself in his brain. A contemptible cheap clap-trap line,

> '*The curse has come upon me, said the Lady of Shalott.*'

Why did memory throw that up from his boyhood? Because the curse *had* come upon him?

> "*Be sure your sins will find you out.*"

There was nothing for it now but suicide. He could not live to be blackmailed.

No, Miranda Burbidge was not a blackmailer. But he could not live in a redoubled fear of exposure.

It was not fair.

It was cruel.

Just when he was beginning to recover, to feel better, to get on terms with life again.

This woman, here, and in his house—the sole

witness of the murder. Why had she come, and what did she want?

But he had sent for her himself . . . Yes, yes. But now, what would happen? To think that *he himself* had actually written, with his own hand, to the one person who could denounce and expose him, and had brought her here, face to face with him, to out-face him!

It was the hand of God.

"*Thou God seest me*"! . . .

Murder will out! . . .

This woman, seated here, in his private sanctum. . . . And Jacintha might enter at any moment.

God help him.

Richard Neystoke buried his face in his hands, which trembled and shook.

"*Richard!*" whispered the woman again. "Don't. *Please* don't."

To her, this was terrible. To think that she, of all people, should bring such dreadful fear and horror upon Richard.

"Don't, dear. *Don't!*" she begged.

If he made that dreadful sound again, she would have to go round to where he sat, and comfort him as though he were a child—as she had so often done before, when he was so terribly ill and weak and depressed. She would have died, sooner than come into his house and upset him like this.

With a great effort, Richard Neystoke endeavoured to gain control of his nerves, to pull himself together, and to meet his fate with what dignity he might.

What could he say to her? How could he ask the question that . . . he must ask:—*What had happened that night—after he fled.*

No, he could not ask that question. He must not think of it. He had always thrust it from him.

"So you married?" he said.

"*Richard!* Of course not! You don't think that I could—after . . ."

"But the name 'Garden'? The boy?"

"I took a different name . . . I had to change my name after . . . When I came out of . . ."

"What made you choose the name Garden? Did you live with a man named . . ."

"*Richard!* Of course not! . . . Don't you remember the garden? Don't you remember the long walk we took from Hampstead Heath that night, and the time we spent in that garden? They were the loveliest hours of my life."

This was dreadful. He must not listen to such talk. Not now. Not here. Why, Jacintha might . . .

With a sudden surging rush of fear, anger, and desperate need to know the truth, Richard Neystoke felt that he must quickly ask the first of the terrible questions that he must put to her. He must. He must know the worst.

"*What happened that night?*" he said, and rose to his feet.

Miranda Burbidge also rose from her chair, and answered his question with another.

"You don't *know*, Richard? You never saw anything in the papers? Or heard anything?"

"No. Never."

"You are married, Richard?"

"Yes."

"You are happy?"

"Yes."

"Children?"

"A daughter."

Miranda paused for a few seconds, searched his face, and answered his question.

"Richard . . . He came round . . . *So I killed him* . . ."

Richard Neystoke sank back in his chair.

"Merciful God!" he whispered.

Wide-eyed, white-faced and aghast, he stared at the face of the woman before him; dumbfounded, scarcely even able to believe his ears, scarcely able to find his voice.

"*You* killed him!" he said, at length. "*You!*"

The woman moistened her lips, struggled bravely, and repressed for ever the terrible yearning to speak the truth, to appeal at last, after these years of waiting, to his understanding, to his sympathy, and, if such a thing still existed, to his love.

That he had loved her, she knew, and nothing could change that fact, nor take away that knowledge.

A passing weakness in a strong soul, a calm spirit.

"Yes, Richard," she said again. "I killed him."

"Why?" whispered the man.

"I was afraid," she answered. "He came round just after you had gone. He said . . . He said he'd spoil my face for me. He said he wouldn't do me in, but he'd make my face so awful that I'd never dare look in a glass."

"And you *killed* him?"

The voice was not so much accusatory, as incredulous.

"He said he'd make me so ugly that people would shudder."

"And you *killed* him!"

He had almost added "In cold blood." For indeed, it seemed a very dreadful crime. But he refrained, for this was not the moment in which to make things more difficult for this poor soul, this poor penitent creature obviously labouring under a deep sense of sin, and painfully striving to keep herself from breaking down.

"You are perfectly certain," he asked gently,

"that he was . . . recovering? That he had not received . . ."

Again, he refrained from saying the words which formed themselves in his mind. No, he would not utter that dreadful phrase "a fatal wound".

". . . a dangerous blow?" he said.

"Oh, no. He was just knocked out. Like Tom Brickett has been, hundreds of times. He was stunned . . .

"That was all, Richard," she concluded.

Richard Neystoke relaxed from head to foot, breathed freely, and felt a warm uprising surge and glow of thankfulness, of relief; an inexpressibly beautiful sensation of release, and of freedom.

He felt that he was like a man who had received a reprieve on the scaffold itself; that this was not reprieve, but something a thousand times better; it was complete and final pardon—nay, it was ten thousand times better than pardon, it was knowledge that he was awaking to find that this appalling horror had been but a nightmare.

He was not a murderer!

He was not a murderer, and the sin that he had committed, now, by comparison, seemed and was venial.

A hasty blow.

What man alive that day, what man who had ever lived since the beginning of the world, had not committed some little hasty act wherewith to reproach himself?

Oh, God be praised and thanked!

The burden of these awful years fell from his shoulders; the burden he had borne since Marindin had unwittingly told him that the crime was *murder*. Almost, he could hear its reverberating crash.

He rose to his feet, feeling a different man, a new man, and a better man.

There was still the woman, however. . . . But she represented a mere venial sin. An error of youth. Just a tiny wild oat.

How had he better get rid of her? He must be as kind as possible, for, really, she had behaved very well; or, rather, she had refrained from behaving very badly. She might have made it dreadful for him; could have told a lie and blamed *him* for the murder; could have made a terrible claim on him; blackmailed him for life.

And now, if she would only go, before Jacintha came to intercede for the boy. She had said she would like to see Itler's mother and tell her that she, personally, believed in him; believed that he was quite innocent; liked him very much, and would do anything she could for him. She had said she would jolly well speak up for him, if there were an official enquiry and he was in trouble. Give him a testimonial as to character.

"Well, Mrs. Garden," he said. "I asked you to come and see me about your boy. We have had a burglary here, and I am afraid that he knows more about it than he will tell us."

"I can tell you one thing, Sir," replied Miranda Burbidge, "and that is that he had nothing to do with it, whatever he may or may not know."

This too was very dreadful for her. This could not be Richard talking to her about the boy—*their own boy.*

"I can't think how you could possibly suspect him, Sir. He's a mischievous young limb, I know, but he'd never do anything wicked, criminal, like that."

"Well, the police . . ."

She sprang up.

"The *police*, Sir?" she cried, in horror. "Let me take him away with me. Let him go, and I'll look after him. He'd never, never do anything like that. Let me take him away. Why, the police might . . ."

Richard Neystoke quite agreed. Of course. That would be the best thing. It would get rid of them both, and he would never see them again.

Police! Why, even now, the thought of police and police-courts made him quail. But that was foolish. The whole thing had been a terrible mistake. He had never been in danger of the Law. He had never committed murder. This woman was his witness.

He must do something for her. How could he help her? She would be offended if she were offered money, if she were still the Miranda Burbidge whom he had . . . known.

An idea. A memory. Yes.

"Do you know, Mrs. Garden, I am in your debt?"

"*You* in *my* debt, Richard?"

"Yes." It was a hateful and horrible thing to have to say, but he must say it. "You slipped some money into my pocket . . . that night."

Miranda Burbidge seemed almost to recoil from him.

"You owe me nothing, Richard."

"I'd like to do something for . . . for the boy."

Miranda eyed Richard Neystoke with a steady level gaze—a long look before which his own fell.

"I shall be able to look after . . . the boy," she said. "And later, he will look after me. We shall do very well."

"Well, Mrs. Garden, if you . . ."

"I'd like to go now, Sir. I'll go at once, please," and she turned suddenly towards the door.

Richard Neystoke's hand went out to the bell,

but then, some feeling of shame overcoming him, he hurried to the door and opened it for her.

(What was it she had said, fifteen years ago? . . . You are so *different*, Richard. So polite to me.)

"Let me show you the way," he said.

Heaven grant Jacintha remained in her drawing room. She was quite capable of coming out and insisting on Mrs. Garden having tea with her, while she talked to her about her boy.

As he opened the front-door, he saw young Itler in the drive, apparently standing about, and waiting for his mother.

Turning to Richard Neystoke, and holding out her hand,

"Good-bye," she said, her voice controlled, soft, and friendly; her smile kind; her eyes alight with love—incredibly unquenchable love. "Good-bye, Richard. I do hope you will always be *so* happy. Don't ever think any more about that dreadful man. Good-bye. And thank you, more than I can say, for all you've done for me."

"Good-bye. And thank you, too," said Richard Neystoke.

Miranda turned away.

As she approached her son, a girl came up the drive and the boy turned quickly at the sound of her footsteps.

"Rosemary," he said. "I wanta tell you . . ."

But, even as the archer with the grey-goose-feathered shaft struck down the grey goose itself, so did Rosemary wing an arrow of pointed speech, barbed with words of Itler's own providing.

"Perishin' stinkin' little swine," she hissed, and passed him by.

A few yards farther on, she turned and made the last gesture of her childhood—a most derisory grimace which included the protrusion of a long pink tongue.

"Who was that, dear?" asked Miranda, as, stooping, she put her arms about his shoulders and kissed him.

"Rosemary. 'Oly Joe's nipper," replied Itler, wriggling from his mother's embrace, but acknowledging it with a friendly punch.

"Oh!" she said, and looked again at the retreating form of young Itler's late friend.

Withdrawing her gaze from the girl, and glancing at the face of her son, she realised that he was in the grip of a strong emotion; that the eyes, so like her own, were refusing the passage of tears, that the hard young mouth was twitching, the chin inclined to tremble.

"Come with me, Son," she said. "Come back to London."

The boy swallowed.

"I'm comin', Old 'Un," he replied. "Don't you fret your fat. Nobody don't want me 'ere."

"I want you, Son," said the woman, and gently patted his back.

"Chuck it," growled the boy.

But the second thump that he therewith bestowed upon his mother was also an expression of love.

EPILOGUE

". . . and on the previous day she had overthrown the idol that had stood so firmly on its pedestal in her heart. And the idol lay smashed in fragments at the base of the pedestal that bore its name. But the effort had been terrible; the experience painful almost unto death; and it had left her weak and wan but strong. Strong, firm, and resigned. She had realised and accepted the fact that love is not all; that duty is almost all; and that unselfishness is everything."[17]

Elspeth Grey sat upon a rock on the secluded beach beneath the grounds of Marstone Park, and waited the coming of Richard Neystoke.

He had written to tell her that he was now really happy, free, and cured of his illness; and that, in spite of this, he was coming back to Dr. Fieldwicke's nursing-home to be her patient again —for he needed a period of convalescence. He needed a time of retreat, seclusion, peace, in which to realise his wonderful healing and recovery—and he needed *her*. He would await her reply.

After a day and a night and a day of mental struggle and earnest prayer, she had written and told him that she could not, of course, prevent his return to Marstone Park—and she had begged him not to return—but that he would not find her there if he came.

Richard Neystoke had then written a full and

---

[17] *Love is not all.*—Camoens.

complete account of his interview with Miranda Burbidge, and assured her that she need no longer shrink from him—(since that was obviously what she was doing)—because his hands were not stained with the blood of his fellow-man; that he was not a murderer, as he had thought; that he was not a fugitive, hiding from the police; that he had done nothing of which she might be ashamed, for his life was as blameless as her own.

To this letter, she had replied that he missed the point entirely; that whether he had committed a murder or not was quite immaterial; that she had no right to receive love-letters from him, nor to listen if he wished to tell her the state of his feelings towards her; that she blamed herself severely, deeply, and unceasingly; and that while she thanked him for what he had done for her—for he had changed her whole understanding of life, and she would never forget him, nor a moment that they had spent together, nor a word that he had said to her—she begged him to believe, understand, and realise that, if he returned to Marstone Park, she would have to go.

And she *would* go, but it would be a dreadful and a painful thing that she should have to leave the place where she had been so happy—so unbelievably happy—owing to his presence there. And this was final. Please would he write to her no more. Would he forgive her, forget her, and . . . *good-bye.*

Next day, she had received a telegram.

I shall be on the sands by our rock at three on Wednesday and shall wait for an hour. Will you not say good-bye to me there?

With high purpose and stern resolve, she had come to say farewell to him, and to her happiness.

*   *   *   *   *

But Richard Neystoke had not come to say farewell. He had come to persuade her, and, only half-consciously, to exercise that charm which had never failed with a woman, and but very rarely with a man.

Almost, he persuaded her. Almost she stooped to pick up the fragments of the shattered idol and replace them on the pedestal.

But not quite.

A life devoted to duty, a life of practice of the Religion of Unselfishness which Richard Neystoke had preached, had strengthened her moral fibre, given her power over herself, power even over Love itself, and now enabled her to be cruel to be kind.

Yet, in the last moments before giving him his final answer, her strength faltered, her heart clamoured with loud insistence that made it more powerful than her head. . . .

"If he accepts this," she thought, "if this does not hurt him unbearably, I shall give way. I shall fail. Fail myself, and, perhaps, him. I am not a nun, a saint; I am human. Why should love come to me at last, if I am not to accept it? Oh, Richard! Richard! Listen, and *you* shall decide."

§2

"Listen, Richard," she said gently, "when you were here, you told me what you called 'everything'. The truth, the whole truth, and nothing but the truth. But you didn't tell me everything, neither the truth nor the whole truth.

"You said you murdered a man in blind rage and fear of him. I respected you for admitting the fear, and I cared nothing that you were a murderer, as you called yourself; I would not have cared if you had killed a dozen men in such circumstances—any more than I would have cared if you had killed them in battle, for I don't call that murder.

"And I didn't understand how what you had done could have so filled you with remorse as to wreck your health and ruin your life.

"But it was not that at all. That was not what you had thrust down into your Unconscious Mind, refused to recognise and admit.

"It was your desertion of the woman whom you left to bear the brunt of whatever might follow; whom you left to bear the blame. You didn't even trouble to find out whether she had been arrested and punished for what you did. For all you knew, she might have been hanged—this woman who, on your own showing, saved your life when you were ill, and gave you her love . . . No, no, let me finish. . . .

"Of course she wanted you to escape. Of course she helped you to do so. Didn't she love you? And that was the return you made for her love, the return you made to this woman who refused to marry you lest she should be a mill-stone about your neck?

"God forbid that I should judge you, Richard, but I am telling you why I will not listen to you, and also why I never wish to see you again.

"I think it would have been better if you yourself had hung a mill-stone about your neck and been drowned in the depth of the sea, than to have so offended against this woman who loved and trusted you. . . .

"No, *please* don't interrupt, or I shall be unable to say what I must.

"I'm *preaching*, Richard, and it makes me feel ill, but I *must* say it.

"You behaved vilely, abominably, and I could never forget it, or forgive it. The dreadful desertion, treachery, cowardice. Richard, you are a weakling, a coward, a cad, and something of a cur. . . . You have a wife who loves you, who has done her utmost for you, for the last fifteen years. . . . Go back to her."

Richard Neystoke rose to his feet.

"I have not been too well, just lately," he said, and went.

How *could* she say such words to him?
Revulsion.
He felt he hated Elspeth Grey.

§3

A woman and a boy, tired, dusty, and far from unhappy, sat beside the highway sharing a stale loaf and a piece of what had been sold under the name of cheese.

"Tired, Son?" asked the woman.

"Chuck it, Old 'Un," replied the boy. "Me wot Tom Brickett's goin' to make fly-weight Champion of England? *Cor!*"

"It's good of old Tom to help us so kindly," said the woman. "But I don't want you to follow the boxing, Dick."

"Lots of money in it. . . . Why! Time I'm feather-weight Champion *of England only*, you'll 'ave a posh fur coat, a motor-car, and a 'ole little 'ouse to yerself. . . . Be in the big money then, we shall. All the dough we wants."

"Dough isn't everything, Son," smiled the woman. "It's a hard rough life; you being knocked about, for a living."

"Naow! It's the other guy as'll get knocked about. Anyway, we'll make out all-right, ole girl. Wot with me in the Boss's string challengin' any boy of me weight and age, and you in the pay-box sellin' the tickets! . . . 'Ow much d'yer pinch?"

"Yes, the Boss has been very good to us. That was for your grandfather's sake, Mr. Horatio Burbidge, the well-known actor."

"Not for your sake, Old 'Un?"

"The Boss? No thank you, Dick. But he's been very good to us, and so has old Tom Brickett and old Bill Munry. Everybody has been very good."

"Blimey, you oughter be good yerself, then. Grumblin' at me boxin'!"

"Well, it's not what I or your father would have wished for you, Dick."

"Father? Wonder where 'e is," mused the boy.

"I've heard about him. . . . He's dead," replied the woman. "Dead to me, anyhow," she murmured to herself, as she turned away to bury in a rabbit-hole the scrap of paper that had been their napkin and table-cloth.

"Well, p'raps I shan't stick to it—the boxin'," said the boy. "I got somethink else in me mind, you know."

"What's that, Son?"

"Join the army when I'm old enough. Fight like 'ell and get a c'mishion. Ride on a norse. And then I'll go to that little dumpling place, Suet Pudding, and I'll ride into the Vickridge grounds, and up the drive to the front-door—you know, callin'; leave a card; give it to the skivvy; and say,

" 'Shove that there card at the missus.'

"Then when she comes out, I'm goin' to salute and shake 'ands and say,

" 'Very pleased to meet you again, Mum.'

And when she ses,

" 'Strike me pink if it ain't Mr. Garden!' I'll say,

" 'Captain Garden, Mum.'

"And when she ses 'You'll like to see Rosemary, I'm sure,' I'll just say off-'and like,

" 'Don't mind if I do. Not very interested'."

The woman put her hand over the boy's fist that lay clenched beside him as he stared into the rosy future.

"Come on, Son. We have got to catch up with the Circus," said she.

"Yes, Old 'Un," replied Young Itler, "and that's wot you got to *do* if you want to get on in Life— catch up with the Circus."

Available P. C. Wren Titles
from
Riner Publishing Company

The Collected Short Stories

Volume One: ISBN 9780985032609
Volume Two: ISBN 9780985032616
Volume Three: ISBN 9780985032623
Volume Four: ISBN 9780985032630
Volume Five: ISBN 9780985032647

The Collected Novels

Volume One: *The Geste Novels*
    Part A: ISBN 9780985032678
    Part B: ISBN 9780985032685
Volume Two: *The Sinbad Novels*
    Part A: ISBN 9780692639382
    Part B: ISBN 9780692639429
Volume Three: *The Foreign Legion Novels*
    Part A: ISBN 9780999074909
    Part B: ISBN 9780999074916
Volume Four: *The Earlier India Novels*
    Part A: ISBN 9780999074923
    Part B: ISBN 9780999074930
Volume Five: *The Later India Novels*
    Part A: ISBN 9780999074947
    Part B: ISBN 9780999074954
Volume Six: *The English Novels*
    Part A: ISBN 9780999074961
    Part B: ISBN 9780999074978
Volume Seven: *A Mixed Bag of Novels*
    Part A: ISBN 9780999074985
    Part B: ISBN 9780999074992

Further information can be found at
rinerpublishing.wordpress.com

2 February 2020

www.ingramcontent.com/pod-product-compliance
Lightning Source LLC
Chambersburg PA
CBHW032249020726
47495CB00001B/27